To a
recent dear friend
and fellow artist...."
a real Southern belle!

The Ring of
the Piper's Tune

Austin Dwyer

iUniverse, Inc.
New York Bloomington

iUniverse books may be ordered through booksellers or by contacting:

iUniverse
1663 Liberty Drive
Bloomington, IN 47403
www.iuniverse.com
1-800-Authors (1-800-288-4677)

ISBN: 978-1-4401-7480-3 (sc)
ISBN: 978-1-4401-7478-0 (dj)
ISBN: 978-1-4401-7479-7 (ebook)

Printed in the United States of America

iUniverse rev. date: 10/19/09

Praise For Austin Augustine Dwyer's
the Ring of the Piper's tune

"I enjoyed *The Ring of the Piper's Tune* immensely and truly regret that it came to an end. Austin Dwyer has done a magnificent job in weaving a completely credible family saga into a fabric of events and characters like J. Edgar Hoover and Joe Kennedy. In my opinion, the book really does stand alongside books like Margaret Mitchell's *Gone with the Wind* and Herman Wouk's *Winds of War*. I have every reason to be extremely confident that it will be a great commercial success, and should make a terrific film."

– RORKE BRYAN, Professor, Fellow Emeritus,
Writer and Past Dean of Faculty, Toronto University

"With the sure hand of an artist, in his first novel, nationally known master maritime painter Austin Dwyer creates unforgettable characters who move through a world of intrigue and suspense to a totally satisfying perfect ending."

– LAURIE FISH GREIMES, 15-year Seattle Times Columnist,
Flying Tiger Lines Publications Editor, International Freelance Travel Writer

"Who but an Irishman like Dwyer could weave a tale of undying, tormented love played out against a background of intrigue which builds to a new take on the origins of the First World War? A love as hopeless as that of Yeats for Maud Gonne drives the central character even as the world collapses into savagery. Dwyer's knowledge of passion and persistence spins out in language as musical as the Irish tones that hum in the streets and parlors of Dublin. Astute readers will not be wrong to think of Pierre Bezukhov and Natasha Rostov."

– DENNIS PETERS, Professor of Humanities Emeritus,
Shoreline Community College

"Early in reading Austin Dwyer's novel, I could visualize Kathleen Barrett as a young woman who would stand her ground until she prevailed. She would bring happiness to the man who either readily yielded to her to keep the peace or brought a dominant power through strong character. In the course of this story her strengths are tested in relationships with William Hamilton, who first meets her during the Irish rebellion in 1916, and Ryan Thornton, who in first seeing her pass in a car in Boston begins shaping strategies to meet her. Kathleen, and scores of other characters, all portrayed with the precise focus of an artist, take the reader through prohibition business in Chicago and two world wars. Dwyer skillfully leads the reader to judge characters whose actions raise the question: How could he do *that*? This is their story. This is what they did. Thanks to Austin Dwyer I have had a good time looking in on fascinating lives."

– DENZIL WALTERS, Editor, Teacher and Writer

Cover Painting | © 2009 Austin Dwyer
Design | Dan Fraser

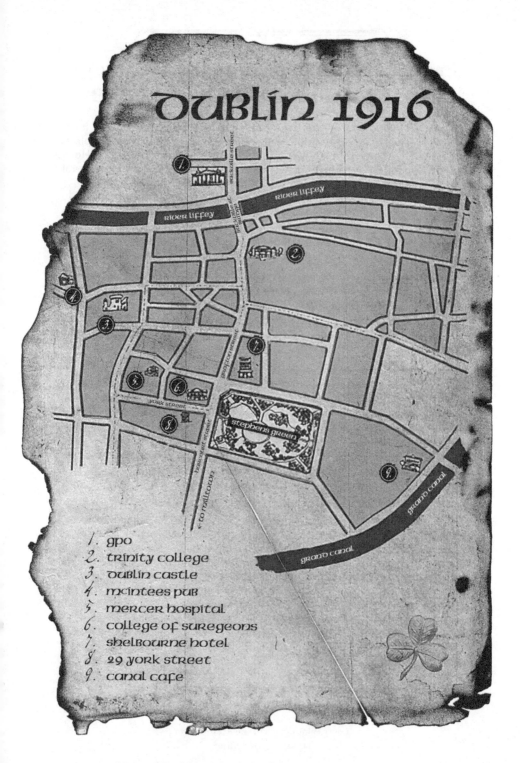

DUBLIN 1916

1. gpo
2. trinity college
3. dublin castle
4. mcintees pub
5. mercer hospital
6. college of suregeons
7. shelbourne hotel
8. 29 york street
9. canal cafe

Map of Dublin in 1916 after the insurrection.

McIntees Public House in 1916.

General Post Office in Dublin 1916
just after the insurrection.

To my mother, Annie Russell

Part One

CHAPTER ONE

New York, 1960

THE CATHEDRAL'S STAINED-GLASS windows, illuminated by the evening sun, cast colors on the otherwise dreary walls. An old woman struck a match to light a votive candle, a prayer for the dead. The smell of incense from a Funeral Mass permeated the air. A small group of penitents knelt and prayed in loud whispers. Deep bells tolled, announcing confessions.

Briskly, he entered the sanctuary from the sacristy. Genuflecting and pausing for a moment, he continued toward the confessional. His features were rugged, shadowy, and tanned. His white hair made him look older than forty-three. He stopped in front of the confessional door.

Reaching deep into his cassock, he produced a nameplate and gently moved his fingers across the black gothic letters that bore his name, Michael Riordan. He asked himself if he would ever hear his new title, Monsignor, without turning to see for himself the priest bearing the elevated designation.

He pushed the nameplate onto the tracks above the door. For an instant, the slap of the plate striking the end of the holder startled the quiet murmuring of the waiting penitents. Embarrassed, he turned toward the pews and mouthed silently, "Sorry."

He had spent the past three years in a monastery in southern Spain, a hot, desolate spot where only the occasional peasant ventured to trade his wares. He had found it difficult to nurture real friendships within the monastic community. The language barrier had not been overcome. For three years he saw no art. The culture was survival level. It was a community without industry. He had chosen this primitive sabbatical to challenge the conviction of his faith. The self-inflicted penance ended when he received a welcome letter from Cardinal Spellman recalling him to his old Archdiocese in New York and informing him that he would be elevated to the office of Monsignor.

Now, in the dark silence of the confessional, he thought about his approaching Celebration Mass and asked himself whether his mother would accept him. In the past three years he had received many letters and had written few in return. Many times he had attempted to put his thoughts on paper, only to lose his courage, extending the lies and terrible secrets. Despite his misgivings, he believed that she would forgive him. He was confident that she would be proud of his becoming a Monsignor. And yes, he was certain that she would be happy to learn that he was home.

His reveries were interrupted by the sound of the door opening and closing. Despite the years, he had little experience on this side of the confessional. Inside the center cell, he fought off his unease in the dark, musty, confined space, where body odors mixed with wood oils. He waited for the person on the other side to kneel and begin his or her confession, and then drew back the door covering the screen.

Even though the screen concealed the penitent, some parishioners tried to disguise their voices.

"Bless me, Father, for I have sinned. It's been two weeks since my last confession."

The dialect could not be disguised. It was unmistakably Irish. The declaration of guilt poured, accusing himself of looking at women in an inappropriate manner. It was more difficult, he admitted, when they wore short skirts. In the case of long skirts, he blamed his impropriety on the wind. He confessed to numerous infractions of Catholic dogma and finally settled on issues regarding his wife.

"We're not gettin' along at all, Father."

"To the best of your knowledge, why is that?"

"It's always about the money, Father."

"Well now, that's not so uncommon. More often than not, money is at the root of most of our problems. What about the money?"

"It's not that I don't make good money, Father. We argue all the time. She says I don't give her enough."

"Go on."

"I give her enough money to live on. She just has problems with—shall we say—some of my contributions."

"I can understand her concern. These contributions of yours—are we talking about a great deal of money?"

"She thinks it is." There was a long silence. The man changed the subject. "Can a person be excommunicated, Father, for being a member of the IRA? There's a rumor that the Vatican —"

Riordan interrupted, "I'm sure that's not a rumor. The Church doesn't look favorably on organizations that condone killing as a solution, for any cause. Why? Is that where the money is going?"

"Well, I'm not actually a member, Father. I send money to help the cause, that's all. I have nothin' to do with the killin'."

"You would if your money is used to buy guns."

"I've been helpin' out the Irish Troubles. How they use the money is their business, Father. I had a feelin' I could be excommunicated for what I'm about to tell you, but I came to you because I felt you might be more understanding, being an Irishman. I mean, yer name being Riordan an' all."

"What's important for you to remember is that I am a priest." There was a touch of hostility in his voice. "Would you feel any responsibility for the killing of a man if you had supplied the weapon or the bullet?"

While the confession spilled out, Riordan thought back to his own life. The delicate conscience of this parishioner reminded him of his own vulnerability. *How responsible am I to God? Could a just God judge this man harshly for wanting a united Ireland? Was he sending his wages to a righteous war or a pointless, never-ending slaughter?*

As the accent behind the screen grew thicker, Riordan became lost in his own memories. He remembered his mother's vivid stories of Ireland and its struggles as if they were told to him yesterday.

CHAPTER TWO

Dublin, 1916

ROUCHED IN THE dark alley, he sighted down the barrel of the German-made Mauser and prepared himself to murder. Mick Barrett studied the features of the young British officer standing under the gas lamp. From less than thirty yards, he could see the other man's mouth move, uttering orders to the small group of soldiers.

Hesitating for a moment, Mick was brought back to reality by the harsh whispers of his companion. "For Christ's sake, shoot the bastard, Mick! Pull the bleedin' trigger!"

Mick froze. As much as he despised the British soldiers, he had no idea that it would be this difficult to kill one of them. It wasn't the case at McIntee's pub, where after downing a couple of pints and a few whiskies, he'd bragged passionately about what he could do to one of them, given the chance. On this night he had lain for hours in the shadows of the dark alley. It was his moment of truth. All the boasting was now lurid detail and his senses adjusted to the inevitable inquiry. *Wasn't this the reason I joined the volunteers?* He had even demanded this mission. Yet, the soldier appeared so young. Mick attributed his weakness to his Catholicity, which forbade him to kill. He felt ill. An instant attack of heavy breathing caused his gun-sight to move up and down. He knew that if he fired he would miss.

"Give me the bloody thing!" his companion ordered.

"Be Jasus, Ned, I'm sorry. I just can't do it."

Grabbing the gun, the young man with the lantern jaw raised it to his shoulder and fired off the 30-caliber round. What Mick saw reminded him of one of those silent pictures. There was no sound. The hat tore upwards, insignia fleetingly glistening in the gaslight as the head of the young officer exploded like a ripe marrow, splattering on the red bricks of the old tenement. Mick's body trembled at the crack of the man's skull shattering. The two of them had followed orders and now faced the frightening reality of capture.

For a moment, the remaining British soldiers were paralyzed. Retching, they wiped blood and pieces of brain from their faces.

"The bloody Irish bastards!" one of them managed to say.

While Mick hesitated, Ned ran.

"There they are!" snapped one of the British, pointing toward them.

Mick followed Ned as he bolted down Harcourt Street toward Stephen's Green. Every stride exposed them as their hob-nailed boots struck the pavement. Mick cursed the boots and wished that they had gone barefoot. Every sound pronounced capture: the screech of a distant railway whistle, the sound of shots fired not far behind, pings striking the road around him. He cursed himself for being overweight—too much of the stout. Their orders suggested a number of escape routes. They could cut through the Green or make it to Bill Elliot's place on York Street.

At the bottom of Harcourt Street, Mick turned left to York Street by the College of Surgeons and Ned turned right toward the Green. Immediately, Mick knew he should have followed Ned, where the grass would mute the pounding of the boots and thick bushes could hide a man. He realized now that the difference between life and death had everything to do with experience. His terror had wiped out all the rehearsals. He should have followed Ned to the dark shadows of the park!

Mick's heart was throbbing in his throat. He could hear the soldiers closing in. Halfway down the street, he stepped into the familiar doorway of the old Georgian house. The four-story, red-brick building had been converted into tenements. He knew that the darkness of the hallway would shelter him for a few seconds. He prayed that his heavy breathing would not give him away. The soldiers were so close that he could hear them calling out orders. The warm moisture on his brow turned into a cold sweat. *If the soldiers are here, Ned must be safe in the park. God, why didn't I go with Ned?* he thought. *My first mission with the volunteers and not only have I botched the job, I am goin' to be killed!*

As his eyes adjusted to the dark, objects began to reveal themselves. He was close enough to the wide staircase to know that the area beneath would provide a hiding place long enough for him to catch his breath. Again, he cursed his clumsy boots that made a tapping sound on the old mosaic floor. The angry voices persisted. Too close for comfort. He finally reached the alcove under the stairs, where he cowered and began to pray.

Our Father, Who art in heaven. Oh God! Thy kingdom come. Oh, my God! I promise I'll stay home with Annie and the kids, if You get me out of this one. Thy will be done. I know I've made these promises to You before, but it was for missin' Mass on Sunday and drinkin' too much an', oh, God, I'm only 37! Who's to care for Annie an' the children if they catch me?

The shouts of the British sounded closer.

Mother of Jasus, help me! The Elliots'. I have to get to the Elliots'!

"We'll get the bastard who did this, even if it takes all night!" The hollered cockney accent grated Mick's nerves.

God help me. God help us all! Merciful God, I promise I'll resign from the movement. I'll quit. I'll not put myself in jeopardy again.

Cautiously, he peered out from under the stairs. How many doors until he reached number 29? He was unsure that they would open their door to him, with the British running up and down the street, shouting commands and free to search anywhere.

Bill and Molly Elliot were in their mid-forties. Although Bill's origins were English, he sympathized with the Irish cause. He was a schoolteacher and taught all grades at the Damer, one of the few non-denominational schools in Dublin. A thin, lanky man with deep, perceptive eyes beneath thick eyebrows, he wore rimless glasses, and the rest of his features were obscured behind the thatch of red whiskers. They seemed an unmatched couple. Molly, inclined to stoutness, was born and raised in Dublin and four years older than her husband.

Mick trembled, blessed himself, and ran for the Elliots'. "Bill, open up, for God's sake! Let me in. It's Mick—Mick Barrett!"

From behind the door, Mick could hear Bill Elliot arguing with his wife. "For the love of God, Molly! If Mick's in trouble —" Bill threw back the bolt. "We're not going to turn him away."

"Dear God, Bill, don't we have more than ourselves to be thinkin' about?" She was referring to their two children. "I don't want him in here!" she whispered loudly.

Mick was frantic. "Please, Bill, they're almost here. I can hear them!"

"Molly, listen!" Bill persisted. "If they catch him now, he'll never see the light of day."

"And if they find him here?" Her tone was severe.

"We can't shut this man out, Molly. I'll not turn my back on a friend of the movement. Please."

She stepped aside reluctantly.

When Bill finally opened the door, Mick rushed feverishly into the room. He slammed the door shut with his back and was momentarily blinded by the two gas lamps burning over the fireplace. Relieved, he looked around the large room and finally felt safe. Bill looked at the sorry figure in front of him.

"So, it's started already, has it?"

Mick's eyes lit up. "You should have been there, Bill. Ned Morriarty shot a British officer."

"Glory be to God! What are you talking about, Mick?" Molly said, making the sign of the cross. "Is he dead?"

"He is."

"Hush now, Molly. Let the man talk. Go ahead, Mick. Tell us what happened."

"Well, Bill, as you know…" Mick hesitated, trying to catch his breath. "At least I was given to understand that you knew. We were all broken down into small groups to create a diversion in the city. Each group was supposed to eliminate key British officers. Ned and I…"

Bill interrupted him, "Where's Ned? Did they catch him?"

"I don't think so. Last I saw him, he was headin' toward the Green. It's my heels they were on." Mick frantically reached in his pockets, finally locating the bent Woodbine, which he lit through cupped hands. He inhaled deeply. The smoke came from his nose and mouth as he spoke. "We have to move now! The time couldn't be better. Maybe I'm not the one to be doin' the killing. God knows I have to do something."

Molly interrupted, "Do you think for a moment that the English are going to give Ireland its independence because they're busy fighting Germans?" She answered her own question. "Absolutely not, Mick." She filled the kettle with water, put it on the stove, and peeked out the window.

Under his breath, Mick whispered to Bill, "God, I could use a little drop of whiskey."

Bill retrieved a pint bottle from the medicine cabinet and poured a little Powers into two glasses. Before Bill had a chance to raise his glass to his mouth, Mick's glass was drained. His whole body shuddered. Bill refilled the glass.

"God, I hope we're right about this, Mick."

"Remember, lads, I'm all for a free Ireland, too, but not your way," Molly said. "There's something to say for the scholar's ink lasting longer than the martyr's blood."

"I suppose Molly has a point there, Mick. We're not unified yet, are we? As we speak, there's more young Irishmen fighting with the British against the Germans than there are in the Irish Provisional Army."

Mick crushed out the cigarette. "The Germans aren't our enemy. England is and any enemy of England is a friend of ours!"

"And what about the Americans?" Bill said. "I hear President Wilson is being pushed more and more toward war on Germany. Are they going to be the enemy then, too?"

"There are a lot of Americans on our side, Bill. Where do you think we got the money to buy the German guns?" Mick said with certainty.

Molly looked over at her two sons. There were two beds in the room. One was occupied by their sons, Frank and Jerry. A divider with a Japanese motif maintained some measure of privacy. They lay quietly, pretending to be asleep, knowing they would hear all the details of the eventual Uprising. At fourteen and sixteen, they looked forward to the excitement. The idea of a united Ireland, without soldiers, was something to hope for.

When Molly was convinced that the boys were asleep, she nervously fussed over the kettle, peeking out the window again. "I think they're leaving!"

Mick looked relieved. "Which direction did they go, Molly?" he asked.

"Back up toward the park."

"God, I hope Ned's all right," Mick said, placing his hands on his head.

Molly looked at the clock on the mantel as it struck one. "With the curfew and all, you'd better stay here, Mick. We'll put you up for the night."

"I knew I could depend on you, Molly." He turned to Bill. "Tomorrow, the whole thing begins. The General Post Office, the College of Surgeons, other strategic locations. We're takin' them all. It's the big day! By Monday, Eamonn de Valera and the Volunteer Army are going to control the city. If the British don't have leaders, we'll have them out of Ireland for good."

Molly overheard. "Not tomorrow, Mick! Good Lord, man, it's Easter Sunday." Her tone was bitter. "You should be in church thankin' God you're alive and askin' forgiveness for that young officer's death."

"Isn't that the sad nature of war, Molly? I think we'll all serve God better when we free Ireland," Mick said, forgetting all of the promises he had made under the staircase.

CHAPTER THREE

A T THIRTY-FIVE, ANNIE Barrett could still turn the heads of men. Her softly rounded curves and firm, ample breasts belied the fact that she had given birth five times and was the mother of teen-age children. Her face was an almost perfect oval. Faintly dusted with freckles, it was remarkably unlined, despite the hard times and the grief she still felt since burying a stillborn baby. Her blue eyes reflected her feelings and could be steely cold or flash with passion or joy. The golden red of her hair was softened by a few strands of silver.

Annie sat by the window, her eyes dark with worry, drinking her second cup of tea. She looked at the clock again. *Half past two in the morning and still no Mick*. She worried a lot about Mick these days, with all the trouble in Ireland. She knew he wanted to play a part in its independence.

She resented the troubled times and the effect on her family. Mick wasn't a fighter. He wasn't callous enough. Their life was simple. Mick's second-hand store provided them with a comfortable home in Milltown, on the outskirts of Dublin. They had land and a garden, luxuries most Dubliners did not have. His older brother, Padraig, was a partner and handled the financial end of the business. Mick was more affable and obliging, so he was in charge of the sales. She was deft with her hands. With a stitch here and some polish there, Annie helped Mick ready his cast-off merchandise for the store and also furnish their home with some nice things. Certainly she was the envy of many of her friends.

Anxiously, Annie watched as the clock struck three. It was beginning to rain and still no Mick! She knew he was meeting Ned Morriarty tonight and that worried her. Ned was a known activist in the Volunteer Army and was always looking for new members. Annie wasn't as influenced by Ned's politics as her husband was. She didn't want Mick to risk his life for a cause she thought foolish because she doubted that it would bring a better way of life to Ireland.

Most Dubliners had heard the gossip of rebellion. The thought that the rumors were true terrified her. She knew that Mick had been involved in peaceful demonstrations protesting the atrocities of the British Army. Indiscriminate killing of innocent men, women, and children rallied the Irish people to their cause for freedom. Instinctively, she wanted to reach for her children. She went into the boys' room first.

Michael, 12, Jamie, 7, and Paddy, 16, shared a room. She looked at each one in turn, Michael and Jamie first, who shared a bed. Annie had to look closely to see which one of the black, curly heads was which. Tawny-faced and blue-eyed, they definitely took after their father. She tried to untangle the arms and legs. Giving up, she pulled the covers over them and kissed each tousled head.

Freckle-faced and ruddy, Paddy had inherited her deep auburn hair. When she reached for Paddy, he rose up on one elbow. Half asleep, he asked, "Is Da home yet, Ma?"

Annie sighed and said, "Go back to sleep. I'm shure he'll be along shortly." She hugged him and gave a reassuring pat. It maddened her to think of the role he would someday have to play in Ireland's independence.

Next, she went to Kathleen's room. This 17-year-old beauty was a female version of Mick. Her coal-black hair curled long around her shoulders and her flashing blue eyes were just like her father's. Annie never ceased to be amazed at how her pudgy raven-haired baby had blossomed into such a beauty. Kathleen was so much like Mick that Annie would watch them with pride and a bit of awe. Mick was a self-educated man, acquiring a great deal of knowledge from reading. Kathleen's education was similar and she had inherited her father's deep love of books. Neither was ever at a loss for an answer, even if the details were inaccurate or fabricated. Kathleen was tall for a woman, two inches shorter than Mick's five-feet-ten inches. Too often they would stand face-to-face, eyes penetrating, each accustomed to being thwarted and opposed by the other, arguing about which river was the longest, which mountain the highest, neither willing to budge until written evidence found one gleaming with mocking self-satisfaction. Sometimes Annie felt they argued for the sake of arguing. She dreaded the time that they might come to such bitter disagreement as to destroy their relationship. They were both so opinionated and stubborn! Secretly, she admired Kathleen's courage when she stood up for herself. Kathleen was not sleeping, having sensed the tension in her mother earlier.

"Why aren't you asleep, Kathleen?"

"How can I sleep? I keep listening for him. I know it's way past closing for the pubs. Sean McIntee said his ma overheard some of the lads talking at the pub. They said there's going to be big trouble soon. It's just a feeling, but I know Ned Morriarty has Da involved in it!"

"I know," Annie said softly.

"That Ned Morriarty is a bad piece of work."

"Hush, child. You'll wake the boys."

"I just know he'll get Da into trouble! It makes me mad sometimes, the way Da goes off and thinks only of himself. He should consider us, for God's sake."

"I'm sure everything is going to be all right, Kathleen. Tomorrow is Easter Sunday, and I know he'll be here to take us to Mass," Annie said, trying hard to convince herself, as well as comfort her daughter.

The knock on the door jarred Annie back to reality. The impatient knocking sounded again before she had a chance to open the half-door.

"Annie, sorry to bother you at this time of the mornin'." The voice came from a husky, broad-shouldered man in his fifties.

Annie's eyes adjusted to the man in the shadow of the door. "Seamus O'Connor, for God's sake come in out of the rain." She didn't give him a chance to answer. "Is it about Mick?"

"Annie, it's more about poor Ned Morriarty. Shure, we don't know where Mick is."

"I thought he was with Ned!"

"I know that, Annie. That was earlier. I don't know if you knew or not, the revolution has started. Mick and Ned had a mission."

"Mission?" she echoed, mockingly. Slowly, she lowered herself to the edge of the used Chesterfield and held her hands to her head. "A mission?" She looked up. "Mick isn't a soldier, Seamus. Maybe they're at Ned's house."

"No, Annie. We're shure Ned's been picked up by the British."

"Oh, Holy Mother of God." She stared down at the old black and white kitchen tile, fixated by the pattern. "They'll hang him won't they, Seamus? His poor mother," she uttered softly. After a short silence she continued, "What'll I do without Mick?" She put her hands over her ears and cried.

Seamus put his hand on her shoulder. "Annie, I'll get you word of Mick as soon as I hear something."

In an appreciative gesture, she placed her hand over his. Looking up at him, she whispered, "Thanks, Seamus."

"Dia agus Muire agat, Annie," he said, leaving.

"And God be with you," she said.

CHAPTER FOUR
New York 1960

R IORDAN WAS BROUGHT back to reality by the voice on the other side of the confessional.

"Father? Father, that's all I have to confess."

Riordan's wandering thoughts of Ireland left him embarrassed; for a moment, he forgot what he was supposed to say.

"Father?" the voice asked again.

"Oh, er, yes," Riordan said. "And is that everything you have to confess?" He thought it a trite response.

"Yes, Father," the man responded. "As well as I can remember."

Riordan admonished the man for putting the illegal organization ahead of his family. "Now, make a good Act of Contrition."

The man recited a perfect Act of Contrition and Riordan responded, *"Ego te absolve in nomine Patris, et Filii, et Spiritus sancti,* Amen."

He absolved him, knowing that this poor soul had done nothing more than he himself might, had the shoe been on the other foot. Riordan pulled a handkerchief from the cuff of his cassock and wiped his brow. The unusually warm evening had him hoping the number of penitents would be few. He didn't have long to wait before the next confession.

The door opened and closed again. After allowing a moment, he once again pulled back the small door.

It was a woman's voice and she sounded apprehensive. "Padre, yo no me he confesado desde hace mucho tiempo," she began.

"Cuando fue su ultima confesion?" he asked.

"I really can't remember," she continued in Spanish. "At least since my confirmation." She was obviously nervous.

"The important thing is you are here now, but it would help if you could give me some idea of how long it has been," Riordan said.

"I would say about eight years, Father."

What crisis has to take place for someone to seek guidance from the confessional? Riordan questioned.

"I don't even know if I should be here now," she said.

"Of course you should be here. This is where a loving God would want you to be. Nobody is judgmental in a house of God. Try to relax and tell me everything that's on your mind."

"I'm pregnant, Father." Her impetuous response startled him.

"I see," he said. "Are you married?"

"No, Father. That's the problem."

"And what about the father of the child? Does he know?"

"He's married, Father!"

"I see. You are, of course, planning to have this baby?"

"Father, that's why I'm here. How serious a sin would it be if I didn't have the baby?"

Riordan paused before he answered. His thoughts turned to his own mother, who must have had the same ambivalent feelings about her pregnancy. Had she been counseled by a priest? Would he have asked his mother the same questions?

CHAPTER FIVE
Dublin, 1916

COLONEL ALBERT LYNCH was a wiry little man with glasses. In his middle sixties, his face was drawn and pale. Although he was slightly balding, his upper lip sported a bushy white mustache, yellowed from tobacco stains.

Since the outbreak of the war with Germany, Lynch had been stationed in Dublin, working with British Intelligence, a position he didn't much care for. He had become a policeman of sorts, investigating conspiracies against the Crown. In his mind, he had been trained for something more important, having to do with the real war. What he called *good intelligence gathering* he prayed would materialize before the war ended. In the meantime, he followed orders. He would be the best policeman that he could be. He had no quarrel with those Irish who joined the British regiments on the Western Front. On the other hand, the Irish Volunteer Army represented home rule and had to be eliminated. They'd gone too far this time. The recent Easter Uprising had lasted only three days, and he was proud of the part he'd played; however, he was not happy with the way it had been handled by what he sarcastically referred to as "The Irregular British Army." He understood that England couldn't afford to use real soldiers to oversee Ireland's dissidents, but this bunch of incompetent misfits was made up of prisoners given the option of serving their term or serving their country. He had heard rumors that some of them had been serving life sentences for murder.

God, what was the Army coming to? he thought. He took credit for the

Irish Volunteer Army surrender. After all, it was his department that had supplied the vital information that intercepted munitions storage areas.

He stood behind an old army-green metal desk, his diminutive body framed by a map of Dublin on the wall behind him. Large red circles ringed the General Post Office and the Four Courts where the Volunteer Army had taken its stand. He shuffled some papers on his desk and addressed the four men in the small, smoke-filled room. The men were all officers, recently assigned to Lynch's department.

"I have all your dossiers and have familiarized myself with your capabilities. The War Department isn't assuming for a moment that this Irish thing is over. We believe most of the ringleaders have been apprehended. However, it is the duty of this department to ensure that all who were responsible are brought to justice. The intelligence information secured by this department was directly responsible for suppressing this bloody uprising and we're going to make sure there are no further outbreaks. Those defiant arseholes may survive without their cabbage and potatoes, but they sure as hell couldn't fight a battle without ammo!"

"Excuse me, sir." The young officer with his hand raised was Lieutenant William Hamilton, a tall, blond man in his early twenties.

Lynch leaned forward, pointing with the baton. "You have a question?"

"Did the sinking of the Aud have something to do with the fact that they ran out of ammunition, sir?"

Colonel Lynch looked directly at the young officer. At first, the query seemed to offend him. He plucked a sheet of paper from the pile on the desk and studied it for a moment. Then the old man smiled wryly. "Lieutenant Hamilton, is it?"

"Yes, sir."

"I see here you're an American."

Hamilton nodded.

"Well, Lieutenant, given the fact that the sinking of the Aud was privileged information known only to high naval intelligence, I am, therefore, quite impressed with your question."

"Thank you, sir. Actually, I happened to read about the sinking in the *Times*."

The comment brought laughter, which was immediately halted by Lynch. "Nothing gets past our bloody press. I should have such good bloody people working for me. Go on, Lieutenant."

"Actually, sir, it was a couple of paragraphs in an obscure part of the paper. The story said that she was seized by one of our destroyers. It was a hunch on my part that she carried supplies for the rebels."

"And a jolly good one." Lynch continued, "The Aud carried twenty thousand guns, artillery and millions of rounds of ammunition. She was a German freighter flying a neutral flag. We also know that her destination was Queenstown, County Cork. Had this bounty landed in the hands of those bloody insurgents, it could have changed the tide of the Uprising. That brings us to your reason for being here." A melancholy twist touched his mouth. "The week before the attempted takeover, their assassination teams were almost too successful, and although many of them will hang this very week, most of the perpetrators were not caught. These rebel bastards had the right idea. By eliminating key British officers, the regular Army regiments would have no real leadership."

William Hamilton nodded in agreement. He reached down into his jacket pocket and produced a silver cigarette case. He spoke as he offered a Player to the Colonel. Lynch waved it away.

"May I?" Hamilton asked.

Lynch waved him on.

"I imagine this assignment is taking us undercover, sir." He seemed keen on the idea. He lit the cigarette and drew on it before continuing. "These killing squads must be part of the Volunteer Army. How about informants?"

Lynch leaned back and folded his arms. "So far, we have no leads. Let me advise all of you that this is not going to be a piece of cake. This bloody police force we have here is not making things any easier. Their indiscriminate mistreatment of the people, in general, has nurtured a strong disaffection toward all of us. Christ, you couldn't even bribe an Irishman these days with a lifetime supply of stout." He was openly pleased with his attempt at humor and made an effort to smile.

This relaxed the tension in the room and everyone laughed aloud.

One of the other three men in the room, a handsome, chisel-faced young man in his late twenties, raised his hand, introducing himself. "Captain Cronin, sir."

Lynch looked once again at the papers on his desk. "Ah, yes, Captain Cronin. You've been with the department quite a while."

"Going on five years, Colonel," he said, easing back on the Bentwood chair. "I gather our assignments are actually going to take us inside the movement? I guess that means acquiring a taste for stout."

"Don't try to keep up with these people. Remember, they've been drinking the stuff for a lifetime. My advice would be total abstinence." Lynch handed each man a nine-by-twelve envelope he produced from the stack of papers on the desk. "Here's the plan. Four of the conspirators are going to the gallows this week. Their remains will be picked up by relatives for the usual Catholic wake and burial. Each of you will attend the services of your selected subject as a friend of the deceased. Introduce yourself, particularly to close acquaintances of your dead host."

He paused for a moment, twisting the end of his bushy mustache. His penetrating eyes traversed each of the soldiers in the room, his voice more serious.

"We feel reasonably sure that those murdering bastards who got away will be in attendance and it's up to you and your good judgment to bring them to justice. Each envelope contains information pertaining to your newly found friend, along with your alias, background and how you met the deceased."

While Lynch sipped his tea the others perused their portfolios.

When the World War broke out in 1914, William Armstrong Hamilton was graduating from Cambridge. He was an only child, but not spoiled. On the contrary, his parents had shown him little affection. His father, a mathematics teacher from Scotland, had immigrated to America in 1890. A man with wide interests, Basil Warwick Hamilton had a great mathematical faculty, took pleasure in the arts, had a love for classical architecture, and was extraordinarily eloquent. He possessed extremely high standards and had no patience for those he referred to as dimwitted, who by most people's standards, might have been ordinary indeed. He had no time for religion, but was understanding of those who did. He chose Harvard to teach and after a year's trial, decided to stay on. He soon met and fell in love with Sarah Armstrong, another teacher, who, like himself, was blessed with a remarkable intelligence and whose background was Celtic.

They had everything in common except religion, which they agreed to discuss without quarrelling over their differences. Sarah was a devout Presbyterian. She was ten years his senior and seemed destined for spinsterhood, had it not been for his proposal of marriage, which she graciously accepted. Shortly after, William Hamilton was planned and in October of the following year, they were blessed with what they'd always hoped for, an heir.

William was a perfect son, showing an inclination for mathematics and logic at an early age. He sailed through his studies at Choate, the prep school, where he was also an outstanding athlete. Throughout his childhood, affection missing in his relationship with his parents was offset by mutual respect. When the time came to choose a college, it would be William's decision. This is what his education had been about, making choices. Good choices, he hoped. His father was delighted at the possibility of William's attending Harvard, but in the tradition of his mother's family, he chose Cambridge in England. He strongly supported England's views on the war and came to despise his own country's isolationism. William Armstrong Hamilton, doing what many other Americans had done, entered the war under the British flag. Because of his quick wit and analytical mind, he was a natural for the Intelligence Branch. A shade under six feet, blond and blue-eyed, with a clean-cut, boyish look, he disarmed the suspicious.

After leaving his small flat on Wicklow Street, he walked a short distance before turning onto Grafton Street. He had selected a dark wool suit for his meeting with the priest. It was five o'clock and the street was alive with people returning home from work. These were troubled times in Dublin and the stress showed on the faces of every passerby. At the bottom of Grafton Street, he boarded the tramcar, ascended the serpentine metal stairs and sat on the open-topped deck. The tram moved slowly. The cool spring breeze was refreshing. His senses were awakened by the sounds of the city, and as the tram rattled over the Carlisle Bridge, he could tell that the tide had ebbed in the Liffy by the pungent odor of seaweed.

The tram hummed and Hamilton thought about his new identity as Liam Riordan. His orders had indicated that he was to meet a Father Michael Donnelly. He had memorized a copy of the letter that had been sent to the priest from headquarters, announcing his arrival. Father Donnelly was going to preside at Ned Morriarty's funeral. There would be a wake, and no doubt he would be there, as would Hamilton.

The parish house in Clontarf had been easy to find, just a few short blocks from where the tram dropped him off. It was a large, two-story, white-stucco house with a black-slate roof. The gray-haired lady who opened the door showed Hamilton into the rectory's parlor. The room, simply appointed, smelled of polish. He walked around the room with his hands behind his back, picturing Father Donnelly.

Father Donnelly moved swiftly into the room. "Good morning." The husky voice made Hamilton jump.

Hamilton moved forward to meet him, his hand swallowed up by the grip of the older man. "My name's Liam Riordan, Father. I trust you received my letter?"

"Indeed, I did, but I'm not sure if I can be of any help, Mr. Riordan." Father Donnelly gestured to a chair. "Please, have a seat."

Hamilton sat down and automatically reached for the silver case. "May I?" He offered the open case to the priest.

"Of course you may. Oh, American. I'd love one."

The men lit up and Hamilton lied to the priest about his grandfather leaving Ireland during the famine and how his job as a magazine writer afforded him the opportunity to come to Ireland and gather information about his family ties here.

"So, is it a story on the Uprising you're doin', or getting in touch with your past?"

"I hope to do both, Father."

"Riordan, Riordan. Well, now, there are a few Riordans around here." Donnelly stroked his chin reflectively.

"My Grandfather was an only child, so I doubt that I have any close relatives," Hamilton said.

"And you say he left during the Potato Famine?" Donnelly inquired. "Shure, we almost lost the whole Irish nation, Mr. Riordan. Lucky for you, at least he made it out of Ireland. You wouldn't be here talkin' to me now, would you? Ah, heart of God, it wasn't the best of times, was it?"

He went on, pouring a generous amount of sherry into his glass. "Would you join me in a little sherry? D'ya mind if I call you Liam?"

"I'd like that, Father. Both, that is."

The men shared a pack of cigarettes and a carafe of Ecclesiastical Sherry, which hastened the friendship. Donnelly expressed his views on the Irish Troubles with the young visitor and left little doubt where his allegiances lay. He told the younger man that he had already been chastised by his Bishop for his outspoken criticism of the British. Hamilton was beginning to question whether Lynch had a file on the priest.

His mission to attend the wake of Ned Morriarty was progressing more smoothly than he expected. The priest seemed genuinely impressed with his sympathy toward the patriots and abhorrence of the British.

"I read in this morning's paper about the execution of a young man," Hamilton said, casually. "Ned Morriarty, I believe?"

"Ah, dear God, isn't that an awful thing," Donnelly said wearily. "As a matter of fact, we'll be saying a rosary for him in the morning."

"And I suppose an Irish wake following?" Hamilton asked.

"Have you ever been to one?" Donnelly perked up.

"Can't say I have," Hamilton conceded. "I'm not a Catholic."

"Being Catholic isn't a prerequisite," the priest said soberly, consuming the last of the sherry. "Yer on then, Liam," he said, scratching the address on a sheet of parish stationery.

Kathleen brushed by Father Donnelly on her way through the room. She had glanced at the tall, handsome stranger Father had with him. *Must be one of Father's drop-ins,* she thought. Father was often host to visitors from America and it was not unusual for him to bring them with him, even to a wake.

"Kathleen," Donnelly said. "I'd like you to meet Liam Riordan from America. He's visiting Dublin for a while. He's doing research on Ireland and I thought we'd begin with some of the sadder aspects."

"Pleased to meet you, Mr. Riordan."

He held her small outreached hand. "Liam, please."

"As you can see, she's a portrait of Irish beauty," Donnelly said, indulgently. Hamilton smiled and acknowledged with a discrete nod.

Not wanting to appear shy, she said, "Have you been in Ireland a while then?"

"Arrived in Dublin just last week."

"I'm afraid you didn't catch us on our best behavior, Liam Riordan." She politely excused herself and hurried outside with her friends, Sean and Bridget McIntee.

"She's a little shy, our Kathleen," Donnelly said to Hamilton. "And her da keeps a close watch on her. She's a beauty, though, and innocent in the ways of men, a state of grace I think her da wishes to preserve."

Mick stood alone, looking down at Ned. They had made arrangements for Ned in the parlor. The room was small, and the coffin, supported by two small end-tables, was directly in front of the hearth. The only light came from the four blessed candles lined up behind the coffin. A small lace-covered table displayed some of Ned's personal possessions. Mick looked sadly at the picture of his friend, the wide, toothy grin and that devilish gleam in his eyes. Mick's eyes traversed to the chalky-faced man in the coffin. The face didn't seem content, as most do after a trip to the undertaker. The large, tanned hands that had once wielded a hurley stick were now white and folded in prayer across his chest. Mick placed his right hand over Ned's. A tear had just appeared when Mick felt a strong hand on his shoulder. Mick wiped away the tear before turning around.

"Don't worry, Mick," said Father Donnelly. "Shure, isn't he in the palm of God's hand this very moment."

"Ah, Father Donnelly. I was just saying my goodbyes." He was embarrassed about his moist eyes. He looked beyond the priest to the stranger.

"Meet Liam Riordan. He's an American."

Hamilton was impressed with Barrett's strong handshake.

Mick pulled a white handkerchief from his pocket and blew his nose.

"You must have been very close," Hamilton said.

Mick nodded. "Indeed," he said.

"I understand he was killed by the British, Mr. Barrett."

"He was indeed. Hanged," Mick said, guardedly. "You can call me Mick. So, you're an American?"

"Yes, originally from Connecticut and recently from Boston."

"Ah, Boston! Shure, I'd love to be able to take the family there someday, maybe even emigrate."

"And who'd be left to take up the fight for freedom?" Hamilton said, putting his hand on Mick's shoulder.

Mick smiled, appreciatively. "Indeed," he muttered and wandered off toward the pantry for a Powers.

Hamilton made a mental note of his first suspect.

"I'll introduce you around a bit, then I'll leave you to your own fate."

Hamilton followed the priest through the crowded house. He raised his voice over the music. "Presbyterian funerals are certainly different than this."

"This has more to do with being Irish, Liam. Shure, I've been to Presbyterian funerals with the same wake."

On the way to the kitchen they passed a table, straining under the weight of the food. Nora McIntee was busy directing the final resting place for the large keg of Guinness. Her son, Sean, with the help of Seamus O'Connor, wrestled the heavy liquid to the countertop in the pantry.

"There, Ma. How's that?" Sean asked.

"Just make shure to hang a bucket on the spigot before you leave. We wouldn't want to lose a drop now, would we?" she said, with a wide, toothless grin.

Donnelly introduced his new friend.

She dry-washed her boney hands and apologized, then she curtsied. "Nora McIntee. Pleased to meet you, sir."

"Nora owns *The Patriot Game*, a pub on Camden Street," Donnelly said. "It would be a great spot for you to learn more about the troubles, if you know what I mean."

"It's my pleasure, Mrs. McIntee," Hamilton bowed. "And I suppose your husband is leaving you to do all the work?" he asked, anxious to meet as many men as possible.

"Dead," she said matter-of-factly, wiping the spigot.

"Nora's husband, Peter—God rest his soul—died of a heart attack just six months ago," Donnelly intervened.

"I'm sorry," Hamilton said.

She smiled vacantly. "Shure, I've been tellin' everyone it was the Guinness that led to his demise—that's how we found him, anyway—in a great pool of Guinness." She turned to the priest. "I swear to God, Father, shure, I think he drowned in the stuff." She expressed her gratification for at least having her children, Sean and Bridget, to comfort her.

Mick drank heavily, looking in occasionally on Ned and picturing himself lying there. He made one of his many toasts that night. "To Ned Morriarty, God rest his soul. A true patriot and martyr to the cause."

"Humph," Molly Elliot muttered from the kitchen. "A dead patriot and but for the grace of God, you'd be there too, Mick Barrett." Molly couldn't look Annie in the eye. She was still angry with Mick for putting her family in jeopardy.

After getting some fresh air, Kathleen returned to the kitchen to find her mother. Her friend, Bridget McIntee, was close behind her.

"Can I help, Ma?" She asked.

Annie was busy washing dishes. "No thank you, child." She preferred to be busy. It helped her keep her mind off Ned and how easily it could have been her Mick lying there with him. And for what? It had failed, like she knew it would. And they were no better off for it.

"Go, Kathleen," she said. "Father Donnelly has a young man he wants you to meet."

"I've already met him," said Kathleen, blushing for a second time.

"Well, go then and join the dancers. Dance with poor Sean. He's been lookin' for a dance since you arrived."

Hamilton, becoming more self-assured, moved over to the pantry to pour himself a drink. He carefully measured a jigger of Powers and added as much water.

A group of men was standing close by. Hamilton had met most of the men earlier and was now close enough to overhear the conversation. He worried about hovering too closely and decided to revisit the dancers.

"Hey, Liam." It was Mick Barrett, his chin wet from the stout. "C'mere, Liam," he slurred. "I'd like ya to meet a few o' the lads."

Hamilton was glad for the opportunity. He nodded to those he had met earlier.

Seamus O'Connor and John Murphy acknowledged by raising their pints.

Bill Elliot moved toward Hamilton. "I haven't had the pleasure," he said, extending his hand. "Bill Elliot."

"Liam Riordan," Hamilton responded, likewise, to the firm handshake.

"He's American," said Mick. "All the way from New York."

"Boston," Hamilton corrected.

Seamus O'Connor didn't remember shaking Hamilton's hand and

shook it again vigorously. "Shure, Mick here has relatives in America," O'Connor slurred. He turned back to Barrett. "Isn't that right, Mick?"

"No, they're Annie's relations."

"What's their name again?"

"Fitzgeralds."

"D'ya know the Fitzgeralds in New York?" O'Connor asked Hamilton.

"Boston," Mick said into his ear.

"Boston, right, d'ya know them?"

"I don't think so," Hamilton said, apologetically.

Bill Elliot smiled at O'Connor's naiveté. "America's a big country, Seamus. Mr. Riordan can't be expected to know everyone." He turned back to Hamilton. "All the same, you're most welcome here, Liam. I am sad to say that your arrival finds the Irish people in very sad times, though."

"I hope the troubles settle soon," Hamilton said.

"Don't we all," said Mick, downing another swig of black stout.

"Are you staying here long then, Liam?" asked Murphy.

"Just long enough to finish a story I'm doing for a magazine back home."

"Oh, a writer," Mick's pronunciation was thick. "I hope —" He took time to swallow the stout, "that you describe us favorably."

"I'll make sure you're not disappointed, Mick."

Bill Elliot was wearing a Harris-tweed jacket with leather patches at the elbows, a fitting attire for his schoolmaster demeanor. "I suppose your article will cover our recent attempt to bring about an Irish Free State?" he asked Hamilton.

"That's what Americans are paying to read," Hamilton responded.

"There's a lot to write about," Bill said, lifting the glass to his mouth.

"Americans should be particularly interested in a story of independence. After all, it was just one hundred and fifty years ago that your country felt the same bitter enmity. And toward the same oppressor, I might add."

Mick raised his glass. "Here's to America," he said. "May Ireland one day..." He hesitated a moment, wanting to impress the American writer, "be emancipated."

"Here, here," they all said in unison, clinking their glasses.

Murphy drained his glass and refilled it from the keg. "Be Christ, I've been to three wakes in the past month. Shure, weren't we busy enough dying before the bleedin' English added to the mortality rate?" he said, filling the glass.

Thinking that he might have missed another wake, Seamus O'Connor was genuinely disappointed. "Anyone I knew, John?" he asked, as a drivel of stout ran down his broad chin.

"Ah, indeed ye did. Wasn't it auld Mister Gianelli?" Mick moved the pint to his left hand and blessed himself.

"Heart of God, Gianelli, the ice-cream man?"

"The very same," O'Connor said, piously. All three clinked their glasses.

Bill Elliot, not wishing to be left out, chimed in and nodded for Hamilton to do the same.

"Who are we toasting now?" Bill asked, smiling disingenuously.

"Gianelli, the ice-cream man. Here's to the auld Italian fart," Mick chuckled. He moved his head closer to them and whispered indiscreetly, "an' may he join his fukken nag in heaven."

Hamilton and Bill Elliot shrugged their shoulders as the other three roared. When the laughter waned, Elliot was eager to be included in their humorous secret. "I can't say I've ever heard of the man—Gianelli?"

Mick put the pint glass on the sideboard, needing both hands to tell the story. "He was an Italian from Swords. A grumpy, mean auld cur that wouldn't give ye a sniff of his ice-cream without copper."

Seeing the confused look, Elliot turned to Hamilton. "A penny," he said. "A 'copper' is a penny."

Hamilton produced a small note-pad from his inside pocket. "I don't want to miss anything."

"It was bleedin' tragic when it happened then, wasn't it, Mick?" Murphy said to them seriously.

"Ah, indeed it was, but didn't yer man deserve it."

"What happened?" Elliot asked.

"The auld bastard was a bit mean with the ice-cream," Mick began. "He used to sell all the way down the hill into Fairview. Shure, on a hot day ye could be dying of the thirst and he wouldn't give ye a lick, mind ye, without a penny."

"He was a right sod," Murphy said.

"Here, here," O'Connor agreed.

"Anyway," Mick continued. "One day—a real scorcher it was—the auld fella is coming back up the hill. The bleedin' auld nag is sweatin' an' fartin' like ye do after a night of the bevy. Anyway, John, Seamus here, and God rest his soul, poor Ned, and meself are watchin' the whole thing."

O'Connor interrupted, "Wasn't he beatin' the be Jasus out o' the auld horse. Remember, Mick?"

Mick reached for his glass. "An' who's tellin' the story anyway?"

"Go on, Mick," Elliot said. "We're all ears."

"Anyway," Mick continued. "The horse stopped in its tracks, let a couple of big rips and dropped."

"Dead?" Hamilton asked.

"Ah, indeed he wasn't. Not then, anyway. Just fatigued. Gianelli gets off his perch on the wagon and starts caressing the auld nag, pattin' her sweaty auld head and consolin' it in Italian. It was Ned that went over an' asked if there was anything he could do. Anyway, Ned suggests that he'll take care of the horse while Gianelli heads back down the hill looking for a vet. Meanwhile, the rest of us joined Ned. We opened the back doors of the wagon and we just ate everything in sight."

O'Connor chimed in. "It would have been a shame to waste it now, wouldn't it?" Mick gave him a look.

"Sorry, Mick."

"Anyway," Mick said. "After we'd had a few cones, we unharnessed the exhausted auld nag and carried her off up the hill to Donnycarney." Mick was beginning to laugh again. "Jasus, we had a divil of a time gettin' her up the hill. Ned was holdin' up the arse-end. Half the bleedin' time we didn't understand what he was sayin'."

All three men began to laugh.

O'Connor took the opportunity to interrupt. "Ned's voice was muffled 'cause his head was up the auld nag's arsehole."

Mick continued, "There wasn't a soul around so we laid the auld nag to rest in the chapel vestibule, where she finally died."

Now Elliot and Hamilton began to chuckle.

"Ned got back to the horseless wagon before Gianelli. Later, the Italian returns with a bleedin' vet and sees the horse gone." Mick looked piously toward the parlor. "Ned—God rest his soul—tells Gianelli that the horse stood up, like some kind of miracle. He tells Gianelli with a straight face that a sign from God suggested he unharness the horse, an' like a divine intervention, the horse proudly raises its head and cantors up the hill toward Donnycarney."

"What happened? Did they find the horse?" Hamilton asked.

"Ah, indeed they did, an' wasn't Father Lane there an' all. Recitin' a litany, they were, to Saint Francis." O'Connor's whole body jiggled when he laughed. "They held a special Mass that evening in honor of the fukken nag. Later, Gianelli donated a stained-glass window of Saint Francis in commemoration of the horse. Ah, what irony indeed. Shure, I heard that he sank his life's savin's on the fukken stained-glass."

"Anyway," Mick said seriously. "He's dead. The auld fukker's dead."

"Did anyone ever find out?" Hamilton asked.

"Find out what?" Mick asked with a wry smile.

"I certainly never heard that one before," Elliot said, shaking his head.

"The window's there, isn't it?" Murphy asked.

"Let's not be forgettin' what we're here for," said Seamus.

Mick looked sad again. "Right," he said. "Here's to Ned Morriarty."

The four men raised their glasses again.

"Hanged, he was, like a dog," Mick continued. "And with no benefit of a trial—and for what?"

Seamus answered, "Shootin' the enemy."

"Come on now, lads," Bill Elliot stepped between Seamus and Mick from behind and placed his hands on their shoulders. "Let's not bore our young American friend with nonessentials."

Hamilton felt good about his cover as a writer. Asking questions was something that came naturally to him, and so far, nobody seemed tight lipped. On the contrary, people were more than happy to share information, especially if they thought they were going to be quoted in an article.

"I want to write the truth about this rebellion," he said, looking at Mick. "I want the American people to feel the kind of oppression that Ireland is experiencing. You know, the men responsible." He paused. "What they're like—the human side."

"You should talk to Bill here," said Seamus. "He's our local historian. He teaches at the Damer."

Murphy piped in, mockingly, "That's a private school, no less."

"Good," Hamilton said with enthusiasm. "I'd really appreciate talking with you. If you don't mind, that is."

"My pleasure," Elliot responded. "How about this weekend?"

"Great," said Hamilton. "Shall we meet at your place then?"

Elliot took a piece of paper from his pocket and spoke as he scratched the address with his fountain pen.

"Saturday night. How does half-six sound to you, Liam?"

"Perfect," said Hamilton.

Hamilton thanked everyone and excused himself. The musicians were now playing *I'll Take You Home Again, Kathleen,* one of his father's favorites. He could overhear Father Donnelly's voice chanting a litany in the small parlor where Ned lay. A handful of women also knelt in front of the casket, their hands adorned with rosary beads and folded in prayer. They responded to the priest, "Hail Holy Queen, Mother of Mercy."

As he leaned against the alcove between the two rooms, Hamilton's attention turned to the dancers. He looked casually at the note in his hand: *29 York Street.*

He circumvented the dancers and drifted over to the musicians, where a small group had gathered and was singing. His gaze intently fixed on

Kathleen Barrett. She was waltzing with a lanky, pimple-faced youth who was holding her too tight. At every turn, she seemed to catch Hamilton's eye, transmitting sensual glances, or it seemed so to him. He questioned whether she was as innocent as Father Donnelly believed.

Bill Elliot came over to Hamilton. "I can see you have an eye for Irish beauty. That's Mick Barrett's daughter and that's Sean McIntee she's dancing with. His mother owns the pub on Camden Street. That's a great place for you to get some local color."

"They're going steady, then?" Hamilton inquired.

"God no, man," said Elliot. "They're just childhood chums. Their families have been friends for years. She's beautiful, isn't she?" He continued, "Why not ask her for a waltz?"

Hamilton was a little startled. He didn't realize he had been that transparent. If he let his feelings for the girl show, how obvious to them was his masquerade as a writer?

"Go on, Liam! Give the girl a dance," urged Bill.

"I thought you said Mick kept a close watch on her?" Hamilton said quizzically.

"He does. But you being Father Donnelly's guest and all, I'm sure Mick wouldn't mind a dance or two, with his daughter that is."

The waltz stopped and Kathleen linked up with her friend Bridget. More than once, she seemed to catch his glance.

Urged on by Bill, Hamilton approached her. "Excuse me, Miss Barrett, er, would you like to dance?"

Startled, but delighted by the request of the handsome stranger, Kathleen nodded her consent and they took to the crowded floor.

When he placed his arm around her tiny waist, he felt her body quiver. That conveyed for him the ultimate expression of confidence. It seemed as if an electric current had passed between them.

"I hope your father doesn't mind the dance, but Mr. Elliot thought it would be all right, since I came with Father Donnelly."

Blushing, Kathleen said she thought Mr. Elliot was probably right.

Hamilton tried to engage Kathleen in small talk, but her answers were terse. He tried another approach. "Did you know Ned Morriarty very well?"

Kathleen replied, "Ned was mostly my father's friend."

Hamilton thought her comment was useful. But his mind wasn't on the questions he was asking. He was busy appreciating her beauty.

"Oh, fishing buddies were they?" he asked nonchalantly.

"Well, not exactly," Kathleen replied. "What brings you to Ireland at such terrible times?" she asked, changing the subject.

She looked up at him and her long black hair brushed his hand at her waist. He was startled at the sensuousness of the feel and found it difficult to concentrate on her question. *She is an innocent girl with an overprotective father and here I am getting lightheaded simply from the feel of her hair.* As they moved, her loose-fitting dress had a tendency to slip under his fingers, leaving his imagination to fill in the outlines of the young, firm body.

"Excuse me, what did you say?"

"I asked, 'What brings you to Ireland?'" Kathleen repeated her question.

"Oh, I'm writing an article on Ireland and its troubles for the people in America. Americans are sympathetic to the Irish cause."

"Is that so?" said Kathleen, looking up at him with the most beautiful blue eyes Hamilton could remember seeing.

"I'd love to have a young lady's opinion of the uprising," Hamilton said. "You'd be perfect."

"Not really," Kathleen said, blushing. She didn't know how to respond. "I don't pay that much attention to war and those things," she said demurely. She looked up at him again with those incredible eyes and bravely tried to change the conversation. "What does your family think of you coming over all this way?" she asked.

"I didn't think to ask them," he said.

She wished that the dance would end so she could politely excuse herself and go to the safety of the kitchen, yet another side of her hoped the dance would never end. She felt so sophisticated and grown up dancing with this incredibly handsome man. She could feel Bridget's penetrating look from across the room. She knew Bridget McIntee would question her relentlessly the minute she left the floor, demanding to know everything that had been said between the two.

"On the other hand, my father thinks that this trip was just what I needed," Hamilton said, continuing to answer her question. "I'm sure that deep down he hopes I will become a professor like most of the men in my family. He thinks I'll be ready to settle down when I get home from this assignment—marriage maybe."

"There's a girl back home then?"

"Not yet." He was elated that she appeared pleased. "Enough about me." Drawing back and looking down into her small, innocent face, he asked, "What about you? I mean, what do you do during the day? School? Work?"

"Actually, I'm a student nurse." She appeared more comfortable now. They could talk about something she understood.

"A nurse," he repeated, impressed. "Well, now, I'm surprised all young Dublin men aren't feigning some malady or other." Smiling, he continued, "You could take care of me any day."

She blushed a little and pulled back. "You keep that up, Mr. Riordan, and me da will make all your dreams come true."

They both laughed and drew closer.

A corpulent couple bumped the waltzing pair and sent them even closer together. She blushed to the roots of her hair. Hamilton was unnerved at his reaction when her firm breasts brushed up against his chest. *My God*, he thought, *I'm worse than a schoolboy on his first date. Why is she affecting me this way? I should be getting all the information I can and instead I'm giddy when she accidentally bumps into me.*

During the rest of the dance, he was content to hold her at a discrete distance and listen to her unbridled enthusiasm of a free Ireland. The waltz ended, replaced by a single chant of the uilleann pipes. Kathleen hummed the tune as they walked toward the door.

"That's grand," he said. "What's that you're humming?"

"Oh, it's just a little Irish aire," she smiled. "I love it when played on the pipes."

"Does it have words?"

"Yes," she said, laughing. "Of course it has words."

"Well?" he asked. He didn't need to prompt her again.

Oh, the ring of the piper's tune,
Oh, for one of those hours of gladness,
Gone, alas, like my youth, too soon.

"That was beautiful," he said. "And sad."

"That's the Irish for ye," she said with a lilt. "Beautiful and sad."

Mystified by the spark they both felt, they looked away from each other's eyes.

"Would you like to join me for a bit of air?" he asked. "I'd still appreciate your point of view."

"I'd really like to, but I'd best help my ma in the kitchen."

"Some other time then," he said.

From the back of the room, a sullen Sean McIntee watched the two suspiciously. It was obvious from the look on his face that if he had any say, Kathleen wouldn't be dancing with this American, even if Father Donnelly did bring him.

Observing the two dancing, the priest thought her father was going to have difficulties in distancing men from such a beauty.

The following morning, Hamilton was awakened by the irritating sound of the alarm clock. Turning it off, he reached for a cigarette. One arm behind his head, he lay back and stared at the ceiling. Taking a deep drag on the cigarette, he blew smoke rings, one after the other. He felt good about himself. He had finagled his way into the wake of Ned Morriarty. He was surprised at his alertness, considering that he had spent most of the night preparing notes about the men at the wake. Still, a lot of the information was fragmentary. He looked forward to his meeting with Bill Elliot.

His thoughts turned to Kathleen Barrett. He was as impressed in the morning as he had been in the evening with her passionate devotion to Ireland and her desire to see it free. He was dancing again, the slow waltz, recapturing her springtime youthfulness—the sweet, pleasant odor of her body. He was displaying a complete lack of forethought and good sense. He had a meeting to get to.

He rubbed his face, questioning if it would be necessary to shave this morning. He wiped the sleep from his eyes and splashed cold water on his face. It would be all right to appear casual for his prearranged meeting at the Shelbourne Hotel. Hamilton had time to prepare his report for the Colonel. He had gleaned a wealth of information last night and narrowed his suspects down to three.

He reached the Shelbourne after a short walk. A young, rosy-cheeked pageboy opened the door for him. He was stunned by the lavish appointments in the lobby. As impressed as he was with the plush red carpet, his gaze was drawn to the extravagant gilded and cut-glass chandelier that hung in the foyer. The contrast with other parts of the city that lay in ruin was overwhelming. Snobbish-looking people in fine clothes moved about the lobby.

"May I help you, sir?" asked the hotel manager.

"I have a meeting with Mr. Lynch in the tea room," replied Hamilton.

"Yes, sir. He's expecting you. Right this way, please."

The colonel sat in a corner of the large room. In civilian clothes he looked every part the old landed squire, meeting a young companion for a spot of tea and innocent conversation. The toast and marmalade he had ordered was delivered on Wedgwood China, and the tea was poured from an ornate silver teapot.

Colonel Lynch stood up to greet him. They shook hands and sat down.

"Good morning, Hamilton," he said.

"Good morning to you, sir," Hamilton responded. "You look, well, let's just say **different**. At least, benevolent, out of uniform, sir."

"Don't let the civvies fool you, Mr. Hamilton. Now, I assume your meeting with the priest went well," Lynch said.

"Much better than expected, actually."

"Good! You got to the wake then?"

"Yes, as a matter of fact, it went quite well," Hamilton responded. "Friendly people, the Irish! They seem to have so much fun at a wake, I can't imagine the time they'd have at a wedding."

"Don't be deceived by their friendliness or their charity for a moment," the Colonel cautioned.

"But, they just seemed so warm and harmless, I suppose."

"Uh-huh, they're so bloody harmless, I'd like to show you what they did to Cronin," hissed Lynch, leaning closer.

"You mean Captain Cronin?" Hamilton spoke a little too loudly to be discreet.

"Not so bloody loud, man!" the colonel cautioned. "And remember, no mention of rank here."

Hamilton eased back in his chair, slightly embarrassed by his show of enthusiasm. "You were saying, sir?"

Lynch poured the tea. "I just came from seeing him. Actually, he's not a pretty sight."

"Then he's already—I mean, he's not..."

"Dead?" Lynch said, stirring three heaping spoonfuls of sugar in his cup, looking up at Hamilton. "Actually, he's quite dead. The Irish constabulary picked him up at Phoenix Park on a bench. They thought he was a vagrant and brought him into Mercer Street Hospital."

"Any chance he might have given them information on the rest of us?" Hamilton was stone-faced.

"No, at least not enough to do any damage. He had no knowledge of anyone's assignment but his own. I believe we're all right there." Lynch continued, "He died just before I got there. They knee-capped the poor bastard. One knee was shattered, just barely attached by a piece of white sinew. The other was completely gone. Then, the bastards shot him in the back of the head."

Hamilton looked pale. "And you're sure, sir, that he didn't jeopardize the mission?"

"Not much chance of that—him talking, I mean. Each of you has a new name, occupation, nationality and mission that only I'm privy to. Period." Lynch slathered marmalade on his toast with the deftness of a plasterer.

Hamilton lit a cigarette. "Why would they blow off his kneecaps?"

"Seems to be their signature. They just strap you down in a chair, like your electric chair back home, I would imagine," he said sarcastically.

Hamilton winced at the colonel's callous attitude. "I think I get the picture."

"It's for your benefit, Hamilton, that I illustrate the *whole* picture," Lynch muttered, extending his finger. "Bang," he said. "At point-blank range, they blow off your bloody kneecaps."

Lynch was staring down at a Player that he was preparing to light. "Now, back to you. What have you found out so far? What about the wake for this arsehole—what was his name?"

"Morriarty. Ned Morriarty," Hamilton said. "And I'm sure his partner was there at the wake."

"Morriarty," Lynch said. His head raised slightly toward the ceiling and he exhaled smoke through his tight lips. "Morriarty. Yes, now I remember. There were two assassins in that case."

"That's right."

Lynch seemed happy now with his ability to recall all the information. "Morriarty was caught at Stephen's Green." He pointed out the window to the park across the street. "Actually, just over there someplace," he said. "The other fellow disappeared by the College of Surgeons."

He thought for a moment and both men said in unison, "York Street."

Hamilton extinguished the cigarette.

"I have a meeting next Saturday night with a Bill Elliot. He was at the wake; he's a friend of Morriarty and guess where he lives?"

"Don't tell me. York Street? Great work!" said Lynch, enthusiastically.

Lynch left a shilling on the table and both men walked toward the door.

"How do you like your flat?" Lynch asked casually.

"Flat!" said Hamilton, raising his eyes. "Are we talking about the same place? I'm not sure that a bedroom and kitchenette qualify as a flat. Besides, I thought I was a big-shot writer for an American magazine."

The same pageboy opened the door for both men.

"Well, now," said Lynch. "Let's just say that you're not such a hotshot, and the magazine is a second-rate publication."

They both laughed, and after making arrangements for their next meeting, walked in different directions.

The Canal Cafe was a small, continental-style restaurant with outside tables and umbrellas. The Baggett Street Canal was across the street. A small pathway for pedestrians at the water's edge was separated from the roadway by a beautiful tree-lined greenbelt. It was noontime and the weather was sunny. Kathleen and Bridget usually went there for lunch. Mercer Street Hospital was a short bicycle ride to the cafe. Bridget, just a year older than Kathleen, worked at a nearby hotel in the kitchen. They had been close friends since grammar school and shared everything. Bridget was far more knowledgeable in the ways of the world than Kathleen. Living above the pub provided her with an unrefined, crude wisdom that sometimes bewildered Kathleen. They sat outside in the noonday sun and ordered two lemonades.

"Well?" Bridget probed eagerly.

"Well," Kathleen responded.

She knew that Bridget would want to hear every intimate detail of the short time she had spent with the handsome American. Bridget was easily tantalized and Kathleen liked to arouse her curiosity. "C'mon, c'mon, I know you like him." Bridget was leaning across the table now, eager to hear all the little intimacies of Kathleen's licentiousness.

Kathleen moved closer to Bridget and clasped her hands. "I liked him. We danced. We talked about his work, that's it!" said Kathleen.

"You can't fool me, Kathleen Barrett. You danced twice and his hands were *all over you*. He wanted to get into your knickers. I think it was obvious to a few people. I know my brother was just a little infuriated."

"Oh, Bridget. You're exaggerating again. We were just dancing, and besides, Sean and I are just friends."

"Friends, is it?" Bridget's voice was melodic. "That's not how Sean feels." Her voice lowered as she drew Kathleen closer. "He's in love," she snickered. "Remember when we were kids and me ma caught him hangin' from the gutter just to get a look at ye? And just the other day when you came by the pub, he was outside, an' I wouldn't dream of tellin' ye what he was doin' to yer bicycle seat! I'm telling ye, the lad's in love."

Kathleen drew back and took a sip on her lemonade. "Is that what you think love is, Bridget? Sniffing bicycle seats and peeping in bathroom windows? I think that's crude and adolescent."

"You don't have to convince me," said Bridget. "Shure, I'd take the American any day. He reminded me of Adonis, you know, that Greek god." She hesitated for a moment. "How was it—dancing close an' all?"

The cafe was getting busier. Patrons were enjoying their Dublin coddle and open-faced ham sandwiches. A barge floated by on the narrow canal. The girls had become more discreet.

Kathleen whispered. "Okay, Bridget. I like the way he treated me. Like an adult, I mean, and you know what?"

Bridget moved her chair a little closer.

"I really think he likes me," Kathleen continued.

"Well, then, did he ask you out?" said Bridget.

"Well, not in so many words. He did say that he'd like to continue our conversation sometime."

Bridget was eager to hear everything. She spoke seriously to Kathleen now. "Sounds like an opportunity to me. I overheard Molly Elliot talking to him at the wake. I know that he was invited to dinner Saturday night."

"You know, he did mention that. Wouldn't I love to be a mouse in the corner."

Bridget thought for a moment. "Why be a mouse, when you can be yourself?"

She moved closer to Kathleen and shared in the grand plan for Kathleen's appearance at the Elliot place Saturday night.

It was six-fifteen and Hamilton was concerned that he was running late. He was dressed casually for his evening meeting with Bill Elliot.

The tall, red-bricked Georgian buildings blocked the rays of the evening sun. The buildings were joined like row houses, and wrought-iron railings surrounded the open basement areas, which were used as latrines by the younger residents.

Hamilton genuinely liked Bill Elliot from the first moment they'd met. It was difficult for him to believe that he could shoot someone. It seemed more likely that Elliot might harbor an assassin. He was sure of one thing: York Street was pertinent to his investigation.

Molly answered the door. She couldn't have been more hospitable. Reaching out to Hamilton with both hands, she pulled him inside. "So nice of you to come," she said.

"And thank you for the invitation," he answered.

As Hamilton entered, Bill Elliot was hastily moving toward him. "Welcome, Liam. Or, as we say in Gaelic—'caed mile failte'—a hundred thousand welcomes. Our home is ever so humble, but Molly here is the best cook in Dublin." He smiled at Molly. "Shure, I love it myself when we have guests." He backed off defensively, "It's the only time we eat well!"

"And you'll be doin' the dishes for that remark," she said. Engaging Hamilton with a look of confidentiality, she continued, "Besides, Bill will probably bore you to sleep with his solutions to Ireland's discontent."

Hamilton, his hands now in his pockets, was moving toward the mantel. "We'll just have to see which of us falls asleep first, then," he responded.

Molly left the men and returned to the large, lace-covered kitchen table. She wanted to impress their young guest from America. Meticulously, she began to arrange her favorite china setting.

"Great old photos," Hamilton said. He picked one up for a closer look. "Your parents?" He was looking at Bill for a resemblance.

"My mother and father," he said, pouring some whiskey and passing a glass to Hamilton. "He was English, a barrister just out of university. After marrying my mother, a Dublin girl, he became very attached to the Irish people. He never returned to England."

Hamilton let the Powers embrace his taste buds before swallowing. He shuddered slightly. "My parents are also devoted to the old country," he lied. "What brought your father to Ireland, Bill?"

"As I said, my father was a young barrister. You call them lawyers."

Hamilton nodded and Bill continued.

"He was hired by an Irish family from Liverpool to represent their son back in Ireland. It was a long time ago," he said remotely.

"When did all of this take place?" Hamilton asked.

"It would have been about the same time that your country was recovering from the Civil War."

Hamilton searched for his cigarettes. "So he came here and stayed?"

"Here, let me." Elliot offered Hamilton a Woodbine. Both men lit up. "Yes," Elliot said on a stream of smoke. "He stayed, but not before trying his damndest to clear the young man who was accused of conspiracy and treason. He was a Fenian. Another uprising bent on a do-or-die pledge to free Ireland. I imagine most of them would have considered it a privilege to die for freedom."

He poured both of them another drink.

"Maybe I should be writing, or taking notes." Hamilton had brought along a small notebook and looked all the part of a reporter. He placed the old photo back with the other mementos on the mantelpiece and seated himself in a worn, overstuffed chair. "This young man, then, was being tried for treason? And your father represented him? Was that difficult for your father? I mean, an Englishman representing an Irishman?"

Elliot shook his head. "Not really. Actually, the lad's family and my father thought that it might do some good."

"And did it?" Hamilton asked.

There was a pause. "Not really, Liam," he said, swallowing the last of the whiskey in his glass. "They hanged him. Oh, I dare say, they could have given him life, but no. Hanged him like a dog. 'A public hanging to set an example,' they said."

Hamilton stopped writing and looked up at Elliot, who was staring down into the fireplace. "And what about his family? They must have been devastated."

"Devastated," Elliot said. "The boy was only fifteen."

Hamilton shook his head despondently. "And your father?" he asked.

"Well, I guess the trial lasted longer than most and Father hadn't exactly spent all of his waking hours devoted to the trial. He lost his first case and met his first love. A Dublin girl. She was a beauty. Anyway, to cut a long story short, they got married and I came along. But, enough about me. You have an article to write and I'm sure your readers don't want to hear this dribble."

"So, this Easter Uprising is nothing new? There have been other attempts to separate from England?"

Elliot nodded, his mouth turning to a half-hearted smile. "The same problems we're experiencing today have plagued Ireland for centuries. In the eighteen hundreds it was the Fenian movement and before that it was Sarsfield and James the Second fighting together for the cause against William. And just a few weeks ago, the Irish Volunteers."

"And another failure for Ireland," Hamilton said.

"Not necessarily." Elliot placed his glass on the mantel and with both hands in his pockets, moved up and down slowly on his toes. He was pensive. "I really do believe that in order to completely subjugate the Irish, the intention was to keep them poor by crushing every iota of natural enterprise. Every scholarly instinct had to be repressed to a state of servile indignation."

Hamilton noticed that with each sip of whiskey, Elliot became more eloquent.

He brought the pen to his mouth and asked, "And having spent just a short time with these people, that doesn't sound like an easy task. If you don't mind me saying so, they seem a bit stubborn. You can't dominate people like that, can you?"

Elliot shook his head. "You'd have to abolish an entire culture as if it didn't exist." He paused and smiled. "Yes, they are hard-headed and every hard-head is filled with a dream of freedom. Basically, take away a people's faith. Can you imagine not being able to practice your beliefs? Take away your land. Take away your language, your games…"

"But, you're not Catholic, are you?" Hamilton asked.

"Actually, I was raised Presbyterian. I have been shamming the Irish for years. Since I don't attend church anymore, all my friends think I'm an atheist." He smiled, "And, for my benefit, a misconception I plan to perpetuate."

"You mean, you're better off an atheist than a Protestant?"

Bill sighed, "Oh, I don't really take it too seriously. I just seem to enjoy the whole idea that I'm not who they really think I am." He paused, then looking directly into Hamilton's eyes, said, "Do you ever do that, Liam? Pose as someone you're not?"

Although Hamilton was writing, another part of his brain was forcing his gestures and his facial expression to react casually to the question. "I suppose we've all had a predisposition to be something or someone we're not."

They talked about Ireland's perpetual rule by invaders: Danes, Norsemen, and now the British.

Elliot raised his head back. He inhaled deeply, refilled the glasses and was about to say something when Molly's ill-timed announcement punctuated the silence.

"Dinner's ready."

When all three were seated, Molly said grace and served the food. Not much was discussed about the troubles. The conversation revolved mostly around the Elliot boys, Frank and Jerry. Hamilton was impressed. He had not eaten this well since he'd left home. Lucky the plates were large because Molly's servings were generous. Three large boiled potatoes were served in a white-cream sauce with parsley, along with steak and kidney pie, fresh green peas dotted with small chips of carrot and finely chopped onions. The small, piping-hot cake, Molly explained, was Yorkshire Pudding. Hamilton was ravenous and savored every mouthful. He was granted permission to clean his plate with a piece of buttered soda bread.

He raised his glass of wine toward Molly. "My compliments to the chef."

Elliot nodded in agreement and the crystal glasses chimed together. "And here's to our guest, William," he said.

Hamilton was momentarily startled. *Jesus, he knows who I am.* He desperately searched for the right words. Had he heard Bill Elliot clearly? He had called him William.

Bill Elliot, seeing Hamilton's confusion with the toast, said, "Is something wrong, Liam? I just called you William and you look like you've been run over by a lorry."

"Oh, no, er, you just caught me off guard." He smiled nervously as he continued, "Why did you call me William?"

"Because that's your name, man. The same as mine—Bill—William and in Gaelic, it's Liam. My God, didn't anyone tell you? Surely your parents would have told you." Elliot smiled. "Amazing," he said, looking at Molly. "Imagine going through life not knowing that your Gaelic name had an English counterpart."

Molly patted a nervous Hamilton on the shoulder. "Oh, not to worry, Liam, isn't it the Gaelic that's important anyway."

Hamilton smiled on the outside. Inside, he was furious. *Why in God's name didn't those assholes back in intelligence tell me that the new name they gave me was my own name in Gaelic? Jesus, what a stupid mistake!* he thought.

Elliot changed the subject and offered Hamilton a drink. "Did you meet the rest of the family at the wake? The boys, that is?"

"Yes, I did," said Hamilton, recovering slightly with a swig of whiskey. "Fine lads you have there. I feel bad that the boys missed a great dinner. I hope their absence isn't because of my being here."

"Not at all, Liam," Molly said. "They're staying the night with their friends, the Barrett boys. You may have met them at the wake."

"Oh, yes. Mick Barrett is their father," Hamilton said, taking advantage of the opportunity to talk about Barrett. "He was a good friend of the deceased."

"A couple of book-ends," Elliot said, reflectively rolling his last drop of whiskey around in the glass. "Best of friends."

"'Course, weren't we all," Molly popped back into the conversation.

Hamilton didn't want to lose the moment. "Ned Morriarty, he was executed for killing a British officer? At least that's what I heard someone say at the wake."

"I believe he confessed to doing that, all right."

"I heard that the British were looking for an accomplice. Actually, I hear that the shooting took place not far from here." Hamilton felt that it was appropriate to ask these questions. After all, he was the writer.

"Somewhere up on Harcourt Street, I believe," Elliot said. "That's where they shot him."

"They? Ned wasn't alone?"

"No, he wasn't," Elliot said. "'Course, that's common knowledge now."

"Have you known Mick for long?" Hamilton was pushing the question.

"Not really. The young lads are close, what with school and all. It was the first time we'd seen them in a long time—at Ned's wake," he lied.

Hamilton noticed Molly's concern as she left the table. "I guess I'll just pick up the delph, while you two make yourselves comfortable," she said.

Hamilton returned to the same comfortable easy chair that he had occupied before dinner. He eased himself into the chair with a sigh.

"Without a doubt, that was the best meal I've ever tasted. I guess I made a bit of a pig of myself."

What was left of the bottle of Powers was now being poured into the two glasses. Hamilton silently scolded himself for being careless with the drinking. Colonel Lynch's words of wisdom began to haunt him. They had all been cautioned at their first meeting. *Don't try to keep up with these people when it comes to drinking.* He glanced down at his watch.

"I really should be getting along. It's half past eight already," he said, as he stood up.

Molly was coming toward the men with a fresh pot of tea and some cups on a tray. "I've made some tea for the both of you," she said, placing the tray on the end of the table.

"Now, you can't leave," Elliot gestured the young man back to the chair. "Besides, you haven't yet tasted the afters that Molly's prepared."

Hamilton sat back down, reluctantly. "Afters?" he questioned.

"I'm sorry, I believe you call it dessert."

"Oh, it's just a little bairin breac and a spot of tea. It's really quite refreshing after dinner," Molly said as she poured. The sound of the tea being poured was interrupted by a knock on the door. "See who that is, will you dear?"

Bill promptly moved toward the door. "That's probably nosey McDade from upstairs. I'm sure he's just curious about our American guest," Elliot said. "Kathleen?" He opened the door wider. "Come in. Whatever brings you here tonight?"

"I'm sorry to bother you," she said with self-reproach. "I just got off work and thought I'd stay tonight at Bridget's. I had a bit of an accident with the bicycle."

"Accident?" he said, considerately.

"Oh, it's nothing—just the chain. It came off and I was hoping that maybe Frank or Jerry could give me a hand to fix it."

Seeing Hamilton, she continued with the act. "Oh, no, Mrs. Elliot! I didn't know you had company. Maybe I can just leave it here. I can walk on down to the pub."

"Nonsense, Kathleen," Molly said. "You'll come in and enjoy a cup of tea and some afters. You remember Liam Riordan? He was at Ned's wake."

Kathleen walked to greet Hamilton, her hand outstretched. "Of course. Father Donnelly's friend," she said.

Hamilton experienced a new wave of exhilaration as he held her hand.

Molly saw the attraction right away. He held her hand long past what was considered customary. Taking her husband by the arm, she walked him toward the door. "You two visit for a while. Shure, Bill can fix the bicycle."

She was even more beautiful than Hamilton had remembered. "Good to see you again," he said, enthusiastically. "I'd be happy to help. I know all about bicycles."

It took Bill Elliot longer than most people to grasp the significance of Molly's wink.

When they returned, Kathleen removed her cloak and sat down. Hamilton was back in the easy chair.

Molly entered, gesturing toward the couch. "Liam, could I bother you to sit there by Kathleen? It's easier for me if we trade places, to get at the tea, that is."

"No problem here," he said, leaving a little space between himself and Kathleen.

Molly poured another cup of tea while Kathleen asked questions about the story. "It's coming along then, is it? I'm shure you could write two books with what Mr. Elliot knows about Ireland."

"I'd still like a woman's point of view, like your work, for example. You see the destitute, the broken bodies, families in pain. That's an angle my book is definitely missing."

"Angle?" Kathleen asked. Her tone of disapproval shook him. "You Americans. Everything has to have an 'angle.'" She mimicked him.

Molly broke in, "There now. Let's not ruin what's left of the evening with talk of politics."

"I agree." Hamilton's eyes thanked her. "I was just interested in your personal opinion."

"Oh, shure, let's get 'the little woman's point of view' for your American readers. Just you remember one thing, Mr. Liam Riordan, us women," she brought her hands to her bosom, "want freedom for this country every bit as much as men. Women have given their sons, and I fix up what's left of them. Oh, yes, we've given dearly, Mr. Riordan, and that is not a bloody afterthought or angle, as you call it."

Hamilton was disheartened. "I'm really sorry," he said. "Truly, Miss Barrett, I didn't mean it like that."

Molly intervened, this time with a cup of tea. "Here, child. I know you've had a hard day at the hospital."

"It's that amputee ward, Mrs. Elliot. Some of them are just boys, like my brothers or Frank and Jerry." Kathleen turned to Hamilton. "Sorry I snapped. I'm not angry with you."

"I apologize, too," he said. "So far, all I seem to do is irritate you when we meet." He stood up. "I really should be getting along," he said to Molly.

"Not 'til you've had some afters," she said. "You promised you'd stay." Molly looked up at Hamilton. She had a pleading expression.

"Please," Kathleen intervened. "I've just arrived and I feel like I'm running you off."

"Well, okay then," he said. Seating himself beside Kathleen, he took her hand in his.

She was unsure of what he was doing.

"Let's start with a new beginning." He was looking deep into her beautiful, blue, innocent eyes. "Hi, I'm Liam Riordan," he smiled.

"Hi," she mimicked him. "And I'm Kathleen Barrett."

They chatted about other things while Molly cut the bairin breac into four small servings. It was the tradition in Ireland to place a gold ring in waxed paper and bake it inside the bread pudding. It was a lucky person who got the helping with the ring inside. Good fortune and marriage would come to the recipient. Molly felt it her duty to give the lucky piece to their young American visitor.

Elliot, having fixed the chain, was washing up at the sink. Molly offered him a towel.

He patted her affectionately on the rear. "I know what you're up to," he whispered in her ear. "Playing little Molly Matchmaker is it?"

"Oh, hush up," she said impishly.

Hamilton had no idea what he'd bitten into. The first two bites were absolutely delicious. Now something was in his mouth that he knew he couldn't swallow. It would certainly be inappropriate to remove it while all looked on.

"Something wrong, Liam?" Elliot asked, with a wide grin.

Hamilton stood up pointing to his mouth. "Oh, it's nothing, er, excuse me. I may have broken a tooth."

He moved toward the sink and extracted the small gold ring from the waxed paper. After washing it under the faucet, he turned to face his three smiling companions. Molly looked much more mischievous than Bill Elliot. Kathleen looked mystified as Hamilton held the ring up between his forefinger and thumb. Although it was obvious to him now that he was the object of a conspiracy, he played along with the game.

"Now, where do you suppose this came from?" he said. "You'd better check your finger, Mrs. Elliot 'cause I'll bet I have your wedding ring."

Kathleen appeared a little embarrassed when Molly explained the custom to Hamilton.

Bill Elliot placed his hand on Molly's knee. "That's how I got this little colleen, Liam—with a bairin breac ring."

Molly pushed his hand away. "And one of these days you'll be getting me the real thing, won't ye?"

Elliot turned to Hamilton with a more serious tone. "Is there someone special back home in America?"

Hamilton didn't say anything right away. He studied Kathleen's face. She turned away from his eyes. He knew by the look on her face that she wanted him to say no.

"No," he turned to Bill. "Not a soul."

"So, what happens now?" Hamilton asked insistently. "When I think I've met the right girl, I present the ring and she falls head over heels in love with me, right?"

Molly turned from Hamilton and looked at her husband. "Be Jasus, the lad's a genius," she said with a contrived Dublin accent.

Elliot glanced at his watch. The British had imposed a state of martial law in Dublin since the day of the Uprising. Anyone on the street past ten o'clock would be routinely incarcerated. "I'm forced by circumstances beyond my control to be impolite to my guests," he said, standing. "I want to leave plenty of time for you to get home, what with this bloody curfew and all."

Kathleen kissed Molly on the cheek. "Thanks for everything, Mrs. Elliot." She gave Bill Elliot a hug. "And thank you for fixing my bicycle."

Hamilton couldn't say enough to express his gratitude.

Molly Elliot, in a final effort to stimulate a relationship, suggested that Liam see Kathleen safely back to Bridget's, where she was spending the night.

It was past nine-thirty when Kathleen and Hamilton left the Elliots'. They turned left on York Street, heading for the pub, about twenty minutes away. A full moon had replaced the setting sun. Dublin, approaching the ten o'clock curfew, was quiet.

A loose rope dangled from the lamp post where the children had played earlier. A fine haze blanketed the city and the soft glow of the flickering lanterns illuminated the street. The tall buildings had become black silhouettes against the occasional burning light of a friendly window. A pungent smell of urine filled Hamilton's nostrils, the price paid for the primary transportation in the city—horses.

Pushing the bike with his right hand, he placed his left arm around her waist. She didn't reject his advances, nor did she respond by drawing closer. He felt awkward and finally made a halfhearted retreat.

"Mr. Elliot is quite the scholar, isn't he," she said.

"I was very impressed with his reasonable sense of patriotism," Hamilton replied. "And his knowledge of global politics is refreshing. He's certainly of the opinion that the pen is mightier than the sword. That probably stems from the fact that he's an anglicized Irishman."

"Are you saying that if you're not anglicized Irish that you have no sense of tolerance and want to solve everything with a gun?" She was confrontational once again.

Hamilton replied, "That's *not* what I meant. I was just talking about one man and besides, I'm not here to pass judgment. I just record what I see and so far, it seems this Uprising of yours has only served to cause a lot of grief and dying."

"Well, Liam Riordan, I can already see the direction of your article!" countered Kathleen.

Hamilton realized his remarks were getting him nowhere fast. Her mild annoyance had turned to anger.

"Believe me, it wasn't my intention to offend you or your country's desire for independence. You have to admit that this—this rebellion of yours hasn't contributed much to the lives of ordinary people. My account of what happened here will tell the truth about this Uprising."

"Well! Excuse me if that concept has evaded me!"

"Look," he changed the subject. "I'd much rather talk about you. Your calling as a nurse, I mean. You're young, obviously dedicated to healing, and if I might be so forward, a very beautiful girl."

"Stop trying to change the subject, Mr. Riordan. It's Irish honor and not my looks we're discussing."

"And both well worth fighting for, in my opinion," he said, in an effort to make up.

"Aren't you the cute one. I'm sure you're this charming with all the girls," she said, her face turning from stern to amiable sarcasm.

"It's just my way of apologizing. And, no, I'm not charming around all girls," he said. "Remember, there are no other girls."

"Ah, yes," she smiled up at him. "Your writing keeps you too busy." He pulled her closer and squeezed her affectionately.

Feeling a little more comfortable with each other, the couple turned left onto Georges Street and headed toward Bridget's. Hamilton noticed a military vehicle parked across the street, next to the curb. He could tell by the red glimmer of the lit cigarette inside the cab that it was occupied. Casually, he looked at his wrist-watch and saw it was almost ten o'clock.

He hoped that Bridget's was just a short distance away. "How much farther to McIntees'?" he asked nervously.

Unaware of the present danger, Kathleen smiled up at him and answered, "We'll be there in five minutes."

When he passed the truck, he sighed with relief, feeling safe with a short distance to go. It was then that he heard the door open, and that cockney ring broke the quiet of the evening.

"Well, now, where are you love birds going this fine evening?"

Hamilton ignored the challenging remark and whispered to Kathleen, "Just keep walking."

He could hear footsteps following them. He could tell there were at least two, maybe three men. He would soon have to turn and confront them. He was more worried about Kathleen's safety than his own. His knees felt a little shaky and Mrs. Elliot's steak and kidney pie was beginning to sour on the back of his tongue.

This time, the same harsh cockney accent sang out, "All right mates, hold it right there!"

Hamilton turned to face the three men. They wore their uniforms slovenly and looked as though they'd been drinking. He stepped slightly ahead of Kathleen and with a show of indignation, demanded an explanation.

"What's the problem, gentlemen?" Hamilton asked, using the term loosely.

The uniformed men found the term "gentlemen" amusing and laughed.

Hamilton realized that his first impressions were accurate when one of the soldiers removed his tam and curtsied to the other two.

"Gentlemen," he snickered, and did a little dance.

Hamilton noticed that each of the men carried a service revolver attached to a black-leather belt. One of them shouldered a Springfield rifle as well.

Obviously, discretion being the better part of valor, Hamilton knew he was going to have to defer to the men in uniform. Although he was concerned about Kathleen, he felt his American passport would bail him out. There was, after all, diplomatic immunity, provided they knew what that was!

The one who did most of the talking wore stripes, indicating that he was in command of this group. He was a gangly man about five-feet-ten inches, with high cheekbones and a big mouth, full of horse-like teeth.

Hamilton backed off when the man shoved the back of his hand in his face. He was pointing to the watch on his wrist. "Can you tell time, mate?" he growled.

Hamilton glanced at the time and then past the wrist to look into the face of the ugly man. "So, it's five after ten. Is there a law about being out after ten?" Hamilton asked, hoping to appear ignorant of the curfew.

"Bloody right there's a law. It's called *martial law*," the soldier snapped.

One of the other ugly soldiers, a short, corpulent man in his late twenties, asked, "What 'ave we 'ere mate, a bloody American?"

Before Hamilton had a chance to reply, the horse-tooth man stepped around him toward Kathleen.

"An' lookie 'ere, mate! The American seems to have a fine taste for Irish arse," he said, running his hands through her long black hair. His hands slipped down from her hair and brushed lightly over her breasts.

"Get your slimy, limy hands off of me, you British bastard!" Kathleen demanded.

Hamilton stepped between Kathleen and the soldier. "Now, look, I'm an American in this country on business and I don't want you men to get into a lot of trouble with your commanding officer. You've had your fun. Now just let us be on our way." He placed the bicycle against a lamp standard and reached into his pocket for his passport. "Just to show you that I am an Amer…"

His hand was still in his pocket when the soldier with the rifle brought the butt up hard against his groin. He wasn't sure anything could feel worse than that until the second blow slammed squarely in his stomach. The pain pierced through him. For a while, everything seemed to float. He could hear Kathleen screaming, but from another world. With glassy, unfocused eyes, he felt more blows to the head. He had to vomit. He could hear other cockney voices swimming in his head. He could taste blood, but he didn't think he'd been hit in the mouth and assumed it was coming from his stomach.

Hunched over the gutter, he swayed back and forth. He was repeatedly kicked, but could no longer distinguish the source of the pain. He endured more than he'd ever thought humanly possible. The only thing that seemed to keep him conscious was the retching and vomiting. He was on his hands and knees, groping around in his own swill.

"Ah, leave him, mates." He could hear the cockney voices in the distance.

"That'll teach the fucker how to tell time."

Their laughter was the last thing he heard as he mercifully lost consciousness.

CHAPTER SIX

THE NIGHT SHIFT was Kathleen's favorite time to work. Day duty at Mercer Street Hospital was hectic. All of the operatories were busy. Doctors and interns rushed from one ward to the next, and patients were pushed about like bumper cars at a carnival. The night shift was more of a vigil, a time when it was easier to detach one's mind from medical care. Most of the patients were given tranquilizers to make them sleep. Although it was a time of quiet, sometimes the misery was more apparent.

The corridors were illuminated with newly installed electric lights. The upper portions of the ward doors were glazed with a translucent dimpled glass and at night the only light inside the ward came from the red-covered votive candles beneath the statue of the Virgin Mary, an area set aside for prayer.

Kathleen left Hamilton's bedside and closed the door gently behind her. She wiped the tears away with a white-lace handkerchief. He had been unconscious for five days, and she had received special permission to nurse him back to health. She didn't understand her feelings about Liam Riordan. She felt compassion for all her patients in a professional way, but this was different. What she was feeling was like the sadness one would feel if a very close friend or family member was ill. More than once, the thought of losing her little brother, Jamie, to a terminal illness brought tears to her eyes. Now it was a virtual stranger whose near-death was filling her life with sadness. She felt helpless and silently recited the prayer placed on the ward door, hoping it would wake him from his coma—*Resurgan—I shall arise*. As she made her rounds, her thoughts were a blending of joy and sorrow, pleasure and torment. There were other patients that desperately needed her help. One such patient on whom she particularly focused attention was a ten-year-old boy awaiting the frightening possibility of losing his leg. His name was Aidan Flynn. He was suffering from a gunshot wound to the thigh. The bullet had exited, ripping apart a good portion of the quadriceps and the wound had become ulcerated. He was slightly built and fair-complexioned to begin with, which when combined with his illness, made him appear even more frail. The freckles on his small face were more prominent now when contrasted against the light pallor of his skin. Rusty curls hung over his brow, almost covering the large green eyes, giving him the appearance of a sad puppy. Even when her shift replacement arrived, she usually returned to his bedside as a visitor.

These days, the doctors at Mercer Street were much too busy to properly administer to the patients, and sometimes a quick cure to save a life meant sacrificing an arm or leg. Kathleen was aware that Aidan's doctor was considering amputation and disagreed vehemently with the surgeon's practice of immobilizing the leg. A splint, in her opinion, would only put off the eventuality of amputation. When she questioned the prognosis, she was informed that challenging the doctor's orders wasn't part of her duties. The leg was immobilized.

Kathleen Barrett, with no medical endorsements, degrees or even another opinion to back up her medical theories, proceeded diligently on the night shift to heal the boy. She was adamant in her belief that what the boy needed was to exercise the wounded limb. She had little doubt that movement, controlled exercise, massage, and hot packs would help the blood to circulate, and she had no doubt that this would hasten the healing process. She knew it was painful for Aidan to move his leg, and each time he cried out in pain it tore at her heart. Nevertheless, she continued the treatments every night, pushing the leg gently to his chest and bringing it back slowly. Watching his face grimace, she convinced the boy that feeling pain was important to his recovery. It was better than feeling nothing. She ended the therapy with hot, moist packs, which he did seem to enjoy. After the treatments, she replaced the splint and prepared to answer Dr. Purcell if he said she was interfering with his course of treatment.

The following morning, Hamilton was showing signs of recovery, and Kathleen didn't leave his bedside, even after she was officially relieved. Several visitors had come by, including Father Donnelly, who had spent many hours at Hamilton's bedside praying for his recovery. Kathleen appreciated Father Donnelly's winsome sense of humor.

"When the young American writer recuperates, he'll have the first-hand knowledge he sought—the hospitality of British soldiers," he told Kathleen.

The small cubicle was screened from the rest of the ward by curtains. The white, sterile atmosphere was relieved only by a window and a slender cross above his bed. The congoleum floors were scrubbed daily and smelled of disinfectant and carbolic antiseptic.

Hamilton had nearly died from internal bleeding, and surgery had been necessary to remove his spleen. In addition, several ribs had been broken by the blows from the boots of the soldiers. His bruises were beginning to fade a little, leaving a palette of yellow and purple hues on his face and body.

Kathleen rolled him gently to one side and while she was making his bed, Hamilton opened his eyes. The sun, shining in the window, made the stark whiteness of the area even brighter. His eyes fixed themselves on the figure in the white dress—her hair black as coal, and for a moment, he thought he was dead. Unable to focus, he tried to sit up. He was reassured in learning that he was alive. When his whole body convulsed with pain, he looked around, confused.

Where was he? How did he get here? The last thing he remembered was lying in the gutter after being kicked by those bastards. He thought of Kathleen. He tried desperately to re-examine his last thoughts, his feeble attempt to protect her. *Oh my God, what has become of Kathleen?* The thought of those barbarians having their way with her made him groan.

"Liam," the figure in white addressed him. "Liam, are you awake?"

With difficulty, he focused on a woman. She was dressed in a long, white, starched uniform over a pale-blue blouse. A wimple headdress covered her hair. She bent down to him, "Liam, can you hear me?"

God, Hamilton thought, *those eyes can only be Kathleen's.*

"Is it you, Kathleen?" he whispered.

"Hush, don't waste your energy," she cautioned him. "Oh, thank God. You're going to be all right." She leaned closer. "I'll be right back! I've orders to notify Sister Monica the moment you wake up."

He was breaking through his blackout. *Good Lord, how long have I been here? What is Kathleen doing dressed as a nun? Oh, God, did I talk when I was unconscious?* He became agitated and tried to sit up. Unbelievable nausea overtook him, and the pain was excruciating.

I have to get out of here, he thought. *I have to get to Colonel Lynch.* He became apprehensive. *Have I implicated Lynch? Why can't I remember?* Gingerly, he sat upright, and turning slowly, allowed his legs to hang off the side of the bed.

The perplexing images permeating his mind were interrupted by the tiny, wizened old nun who came scurrying into the room. She barely reached five feet tall and reminded Hamilton of an Emperor Penguin. What she lacked in stature, she more than made up for with her sharp, shrill voice.

"Young man—now lay back down and don't move an inch until you've been given permission to do so. That's a good lad!" She introduced herself and positioned him back in the bed, drawing the covers over his half-clad body.

Hamilton tried to sit up again. With a moan he lay back down. "How did I get here?" he inquired.

"Sean McIntee and Nurse Barrett's father brought you. Lucky for you, they got you here before you bled to death. The doctors operated immediately. We were all very concerned about you, Mr. Riordan. Particularly Nurse Barrett here," she gestured behind her to Kathleen.

"Was that yesterday, Sister?" Hamilton asked.

"Good Lord, no, Mr. Riordan. It was five days ago and you've been napping here like a baby ever since. You've had visitors, Nurse Barrett's father and a Mr. Elliot. Oh, and that man from your magazine, Mr., er, what was his name?" She was straining very hard to remember when Kathleen intervened.

"That would be Mr. Lynch, Sister," she said.

"That's right. Mr. Lynch," echoed Sister Monica. "He's a pushy one, that fella. Thought he could come in here and rule the roost." She turned to Kathleen.

"I showed him who's the boss, didn't I, nurse?"

Kathleen acknowledged with a nod.

Hamilton wouldn't have put it past the colonel to slip him some arsenic to protect the operation.

Sister Monica turned back toward Hamilton with a more serious tone. "Now that you've regained consciousness, we'll be wanting that bed for someone who really needs it. You should be grateful, you know. Not everyone who the British have a go at fare half as well as you."

"Lucky, you say!" an exasperated Hamilton barked. "Lucky to feel like a truck ran over me? I'd like to see someone you'd consider unlucky."

"Nurse Barrett," Sister commanded. "Get Mr. Riordan here to a wheelchair. I'm going to show him just how lucky he is. Why, a little surgery and a few broken ribs and the man thinks he's injured. It's time he found out what happens to the real victims of our British friends," she said sarcastically.

"Sister, I don't think he feels well enough to get into the wheelchair," Kathleen protested.

Hamilton admired her defiant protective stand against the little penguin dictator. *She must really care for me,* he thought. *Somehow, though, I don't think Kathleen is going to win this battle.*

"Are you refusing to follow orders, Nurse Barrett?" Sister Monica snapped. "He's fine, I tell you. A little weak maybe, but we're going to give him a ride. Remember, Mr. Riordan, one real experience will stay longer in your memory than somebody's telling. This will give you something else to write about in your article."

Kathleen managed to get Hamilton into a wheelchair in spite of his moans and groans. As her arms wrapped around him, she sensed his misery, and rather liked this over-sensitive apprehension she felt for him.

"We'll not be needing you for a while, Nurse," Sister Monica said. Then her stern face turned to an appreciative smile. "Why don't you go home, dear, and get some rest. You really can trust us to take care of your patient." With that, she grabbed the handles of the wheelchair and swept out of the curtained area.

Her first stop was the bed close to where Hamilton had lain unconscious for five days. A boy of about twelve years lay motionless. His arms and legs were bandaged, and his eyes were covered with surgical gauze.

Sister Monica didn't have to lean far to find Hamilton's ear. "James Sullivan," she said gently. "How are you today, James?"

A broad smile appeared on his small, innocent face. "Just fine, Sister. I think I'm much better today. Do you think I can take the bandages off me eyes yet?" he asked in a pronounced Dublin accent.

"Probably not today, James. You must be patient, you know. Doctor will be in to see you soon."

She pushed Hamilton away from the bed. When they were out of earshot, she said, "It's not going to do him a bit of good to have the bandages removed. He's lost both eyes. It happened when the British raided his house, looking for the boy's father. They tossed two grenades through the window." She hesitated. "As if *one* wasn't enough. Thank God he hasn't remembered much of what happened to his parents." She snapped her fingers. "Gone, just like that."

Hamilton looked back at the boy sitting up in bed, still smiling.

"How do you tell him?" he asked thoughtfully.

"With all the love we can muster, Mr. Riordan." Her true colors were beginning to show.

God, she really is human, thought Hamilton.

The next bed held a young man who didn't acknowledge their arrival.

"This is Aidan Flynn. He saw his whole family go down under the rifles of the British. One of the bullets entered his thigh. We had to remove most of the muscle. He hasn't spoken a word since—just lies there and hums to himself. No one, so far as we know, has gotten him to speak a word, except Nurse Barrett. She's the only one who seems to be making any progress with the lad. Between you and me, if it wasn't for Nurse Barrett's unique caring methods, I don't believe he'd be with us today. Although we've repaired him physically, he still stares right through you with those glassy eyes."

She continued her tour around the ward, stopping at each bed with a reassuring pat or smile for each of the wounded men. It was a stretch calling them men because some of them were just boys, barely into their teens. Hamilton felt nauseated. He didn't know if it was his weakened condition or the simple injustice of this carnage. Healthy young men, innocent bystanders, lay silently, their arms and legs swaddled. Some of the injured were being treated, only to face a firing squad later.

"Sister," he said. "I've seen enough."

"We're going to visit the amputee ward now," she said, ignoring him. Down the hall, she steered him into another antiseptic room. The men in these beds were all amputees with bandaged stubs where arms, legs or feet used to be. The sweet, sickening odor of fresh blood filled the ward as many of the wounds had not yet healed. The sulfur powder poured on the mangled stumps added to the putrid smell.

One bed in the far corner of the room had Hamilton curious. Two British soldiers guarded the precious quarry. *As though the poor soul in the bed is going someplace,* thought Hamilton. The man seemed unconscious. His face was a yellowish color and his mouth was drawn back and partially open. What was left of his leg was bundled up in a bloody mass of bandages. The stub seemed to pulsate and reminded Hamilton of a cocoon.

"Who's the celebrity, Sister?" Hamilton inquired.

"Ah, shure, that's one of the noblest men in Ireland, James Connolly. He was one of the signatories of Ireland's Proclamation of Freedom. Also, he and Pearse led the fight against the British." She raised her eyes upwardly and said in a saintly manner, "Mother of God, I don't know why they just can't leave him alone to die."

"He's dying?" Hamilton asked dubiously. "Why in the hell—excuse me, Sister." His face reddened slightly.

"That's all right, Mr. Riordan," she interrupted. "Shure, haven't I heard that—and more—before."

"I guess what I'm trying to say is, if he's dying, why the guard?"

"He's going to be shot, Mr. Riordan," she said firmly. "And we have to save his life so that they can take it." She left no doubt who *they* were, pointing at the soldiers.

Sister Monica informed him of other men in the ward being healed only to face a firing squad or the hangman's noose. One boy was only sixteen and reminded Hamilton of Bill Elliot's father and his first case against these injustices fifty years earlier.

"Sister, I think I'd better go back."

"All in due time, Mr. Riordan. I certainly want to give you enough to write about."

"I've seen enough to last me a lifetime, believe me. I promise I'll write of every brave man I've seen here and of the bloody war that seems to have no end."

Trusting that this was one man who was certainly more empathetic than when he'd started, she kindheartedly wheeled an exhausted Hamilton back to the safety of his bed.

CHAPTER SEVEN

T HE REMAINING DAYS at Mercer Street were a blur to Hamilton. Colonel Lynch had dropped by and declared that it was brilliant of him to get on the good side of the Irish by being beaten up. That confused Hamilton. He thought it was indefensible the way the Irish were being treated. These were people for whom he was developing a liking. Hamilton knew that what he needed was to reconcile his feeling of compassion for the Irish with the reason for being here in the first place—to come to grips with his assignment. After all, he was a British officer and had a job to do. *Damn it, pull yourself together, Hamilton.* He reprimanded himself for losing sight of his duty.

Annie awakened him when she came into the room. This was Hamilton's second day of convalescence at the Barrett home in Milltown. The doctor had quietly suggested that the American should really stay with somebody while he was recovering. Hamilton remembered the hushed conversation beyond his cordoned-off bed.

Mick Barrett had graciously offered his home. "Shure, I'm the one that got him here, and being the responsible man that I am, I'll see that he's taken care of."

Kathleen's voice was just as memorable. "And I can continue with his nursing needs, Doctor."

So, here he was at Kathleen's home, astonished at the family's hospitality. Even little Jamie found the American visitor exciting. Yesterday, after arriving, Hamilton had no sooner been transferred to the bedroom when Paddy and Michael stopped by. The questions were unending. Questions about America. They were particularly interested in cowboys and Indians. Hamilton enjoyed their curiosity, their simple naiveté. When he stretched the truth a little, their eyes grew wide and their mouths hung open; they were eager to hear more.

Annie Barrett's words amplified in his ears. "The doctor said that you could have some solids today. I made some chicken stew."

Hamilton slowly eased himself up into a sitting position. "You really shouldn't have," he said. "I'm a little embarrassed, needing all of this attention."

She interrupted, "Never mind that. It's nothing special. You're just eating what the rest of the family is having for dinner. It was no bother at all." She smiled as she spoke. It was Kathleen's smile. "We're going to make you all well," she said, placing the tray on his lap.

"It looks delicious," Hamilton said as he brought the dumpling-filled spoon to his mouth. It was the only real food he had eaten in a week. His whole body shuddered, and his mouth ached with the first taste.

Annie was waiting for a more positive reaction to her culinary efforts. "Are you all right, Mr. Riordan?" she asked softly. "Dear God, I should have warned you that it was hot!"

Hamilton's body didn't take long to adjust to the taste of real food. "No, no. Really, I'm just fine. It's delicious," he smiled. "Look." He devoured another spoonful. "It's perfect!" he said with a full mouth.

"Oh, I'm glad you like it!" Annie said enthusiastically.

"You know, I'm not sure I'll be able to go back to the way I've been living. You Barretts have done nothing but pamper me since my arrival."

"That Kathleen of ours is a real Florence Nightingale." Her eyes sparkled when she spoke of Kathleen. "And she seems to be a little taken with you, Liam." She hesitated. "I hope you don't mind me calling you Liam?"

"I'd be disappointed if you didn't...Annie."

They smiled together.

"And, if you don't mind me saying, I think your daughter is one of the most beautiful girls I've ever met."

"You eat up and get well. I'll leave you be now," she said, closing the door gently behind her.

CHAPTER EIGHT

T HE DAYS PASSED slowly for Hamilton. He was able to get around now
without his ribs aching. He had become something of an attraction.
All of the neighbors had stopped in to pay their respects and deride
the British soldiers for his suffering. Father Donnelly had also come by.

Hamilton wasn't sure about Donnelly. For a man of the cloth, he was
very headstrong about the British being in Ireland. He was the consummate
martyr and blamed himself for Hamilton's misery.

"Shure, if I hadn't taken ye to the wake, you wouldn't have met Bill
Elliot. You wouldn't have been in York Street and, that being the case, you
wouldn't have been out after hours. Shure, when ya look at it that way,
now wasn't I to blame?" Hamilton was relieved to see the priest leave.

Afterward, Sean McIntee dropped by with his mother. He didn't even
get out of the old van. He chose to sit where he did not have to hide his
hatred for Hamilton. Annie was sitting with Hamilton at the kitchen table,
and they had a clear view of the woman now walking up the drive.

"Dear God, you mustn't think bad of me for saying this, but here
comes one of my very favorite people," Annie said sarcastically.

Hamilton smiled.

Nora knocked and entered without waiting for someone to answer.

"C'mon in, Nora," Annie said pleasantly.

"How are ye?" Nora asked. "And how is the wounded American?" She
came toward Hamilton, her hand extended. "Takin' the British on single
handed, I hear."

He shook her hand. "You guys took a shot at them. I felt it was my turn. Neither of us did so well."

"Well, you're everyone's hero at the pub," she said. "Almost everyone's anyway," she continued. "It's Sean." Nora made a slurping sound as she tasted the tea. "Ah, shure, you know how him and Kathleen are. They've always been the perfect little couple." She turned to Hamilton. "And now with Mr. Riordan moving in an all…"

Annie stopped her. "Excuse me, Nora, Liam, er, Mr. Riordan, is only here until he gets well. Besides, Nora, Kathleen and Sean are just good friends."

Hamilton opened the silver case and held it out to Nora. "Smoke?"

She delicately slipped one out from under the band in the case. "American?" she asked.

"No, English. Players, as a matter of fact."

When Nora removed the old black flannel coat, Annie knew it was going to be a three-cup visit. Wearing a stained, white apron, Nora leaned toward Annie, a cigarette dangling backwards from her bony fingers and a cup of tea in her left hand. She looked all the part the owner of the house. Annie hated the way she put on an upper-class Dublin accent for Hamilton's benefit. It took close to an hour to hear all the gossip.

The house was finally quiet except for the ticking sound of the grandfather clock in the hall. Hamilton sat on a bay-window seat watching the rain through the French panes. His thoughts turned to the pony and trap coming up the dirt driveway.

Mick had picked up Kathleen at the hospital. *I'll bet it's that damn bicycle chain again*, thought Hamilton, as they came through the door.

"The chain again?" Hamilton said, taking her shawl.

She looked at him, confused, "Chain?" It was then that she remembered her planned intrusion at the Elliots'. "Oh, the chain. No, no, it's fine."

She was momentarily embarrassed. After all, if she hadn't been at the Elliots' that night, he might not have been hurt. She hastily excused her regret. *Well, he's all right now, and he's at my home.* It was more than she'd hoped for.

"I took her to work this morning," Mick said, taking off the old overcoat.

"It was raining cats and dogs—no weather for bicycling." He moved slowly into the kitchen, leaving Kathleen and Hamilton in the front parlor.

They didn't speak for a while. They just sat looking at one another.

"Are you all right?" She placed her hand on his wrist.

"Yes, and if you're looking for a pulse, it should be racing a bit," he said.

She gave him a professional smile. "I think you're going to be just fine, Liam Riordan."

Later on, Mick and Annie were in the kitchen. Mick was sampling the cauliflower and white sauce. "Delicious," he said, putting his arms around Annie's waist. "Ah, shure, 'tis a darlin' and a great cook that you are, Annie Barrett. And what pray tell is that fine piece of meat you're cookin'?" He became serious.

"Steak," she said, turning to his broad, serious face.

Most of the people in Ireland were eating mutton and ham these days because of the war. All the beef was being shipped out to feed the warriors at the Western Front. What was left was rationed stewing meat. But these were fine steaks that Annie was frying.

"Where in God's holy name did you get them?"

"I just thought it might be nice for Liam to have steak. After all, isn't that what Americans eat?" she said.

"I suppose so," he answered. "But where did you get it?" he persisted.

"It's a bloody horse," she whispered. "So there!"

"Horse?"

"Sshhh, Mother of God, would you shut up!" she scolded him. "Shure, more people are starting to eat horsemeat, Mick. I hear it's just like beef."

"Well, I'll give it a try," he said quietly. "I'll bet it's the horse I lost a bet on last month!" He joked while holding the fork to his mouth.

After Mick sampled the meat, he gave his approval and moved into the parlor. Paddy, Michael, and Jamie were playing a board game. Kathleen and Hamilton were sitting on the piano bench. When Kathleen played and sang *Boulavogue*, one of Mick's favorite ballads, tears came to his eyes. Again he saw the heather blazing on the meadows of Shelmaliar, and the boys of Wexford charging the regiment of King George in the fight for the green.

Hamilton could feel her closeness, the warmth of her leg next to his. He was beginning to feel vulnerable again.

"Dinner is being served," Mick said, imitating a haughty English butler.

They sat at the table, Kathleen next to Hamilton, and Mick said grace. "And these Thy gifts which we are about to receive from Thy bounty, through Christ our Lord."

They responded together, "Amen."

Annie was busy putting portions on everyone's plate. "I'm sorry, Liam. I should have asked if you felt ready to eat," she said.

Hamilton had already filled his mouth with a piece of meat. "I must be getting better," he said. "I'm so hungry, I could eat a horse."

Annie looked at Mick, their smiles turning to laughter.

There was an air of excitement at the Barrett house. To help Hamilton celebrate his recovery, the family was going on a picnic. Tomorrow he was returning to his lodging on Wicklow Street. He had also arranged to meet with Colonel Lynch during the same week. Lynch wasn't going to be too thrilled. Hamilton knew what the colonel's reaction would be with his decision to resign from the case. He consoled himself with the thought that this wasn't exactly what he had expected of the intelligence service. He belonged in Germany, working against the real enemy; besides, that's why he'd joined up.

Investigating ordinary, friendly people who had committed no sin other than trying to free their country did not contribute to his civic or national pride. The colonel would probably have him drawn and quartered for yielding to the rebels. Lynch would say that he had become the enemy. God, how was he going to tell Kathleen? Explaining to her was going to be even more difficult. He was determined to resolve this soon. Being everybody's traitor wasn't his idea of fun.

Annie and Kathleen spent the morning cooking and baking. Mick had brought home the company lorry for the outing.

"Ma," Jamie cried. "Can I ride beside Liam and Kathleen?"

"Ah, be quiet, ya baby," Michael admonished. "You're going to ride up front with Ma and Da where ye belong."

"That's not fair!" wailed Jamie. "Just because I'm the youngest, it don't mean I'm a baby."

"Doesn't, baby. You can't even talk right. Baby, baby, baby."

"Michael, stop tormenting your brother," Annie said. "There's time enough to decide the seating order. Maybe Da will let you drive," she said, joking.

"Yes! Yes! I'm riding with Ma and Da and I'm going to drive the lorry."

Annie's attention turned to the pony and trap coming up the drive. It was Padraig, Mick's brother, accompanied by a man on the other side.

"Glad I caught up with ye before ye left," Padraig said, stepping off the cart. "Where's Mick?" he asked hurriedly.

"Is something wrong, Padraig?" Annie asked.

"Not at all, Annie. This is Mr. Connors."

Connors, an older gentleman, tipped his hat to Annie. She curtsied and turned toward the house to find Mick.

"Ah, shite," Mick grumbled under his breath when Annie told him who was outside. "Wouldn't ye know it. Just as we're ready to leave. Shite!" he said again, as he left to see his brother. "What's up, Padraig?" Mick asked.

"Sorry to bother ye, Mick, what with your picnic and all." Padraig made the introductions. "Mr. Connors has an estate full of furniture and he'd like us to put it in the store on consignment. Top o' the line furniture." He turned to Connors. "Isn't that right, Mr. Connors?"

The older man nodded.

"I'm afraid I'll be needin' your help—and the lorry," Padraig said. "That's all right, Mick, isn't it?"

Mick was aware of the opportunity. The store hadn't been doing well since the Uprising. It was hard to find anyone willing to part with good second-hand furniture.

"Very well, Padraig. I'll be right back with ye." Walking back to the house, he turned his head, "I'll just let Annie and the kids know. Be right back."

"I understand, Mick. Don't worry, we'll do it another time," Annie said, disappointed.

"I'm sorry, darlin'." He kissed her on the cheek. "Would ye explain to the kids?"

"I will." She waved as the lorry moved down the drive, followed by Padraig and Mr. Connors in the trap.

CHAPTER NINE

"**H**ILL O' HOWTH!" the weary little conductor hollered from the back of the tram.

Kathleen readied herself. "Well, Liam, here we are." She was in control now as she stepped off the tram with both picnic baskets.

"I'll bet the boys had a great time on top of the tram," Hamilton said, appropriating the baskets.

Paddy and Michael came down the winding stairs, two at a time, carrying parcels of food.

"Shure, 'tis too bad Ma and Da couldn't come," Michael said to Hamilton. "She loves it here at Howth. It's where we always come for outin's."

Kathleen agreed and explained to the boys again the importance of their father's business and Annie needing to stay home with Jamie.

"She doesn't trust us to watch after him, Liam," Paddy said.

The boys ran ahead, anxious to reach the summit. The tram terminus left them a mile or so from the top of the hill, and although the incline was steep, they walked briskly. They couldn't have asked for a better day in County Dublin.

Hamilton was awestruck. The top of the hill was a rolling plateau of green grass, occasionally interrupted by large jutting rocks. The grass landscape ended abruptly at the edge of a precipitous cliff to the raging Irish Sea below.

Hamilton and Kathleen stood motionless, captivated by the awesome Irish seascape. With their hands clasped together, they silently shared the natural beauty that surrounded them. Each seemed to enjoy what the other was enjoying, feel what the other was feeling. Hamilton and Kathleen were unavoidably falling in love.

While Paddy and Michael went off scouting for tern nests, Kathleen sought an appropriately secluded area to lay the white tablecloth. A large rock obstructed the breeze and afforded them some privacy. Hamilton was close by, sitting on a rock, enjoying the scenery. He removed a Player from the silver case and lit up. He took a deep drag and fixed his gaze on Kathleen. She had removed her jacket and was busy organizing the food. She stood up for a moment, her back toward Hamilton, looking for the boys. The light from the sun illuminated her youthful symmetry through the white chiffon dress. Her well-proportioned curves held his attention longer than he felt appropriate. He thought that he was invading her privacy and silently scolded himself. With some self-control returning, he filled his lungs with more smoke and looking out to sea, contemplated his own homeland.

"What are you thinking about, Liam? Home?" she asked perceptively, walking over to where he sat. "Because if you are, you're looking the wrong way," she said, smiling. "That's England over there." She was pointing in the direction he was scanning.

"I know where England is, Kathleen Barrett," he smirked back.

She had discovered his more serious side and thought that it might be interesting to taunt him a little more. He obviously didn't like to be teased, especially about the invariable manly distinctions like science, motor cars, and geography.

"Shure, you know where England is, but it was America you thought you were lookin' at."

He stood up from his perch as she continued to taunt him.

"C'mon," she said, bending slightly to raise the long skirt, just enough to run. "Show me the way to America."

He ran to catch up with her, and with his arms enveloping her small waist, he brought her gently to the grass. He could feel the heavy breathing of her bosom as he lay on her. With one hand he bridled her hands back over her head and his free hand tickled her face with a blade of grass.

She had become subjugated to his wishes. "I give in," she said, laughing hysterically. "Please, I'll do anything, please!"

He stopped tickling her. "Okay, okay." He thought for a moment. "Tell me I'm the nicest guy you've ever met." His hand held the grass delicately close to her neck.

She stopped laughing and looked directly into his steel-blue eyes.

"You, Liam Riordan, are the nicest guy," she said, mimicking him, "that I ever met."

"And you, Kathleen Barrett, are the most beaut..." He stopped midsentence.

"Hey, what's to eat, Kathleen? We're bleedin' starvin'!" It was Paddy, completely indifferent to their intimacy. Michael nudged Paddy knowingly.

"Lucky we got back in time—shure, they might have kilt one another," he said with a broad Dublin accent.

Kathleen rose and straightened out her wrinkled dress. That's when she noticed Hamilton's cigarette case. Picking it up, she turned back to where he was standing.

"Oh, and by the way, I'll be keeping this for you," she said, holding up the case. "I'll be doling out the cigarettes from now on. They're not good for you, and I'm still your nurse."

He nodded in agreement and followed her back to the picnic area, hoping they would soon be alone again.

They all blamed the fresh air for their hunger. The boys ate most of the sandwiches and drank all the ginger ale, while Hamilton and Kathleen shared a bottle of wine. There was a carnival in the town of Howth that day and all had planned to attend.

Kathleen told the boys that she had a slight headache. "It must be the wine," she said. "The last thing I need now is a ride on a chair-o-plane."

Hamilton assumed that she did have a headache, but thought that she could have another reason to let the boys go without her.

"Take your time, and have fun," she hollered after the boys.

They were alone again. Things had to be said, and yet both nervously attended to insignificant matters. Kathleen packed the basket for the return trip while Hamilton disposed of the empty bottles and wrappings. When finished, he begged for a cigarette. She allowed him one. He lit it and reclined, supporting his head with one arm.

She placed the case back in her purse and sat beside him. "Shure, they're awfully bad for you, Liam," she said seriously. "You smoke a lot, don't you?"

"Things on my mind," he said.

"Is it your article?" Kathleen probed.

"Article?" he said curiously.

"Your story, Liam."

"Oh, that," he said. "No, not really. Frankly, Kathleen, I've, well, been thinking about us." There, he said it. He wanted to tell her everything.

When he wasn't with her he was miserable. His thoughts centered on love.

Her hands were resting in her lap and he placed his hand over hers. "I think about you all the time," he whispered.

The wine had made her brave. She didn't pull back. Her whole body shivered when he touched her. "I know," she said softly. "I feel the same way. Ever since I met you, Liam, you're in my thoughts. Even when I'm working, I think of you."

He looked into her deep-blue, smiling eyes. "There's so much you don't know about me," he said. "Who I really am and…"

She stopped him, placing her fingers to his mouth. "Sshhh," she said, pursing her soft lips. "We have plenty of time to talk."

She leaned over. He caught a glimpse of the white strap of her petticoat. He could smell her delicate fragrance as his hand reached for her shoulder. He drew her to him, their faces almost touching. He eased his face closer to hers. Her eyes closed as he paused to revere her beauty. It was a long kiss, and as they embraced, he gently moved her to her side, then to her back.

His hand moved slowly from her shoulder. Her hands wrapped around his head, pulling him even tighter on her open mouth. She felt him touch her breast through the loose petticoat. Nothing else mattered now as his mouth moved to the side of her neck. She could see past him to the blue sky above. In ecstasy she was reminded of the Holy Spirit as the seabirds held motionless by the tempestuous Howth breezes screamed. His gentle hands explored, exciting the most intimate regions of her body.

They took the five o'clock tram back to Dolier Street. On boarding, the boys headed immediately to the top of the tram. Hamilton and Kathleen stayed on the first level and moved out of earshot of the conductor. Hamilton tried to convince himself that their love would weather all the lies. It was too soon to discuss anything with her now—maybe in the next few days, after submitting his resignation to Colonel Lynch.

"Do you still love me, Liam? I mean, now that we've—well, what I mean is…"

He stopped her words with his lips, kissing her softly. "I love you more every moment," he whispered. "And to prove it," his face illuminated, as he remembered the ring. Whatever had possessed him to put the bairin breac ring in his pocket this morning earned his thanks. He took her small, delicate hand and placed the ring on her finger. "What do you say we get married, Kathleen?"

Her eyes welled up. It was the first time he had seen her tearful.

"Well?" he said. "And I promise we'll have lots of pretty children."

"Oh, God, Liam, yes! I'm so happy, and all this time coming back I thought you'd think less of me." She threw her arms around his neck. He placed his hands on her shoulders and held her back.

"There are some things we have to talk about," he said.

"Oh, I know. Don't worry about Ma and Da. Shure, they love you too, Liam. They'll be all for it."

"That's not what I'm concerned about," he said seriously. "It's me. I, well, I may have to go away for a while."

"I know that, Liam. I know that you have to go back and finish your article. She became more excited. "Shure, maybe I could come with you?"

"No!" he interrupted. "No," he said softer. "It's not that—you coming with me—I mean. What I mean is that would be all right." He searched for some temporary excuse to help soften the truth. "Look, I have something to straighten out in my life, but I promise you one thing. You are the only woman I have ever loved. You are the woman I want to marry, and you are the woman that will bear our children."

The noise of the tram reverberated in his ears as she clung to his arm.

"Oh, Liam. As long as we love one another, we can solve all our problems. Oh, yes, and we will have babies. Just think of it, Liam, a baby."

CHAPTER TEN

New York, 1960

"**B**ABY, BABY. THAT'S all I ever hear. What about me, Father?" The young woman had poured out her heart.

It was becoming more evident, however, that Father Riordan was asleep or in a state of contemplative repose.

"Father Riordan?" her voice arose to a full whisper.

"I can hear you, young lady. My hearing is exceptional and there's no need to raise your voice. Now then, let's see what we have here. The reality is that you're carrying a married man's baby. The man wants nothing to do with you, or for that matter the child's welfare. You are probably in your early twenties and in good health. Right so far?" he asked empathetically.

"I guess so, Father," she said.

"It's true, isn't it?" He wanted her to repeat after him. "Isn't it true?"

"Yes, Father. So far, everything you've said is true."

Riordan continued, his mind probing, searching for the advice that was expected of him. "Look here," he said. "You sound to me like a conscientious young woman, or you wouldn't be here, would you?"

"I suppose so, Father."

"Do you realize that this baby that you're carrying might be destined by God to do great deeds? Your baby could be preordained to be a great missionary and save souls, or maybe even a general and save the free world from Communism. What if it was meant that your baby should be born to be a great president?"

Riordan felt he was on a roll now. He was using every trick in the book. The confessional was quiet. It was the quiet that made him realize how thunderous his voice had become. It was then that new images of what might be filled his mind. *What if the little bastard grew up and became a serial killer, what then?* he thought. *Jesus, wouldn't that be something. If Hitler's mother had solicited advice in the confessional, what would the priest have said, given the course of history?*

"It's a sin against God not to have this child." He was more tender now. "You can always give the baby up for adoption. Don't deprive your baby of life. Even as saddened as we become with life, we wouldn't want to end it, now would we?"

"Thank you, Father. Thank you. I really do understand what you're telling me," she said, bravely.

"Good," he said. "Now, make a good Act of Contrition and think good things for your baby and say five Our Fathers and five Hail Marys."

When she left, he relaxed for a while before acknowledging the next penitent. The odor of the confined space was oppressive. He hoped that the number of persons waiting in the penitential pew to relieve their guilt was dwindling. *Dear God, let their sins be uncomplicated and their confessions short*, he prayed silently, as he slid back the door.

"Bless me, Faddah, for I have sinned. It's been a long time since my last confession, er, maybe six years or so."

"I see," Riordan said indulgently. "What was it that finally prompted you to feel the need to talk to a priest?"

"Well, actually, it's nothin' I did, er, recently dat is. I've been haunted, Faddah—by somethin' I did, like—six years ago. Just lately, I've been feelin' woise. I got a family. I'm in a nice parish. The kids go to Cat'lik school. Oh, I go to Choich, Faddah." He hesitated. "But, I don't receive da Sacraments. You know what I mean?"

"I know what that must be like. Why don't you just tell me what sin you committed six years ago?" Riordan asked, looking at the luminous dial of his watch.

"I grew up in Brooklyn, Faddah."

Riordan smiled. He imagined the man with the obvious Brooklyn accent saying, 'I grew up in London, Faddah.' The man also spit out the words with a slack mouth, and Riordan was happy for the screen.

"I had a deprived childhood, Faddah. So, naturally, when I was old enough—well, I—well, let's just say I was industrious. You know. I found ways to make some moolah, Faddah."

Riordan was becoming more interested in the gangster-movie vernacular and moved closer.

"I understand," he said compassionately. "I know what 'industrious' means. Please continue."

"Everything was goin' great. I had a goil. Oh, sure we did some illegal things an all, but I ain't never—well—taken someone out, if ya know what I mean."

"Good, that's good. Please go on."

"This friend of mine—Bonnello—he like puts da make on my goil. Look, Faddah, no matter what ya hear about the mob, when it comes to our women—well, let's say dat we have a deep sense of honor for another man's woman."

He blew his nose, and Riordan hoped the man used a handkerchief.

"This man, Bonnello, you didn't harm him—you didn't —"

The voice interrupted, "Kill 'em? Jeez, Faddah, wha'da ya think I am, anyways? I just told ya, Faddah, I never kilt *no one*. Well, I suppose I may's well have. I put 'em away."

"Away?"

"Yeah, ya know. Away—da clink, da slammer. I sang like a canary. I knew enough to put 'em away for a long time, Faddah, and it didn't seem like a bad deal at the time—ya know. I, er, got my goil back, for starters. I got some cash." His voice was becoming more enthusiastic. "I also got a new life. Not bad, uh? Anyway, Faddah, da whole thing still haunts me. Ya know what I mean? Like I'm some kinda Judus or somethin'."

"So, you were taken care of by the government?" Riordan asked.

"Yeah, da wife, too. We got new noses outta da deal, and I grew a beard. Now we got kids an all."

"I understand your reasons to put the man in prison. I'm still waiting for this sin you've committed. Is there something else?" Riordan asked.

"Sometin' else? Faddah! I was a snitch, an informer—a Judus! God, Faddah, I got money." The man sounded confused. "Isn't dat a sin, Faddah?"

"I'm afraid I don't see the sin against God by turning in a criminal. Judas betrayed an honest man for *his* thirty pieces of silver. You may have broken some underworld ground rules, I'm not even sure you've done something unethical, but I am sure in this matter, you haven't committed a mortal sin."

The confessional was quiet.

"Ya mean, all dese years, I've been carryin' dis boiden?"

Riordan interrupted, "Have you any other sins to confess?"

Riordan helped the man remember other indiscretions: sins of stealing, lying, cheating, and impure thoughts.

He asked the man if he remembered how to make a good Act of Contrition. While the man with the slack mouth reconciled himself with his God, Riordan put a question to himself: *What if Judas had asked for absolution?* His thoughts returned to Ireland.

CHAPTER ELEVEN
Dublin, 1916

D UBLIN CASTLE WAS renovated to provide the British Army a cover for the intelligence officers and other high-ranking officials. Sir John Maxwell's office was on the second floor of the castle. He was tall and slender, in his early sixties, with thinning white hair. His weathered face displayed a red hue, the result of high blood pressure. As the Commander of the British Army and Intelligence in Dublin, he was responsible for suppressing the recent uprising. Initially, the Prime Minister had congratulated him for his prompt resolution of the Irish Problem. Now, there was some concern in Parliament about the treatment of the recalcitrants. These secret trials and executions had to stop, he was told. England had loudly criticized the German Army for inhumane treatment of the Belgian people. Now the Americans and the French were condemning the British for their treatment of the Irish. Sir John Maxwell's face was redder than usual as he slammed down the phone.

"Damn," he muttered through tight lips. "That bloody Lloyd George can be a real arsehole sometimes."

A young captain was in the room acting as aide and secretary. He was working his way up the ranks.

"I'm sorry. You seem to be taking a lot of flak on this Irish trouble," he said apologetically. "By the way, Colonel Lynch is here to see you."

"Oh, good. Do send him in, will you, Jennings." He pushed the large upholstered chair back from the desk and stood up. "Oh, and Jennings, be a good chap will you, and wait outside. We won't be needing any written accounts of this meeting."

Jennings showed the colonel in and closed the door.

"Ah, Lynch. Good to see you. I hope you have good news. My bloody tit's in a wringer with the boys upstairs. I'm afraid not too many people are happy with our losses. Over two hundred and sixteen troops killed and wounded in this Irish thing. That's just as bothersome to me as what we lose in a week on the Western Front. I know these Irish bastards are in with the Germans. You know, the Germans shelled the English coast at the very same time that these Irish arseholes were having their rebellion? Don't tell me *that* was a coincidence. You know the punishment for treason as well as I do, Lynch. They don't even deserve to be shot. Hanging is too good for the bastards." Maxwell bit the end off a cigar and sucked until it formed a perfect round glow from the gold lighter. "All of our fine young men that died," he muttered. "I didn't know it was going to come to this."

"It came to this the moment we set foot in this country with the intent to own it," Lynch said. "And that was eight hundred years ago."

Maxwell offered the colonel a cigar. "I don't need a fucking history lesson."

Lynch ignored the remark. "Well, Sir John, with the help of informants and our special undercover teams, we've captured all but one of the killers," Lynch said proudly.

"Not bad, not bad," Maxwell mused. "And I hear you lost only one man. Jolly good work. I do want you to find this last bastard within the week, though."

Lynch let pass Maxwell's apparent lack of remorse at losing an officer.

"Actually the man we have in place is getting close. An American chap. I'm sure he would have been further along if he hadn't been mugged."

"Mugged?"

"Yes, sir, by one of our own."

"Bloody hell." Maxwell was shaking his head.

"Some of our curfew lads picked him and a girl up after hours. They gave him a pretty bad time before leaving him for dead in the gutter." Lynch stuck the cigar back in his mouth.

"And he's one of our inside fellows, eh?" Maxwell asked.

"Yes, he's back on the job now, and in a better position than ever, I might add. It turns out that the little Irish girl he's seeing is related to his prime suspect. Don't ask me how he managed to achieve this, but he's actually staying at their home. The man's a bloody marvel."

"Good show," Maxwell said in a more affable manner. "I want this bloody mess wrapped up, Lynch. In case your man is not on the right track, I've come up with this."

Maxwell unfolded a large poster. The big gothic letters dominated the space: **Thirty pounds reward**. The photo of Morriarty wasn't a good likeness. It was taken in prison, and the tired, deep-set eyes suggested a resignation to his fate. He had been tortured, but it was his silence that necessitated the words below the photo: *For information leading to the arrest of this man's accomplice*. In smaller type at the bottom, assurance was given that all information would be handled in confidence.

"There," Maxwell said. "This should bring some informants out of the gutter."

The colonel showed disapproval. "Sir, I really do believe we're close here. If this hits the streets, we could be inundated with suspects. Deciphering the information could take weeks." His face was showing signs of perturbation.

"You don't seem to understand, Lynch." Maxwell's face was reddening. "I don't give a bloody good fuck who did it. I want to hand this last Irish arsehole over to the gallows and I could care bloody less about his innocence or guilt."

Lynch stood. "I'll do what I can, sir, to hurry this thing up," he said mechanically.

Maxwell softened a little. "Frankly, I believe whoever we hang this on will have had something to do with this uprising anyway, right?"

"I suppose so, sir," Lynch said, saluting.

Rotating like a soldier, he left the room.

CHAPTER TWELVE

T HE DART GAME was practically over. Sean McIntee stood the required distance on the sawdust-covered floor and needed a double three to win. There was an eerie silence in the public house as McIntee aimed through the dart at the small board on the wall. Back and forth, his right arm swung mechanically like the pendulum on a clock. The dart didn't vary an iota on its course to the target. The thud, as it found its mark, was accompanied by a loud cheer. McIntee's team had won the tournament.

"Drinks on the house, lads!" Seamus O'Connor said, throwing his arms around the pimpled-faced boy.

"Sean, me boyo, shure, aren't you the finest dart player in all of Ireland!"

Sean McIntee liked the attention as he was dragged up to the bar for a tumbler of porter. As the evening wore on, a group sang a come-all-ye of love ballads and the men spoke in hushed tones about the troubles. Seamus O'Connor had an ugly habit of spitting after each sentence. He used his hobnailed boot to mingle the spittle with the sawdust on the floor, making a small mound until it dried into a wood pulp-like mixture.

Sean took a good teasing from some of the professional women who came by the public house for rest and recuperation.

Mr. McDade put an arm around Sean, while the other arm raised a pint of stout. "Here's to Sean McIntee. He has an eye for the darts." He winked at Seamus. "And an eye for the tarts."

Everyone laughed and drank to Sean. Mr. McDade smacked his lips and wiped the foam from his mouth with his sleeve. By nine-thirty, the pub was thick with smoke and smelled like an old ashtray. Everyone was beginning to leave before the imposed curfew.

"Good night, Nora. *Agus slan leat,*" Seamus mumbled, staggering into the darkness.

Sean stood in the quiet twilight, breathing in the damp, fresh air. The clippity-clop of a horse pulling a carriage mingled with the voices. A younger woman waved to Sean from the coach window. She was accompanied by an older man. Both had been drinking earlier in the pub.

"Good night, Sean," she said, blowing a kiss in his direction.

The man pulled her playfully back into the coach and the woman's giggling died off as the man rolled up the coach window. Sean snuffed out the used Woodbine with his foot and turned to go back inside. It was then that he noticed the poster stapled to the outside wall of the pub, illuminated by the gas lamp on the street.

Sean had no doubts about who was with Ned Morriarty that night. Bridget had mentioned Kathleen's concern about her da, after he hadn't even made it home that Saturday night. Sean ripped the likeness of Ned Morriarty from the wall. His body froze as he made an effort to toss the wrinkled poster in the gutter. His thoughts turned to Liam Riordan. Mick Barrett was favoring the American over him for Kathleen's hand. *What about my feelings? Nobody gives a good riddance about how I feel.* He slowly straightened out the wrinkled paper. *Thirty bleedin' pounds. And for what? Turning in a traitor to the Crown. A traitor not only to the Crown, but to me, Sean McIntee!*

CHAPTER THIRTEEN

A S ANNIE STARED blankly through the French-paned kitchen window, her thoughts were on Kathleen. A week had passed since Liam Riordan had returned to his lodging. Although she liked Liam, there were some things about him that made her apprehensive. Kathleen had shared almost everything and still they knew so little about him. He never spoke of his family, and although he confessed to being a Catholic, he seemed awkward and unknowledgeable. She did believe that he genuinely loved Kathleen, and she hoped the love went beyond physical desires. She wished for her daughter the love that she had for Mick.

Her thoughts turned to her husband; she focused past her reflection to Mick and Jamie in the garden. Mick formed a mound of rich, black soil with the spade over the potato roots that Jamie was planting a short distance ahead. In times like this, seeing them together, she felt vulnerable.

Her eyes moistened, something she couldn't allow in front of the family. She knew that Mick loved all the children equally but it was just since Jamie's birth that he had time for the children. Still, she never deprived him of the occasional constitutional to the local pub. Jamie was the lucky one. Mick found it easier to share his love with the lad. It was simple and uncluttered. When the other children were young and Mick was busy at the store, their emotional needs were fulfilled by Annie. Mick's love now was transmitted vicariously through Jamie.

The weather took a change for the worse. Annie could hear the beginning of rainfall on the slate roof. She also heard the sound of the lorry's motor in the front driveway and thought it was Padraig coming to pick up Mick. It was the loud unfamiliar voices that first frightened her. The demanding British voices were coming from all directions. She stood frozen while the soldiers surrounded Mick and Jamie. She wished desperately that she was dreaming and would awaken soon from the horrible nightmare. One of the soldiers trying to remove Jamie was felled by the blade of the spade. She could see the fear on Mick's face. Throwing aside the spade, he reached for his son. The stock of the rifle snapped off as it slammed across his back.

The drama outside was reeling in seconds, though it seemed like time had stood still for Annie Barrett. Other invaders were in the house now. Doors loudly opening and closing. Nothing was private as the foreign accents barked orders, desecrating the sanctity of her home. She had to help Mick! She had to save her son! Breaking away from the grasp of one of the soldiers, she rushed down from the house. Four soldiers had Mick restrained while another, obviously the officer in charge, his face red with vicious rage, held a service revolver to Mick's temple.

"Move a bloody muscle, you Irish bastard, and I'll blow your fucking head off!"

Jamie was clutching the man's leg, screaming, "No! No! You leave me da alone!"

Annie was given time to remove her shrieking son. The lament continued, ringing in her head. The rain was now beating incessantly, like transparent bullets, and for a moment she stared at the erosion of newly formed mounds, exposing the fresh seedlings.

"Why?" she screamed. "Why are you doing this?" Her voice trailed off and she could see the blind panic in Mick's eyes as they dragged him to the waiting lorry. Annie followed, pleading to the man with the gun.

"You'll be informed of your husband's whereabouts, Missus." He holstered his pistol and wrestled Mick into the back of the truck.

Annie held her whimpering son tightly. She heard only the lashing rain around her while the only man she'd ever loved disappeared through a curtain of water.

As the truck left, Mick could see Annie and Jamie through the glass panel in the lorry door. They soon faded into the rain. His mind turned to himself. For their sake, he had to survive. His hands were shackled behind his back and his legs manacled to a bar at the base of the wooden seat. His nose and right eye were numbed by his brain to eradicate the pain. He felt a strange itching sensation on his upper lip and used his tongue to investigate the area. The familiar taste of the heavy sanguineous fluid suggested that he was in for discomfort. If he lived that long. He tried to determine what he was feeling. At least he was alive.

I'm obviously here because I was with Ned that night. All right, all right—just relax, now. Don't they have to prove that I was there? I mean, just because I may have been seen with Ned at the pub doesn't mean that I was with him when he killed that British officer. And what about the poster that I saw?—the one offering the reward? Shure, Ned hadn't talked or they wouldn't need a poster: 'Looking for this man's accomplice'—the reward.

His thoughts sprang to life. "That fukken Bill Elliot!" he hollered, hitting his head on the roof as he sat upright. "He told ya, didn't he."

One of the cockney soldiers pushed him back down with the gun stock. "Hey, watch it, Paddy—make any trouble for us, mate, and you won't make it to Kilmainham alive."

The resentment he felt for Bill Elliot turned to diffidence. What if they... He didn't like to think about death. He wished that he could be holding Annie and little Jamie right now. He must be strong for them. He had to get word to Commandant Roach. That Protestant informing bastard had to be 'rewarded.' The soldiers were surprised when the vacant look on their prisoner's face transformed into a wry smile.

The downpour came as Michael sent the winning point over the crossbar. As the lorry left Phoenix Park, the team was packed into the back like upright sardines.

With their hurleys held high, the victorious shouts waned as the lorry disappeared down the quay. Paddy, Michael, Frank, and Jerry elected to take the long walk back to the schoolyard.

"Be Jasus, that was a close one," Paddy said, taking a drag on his Woodbine. "Won by a bleedin' point."

"Well, we won anyway, didn't we, Paddy? Shure, it doesn't matter if ye win by one or ten points, does it?" Michael said.

"I suppose, if ye look at it that way," Paddy mused.

"How's your head, Frank?" Jerry gestured to bandages over dry blood stains where Frank had been hit with a hurley stick.

"Aw, shure, I'm fine. The St. John's lads said that I had a slight—con..." His mind searched for the name of his malady.

"Concussion, Frank," Paddy said. "Shure, isn't one of the first signs loss of memory?"

The boys laughed.

"Gimme a fag, will ye, Paddy?" Jerry asked as they crossed the street.

Ha' Penny Bridge spanned the Liffy and was a shortcut back to the school. In years past, it had been a toll bridge and Dubliners had paid a ha'penny for the right to cross.

Colonel Lynch was still in his uniform as he left the castle. He knew staying in uniform wasn't prudent, but he was running late for his meeting with Hamilton. A couple of days had passed since his urgent meeting with Sir John Maxwell. Later that day, Lynch had received a written order. The posters were distributed immediately. All respondents would be channeled through the local constabulary. He knew the reason that Maxwell was disinclined to do it his way. It would take too much bloody time, and God forbid we might get the right man. Maxwell had a "no questions asked" policy; just hand over a sacrificial lamb. Lynch still felt that he knew these people. Sure, thirty pounds was a lot of money, but not enough to carry the burden of traitor after your name. These days in Dublin, a man betraying the cause was committing one of the seven deadly sins. He was momentarily content with the idea that he still had some time. It would be only a matter of days before Hamilton brought him the real perpetrator.

It went against his better judgment to wear his uniform. What if someone recognized Lynch, the publisher, in a British uniform? He knew, however, that the Grafton Street Coffee Shop had private booths. He was becoming more at ease now with the reality of privacy as he walked down the quay toward College Green.

Michael recognized him first. "I'm just after seeing a double of that man who's a friend of Liam's."

Paddy looked back at the British soldier. "Who are ye talkin' about? What friend?"

"You know, Liam's boss. The one at the hospital," Michael said. "Shure, hasn't he been at the house, too?"

"You mean Mr. Lynch?" Paddy asked curiously. "Shure, what would he be doin' in a British uniform?"

"Impersonatin' an officer?" Michael asked.

"Maybe," Paddy waited. "Impersonatin' a publisher. Are ye shure it was him?"

"Pretty shure, Paddy. Why don't we follow him. You'd recognize him, wouldn't ye?"

"I would indeed," Paddy said with assurance. "Let's go, lads."

The boys stayed a respectable distance behind Colonel Lynch. Lynch's mind turned once more to the uniform. The role of publisher gave him little gratification. He pulled the hat down farther to cover his bushy eyebrows. The lowered hat didn't fool the three inquisitive boys for a moment.

Lynch turned the corner at the bottom of Grafton Street. He looked back, distrustfully, before entering the coffee shop. That's when Paddy confirmed Michael's suspicions.

"Let's wait an' see what he's up to, lads," Paddy said covertly.

He was on his second cup of coffee when he spotted Colonel Lynch, whose sharp, beady eyes surveilled the few patrons before he acknowledged Hamilton's presence. When he got to the booth, Hamilton made a clumsy effort to stand and Lynch gestured him down.

"Sorry about the uniform. I'm running a bit late," he said breathlessly. "Anyway, it doesn't make a lot of difference anymore." He looked around impatiently. "A cup of bloody tea would hit the spot, though."

Hamilton interrupted, "What exactly do you mean, Colonel—it doesn't make a lot of difference? What about my cover?"

"Oh, your cover. No need to worry, ol' chap. It's over. We do have to be a little concerned, until we get you back to London."

"London? It's over?"

"Yes, Lieutenant. It's over. We have our man and you were right all along. We should give you a bloody medal."

Hamilton's jaw dropped. His eyes had a frightened look. "You mean you've already arrested someone?"

His mind begged for a sign that he was dreaming as his plans for him and Kathleen became more distant. "Who? Who did you bring in? Was it…"

The Colonel's face gleamed proudly. "Yes," he said. "Barrett. You were right on, ol' chap."

"But, I haven't finished my report. Mr. Barrett is still just a suspect. There's no real proof. I have to know for sure."

Lynch opened a pack of Players, offering one to Hamilton. "Cigarette?" He paused to light his own. "Look, it was a combination of things," Lynch said on a stream of smoke. "Actually, it was a tip on that poster I told you about the other day. I must admit, I had my bloody doubts, but when an informer identified Barrett as the assassin—well, I felt it was asking too much to be a coincidence."

Lynch noticed Hamilton's downcast expression. "What's the matter, man? You look like you've lost your bloody best friend. You should be celebrating—it's over!"

Hamilton placed his hands on the sides of his head, elbows on the table. The men were silent as the waitress poured the colonel a cup of tea.

"More coffee, darlin'?" she asked Hamilton.

His mind was elsewhere.

"Coffee, sir?"

Lynch waved her away. "What is it, man? You look bloody awful."

Hamilton poured out his heart to the older man, hoping for some indication of understanding. He knew it wasn't the soldierly thing to do.

Lynch had grown attached to Hamilton, and although he had never married, under other circumstances, Hamilton might have been the son he'd never had.

"Christ almighty." He was genuinely concerned for his young subordinate. "You realize that your life won't be worth two-pence if you try to explain yourself to these people. They'll never believe that it wasn't you who turned him in. After all, that was your bloody mission, man."

Hamilton's eyes widened. "That's it! Who turned in Mick Barrett? I'll be able to give them the name of the real informer. My God, he's probably someone they already know. They'll believe me if I…"

Lynch interrupted him disconsolately, "It's no good, William." It was the first time the older man called him by his first name. "They won't believe you. Why should they? You've lied all along. Besides, we don't know his name. The man was protected. It was done through the Irish constabulary." Disappointed, he shook his head. "The whole thing was designed to get results. No questions asked."

Hamilton became annoyed. "Damn it. Someone must have recognized the informer. I'll inquire myself. I'll…"

Lynch answered Hamilton's annoyance with the same level of anger. "Look here, man, I've bloody-well told you." Slowly he mellowed. "I've just told you. We don't *know* the informer. As I understand it, he asked to wear a disguise. One of the guards met with him. He gave us the names, the events, everything. I verified his story. It all matched perfectly with your report."

"Where is he now? I mean, Mick Barrett. Has he already been picked up?" His mind turned to Kathleen, her mother, and their agony.

Lynch put out the cigarette. "He's probably in Kilmainham as we speak." He looked up from the smoldering ashtray. "Look, ol' chap, I'm really sorry about this whole bloody mess, but you have to think about yourself now. If you tell this Kathleen girl who you really are—well, if I were in her place—I'd probably kill you myself."

Hamilton wasn't listening. He was about to stand up when Lynch pushed him down in the seat.

He became the officer in charge again. "Look here—you're being shipped out—it's over!"

"But, I love her! You don't understand. I was going to inform you of my resignation today. We're going to be married." He placed his hands again on the sides of his head.

"I'll expect you back at my office within the hour. That should give you enough time to pack. I forbid you to contact any of these people. Do you understand?" Lynch stood up and leaned over the table. "For what it's worth, my tenure was also terminated. Next week I return to London, and you, my friend, have orders cut for Belgium. Remember, my office—and don't be late. Belgium beats jail." He turned and left.

Across the street from the coffee shop, the four boys crowded in a bricked doorway next to a busy store. The late afternoon was still gloomy from an earlier downpour.

"Shure, isn't it him, Paddy?" Michael asked.

Paddy looked over his cupped hands as he lit the Woodbine. Between the cars and the trams, Paddy recognized Lynch.

For a short man, Lynch took long, determined strides, and since meeting with Hamilton, he had less regard for his disguise. He was the colonel once again, and Hamilton had been informed of his new assignment. The last of the assassins was accounted for and he was going home.

"Be Jasus, it's him all right," Paddy said.

"It's Lynch! Wearin' an English uniform. Some fukken publisher, eh?" Jerry held the boys in the doorway. "Let's wait an' see who he might have been with. My guess is Liam Riordan. Then again, what if Liam Riordan doesn't know that his publisher is a British soldier?"

"Are ye kiddin', man?" Paddy said, wetting the end of the Woodbine so it wouldn't stick to his lip. "Were you born bleedin' yesterday? Of course he knows. Shure, it wouldn't surprise me a bit if he…"

Michael pulled the boys back in the doorway. "It's him!" he whispered loudly. "It's Liam Riordan."

Hamilton walked obediently from the coffee shop toward his flat on Wicklow Street.

Paddy made a low whistling sound through closed teeth. "So, that's it. Lynch, the soldier, and Riordan. I'd give ye a fukken tanner if they were talkin' about publishin'."

"Wait till Da hears this," Michael said excitedly.

Frank pulled anxiously on his big brother's sleeve. "We should tell them, Jerry, shouldn't we? I know me ma said…"

Jerry interrupted, pulling his arm back. "Ah, shut up," he admonished Frank. Although he was angry with his brother's attempt to disclose their secret, he knew that the Barrett boys had to be told, especially now. He looked into the questioning face of Paddy Barrett.

"It's about yer da, Paddy."

Paddy looked at Frank, then back to Jerry. "What should ye be tellin' us? What's Frank talkin' about anyway?"

"We swore on me ma's Bible we wouldn't tell a soul…" He hesitated as Michael moved instinctually closer to Paddy, anticipating the bad news. "Yer da was at our house the night that Ned Morriarty kilt that English soldier up on Harcourt Street. Frank and meself were in bed. They thought we were asleep. Shure, didn't we hear it all."

Paddy placed his hand protectively on his younger brother's shoulder and although he tried to appear brave, his voice was tremulous. "What did ye hear?"

"We heard yer da talk about him and Ned shootin' yer man." Jerry picked nervously at the mortar between the bricks. "Yer da didn't do the shootin', though. We were sworn to secrecy, not to tell a soul. 'Course ye know why it is we had to say something."

Michael's eyes were welling up as he looked at Paddy for assurance.

"Da'll be fine," Paddy said, unconvincingly.

Frank nodded. "Shure, that's why we had to tell ye. This fella, Riordan, probably isn't who he says he is and, God forbid, what if he's on t'yer da?"

Paddy remembered seeing the poster of Ned Morriarty that was plastered all over Dublin. "I think that we'd better be gettin' home, Michael. Da'll know what to do with Liam Riordan."

It was beginning to sprinkle again when the boys said their goodbyes. Rather than returning to White Friar Street, Paddy and Michael went home in silence, each conjuring images of pain, confusion and embarrassment. Michael wept and was thankful for the rain while Paddy fought back tears of rage.

Hamilton had packed his belongings. Instead of putting his service revolver in the suitcase, he tucked it reflectively into his belt. To look more native, he wore a brown corduroy jacket with tan pants and an open-neck shirt. He slung a Mackintosh over his shoulder and put on a cap. It had taken about an hour, and although the colonel had demanded his presence at the castle, he was determined to see Kathleen. He left the bags in the foyer, paid the landlady, and left for the Barretts'. He thought it better to walk since he needed time to formulate the delicate explanations. It was going to be difficult, at best.

Especially now that Mick had been arrested. *How am I supposed to act? With raised eyebrows, dumbfounded? Totally surprised and depressed?* At the end of Harcourt Street, Hamilton stopped. He waited a moment and turned around, overcome with guilt and frustration. His love for Kathleen prevailed, compelling him on toward Milltown. He opened a new pack of

Players and lit a cigarette. He put the pack in his pocket and glanced at his watch.

He thought how timely if Kathleen were to ride by. *It is already past four-thirty. No such luck. She's probably home by now. Wait until tomorrow.* He chastised himself, his stupidity. *Christ, she knows by now that her father's been arrested. How can I tell her who I really am without her assuming that I had something to do with it? That was my goddamn mission, to arrest her father. Did I fuck things up?*

Lynch was right. He could be court-martialed by his own people or knee-capped and executed by his new-found friends. As he crossed the canal bridge, two white swans flew by and gently descended to the protected rushes in the quiet water below. He found this serenity inconsistent with the loathsome hatred that people felt for one another. Irish against English, French against German, Catholic against Protestant, rich against poor. He decided that the best way to approach the Barrett family would be to maintain the masquerade. Continue the lie. They do not know about William Hamilton. *That's what I'll do,* he thought, *I am Liam Riordan. I can console Kathleen and the family. When everything is settled down, she might be more understanding.* He would explain when the time was right. He pushed aside thoughts of Mick's execution as he reflected on the idea of perpetuating the "Liam Riordan" disguise.

The rain had let up and the late afternoon sun illuminated the cotton-like tops of the dark clouds. A rainbow contrasted the bleak, blue-gray landscape, and Hamilton hoped that it was surely a good omen.

Twenty long, painful minutes passed before he reached the Barretts'. Although he was familiar with the surroundings, it was as if he were seeing things for the first time. He stood by the gate for a while, putting off the inevitable. He held the awkward latch and stared at the crooked sign that read, *Barretts, Bogside, Milltown.* He had passed through the gate on happier occasions. He prepared himself for continued deceit. At the crest of the dirt driveway, Paddy and Michael appeared from the side of the house. They stopped when they saw him and without saying anything, turned and ran inside.

"Hey, Paddy! Michael!" They had seen him. It worried him that they didn't acknowledge him, but he rationalized their hasty departure; they ran because they were confused. When he reached the door, it opened before he had a chance to use the brass knocker. Seamus O'Connor's big frame filled the doorway and John Murphy loomed behind him. Their expressions were anything but friendly as they eased Hamilton back and gently closed the door. Hamilton didn't take his eyes off them and gingerly backed away.

"Well now," O'Connor said with a twisted smile. "If it isn't Liam Riordan."

"Or whatever yer bleedin' name is," Murphy said, distancing himself from his companion.

Hamilton stopped and extended his right arm as his left hand pulled back the jacket, exposing the revolver. "I'm not here to give you men any trouble. I just need to talk to Kathleen."

"I think you've talked enough," O'Connor said.

"I don't know what you mean," Hamilton said insolently. *Jesus, they know who I am. But how?*

"I see you have an Army issue British revolver there," O'Connor said, unconcerned, while Murphy continued to move around Hamilton.

"I wouldn't do anything stupid," Hamilton said, turning to Murphy.

The larger man tried to draw his attention. "Haven't ye done enough damage, man, skulkin' around? Our friend's in jail now because of you an' they probably gave ye a bleedin' medal."

"I just want to talk to Kathleen. That's all. I owe *her* an explanation, not you. Now move aside."

If he drew the weapon, he was going to have to use it. He reconciled himself to the truth. Kathleen was going to hear everything. That was all that he had left. No more deceit, no concocted stories, and no lies. She would finally know who he was, know he loved her, and intended to marry her. That's all he could do now: tell the truth.

His rambling and inattention to the danger at hand was the mistake that John Murphy needed. Hamilton was too slow drawing the revolver. Murphy seized his armed hand in a viselike grip. As O'Connor fired the right cross, Hamilton drew on every ounce of strength to hold on to the pistol and ducked, allowing the big fist to graze his head. The forward motion of O'Connor continued, sending the big man past Hamilton to the ground. As Murphy drew Hamilton's left arm toward him, Hamilton moved with him and in martial arts style, drove a flat, open palm upwards under Murphy's septum. He could feel the cartilage collapse. At the same time, he stepped alongside and slightly behind Murphy. Hamilton's sweeping right leg took Murphy's right leg, sending the man to the ground in a full-point osoto gari. O'Connor, attempting to stand, didn't see the round-house left hand, still brandishing the revolver. It was a lucky swing. The big man's forehead split under the impact.

Hamilton didn't feel in control; his anger directed his movements. O'Connor was still standing, blood gushing from the open wound.

Hamilton held the man up with his right hand and rammed the revolver under his chin. O'Connor was resigned to die and Hamilton was more than ready to accommodate. He was tired of being pushed around. He heard Annie Barrett's voice and realized that she had been screaming orders, to no avail.

"Stop it—now! There's been enough killing!" She stepped between the men. She stared glassy eyed at the gun. "If you don't mind, Mr. Riordan—or whatever your mother calls you—put that thing away and leave! Heart of God, haven't you hurt enough people?"

Hamilton put the gun away. "I'm really sorry. I didn't mean for things to turn out this way." *Jesus*, he thought, *how inane.* "Can I see Kathleen, Annie?" He spoke like a child asking for someone to come out and play. "Please?" he begged.

"Kathleen has nothing to say to you. As a matter of fact, she loathes you for what you've done to this family."

"But I want to tell her…"

Annie interrupted him. "Just leave! No explanations will bring back my husband, do you understand? Now, please go!"

Her face was drawn and determined. The usually pretty mouth was taut, resolute, and as he turned away, he remembered her eyes: unforgiving, devoid of any friendship or love.

There was an uncomfortable silence in the Barrett household. O'Connor and Murphy were speaking in low tones while they washed away the bloody evidence of their fight with Hamilton. Across the room, Annie sat and quietly waited for them to finish. Kathleen had closed herself in her room, and Jamie had fallen into an exhausted sleep. Paddy and Michael were kicking a soccer ball back and forth, driftlessly, in the back yard.

"What'll happen to Da, Paddy? D'ya think he'll be all right?"

"Oh shut up," Paddy said. "I'm thinkin'."

Inside the house, Annie broke the silence. "Mr. O'Connor," Annie said irritably, "I'm well aware you and Mr. Murphy are with the movement. Mick's never confided in me. Not about his activities involving the rebellion anyway. I don't know why in God's name they took him away. The boys told me that Mick might have been with Ned. They heard it from Frank Elliot. I know you know more than I do. Please?"

Murphy looked quickly at O'Connor and then back down at the towel on his arms. He avoided making eye contact with Annie.

"I'm not asking you to own up to anything," Annie continued. "But you must know someone who can help Mick. Legally or illegally." She was beginning to sob. "You—you must know."

"There's no escaping the bloody bastards once they've taken someone. Begging your pardon, Missus," O'Connor replied, looking quickly at Annie.

"We haven't had much luck, Annie," Murphy said, placing the towel on the drain board. "Gettin' anyone out, I mean."

"But Mick's innocent. He couldn't shoot anyone. I know that, even if you don't," Annie protested.

"Makes no difference to the British," O'Connor said. "You can't get much more innocent than the women and children they kill with their bombs."

"That's right, Annie," Murphy intervened. "Shure, it's not innocence that determines your fate. It's luck, isn't it?" He stared blankly at the floor. "If they reckon he was Ned's accomplice…" He silently shook his head.

"I'll not hear that!" Annie said with icy composure. "Mick's always been a good, decent man. I know he couldn't kill anyone. That I know! I'm counting on you two"—she pointed at each of them—"to see that word gets to the proper sources. I want my husband back." Annie saw the two men to the door.

She walked over to where Jamie was sleeping. *Poor little lad,* she thought. *Bad enough having to grow up in these times. Now he's seen the troubles first-hand, his father shackled and dragged away like some animal. Lord God, don't let that be the last time he sees his father alive.*

Annie heard a muffled sob coming from Kathleen's room. She quietly knocked on the door and went in.

"Oh, Ma, what are we going to do?" Kathleen wept. "What can be done to help Da?"

Annie sat down on the bed and gently took Kathleen into the security of her arms.

"I can't believe it, Ma—I—I mean, Liam couldn't have done that to Da." Her body heaved between sighs.

"We won't talk about it now," Annie said in a solemn tone. She sat and gently rocked her daughter, letting the grief and tears pour out.

CHAPTER FOURTEEN

"WHERE DID YOU get the money?" Nora was quizzing her son. "You were buying everyone drinks tonight with fresh one-pound notes. Now where in God's name did you get the money?"

Sean pulled away from her grip. "Who cares where I got it? I worked for it. I saved me wages," he lied.

"Jesus, Mary and Joseph, son, I know you're lying. Now tell me where you got the crisp notes."

Sean was frightened and confused. Earlier that day everything had seemed justified. The Barretts had no right accepting a lodger over him. It had been predestined that he and Kathleen would one day be married and have a family. As he sat on the edge of his bed, his hands covering his face, Nora continued to question him. She was beginning to believe her worst suspicions.

"Did you get that money for turning in Mick Barrett?"

When he looked up at her, tearful and frightened, he was still her little Sean. He sighed, "I'm sorry, Ma! It's just that Kathleen…" He didn't have to finish the sentence.

Nora held him. She couldn't scold him. He was just a lad, and he had been hurt. "There, there," she said. "Your ma is going to make everything all right."

"They'll kill me if they find out, Ma, won't they?" he asked fretfully.

"Nobody's going to hurt you, son." She needed a plan, and she needed one fast. She thought as she rocked her son back and forth.

CHAPTER FIFTEEN

T HE CENTER OF the courtyard was dominated by a high, wooden platform, the support for a sturdy scaffold. The full moon clearly illuminated the gallows and cast long shadows on the cobblestones below. A long corridor outside the cells was separated from the yard by steel-framed, wire-glassed windows so that all those awaiting execution had a view of the gallows. The cells were small, and rumor had it that the whitewashed plaster-coated walls were over two feet thick. A brown, army-surplus blanket covered a black, metal-framed bedstead, the only furniture in the room. An unattended galvanized bucket stood in the corner. Its contents defiled the air. A candle supplied light and warmth.

Mick clenched the bars next to his face and gazed aimlessly through the glass to the wooden structure beyond. Though the terror of the gallows was an awesome reminder of the arena of death, the yard beyond the glass offered an opportunity for freedom. Occasionally, Mick's focus fixed on the surface, which reflected an image of the young prisoner in the next cell. Mick could tell he wasn't sleeping by the glow of the cigarette.

"How long have you been here?" Mick asked the image.

The glow came closer.

"I've been here about a week. I was at Mercer Street Hospital for a while," the voice said. "What's yer name?"

"Mick—Mick Barrett."

"My name is Kevin." The voice was tremulous.

"How old are ye, Kevin?"

"Sixteen. I'm almost seventeen, though. I was at the post office with

90

Mr. Connolly." The voice was becoming bolder. "God, he's a great man. Shure, I don't mind dying when he tells me what I'm dying for. Ye know, Mick?"

"I know," Mick said, not disparaging the young man's justification for dying.

"By any chance, do ye have an extra fag, Kevin? They took mine away."

The boy stretched between the cells with the cigarette. "Do ye need a match?"

"If ye don't mind," Mick said. He lit the cigarette and took a deep drag. "Did you have a visitor earlier?" Mick asked, hoping that he might also be allowed to see his own family.

"Visitor? Oh, yes. Well, it wasn't exactly a visitor—it was the priest."

"The priest?"

"Yes. They allowed me my last confession and Communion."

As the boy spoke, Mick's thoughts strayed. He was beginning to feel weak again, a weakness soon to be accompanied by fear and cowardice. He remembered how he had prayed before, under the staircase at York Street. It seemed like yesterday. He'd prayed to God, and God had let him down. God let Annie and his family down. *Fuck God. God's no fukken help.*

The young man, rambling in and out of his thoughts, was right. You need something tangible to believe in, like freedom. Ireland's freedom. Not for God. For Ireland. That's something he could leave for his family. The martyrs' legacy. He died for his country. Who the fuck dies these days for God anyway? His mouth twisted, distorting his smile.

"So, that was the priest you had with ye then? When is it going to happen?"

"In the mornin'—early, I'm shure." After a long silence, the boy continued, "Would ye mind stayin' up with me? Talkin' an all—ye know what I mean."

"I know." Mick needed to be more reassuring now. "We'll talk 'til they come, lad."

The boy was from Donnycarney and had gone to the Christian Brothers at Marino. He had been attending St. Joseph's Secondary School when he'd joined the Volunteers. He was the oldest of five children. He talked about his capture. The British had bombarded the General Post Office for four days. The roof was gone. The food was gone. The ammunition was gone. They had fought without cessation and had sung songs of freedom. Padraic Pearse stood beside Connolly. He vaguely remembered their words. *No one should be afraid to face the judgment of God or posterity.*

Mick, finally talking to someone who had been there, asked him about the surrender.

"Why? Why did Connolly surrender to those bastards?"

"They said it was to prevent the slaughter of unarmed, innocent lives. We were outnumbered, just sitting there. Oh, I guess we could have thrown stones."

They smiled.

"I'm shure Mister Connolly didn't believe that we'd be shot or hanged without a trial or hearing of any kind."

"You mean no one's had a trial?"

"Well, not that I know of anyway," the boy said. "Shure, I'd rather have died there. They're just killin' prisoners here. Ye didn't know?"

"No," Mick said, discouraged. "We didn't know."

"I hear ya spoil yerself," Kevin said, changing the subject.

"What's that?" Mick asked.

"Shite yer pants. When they hang ye, ye shite yer pants."

"I didn't know that," Mick said.

"Well, that's what they told me. The officers here askin' the questions—the eh…"

"Interrogators," Mick said.

"Yeah, interrogators. They wanted me to name other men in our battalion. I wouldn't tell the limey bastards anything! Then they went on about this hangin' business. *You'll crap your bloody trousers, ole' boy, and your neck will stretch when the bones snap apart,"* he mimicked them. "Then, one of them grabbed me mickey. *It'll stretch this far on its own when they drop your arse.* Anyway, I didn't believe any of that stuff. Mister Connolly said either way, hangin' or shootin' is fast and ye don't feel a thing."

There was a silence.

"He's right, ain't he? I won't feel a thing—I mean, none of that stuff they talked about?" he asked, looking for reassurance.

"It's very fast," Mick said. *Jasus Christ, who am I trying to convince?* So far, he'd learned that he would have no trial. He thought about Annie. "Did they let you see your family, or will you see them in the morning before you…"

"No. They already told me if I gave them some names they might consider it. I'm tellin' them fuck-all!"

Barrett couldn't believe that the bastards wouldn't let the boy see his family before he died.

It was six o'clock when they came for Kevin. He walked out like a man. Mick stared at the young, brave, innocent face, a black shock of hair tumbling down over his blue eyes.

"Goodbye, Mick," he said, nervously. "See ya in Heaven."

Mick didn't want to watch, but he felt that it was his responsibility to witness the last moments in the life of the young martyr for Ireland. The boy refused the black hood and sang the "Soldier's Song" until the slam of the trap door silenced the brave words in the damp spring morning.

CHAPTER SIXTEEN

"I'LL SEE YOUR ha'penny and raise you a farthing."

The man threw the three farthings into the pile of coins and drained the last of the whiskey in his glass. Hamilton glanced over his cards to the poker-faced man sitting across from him. James Scott was in his late twenties, tall and powerfully built, with a shock of curly red hair. His walrus mustache was waxed at the ends and turned upwards, suggesting a perpetual leer.

Hamilton was billeted at the castle while he awaited orders. He would be leaving for London next week for indoctrination and then on to an assignment in Belgium. Colonel Lynch had already gone. He had come to like the irascible colonel even though he had received a scathing tongue lashing for his visit to the Barretts. His showing up had fortified the family's hatred for him, and thrashing the neighbors didn't help.

"Well, what'll it be, ole' boy—are you in or out?" Scott asked, refilling their glasses.

"In," Hamilton said, flicking the farthing with his thumb, launching it into the pile.

"Well, Captain Scott, let's see what ya got."

Scott twisted the end of his mustache and turned his cards face up. "Can you beat two pair, Willie, ole' boy?" he asked with an Oxford accent.

"Those two I can," Hamilton said, laughing. Hamilton stacked his winnings next to him. "Want to try one more deal?"

"One more then, and that's it for me."

"You deal," Hamilton said.

As the ruddy-complexioned officer dealt the cards, Hamilton was thinking about his last meeting with the colonel. Lynch had no doubt that the movement would seek retribution. Lynch had demanded that he not leave the castle, at least until he was ready to depart for London. The colonel had made him swear on his honor as an officer and a gentleman. Hamilton knew that Lynch was right. He knew that he had to forget the Barretts. He even knew that he had to forget Kathleen. As he placed one card after the other, fanning them in his hands, he could see her face. It hurt to think about how much she despised him. There was nothing he could do to change that. Not even reuniting Mick with his family, something he could not do. Scott's demands returned his thoughts to the game.

"Ante up, Will—ante. Still thinking about that Irish girl, eh?"

"Sorry," Hamilton said, flicking another farthing. "I didn't think it was that obvious."

"Jacks or better. Can you open?" Scott asked.

Hamilton had two aces among the five cards. "Two-pence," he said, throwing the two pennies on the table and discarding three cards.

Hamilton liked his new companion, his roommate for over a week. Captain James Scott was also awaiting new orders. He was a good listener, and both men shared their disillusionment with their duties in Ireland. He worked in the same branch of intelligence as Hamilton. He was in charge of files and records, which included names of people suspected of or belonging to illegitimate or anti-Crown organizations. Scott had even trusted Hamilton into his enigmatic world of paper files, and when he asked Scott if he could see the Barrett file, it was handed to him. Scott knew what Hamilton wanted. Any information recorded by the guards who'd questioned the informant. As he thumbed the pages he recognized his own notes. He remembered stopping at the pages describing Mick's arrest. He visualized Annie and Jamie and the abominable treatment of his innocent friends. The thought of their horrendous fear made him shudder. It's clear why they hated him! He continued turning pages and found no evidence that would incriminate the informer. Once again, Scott brought him back to reality.

"I see your two-pence and raise a farthing," Scott said, discarding one card.

"Well, you got a straight or a flush there?" Hamilton smiled as Scott gave himself the card.

"Or I might be going for a full house," Scott said. Hamilton's three new cards still left him with just two aces.

"It's gonna cost you to stay in," Hamilton said, tossing in a thruppence.

While Scott occupied his mind on how best to deceive Hamilton into believing he had drawn the card he'd needed, Hamilton's thoughts turned to Father Donnelly. He had considered seeing the priest, and, although the idea seemed risky, Hamilton was giving the notion more consideration. On top of everything else, he would have to tell the priest that he was an Episcopalian.

"Three pence it is," Scott said. He dropped another coin onto the table. "And it will cost you the same again to stay in." He lit a cigarette.

"Sorry," he said, offering one to Hamilton.

Hamilton tapped the end of the cigarette on the table and placed it between his lips.

Scott reached over and lit it. "Want to talk about it?" he asked.

"Huh?" Hamilton mumbled, looking up from his cards. "The game takes my mind off my problems."

"Sure," Scott said.

"Then let's play, ole' boy. If you want to stay in the game, ole' man, deposit three pennies."

"Oh, er, sure," Hamilton said, calling Scott's bet. His face became resolute. "What if I told you that I was thinking of seeing the priest?"

"What?"

"The priest," Hamilton said, more earnestly. "I could tell the priest everything—that my intentions were to protect Mick. Even how I planned to resign and marry Kathleen. I, er, do have proof that someone else turned him in," he said, referring to the files.

"Only if I let you," Scott said. "Besides, he'd never listen to you, ole' boy."

"He would if I went to confession."

"But you're a bloody Protestant!"

"*You're* a Catholic, Scott—you could help me. I —"

Scott interrupted, "You're not only obstinate, you're also bloody stupid."

"It will probably be a first time for Donnelly, too," Hamilton smiled.

The next day was Saturday; Hamilton had been up for an hour. He was bored with his seclusion. It was impossible to think about anything but Kathleen. He told himself to forget her. He tried reading and stared, fixated on the open book, her image pervading the gray pages. His need to share the truth with someone who knew them both dominated his thoughts. He knew his foolishness was winning, but he didn't care. The likelihood that he would visit Father Donnelly was becoming a reality. The knock turned his attention to the door.

"Yeah," Hamilton said. "It's open."

Scott entered, his imposing frame clad in rumpled pajamas. The sleep was still in his eyes and his red, unkempt hair gave him the look of a rag doll. He held a mug of tea in one hand and an envelope in the other, his usual high spirits replaced with a grim face. He collapsed into the easy chair. Hamilton offered him a cigarette, which he waved away.

"Did we drink last night or what?"

Hamilton lit a cigarette and smiled. He pointed to the table with the stacks of copper coins. "You also lost a little change."

"It's not my game, ole' boy. Next time we'll play pontoon," Scott said, attempting to smile. "Anyway, that's not why I came by. I know what you're going through—this Barrett thing and all. Frankly, I wish England would just give this bloody country back to the Irish."

Hamilton went over to the kitchenette, where he had been boiling water on a Primus. He poured the water into a cup and added two teaspoons of liquid Turkish coffee. "Want some?"

"I'm drinking tea," Scott said. "Thanks anyway. Look, I'd be bloody well court-martialled for what I'm about to show you, and so would you just for listening. In a short space of time we've become—well, friends. Right?"

"Right," Hamilton said. His face looked painful from the first sip of the black concoction. Scott looked inquisitively at Hamilton, waiting for more confirmation.

"Right?" Scott asked. This time he was more demanding.

"Right," Hamilton acknowledged "You're probably the only friend I have in Ireland right now." Hamilton continued, with his arms extended, "Hell, in the whole world."

"I'm serious, Will," Scott said. "I mean we're talking conspiracy here—treason. Showing favoritism toward the enemy."

"What the hell are you talking about, Scott? So you showed me some goddamned records. Hell, those are my reports too. Don't go getting sensitive on me."

"I know that—but I have complete files that involve Senior Officer input, even as high up as Sir John Maxwell. You know as well as I that two signatures are required to review records."

"So that's it." Hamilton was becoming annoyed. "You're having second thoughts about showing me the goddamn files?"

"No, Will, it's not that. It's what I'm about to show you." He held the paper toward Hamilton. The letter had a broken red-wax seal.

"I'm sorry," Hamilton said nervously, taking the folded letter from his friend. "Look, Scott —"

Scott waved his hand. "That's all right, ole' boy. I know what you're going through."

As Hamilton read the letter, Scott continued talking.

"It came in yesterday afternoon. I wanted to tell you last night. I thought it best to wait until I was sure. Until I was sober. I wanted to be accountable."

Hamilton wasn't listening. His mouth moved, uttering silently the words he knew one day would be inevitable. The dreaded words that turned his blood cold. His breath became short as his chest moved visibly from the shock. When he finished reading, he read it again and looked at Scott. His expression showed the melancholy of a person bearing the pain that comes when someone close dies.

"Thanks."

"You can see, ole' boy, why I didn't want to show you this. This goes against everything we stand for. This letter indicates that there have been secret inquisitions. No trials. Executions in the name of the Crown. Because the Irish Volunteer Army yielded to the authority of the Crown— falls under British dominion—I expect they're calling it treason. Especially given the fact we're in a war."

"Executed," Hamilton whispered, not acknowledging Scott's comments. "Mick's hanged Wednesday morning and I ship out that same night. That's not a lot of time to plan something. The bastards couldn't have timed it better.

"Damn!" he shouted, slamming his fist on the table, upsetting all of the stacked coins. "They're not getting away with it," he said deliberately. "When are you leaving, Scott?"

Scott didn't like the look on his companion's face. "As of tomorrow afternoon, I'm relieved of my duties. I leave for London Thursday. Why?"

"Hmmm, that gives me just four days." Hamilton handed the paper back to Scott and led him toward the door. Scott was reluctant.

"I don't like that look on your face, Willie, ole' boy."

"Stick around Scottie—I think I'm gonna need your help," Hamilton said, closing the door on his bewildered friend. He removed a small black book from the bureau and allowed the pages to flutter off his thumb. He stopped the pages by inserting his pen. His mouth moved silently, mumbling the priest's name, "Donnelly—Donnelly." He wrote the number on a piece of paper, left the room and used the phone at the end of the hall. "Yes," he said. "Could you tell me when Father hears confessions tonight?"

CHAPTER SEVENTEEN

HAMILTON WAITED FOR the last person to enter the confessional. He was listless, and his thoughts alternated between anxiety and optimism. He had begun to chew his fingernails when he heard the door nearest to him open. An older woman, wearing a knit shawl, held the door. She looked up at him and the wrinkled, toothless mouth smiled gracefully. He thought of sins she had perpetrated against her God or the Crown. He imagined her leaving a shopping bag with a bomb by a British garrison. The innocent antiquity was a tremendous asset when it was needed. He dismissed the improbable notions, thanked her, and moved into the dark confessional.

He knelt on the wooden kneeler and clasped his hands prayerfully, staring at the small closed-off screen. He was terrified. He could hear the murmurings of the person on the other side. He recognized Father Donnelly's indulgent voice.

Hamilton was repeating over and over in his mind the opening words. *Bless me Father, for I have sinned.* James Scott had tutored him well. The noise of the door sliding on its wooden rail seemed to last forever. The thud as it stopped was accompanied by Father Donnelly's opening acclamation.

"In nomine patri et fili et spiritu sancti."

Hamilton was dumbfounded. *Sweet Jesus*, he thought *I've forgotten everything.* Just one word to begin the opening dialogue—the rest would come—he knew it. *Relax. Just relax.* He opened his mouth to speak and nothing came forth.

"Yes?" Donnelly said impatiently. "Please begin."

"Father—I—" Hamilton shuddered.

"Is this your first time?" Donnelly asked, his voice turning more sympathetic.

"Yes, Father, it is." He dismissed everything he had learned from Scott. It would be more comfortable being himself.

"My first time—and I'm not Catholic. But I do need to talk to you, Father, I…"

"Riordan?" Donnelly whispered loudly through the screen. His voice faltered, tripping over his tongue—"Li—Liam Riordan? You traitor—you, you used me! Used me to destroy a good friend. And you have disgraced this Holy Church by your presence!"

"Father Donnelly, please…"

Donnelly wasn't through with him yet. "What in God's holy name compels a man like you to inform on people that have given you their love? They took ya in, man—into their home and hearts! Now it's me you're probably after. Is there no shame in yer…"

"I'm not here to arrest you, Father. Please listen to what I have to say. I didn't intend for things to turn out this way. The truth is…"

"Truth?" Donnelly enunciated the word loudly through the screen.

"Truth, is it? I'll tell you what's true—it's true that you're a smug, hypocritical, worthless excuse for a human being." Donnelly took a deep breath and sat back. Hamilton could see the shadowy profile of the priest. The large nose almost touched his upper lip. His mouth was open. He could hear the priest's heavy breathing. Hamilton took advantage of the quiet.

"I want you to forgive me, Father. I need desperately to talk to you."

"You're making a mockery of the confessional, son—a mockery. Why, you're not even Catholic. You said that, didn't you?" His voice had returned to the soft, velvety, complacent tone. He assumed that Hamilton was going to arrest him.

"Look, Father—didn't Jesus sit with whores, tax collectors and non-believers? Jesus didn't ask for credentials. He didn't repudiate sinners because they were not of His faith."

"You're making a mockery of this sacrament, Mr. Riordan—or whatever they call you. I can't give you absolution."

"Hamilton. The name's William Hamilton, Father, and yes, you can forgive me. If you can't do that, Father—well, I guess you're the one who's making a mockery of the confessional. What would Jesus do?"

"I'm not Jesus, Mister Hamilton. All I know is that you've done a despicable thing, and I don't find it that easy to forgive."

"Look, Father, you must believe me when I tell you that I really love the Barretts."

Donnelly found his comment amusing. He chuckled. "Well, you certainly have one interesting way of showing it. Mick was dragged off in front of his wife and son—'course you already knew that, didn't you?"

"That wasn't my doing, Father."

"Whose was it then?"

"Someone else informed on Mick—one of your people."

"My people? My people, is it? An' what makes ya think I'm an insurgent, eh?"

"What I mean is, someone that knew Mick. Knew where he was—knew he was with Ned Morriarty."

"And I suppose I'm to believe you—a known British spy, an informer yerself?"

"Father Donnelly, please, if I wanted to arrest you I'd have done it a long time ago. Look," he hesitated. "I'm not a very religious man; however, I do respect you and everything you stand for. As God is my witness, I didn't turn Mick over to the constabulary. The truth is I'm also here to see if there's something I can do. Information—you know—a plan, if you will—to release Mick."

The confessional was quiet.

"How can I be sure you're tellin' the truth?" Donnelly asked.

"With all due respect, Father—don't you think that I'd be after some bigger fish?"

Donnelly didn't lose any time taking advantage of the moment. "Ya mean like ya did before?" he asked. Contempt registered in his tone.

"Touché, Father," Hamilton said, meaning it as an apology. "Look, Father—you don't have to tell me about your friends—why can't we just concentrate on saving Mick?"

"We have a plan to get him out next week," Donnelly said, reluctantly. "Mother of God, why am I talking to you? May God forgive me," the priest said, blessing himself.

"Next week will be too late."

"What do ya mean? Too late?"

"By next week, Father, Mick will already be dead."

"Dead?"

"Dead, Father. I'm shipping out in a few days. Wednesday night. Mick's execution is set for early that same morning. We have to do something before then."

"Holy Mother of God," Donnelly repeated, making the sign of the cross. "Look, Mr. Hamilton…"

Hamilton interrupted, "Call me William—please."

"Look, William," he hesitated. "Maybe we should continue this conversation in the rectory."

"I'm glad you're beginning to trust me, Father. It means a lot."

Donnelly moved closer to the screen. "Don't count your chickens, Mister Hamilton. We'll take one thing at a time. Trust? Well, that's something you're goin' to have to earn. Now leave and go through the back of the church into the rectory, an' cover yer face or somethin', or whatever it is ye spies do."

"Thanks, Father," Hamilton said and left the confessional.

CHAPTER EIGHTEEN

HAMILTON REACHED THE motor pool in uniform and carrying a brown briefcase a few minutes after six. A garment bag hung over his right shoulder. A warm afternoon shower had left a reflective mantle of water on the street, and the city was still dark with ominous black clouds. In the distance the verdant hills that formed the base of the Dublin mountains were illuminated with intermittent rays of sunshine.

Hamilton's gaze momentarily fixed on one hill in particular. A dark, gloomy, rain cloud hung over Hellfire Hill, baptizing the uninhabited house at the top in a watery veil of superstition. Hamilton remembered Kathleen's story about the old house at the top. At one time the house had belonged to an unfrocked priest. Apparently he had favored the black mass and Satan over Catholicism and suffered through a scandalous excommunication. Hamilton remembered Kathleen had stopped melodramatically. *He had the cloven feet of the devil,* she'd said. Hamilton was once again becoming obsessed with her innocent face when his meditation was interrupted by the lance corporal at the entrance.

"Evenin', sir," he said, with clicking heels and a rigid salute.

Hamilton's pensive face turned to a cursory smile. "Good evening, corporal," he said, returning the salute.

He crossed the cobblestone courtyard and opened the door to the motor-pool office. When he entered, a sergeant came to attention. Hamilton casually returned the salute.

"I'm Hamilton. I called earlier for a staff car."

The sergeant shuffled papers on the desk.

"Yes, sir, we've got it handled—just need some identification and a signature."

Hamilton produced an identification badge, and as he signed the release for the car, the sergeant scrutinized the wall of keys. He unhooked a key from a numbered fastener and turned toward the door.

"I'll show you to your car, sir," he said. "It's a Rolls. It'll need a bit of a crank."

Hamilton was finally on his way to Clontarf to pick up Donnelly. He was on a mission of mercy to liberate from prison, from death, a man put there by *his* circumstantial evidence. He turned left at College Green and headed toward Sackville street. He dismissed the notion that his adventure had its basis in stupidity. Even the good Father thought that the plan was hopeless. Hamilton hadn't thought much of Donnelly's strategy to free Mick either.

An arrangement had been made through the Church allowing Barrett to see a priest. He would be granted his last confession, and Donnelly had been appointed Father Confessor. Donnelly and Mick, being of similar build, were to exchange clothes, and when it came time to execute Mick Barrett, they'd find the priest. Donnelly didn't appreciate the thought that Mick would have to beat him into unconsciousness. It's the only way that Donnelly's story would be accepted.

Hamilton remembered asking the priest about their differences—the priest was older. They didn't exactly look like twins. Donnelly's response was a work of the stage. He would wear a disguise, wire-rimmed glasses and a mustache. Then transfer the glasses and mustache to Mick. Hamilton remembered quizzing the priest. *Excuse me, Father, but what if Mick has a two-week beard? Supposing he has lost weight and you're not the same build anymore? What if the guard has orders not to let you out of his sight? Jesus, Father—excuse me, but your plan stinks.*

Hamilton was remembering the priest's bewildered look. It was obvious to both of them that Hamilton was right. The more he thought about it, the more Hamilton preferred his own plan. After all, he was the officer in charge of the case. It was his testimony that had put Mick there. Now it would take just two signatures to get him out. The briefcase contained Scott's files on Mick Barrett, and at this very moment, Mick Barrett failed to exist, as far as the British were concerned. Earlier in the day Hamilton had paid a visit to the prison. All military prisoners were overseen by British guards and the local constabulary.

He spent most of the afternoon with a young officer in charge of the prison. He was impressed with Hamilton's involvement in capturing Mick Barrett. Scott's files helped confirm his authenticity. He reminded the captain that although his prisoner had been found guilty in a hearing, Barrett was far more valuable alive, at least until Sir John Maxwell's office had more time to interrogate the prisoner. Hamilton remembered his conspiratorial tone when he leaned over the young officer's desk. *It would be easier to question the prisoner at the castle.* Hamilton convinced him that Barrett had information that might even lead to the arrest of the hierarchy within the Church. *Bishops yet—can you imagine that!* He said that he would return with the captain in charge of Sir John's affairs and the necessary papers.

Father Donnelly's role was of concern to Hamilton. There hadn't been a lot of time to transform the Irish priest into a British soldier. He hoped that Scott's uniform would fit the priest. He thought that Donnelly was a little shorter. Hamilton could see the priest now, sitting on the park bench where they had planned to meet. He wore an old tan raincoat and a peaked cap, pulled down over the tawny eyebrows.

When Hamilton stopped the car, Donnelly looked about apprehensively while approaching it. He leaned on the door and popped his head in the open window.

"'Ello, sir," he said with a contrived cockney accent. "Got somethin' for me?"

Hamilton smiled and handed Donnelly the garment bag. "That accent will get us both shot," he laughed. "Remember, it's 'Good evening, ole chap,' *not* ''ello.' We'll work on the Oxford accent when I pick you up."

"Oh, jolly good show," Donnelly said, mocking the contrived role. "It's going to be *so* charming to have my bloody arse shot off."

"That's better," Hamilton said. "By the way, there's also a false mustache in the bag and a jar of rouge. All those British captains and colonels seem to have high blood pressure. I'll pick you up here in about half an hour." Hamilton checked his watch. "Seven-thirty sharp," he said, and drove away.

It was beginning to rain again as he drove along the Bull Wall toward Sandymount. The tide had ebbed and the odor of seaweed filled his nostrils. Hamilton silently admired the manicured forest-green lawns, complemented by serene, pastel-colored cottages of peach, rose, and pale blues. Occasionally the low sun found an opening in the clouds, illuminating the harmonious little houses. It was incongruous and regrettable that, just fifteen miles away, Dublin City was in shambles.

Hamilton's reveries returned to reality. He was taking a detour because he understood the priest's need for discretion. It wouldn't have looked good to have a British staff car parked outside the parish house. Donnelly had given his house-keeper the day off. He would make the transformation to

Captain Montague in the obscurity of the rectory and pray to God that he wasn't confronted by a wayward parishioner in the short walk to his car. On their return, Mick would stay at the rectory while Donnelly returned the uniform. Hamilton knew the plan would work. It would be successful because he was a trusted British agent, genuinely privy to every detail of the case. *It will work,* he assured himself.

He reaffirmed the naturalness of Mick's transfer. The planning would bring the result sought. He glanced at his watch and noticed that fourteen minutes had passed since he'd left the priest. It was time to turn around and pick up the captain. *It will not be long now,* he thought. By eight-thirty, Mick Barrett would be sitting in the back seat, plucked from the hangman's noose. The alternative made his body shudder.

He reached for a cigarette. He drew the smoke in until the tip glowed. That helped him relax. He couldn't dwell on failure. Not now. In his mind he envisioned the details of the plan. He would prevail. He would be vindicated. Kathleen's love could even be revived. The rain came harder now and turned to steam off the hood. Through the fine haze, he saw the soldier holding the black umbrella. Hamilton stopped the car and flung the used cigarette out of the open window. He smiled as Donnelly laboriously pressed himself into the passenger seat.

"Fantastic! You look great, Captain Montague—sir."

"I feel like a fish out of water," Donnelly said.

Hamilton was pleased with the priest's disguise. He ground the gears and headed for Kilmainham. On the way, Donnelly practiced his Oxford dialect. As they approached the somber gray prison, the 'jolly good show,' 'eh what' and 'bloody hell, ole' chap' became Irish again, more indulgent, almost whispering, for it would have been blasphemous for the priest to pray with an English accent.

The visitors were escorted into a lofty vacant room. Two soldiers guarded an oversized steel door, obviously the entrance to the cell blocks. A stout middle-aged sergeant reclined behind an oak desk upon which he rested his feet. He was in the process of devouring the last morsel of a tomato-and-lettuce sandwich when the escort left the room.

"Tenshun!" the sergeant hollered, rising to his feet at the second syllable, so powerfully enunciated that pieces of unchewed lettuce and tomatoes hurled across the desk. The lance corporals, armed with Enfield rifles, snapped to attention and saluted. Hamilton and Donnelly returned the courtesy.

He introduced himself, and gesturing toward Donnelly, acquainted the stout sergeant with Captain Montague.

"At ease, Sergeant."

"Street, sir," the sergeant stuttered. "'arry Street."

Hamilton placed his briefcase on the desk. He removed some papers and motioned for Street to sit.

"I hope you're properly acquainted with the mission here, Sergeant," Hamilton said. "You can well imagine the need for confidentiality."

"Sir?"

"Secrecy, Street. We instructed your superiors to have the prisoner, Barrett, ready for transfer."

"We 'ave 'em ready," Street said. "Other than that, sir, we don't ask questions 'bout the whys and wherefores—if you know what I mean."

"That's the spirit. Just do as you're asked," Donnelly said in his best English inflection.

"I, er, spoke with your commanding officer earlier," Hamilton said. "A Captain Harrington."

Street appeared eager to please and enthusiastically confirmed the earlier visit. "Captain 'arrington, that's right, sir. The captain did mention 'bout the need for tight lips an' all that." Street's large, globular head rotated from side to side and finally settled squarely on Hamilton's face. "'E told me you were one of those cloak-and-dagger chaps."

"Oh, he did?" Hamilton's tone was more serious. He handed the sergeant a document with Sir John Maxwell's personal wax seal. The forged paper detailed the release of the prisoner, Michael Barrett, into the custody of Captain Charles Montague and Lieutenant William Hamilton of the Intelligence Service.

Street was reveling in his importance as he glanced over the document. He put the paper down and opened the desk drawer, producing a file folder. He opened the folder importantly and studied the photo clipped to the right corner of the face page.

"I was told by Captain 'arrington to make sure that I make a proper identification." He glanced at Hamilton and then back to the photo. "Unless you got a twin brother, it's you all right." He looked inquisitively at Donnelly, then turned the pages over slowly.

"If you're looking for something on Captain Montague, I'm afraid you'll come up empty-handed," Hamilton said. Street closed the folder.

"Captain Montague is newly assigned as Special Interrogator in the Irish problem. He, er, speaks the language—and not just dialects. He also speaks fluent Gaelic."

The stout sergeant was genuinely impressed.

"Blimey—I 'aven't ever 'eard of anyone outside this miserable country speakin' that gibberish—particularly an Oxford gentleman like yourself, sir."

Donnelly smiled, "Is that a fact now," he said in his natural tongue, happy to indulge the sergeant. *"Agus conas ata tu?"*

Street reached out to shake Donnelly's hand and the captain obliged.

"Remarkable—bloody remarkable—er, excuse me for swearing, sir, but that's—that's bloody remarkable. I've 'eard that inside every Irishman is a bloody Englishman, trying to get out. But this takes the bloody cake, eh? I mean a proper Englishman like yourself, sir, speakin' that gibberish."

Donnelly didn't care for the comment, but found it unsurprising.

Hamilton was pleased with Donnelly's dramatic abilities, especially now that he had an admirer. *A little of this goes a long way,* Hamilton thought, and returned the dialogue to the subject of Mick's release.

"I hope you grasp the importance of this transfer, Sergeant. He's not just an ordinary prisoner. He has information involving more important people. All paperwork has to be returned to headquarters. We want no records—no trace."

"I've been told to accommodate you, sir," the sergeant winked. "As I understand, sir, we're trading a little fish for a big one, so to speak, sir?"

"That's exactly right. I couldn't have said it better," Hamilton agreed. "Now, where's the prisoner?"

As Street moved in the direction of the guards, Hamilton boldly placed the sergeant's files in his briefcase. "I'm returning these records to the castle archives."

Street turned to Hamilton, "I don't imagine we'll be needing signatures, sir," he winked again. "This Barrett chap is probably going to get hurt trying to escape from your custody. When 'e tells you what you need to know, I mean. Captain 'arrington informed me that the prisoner was never 'ere, if you know what I mean," he said again.

The guards unlocked the steel door and allowed Street and the officers into a dimly lit corridor.

Hamilton turned to Street, "I believe you have the wrong impression of us, Sergeant—we don't eliminate prisoners, you know—when we get what we want out of Barrett, all we need to do is spread rumors in the right circles. He'll be taken care of by his own people—if you know what I mean." He winked at the sergeant.

They both laughed as their heavy footsteps echoed through the long hallway. They stopped at the end of the corridor at an even more imposing steel door. Street had to stand on his toes to speak through the small, barred opening at Hamilton's eye level. A gaunt white-faced man stared back at the sergeant.

"Is the prisoner prepared for the transfer, Private?"

"'E's all ready, Sergeant."

"Open up then," Street demanded. "Some officers are 'ere from headquarters for pick-up."

"Sir," the voice said, accompanied by a loud clashing of heels.

The door needed oiling. The screeching of metal against metal reverberated in the empty corridor. The odor of urine and unwashed bodies filled Hamilton's senses. The only light came from outside. As the mantle of evening absorbed the last rays of the setting sun, the gas lanterns seemed ineffective. To his right, his attention fixed on the gallows through the thick safety windows running the length of the cell blocks. The concrete floor sloped from the cells on the left to a trough just under the windows. The floors had recently been hosed down and Hamilton could see fragments of feces floating toward an open drain. Every cell he passed was unoccupied. Hamilton felt nauseated and remarked to Street about the cramped quarters.

"Don't want to make it too nice for 'em now, do we, sir," Street said mechanically.

"You're sure that the prisoner is hooded and shackled?" Hamilton asked, imagining the surprise of Mick, seeing himself and Donnelly in British uniforms.

"'E 'as no idea where 'e's goin', Lieutenant, but believe you me, 'e's just as you asked," Street declared.

When they stopped at the cell, Hamilton saw the silhouette of a man in the small, murky room. He had to know that they'd come for him, yet he didn't move from his hunched-over pose on the bed. In the short period of his incarceration, Mick Barrett had been conquered, defeated, resigned to die without seeing his family, without a priest. The broad frame was bent. Under the prison shirt, the crumpled body breathed fast and shallow.

"Stand up!" the private shouted.

Mick stood slowly, his head downcast. His hands were locked behind his back, his legs were shackled and his head was covered with a black hood. He reeked of body odor and urine.

"Jesus Christ," Street muttered, stepping back. "'E's bloody well pissed on 'imself. What a bloody stench!"

Hamilton looked at Donnelly. The priest's eyes were moist. *And you thought you could change places with this poor soul.* Hamilton was trying to convey his thoughts to the priest. Donnelly looked as if he understood. He was hoping that the private and Street would tell the prisoner that he was being transferred, not taken to the gallows. They did not. Mick, accepting his fate, did as he was told.

Donnelly, walking behind Mick, thought he could hear him

murmuring. "Hail Holy Queen, Mother of Mercy —" Donnelly silently said the rosary with his friend as they walked toward the large steel door and freedom.

Other than thanks and the usual farewells, nothing was said until they were in the safety of the car. Donnelly sat beside Mick in the back seat as Hamilton cranked the engine. The car sputtered. A call to the motor pool for help was out of the question. He turned the crank furiously. The engine turned slowly, then worked itself into a fast idle. Hamilton lost no time leaving the prison facility. He could clearly see his two passengers in the rear-view mirror. Mick sat lifeless, not showing a sign of curiosity about where he was being transported. Donnelly, who had been given the keys by Street, was taking his time removing the handcuffs.

"It's goin' to be all right," he said.

Mick moaned as he gingerly brought his hands around and placed them in his lap. He didn't acknowledge Donnelly's remark. Gently he rubbed his wrists. The open, festered abrasions oozed pus and looked agonizingly painful.

Donnelly carefully untied the black hood. He wasn't surprised by the appearance of his former parishioner. In the ambient light of the late evening, his face was colorless. Earlier wounds had scabbed over. The thick, black curly hair was long and matted. It tumbled over Barrett's broad forehead. A salt-and-pepper growth covered his lower face. It was the vacant stare that Donnelly noticed more than anything else. A putrid stench filled the car. Hamilton opened the windows

At least he's alive, Donnelly thought—*at least I think he's alive.*

"Mick, Mick—it's me, Father Donnelly."

Mick stared blankly at the man in the uniform. Donnelly threw the military cap on the floor. He removed the wire-rimmed glasses, and taking a corner of the walrus mustache, he swiftly ripped it from his upper lip. Mick's lifeless eyes lit up. His mouth attempted to smile. His hand touched Donnelly's face as if to confirm the apparition.

"Be Jasus—is it really you, Father? Be Christ—I must be dreamin'."

"You're not dreamin', Mick."

Mick's smile became broader.

"I'm not—am I? Pinch me—Jasus, I know I must be dreamin'."

Donnelly was smiling with Mick now. He pinched Mick's forearm.

"There," he said. *"Cogito, ergo, sum.* See, you really do exist." Donnelly ignored the fetid odor as they held one another.

Mick pulled away to see the priest's face. "How's Annie?"

"Fine, Mick—Annie's fine."

"An' the kids?"

"The kids too, Mick—they're fine."

"They don't know about your release, Mick—it's goin' to be a surprise. You'll be coming back to the rectory with me. After you've cleaned up and gotten some rest, we'll take ye home in the mornin'."

"God, I don't believe it, Father…" Mick's body shuddered as he exhaled a great sigh of relief. He was becoming more talkative, recounting stories of his captors, the torture. He stopped, silently gesturing to the driver. His inquisitive expression asked the question.

"It's William Hamilton," the priest said. Hamilton shook his head at the mirror and the priest corrected himself. "Er, alias, Liam Riordan."

"No—it isn't," Mick said, in disbelief. "Liam Riordan—I would have expected Murphy or O'Connor—but you—shure, ya hardly know me, an here ye are, riskin' yer life."

"Relax, Mick," Donnelly said softly, reaching for a cigarette.

"Here, have a Wooley Woodbine."

Mick took the cigarette and passed it under his nose as if it were a fine cigar. He allowed Donnelly to give him a light, and he inhaled deeply.

"Ahhh—isn't it amazin' how appreciative we become of the small things in life. Bedad, it's bleedin' amazin'," Mick said on a cloud of smoke. "Amazin'—the uniforms an' all. Now tell me, whose idea was it anyway? Was it yours, Father, or Roach and the boys?"

"Not at all," Donnelly interrupted, not entirely trusting Hamilton. It wasn't necessary that Mick know Hamilton by his real name, yet he wished Mick to know that it was the American who had saved him from execution. "It was Riordan's idea. Riordan and meself it was, Mick."

Mick patted Hamilton's shoulder again.

"I'm indebted to ye, Liam," he said thoughtfully.

"An how are ye an' Kathleen gettin' along?"

"I guess she's fine. I, er, I haven't seen her in a while. Look, Mick, when I drop you off, you and Father Donnelly are taking his car back to the parish house. I, eh, won't be coming along."

"Ahh, for God's sake, ye have to." He turned to Donnelly. "Tell him, Father. You tell him he has to come…"

Donnelly searched for an excuse. "Liam's right, Mick. It's better if he takes care of some of the final details—well, like the car here—he has to get rid of it."

"Bedad, it's an Army car all right—did ye steal it? Shure, an yer a hard man, Liam Riordan. You are. Why, I would have thought ye…"

"Look, Mick, we're almost there," Hamilton interrupted. "And I don't have a lot of time to explain things. Father Donnelly has a folder that

I gave him. He'll explain everything. I'm leaving for London tomorrow night and I won't be returning for a long time."

"This may not be the best time to do this, ya know," Donnelly said.

"This is the only time I have, Father—then it's up to you to speak in my behalf, maybe."

"What are ye two talkin' about?" Mick said, impatiently. "What's all this blabber about leaving an' not comin' back an' speaking on my bleedin' behalf about anyway?"

Hamilton stopped the car. "We're here," he said. Donnelly's car was across the street.

Hamilton turned around and saw Mick for the first time since they got in the car. He reached out and placed his hand on Mick's shoulder.

"Before you leave—promise me just one thing."

"Anything, man," Mick said seriously. "Anything."

"Just have Kathleen meet me tomorrow night at Alexander Basin. My ship leaves at seven o'clock. Please, whatever you hear about me is going to be mostly true, but I do love Kathleen. You have to know that I wouldn't harm her or your family for the world."

"I believe ya, Liam. Shure, don't I already know that?"

"Both of you have to get going now. I don't want you caught again because of some goddamn curfew infraction."

The men got out and Father Donnelly closed the door. He came around and leaned in the open window.

"How about the uniform?" he asked, smiling.

"Keep it. I'll buy Scott a new one." They shook hands vigorously.

"It's up to you, Father. You have the file folder?"

"I do indeed, Liam."

"I hope Kathleen can make it. Will you put in a word?"

"I will—and—thanks again. For a spy, you're not really a bad sort," he said, and left.

CHAPTER NINETEEN

IT WAS A warm, sunny morning. Dubliners were busy going about their business as Donnelly and Barrett drove across Carlisle Bridge.

"Ya know, Mick, this bridge is one of the only bridges in the world that's wider than it is long," Donnelly said, trying to make conversation.

"I didn't know that," Mick said wistfully.

"Look, Mick—I'm not mad at ye or anything like that—it's just that, well, if ye could just find it in your heart to forgive the man. I mean…"

"Father, if ye don't mind me sayin' so, it's your job to forgive people like Riordan—or Hamilton, but I don't have to."

"If it hadn't been for him, Mick, shure, ye'd still be in prison," Donnelly said. Then looking contemplatively at his watch, he said somberly, "Correction, you'd probably have been shot or hanged by now."

Mick didn't respond. Instead, he stared at the busy crowds and experienced an inner quiet jubilation as he listened to the sounds the city yielded. He was grateful for the summer breeze washing away the stench of Kilmainham. His reveries turned to happier thoughts of Annie and Jamie and the other loves of his life.

Donnelly turned the car right at Stephen's Green and drove to Milltown. When they passed York Street, Mick thought about Bill Elliot. He regretted his accusations of Bill when he was arrested. *And all the fukken time it was that bastard, Riordan,* he thought. He didn't appreciate Father Donnelly's attempt to influence him into accepting the American. *Just because he master-minded my escape—wasn't it that fukker that put me there? Oh, shure, supposedly there was another informer, a paid informer, but that could have been anyone lookin' for a quick bob or two. No, there's no bleedin' doubt—Riordan did a job all right, an' that's the likes that Father would have my Kathleen to go with, even marry maybe, a fukken English spy yet!*

Father Donnelly was asking himself questions about Mick's unwillingness to accept Hamilton as a friend. In talking last night, Mick had asked about Annie and the children. His family was all he had time for. Efforts to convince Mick of Hamilton's remorse and his intentions to smooth things over with Kathleen had been ineffective. Hamilton had risked not only his career, but his life. Donnelly had shown Mick the file and asked him to read the guard's report on the actual informer. For someone that had just been pardoned, freed from the noose of death, Mick Barrett was incredibly stubborn, spiteful and uncompromising.

"I'll not read that shite, Father. The man's a British spy, for Christ's sake, and I'll be thankin' ye not to mention his name around me again— and get rid of that bleedin' file. As far as I'm concerned you're the one that got me out of there—you, Father, alone."

Donnelly vividly remembered Mick's vehement tone. He knew Mick was serious when he slammed his big fist down, almost breaking a precious Louis XIV coffee table. He sensed that it was time to drop attempts to exonerate Hamilton. He would place the files that Hamilton had given him in a safe at the rectory. The files that could help prove what really happened that night would be preserved. But he would try to forget that William Armstrong Hamilton ever existed.

After Mick had bathed, he dressed himself in some of Donnelly's older clerical garments. The priest fixed him a slab of rashers and eggs. He ate heartily and shortly after, vomited up the breakfast. Still, he felt much better. The rest of the evening was spent outlining Mick's and the family's departure to a safe house, to stay until things settled down.

Donnelly's rambling thoughts returned to reality as he stopped the car by the closed gate. "Well, we're home, Mick!" he said excitedly.

Mick wasted no time exiting the car. He opened the gate for Donnelly to park closer to the house and walked briskly toward the front door. Before he was halfway up the drive, Annie had opened the door and was running to meet him. Her face was jubilant and tears of delight filled her eyes.

"Mick! Mick!" She cried. "God, it's really you!" Her arms stretched out and her fingers extended; she knew that within seconds she would be in his arms. Donnelly stopped the car again within a few feet as they embraced like young lovers. Annie put her hands on Mick's head, kissing one side of his face and then the other. She could feel the throbbing of his temples through her fingertips. She touched his dry lips and kissed him tenderly. Tears flowed generously as the children streamed from the house.

"Da, Da!" Jamie cried, outrunning Paddy and Michael. Reveling in every moment, they took turns touching Mick as if he were an apparition about to vanish. Finally, they walked awkwardly back to the house, seemingly tied together with an invisible rope.

When they got inside, Annie ministered to her husband's needs, changing the pus-ridden bandages that Donnelly had applied the night before. She applied a hot-bread poultice to each festered wound.

"There, Mick," she said. "We'll have you back to normal in no time at all."

She put the kettle on for tea, and Donnelly, Mick, and the boys sat around the kitchen table. Mick told them of his ordeal in prison and described at length the story of the young, gallant martyr who had died to save Ireland. He held the attention of his eager, young listeners until Annie returned to the table with a cozied teapot and three large mugs.

"Be off with ye now," she said seriously. "Leave your father alone. Go on outside now. Father Donnelly and myself want to spend some time alone with your father." They didn't heed right away and she insisted, "*Now,* I said."

When they left, Mick asked about Kathleen.

"She's working this morning," Annie said. "This has been a hard time for her, too, Mick. Our little Kathleen was madly in love with the American, or the Englishman with the American accent." She used the word 'American' in lieu of saying his name. She swore that his name would never be mentioned in her house again.

"God, she'll be so happy to see ya, Mick." Her eyes teared up again. "I can't believe it myself," she said, resting her hand on his. "Father, it might be a good idea if you could talk to her. After all, we have Mick back; I know that she'll be elated." She turned to Mick. "He even asked her to marry him. Dear God, how can a man stoop that low? He broke her young heart, Mick—and God only knows where he is now. Gloating, I dare say, with his triumph over a young girl."

Donnelly looked sternly at Mick, knowing that now would be a good time to tell the truth about Hamilton. Mick had promised the young man 'anything.' Hamilton would be expecting to see her tonight to explain everything. Mick Barrett was easy with his promises and short on delivery. Without Hamilton, Mick would be dead. The priest was certain that Roach's plan would have failed.

Donnelly waited for Mick to respond, hoping.

Mick held Annie's hand tightly. "Let's not talk about him. I'm shure he thinks I'm dead by now," Mick said. "And as far as I'm concerned, he's a dead issue." He knew the priest was staring at him. "Anyway, 'tis Father here we have to be thanking—isn't it him that's the hero—the man that got me out." Mick raised his mug of tea. "Here's to Father Donnelly," he said, smiling.

Annie acknowledged Mick's toast. "Father, how can we thank ye? How can we ever thank ye?"

Donnelly stood up to leave. "I'll be leaving you two alone now—you should be thinking seriously though about leavin' Dublin, at least until all this British retaliation is over."

"I'll not be kicked out of me own house."

"Now, now, Mick," Annie interrupted. "I think Father's right. It'll be just for a while, 'til things settle down. Isn't that right, Father?"

"Right indeed, Annie," Donnelly said.

"Thanks again, Father."

"I was happy to do it, Annie," he said with a confiding tone. "I had the distinct feeling though that someone was there with me, guiding me through things, if you will," he said, turning his head in Mick's direction.

"I know," she said knowingly. "Like God was with you."

Donnelly hesitated and smiled. "Something like that," he said, closing the door behind him.

CHAPTER TWENTY

G OOLDS CROSS RAILWAY Station was in County Tipperary. Back twelve feet or so from the platform's edge stood a small, stone-fabricated building with a slate roof. The men's and women's facilities were at opposite ends, separated by a ticket window and a sparsely furnished waiting room. Tin-type posters decorated the outside walls. One poster illustrated a British soldier handing a young farm boy a rifle while a phantom image of a German soldier desecrated a Celtic cross. The logo was in Gaelic. *Help us save your country.*

Larry Fitzgerald stood alone on the elevated platform above the tracks. He was of medium build and was dressed in a well-worn suit. Larry was in his early forties, and his round face was brown and weathered with deep lines resembling a busy road map. The last of the Fitzgerald line, he knew that it would end with him. He had never been attracted to women, not in a sexual way, that is, and he knew that he would remain celibate. Earlier, he had entertained the idea of becoming a priest.

He had two sisters, Madge and Annie. Madge, the younger of the two, had been sent to Boston to live with relatives when she was ten. Larry was a surviving identical twin. His brother, Michael, died in his early twenties in a hunting accident. Larry never forgot that gray, overcast, breezy October day. All the following days had become an endless duration of somber indifference. Michael, for whatever reason, had had the safety off on the old shotgun. Larry'd crossed over the barbed-wire fence first and held it down for Michael. As he straddled the wire, Larry remembered his joking, "This is as close as I ever want to come to tearin' me bollix off." His smile turned to a gaping, confused mouth when the gun exploded, triggered by an ill-fated barb. While Michael lay on his back in the tall straw-colored grass, Larry pulled clumsily at his clothing and tried to stop the pumping blood with his hands. As Michael's life fluids squeezed through his fingers, Larry cried to God for help. Reaching up, Michael motioned for Larry to come closer.

"I can't—see," he whispered laboriously.

"Ssshhh," Larry mumbled. "Don't try to talk now."

"Get—get me a—a priest, Larry."

"I promise, Michael—I'll be back with the priest."

Larry was remembering the last words he'd said to his brother. He remembered running across the fields as if in a dream, never fast enough. By the time he reached Cappamura, his heart was pumping in his mouth. Finding the priest, all he could gasp was "Michael—Michael." When they returned, his brother lay quiet, his face white and drawn.

"He's at peace now," Father Condon said. He proceeded to the incantation, the unintelligible, mysterious Latin murmuring of the Last Rites.

"Michael is with the Holy Saints in Heaven," he assured Larry.

A few years after Michael's death, Larry's parents passed away within a year of one another. What to do with the land had become a concern now. Twenty acres had been passed down from one generation to the next as far back as he could remember. His ancestors had fought and died for the land, and it was up to him to keep it in the family.

You could see forever in either direction; Larry focused on the black wisp of smoke on the horizon. He knew that very shortly he would be seeing his sister, Annie. She was the only woman he'd loved besides his mother. From the time they were children he'd always taken care of her and now he was given another opportunity to help her, particularly now that her family was in trouble with the British.

The letter did not say much, just that they needed his help.

CHAPTER TWENTY-ONE

T HE H.M.S. FARRADAY was a twenty-thousand ton dilapidated merchant ship that had recently been refurbished and commissioned to ferry troops and military supplies. To protect her against U-Boat attacks, she was retrofitted with five-inch guns, one on the prow and the other mounted at the stern. They were fitted inconspicuously into inverted steel pillboxes and, like the rest of the ship, were painted gun-metal gray. The Farraday, one of the first freighters with the guns, already had two U-Boats to her credit.

The captain, a short, wiry, steely-eyed Scotsman, was proud of his crew. He watched as four able-bodied seamen assiduously secured the midship hatch. The cargo in the hold was heavy and unwieldy, consisting of thousands of rounds of ammunition, heavy artillery, armored vehicles, field pieces, horses, and explosives, which lowered the Farraday precariously below the waterline.

More than one thousand troops had been distributed throughout the ship, most of them occupying the steerage section. They were part of the returning task force that had been deployed to suppress the insurrection. Soldiers leaned over the portside rail, waving to small groups of civilians crowded on the quay. Most of them were young girls who had befriended the soldiers during the Occupation. They screamed, hollered their goodbyes, cried and waved handkerchiefs as a regimental pipe band played *It's A Long Way To Tipperary*.

Hamilton looked around the room one more time before leaving. Although he had said his farewell to Jim Scott, he handed the sergeant on

119

duty a letter. It was easier for Hamilton to say thanks in writing. He threw his bag in the back seat of the staff car and joined the lance corporal in front.

"Alexander Basin, Corporal," he said sternly. "We're looking for a merchantman named H.M.S. Farraday."

The fanfare confused Hamilton. He moved quickly through the crowd, looking for Kathleen. His anxiety increased and his movements became more frantic. Mick had promised him. At least he promised that he would tell Kathleen of his need to meet with her. *Did I tell him the right pier, the right time, the right day?* Maybe she didn't want to have any part of him. Finally he saw her—the nurse's cape, the long black hair. Her back was to him, and she was speaking to another girl he didn't recognize. *Thank God!* he thought as he grabbed her arm.

"Kathleen?" he said enthusiastically. His disappointment surpassed his embarrassment.

"Do you mind?" The unfamiliar face looked bitterly into his eyes; she pulled her arm from his hard grip. She was a much older woman with hateful eyes and a slit in place of a mouth.

"I, er, I'm really sorry—I thought you were someone I knew." He stuttered ambiguously, his mouth agape. The woman turned back to her friend, muttering something under her breath.

"Damned English."

"I really do apologize," he said, regaining his composure.

The bo's'n's hollering jarred him. "All aboard that's goin' aboard!"

Hamilton waited as long as he could and was the last to board the Farraday. He walked slowly up the gangplank, looking back from his loftier position, scanning, waiting, hoping. He knew she was not coming. The bo's'n detached the gangplank; it seemed to symbolize their separation. He felt totally isolated as the burdened vessel eased slowly away from the pier.

Distanced from the crowd and the pipe band, Hamilton's blank gaze focused on someone beyond the crowd. The form walked briskly toward the ship. As it came closer, he knew it wasn't a woman's form. The man pushed his way through the crowd to get closer. He appeared to be waving at Hamilton, and the black clerical suit and broad smile became recognizable.

"Goodbye, William," Donnelly yelled through cupped hands.

Hamilton leaned as far as he could, straining to hear the priest.

"Kathleen didn't know about your sailing—Mick never told her!" The mouth moved but the voice was inaudible, muted by the screeching of the pipe band and the thunder of the ship's engines.

Hamilton stayed on the fantail until the priest became a black speck.

At the mouth of the channel, the Farraday made a hard to port on a northeasterly heading, toward Liverpool. The ship's claghorn made a scratching sound predicting the upcoming announcement.

"Now hear this!" The captain's Scottish accent cut through the silence. "Now hear this! All officers and lookouts to the wardroom—on the double!"

The officers' mess doubled as the wardroom. The room was small, with one large table in the center and a galley at one end. Around the table, five men sat drinking tea from white porcelain mugs. The two officers and three able-bodied seamen discussed the possibility of King George's visit to Ireland.

"It'll never happen," the second officer was telling the rest. "Not now, not with this Irish trouble. No monarch in his right mind would visit Ireland."

One of the seamen, a tall, gangly, young, blond man, seemed more interested in the topic than the others.

"Ireland is part of England, right?" He asked.

"Well, technically speaking, I suppose," the older officer replied. "Why?"

"Well, has any King or any Queen of England ever visited their subjects in Ireland?"

A rotund, ruddy-faced man wearing a chief petty-officer's uniform interrupted, "Look, lad—you've just come from the bloody place. They're a bunch of bloody ingrates, if you ask me—animals, that's what they are. No monarch in his right bloody mind would visit that country."

The second officer moved his chair back noisily and went to the galley to replenish his mug. "I feel that we should give Ireland back to the Irish," he said. His tone was serious, moderate.

The conversation changed to a more immediate concern: the number of freighters going to the bottom, casualties of the U-Boats.

Early in the war, the German submarines surfaced within megaphone range of a burdened vessel and issued a warning. It was a gallant gesture on the part of the U-Boat commanders, allowing the crew to abandon their ship, before sending her to the deep. Some luminaries at the Admiralty decided to outfit the freighters with bow guns so that they could take advantage of the surfaced U-Boat's vulnerability. The unsuspecting submarines didn't stand a chance against five-inch shells at close quarters. Soon the wolf pack learned that most merchant ships were armed, and therefore fair game, with no civilian privileges. In a short time the U-Boats would be unwilling to surface, content to stalk their prey with unparalleled destruction.

All conversation ended when Captain George Russell entered the room. Before they had a chance to come to attention, he said, "At ease." He wore a white shirt with his military black tie. He poured a mug of tea and walked nervously back and forth.

"No doubt you've heard rumors that the German submarines aren't showing their colors anymore before firing their torpedoes."

The men murmured and nodded.

"If that's the case, these bloody guns are going to have to be replaced with something useful, like depth charges." Russell sipped on his tea and put the mug on the table. "Tastes like bloody piss." He motioned to the second officer. "Tell Cookie we need stronger tea." He unfolded the piece of paper from his pocket and cleared his throat.

"Prior to departure, I received a telegram. The message is brief." His eyes focused on the paper. "Caution: We feel it necessary to inform you that U-Boat activity has been observed in the Irish Sea." He put the paper away.

"I want to double the lookouts, and oh, by the way, Sparks…" he looked seriously at the young radio officer, "I want someone on that radio at all times. Keep me informed of any signals or sighting of anything—and I mean *anything*—unusual. That's all," he said. Halfway through the door he turned his head. "And do something about that piss you call tea."

Hamilton moved awkwardly to the steel ladder leading to the lower deck. He entered a narrow companionway through a steel door and headed toward his cabin. He had been informed that he was sharing space with a member of the crew. Upon arrival, Hamilton could see that he was the intruder. The room was small, with two made-up narrow steel bunks attached to the bulkhead. Above the top bunk the thick-glass porthole had been covered for security. Everything was painted with many coats of white enamel. The hinges and fastener bolts on the porthole suggested it hadn't been opened in many years. A small desk, chair, and end table were the only furniture. A built-in curtained closet held some civilian shirts, a houndstooth jacket, and a navy-blue, junior-grade officer's uniform. A shelf above the desk displayed a dozen or so books held in place by a two-inch lip across the front. Hamilton inquisitively perused the titles, clues to his companion's personality.

Most of the books were on the subject of radio. Marconi, Morse, books on radio-telegraphy and the making of the two-valve receiver. *Under Two Flags* and Richard Henry Dana's *Two Years Before the Mast* seemed proper enough for a young, career-Navy man. Hamilton's attention fixed on the worn-leather spines of several books:

The Complete Works of William Shakespeare. He took one of the books and carefully thumbed through the yellowing pages. Some sentences were underlined with red ink. One such sentence was marked bolder than the rest. *This above all; to thine own self be true, and it must follow, as night the day, thou canst not then be false to any man.*

Sound advice, he thought, *for a young man leaving home.* He carefully replaced the book. One end of the table held a new gramophone and a short stack of well-used records, all of them operatic. A hand-colored photo of a handsome couple sat on the small table by the bunk. Obviously his parents, Hamilton thought. Hamilton was taking his investigative curiosity to a more comprehensive level when the door opened. The young man he already knew so much about seemed happily surprised.

"Captain Russell told me I'd have a cabinmate on this trip," he said, extending his hand.

"Hamilton, William Hamilton. Pleased to meet you. Hope I'm not putting you out here."

"You're an American. Great!" he said. "My name's Tim Willows, radio officer."

Hamilton smiled, knowingly. Tim sat on the bunk.

"I don't understand the uniform," he said. "You *are* American, aren't you?"

Hamilton shrugged. "It's a long story," he said.

Tim Willows was genuinely enthusiastic with Hamilton's company. He was full of questions about America and why she was taking so long coming into the war.

"That's what I want to know," Hamilton said.

"I want to get into the war," Willows said. "I've already applied for transfer to cruisers or battleships or anything but a merchantman."

Tim Willows was short and well proportioned. The broad smile displayed bright, even teeth. He smiled when he spoke, and the black, wavy hair was well groomed. His face was animated, and the dark eyebrows raised inquisitively every now and then, making his brown eyes appear like black marbles. Overall, Hamilton thought that his temporary cabinmate had an honest face.

"Like opera?" Tim asked, wide-eyed.

"Love it," Hamilton lied.

"My favorite is 'Madam Butterfly,'" he said. "And yours?"

Hamilton stuttered; the thought crossed his mind never to lie about something he didn't know anything about. However, his training in the art of deception prevailed.

"Isn't that a coincidence," he said.

"You mean—that's amazing," Tim said excitedly. "You like 'Butterfly'?"

"One of my favorites," Hamilton said again, appearing sincere.

Hamilton sought permission to smoke and Tim Willows wound the gramophone until it was tight. He listened attentively to the Aria, *Un Belle Di,* while Tim related his views about the American officer that came to Japan, fell in love with the young Butterfly, and left, breaking her heart. He thought it was the saddest of any of Puccini's operas. He asked Hamilton what he thought. The story was too much for Hamilton and he excused himself.

"I think I'll just go up top for a little air."

"You look a little peaked," Tim said. "Happens to most of us 'til we get our sea legs."

The Farraday had been underway for almost an hour and was beginning to roll gracefully as she approached deeper water. Hamilton was alone on the stern, staring vacantly into the distance. Ireland had disappeared into the soft haze of the setting sun. He took a last drag on the cigarette and flicked it into the red wake. His thought receded to the moment on the pier when the ship pulled away. The frustration. Questioning why she hadn't come.

The propeller labored noisily under the strain of the hard-right rudder. The Farraday shuddered and Hamilton's balance was shifted as the powerful ship began her first zig-zag maneuver. The sudden change in course ended Hamilton's musings. What he saw he didn't want to believe. The white streak cutting across the Farraday's wake could only mean one thing. Torpedoes.

He found himself shouting. He held fast to the steel rail. *The captain has to know or we wouldn't be trying to avoid the goddamn thing,* he thought. *What if the U-Boat has fired off a pattern of torpedoes?* He ran awkwardly to the starboard rail. He saw the two wakes and deduced that in a moment he would be dead. Adding to the confusion, the Farraday claghorn continued to scream.

The Farraday was thrust upward, as if lifted by some giant hand. Hamilton held fast. He didn't hear the explosion right away. His breath was sucked from his lungs, and for a moment he felt a bizarre tranquillity. He imagined himself in the eye of a hurricane. The heat came. The great hellish fireball was accompanied by a roar completely disintegrating the superstructure. More followed when the magazines and powder exploded, showering the area with fragments of wood, iron, and molten metal.

Hamilton's eyes burned with noxious smoke and heat. He felt his body moving through space.

The experience wasn't entirely unpleasant. In a semi-conscious state, he floated, waiting for the final impact of death that never came. Instead, he felt pressure on his head. He wanted desperately to breathe, but his lungs drew no oxygen. His mouth opened to draw air, but his limp form was face down in a muck of oil and salt water. His body repelled the salty, black concoction, gagging, then retching. He rolled over. His open mouth made a sucking sound. Hot air filled his dying lungs. He tried to open his eyes. They wouldn't. *Jesus, I'm blind!* Moving his hands to his face, he rubbed the slimy, black mixture of oil and saltwater from his eyelids. Through painful slits, he saw a red glow. It stung to open his eyes but he could see. *Thank god!* He could breathe. Not well, but he could breathe.

His mind told him it would be a good time to take an inventory of the rest of his body. He touched every part he could reach, starting with his feet. He smiled when he realized his penis was still there. Right now it seemed the least important of his extremities. Only a man would appreciate the significance of the short-arms inspection. His predicament reminded him of so many tasteless jokes. He was beginning to communicate with every part of his body. Each breath and touch signaling new life. The inspecting left hand stopped just below his right shoulder. His fingers discovered a soft indentation. The fingers continued investigating through the hole in his chest, and for the first time, he could feel the pain. It hurt to breathe now, while his fingers invaded the cavity of his lung.

He lay quietly in the black pool and took stock of his surroundings. The ring of fire and black smoke was burning close. He knew that he had to get the hell out of there—and fast. His sore eyes scanned the fiery wall, looking for the least volatile area that he might swim under. He picked a section, swam as close as he could without burning, painfully filled his good lung with air and dove into the black slime. He emerged with air still in his lung, just outside the wall of fire.

He could hear men screaming and moaning. Through the gray haze, the stern of the Farraday was still, like some ominous black monument. It tipped forward and the big screw was visible above the waves. Some of the voices seemed to make sense.

"Over here! Try to swim over here!" It was the chief petty officer, accompanied by some of the crew. By some miracle he had managed to find a lifeboat.

Hamilton raised his right arm, but pain forced him to lower it. He tried to holler. His scarred throat allowed a feeble, "Help—I can't move." The heavy, black swells were strewn with flotsam and dead soldiers.

The men in the lifeboat rowed and pulled him aboard. The pain in his chest was unbearable when they pulled on his arms, dragging his wounded body over the hard gunwale.

"Jesus Christ," he heard someone say. "This one's got a bloody great hole in 'm!"

They laid him on his back, stuffed the hole with oil-drenched rags, and watched as what was left of the Farraday slipped into a gurgling, black foam.

CHAPTER TWENTY-TWO

FATHER DONNELLY AWAKENED to a sun-filled room, stripped off his pajamas and put on his shorts. He caught a glimpse of himself in the long wardrobe looking glass and stopped for a moment. He turned sideways and depressed the middle-aged bulge at his waist with both hands. He smiled. *Not bad for an old codger in his fifties*, he thought. He finished dressing and continued downstairs. The aroma of fried bacon filled him with anxious appreciation. He looked forward to breakfast more than any other meal. The morning paper, and a cigarette afterwards with a cup of tea, was the way to start the day.

"Good mornin', Father."

"And a good mornin' to you, Missus Costello."

"Yer breakfast's on the table. I'll bring you a spot of tea and the paper as soon as the kettle boils."

"Shure, it's too good to me you are," he said, sitting down.

"An' am'nt I the one that knows it," she said insolently, walking toward the kitchen.

He said grace and began to eat. He went at his plate methodically, first cutting a mouth-sized piece of rasher. He put the morsel aside and attacked the hard-fried egg, plastering a small piece on the fork. This was followed by fried potato, tomato, and finally to hold it all in place, the piece of bacon. After filling his mouth, he took a bite of toast, the last ceremonious gesture. When he finally swallowed, he began the orderly process over again.

Mrs. Costello brought him the morning paper, placing it so he could

127

read the articles at the bottom of the front page first, as he favored. He propped the folded paper against the milk carafe, read the reports on street rumblings and motor-car accidents, then turned the front page up. His eyes galvanized and his body stiffened in horror as he read:

HMS FARRADAY SUNK
ALL CREW & PASSENGERS LOST

Slowly he laid his knife and fork on the plate and drew the paper closer. His lips moved though he read silently.

> *Her Majesty's Ship the Farraday sank in the Irish Sea Wednesday. She was on a return voyage from Dublin transporting supplies and munitions considered unnecessary since the short-lived Irish rebellion has been crushed. Vice Admiral Newport of the Admiralty said, "Over one thousand brave young British soldiers and officers perished" in the sinking. The Admiral said that a left-wing faction of the recently disbanded Irish Volunteer Army was responsible.*
>
> *Newport said that sabotage was obviously the result of a disappointed coup. The Admiral expressed little hope that any members of the crew or passengers would be found and rescued by search teams. He said, "As of twenty-one hundred hours Wednesday, we lost all radio contact with the Farraday and the likelihood of anyone surviving the massive explosion is doubtful."*

"How about another cuppa, Father." Mrs. Costello's voice fell on deaf ears.

Father Donnelly stared blankly at the paper. He was trying to understand his sense of loss. Naturally, as a priest, he was sensitive to the feelings of others, but there had been something he deeply appreciated in William Hamilton. Maybe it was the time they'd spent together, culminating in planning the happy ending that had returned a condemned man to his family. Lies turned to truths. He realized that he had spent more valuable moments in the shortest time with this young man than with any other person. That was it! He had challenged death, endangered his own life for a friend. And Hamilton had made that possible. Mick Barrett didn't allow him to give credit to Hamilton. For that he felt guilty. Hamilton was the sainted hero; he had planned the escape. He had returned Mick to his family. Today Father Donnelly would pray for his friend—and some humility.

"Tea, Father? Father?" Her voice invaded his musings. "Father?"

"Oh—yes. Thank you very much, Missus Costello," he said, holding the cup toward her.

"You look like you've just seen a ghost. Are you all right?" she asked anxiously, pouring the tea.

"Oh—I was just thinking about this article. It seems that another ship has been sunk. Over a thousand young British soldiers lost. Terrible..."

"Forgive me for sayin' so Father, but I wouldn't be grieving for those that have been slaughtering our own young boys."

"Now, now, Missus Costello—remember, in God's eyes *all life* is sacred. Remember to forgive. The last words that came from Jesus on the cross—Father, forgive them, for..."

"They know not what they do. I know. I know, Father..." her voice trailed off as she left the room.

He neatly folded the newspaper down to book size. He held it with one hand while the other brought the cup to his mouth. He sipped the tea and read the account again—*the likelihood of anyone surviving the massive explosion is doubtful.*

CHAPTER TWENTY-THREE

S EVERAL WORRISOME WEEKS had passed since the family's departure to the country. Most of Annie's depression resulted from fears centered around her husband. She had reason to be concerned. Mick had told her everything. Everything, that is, except Hamilton's involvement in his escape. He feared that she might acquiesce to Kathleen's foolishness. Annie was more forgiving of her daughter than Mick. In Mick's mind, Hamilton had betrayed a trust and used his innocent Kathleen to strike a blow at him. Mick thought that his daughter's involvement with a British soldier would bring dishonor to his family. Nothing was worth that, not even his daughter's happiness. No. That would be his and Father Donnelly's secret. Annie still worried that soldiers might return for her husband. She couldn't go through that hell again. If that ever happened, she'd kill before allowing the British to hurt her family.

She believed that time would heal things, and the longer the family stayed unnoticed, the sooner all this would be forgotten.

There was an adjustment to make to living in County Tipperary. Dublin's faster pace was missed initially by the whole family. Recently, though, it appeared that the boys were beginning to like their new surroundings. Communication with the city was kept up by an occasional letter from Padraig or Father Donnelly, the only people aware of their exile. Since no one knew of Mick's escape, friends of the family assumed that Annie had moved away with the children for the summer. Padraig was looking after the Barrett home, and his last letter had included money, Mick's quarterly share in the store's profits. He wrote of a growing anti-British sentiment, even in England, over the atrocities in Dublin's prisons. Some dignitaries were being considered for release, Eamon de Valera among them. The good news was that so far he hadn't heard or read anything in the papers about Mick's escape.

"It's as if ya didn't exist, Mick," Padraig had written. A postscript said that Sean McIntee had left over night for America.

Larry Fitzgerald was happy for the company and help with the everyday chores. The Fitzgerald Estate was enormous, and the fine two-story house was large enough to provide the privacy that everyone needed.

Annie hadn't remembered so many modern conveniences. Central heating was provided by a copper water pipe that wrapped the chimney flue. Annie didn't care much for the radiators since they hissed, spit, and made loud hammering sounds. She did, however, enjoy hot water at the sink and occasionally luxuriated in a hot bath.

Paddy was a big help to Larry. He milked cows, something he'd never done before, cleaned chicken coops, and planted potatoes. He missed his studies at secondary school, but he liked the small stipend that Larry paid. It also made him happy that he had met a girl he liked.

Michael was also adjusting. At first the idea of a new school was intimidating. He missed Frank and Jerry, and he wasn't allowed to write to anyone, at least not for a while. He understood. Lately, though, Michael seemed anxious to attend school. The small school house was a paradise compared to White Friar Street. He was studious, disciplined, and more informed. He was a product of the Christian Brothers and proud, something he would never admit when he had attended White Friar Street. He was held in high esteem by his fellow students and teachers. At first he was uncertain whether he would like the idea of co-educational classes. After a few weeks he was convinced it was a more exciting way to learn.

Paddy was ecstatic. Friday'd finally come. He couldn't wait to finish the pan-fried roe and boiled potatoes. In half an hour he'd be walking hand-in-hand with Cora Jamison. If he was lucky, they'd visit the barn. Having a girl for a friend was new for him, and he lacked first-hand experience. Silent flickers hadn't come yet to County Tipperary and there were no music halls, so they spent most of their time walking, and on braver occasions, sought the privacy of Billy Green's barn, sitting, talking, and just holding hands. Tonight would be different. He was determined to ask her to be his girl, even kiss her. Lost in his reveries, he put the plate on the drainboard.

"Paddy, you haven't finished your dinner. Paddy?"

"What's that, Ma?" Paddy knew his mother had said something.

"Are you all right?" She gestured to the half-finished roe.

"Oh, that's all right, Ma, I'm not hungry—I, eh, think I'll just go outside for a while."

Annie shook her head. She mumbled something to herself as she cleaned the plate. "Youth—they'll be the death o' me yet!"

Cora Jamison was an only child. Her father was killed felling a tree when she was six. Her mother, Mary, had too many problems of her own to bring Cora up with feminine refinery and other necessary social amenities. Mary acquired diabetes after Cora's birth and was confined to a wheelchair after losing a leg to bad circulation.

Paddy liked Cora's mother. She didn't ask a lot of questions and treated him more like an adult. Any relative of the Fitzgerald family taking out her Cora was a pleasant change from the local spalpeens, she told him. Paddy could tell that she took a little nip now and then and even used sailors' obscenities in his presence, which enamored him even more. The second time he stopped by she even showed him her stump. Cora said she didn't do that for just anyone.

Cora was beginning to like Paddy, too. She was seventeen, just a year older than Paddy chronologically, and years ahead physically. She was a bosomy girl with a soft Rubenesque body. Her hair was long and blond. Her blue, lively eyes captivated Paddy, as did her small sensual mouth. She had a habit of pursing her lips when challenged intellectually, resembling a perverse cherub. Paddy Barrett was in love for the first time in his life.

The bales were stacked almost to the rafters. It was especially warm next to the uninsulated roof. Cora wore a light pink and white-striped cotton dress that buttoned down the front. Paddy lay on his back and chewed on a piece of straw. Cora sat upright beside him. She asked him questions about Dublin. What were city girls like, the music halls, and had he ever been to the moving picture shows? She had read that moving pictures were what the future was all about. She asked him about the revolution and if he had been involved. He told her that his family wouldn't allow him to join the volunteers, but he was with the revolutionaries in spirit. She was impressed with his stories of the post-office siege and every so often pursed her small red lips when she didn't understand something. She was beginning to drive him crazy. He was desperate to kiss her. It had to be her choice. He couldn't handle the embarrassment of rejection.

"God, it all sounds so exciting," she said, melodramatically. "My heart is pounding just—just thinking about it—here, feel."

She took his hand and moved it to her rising bosom.

"I can't feel any…" She moved his hand inside her dress.

"There," she said, looking away as if listening herself.

He groped clumsily at her full breasts, first one, then, more confidently, the other. How fantastically lovely. She was gorgeous. In all his impure fantasies it was never this exciting. She helped him explore, unbuttoning her dress and pulling his panting face to her unscented cleavage. He was rigid with expectation. They kissed. A long, hot kiss to the soul made his whole body shudder; this exceeded everything he had dreamed.

Nothing mattered now. Foolish blood waned. He was in love.

He came down the ladder first and she followed. Looking up, he momentarily caught a glance of her thighs and looked away, embarrassed. It was a short distance to the road and freedom. Billy Green was an old crotchety man in his eighties and had been known to fire his shotgun at trespassers. The country road was separated from the green fields on either side by hedgerows interrupted occasionally by uneven stone fences. The warm evening sun bathed the country landscape with marigold hues, and amber haycocks dotted the olive pastures. Jerseys, Guernseys, Black Angus, and Short Horns grazed their final meal of the day. Sometimes a curious animal approached the pair as close as a fence would allow.

Paddy was also curious. He hadn't had much opportunity in Dublin to touch, or even see, a large animal this close. He mimicked them and laughed loudly when they responded. He fed them clumps of grass and pulled away, fearful of the rasp-like tongues. All the while, Cora was quietly amused by the whole charade. She finally took his hand and they walked into the wind. The cool summer breeze was a welcome relief from the hot confines of Billy Green's barn. Holding his hand, she skipped to his long stride.

"Did ye enjoy yerself, Paddy—I mean was it fun for ya?"

"I didn't know anything could feel that—that good—ye know so much, Cora, where did ya..." He hesitated, embarrassed by what he was about to ask.

"Oh, that's all right, Paddy. Shure, I've been doin' it for about a year. I'll have ye know, though, that I don't do it with just anyone." She held him closer, "Ah, Paddy, shure, you're me one and only—next time," she said.

"Next time?" Paddy asked.

"Next time, Paddy—I'll let ye go—all the way."

He wasn't sure how to respond and muttered, "Thank you, Cora. And don't think I'm not appreciatin' it or anything like that, but how—how d'ye go about tellin' the priest, Cora? I mean, I know it's in the confessional an' all, but—I think that he'd be mad an' all—the priest, I mean."

"Not at all, Paddy, shure, he's just like any other man. I see Father Donahough," she giggled. "I'm tellin' ya, Paddy, one day he'll have heart failure on account of me."

"Cora—the confessional is a sacred place, and the priest isn't just any man. God, Cora, that's a blasphemous thing to be sayin'. He's an ordained minister of God!"

"You don't know this priest like I do, Paddy Barrett. He gets into me personal life an' all."

"He's supposed to," Paddy said sanctimoniously.

"Well, Father Donahough likes to spend more time on the sexual stuff, if ya know what I mean."

"Sexual stuff?"

"That's right! I know he knows who I am—when I come in, I mean, not me name or nothin'. 'An' have ya had impure thoughts or deeds?—An' tell me, my dear—does the young man touch you in your private parts?' 'Yes,' I say—'oh, yes, Father, he does.' 'An' where does he touch ye?' 'In the haycock,' I say. 'In Billy Green's barn.' 'No,' he says, 'does he touch your body—your private parts?' 'Oh,' I say, like I didn't know what he meant. 'He does, Father.' 'An' tell me, do you, er—touch him?' 'I do, Father—I touch his, er, ye know, Father.' 'His penis?' he says. 'It's all right. You can say that.' I can hear him beginning to breath heavier, as if he was exercising, or doin' pushups."

Paddy, listening intently, was finding Cora's dissertation hard to believe and sacrilegious, but he didn't stop her.

"What happens then?"

Cora continued with her imitation. "'Yes—yes, go on,'" he says.

"'There's not much more to tell, Father—I mean, he finally goes limp.' I'm tellin ya, Paddy, I'd swear the man stops breathin', and the confessional is no longer thumpin' or shakin'."

"Cora!" Paddy exclaimed. "Cora, that's sacrilegious—you'll go to hell for that, Cora!"

"Shure, I'm not the one wankin' me mickey, Paddy. I'm tellin' ye, priests are men first—they're just human, Paddy. I really get a rise, pardon the expression, outa' the way he says to me—like when he's all through an' all. 'Now then darlin', is that all the sins ye have to confess?' Like *I'm* the only feckin' sinner here! Sometimes I'd like to say, 'Shure, I'm done, Father—if you are.'"

CHAPTER TWENTY-FOUR

NNIE WAS FEELING depressed with her inability to help her daughter. She knew that Kathleen's suffering would heal only with time and patience. Annie was the patient one now. She would be there when her daughter needed her. Her happy, outgoing Kathleen had become a recluse, and although she'd found a part-time job with a doctor in Cashel, most of the time she stayed in her room. When she would finally come downstairs for supper, Annie could tell she'd been crying. She knew her daughter missed the hospital, her friends, and most of all she grieved for the American.

Kathleen had no idea where he'd gone. She only knew why he'd gone. He was a British soldier, a spy even, and although her father was the subject of his investigation, she felt there were times when he'd wanted to tell her. If only he had. Many times the thought crossed Kathleen's mind. Would things have turned out differently had he been honest? She knew the answer only too well. No. No. Her parents and her friends would never have condoned their marriage, nor a priest blessed it. What really hurt Kathleen was that she'd given so much of herself to someone she knew so little about.

It was Saturday evening, and Kathleen, as usual, had spent most of the afternoon in her bedroom reading. She enjoyed reading, and during these long unhappy days, it had become a perfect diversion. Kathleen knew her mother's distinctive tap on the door.

"Kathleen?" She knocked again, this time more assertively.

"Kathleen—why don't you come down now for supper? Your Uncle

135

Larry's selected a fine piece of bacon that I've boiled with some cabbage and potatoes."

"Be right down, Ma."

"Don't keep us waiting," the voice trailed off.

Larry sat at the head of the table. He said grace. The oversized hands folded in prayer, his head bowed and a shock of red hair tumbled into his plate. After the 'Amen,' the room became animated with voices and clinking dishes. Annie passed Larry the large boiled ham and Mick dug into the bowl of potatoes. The table was banquet style, more than comfortable enough for the seven diners. The dining room was spacious, with a great bay window facing westward. The coffered ceiling had massive walnut beams, and a great chandelier hung from a decorative rosette above the table. Annie had lighted the candles, although it was unnecessary with the evening sun streaming through the lace curtains.

Next to Mick, Paddy was usually the big eater. Sometimes it was a toss-up as to who ate the most, so it didn't go unnoticed that he just played with his food, pushing a cube of ham around on his plate. His reveries carried him to Cora Jamison in Billy Green's barn.

Annie sat between Paddy and Mick, and in a motherly way she nonchalantly touched Paddy's forehead with the back of her hand.

"You don't have a fever—are you feeling sick, Paddy?"

"Love sick," Jamie said, smiling.

"Is it a hangover ye have, Paddy?" Michael said.

Annie looked at Paddy. Her face was stern. "You haven't been drinking—is that the reason you're not eating your supper?"

"I think he's had too much of the Jamison, Ma," Michael scoffed.

The adults were the only ones not laughing. Mick particularly didn't think that his son's drinking was a laughing matter.

"I'll thank ya all to be quiet now—and you, Paddy—go to yer room—I'll talk to ya when…"

"'Jamison,' Da—we're talkin' about *Cora* Jamison," Kathleen interrupted. Mick looked confused. Annie patted his hand soothingly.

"It's all right, darlin'," she said, smiling. "Our Paddy's been seeing the little Jamison girl."

"Little?" Michael interrupted, holding his hands to his chest, cup-shaped around invisible breasts. "Little? Have ye seen her…"

"Michael!" Annie said, disapproving.

Paddy was becoming embarrassed and moved his chair from the table.

"I'll thank ye not to be talking about the girl I happen to like."

"Who's Cora Jamison?" Mick asked, more politely now, trying to overcome the earlier outburst.

"She works in Cashel," Annie told Mick. "At the bakery."

"I thought she worked at the dairy," Michael said, still laughing.

"You'd better shut yer gob, Michael, or I'll be closin' it for ye," Paddy said, rising from his chair. His face was getting red.

"Can't you take a joke, Paddy? We're just having a little fun now that you're courtin'," Kathleen said.

"No one made fun of you, Kathleen," he said, through tight lips. "I didn't take the Mickey out a you when you were gallivantin' around with that—that spy, did I?"

Annie saw the hurt on her daughter's face. "Sit down, Paddy, and finish your supper." She held his arm tightly, "Please."

Paddy knew that look. He felt the solid grip on his arm and sat back down. Mick shoveled a heaping portion of ham, cabbage, and potato into his mouth. "I'll not have his name mentioned in this house," he garbled.

"No one made mention of his name, Da," Kathleen said, firmly. She turned back to Paddy. "And he's not a spy."

"Don't, Kathleen," Annie pleaded.

"Your mother's right, Kathleen," Larry said, finally sensing an opportunity to talk.

"How can ye still care about the man that put Da in prison?" Paddy said, changing the subject to Kathleen's improprieties. Kathleen's eyes widened with anger.

"He wasn't responsible for that—you have no bloody idea what you're talkin' about."

Larry was becoming more assertive. "Please," he said, loudly. "If we're going to discuss family problems...the dinner table is not the place. Besides, your mother made a fine meal and..."

"Who in Christ's name do you think put me in prison?" Mick asked loudly, ignoring Larry's attempt to quiet the conversation.

"It wasn't Liam Riordan," Kathleen interrupted.

"I knew him better than anyone here and..."

"That wasn't even the bastard's real name. You loved a fukken specter." Mick's face was beet red and displayed the same fiery eyes as his daughter's.

"Mick, please—I'll not hear that language in front of the children," Annie demanded.

"Nor I—tis my house, Mick Barrett, and..."

Kathleen wasn't listening to Larry or her mother. This was a battle long overdue between her and her father.

"I don't care what his name is, Da. I love him, and if I—**when** I see him again, we'll be married," she said. "There, I've said it." She was finally venting all of the pent up emotions, her unmentioned private thoughts.

Mick wasn't paying attention to anyone else but his daughter. Her choice in men angered him.

"Marry him is it! Well now, I don't think ye will, Kathleen." Mick stood up, making a loud noise with his chair. With tight fists on the table, he leaned forward inches from her face across the table. "As a matter of fact—I know ye'll not be seeing him." He was emphatic. "Never again."

"You can't stop me, Da." Now Kathleen was also standing.

"Boys," Annie said, picking up the half-finished plates. "Leave us be now—outside with ye."

"Oh, Ma, we're part of this, too," Paddy said.

"I won't have to stop ye," Mick was gloating now. "The bastard's already gone."

"He'll come back! I know he will! He told me." Kathleen was beginning to sob.

"He's dead, girl!" Mick's loud announcement was followed by an inexplicable silence. All eyes were on Kathleen. In the silence, she closed her eyes.

'*Dead, girl—dead, girl*' reverberated in Kathleen's head.

Mick's face softened, the eyes returned to their usual sparkle, only this time the sparkle was a tear. He had never seen his daughter so dejected, so completely overwhelmed with sadness. This was a moment Mick Barrett would regret.

"Gone?" was all she could whisper. "Liam's dead?"

Mick slowly unfolded the letter from Father Donnelly. Annie picked up the newspaper clipping that dropped on the table. She read the headline and turned to Mick.

"What does this sinking have to do with…"

"He was aboard the Farraday." He turned to Kathleen, "I'm sorry, Kathleen, I…"

"What are ye talkin' about—aboard the what?" Kathleen's voice trembled.

"The Farraday," Mick said quietly. "Liam Riordan was returning to England. Father Donnelly saw him off—the Farraday was the name of the ship."

"And you knew this—you knew this all the time?"

"Kathleen, I…It's maybe just as well that he's…well, I mean it wouldn't have worked out…"

Kathleen screamed the words. "You knew? You bloody well knew and you didn't let me see him!"

Annie reached out to embrace her daughter, but Kathleen pulled back.

"Kathleen, darlin', you'll get over it—trust me—time will heal your sadness."

"Your mother's right," Mick interrupted. "In time you'll forget he even existed."

Kathleen took advantage of the quiet. She wanted them both to hear clearly, deliberately what she had to say. "And will time take care of the baby? His baby!"

CHAPTER TWENTY-FIVE
Boston, 1916

MADGE NOONAN, TWENTY-EIGHT years old, lived in a red-brick, four-story house in Louisberg Square, the rich section of Boston. Born Margaret Ellen Fitzgerald, she was sent to her uncle's home after her mother died. Her older sister, Annie, had just married a Dubliner, Michael Barrett, and Larry had hit the bottle, blaming himself for his brother's death. Madge was ten years old. Not understanding Larry's recurrent bouts with the drink and Annie's preoccupation with Mick Barrett, Madge was happy to leave Ireland. In Boston, Paddy and Noreen Fitzgerald had no children of their own and welcomed her with open arms. Paddy was delighted with his brother's little girl, and since she bore the same name and had the Fitzgerald's distinctive features and auburn hair, people who didn't know the family mistook her for Paddy and Noreen's daughter.

At seventeen she met Dennis Noonan, her first and only love. Dennis was a hero of the Spanish-American War, a Rough Rider who helped take San Juan Hill in the famous charge with Teddy Roosevelt. She met Dennis at a political fund-raising dance for Mr. Roosevelt. Her aunt and uncle were admirers of Roosevelt and had her accompany them in the hopes of meeting up-and-coming young men worthy of their beautiful niece. She had immediately fallen in love with Dennis Noonan, who was introduced as the youngest hero of the war. He was twenty-six, a little old for her, she thought at the time, tall, handsome, articulate, Irish, and more importantly, a bachelor. After a short courtship, Madge became Mrs. Dennis Noonan.

He was a partner in a respected law firm. They had two children, James and Anne, who were now eleven and nine.

Madge stood in the beautifully appointed sun-filled drawing room. All of the furniture was made of polished rosewood, especially for the family. The open beams in the ceiling were paneled and trimmed in matching wood species. A Venetian chandelier with tiny electric lights graced the center of the room. Expensive Irish-lace curtains were tied back with green velvet swags. A green floral-patterned valance crowned the French panes. This was Madge's favorite room.

The children played outside, and Dennis was still at work. She was alone, reliving those fearful years after her mother had died. She was always happy to hear from her sister Annie, but her letter this time was full of sadness. She had barely mentioned Mick's problem with the British; it was the last paragraph Madge read over and over. It said:

> *Kathleen needs desperately to get away from Ireland. She married an American boy named Liam Riordan. He was lost at sea when his ship was torpedoed by a German submarine. It's times like this, Madge, that I feel so inadequate as a mother. There's nothing that would make me a believable confidant for her right now. That's why I'm writing to you. She's pregnant, Madge, and needs a new beginning, for herself and her child. I guess the baby is due after Christmas. Mick and I would be indebted to you if you could see your way to sponsor Kathleen. If anyone would understand a need for new beginnings, I knew that you would.*
>
> *Your Loving Sister,*
> *Annie*

Kathleen was becoming impatient. Bridget was already fifteen minutes late for their meeting at the Canal Cafe. She stared wistfully at the bairin breac ring on her left hand.

"Missus Liam Riordan," she whispered to herself.

It was her mother who had suggested the idea. Once the shock of Kathleen's having a baby evolved into recognition of an inevitability, the family had to contrive a plan. To an Irish Catholic, having a baby out of wedlock was shameful, a disgrace to the family that brought dishonor, not to mention the hardships the child would have to endure. No, Kathleen would have a husband and since she didn't have time nor the inclination for a live one, Annie decided that a deceased one would do.

Annie and Kathleen had no problem with Liam Riordan; however,

Mick was another story. It was all very logical to Kathleen; after all, the baby was conceived in love by the man whose name it should bear. She was convinced that her father would come around, at least when he became a grandfather.

She had arrived in Dublin two days earlier and was staying with her Uncle Padraig. Mick had given her strict orders not to see anyone but Padraig and Father Donnelly. She was to purchase a ticket for America then return to Tipperary immediately. Kathleen looked at her watch. It was almost half-twelve.

Why can't people be on time, she thought. She was anxious to see her friend. So much had happened since they last talked. She knew she was disobeying her father by seeing her friend, but Bridget wasn't just anyone. She was a good friend and right now she needed a confidant.

While she waited, her thoughts returned to her visit with Father Donnelly. Everything had gone so well. Annie had written Father Donnelly to ask a very special favor: a marriage license for her pregnant daughter. The priest's returned letter was understanding, sensitive. 'It wasn't an unreasonable request for a friend,' he wrote back. After all, the name she wished to take in marriage was a man already dead, and as far as Father Donnelly was concerned, Liam Riordan was a man who really hadn't existed to anyone but himself, Kathleen, and her family. He would be happy to oblige.

Kathleen was also surprised at the priest's willingness to commit a breach of his Holy Office. He would most surely have been defrocked, or at the very least, severely reprimanded, had the Bishop discovered the deception. She knew that the priest was in the business of forgiving people, and she sensed that he really liked Liam Riordan. Donnelly told her that deep in his heart Riordan was honest, but like most young men these days, was caught up in a bloody, unholy war. He had spent enough time with Liam Riordan to realize that he loved Kathleen. He also told her that he believed it might have been someone else that turned in her father, not Riordan. She wished she hadn't pressured him now. He might have told her more. She was remembering his final words. *It's not important, Kathleen, that you know everything about him—all I can tell you now is that I know he loved you.* The priest had stopped mid-sentence. She knew he didn't want to continue. She felt that for some reason he had already said too much. She guessed the priest's reluctance to share was based on some promise he'd made. A secret maybe, or something Liam had told him in private. She concluded that the priest's inexplicit rambling might even have been something that Liam told him in the confessional. He did go on to say that one day she would know more. He promised. One day.

She smiled openly and her blue eyes stared vacantly at the ring on her left hand. Her musings were jogged to reality.

"What are you smilin' at, Kathleen Barrett?"

"Bridget!" Kathleen stood and they embraced.

Bridget held Kathleen at arm's length. "God, it's so good to see ye—shure, we thought you'd died an' gone to heaven."

"There were times, Bridget, that I wish I had!"

"We all feel bad about yer da an all—I hear he's all right, though."

"He's fine, Bridget. Oh, Bridget. It's been horrible these past weeks. We're all in seclusion—exile. No friends or neighbors. Can't talk to anyone—I'm not even supposed to be talking to you. Ma says it won't be long, though."

A young waiter with bulging, black eyes asked for their orders. They each had a bowl of Dublin coddle and a ginger ale. Bridget changed the subject.

"How are the boys?"

"Fine, Bridget—they're adjusting better than me—and Paddy has a girl already."

"Go on with ya," Bridget said.

"We heard that Sean left for America?" Kathleen's inflection made the statement a question.

"That was me ma's doin', Kathleen. She knew there were more opportunities for a young man like Sean in America," Bridget said. "Oh, and Kathleen—we heard all about yer man—the American."

She touched Kathleen's hand affectionately. "I'm awfully sorry—shure, weren't we all taken in, and you more than any of us."

Kathleen's right hand mechanically moved to her left hand, rotating the bairin breac ring with her thumb and forefinger.

"Bridget, if you only knew the real truth."

"Kathleen Barrett, the man was an ingrate! After all your family did for him—an' him turnin' in yer da, it's a bleedin' good thing for him the English got him out. Shure, the movement would have had him killed..."

"He's already dead, Bridget," Kathleen interrupted. "And I'm pregnant."

Bridget was stunned. She noticed Kathleen's preoccupation with the ring.

"Yer married!" she exclaimed.

"Yes."

"And yer pregnant, ye say?" Bridget's face turned from curious amazement to sadness. "Aw, dear God—an' he's dead? I'm really sorry, Kathleen. I know ye loved him an all but I didn't know ye married him."

She hesitated and the tone in her voice changed. "How could ye marry the man that turned in yer da, Kathleen? He was working for the British. We heard he was a soldier—a spy yet!"

"I don't believe that," Kathleen said firmly. "He **didn't** turn in me da. I just came from seeing Father Donnelly this morning, and he as much as told me that he believed it to be someone else, Bridget."

Bridget's face paled. "Did he, er, say who it was?"

"No. Oh, but I have a feelin' he knows and won't say—shure, I think it might have been —" she leaned across the table —"one of our own," she whispered.

Bridget clasped and unclasped her fingers. She knew that her brother was responsible. Her mother had told her everything before Sean left for America. Nora made her promise on her father's grave not to tell anyone. Her brother wouldn't be safe, not even in America. An act of betrayal by the enemy could be understood. One by your own could not. An informer was the lowest excuse for a human being, a low life. Bridget understood that Father Donnelly was in the movement and would surely report anything he knew—unless he had heard it in the confessional. *Her mother,* she thought, *would have wished to cleanse her soul. Oh, shure, she has to swear to God and their father's grave that she won't tell a soul and her mother blabs everything to a priest in the movement. How else would he have known?* She scrutinized Kathleen's face for some sign of uncertainty. *Kathleen didn't seem to know who the informer was. Kathleen couldn't have concealed that.* Bridget was pleased again, knowing that her brother's secret was safe.

The young man with the bulging eyes brought their soup. Kathleen waited for the hot coddle to cool down. Bridget immediately filled a spoon and brought it to her pursed lips. She blew on the broth and made the loud sucking sound that always embarrassed Kathleen.

"When did ye get married?" she asked, with a twisted hot mouth.

"This morning," Kathleen said, smiling.

Kathleen explained to a shocked Bridget about the marriage license, and the Hill o'Howth when they made love and he proposed to her. She talked about the horrible argument with her father and her having to leave for America. After lunch the girls walked down Baggett Street to Stephen's Green. They strolled in the park and talked about America and asked if they would ever see each other again. They cried and revealed each other's secrets, all except Sean McIntee's betrayal.

On the day of her departure, Kathleen and her family, including Uncle Larry, traveled to Queenstown. The small seaport was at its busiest, playing host to the hoards of emigrants awaiting their boarding the Cunard Line steamship, Carpathia. The ship was berthed in the harbor, taking on provisions for the long trip. Friends and family of the passengers were allowed on board to say their farewells and tour the ship. Annie had booked a cabin-class ticket for her daughter, a luxury Larry's money helped purchase. The enormous ship catered to four hundred first- and cabin-class passengers, and over a thousand in steerage. Michael and Paddy were more excited by the bo's'n's dissertation on lifeboat drill than sorrowful at their sister's departure. Annie, Kathleen, and Jamie stood at the rail just below the wheelhouse and looked down at the masses of poor, common, Irish emigrants who filled the ship's prow. Not a square inch of the ship's deck was visible. Men held children on their shoulders, waving at relatives on the pier.

Mick had left them at the rail to find the captain. It was unusual for a young woman to travel alone, and he wanted to make sure his daughter was looked after.

A sign indicating that passengers could not pass this point stopped Mick momentarily. As he was about to remove the chain across the stairway leading to the wheelhouse, a firm hand grasped his shoulder.

Captain Nicholas Peters was a tall, medium-built man in his mid-fifties, and the early signs of a middle-aged paunch didn't take away from his smart appearance in navy whites. He wore a well-groomed salt-and-pepper imperial mustache. His chin was square with a dimple, and beneath the peaked cap with the embroidered insignia, lively deep-set hazel eyes smiled, even though the voice was demanding.

"That's all right, Mr. Fellows, I'll see the gentleman. This way, Mr...?"

"Barrett, sir—Mick Barrett," Mick said, ascending the narrow steel stairway.

"It's about my daughter, Kathleen Bar—er—Riordan. She's a passenger."

They exchanged handshakes and the captain introduced himself before turning back inside the wheelhouse. Mick followed him through the steel doorway. Inside, Mick was taken aback with all the instruments.

"They're not so magical when you know what they're all about." Peters gestured to the array of electronic and mechanical instruments. "I wouldn't want to concern you, but there's only a few that we really have to watch carefully."

"You're an American?"

"Yes."

"On a British ship?"

"Is that a problem for you, Mr. Barrett?"

Mick was embarrassed for asking the question. "Not at all, sir—it's just that I thought you'd be..."

"British?" Captain Peters intervened, smiling. "Anyway, about this daughter of yours, Barrett—she's married?"

"Yes, er, well, widowed. He—er, her husband, was killed by a torpedo—his ship, that is."

"I'm sorry to hear that. Is she traveling alone—any children?"

"No," Mick said. "I'd be obliged if you'd look in on her once in a while—if you could find the time, I mean."

"The pleasure would be mine," the captain replied. He took a pad from his pocket and spoke as he wrote. "Kathleen Riordan."

Mick thanked him. He turned halfway through the door, "By the way, she's in cabin-class," he said proudly and left.

He joined his family and told Kathleen and Annie of his visit to the bridge. His words were drowned out by the ship's blast, indicating it was time for visitors to go. Kathleen felt the stab of grief. Leaving Ireland and her family was moments away. The thought of not seeing her mother, father, and the boys was punishment enough, but what if she never saw Jamie again? Tears welled in her blue eyes. She'd helped take care of him since his birth and held a special love for him, not unlike a mother for her child. She said goodbye to the boys and hugged Jamie for the longest time.

Annie hugged her daughter. All she could think to say was in a whisper, "Write, darlin', be sure to write." She turned and left with her tearful sons.

Mick stood looking at Kathleen with outstretched arms. "Well, Kathleen—I guess this is it."

She rushed to his arms, strong and comforting. Her body trembled and she managed some words between sobs, "Oh, Da—how can I go—I don't want to."

"Oh, darlin'—shure, an' it's the only choice for you an' the baby—you'd never find acceptance here. Just think of this whole thing as a great opportunity—a Godsend for you an' your baby."

Unable to deal with the grief in her eyes, Mick simply held her close momentarily, then walked away. She dried her tears and found a place at the rail. Everyone on the pier looked the same to her. The large crowd waved and screamed names of departing passengers. She didn't see her family right away and was becoming panicky when she caught a glimpse of Mick. He was the last one off the ship. Her eyes carefully followed him to where her mother and the boys stood. They had seen her and were already waving. The ship finally eased away from the pier. She waved to the beloved until they became disappearing specks on the dock.

CHAPTER TWENTY-SIX

O N THE THIRD day, Kathleen sat in her cabin thinking about her past and what the future would hold for her and her baby. She looked forward to seeing her American aunt and uncle, and the prospect of working in a hospital in America excited her too. She was unsure whether her skills were enough to qualify her. Certainly her recent experience with victims of the uprising would be beneficial. She opened her valise and took the well-worn envelope from its secure pocket. Inside the envelope were ten one-pound notes and the letter from her Aunt Madge. The paper was made of fine linen. The Noonan and Fitzgerald crests were embossed and colored at the top of the page. She rubbed her fingers over the raised images. *How impressive*, she thought. *Aunt Madge must be very rich.*

The letter read:

Dear Annie,

Having received your letter, I am deeply saddened by all the problems you and your family are experiencing. We are doing our best to help the cause by raising money. I don't ask Dennis what it's used for. I can only hope some of it goes to feed and clothe the less fortunate. Dennis is very politically active these days and is determined to see that the "bungling school teacher" as he calls him, is a one-term president. We're all very upset with Woodrow Wilson. He's not Catholic, you know. As a matter of fact he has publicly denounced the revolution and complimented the

British on their handling of the situation. God willing, Annie, we'll see a free Ireland in our lifetime

Regarding my niece Kathleen. We welcome her with open arms. The whole thing reminds me of my arrival in America. I have first-hand knowledge of what Kathleen is going through and what she'll encounter when she gets here. You can rest assured, Annie, that we shall treat Kathleen as our own and that goes two-fold for the baby.

Your loving sister,
Madge Fitzgerald Noonan

A tap on the door roused her. She quickly folded the letter, returned it to the pouch inside the valise, and placed it under the bed. After straightening her skirt, she quickly approved her looks in the mirror and answered the door.

Captain Peters doffed his cap. "Sorry to bother you, Missus Riordan, but there's a young woman in steerage that could use your help."

"My help?"

"Yes. Your father told me that you are a nurse. Is that right?"

"Well, yes, but…"

"I'd be indebted to you if you could assist the ship's doctor," he cleared his throat, "in a delivery."

"I'd be happy to, Captain." He stepped aside as she self-assuredly moved past him. "Is the doctor with her now?"

"Yes—but…"

She stopped him mid-sentence. "Lead the way," she said, gesturing.

Walking briskly ahead of her, he turned his head. "It's about the doctor, Missus Riordan."

"Please, Captain—call me Kathleen. Missus Riordan makes me feel so old!"

"Kathleen," he said. "Yes—well, this is his first delivery. In fact, this is his first *anything*. He's just out of school. He seems hesitant to me."

"Captain Peters, babies are my forte. I'll try not to embarrass the ship's doctor too badly."

After descending a number of steel stairs and narrow companionways, they reached the steerage sleeping quarters. The smell assaulted Kathleen—body odors, human waste, and vomit. The room was massive with a low, steel-girdered overhead. Bunks stacked three high lined the bulkhead. The only light came from the open portholes; all had been painted black to shield the ship from submarines at night.

She pushed through the crowds in the direction of the woman in labor.

Each cry grew fainter. Kathleen saw a very pregnant woman on a bunk. A young man with a stethoscope, presumably the doctor, was checking the woman's heart rate. A tall, gaunt man leaned over the patient, holding her hand. He looked at Kathleen with tired, deep-set brown eyes. She assumed he was the husband.

"Are you the nurse, Miss?" he asked. He had a Kerry accent, fast and well enunciated. "My name is John Duggen. This is my wife, Mary. I'm afraid her time has come," he said grimly. "We were told the baby wouldn't be due for another month—at least."

"It appears that someone forgot to mention that to the baby," she said, smiling.

Kathleen was introduced to the doctor by the captain. For Dr. Richard Matlick, newly graduated from Johns Hopkins, this was his first appointment, second voyage as a ship's doctor, and not only his first delivery, but a breached one at that.

"Dear God," Matlick whispered.

"What's the matter?" the father asked.

The captain placed his hands firmly on Duggen's shoulders. "Your wife is in good hands. Your children need you more than your wife right now," he said softly. The man looked bewildered as he was gently moved to where two teenagers held a cowering five-year-old girl.

"Will me ma be all right?" one of them asked anxiously, obviously the older one, with a shock of red hair tumbling onto fair eyebrows and green eyes.

"Your ma's in good hands, Anthony," the father said. His voice indicated he was trying to convince himself.

"Dear God," Matlick said again, his hand groping awkwardly inside the woman. "I feel feet—we're going to have to rotate the baby."

Kathleen had been handed an apron by the ship's cook, who had flunked veterinary school. After somebody quipped that too many cooks spoil the soup, he left in a huff.

"Do you mind if I try, Doctor?" she asked modestly.

The woman was writhing in pain. Kathleen knelt and eased her hand gently through the birth canal. Casually, she turned to Captain Peters, who was still standing by.

"We'll need lots of hot water and clean bed sheets, Captain," she stated. "And a little privacy would help." Her eyes scanned the curious spectators. "An animal in a barn has more privacy."

Captain Peters was impressed with Kathleen Riordan, her sense of order; so professional she was for someone so young. Certainly more impressive than his ship's doctor.

"Please," he said. "Let's give Missus Duggen some privacy." The cook returned with two helpers carrying cauldrons of boiling water and stacks of freshly laundered sheets.

"Take some of these sheets and cordon off this area."

"Yes, Captain," the cook said.

"Mr. Duggen, why don't you take the children topside—get some fresh air," he said firmly. "And don't worry, your wife is in good hands—trust me."

"Yes, Captain," Duggen said, eager to leave the birthing to his wife and the professionals.

At ten o'clock that night she left the small cabin. She couldn't sleep. She stood alone at the rail and looked toward America. The steamer rolled gracefully, calming her. She was proud of the way she'd handled herself this morning; so was everyone else, including young Dr. Matlick. He thought that the baby might have died had it not been for her.

Staring at the deck below, she thought about the passengers she had seen earlier. They filled the steerage section, fore and aft, burdened with the noise of the ship's anchor chain and the monotonous growl of the ship's screw. She thought about the steel bunks, row upon row, stacked deck to ceiling, each with a scrawny straw-filled mattress and a blanket, the only protection against the cold Atlantic nights. A husband and wife's most sacred conversation was privy to all. In the dark, the cries of a baby and the weeping of a woman brought everyone to think of the lives left behind and the days ahead.

She felt proud of how the Irish made the best of an abominable situation and could spin charming tales or sing a ballad. The food was meager, the meal consisting of a bowl of barley or potato soup with a piece of dry bread. Fish or canned beef in a gelatin mold was a culinary treat. The promise of a better future lifted their spirits beyond present conditions: all were going to a far better place.

"Good evening, Kathleen." She knew the voice well by now. She turned toward the sound, smiling.

"Good evening, Captain."

He stood by her, holding the rail with both hands. He was looking up at the star-filled, black, moonless night.

"Mind if I join you?"

"I'd be delighted," she said. "I've just been admiring the stars."

"That was a wonderful thing you did this morning."

"Thank you, Captain. It's certainly times like that when I really do love my work."

"I can imagine," he said enthusiastically. "You're a good nurse—controlled—firm—and, I might add, qualified."

She looked up at him and smiled. "Like you, Captain?" she said.

"Now that you mention it, I did see a 'take command' quality about your demeanor," he said, smiling. As if to avoid the reaction on her face to his next question, he looked up at the stars. "Your father told me that you are recently widowed?"

"Oh, he did, did he?" she said facetiously. "And what else did he tell you about me, Captain?"

"Only that he thought you needed looking after. I believe he underestimated your capabilities," he said, looking down.

"Don't all fathers?"

"I guess so."

"Are you a father?"

"A grandfather," he said proudly. "And you're soon to be —"

"Soon to be a mother," she sighed. "Today just reminded me of my own fate. I certainly hope I'm in better surroundings."

"You saved the baby's life this morning—and probably the life of the mother, too."

"Oh, I wouldn't say…"

"It's true!" he said, firmly. "Dr. Matlick told me. He said he didn't think he could have done it without you. He said he was like a big-handed farmer trying to fix a fine watch."

"Thanks," she said. "Tell him thanks."

A shooting star lit up the black sky. Kathleen became excited. "Oh, did you see that!" she exclaimed. "Quick, you must make a wish!"

"It's your star," he smiled. "I had it arranged just for you, Missus Riordan. It's your wish."

She closed her eyes and crossed her fingers like a little girl at a birthday party.

"Do you know much about the stars, Captain? I mean, you must have studied how to get from one point on the globe to the other."

"At night, Kathleen, it's sometimes a good cross reference. I don't always trust the instruments."

"Where's the North Star?" she asked. He pointed to Ursa Major and followed the grouping. "There," he said. "See it?"

"So *that's* the North Star. What sign are you, Captain?"

"Sign?"

"Sign—you know, the Zodiac?"

"Oh, I'm a Leo," he searched with an extended arm. "There's the constellation of the lion. Now, what's your sign?"

"Gemini."

"Oh, the twins," he said. His keen eyes scanned the general area where he knew the Gemini constellation to be. "There, Kathleen—there's your sign—Gemini."

It was difficult for her to interpret at first. She had no desire to affirm the arrangement of the stars if she couldn't see them. She genuinely wanted to see what he was pointing out. Finally she was pointing excitedly.

"Yes, I do see it." Then, somberly, she said, "They're not very easy to distinguish—I mean, one constellation from the next, are they?"

"No—not even for an old sea-dog like me. Early seafarers, however, were very familiar with celestial navigation. They could also spin a tale or two about their authorship."

"You mean there's a story behind each of them?"

"The Greeks had a story for everything."

"And what about Gemini?"

"Twins," he said. "There's at least one story, as I remember. A tale of good and evil."

"How fascinating," she said excitedly, "like Cain and Abel—that's interesting; maybe the Greeks stole the story from the Old Testament?"

"I wouldn't know that, Kathleen."

"Do you remember how it went?"

"Vaguely."

"Well?"

"You really want me to bore you with some Greek tragedy?" He smiled, taken with her inquisitiveness. "As I remember, it was a tale about a shepherd's daughter. She married a young warrior and soon afterwards he was called away to battle. He never returned—killed or lost at sea. She had his babies nine months or so later."

"Twins," she said enthusiastically.

"Yes, identical twins."

"Good and bad."

"Not so fast, Kathleen." He smiled at her sense of genuine, whole-hearted, enthusiasm. "It was the duty of the gods to imbue every newborn with a presence of good and evil. A sense of right and wrong, if you will."

"Like what we Catholics call 'free will.'"

"Yes, something like that," he said. "There was a mix-up. One of the babies got all the good characteristics, and the other became the aggregate of everything that was evil. The Greeks felt that the good had to be tempered with a little evil. Self-sacrifice made the whole person."

"So, they grew up?" she asked eagerly.

"Yes—and the evil brother totally absorbed the good brother, controlled him, and finally killed him."

"Just like Cain and Abel—I told you, it's the Old Testament."

"Kathleen, I suppose you're going to have me change this old Greek tale with a Biblical version—'Gemini, the story of Cain and Abel'?"

"I'm sorry," she smiled. "You're right—I like your story better than mine."

CHAPTER TWENTY-SEVEN

D ENNIS NOONAN WAS in his late thirties. He was tall with thick, black, wavy hair. His eyebrows were heavy and almost joined in the center. His dark eyes were probably his most impressive feature. They were deep-set and genuinely smiled. Small bags had formed underneath and crows feet added a sense of maturity and hospitality. Dennis personified what it meant to be American Irish. He despised the English government for their treatment of his ancestors. His adamant behavior would lead one to believe that he, personally, had borne the brunt of British brutality.

His father and mother left Ireland during the Potato Famine, which Dennis also blamed on the British. He quoted British atrocities of the early eighteenth century as if they had happened yesterday. The dreaded Penal Codes were his favorite topic. It was hard for him to imagine how one country could impose such inhumane restrictions on another. It was against the law to practice your religion or speak your own language or own your own property. No Gaelic games were allowed. A Protestant, even if he liked a Catholic, could not bequeath land to him or his family. Dennis Noonan's face usually reddened with rage as the penalties continued to haunt him. He took everything that happened to the Irish personally; there was no place in his mind for negotiation. Revolution and sedition, those were his answers to the Irish problems. When he was really upset he had a habit of rubbing his right ear lobe between his index finger and thumb. Those who knew Dennis were cautious not to arouse his anger when his hand reached for his right ear.

155

He was meeting tonight with newly appointed board members of the Irish Republican Brotherhood. He was its first American chapter president. The board consisted of five officers besides Dennis: a vice president, secretary, treasurer, Irish liaison and a representative to the general membership. They were meeting tonight at the home of Ernest Conway, a portly man in his mid-fifties, a certified public accountant and the group's secretary.

"How much do we have left in the coffers, Ernest?"

"I'm afraid not much, Dennis," Ernest said, shuffling through the papers on the table in front of him.

"Five thousand," he said, looking over his wire-rimmed spectacles.

"Five thousand," Dennis repeated. "That's about what we spent for the last hold of guns and ammunition, isn't it?" He was asking Anthony Creehan, a tall, thin, Limerick man in his thirties. He had thinning, mousy-colored hair, expressive blue eyes and a broad, white, toothy smile. Creehan wore a short-sleeved, white shirt without the plastic collar. His forearms were enormous and covered with light-blond hairs.

"That's right, Dennis—actually it was a little bit less. That also included the cost of getting it to Cork from Hamburg. The captain of the ship, a Norwegian, told me everything would have been all right if they hadn't made so much hullabaloo—exchanging the ordnance to smaller boats."

"I heard," Dennis said despondently.

Creehan shook his head as if to take some of the blame. "The British gunboats had a bleedin' field day. A lot of Irishmen died that night," he said. "Maybe we should be lookin' at another source for guns, like Russia."

"There's no way Russia would help Ireland, not while we've cast our lot with the Germans," Dennis said.

"I can say this with some authority: shure, the Irish don't care for the bleedin' Germans any more than the British. I say, let the two arsehole grandsons of auld Victoria go at one another like they already are and us Irish concentrate on the problem at hand—the English—anyway, Dennis. That whole bleedin' exchange of merchandise was a fiasco."

"And a lot of money was wasted," Ernest declared.

"God, they could fuck up a wet dream," Dennis said, shaking his head, "Unbelievable. What the Irish need is some leadership—real leadership. Soldiers with experience. What do you think, Chuck?"

Charles Michael Boyle was Old Boston Irish. He was the same age as Dennis and had served with him in the Rough Riders. He was happy to serve as the group's vice-president. Being president would have made him happy, but he always did come second best to Dennis Noonan. He didn't resent it; it was just a fact of life. He was proud that Dennis trusted him.

"If you and me had been there, we'd—ah, be celebrating Ireland's freedom by now, eh, Dennis?" He turned to Creehan. "They do need training. We can't, ah, keep sending guns just to be, ah, picked up by the British."

"They have spirit, Chuck!" Creehan said, adamantly. "The Irish have a great spirit!"

"You can't win a war with, ah, spirit," Boyle responded.

"That's right, Anthony," the squeaky voice came from Tim Fagan, a slight man with a face like a rat. He was there to pass the board's considerations to the general membership.

"Somebody should be training these farmers. In the fine art of warfare." Creehan, a towering, great figure of a man, stood up. His eyes flared down at Tim Fagan. "I happen to know *for a fact* that those that died were brave fightin' men. *Twice an' three times the little shite that you are!*"

"All right, all right; settle down now. *The British* are the, ah—the enemy," Chuck said.

"That's right," Dennis said. "Sit down, Anthony. We'll work something out."

Anthony's face was red, but he knew better than to disobey Dennis Noonan.

"How about money for special squads, Anthony? Training. Hit major targets in Britain, you know. Army barracks, train depots, ammunition plants. That sort of thing," Dennis said.

"That's, ah, a real good idea, Dennis," Chuck said. His enthusiasm brightened the others.

"I'll look into it," Creehan said, reaching for a cigarette. They all smoked, with the exception of Tim Fagan. He had asthma, but no one seemed to care, even when he wheezed.

"Any new business?" Dennis asked.

"Just that this country is heading for, ah, war," Chuck said.

"Someone should be takin' out that fuckin' school teacher," Dennis said, smiling sarcastically. "I read an article in *The New York Times* yesterday. Senator O'Gorman was being interviewed; he was asked if America was coming into the fight. He mentioned something to the effect that the idea wasn't inconceivable and if certain unmentionable countries had anything to do with it, America would go to war. I don't think Senator O'Gorman cares for Wilson."

"He doesn't like, ah, Lodge or Roosevelt either," Chuck said. "If we do go to war, Dennis, where will that leave the Irish Republican Brotherhood?"

Dennis Noonan shook his head slowly. "You shouldn't even have to ask that, Chuck. America has always come first. We'd fight Germans to protect American interests," he said diplomatically, "and we'd continue to fight England for Ireland's freedom." A chorus of 'Amens' followed.

A light tap on the drawing room door quieted the group.

"Yes," Ernest asked. It was his wife. She was heavy-set with graying hair tied in a bun at the back.

"Tea, gentlemen?" She was holding a tray with five cups, a teapot, cream and sugar.

"Thank you, Missus Conway," the voices said in unison. She laid the tray on the table and exited gracefully. "Don't be up too late, Ernest," she said before leaving, "and remember, just one cup. You know how it keeps you up."

The men drank and talked of other things. Dennis talked about his niece and her famous father. He was proud of Mick Barrett. He appeared to know even more than Annie's letter had outlined.

CHAPTER TWENTY-EIGHT

K ATHLEEN AWAKENED TO a buzz of activity. The ship's whistle sounded at least twice and loud; excited voices outside her cabin announced the ship's arrival into the wide port of New York Harbor.

"There she is!" And "Over there. It's the lovely lady!" The voices of varying dialects came from women and men. "New York at last—America."

"America," Kathleen whispered. "America—finally."

She dressed quickly, put on a bonnet and anxiously went outside. A large crowd had already gathered at the rail. She pushed closer. A polite man in a tweed overcoat moved aside to allow her a place. She thanked him, making herself as thin as possible.

They were just outside the harbor, and in the distance through the mist she could see the Statue of Liberty. The formed-granite base seemed to grow out of the rock on which it stood. The burning torch looked as though it was directing the ship. Straining her eyes, she could see land on either side of the ship. The mist was trying hard to turn to rain, and the sky ahead was dark. Behind the ship the sunrise was spectacular. The sea on the horizon edge shimmered with tiny speculars of light, a fantastic contrast to what lay ahead in the harbor.

Below Kathleen on the foredeck, the steerage passengers had assembled to get a glimpse of their new country. They clammered, shoved, and even took turns on each other's shoulders to see what lay ahead. The stronger won over the weak to secure a position at the railing. All the dialects were blending into one great noise, a chorus of accents from Cork,

Kerry, Dublin, and Belfast. Occasionally a perceptible exclamation made it past the confusion.

"There! There, the Statue of Liberty and look, Ellis Island!"

Soon she was standing inside the largest building she had ever seen. It was the culmination of bricks, granite, steel, and glass. Ambient light came from the skylights in the curved ceiling. Halfway up, the lofty walls were girthed by a mezzanine accessed by a wide staircase. Mostly she noticed the noise. People were being herded like cattle through waist-high dividers. Uniformed men directed the hoards through the steel maze. They moved slowly and awkwardly, dragging trunks and twine-wrapped cardboard suitcases. The immigrants were handed slates on a string that hung around their necks, not unlike the brown scapulars that most of them wore under their clothes.

Captain Peters had prepared her for what she was about to experience. One inspector processed up to five hundred people a day; two out of ten immigrants were sent back, returned for incurable maladies that would prevent them from being self-sufficient in the new world. For those unfortunate few, there was no forgiveness, no compassion, no entry. The eye doctor, she was told, was most feared of all. Kathleen was familiar with the culprit. Trachoma. It didn't take long for Kathleen to hear the first outcries of rejection. Not far from her, a guard was quietly suggesting that a young lad of about ten accompany him up the wide staircase. The chalk mark on the slate was a large letter "T." The boy's eyes were tear-filled and wide.

"Ma—Ma, where are they takin' me?"

"You may come with the boy, ma'am," the guard said, calmly. "It's just that we need further testing. Please follow me to the nursery."

The woman, who had two other children clinging to her dress and a confused husband holding a two-year old, went obligingly. Kathleen saw in their faces fear and utter dejection.

Kathleen was briefly examined and finally reached the long table where she would receive the colored landing card. An older woman wearing glasses asked questions and systematically punched holes in a stiff-paper card.

"Name?"

"Kathleen Riordan."

"Married?"

"Widowed."

The woman said, "Single," and continued with the litany:

"Age?"

"Eighteen."

"Sex?" She answered herself, "Female." … "Nationality?"

"Irish," Kathleen said.

When the woman finished punching out holes where numbers were printed in outlined circles, she placed the card in a box behind her.

"Next," she said mechanically, gesturing for Kathleen to move to the next table. The woman did not inquire about her being pregnant. That suited Kathleen. She waited patiently for the next barrage of questions.

"Where are you staying in America?" The voice came from a stocky man in his mid-forties. His thin mustache hovered over a pleasant smile. His eyes, peering over large bags, seemed friendly.

"I'm going to Boston. I'm staying with an aunt and uncle there." She produced the letter from her Aunt Madge. The man read the letter and handed it back.

"You'll find information at Jersey Central Railway. A ferry will drop you off. Please wait through that door there," he said, pointing at a bright-colored double door. "And failte," he smiled. "Welcome to America, Missus Riordan."

Kathleen arrived at the New Jersey Railway Station. Wishing to see all of America she could, she decided against the Pullman sleeper. She purchased a first-class ticket to Boston and was informed by the ticket agent that the trip would take about three-and-a-half hours. He told her that the train would make stops in New York and Connecticut before reaching Boston.

Just two weeks before, these were mysterious places in her World Atlas. She thanked him and waited in a restaurant until her departure was announced. A large slatternly waitress loomed over her table. She seemed very unhappy. She had a stern face and her mouth chewed constantly as she spoke. Kathleen wanted to know how she could chew anything that long without swallowing. There was nothing on the menu that she understood or cared to order. The surly waitress tapped her fingers impatiently on her pad.

"Make up your mind, honey. I don't have all day."

"Yes, well, er…" Kathleen was frightened and confused by the woman's attitude and thought that surely something horrible had to have happened to her this morning to make her so angry.

"I would like to have a boiled egg and some toast, please."

"If it's not on the menu, honey, the cook ain't gonna make it. You must be just off the boat?"

"Yes, as a matter of fact, I am."

The dismal woman interrupted, "I thought so. First thing you have to learn, honey, is how to order off the menu. You'll find everything in America is based on the dollar. We don't make things for the elite, we make 'em for the masses. And we make 'em for less than any country in the world. Now take your boiled egg, for example…"

Kathleen decided against the egg.

"I'll just have the toast, if that's all right—oh, and a cup of tea."

Whatever she was chewing, Kathleen concluded, must have been very difficult to masticate.

"Never seen one done right yet. They always come back. Too hard or too soft." The woman turned away, writing vigorously on the pad, mumbling something about foreigners.

Kathleen was embarrassed by the woman's attitude. People were beginning to stare. So far, she didn't like America, and from the looks of things, she wasn't sure about the people.

In the foyer, the grandfather clock's Westminister chimes struck two. It was Friday, the fourteenth day of July, and Boston was having a heat wave. Dennis had left in the family Ford to pick up Kathleen at the South Railway Station. Today, Madge was concerned for her niece's comfort. She knew Kathleen wouldn't be used to the humidity. She had the housekeeper open as many windows as possible and position the new electric fans to create a cross breeze.

The children were just as anxious as Madge to see their cousin from Ireland. James would have been a lot happier if he hadn't had to dress up. His black pants, although made of light, summer material, tucked into long, knee-high white stockings, felt restrictive and uncomfortable. He wore his Sunday patent-leather shoes and a white shirt embroidered in the front and buttoned down with mother-of-pearl fasteners. He would prefer to be wearing his regular after-school clothes.

At least, in those clothes, he could put his hands in his trouser pockets occasionally. He missed the feel of his pocket-knife, the small tin box that held his change. They were also a safe haven for his half-eaten candy bar and sometimes a frog or garden snake. Like other boys his age, he tested adult tolerance by being mischievous at times.

He was extraordinarily handsome, with black, curly hair and dark eyes with small bags beneath them that gave them character. When he became excited, they were most expressive. He was tall for his age and belonged to a neighborhood boxing club. His father was proud of his performance in matches. Outside the ring, James was very sensitive to the feeling of others. He wasn't belligerent or arrogant. In the ring he was something else again. He boxed as a predator stalks its prey, skillfully, with patience and determination. James Noonan was extremely competitive, and, like his father, didn't lose many contests.

Anne was like Madge. She was a Fitzgerald. Her face was heart-shaped with lively hazel eyes. She had a beautiful nose, and the edges of her mouth turned upward, always suggesting a smile, and aligned perfectly with her large pupils. She was studious and had an unrelenting inquisitiveness that usually annoyed people who couldn't answer her curiosity. She attended a Catholic elementary school where the nuns considered her something of a rarity. Today her auburn hair hung about her shoulders in ringlets. Anne was sensitive like her mother and thought that one day she would be a nurse just like her cousin. She had looked forward to this day with such enthusiasm she could hardly contain herself. For nearly an hour she had been sitting on the bay-window seat, waiting patiently for her father's return with her new cousin.

Dennis arrived at the station fifteen minutes early. He lit a cigarette and read the headlines of the papers in the newsstands. America's involvement in the war was becoming inevitable. He thought it was ironic that Wilson was campaigning on the slogan, "He kept us out of the war." Now he espoused freedom and democracy for all countries. America was beginning to show signs of entering the war so that small nations might be free. He hated the fact that Ireland was never included. He was pulling furiously on the lobe of his ear when the train slowed to a stop, sending smoke and steam up to the curved glass ceiling.

Dennis recognized her instantly. Lucky for her, because she would definitely have missed him. They embraced and he collected her suitcases from the porter.

"The car's this way, Kathleen," he said. "I can't tell you how much your coming means to Madge and the kids—that goes for me, too." They walked the short distance to the car. "Did you have a pleasant trip?"

"I did," she said, enthusiastically. "I even got to work."

"Work?" he asked, looking down at her curiously.

"Yes," she said. "I delivered a baby."

"Sounds exciting," he puffed. "You'll have to tell us all about it when we get home."

He placed the luggage carefully in the trunk and came around the passenger side to let her in. He gave her another big hug and opened the door.

"God, you're more beautiful than all the photos Annie sent us."

She blushed. "Uncle Dennis, I've a feelin' there's a lot of the blarney in ye—but thanks anyway. I'm sure I look a sight."

He closed her door and quickly returned to the driver's side. "How's your father?" he asked, seating himself behind the wheel.

"Did me ma mention anything in the letter?"

"Oh, we know that the British put him in jail. Your mother did say that he was released. She didn't elaborate in the letter. He was involved in the uprising?"

"Indeed, he was. I'm afraid, though, that there weren't enough like him, Uncle Dennis."

"That's what really surprises me. I mean, that so few men participated," he said. He started the engine and eased the car into a line of motor vehicles, and horse-drawn carriages and carts.

"I'll tell you, if it took place today, things would be different," she said. "Since the uprising, the British have become even more brutal. Even the clergy are taking a more militant stand."

"That's the same information we're reading here in the paper. They're treating every Irishman like he's a threat to the throne."

"Even my—" she hesitated, "late husband—was almost killed. We were returning home from a friend's house a few minutes after the curfew. Three soldiers beat him to a pulp. He was in the hospital for weeks with broken ribs and a concussion."

"Wasn't he an American?" Dennis asked, momentarily taking his eyes from the road.

"Yes, but that didn't help matters at all—shure, the British can't forgive the Americans for not coming into the war."

"But I thought Annie mentioned that he was in the British Army—and they beat him up just the same?"

Kathleen knew that Dennis didn't approve of Americans or Irish fighting for the British. "He realized too late, Uncle Dennis—he came to love Ireland."

"Bastards," he said under his breath. "If it was up to our English-loving president we would have been on the Western Front a long time ago, losing young Americans to support the English cause."

He stopped the car for a pedestrian. "Madge is really excited about your coming," he said, changing the subject. "Even though I'm not a blood relative, I feel very close to your family. If there's anything you need—anything, I want you to know that you can always count on me. Okay?"

She looked at him and smiled politely. "Okay," she mimicked. "And thanks, Uncle Dennis."

"I mean that," he said seriously. "We're all one big family. Good or bad, if it happens to you or the family back home, it happens to me."

"It's true then, that Americans are more passionate when it comes to their Irish heritage."

His answer was immediate and serious. "To the death," he said.

The ride from the station took about thirty minutes. The windows were open because of the sweltering heat. The warm breeze brought an unfamiliar odor. Although she was fatigued from the trip, Kathleen was intoxicated by the charm of the city. Tall, official-looking red-brick buildings, department stores, even burlesque and the newer picture houses created an interesting mix of architecture. Signs with colorful illustrations and clever slogans were everywhere.

Dennis stopped the car at a busy intersection. Pedestrians bustled in front of them and a clanging trolley car crossed. The driver waved appreciatively at Dennis, and he acknowledged with a two-fingered salute. A policeman walked past, his discourteous gaze frozen momentarily, enchanted by the beautiful passenger. Kathleen's eyes caught his and for a moment it was as though they knew each other. She looked down, embarrassed by her obvious unladylike indelicacy, and as the car resumed speed, she looked up once again. He was standing still, fixed in place. Even after the car left his sight, he continued staring past the empty space to the busy street beyond. Officer Ryan Thornton continued on his beat, thinking about his attraction to the beautiful young woman. *Maybe it is her seeming preoccupation with me that excites me,* he thought. He wrote it off to one of those unusual, instant, friendly encounters. Whistling, he crossed the street, swinging the black billy-club.

Moments later the car turned on to Louisberg Square and stopped outside the large, red-brick house. The cobbled street was separated from the house by a wide pavement. Every twenty feet or so low, red-brick planters protected fruit-laden plum trees. While Dennis got the luggage, Kathleen sat admiring the tall, green doors with stained-glass windows. The doors were framed on either side by white, square, decorative pillars that supported a broken pediment. She instantly recognized the two heraldic symbols designed into the center of each window. Across from the house, a black wrought-iron railing surrounded the park in the middle of the square. Weeping-willow, vine-maple, and cherry trees dotted the beautifully manicured lawn. She knew she was going to love her new home.

Madge held Kathleen for the longest time. They laughed and cried. Finally, holding her at arm's length, Madge talked through the tears.

"You're—you're the spit an' image of your mother—I can't believe it! You're exactly as I remember her when I left Ireland."

Kathleen couldn't think of anything to say. Her lips tightened in a smile, high-lighting her dimpled cheeks. She tried desperately to hold back the tears.

"And you must be James?" At last, she could talk without crying. "James." She hugged him. "What a big lad you've turned out to be."

She looked over his shoulder to where Anne stood patiently waiting to embrace her cousin from Ireland. Kathleen's face lit up.

"Anne—Anne, come here. I want to get a good look at ye." Anne rushed over and the three embraced.

"Come on now, children," Dennis interrupted. "Give Kathleen a little air. I'll take your bags to your room. Why don't you two just sit and talk for a while? Here, James, give me a hand with these."

Madge, Kathleen, and Anne went into the drawing room. Madge gestured for Kathleen to sit on the sofa. Kathleen was dazzled by the opulence. *The chandelier alone must be worth hundreds of pounds,* she thought. There was a light tap on the door.

"Come in," Madge said.

A middle-aged woman dressed in black and wearing a tiny lace apron entered with arrowroot biscuits and tea on a silver tray. Kathleen felt that she seemed a little severe.

"Thank you, Missus Dunne," Madge said. Mrs. Dunne placed the tray on the rosewood coffee table in front of Kathleen.

"Will that be everything, Missus Noonan?" she asked politely.

"Yes—and by the way, this is my niece from Ireland, Kathleen—Kathleen Barrett."

"Riordan," Kathleen smiled.

"Oh, dear! I'm awfully sorry, Kathleen. I'll get used to your name. Just give me a little time."

"Nice to meet you, Miss Riordan."

"*Missus* Riordan," Kathleen said, still smiling. "Why don't you call me Kathleen. That should make it easier for everyone."

"Kathleen it is then," Mrs. Dunne said and left.

"Missus Dunne's a little stuffy but she's a good sort. Her husband works for one of Dennis's clients—a foreman with a construction firm."

Dennis joined them later and they talked into the late afternoon. They talked of nursing, Ireland, the revolution, politics, and the Catholic Church. They talked until it was almost time for dinner.

"Come on, Kathleen," Madge said. "Let me show you to your room." She turned to her son. "James, why don't you draw a bath for your cousin."

Madge was still talking excitedly when they left the room.

"When things settle down, we'll slowly introduce you to the rest of the family. Your grand-aunt and -uncle are looking forward to seeing you. Also, there are lots of Fitzgerald cousins and distant relatives you'll just have to meet. You'll enjoy Rose. She married a handsome Irishman." She stopped at the bottom of the staircase and looked pensively at Dennis.

"Joe," he said.

Madge was still deep in thought. "Hmmm, what is his name?"

"Joe," Dennis said again, walking toward the den, cocking his head back. His name's Joe Kennedy."

Madge was walking upstairs, followed by Kathleen. "Yes, Joe Kennedy. They just had a baby. We'll have to attend one of their parties. They just love to party."

Kathleen's room was on the third floor. It was a large room with tall, angular ceilings. The dormer window was embellished with lace curtains that moved slowly, influenced by the electric fan in the open window. A white-canopy bed with a matching dresser and night table occupied most of the space. Sliding mirrored doors concealed the walk-in closet. An overstuffed chair, parson's table, and floor lamp engaged space by the window. Book shelves lined the wall behind the chair.

Madge and the children went downstairs. Kathleen quietly closed the door and dropped backwards onto the soft eiderdown. She stared at the underside of the canopy, appreciating the hospitality of her aunt and uncle. This room was decorated with her in mind. She knew that she was going to spend many happy moments in this room with her baby.

She moved off the bed and undressed. She removed her shoes and stockings first. After taking off her blouse and skirt, she caught a glimpse of herself in the full-length mirrored door. She turned sideways and studied her figure. It was the corset that produced the hourglass look, pulling at her waist *like one sewed a stuffed turkey* or *wrapped a roast,* she thought. She removed the corset and the rest of her underwear, feeling free at last. Her hands rubbed her stomach, which, without the aid of the corset, was beginning to show early signs of distention.

A light tap on the door made her reach for the robe that she had laid on the bed.

"Coming," she said, hurriedly. "I'll be right there."

"Kathleen," the voice said. It was James. "I've drawn your bath."

She opened the door. James stood there diffidently, admiring her like an orderly awaiting further instructions.

"Come in, James," she said, sitting on the edge of the bed. With one leg over the other, she placed a slipper on her foot.

"You and I are going to have so much fun, James. You can show me Boston."

"I'd like that very much," he said, thinking how lucky he was to have such a beautiful cousin. "If you wish, I'll show you to your bath."

They went down one flight of stairs, and James opened the door for her.

"Thank you, James," she said, kissing him in a matronly way on the forehead. His face turned a deep shade of pink. "You're welcome, Kathleen." He turned and hurried down the staircase, taking two steps at a time.

CHAPTER TWENTY-NINE

OMINE, NON SUM dignus, ut intres sub tectum meum; sed tantum dic verbo, et sanabitur anima mea.
D The priest faced the intricately carved altar and extended the host, holding it between his thumb and forefinger. The congregation of the Holy Name Cathedral recited the prayer along with the priest. Kneeling with bowed heads, they struck their breasts three times with clenched right hands. It was a prayer of humility, intoned just before receiving Communion, and no one felt more unworthy this Sunday morning than Sean McIntee.

He had been in America just over three months, and until recently he'd been in New York. Nora had arranged for Sean to stay with a second cousin of hers who lived in Brooklyn, but Sean had other ideas. He didn't like New York. Chicago. That's where he had always dreamed of going. Not wishing to offend his relatives and especially his mother, Sean McIntee stayed in New York for what he considered a generous length of time. Even though he had plenty of money, certainly more than most immigrants, he went about finding a job.

With his background it was easy to find work tending bar. He was given an opportunity at Kelly's Bar and Grill in Brooklyn, and although first impressions suggested a lack of maturity, McIntee knew how to pull a good pint of stout and was blessed with the gift of the gab. The patrons, most of whom were American Irish, were taken with his Dublin brogue. He knew they were anxious to hear first-hand stories of the Easter Uprising and the bloody persecutions that followed. McIntee's elucidation of the

Five Days of Easter became more embellished with every recitation. When recounting Pearse's and Connolly's surrender at the General Post Office, instead of the usual *'they'* were out of ammunition, it was, *'we'* were out of ammunition. He loved the attention.

In America, he was already becoming 'someone,' especially behind a bar, where he could control the conversation with over-intoxicated patrons who told tall tales and listened to over-rated anecdotes. After the last patron left, usually a little after two in the morning, McIntee spent the next half hour cleaning the bar before he locked up and walked home. Francis Patrick Kelly, the proprietor, knew he had a good worker for slave wages. Kelly took advantage of McIntee. He worked him long hours, seven days a week.

Sean wasn't given time to explore New York and resented Kelly for not giving him a day off. Kelly trusted him to close the till and lock the contents in the safe before he left each morning. The few dollars McIntee kept back each night he considered fair payment for his unparalleled loyalty and unrestrained labor. The money was not missed. When it was time to say goodbye to his job, taking with him a healthy self-administered profit-sharing plan, he also walked away with impeccable references from Francis Patrick Kelly.

He liked Chicago much better than New York. He was staying with an Irish landlady on Chicago's North side, known as "Little Hell." The tenement district reminded him of Camden Street in Dublin. It was overrun with saloons, whore houses, and burlesque theaters. He had inquired at a number of bars about work, and so far he had managed one appointment at McGovern's Cabaret on the corner of Clark and Erie. He prayed that his appointment would go well tomorrow.

He knelt at the communion rail, his hands folded in, and with his tongue extended, waited for the Host. After a moment he returned piously to his pew, being sure not to allow the dry wafer to touch his teeth. He was still deep in thought, trying to remove the sticky dough from his pallet, when he heard the priest's final blessing, telling everyone to go in peace and inviting the congregation, new parishioners and visitors, to a pancake breakfast in the gym. This week it was sponsored by Saint Theresa's Women's Guild. Sean McIntee wasn't known to turn down a free meal.

The gym was a large, wood structure. Long tables covered in white butcher paper filled the court, and although it looked sparse, an attempt had been made to incorporate an intimate atmosphere by placing colorful centerpieces on each table. He selected a quiet table under the basketball hoop, away from the crowd. It wasn't long before the gym filled with parishioners. A young man accompanied by an older man and woman approached Sean.

"Mind if I join you?" he asked, drawing back a chair.

Sean McIntee had the feeling it didn't matter what he thought, the stranger was going to do exactly as he pleased.

"No—not at all," McIntee said.

"You're new around here, eh?"

"I am. I, eh, I'm Irish."

"Yeah—I'd never of guessed." The man stuck his hand out. "The name's Weiss, Hymie Weiss. I'm Polish, Polish-American, that is."

"McIntee, my name is Sean McIntee. Pleased to meet you."

Hymie Weiss introduced his parents. He was well dressed and looked much older than his eighteen years. He was the youngest member of the North Side Mob, and though he attended Mass regularly, he had a very ugly disposition and was in the business of safe cracking, hijacking, and extortion. He had been known to kill without qualms. Not much was said during the breakfast of sausages and pancakes. When the table was cleared, an older woman poured coffee for the four. Hymie Weiss offered McIntee a cigarette.

"Thanks."

Weiss pulled an expensive gold lighter from his inside pocket. It was shaped like a gun. He pointed it at McIntee's face.

"Bang," he said, smiling cynically, lighting the cigarette.

"That's cute," McIntee said, drawing in the smoke. "Real bleedin' cute. Ye could scare someone with that thing."

"Don't be so serious, Irish." He saw that McIntee was embarrassed.

"It's just a joke. Believe me—people in this district know this piece of shit from the real thing."

McIntee's look showed his disapproval.

"Don't worry," Weiss gestured toward his parents. "They don't speak English. They don't even try to speak the goddamn language. I have to do everything for them." He reached under the table and pulled at his pants.

"Take a look at the real thing," he whispered. McIntee discreetly glanced down and saw the small handgun strapped to Weiss's leg. McIntee was impressed.

"How long 'ya been here, Sean? In Chicago?"

"It'll be a week tomorrow. I have an interview in the morning for a job."

"Job—you mean, like work?"

McIntee looked beyond the young, white-faced man to the priest coming their way and recognized him as the priest who celebrated the

Mass. He stood behind Hymie and placed a large hand on his shoulder. The priest acknowledged Hymie's parents in their native tongue. Delighted, they said thank you.

"Good to see you at Mass, Hymie," he said, reverting back to English. Hymie looked up briefly and glanced downward again.

"I may be accused of a lot of bad things, Father, but one thing I don't do—is miss Mass."

"Speaking of bad things—I'm a little worried about some of the things that I'm hearing, Hymie." His voice was low-toned and firm. "Things about you and Dion O'Bannion." He hesitated. "And George Moran."

"I wouldn't believe all that I hear, Father," Hymie said, feeling challenged by the priest.

"What I'm hearing, I don't want to believe, Hymie. Did you listen well to this morning's sermon?"

"Why? Was it just for me?" He laughed nervously, trying to manifest a display of authority. The show was for the Irishman, but McIntee was becoming more embarrassed for Hymie.

"Well, now that you mention it, I did have all of you in my thoughts this morning. You know, in order to really experience God's love, you must feel what it is really like to be deprived of it." He smiled at Mr. and Mrs. Weiss. "Like your fine parents here, Hymie. They left Poland to find religious freedom."

"Oh, I get it, Father," he looked upwardly, his face displaying a devout expression. "To really experience freedom—" his eyes squinted thoughtfully, "I should spend time where there isn't any, right? Like Poland?"

"Well, Hymie—you wouldn't have to go quite that far. I was thinking of someplace a little closer," he paused, "like Bridewell Prison."

Hymie didn't like being bested by the priest. He pushed his chair back abruptly and stood up. Still a full head shorter than the man in the black cassock, he focused his eyes on the priest's chin.

"Yes, Hymie?" the priest asked contentiously.

Hymie's pasty face took on a deep shade of crimson, the lips closed tightly, becoming a prudent slit, and he stared viciously at the priest before turning to his parents. He said something in Polish. His father shrugged and mumbled something back. As he turned to leave, the priest held his arm tightly.

"And I'd appreciate it if you'd do your recruiting someplace else, Hymie!"

He pulled from the priest's grasp and before leaving turned his gaze to McIntee. "I'll see ya later, Irish."

McIntee nodded.

"I'm sorry for the intrusion. I don't want you to think I treat all my parishioners badly," the priest said, extending his big hand toward McIntee. "I don't know where my manners are. I'm Father Potocsnak, Jim Potocsnak."

The Irishman stood. He had a feeling that this was one priest for whom he was going to show some respect.

They exchanged handshakes. Their casual conversation was soon interrupted by one of the gray-haired ladies from Saint Theresa's Guild. McIntee excused himself and returned to his lodgings on Chestnut Street.

His room was situated on the top floor of a converted single-family dwelling, a boarding house. Each of the four bedrooms was rented to young men thoroughly grilled by Mrs. O'Leary before they were accepted as boarders. She was widowed and lived downstairs. She cooked their meals and did the washing. McIntee hung his jacket in the wardrobe and lay on the bed. He lit a cigarette and thought about how lucky he was to have met a new friend. For the first time since he'd arrived in America, he felt happy. He reached for the open envelope on the nightstand and read again the letter from Bridget.

> *Dear Sean:*
>
> *Everyone asks after you here in Dublin and they feel the same as me and ma do, that if anyone can make it in America, sure you can. Nobody is any the wiser about why you left so fast. I know you were hurt by Kathleen and that didn't justify what you did to Mick but ma and I know that you weren't in your right mind. Anyway, you'll be glad to know that Mick Barrett is out. There are rumors that the movement was involved, anyway, I knew you would be happy to know that he is safe.*
>
> *Speaking of Kathleen, she's living somewhere in America now. Boston, I think. When she writes, I'll keep you informed. Before she left, we had lunch at the Canal Cafe. She's pregnant by that British spy, Riordan. I think she's really foolish for taking his name. They weren't even married! Ma said to be sure and tell you to get to mass. Write soon.*
>
> *Your loving sister,*
> *Bridget*

He put the letter back in the envelope, placed it on the night stand. His mind wandered to Kathleen. *If things had just turned out differently, I probably would have been engaged by now, if not married. The baby would be mine*. He lapsed into a deep sleep.

The warm July days passed, and each one of them was filled with new and exciting experiences for Sean McIntee. Monday, the day after his bizarre meeting with Hymie Weiss, he rose early. He dressed in his best suit, ate a light breakfast and walked to McGovern's Cabaret on the corner of Clark and Erie. The interview for the job as bartender went well, mostly on account of the excellent references from Francis Patrick Kelly.

When he returned to the boarding house, Mrs. O'Leary told him that a young, well-dressed man had called on him. She handed him a calling card, which he read eagerly. The card was from Hymie Weiss. He touched the raised type on the card and thought it was exquisite. He was even more impressed with the title, "Safe and Lock Specialist." *What a splendid title*, he thought.

The back of the card had a message scrawled in atrocious penmanship: *Sean—meet me at two-thirty this afternoon across from the church—738 North State.*

It was signed *Hymie*. McIntee was exhilarated.

The afternoon was hot and muggy. Both young men wore short-sleeved white shirts. Most of the afternoon was spent exploring the waterfront. Late afternoon brought a refreshing breeze from the lake. McIntee had never been introduced to so many people in such a short time. The early evening was a good time to get indoors. Saloons and brothels filled the agenda. Most of the bars were supplied with booze hijacked by the O'Bannion gang. According to Hymie Weiss, there were no great economic rewards to owning a brewery; it was much smarter to let someone else, like the Italians, make the stuff. Then you could steal what you wanted from them.

During the next few days, Weiss became McIntee's tutor, and he couldn't have selected a more enthusiastic student. Every experience was new for McIntee. It was even his first exposure to a brothel. He didn't confess to his mentor that this was also his first time with a woman.

"The Boss won't have nothing to do with prostitution." Weiss was emphatic. "Remember—when you do meet the Boss—no mention of the brothels."

McIntee nodded affirmatively. It was true that O'Bannion had high standards when it came to women. He was much too pious to take advantage of a prostitute's immorality, although he had no qualms about killing them when it served his purposes.

Before the week ended, Weiss had convinced McIntee of the futility of working for a living. Thursday evening was his first and last shift at McGovern's. The following morning, Weiss came by the boarding house early. He had a simple job to execute at Johnny Torrio's construction company on the South Side and wanted to include his new friend. McIntee protested, sitting up and rubbing the sleep from his eyes.

"For Christ's sake, Hymie—it's five in the morning."

"Let's go—this is fun. This'll be the best kick you've had yet." He threw McIntee his pants. "Let's go," he said.

McIntee kicked the covers back and slowly eased himself into a sitting position. "Do I have time for a piss even?" he asked sarcastically. They laughed.

"Yeah—but make it fast."

By five-thirty they were outside the entrance of the construction site. The large, unfinished concrete structure was surrounded by a cyclone fence. Weiss parked the car.

"Well—this is it," he said. "It's going to be a new brewery. 'The Torrio Brewing Company.' Torrio is also the contractor. This is payday," he winked. "Let's go, Sean. You just keep your eyes peeled."

"Peeled?" McIntee asked. Within seconds Weiss had opened the padlock on the gate.

"Ya know—peeled, er, look out for suspicious people, like cops, workers—anyone," Weiss said, closing the gate behind them.

Weiss went directly to a single-story office. It looked temporary and was supported off the ground with large timbers. Once again Weiss opened the door with one of his manufactured picks. Even in the dim light Weiss knew exactly where everything was. He moved to a set of doors below a shelf weighted down with construction binders. McIntee was amazed at the skill with which he opened the doors and the safe beyond. Weiss stuffed his pockets with dozens of small manila packages.

"Here—quick, Sean—take some of these, will 'ya?" he whispered.

There was a confidence to his voice and actions that gave McIntee some comfort. As he began stuffing his pockets, a strange voice coming from behind caused him to freeze. His jaw dropped and his knees buckled.

"Are you about done, Hymie?" the voice asked.

McIntee turned his head in the direction of the interruption. The man, in his late sixties, wore a night-watchman's uniform.

"Aw geez, Leo," Weiss said. "For Christ's sake, don't scare us like that." McIntee was still white faced and speechless.

"It's startin' to get light, Hymie—the general usually gets here around six-thirty or quarter to seven."

"Okay, okay, Leo—we're just about done," Weiss said, placing the last envelopes in his pockets. Weiss stood up and with his hands on his hips, arched his back. He gave a deep sigh. "Geez, Leo—I'm gettin' too old for this shit."

"Me too," Leo said.

McIntee, who had been unmindful of the night-watchman's involvement, impulsively pushed Weiss hard on the shoulder.

"You could have told me about him!" he shouted, pointing at Leo. Weiss smiled and placed his forefinger to his lips.

"Shhh," he said. "Not so loud, Sean."

"You're a fukken arsehole, Weiss," McIntee said louder. "You almost gave me a heart fukken attack!"

"I forgot—okay?" Weiss said, dismissing McIntee's worries. "Now quiet down. We have one last thing to do before we leave." Weiss lifted his pants leg and produced a long, black night stick.

"Be Jasus, Weiss, you have a fukken arsenal attached to yer legs," McIntee said, adjusting better to the situation.

"And between my legs," Weiss laughed. "Are you ready, Leo?"

"I'm ready," the older man said resolutely.

He knelt and bowed his head toward Weiss. McIntee was confused by the ceremonious behavior. Weiss raised up on his toes, and in an effort to be as compassionate as possible, brought the club down swift and hard. The old man slumped forward and for a while lay motionless. Weiss put the club back in his sock and tugged at the man's shoulder.

"Hey, Leo—you okay? Leo?"

Slowly the old man opened one eye. Blood had already closed the other. His mouth cracked a smile.

"It—it really doesn't—hurt, Hymie. You'd better—get the hell—outa here."

Weiss tapped the old man on the shoulder. "See 'ya."

Five minutes later they were in the car driving down State Street with Johnny Torrio's payroll.

"Why did he let you hurt him like that?" McIntee asked, opening an envelope. Fives, tens, and twenty-dollar bills scattered about his lap. He didn't wait for an answer. "Be Jasus, I've never seen so much spondulix in me life!"

Weiss was laughing. He lit a cigarette with his gun lighter and offered one to McIntee. "Leo was in on the heist."

"Heist?"

"Yeah. You know, the job, caper, heist. That's what we call an *inside job*. Believe me, Sean, for that knot on his head—he was paid almost a year's wages."

"I guess that's different then," McIntee said.

"Yeah," Weiss said, exhaling a cloud of smoke. "I did Leo a favor."

"We came close to being caught—didn't we?" McIntee asked.

"Yeah, but we didn't."

"Still—it was a close call. Why didn't ye do the job at night, when no one was around?"

Weiss flicked the used cigarette out of the car.

"See, Sean—that's why I'm in charge of this caper. Think—a car on the street right by the job would be suspicious, and we don't have the fix with the cops in this area. Also—I didn't fancy leavin' Leo to bleed to death. Shit, I know the family."

He cleared his throat and spat out the window. He reflected awhile and took his eye from the road to look at McIntee as if to emphasize his next point. "Ya know what really gets to me, Sean—I mean really does it for me—it's the, eh, element of risk. I really feel high right now—safe, alive, and not to mention—richer," he laughed.

"I think I know what you mean, Hymie. It's like riskin' yer life—and winning."

"Exactly," Hymie said. They drove along quietly for a while. McIntee broke the silence.

"Ye know, Hymie—I believe that's what Father Potocsnak was talkin' about last Sunday when he stopped by our table."

"How's that?" Weiss asked.

"Well, right at this moment—I feel alive! Only because I risked my life. He's saying the same thing about God—when you're deprived of God's love, I guess you want it more."

"Yeah, well—we don't have a problem with that, Sean, 'cause God loves us all," he laughed. "Even us fuckin' sinners."

They turned on Delaware Street and stopped outside the boarding house, still laughing.

Dion O'Bannion's flower shop was situated conveniently across the street from the Holy Name Cathedral. The bell attached to the door announced the two men's arrival. The woman behind the counter was in her late thirties; in an effort to look younger, she wore too much make-up and ruined her natural dark hair with a peroxide. She was a little overweight for the tight blouse. Complacently, the woman continued filing her long nails and didn't bother to look up right away.

"Can I help? Oh, Hymie." Her initial indifference turned to a more charitable demeanor.

"Good to see you." She looked past him to Sean McIntee, who was taller and more intriguing. Her black, inquisitive eyes passed slowly from his feet to his face.

"Hi," she said sensuously. "And who do we have here?"

"His name is Sean McIntee—he's right off the boat and ready for some action. Sean, meet Lorna—'The Rose of the North Side.'"

Sean held his hand out politely. "Hello, Lorna. Nice to meet ye."

"Ready for action, eh, Sean?" She winked.

Weiss separated their hands.

"Not *that* kind of action, Lorna. Is the boss in?" he asked, gesturing to the door leading to the back room.

"They're all back there. Is somethin' big goin' down, Hymie?" He ignored the question and walked toward the door.

"Follow me, Sean. I'll introduce you to the big man."

Lorna pushed a button under the counter, using a series of long and short signals. Soon the sound of dead bolts being drawn back filled the quiet shop, and the visitors quickly vanished, the door closing behind them.

Dion O'Bannion was almost twenty-four years old. He was short and slight of build, a diminutive physique with narrow shoulders making his head look too large for his body. His size was not to be confused with diffidence or lack of brutality. His business was crime, and nobody in Chicago knew the fix better. The annual cost of doing business in the 42nd Ward, better known as the North Side, was over thirty thousand dollars. Protection money: payments to city officials, politicians, judges, prosecutors, all the way down to the cop on the beat. All were in the employ of Dion O'Bannion, or as friends and family called him, Deanie.

The last time O'Bannion saw the inside of a jail had been eight years ago. He was just sixteen and had been picked up on charges of possessing firearms. When the police strip-searched him at the station, they found knuckledusters, knives of various sizes, a blackjack, and three guns. He was fined twenty-five dollars and spent ninety days in Bridewell Prison. After his release, he took up a new career as a singing waiter. He was blessed with a beautiful Irish-tenor voice and had sung in the church choir as a young boy. He always laughed when admirers told him that he sang like an angel.

"As long as I don't sing like a bird," he would respond with a chuckle. His first attempt at honest employment was in a saloon on Delaware and State. Everyone loved O'Bannion when he sang love songs and Irish ballads. The soft, gentle, Irish singer brought tears to the eyes of the patrons. Even the big, rough, unemotional louts succumbed. It didn't take long for O'Bannion to realize that the real profit was in the grift. It was fertile ground for a pick-pocket operation. While he sang, he scrutinized the audience for the out-of-town suckers. He was quick to learn how to separate the drunks from their wallets or roll of bills.

"It's like takin' candy from a baby," he once told Bugs Moran. By the time O'Bannion was twenty, he was boss of one of the most feared gangs in Chicago. Now four years later he owned the North Side. Bugs Moran, his second in command, was a ruthless killer who still lived with his mother and never missed Mass. Between them, Moran and O'Bannion had killed over twenty-five people. O'Bannion carried rosary beads in one pocket and at least three guns in other locations in his clothes. He had an obsession with guns. One of his favorite pranks involved stuffing the barrel of a shotgun with clay and challenging some unsuspecting soul to a shooting contest. This usually resulted in permanent brain damage and sometimes required funeral arrangements on which he made a bundle.

Although O'Bannion had the police somewhat under control, he still had a more formidable enemy: the Sicilians from Little Italy—the Gennas, Al Capone and Johnny Torrio. All of the gangs, whether they were Irish, Italian, Polish or Jewish, were beginning to realize the need for legalized fronts. Cabarets and saloons were fronts for prostitution, drugs, and hijacked booze, the latter being the specialty of the O'Bannion gang.

O'Bannion, known as "Boss" to his hirelings, sat behind a large desk, the front of which had a small hole, chest high, aimed at whoever sat in front of the mobster. A shotgun under the desk was operated by O'Bannion's right foot. The small room had no windows. Besides the large desk, which occupied most of the space, a liquor cabinet, some chairs and a couple of end tables furnished the room. The wall behind him displayed photos of him, his mother, and other family members, suggesting a more sensitive side to the mobster. Today the room was crowded. Bugs Moran, "Two Gun" Alterie, "Dapper Dan" McCarthy, Frank Gusenber and "Schemer" Drucci waited for Hymie Weiss and his new recruit.

Hymie made the introductions. O'Bannion respected Hymie's judgment. McIntee sat in front of O'Bannion as a precaution. The room was quiet as O'Bannion sized up McIntee. He reached into one of the desk drawers and pulled out a large Cuban cigar. He bit off an end and broke the silence, spitting into the wastebasket. Almost immediately Weiss reached across the desk with his gun lighter. He held the flame until the cigar glowed red. Weiss sat down and O'Bannion's musical voice began the interrogation.

"So—Hymie tells me you're from the 'ole sod?"

"Yes, sir—born and raised in Dublin."

"Too bad, about the Troubles, I mean."

"Yes, sir."

"You can cut the sir. Sean, is it?"

"Yes, sir—I mean, Boss."

Everyone laughed. McIntee's nervousness was refreshing. Moran couldn't resist the attempt at humor.

"Yez, suh, Boss," he mimicked. The room filled again with laughter, slowly subsiding when they realized that O'Bannion wasn't joining in the festivities. The last to stop laughing was Bugs Moran.

"Sorry, Boss," he said, apologetically. O'Bannion wasn't pleased and severely chastised Moran with a contemptuous glare.

"Makes ya a little mad when people make fun of ya—eh, Sean?"

"I—I guess so. Yes, it does."

"Enough to wanna hurt someone—does it?"

"Well, I guess," McIntee said. He didn't know what to do with his hands, and he was beginning to fidget nervously.

"Enough to wanna kill," O'Bannion said, casually opening a drawer and producing a 45-caliber pistol. He tossed it to McIntee, whose reaction was slow; however, he caught the gun clumsily with both hands.

"Now, I want ya to carry out my first order, kid. You're pissed off, right?"

"Well," McIntee shrugged, flustered by the pressure. "I'm not that upset—really…"

"These guys are makin' fun of 'ya, kid—especially this asshole here," he said, pointing at Bugs Moran.

"Eh, look, Boss—I'm just havin' some—"

"Shut the fuck up, Moran! Now, kid—are 'ya pissed off enough to shoot someone? Go ahead!" O'Bannion gestured to Moran.

"Like Moran here—go ahead, someone makes fun of ya—ya shoot the fucker."

McIntee was confused. The blood was draining from his face rapidly, leaving a white mask. His mouth was dry and he could hear his heart pumping.

"Er, that's all right, Mister O'Bannion, I, eh…"

"Boss, dammit—I said ya could call me 'Boss,' not 'Mister O'Bannion,'" he mimicked. With an unexpected motion, he stood, slamming the chair against the wall behind him. He leaned forward, aiding his stature by pushing upwards on the tips of his fingers. His boyish face with slicked-back, dark hair stretched forward, the blood vessels in his head and neck bulging, transforming the pasty complexion to a shade of pink.

"I don't like this son-of-a-bitch either," he said, furiously, his finger extended at a cowering Moran.

"Geez, Boss—I was just havin' a little fun…"

"Shut the fuck up!" O'Bannion hollered. The red face turned toward McIntee again.

"If you want to be a part of this organization, kid, we have to make some room." McIntee could feel the stale cigar breath on which O'Bannion's words streamed. It was as though he were playing a role in a bad dream. O'Bannion's voice echoed over and over.

"Shoot the fucker—*now*. Shoot the fucker!"

The gun was pointed in Moran's direction, the trembling body forcing the weapon to oscillate back and forth. Everyone moved away from Moran, fearful for their lives.

"Now!" O'Bannion said, louder than before.

McIntee held the gun with both hands to steady the weapon and with outstretched hands, made an effort to hold the weapon as far away as possible. All of the blood had drained from his face. The last thing he saw before he closed his eyes tightly was Moran's frightened stare. The click of the hammer striking the pin in front of the empty chamber was the only sound breaking the silence.

McIntee opened his eyes and stared blankly at the face of Moran, who wore a big, soundless grin. The laughter began slowly, first with Deanie O'Bannion's thunderous horselaugh, which was the signal everyone needed. Even Hymie Weiss reeled back, howling. O'Bannion fell backwards into the chair. He had pulled off another of his favorite pranks. He pointed a finger at McIntee, trying to say something between hysterical convulsions.

"If—if it was—loaded—it—it would have hit—hit the fuckin' ceiling."

Although McIntee was the butt of O'Bannion's amusement, he began to see the humor. Tears streamed while the frozen arms pointed the unloaded weapon at Moran, who was still laughing.

"Hey kid—point that goddamn thing somewhere else." McIntee's arms dropped loosely. Soon, he laughed with them and felt triumphant because he had done what he was told and ecstatic because he hadn't had to kill someone.

When the laughter died down, McIntee slumped into the chair. His hands loosely held the automatic Colt pistol in his lap, and his head fell back, fixing his glassy eyes on the ceiling. Had the weapon been loaded, there was no doubt that Bugs Moran would have been dead or severely wounded. The idea of killing another human being made his body shudder. His stomach reacted with wet gurgling sounds, dredging a sour concoction into his mouth. He swallowed, trying desperately to suppress his need to vomit by clenching his teeth.

O'Bannion quickly pushed himself from harm's way.

"The son-of-a-bitch is gonna puke!" he shouted.

Hymie Weiss grabbed a wastebasket and thrust it under McIntee's face just in time to collect what was left of his boarding-house breakfast. His body convulsed, heaving until there was nothing left in his stomach and his throat was dry. The offensive odor didn't seem to bother Weiss. He had seen and even been responsible for worse. It wasn't often that he showed compassion for anyone.

"Are you all right, Sean?" he said, placing a hand on McIntee's shoulder.

"I—I'm sorry," McIntee muttered, holding his head down, concerned with what O'Bannion was thinking. *Christ what an arsehole—what an impression I'm making*, he thought. His misgivings didn't last long.

"That's okay, kid—I got sick when I made my first hit—at least I think I did," O'Bannion said. The cigar was stuck in the side of his mouth. "Maybe I just felt bad. Anyway, you passed the test, kid—you're in."

"You're in." The two words McIntee wanted to hear. He was finally a member of one of the most feared gangs in Chicago. It would mean no more long hours working, tending bar. No more pandering to drunks, no more cheap saloon owners deciding on how much and when he should be paid. No. Sean McIntee had finally arrived. He had no heroes. He had advanced himself from an ignoble informer to an even lower life form.

CHAPTER THIRTY

THE FIVE O'CLOCK commuter train from London labored into Putney Station on a cloud of smoke and steam. The massive cylinders pushed the piston rods in slow motion, making great hissing sounds. Even before it stopped, the clattering of carriage doors reverberated through the empty station and soon the platform filled with scurrying workers returning from their jobs in the city.

Ordinarily these Londoners were civil and friendly, but not now. The long day at work and the cramped train ride left them hurrying and shoving. The narrow exit gate at the platform's end, manned by a soon-to-retire lanky ticket inspector, contributed to the pandemonium. Captain William Armstrong Hamilton remained on the train, waiting for the crowd to dwindle. No sense leaving while the impatient, hungry crowd stood motionless outside the carriage window. Eventually he disembarked and trailed the last persons through the gate. He flashed his ticket and the uniformed inspector saluted.

"Good day, guv."

Hamilton switched the cane to his left hand and gallantly complied by returning the gesture.

"And a good afternoon to you, Inspector." He hesitated past the gate and turned his head. "By the way, could you direct me to Roehampton?"

"It's a bit of a walk from 'ere, Captain," he said, glancing down at Hamilton's right foot, "'specially for some'un with a gammy leg."

Hamilton transferred the cane back to his right hand, "Oh, this."

He tapped the cane to his foot. "It's really nothing, just a small fracture. Actually a walk would do me some good—or so the doctors say anyway."

"The Front, guv?" The inspector asked sympathetically.

"Excuse me?"

"The Front?" he reiterated, pointing to Hamilton's leg. "Did you get it at the Front?"

"Oh—the leg," Hamilton exclaimed, slapping it self-assuredly. "No, it's a long story." He didn't wish to be brusque with the older man, but he was tired of relating the account of the Farraday's sinking, and besides, he wanted to be on his way. It was a soldier's privilege to be uncommunicative in such matters and that was accepted by the inspector.

"Well then, if it's a walk you want, guv, first 'ead up the stairs 'ere and make a right. That'll put you out on the 'igh street. Make a left at the King's Arms—that's a pub, guv."

"Yes, I know," Hamilton said, smiling.

"Well then," the inspector continued, "go on up the 'ill an' make a right at the Green Man—that's a..."

"I know—pub."

"Right, guv. Anyway, the Commons will be on your left—just continue on down the 'ill 'till you come to the bottom—there's a fountain."

"Yes?" Hamilton nodded.

"That's it, guv, you're there, Roe'ampton."

"What, no pub?"

"As a matter of fact..." The old man cocked his head. Hamilton cut him off, smiling.

"Thanks," he said, moving in the direction of the stairs.

"Welcome, guv."

Turning to his duties, the old man removed his cap and scratched his balding head, muttering under his breath.

The walk felt good after the long, cramped ride. It was a typical English summer day, with white clouds occasionally blocking the sun. The breeze was refreshing. He cursed the heavy uniform. At the top of the hill, he passed the Green Man. He crossed the street to the Common's side and continued down the hill. Soon the reality around him became lost to the images that continued to haunt him: reveries involving events he knew only through accounts of others. He was told that the lifeboat had drifted south, toward the Isle of Wight. A fog had rolled in and by the time a rescue ship had reached the area, all they'd found were pieces of flotsam and bloated bodies, human and animal, attached to wooden hatch covers. When the fog lifted they had continued the search, and not finding anyone alive, assumed that all hands were lost. It was forty-eight hours before they were picked up by a fishing vessel registered out of Portsmouth.

Hamilton, Captain Russell, the bo's'n, and the ship's cook were the only survivors. He vaguely remembered some periods of wakefulness when they'd prayed together. A piece of shrapnel had entered his chest, breaking two ribs and puncturing his left lung. The sucking chest wound was dutifully attended to by Captain Russell, who had stuffed the opening with fresh rags, removing those that had become blood-soaked. More painful now was his right foot, which was missing a toe, something he didn't often admit to, given the number of combat soldiers' admissions of similar maladies, often considered to be self-inflicted. He was sad to learn that young Tim Willows hadn't made it and vowed to contact his parents.

During his days of recovery, he had written letters to his own parents and also to Kathleen. All had been returned with no forwarding address. It was impossible to explain everything in a letter, particularly events of Mick's escape. He knew that all correspondence was being screened. For a while he considered writing to Bridget McIntee or Father Donnelly, knowing that if anyone knew of Kathleen's whereabouts, they would. Finally, his new assignment forbade his communicating with anyone.

Originally his orders had him assigned to Belgium and France. He was informed that there were other agents involved. Their duties included establishing an inter-allied network of watching posts to observe enemy troops and artillery movements and they were given the code name Frankignoul, after one of the chief organizers of the plan. It would have been Hamilton's role to see that information got back to Allied Intelligence. Among some of the methods of communicating information, the idea of using carrier pigeons failed to appeal to his sense of good judgment. He wasn't going to find out how well the pigeons worked because he wasn't going. He was informed that because of his disability, he would not be taking part in "Frankignoul." They had instead given him a medal, rank of captain, and a new, very hush-hush, appointment. The orders came from the Naval Intelligence Division. They didn't impart much information, only that he would be sequestered for an indefinite period at a house in Roehampton, and at a future date and time he would be further familiarized with his duties.

As was the custom with M15, he had committed the directions of his destination from Roehampton Square to memory and destroyed the orders. The password was "Mousetrap." Every day he made it a point to scribe the word in his mind. "Mousetrap," he whispered as his eyes fixed on his surroundings, storing his ambiguous reflections for another time. Based on what he remembered of the directions, he knew it wouldn't be long now before he arrived. There was no more sidewalk, just a narrow country road. Large columnar cypress blocked the sun's rays, and as if that didn't afford enough privacy, a ten-foot-high stone wall with concertina wire on top loomed behind the trees.

Soon he was standing outside a set of massive wrought-iron gates which formed an arch; letters shaped in iron across the top read *Roehampton Estate*. A winding dirt road stopped at a tall, brick-Tudor mansion festooned with ivy. There were no trees to speak of around the house, giving it an eerie, haunting appearance. Hamilton would have assumed that it was vacant had it not been for the grazing Guernseys. He tried the gate, but it was locked. One of the stone columns holding the gate had a bell, which he pushed. When nothing happened, he continued to press impatiently. Two Royal Marines came from nowhere. They saluted, and after he gave them the password, they allowed him through. Once on the property, the illusion of the quiet mysterious mansion soon disappeared. The other side of the stone wall masked blockhouse security shelters every twenty feet or so. Each fortification was manned by at least two Royal Marines armed with Thompson sub-machine guns. One of the sentinels, a great burly lance corporal with a handlebar mustache, escorted Hamilton up to the house.

The door was opened by a young naval lieutenant with a slight build and an ashen face. As Hamilton entered, the soldier snapped to attention, saluted, clicked his heels, turned smartly and took off with a long stride. Once inside, Hamilton introduced himself. The lieutenant was cordial.

"This way, sir," he said, walking toward a pair of lofty walnut-stained doors. "They're expecting you," he said curtly, glancing at his wristwatch. "You're a little late."

"Yes, well," Hamilton didn't have a chance to finish.

"The Colonel doesn't like tardiness," the lieutenant said.

"What's your name again?" Hamilton asked, irritated with the man's attitude.

"Poole, sir—Lieutenant Reginald Poole."

"Just remember, Poole, *I* answer to the colonel, not you. Got it?"

"Got it, sir," Poole said, his expression unchanged. Poole opened the doors and closed them quietly when Hamilton was inside.

Nothing in the Great Room was as he had expected. The lofted ceiling was painted white, and a decorative rosette where a chandelier had once hung now embellished a single light pendant supporting a white conical reflector with a lone light bulb. The walls were covered with blackboards, maps, and large sheets of paper portraying unrecognizable ciphers and codes. Perimeter tables supported telegraph equipment and various other decrypting and wireless devices. An opening in one of the walls led to the library. A long table in the center of the room was covered with random papers and surrounded by chairs. The only thing in the room that retained any sense of the tradition of the Tudor mansion was the fireplace mantel. Dark-stained walnut panels bordered the fireplace and decorative wood finials supported an ornate mantelpiece of moldings in various shapes. A ceramic gas insert sat in the middle of the large opening where once friendly wood fires blazed. A brass screen covered the flame.

Although the gas wasn't operating, five older men in civilian clothes sat around as though the fire were radiating warmth. They didn't seem aware of his presence until Poole closed the door. Hamilton moved closer and introduced himself. The group arose almost in unison. One of the men had his back to Hamilton, and as he stood, Hamilton's face dropped. Before the man could turn, Hamilton recognized the small, wiry, balding man with the glasses. It was good to see a familiar face. The white, bushy mustache was still tobacco-stained. The older man smiled and held out his hand. The unexpected reunion left Hamilton almost speechless.

"Colonel Lynch!"

"William, ol' boy, good to see you again," Lynch said, shaking Hamilton's hand vigorously. "And so glad to see you made it through that awful Farraday misfortune."

Hamilton smiled at the colonel's ability to choose words that understated catastrophic events. *Thousands of men lost, and he refers to this as a 'misfortune.'* Hamilton dismissed his silent criticism.

"Colonel Lynch—I—I thought you'd retired."

"Retired—and you believed that tommyrot. I don't look that old, do I?"

"Well no, Colonel, it's just that I thought it was something you wanted to do."

"It was all a good bloody ruse, ole' man." He gestured to the other men who were waiting patiently to be introduced. "Here, I'd like you to meet some very special friends of mine."

First he met Sir Nevil MacLeod, a remarkable Scot who was responsible for deciphering and translating German texts. Macleod, also in his mid-sixties, was a tall, thin man with an unusually long nose framed with high cheekbones. His eyebrows, black and bushy, hovered over deepset, inquisitive eyes. His furrowed brow and a wild, unruly shock of white hair gave him an air of eccentricity.

Next he shook the hand of Robert French. He was the younger of the five and looked the oldest. At the outbreak of the war he had volunteered from the Secret Intelligence Service into the Duke of Cornwall's Light

Infantry. He was eventually transferred back to M15 after he was severely gassed at Flanders. This accounted for the raspy voice. His lungs had little capacity; when he inhaled, he made loud wheezing noises. It was a malady that made people he conversed with nervous and instilled an impulsive need to punctuate.

Colonel Lynch introduced another man, a Major Steven Sullivan. Sullivan had just turned fifty. He was a bright cryptoanalyst fluent in French, German, and Latin. Before the war, he'd taught at Eton and for twenty years had been a Catholic priest. He also liaised closely with the Belgian Intelligence Service, led by Major Mage and General Dupont of the French Deuxieme Bureau. Sullivan's piracy from Naval Intelligence was complicated. Because he was a gifted decoder, he worked in the political section of intelligence, in the highly secretive Room 40 of the Admiralty Building. He was chosen by Lynch because of his familiarity with the German Diplomatic Code, which had become numerically known as 13040. This was the grouping of numbers that the Foreign Office in Berlin used initially to transmit secret documents. Sullivan's parents were Irish, but he was born and raised in England. Although he didn't dwell much on his Irish ancestry, he was unimpressed with England's handling of the Irish Uprising. He despised the German rape of Belgium and the atrocities that followed. With a stout build, he was shorter in stature than the others. He had a healthy looking head of black, curly hair with a little gray at the sides. When he spoke, the voice was velvet with a London accent.

Then came the Professor. Rudy Czernikow was a Jew and a professor of science and mathematics. He was brilliant when it came to ciphers. Some of the early German telegrams and telegraphy transmissions used numbers in place of letters. Rudy Czernikow worked for the Naval Intelligence Division during this time and was responsible for interpreting radio transmissions and telegrams that pinpointed enemy naval positions. He was missing a leg because of the car accident in which his wife had died. They had just bought the car and he had allowed his wife to drive them home from a party. At full speed the car hit a concrete bulkhead. His leg was pinned under the overturned vehicle, and although he was in great pain, he feared more for his wife, whom he could hear calling him in the dark. She screamed for him to help her, and finally, in order to extricate himself from the wreck, he hacked off what was left of the pinned leg with his penknife. When he reached his wife, she was dead. He wore a new leg now, thanks to the amputee hospital at Roehampton.

Hamilton sat down as Lynch gave the group more insight into the captain's background. The small talk that followed was accompanied by tea and biscuits. They talked about Ireland, the Farraday, and his weeks in the hospital. At the appropriate moment, Lynch changed the conversation.

"Well, William—by the way, we don't stand on military rank around here. You may call Professor Czernikow, Rudy. Major Sullivan, Steven. Then there's Robert, here, and Sir Nevil MacLeod—you may call him—well—Sir Nevil, I suppose?" He looked to MacLeod for reassurance.

"Actually, Nevil is fine with me."

"Good, then, Nevil it is. And you may call me Colonel. How's that then?"

"Fine with me—Colonel," Hamilton said, smiling.

"Good, then. Let's get down to business. You are here because you're a Latin scholar, you speak fluent German, and not the least of which—you're an American." Hamilton reached for a cigarette. "If you don't mind, ol' man," Lynch gestured to his throat, then to French, who was sitting with his head resting on the back of the over-stuffed armchair, staring at the ceiling.

"Oh, I'm sorry," Hamilton said apologetically, returning the pack to his pocket.

"I hope it's obvious to you what we're all about here, William." With youthful agility, Lynch jumped up from the chair and began walking around the room, pointing at charts, maps, numerals, letters and mathematical icons. "This is where we'll win this bloody war," he said ebulliently. "Right here! We are five strong, and now with you, we make six. Six minds endowed with enough knowledge to manipulate Germany into making enormous blunders.

"Telegrams and telegraph messages—gathering and decoding information, not to mention forcing our opponent to move based on false information. Once we break one of their codes, we have ways to transmit or courier erroneous information to the Hun." He turned to Steven Sullivan, who was sucking on an unlit pipe. "Right, Steven? You explain to William how we do things."

Sullivan produced a telegram from a stack of papers. "To begin, we can't assume that all military information is relayed through military formats. Apart from decoding the usual military stuff, we are taking a very serious look at civilian transmissions. Hundreds of telegrams are sent every day. From London to America—to Holland, France, et cetera. We have military censors reading all of these domestic telegrams. Sometimes even the most simple message warrants investigation."

He passed the telegram over to Hamilton. It read, **Mother is dead.**

"Seems harmless enough," Hamilton said.

"Yes, doesn't it though," Lynch said enthusiastically. Hamilton sensed that he was being tested.

"Is it a code?" he asked.

"As you know, William," Sullivan continued, "there's no sense spending valuable hours until we're relatively sure that it *is* a code."

Hamilton handed the telegram back to Sullivan. "How did you know it wasn't the genuine article?"

"Actually, we weren't really convinced, so we just exchanged the word 'dead' with 'deceased' and sent it on."

"How clever," Hamilton mused.

"Here's the clincher," Sullivan said, handing Hamilton another telegram. "An almost instant return."

Hamilton read the message out loud. "*Is mother dead*?" He smiled, "*or deceased? Sounds to me like mother was being canceled—or discontinued. Now all you have to do is decode *mother* and you have a receiver for the distribution of—misinformation."

"Exactly," Lynch said. "And what's really bizarre, William, is that this also includes interfering with diplomatic messages to include misinforming not only German ambassadors in every neutral country." He shook his head as if repulsed, "But even our own country."

"I'm not sure I understand, Colonel, why would we misinform our own government?"

"Politics, ol' man. When you want information to leak, let the bloody politicians get hold of it. And remember, Naval Intelligence is still responsible to inform Whitehall, and ultimately the politicians. That's why this group is so important—no bloody scruples, eh what? Just win the war at any cost. Anyway, that gives you some idea of our task at hand." He turned to the professor. "Rudy here has been working with the development of invisible crystals. Show William the results of some of your chemical magic, Rudy, ol' boy."

Czernikow handed Hamilton a letter. Hamilton read the ink-drafted pages. They looked harmless enough.

"I don't see anything unusual," he said, handing the letter back to Czernikow.

"Vatch dis, my young American friend—chust you hold da letter, okay?"

Hamilton held the letter with both hands while the professor placed a lighted match under the paper. As he slowly drew the heat down the page, new words began to appear between the inconsequential lines of the letter. Hamilton was awestruck. *What a spectacular idea!* He grinned. The thought crossed his mind that this was what he needed to get past the censors for his letter to Kathleen. He dismissed the idea almost immediately.

"It's perfect—absolutely perfect—I've seen invisible ink before but never this—well—it's just perfect."

Lynch dropped some crystals into Hamilton's hand.

"Oxycyanine de mercure or a commonly known antiseptic dissolved in milk, mercury, and potassium. After you've written and the ink dries, it disappears. Reheat it and the words return."

"Fantastic," Hamilton said.

"I know," Lynch said, offering Hamilton his hand. "Well, then, what do you think?"

"I think I'm going to like this job, Colonel." Lynch grasped his hand with both of his own.

"Jolly good show—well, then, let's get down to business."

Time passed quickly for Hamilton. No one left the premises. They ate and slept very little, most of their waking hours spent in the 'code room,' as Lynch called it. It was late in September and the war didn't seem to be going in anyone's favor. Newspapers headlined painful stalemates with thousands of lives lost on both sides. One moody overcast afternoon Lynch asked Hamilton if he would like to come for a walk.

"In the pastures—Let's get some cow shite on our shoes, do something dangerous, eh what?"

Hamilton placed the pencil in his folder and rubbed his eyes. He had been up since four-thirty. "Ya know, Colonel, that sounds like a great idea."

Outside the big house they breathed in the cool evening air. A soldier snapped to attention.

"At ease, son." Lynch waved off the return salute. They walked silently awhile on a dirt path. Hamilton knew that when the time was right the colonel would say what was on his mind. "Look, William." Lynch had his hands behind his back. "I'm going to be perfectly blunt with you. Things, well, things aren't going our way. The Hun is scrambling our messages and we're scrambling his. Our fighting men are mired in the mud at the Somme. We're losing almost a hundred thousand men a month. If Russia makes peace with Germany, and we have reason to believe that this would be beneficial to them both, it would send millions of new German troops to the Western Front—I believe the war would be over for France—and, well, I imagine we'd lucky to negotiate peace to save our own arses. And, as if that isn't bad enough, I—well, I have more bad news."

Hamilton hadn't seen the colonel this serious since the talk in the coffee shop in Dublin. "Bad news, sir?"

"Yes, well, it seems that Frankignoul has failed—all of our agents involved have been arrested. At least ten, anyway."

"That was my assignment," Hamilton said. "I—I don't know if I should count myself lucky. I suppose the poor bastards will be executed?"

Lynch lit a cigarette and offered one to Hamilton. "Sorry," he said. "I seem to be forgetting my manners as I get older."

Hamilton waved the cigarette away. "What'll happen now, Colonel?"

"I knew most of them, William—their wives, children. What will happen now is that we've lost a vital link to winning this war. All of our spotters from Holland to France have been captured. It will take us months to rebuild an espionage system like that again."

They stopped by a wrought-iron bench under a large oak.

"Let's take a respite, eh what," Lynch said, sighing as he sat down. "Some of the agents were women too—I've no doubt whatsoever, they'll all be executed..." He hesitated, "But not before the Hun does everything brutally possible to extract information."

Hamilton pulled a cigarette from his own pack, struck a match on the arm of the metal bench, and cupped it between his hands. He drew in on the cigarette and flicked the match. "I don't suppose there's any way of getting them out?" he asked, dejected.

"I'm not usually so fatalistic, but in this case..." Lynch shook his head.

"Do you think any of them might have had a chance to swallow a capsule?"

"The cyanide? Not everyone wants to go that way, William. Anyway, we're not sure how many are still alive, not that they'll be that way for long."

"They're still prisoners of war!" Hamilton said angrily.

"Once they get what they want, and even if they don't," Lynch said resolutely, "they'll be executed—no trials, not even a hearing, I imagine."

There was a short silence, which Hamilton broke. "If you'll forgive me for saying this, Colonel—but isn't that what we did to the leaders of the Irish Uprising—I don't remember any trials." After he made the comment, he was regretful. *It was a stupid thing to bring up*, he thought. *What if the colonel knows that Mick Barrett was released and is just waiting for an opportunity to question me?* And even if he didn't know, it was a spiteful comparison.

"You're absolutely right, William—I'm not proud of our handling of the Irish Problem, either. Sometimes a soldier has to comply with directives from his superiors that contradict all that he considers ethical, moral—and even a soldier's sense of what's just."

Hamilton was beginning to see the colonel in a new light and appreciating the more human side of the older man, when Lynch said, "The fact that they deserved to die shouldn't deprive them of the right to a trial—for all intents and purposes, they were guilty of treason and sedition. By the way, how did you leave it with that girl—the daughter of the one we…" he stopped, then continued, "the fellow who shot one of ours, what was his name?"

"Barrètt," Hamilton almost whispered the name, not wanting to continue the subject, even though he sensed that Colonel Lynch didn't know about Mick Barrett's release.

"Barrett—yes. I was sorry that you had to fall victim of the oldest cliché in the book, ol' man—falling in love with the daughter of an enemy agent—anyway, it's over now, right?"

"Yes, Colonel—it's over." *Thank God*, Hamilton thought, *at least I can rest easy; he really doesn't know.*

"William, I'm getting tired of pulling at bloody straws," Lynch said, changing the subject. "What we need is—is some new blood. We need America in the bloody war. That's what we need."

Hamilton was leaning forward, his hands on the sides of his head, elbows on his knees. "Yes, that would be nice. I can't say I'm very proud of my own country right now, sir."

"I don't think you mean that, William. I just wish I knew what it would take to get Wilson and Congress mad enough to enter the war," Lynch said, shaking his head. "We certainly tried to appeal to their sense of humanitarian justice when we distributed still photos and moving pictures of women and children massacred in Belgium." He rubbed his chin pensively. "And how about the Lusitania! Christ, I should have thought that would have raised a few tempers! This President of yours must be an awfully cool customer."

"An idealist," Hamilton said, reflecting disappointment.

"What do *you* think? You're American. What unholy circumstance is it going to take to bring your country into this war?"

Hamilton already had an opinion. For two years he had rationalized America's isolationism. If German atrocities and attacks on American ships weren't reasons enough, he knew that the one thing no one had attempted yet would surely have Congress screaming bloody murder. A threat to American soil. He had no doubt that Congress would declare war if America was threatened.

"The Monroe Doctrine," he asserted.

"By God, that's it! The Monroe Doctrine." Although Lynch wasn't familiar with the reference to the doctrine, he guessed that the President had left a legacy pertinent to solving the issues of the day. Lynch was curious as Hamilton jumped up and turned in his direction.

"That's it! Look, it's like this, Colonel: America gets really paranoid when other countries get too close to her hemisphere." Hamilton was becoming more excited. "We ran Spain out of Cuba twenty years ago—and during our Civil War, Secretary of State Seward warned France to evacuate the newly established French Maximilian as Emperor of Mexico. Texas didn't stand for that crap." He couldn't think of any other situations having to do with America violated.

Lynch was pensive. He was genuinely appreciative of his young friend's zealousness.

Hamilton sat back down, somewhat drained, his zeal turning to despair.

"Great! Oh, that's just great. And how the hell do we get Germany to attack America?"

"Not so fast, my young friend." Lynch put his hand on Hamilton's shoulder. "Maybe we won't have to wait for Germany to attack America." He paused. "Supposing that just as the French gained favor with Mexico during your Civil War..."

Hamilton snapped his fingers. "That's it, Colonel—Mexico."

"Right, William. Mexico and Germany—and if I'm not mistaken, isn't Mexico's President—what's his name, er..."

"Carrenza," Hamilton said, encouraged again.

"Yes—President Carrenza," Lynch cocked one eyebrow. "Lately the news from your country is that he is having difficulty controlling General Villa. The reports speak of border skirmishes with American troops."

"This is true, Colonel. General Pershing is conducting his own war of sorts against Mexico."

Lynch seemed no longer ambivalent. He smiled. "Considering Mexico's hostility toward the United States, it probably wouldn't take much to convince the Americans that a secret pact was in the making with Germany, would it?"

"Probably not."

"And let's not forget Japan," Lynch said. "I know Japan is an ally of England and France for now, but I believe their sentiments would change if America declared war on Germany."

Hamilton whistled.

"Geez—Mexico and Japan; an unholy alliance. Alliance in exchange for land. The thought of losing Arizona, New Mexico, California," his voice raised, "and how about Texas? Christ, *the Texans alone* would march into Berlin and bury the bastards!"

"I love it, William!" He grabbed Hamilton's hand. "You're a bloody marvel, my boy. I knew I made the right decision when I requested you for this assignment. A bloody marvel! By the way—although you should get another bloody medal, I'm afraid that's out of the question. This is going to be the most bloody hush-hush intelligence dodge ever."

They were oblivious to the downpour when they started back to the mansion. All they had to do now was transmit misinformation from the foreign office in Berlin to their own secret intelligence at the Admiralty. Then they discussed leaking the information to the American press. They were ecstatic by the time they reached the house.

Somehow they were going to bring America into this war, come hell or high water.

CHAPTER THIRTY-ONE

RYAN THORNTON'S BEAT took him from the precinct by the Charles Street Jail, down Tremont Street, almost to the Common. He turned right on Park Street and returned up Beacon Street. Although his beat didn't include the Public Gardens, lately he had been continuing not only to the Public Gardens, but through it, until he reached the playground. He dutifully stood awhile before returning to his designated beat. He had gone to the Gardens with a purpose. He was hoping to see *her* again, the young lady with the gorgeous face. He had become infatuated with her. His heart beat faster and his whole being took on a renewed vitality.

She came at the same time and usually read while the boy and the girl played on the swings and fed the swans. Every Saturday morning for the past four weeks she'd arrived promptly at nine. Regardless of the cold, she read for a while and played with the children. An older sister wouldn't find much joy playing with her younger brother and sister. No, she had to be their governess. At ten-thirty she left as promptly as she had arrived. For Ryan Thornton the rest of the week dragged endlessly. He reproached himself for not mustering the courage to talk to her. He was falling in love at a distance, not knowing if she was married, engaged or single. If he could get close enough to say 'hello' or 'good morning,' he would surely find out if she was wearing a ring. Again he told himself that she was a governess. He wasn't sure why he believed that. *Maybe*, he thought, *it is because she appears much too young to be their mother. What a disappointment it will be if she is married!*

He would just have to cross that bridge.

This Saturday morning, his mind was making excuses. *If she's married, I'll tip my hat and leave,* he thought. *After all, looks aren't everything. What if she has a terrible personality?* His imagination continued to justify her rejection. *It will not be much of a let down if she has a squeaky voice, or bad teeth, or an uneven temper. Maybe she is a foreigner,* he thought, *and doesn't even speak English.* Although he was a little bothered by his uncertainty, he took a deep breath and pushed out his chest. He was feeling comfortable with the notion that if the young lady was married or somehow flawed, he would not be disappointed.

As he passed people he knew, he offered a 'good morning' or tipped his hat to the ladies. This was his fourth year on the force and his third year on this beat. The merchants knew him well. They felt safe and trusted him.

"Good morning, Officer Thornton," called Joey Manelli, proprietor of the neighborhood grocery and produce store. He ventured from the store's warm glow to toss Thornton an apple. Ryan didn't wish to eat it right away, so the little Italian provided a brown bag. "For youra mama, then," he said.

"Thanks, Joey," Thornton said, placing the large red apple in the bag and continuing toward the park and his destiny.

Mike's Barbershop was a favorite stop, especially on Saturdays. The shop was closed Sundays and Mondays, which coincided with Thornton's days off, so two Saturdays a month he set aside fifteen minutes on the city's time for a haircut, for which he diligently worked an extra hour at the end of the day. He liked Saturdays because that's when the quartet practiced. Mike, the owner, sported a great handlebar mustache and sang bass. Barbershop quartets were the rage in Boston and competitive. A barbershop wasn't complete without one. Above the other noises of the city, the street-car bells, honking horns, horses pulling wagons with clattering steel-rimmed wheels, Ryan could hear the familiar melody wafting through the city's din. The four-part harmony reached its climax as he approached the open door. *Bye and Bye*—the last 'bye' coming to a great harmonic crescendo before cutting abruptly. Ryan waved from the sidewalk as he passed by the big glass window. He could see Mike clearly through the ribbon-like graphic design in gold leaf across the glass. Underneath the gaily painted letters, a slogan read: *Steady Customers Welcome—Established 1890.*

His right hand swung the billy-club from a leather strap. He couldn't get the melody out of his mind and whistled. Occasionally he came across a wrought-iron rail in front of the brownstones and pulled the stick along the rails like a metronome for his whistling, *"Wait 'til the sun shines, Nelly."* He crossed Park Street and headed for the Common.

Ryan Thornton, twenty-four years old, was handsome, his face tanned. Although he was five-foot-ten, his broad, muscular body made him look shorter. His parents, John and Katy, had one other child, Deirdre, four years older than Ryan. He remembered fondly his early years when the family was together. He couldn't have asked for more pleasant memories. It wasn't until he was thirteen that everything began to go wrong. His father was accused of embezzling money from the bank where he worked. He pleaded innocent and opted for a trial by jury. The trial was short and ended badly for the Thornton family. Ryan's companion, his mentor, his father, was sentenced to twenty years at Walpole State Prison. After that his sister left. She'd married and lived somewhere in Montana. At fourteen Ryan left school to help support the family. He took a job in the factory where his mother worked as a typewriter operator. Although she was grateful for the support, she insisted that young Ryan continue his studies. He worked hard at night school and finally graduated when he was nineteen. At twenty he joined the force.

Those who knew Ryan Thornton found him a personable young man with a perpetual smile. He could afford to smile because he wasn't easily intimidated. He believed in the law. He was revolted by those who broke it, particularly career criminals. He had no time for men who disgraced their families. He knew that there were many opportunities for officers to make extra money. More than once he had been approached by unscrupulous low-life, scurrilous vermin offering him gratuities just to turn his head the other way. Those who offered such arrangements presented them as a hypothetical so as not to directly suggest a bribe. Thornton, though not on the force long, was a well-seasoned police officer, one whose scrupulous ethics antagonized criminal organizations. The mob didn't frighten Thornton half as much as the mission before him now. He was determined to strike up a conversation with the beautiful young woman in the park.

Kathleen liked America. She couldn't keep track of all the gracious people she had met, distant relatives and friends. She had especially enjoyed meeting her grand-uncle and -aunt. Aunt Madge was happy that she had arrived at the beginning of summer. The warm afternoons were a perfect time to introduce her niece to Boston's wealthy, notable women. At first Kathleen thought that they might be stuffy and pompous, but they weren't the least bit self-righteous. On the contrary, she found the Lodges, Roosevelts, and the rich Fitzgeralds, as Madge called them, rather fun.

During the short summer, Madge had become a close friend and confidant. She hardly seemed to share as much with her husband, Dennis. Kathleen began to sense this when Madge found it necessary to deceive Dennis about where they'd spent the afternoon, especially when it was with the Lodges or the Roosevelts. Teddy Roosevelt had referred to Dennis and his Irish Brotherhood as anti-American and subversive. Dennis never forgave his old hero and even forbade Madge to have anything to do with those 'Wilsonian and English-loving bourgeois.' Kathleen certainly didn't see their wives that way. They seemed more interested in the rights of women to vote and make decisions about women's issues than the war in Europe. That was too far away for them when they had so many important issues to deal with at home. Madge was even teaching Kathleen how to drive the family car. Kathleen was so busy learning new things that she didn't miss Ireland, at least not during the day and early evening. Sometimes, falling asleep, she thought of home and her family. It seemed so long since she'd played with Jamie. Only then did she cry herself to sleep.

Autumn came and went. Now the days had become short and cold, and Kathleen, although eight months pregnant, didn't look enormous like some women she'd known at this stage of pregnancy. Her diet had changed to dill pickles and pickled beets. She desperately missed nursing and caring for people's needs. She told the family doctor that she wanted to continue with her career after the baby was born. He liked Kathleen and more than once confided in Madge that Kathleen was going to make a real contribution to the field of medicine. Kathleen had also come to love James and Anne. James was infatuated with his older cousin. She was his first love. Kathleen knew this. She was sensitive to his feelings and often imagined Jamie or even Michael going through the same difficult period. She spent many hours alone with James, explaining family responsibility, the difference between love and infatuation, and the Church's views on impure thoughts. It took her almost the whole summer to convince him that what he was feeling was natural and that those feelings would soon turn into a very special love, the love that a brother might feel for a sister.

Every Saturday morning she took James and Anne to the Commons to watch the boaters. Sometimes they both listened while she read to them, and occasionally, when James became bored, he played kick ball. She was also aware that these last few Saturdays the same policeman patrolled the park, swinging his billy-club. She could hear him whistling, but he never came close enough for her to acknowledge his presence.

It had been freezing all week. Although it was cold, on this Saturday in December it looked like the sun might appear. James had pestered Madge to allow him to skate. Dennis had bought the ice skates early in the fall, too early to presume forbearance on the part of this anxious young skater. Reluctantly, Madge gave him permission to skate and the threesome left for what was going to be their last Saturday outing until Kathleen had her baby.

The sun seemed small and distant, not warm enough to melt the new snow. Kathleen and Anne sat bundled on the bench, their pink faces exposed. Kathleen opened the book at the marker, an illustrated card of the Virgin Mary. Anne looked forward to these Saturdays when Kathleen read to her. She rocked Mrs. Bee in the small perambulator as Kathleen read about Ebeneezer Scrooge. Small impressions in the snow leading to the lake's edge identified the clumsy form on the ice. It was James. He had the whole lake to himself. This was his second year skating, and he still extended his arms to keep his balance. Every now and then he reeled precariously but never fell. It was time to impress Kathleen. He was warmed up and ready for grand maneuvers.

"Look at me, Kathleen!" he shouted, proud that he hadn't fallen. Kathleen looked up. She worried that he was alone on the ice. Her gaze was so fixed on the teetering figure that she didn't notice the passing policeman.

"Be careful, James—be careful!"

He walked slowly past the park bench where they sat. He knew that her attention was taken with the young boy on the ice. He stopped a few yards past and turned his head.

"Er, excuse me, Miss…" He tipped his cap. "I'm Officer Thornton, Miss."

She looked a little startled and closed the book.

"Oh—I was just telling my cousin to be careful—I'm sorry." She smiled. "My name's Kathleen—Kathleen Riordan." He thought that she was the most beautiful woman he'd ever laid eyes on. Long, black curls hung down on her forehead from under the dark-green velvet hood. Her skin had a youthful freshness, a peach color with natural rouged cheeks.

"Cousin?" he gestured to the shape on the ice. "If that's your cousin, Miss, I'd suggest you make him skate closer to the shore." He tried to be cheerful. *Cousin,* he thought. *The children are just cousins and she's beautiful. She has a beautiful smile and speaks English with a delightful accent, probably Irish,* from what little he'd heard. His reveries were short lived.

His disappointment when she stood to shout to James was obvious. She knew what he was thinking. In a way, she was enchanted by his disillusionment. *He is hoping that I am single, and now he assumes I'm married,* she thought.

"Missus Riordan," he tipped his cap again.

She smiled unpretentiously. He turned around in the direction of Charles Street. He could hear her calling to the young boy.

"The officer says to skate closer to the shore!" Her voice echoed in his head. He wasn't as carefree now and didn't whistle or casually swing the billy-club. He was devastated.

When he heard the crash, he ran toward the lake. He ran hard through the heavy snow, throwing off his hat and removing his coat. He could hear Kathleen behind him.

"Mary Mother of God—don't let him die."

By the time Thornton hit the frozen pond, James was gone. Chaos followed. Thornton ran as fast as his legs could take him, stumbling forward, using his arms and hands to keep his momentum. When he hit the ice, it collapsed, plunging him to his waist in the freezing water. He felt nothing. No cold, no pain from the slashed knee, just frustration.

He rolled himself to the surface, and in one continuous motion he was on his feet moving forward. His left foot broke the ice again, this time dropping him to his right knee. The ice held. Gingerly, he tested the frozen block of water between him and the place where James had disappeared. Slipping beneath the ice, still ten yards to go, he threw himself toward James. The chaos was over.

Anne clung to Kathleen's coat, tears streaming down her pink cheeks. Kathleen was too frightened to cry. She prayed that Officer Thornton would find James. She counted the minutes. She hoped that the freezing water would slow his heart rate. She had heard of such cases and hoped that it was true. She bit her lip and held Anne tightly.

She felt nauseous. Her stomach was hurting. She hoped the warm liquid in her loins was water. She dropped to her knees. The snow was refreshing. She bowed and prayed for James, Officer Thornton, and her baby. She felt time stretch beyond measure.

Certain that they were still trapped beneath the frozen lake, she raised her head, hoping desperately to see them. Still nothing. Just the cold and empty silence. Her head dropped again, triggered by another cramp so severe it pulled her torso forward until her small, pink nose almost touched the snow. Her body stayed motionless. She hoped the pain would subside. Anne pulled her back.

"Kathleen! Kathleen!—It's James. The policeman—he's saved James!" The little girl was delirious, pulling at Kathleen to look at the pair on the ice. Kathleen was weak, but she managed to stand with Anne's help. She would remember this moment. Ryan Thornton cradled James in his arms and walked apprehensively across the frozen lake, making sure that each step would support their weight. James looked lifeless; his head hung back, his limp arms dangled. Just before reaching the bank, a great cracking sound forced Thornton to stop. He stood for a moment, unsure about proceeding.

Kathleen, standing ten feet from the edge of the lake, opened her arms.

"Please, God, don't stop now—we don't have much time."

Thornton made two great leaps before the ice collapsed beneath him. His feet touched the bottom immediately. The water was up to his waist. When he reached the embankment, he placed James on his back in the snow. Kathleen immediately covered him with Thornton's coat and her cloak. She looked for a pulse. Thornton watched her face anxiously. Soon the serious, still mouth turned to a smile.

"He's alive," she said. "Mary Mother of God, he's alive." She clutched Thornton's arm tightly with both hands. "And you did it, you…" It was another cramp. Her face twisted in pain. "You—oh, dear God—I think I'm going to have my baby." Anne was confused. She threw her arms around her cousin.

"Oh, Kathleen—is James going to be all right?"

"Yes, darlin', James is…" She never finished the sentence. Thornton told Anne to stay with Kathleen while he sought help. He carried James with him, knowing the boy would surely die if he didn't get help immediately.

Later that afternoon, Thornton was released from Boston Hospital, where he was treated for hypothermia. Although James had made a remarkable recovery, the doctors suggested he spend the night as a precaution. Kathleen was placed immediately in a maternity ward. She was heavily sedated to prevent contractions since she was at least four weeks premature. Dennis and Madge spent the night at the hospital, taking turns with their son and niece.

Dennis parked the car by Park Street Church, where William Lloyd Garrison had preached against slavery. He walked the short distance to Nelli Pickford's cafeteria. It was a little before noon, and judging from the white plumes of each breath, he knew it was below freezing. Three days had passed since James had fallen through the ice. It hadn't taken long for him to recuperate. His memories of the accident were dim. Kathleen was another story. The shock of James's accident had forced her into a premature state of delivery. She was eventually allowed to go home after the contractions had subsided. The family doctor informed Madge of her responsibility. The baby's health depended on Kathleen's staying in bed. It was important to delay the birth as close to the due date as possible. Dennis and Madge had relinquished their bedroom to her. They were adamant that a miracle had taken place. They didn't believe it was a coincidence that Officer Thornton was just passing by. The ambulance attendants praised Thornton's heroic rescue. Kathleen also praised the gallant policeman. Without him, she believed, two tragedies would have taken place.

She knew she hadn't seen the last of Officer Thornton.

Dennis crunched through the snow, thinking that today he could easily have been attending a double funeral. The thought shook him. His vivid imagination conjured images of death. Ugly thoughts left him feeling empty and vulnerable. Life would be meaningless with the loss of any member of his family. He thought how much easier it would be not to love anyone. He instantly dismissed the notion. He loved his family and that was that.

His musings returned to reality when he smelled the aroma of home-cooked pot pies. He could see the flag-mounted sign with the scrolled letters reading *Pickford's Cafeteria*. It swung lightly on its mounting. Pickford's, famous for its pot pies, was frequented by lawyers, policemen, and other public officials. The desk sergeant at the Charles Street Precinct told Dennis that he could find Officer Thornton at Pickford's, where most of his patrolmen ate. The sergeant also mentioned that Thornton was being considered for a citation. Dennis wanted to meet the man who had saved his son. He hadn't decided the reward he should offer. There was no doubt in his mind that *no* reward would ever be enough. The cafe was crowded. A brusque, elderly woman offered him a table or a place at the counter. He chose the counter and she handed him a stained menu.

"Something to drink while you're deciding?"

"Coffee, please." She immediately placed a large, white mug on the counter and began pouring.

"Haven't seen you in here before, dearie?"

"Actually I am looking for someone. A policeman."

"Take your pick," she said, gesturing around the room. "The plain-clothesmen are harder to spot."

"The name's Thornton—maybe you know him?"

"Ryan hasn't come in yet. Are you meeting him?"

"Well, no—not really. Would you point him out when he comes in?"

"You'll want to order then?—I mean, when he comes in?"

"Er, yes, thank you." He was on his second cup when Thornton walked in alone. Dennis knew it was him before the waitress spoke.

"That's him."

"Thanks," Dennis said, sliding off the stool. "Officer Thornton?"

Dennis extended his hand. Thornton returned the courtesy inquisitively.

"Yes?"

"Noonan—Dennis Noonan. You saved my son's life—and my niece from a premature delivery. I hope this isn't a bad time. I've already been to the station. The sergeant said I'd find you here. Do you mind?"

"Not at all. There's not a lot I can add. I don't know any more than I put in my report."

"I know enough, Officer Thornton. I just wanted to meet you and thank you personally. Thanking you and shaking your hand will never be enough."

"I know how you must be feeling, Mister Noonan, believe me. For me, just knowing that everything turned out all right is my reward."

"Would you two like a table?" The elderly woman gestured to a booth toward the back.

"Thanks, Nellie," Thornton said.

"Do you mind?" Dennis asked.

Thornton said, "Fine." After they were seated, the waitress brought them coffee. Dennis reached into his pocket.

"Cigarette?"

"No, thanks," Thornton said.

"Mind if I...?"

"Go ahead—doesn't bother me."

"Are you married?" Dennis asked, snapping the lighter shut and inhaling deeply.

"No."

"You don't know then what it's like to almost lose a child?"

"Not as a father."

"I don't understand," Dennis said curiously.

"I'm a police officer, Mister Noonan—I've had to deal with lost children—even—even tragic accidents—I don't have to be a father to feel—well, that sense of loss."

Dennis nodded in agreement. "I see," he said. "I've never felt so vulnerable. If anything happened to my son—I don't think I would want to live."

"I can understand how you feel, Mister Noonan. I was just..."

"Please, my name's Dennis."

"Well, look, Dennis, I was just doing what any other man would have done. Really, Mister Noonan—Dennis, you've thanked me sufficiently." Dennis could see that Ryan was uncomfortable with the conversation.

Dennis did most of the talking over lunch. They talked about family, politics, the war, and Ireland. Thornton talked about his father being from Ireland without divulging his present living quarters. They talked for an hour and both refused the final refill of coffee.

"Missus Riordan's all right then?" Ryan asked, seeing an opportunity to present a question he had delayed through the lunch.

"Well—at least she hasn't lost the baby—thanks to you. Look, I know—I know you feel self-conscious about this whole thing, but my wife and I would really like to have you come by—for dinner, so you could meet the family. What do you say?"

"Well, I really don't…"

"Look, it would be an honor—you'd be doing us a great service. It would be just my wife and myself and the children, James and Anne. Besides, how could you refuse to see a boy who's very anxious to meet you? How about it?"

"Kathleen, er, I mean, Missus Riordan, wouldn't be there?"

"She certainly wouldn't be far away. My niece is staying with us; however, she's confined to bed. We have to follow the doctor's orders. I'm sure she'll send down her best regards though."

"Then what about Mister Riordan?"

"Mister Riordan? Oh, I'm sorry, I forgot to mention—Kathleen's a widow. Her husband was killed in Europe. His ship was torpedoed."

A pleased expression that Thornton hoped wasn't too obvious crossed his face.

"Excuse me—did you say widow?" Dennis could see the sudden elation in the young policeman's disposition.

"Yes, Officer Thornton, my niece is a widow."

"If I can call you Dennis, then please call me Ryan."

"Well, Ryan—how about this Friday night for dinner?"

"Would it be proper to bring flowers—for Missus Riordan, I mean?"

"I believe she'd enjoy that," Dennis said confidently. Ordinarily he would have been protective of his niece. Now he felt gratified that this young man wished to call on her. "Friday evening then?"

"I'd be honored."

"You will be," Dennis said, leaving his card on the table.

Friday finally came. Ryan left the precinct early to catch the four-thirty streetcar to South Boston. The city wasn't at its busiest yet and soon he was hopping off by the red-brick rowhouses of Roxbury. He lived there with his mother in a two-bedroom flat on the second floor of one of the Georgian buildings. Normally he would have showered at the station and changed from the uniform to casual clothes, but not tonight. Tonight he would take a quick bath at home, shave, apply a little aftershave and don his best and only Sunday suit.

He took the stairs two at a time, hoping his mother had brought home the flowers he would take to Mrs. Riordan or Mrs. Noonan. His mother would advise him of the appropriate recipient. Reaching the second floor landing, he hesitated. From his trouser pocket he produced a quarter. He placed it in the gas meter and reset it, giving hot water to draw the bath. He unlocked the door and stepped into a large sitting room.

Lace curtains covered a double-hung window at one end. The room was cozy, warmed by the gas fire. The Georgian-style mantel displayed a large clock, a statue of the Virgin Mary, and family photos. Gas sconces on either side of the mantel provided a comfortable light. An aroma of fresh floor wax testified to the sense of order. Other furniture consisted of a low table, plush-cushioned divan and chairs, and finally, a chest of drawers, the top serving as a display for Katy Thornton's memorabilia, a silver-framed sepia of the family the focus of attention. The Kohler and Campbell spinet was open and held sheet music turned to a Chopin etude. Katy Thornton found release from the long arduous day in music. After dinner, when things were put back in order, she sometimes played and sang for hours, but not this Friday night. She had come home early to make sure that Ryan would be prepared for his evening at the Noonans' home. She was proud of her son, and for eleven years had devoted all of her energy to him.

Katy Thornton's shoulder-length auburn hair was streaked with gray. Her skin was smooth except for small wrinkles at each side of her mouth that deepened when she smiled. Her figure was intact, and over the past decade of her 48 years she had added a little weight. Many suitors had wished the company of this attractive woman, thinking that she might be a widow. Turning men away wasn't difficult for Katy Thornton because she still loved her husband. She never missed a visit. The eleven years had taken their toll on John Thornton, and Katy knew she would never see her husband a free man.

Ryan's refusal to visit his father, his reluctance to show any feelings, tore at her heart. She respected her son's merciless drive in the pursuit of law and order and sensed that it was directed at his father. She knew that every time he helped convict a felon he was reprimanding his father. Her prayers, her efforts to reconcile her son and her husband, had become the focus of her existence.

She was in the kitchen and had just finished pressing his pants when she heard the key. She worried so about his safety. She relaxed each night when she heard the key in the door.

"Hi, Mom, did you get the flowers?" He hardly looked her way as he spoke, hurrying toward the bedroom.

"Ryan Thornton, since when do you come barging in without saying a proper hello to your mother?" Willingly he stopped at the bedroom door and turned back to where she stood. He kissed her on the cheek. It was a tender, apologetic kiss.

"I'm sorry, Mom." He put his arms around her and squeezed, as always, a little too tightly, until it seemed to take her breath away.

"Enough," she gasped, "a little recognition will be quite enough—and yes I did get the flowers," she said. "In fact, I also got a get-well card. And don't forget to say something personal. At least sign it."

"Mom, you're just too good to me." He pecked her once more on the cheek and walked more slowly, this time to the bedroom.

Katy Thornton had no idea of her son's infatuation with the pregnant woman he had helped. She felt proud that whoever it was that wished to thank him saw her son as someone special. Although she instantly dismissed the idea of his accepting any kind of reward, Katy was excited that her son had been invited to dinner and was curious enough to have checked into the Noonan family background. She knew Mr. Noonan owned a very successful law firm and could be beneficial to Ryan. He would certainly have friends in the right places. The idea of a job with higher wages would be too much to ask ... Yet, she hoped that Mr. Noonan wasn't asking her son to dinner without something in mind. *Oh what's the use?* she thought, *Ryan will never accept a reward. Accepting a gift is against his values. Even if department policy allowed it. Maybe he will be offered a position with the law firm.*

She dismissed her thoughts, folding his pants automatically through the wooden hanger, and for a moment smiled. The idea of her son working in the safety of a fine company with no risk to his life pleased her. Her smile grew broader, her silent musings jogged to the present by the sound of his off-key tenor voice. She felt sorry for anyone who wanted to sing and couldn't carry a tune. In Ryan's case, the failure was the result of a defect passed on by his father. His passion to sing was inherited from her.

Down lovers' lane we'll wander, sweethearts you and I—Wait till the sun shines, Nellie, bye and bye.

He returned to the living room, dressed except for his shoes, and sat on the edge of the sofa.

"I visited your father today," she said nonchalantly. "He asks about you. He always wants to know how you're doing."

"That's good," Ryan said, inattentively tying his shoelaces.

"We were reminiscing about the time you and he went fishing. It was your first time fishing, remember? Here he was showing you how to bait your hook, cast your line, and you brought home the biggest..."

"Mother, please!" He called her *mother* only when he was upset. "Look, Mom—it's been a long time, all right? I haven't seen my father in over ten years. I've forgotten most of those things—I've forgotten him."

"You can't forget your own father, Ryan. You just don't dismiss those years we had together like—like they didn't exist." An uncomfortable silence followed.

He was the first to speak. "I don't love my father, it's just that simple."

"Well that's too bad, Ryan Thornton, because he loves you. It's not normal for a son not to love his father."

Ryan stood unceremoniously and put on his jacket.

"Mother, I loved my father, past tense—no, I *adored* my father—he was my idol. He was all I ever wanted to be. *He* was the one who left, remember? It wasn't you, Mother. It wasn't me—it wasn't Deirdre. It was him." He held her at arm's length and looked into her teary eyes. "He's the one who stole money from his own bank, and when he did that he may as well have cast us aside."

"He didn't steal anything. I believe him, and he insists he never stole anything from his bank, not a penny, and he still loves us," she persisted. "He's never stopped loving you, Ryan. Every time we visit he asks about you—how you're doing. Ryan, he's just as proud of you now as he was..."

"Mother, stop it! He's a common criminal, a thief! Can't you understand that? A jury found him guilty, remember?"

She stopped him with a hard slap on the face and pulled away. Devastated by what she had done, she dropped into the easy chair and placed her hands on her head. *Why can't you see that this whole thing is tearing at me, deep down to my soul? Love for you and your dad pulls at every fiber of my body.*

He knelt down beside her and drew her hands away from her wet face, and for the first time he could sense the anguish.

"I'm sorry, Mom," he said. "Look, let's go somewhere tomorrow, just the two of us. To the country maybe, let's..."

She placed her hand against his lips. "He's dying, Ryan," she said. "He's dying."

An hour later he was glad to step from the streetcar. He felt awkward, as if people were staring at him, looking at his black-wool overcoat and the bouquet of winter roses. Darkness had replaced the twilight, accompanied by a winter breeze. Most of the snow had melted, leaving behind occasional dirty white mounds. In Louisberg Square he found the house and stood awhile by the imposing green door with the interior illuminated side panels. It was a full minute before he took a deep breath and finally brought the brass knocker down three times. Dennis Noonan's voice was distinct through the door.

"That's all right, Missus Dunne, I'll get it." Noonan opened the door, his exuberant expression barely visible to Ryan. A great crystal chandelier in the foyer and the Christmas tree, lighted with dozens of tiny flickering candles, turned Noonan into a silhouette. The house was warm, friendly, and gaily decorated, and although Christmas had passed, Ryan thought that these were Catholics who celebrated the holidays until the Epiphany. Noonan shook his hand vigorously, pulling him inside like some long-lost brother.

"Ryan, come in, I'm so glad you could make it! Actually I wasn't sure you would come. I'm very glad you did though. Come in, please."

"I didn't want to disappoint the boy. James, isn't it?"

"Yes," Noonan smiled back. "James," he said, knowing that Ryan had other intentions and that unfortunately those desires would not be gratified because Kathleen couldn't grace them with her presence tonight.

"And how is Missus Riordan?" Ryan asked, not the least bit hesitant.

"The doctor feels that as long as she stays in bed there's a good chance she'll have a healthy baby."

"That's good news," Ryan said.

"Welcome—meet the family. Here, let me take your coat—I'll have these put in water," he said, taking the flowers.

"They're for Missus Riordan," Ryan said awkwardly. "There's a get-well card—I thought it would be okay."

"It's okay," Noonan smiled. "Matter of fact, it's very thoughtful. I'll have Madge take them up. She'll know how to convey your thoughts, so to speak."

From the foyer they entered through massive double doors to a large drawing room. A middle-aged couple sat on a plush sofa. Ryan thought they had been there for a while, judging from the almost empty glasses and half-eaten hors d'oeuvres on the coffee table. A log fire roared in the fireplace. Across from the couple, Madge Noonan stood up, eager to meet the young man who had saved her son. In a gesture of sincere appreciation, she shook his hand firmly with both of her hands.

"I'm Madge Noonan," she said. "We're grateful and will always be in your debt. May I call you Ryan?" Her eyes looked directly into his. "After all, you are off duty now." She looked at the flowers Dennis was holding and then back to Ryan, "And how nice of you to bring roses! They're beautiful, thank you."

"Of course," he said, embarrassed by her display of gratitude. "I mean, you may call me Ryan—and, er, the flowers…"

"The flowers are for Kathleen," Dennis said, avoiding further discomfort for Ryan.

Ryan looked past her to the tall, thin man with gray hair spread sparsely over a white dome. He stood, waiting for Madge to make the introductions. Charles Michael Boyle showed little expression when he shook hands. Florence Boyle stayed seated and demurely elevated her right hand. Ryan was directed to an armchair between the couples, a place of honor, and Dennis poured him a generous portion of whiskey and soda. It wasn't a relaxing time for someone as diffident as Ryan Thornton; however, the whiskey helped. For the most part, he gave simple answers to their questions. The initial necessary small-talk soon melted. They happily settled into easy friendship; because they were all Catholic and Irish, religion and politics were easy to discuss. Chuck held the half-empty glass motionless above the table. He was more garrulous than the others.

"If Ireland is to become independent of England, we Irishmen and, ah—that also means the, ah—clergy, and particularly the Bishops, have to unite. If the Church could get together with us on this, I, ah, really believe it would lend credence to our cause, bolster the, ah, political arena in our favor, bring about an independent republic."

"I have to agree," Dennis said. "It's worth fighting for."

"That's my cue to avoid talk of war. Excuse me while I take these beautiful roses to Kathleen," Madge said.

"Fight? Is that all you men think about?" Florence was careful not to appear too critical, especially of her husband, and partially smiled when she spoke. "Personally, I think that the prospect of losing a husband is too dear a price to pay for any country." She placed her hand affectionately on Chuck's knee.

"How can you argue with a woman like this?" Chuck said.

"Maybe it's women like Florence you should be recruiting to represent Ireland's cause in the Parliament," Madge said as she left the room.

Meanwhile, Kathleen sat propped up in bed, trying to read. Her mind wandered from the muffled voices downstairs to thoughts of home. Earlier she had begun to write to her mother. She missed Ireland and her family much more now that she wasn't as active. Her eyes gazed vacantly at the open pages, seeing Michael and Paddy, thinking about what they were doing now—and Jamie; the thought flashed across her mind that little Jamie was probably going to forget her. Tears filled her eyes.

She realized that she was just staring at the pages and put the book aside. She was frustrated and listless, having to stay in bed. The thought of two weeks of this brought on more tears. Even if she did hold on for two weeks, her baby would still be early. She wished the door was open so that she could concentrate on the voices downstairs. She tried to distinguish Officer Thornton's voice from the others, but all she heard was her Uncle Dennis. "She'll love these," she heard Madge say, her voice louder as she ascended the stairs. When Madge entered with the roses, Kathleen was overjoyed.

"They're from Ryan Thornton," Madge told her, placing them on the night table. She sat on the bed. "Oh, dear," she said, seeing the tears.

"Oh, I'm just feeling sorry for myself," Kathleen shrugged. Madge wiped away her tears.

"It's all right to cry, Kathleen. I know you come from sturdy stock. I know because I'm a product of that same proud blood, but sometimes problems seem insurmountable. That's when we need to think about the blessings God has given us—like your baby. You need to stay healthy for that reason alone and that means avoiding thoughts that create stress. Which reminds me—there's a card, too."

"That's awfully thoughtful of him, isn't it?" Kathleen asked, opening the envelope.

"Mind if I hear what he has to say, Kathleen?"

"Not at all—and what would there be to hide?" Kathleen said impishly. Then, ever so slowly, teasing Madge, she removed the card from the envelope. Her eyes scanned the message and her mouth moved, uttering no sound.

"Well!" Madge said anxiously.

"*Dear Missus Riordan…*" Kathleen paused, looking over the top of the card. "How's that for a romantic preface? I sound like a granny!"

"Please," Madge said, pleading, "would you just read the card, Kathleen Barrett Riordan before I…" Kathleen pulled back playfully from Madge's reach.

"All right—all right, I'll read it to you. *Dear Missus Riordan…*"

"I heard that."

Kathleen continued:

I hope you don't think me too forward bringing you roses. I hope that you will get well soon and have a healthy baby. I also hope that when that happens you'll return to the Public Gardens to show him—or her—off.

P.S. I have your book in my locker at the station. I'll get it to Mr. Noonan.

Ryan Thornton

Madge took the card and placed it by the flowers.

"He's handsome and seems very nice," Madge said.

"I didn't have much time to notice—besides, things were happening too fast. I saw so little of him up close I doubt that I'd even recognize him."

"It sounds to me like he's pursuing an opportunity. I think he'd like to call on you."

"Oh, Madge," Kathleen said, "you're reading too much into a simple get-well card."

"We'll see," Madge said, "I'd better be getting back to my guests. I'm really sorry you can't join us downstairs, Kathleen. I'll send Anne up so you don't have to be alone."

"Madge," Kathleen's voice stopped her at the door.

"Yes?"

"Do you think it would be improper of me to respond—maybe a short note thanking him for what he did and all?"

"It would appear ungrateful if you didn't, Kathleen."

"Oh, please, Madge—don't close the door."

Downstairs, Madge poured herself a much-needed glass of wine. She wasn't listening to the conversation; her thoughts were on Kathleen. She prayed silently that everything would go well. A soft tap on the double door preceded Mrs. Dunne's entrance.

"Excuse me, Mister Noonan, it's James and Anne. They're a bit anxious to meet…" Without waiting, the children pushed past Mrs. Dunne, Anne being a little more hesitant. James came to his mother's side, knowing she would be more approachable. He concealed something behind him with his right hand.

"Mother, you promised I'd get to see Officer Thornton."

Since the accident, Dennis Noonan had made allowances for what he now called minor transgressions. He considered the intrusion normal behavior for a growing boy and obviously the result of a healthy, inquisitive, developing young mind. Too bad that James didn't recognize this change in his father's attitude, for it was Madge that reprimanded him.

"James! How many times have I told you that it's impolite to interrupt!" It was more of a statement than a question. James put his head down and dropped his lower lip.

"It's all right, Madge," Dennis said. "The boy's just anxious to meet Officer Thornton. These are unusual circumstances, besides…" Dennis stood and walked over to James, placing a hand on the boy's shoulder, "he has something for Officer Thornton." James looked pleadingly at his mother.

"Please, Mother—may I?" He produced a small package from behind his back. "Father took me shopping today for…"

Dennis broke in. "It was James's idea, something he wanted to do." James shyly handed the package to Ryan, who had put his glass on the table to accept it.

"He even picked it out himself."

"Thank you, James." Ryan acknowledged the gift graciously. "This is very thoughtful." Ryan rotated the small package in his hands.

After a moment of quiet, Madge said, "I for one would like to see what my son would consider an appropriate gift for you, Officer Thornton. I'm sure Dennis knows—how about you, Charles? Florence? Shall we ask Officer Thornton to show us what's in the package?"

James was eager to see what Ryan thought of his gift.

Ryan carefully removed the wrapping and opened the black velvet-covered package. Even before he managed to open the box, he thought it was something expensive. He was right.

"I—I don't know what to say." His voice was choked. Gingerly he removed the watch and displayed it to the rest of the group.

"A wrist watch—it's—it's beautiful. I've never owned a wrist watch!" he exclaimed.

"Ooh," said Florence. "It's gold! The black strap goes so well with the black numerals and the gold. And look at the mother-of-pearl face and the decorative bezel. I like it."

Chuck said, "Ahh."

"Look at the back," Dennis said. "James wanted it engraved."

"It was my idea, wasn't it, Father?"

"Yes, James. I said it was, didn't I?"

Ryan rotated the watch and held it closer and toward the floor lamp beside him as he read aloud.

To Officer—he cleared his throat—*Thornton, for being where you were and who you are. Thanks, James Noonan, January 1917.*

"It's beautiful," he said. "Thank you—I'll treasure it as long as I live."

James felt very special. He was glad that Officer Thornton liked his gift. "It really was my idea, and I picked it out," James said proudly.

"James, please," Madge said, "we don't give gifts to receive praise. God forbid you should have to give something anonymously." Everyone laughed.

"What does *anom...anomon...*?" Dennis stood up and put his empty glass on the table.

"The word's *anonymously*, James. It means," he turned his face momentarily, "it would be like giving something of value to someone without them ever knowing it was you that gave."

"I see," James said. "Like when Mother puts money in the poor box at church. When I grow up I'm going to be a policeman."

"That makes me feel very proud, James—but you really should talk to your parents first. They might have something else in mind for you," Ryan said.

"It's all he talks about, isn't it, Dennis?" Madge said.

"That's right. I think it's fabulous that a boy his age has a desire to aspire to anything," Dennis said.

"I can box." James stepped back and took on his boxing stance.

Ryan sparred playfully, his arms extended, hands spread and upright, offering James moving targets.

"That's enough, James—I'm sure Officer Thornton sees sufficient violence during the day without your impertinence. Take Anne now and go play."

"Oh, Mother," he pleaded, "I have so many questions to ask..." Then looking back to Ryan, he asked, "Have you ever shot someone?"

Before Ryan could answer, Dennis responded by standing and for a moment, displaying his pre-accident demeanor. His voice raised slightly.

"James. Now, you heard your mother."

"Yes, Father." He reluctantly took Anne by the hand. Before he exited, he turned his head. "Thank you, Officer Thornton—for saving my life."

Ryan smiled and nodded.

"Kids sure ask the, ah—the craziest questions, don't they?" Chuck said.

"Sometimes they can be embarrassing," Madge said. "Ryan, I hope you don't mind my son's enthusiasm. I suppose it's only normal that he would consider you an idol, and the gift really was his idea," and as if for assurance, she looked at Dennis, "It's true, isn't it, Dennis?"

"Indeed, it was," Dennis said. "Now let's eat."

All sat in pre-arranged places at the table. Ryan sat between James and Anne. Chuck and Florence sat across from him. Dennis occupied the head of the table, facing Madge. The salads were already in place and Dennis Noonan said grace.

"From thy bounty through Christ our Lord." His voice continued over the 'Amens.' "And this, Lord, is a particularly special time for us to give thanks...thanks for returning our son to us, by sending a young man who didn't hesitate one instant and personally risked his own life so that we might enjoy this moment with our whole family and very close friends." The silence seemed lasting enough and once again they repeated the 'Amen.' "And something equally as…" Dennis continued.

"Oh, Dennis," Madge said, laughing, "if you want to make a speech, why not wait until everyone's at least eaten?"

Ryan was happy that Madge had intervened, adding a touch of humor, since the topic of his noble actions was becoming an embarrassment.

"I just wanted to mention Kathleen; after all, the baby would surely have been lost had it…"

"Please, Dennis, I'm sure Officer Thornton would rather just eat." Dennis sat down, realizing he had had enough to drink.

"You're absolutely right, my dear—let's eat!"

"By the way, I took the flowers and get-well card up to Kathleen." Madge looked directly at Ryan. "You couldn't have brought her a more rejuvenating gift. I don't know what the card said," she lied, "but she's up there beaming, wishing, of course, she could be down here."

"I'm glad she liked the flowers—the card too," he said.

"Actually, she's writing you a short note and said that you shouldn't leave without it."

"Thank you, Mrs. Noonan."

"Madge, please, you call me Madge and I'll call you Ryan."

"A deal," he said, more at ease. Dennis chewed a piece of meat off to the side of his mouth. "She's a remarkable girl, Kathleen. I'm sure she loved the roses. It reminds me of a poem I've read someplace about Connolly:

'They need to be watered,' James Connolly replied,
'To make the green come out again
'And spread on every side,
'And shake the blossoms from the bud,
'To be the garden's pride.'"

"That's beautiful," Florence beamed. "Beautiful. It sounds like Yeats…"

Dennis broke in. "Kathleen took care of James Connolly before they shot him, you know." He knew that Ryan Thornton glowed when her name was mentioned. "She was close to many of the martyrs—even her father, Madge's brother-in-law, was in Kilmainham awaiting the noose. He was rescued by a priest, no less."

Boyle's gaze was riveted on Ryan. "And what do you think of the trouble in Ireland, Ryan?"

"I'm afraid I know only what I read in the papers."

"Thornton's an Irish name, isn't it?"

"Yes—I believe so—my grandfather was from Limerick."

"Are both your parents, ah—still with you?"

"If you mean alive, er, yes—well, actually my father isn't with us. It's just my mother and myself."

"Enough questions, Charles," Madge said. "Let the man eat his dinner."

Ryan was still looking a little flustered when Florence spoke. "Charles asks questions constantly. Well, let me tell you that sometimes it gets downright embarrassing—our daughter's boyfriend won't come by anymore because of Charles."

"That's not so, Florence," Boyle said.

"A father is supposed to ask questions of his daughter's suitors, Florence," Dennis said. "Chuck's problem is that he should learn to separate his business from leisure conversation. Everything ends up becoming a deposition. What makes you think he'll stop now?"

"That's all right, I really don't mind," Ryan interjected. "My mother is of Russian descent. She'd be the first to tell you right now of her disappointment with Germany."

"Do you think we should declare war on Germany?" Chuck asked.

"Actually I—don't like what…"

"Excuse me, Ryan, could you pass the dressing?" Madge asked, attempting to arrest the conversation. Boyle paid no attention to Madge and continued with the questions.

"And what's your opinion of this, ah—war, Ryan?"

Ryan waited to answer while he swallowed. "Well—it's my belief, Mr. Boyle, that war should be avoided." He paused before continuing. "I guess unless one is absolutely forced into it."

"That's an interesting viewpoint—particularly coming from a policeman."

"Remember, Mr. Boyle, a policeman is also called a peace officer."

"Touché, Ryan," Dennis jumped in. Chuck Boyle didn't like being outrivaled. It was obvious that Ryan's answer was popular at the table. Boyle ignored his host's annotation.

"So you believe in Wilson's philosophy that we should have peace without victory to either side? Do you know what will happen to Ireland if England wins, Ryan?"

"I don't imagine things will change much for Ireland," Ryan said, feeling a little pressured.

Florence interrupted. "Why don't we talk about something else, something more pleasant, how about...?"

"How about the prospect of, ah, Germany winning this war?" Boyle pursued Ryan, more eager now to get his point across. "Ireland would be freed from the clutches of England. Isn't that so, Ryan?"

"Yes, I guess you could say that," Ryan said, also wanting to put an end to the conversation.

"That's all I wanted to impart, Ryan. England would no longer control Ireland." Ryan didn't care much for Charles Boyle, the big-shot District Attorney, and for a moment decided not to leave him with the last word.

"May I ask one last question before we conclude this conversation, Mister Boyle?"

"Of course you may, Ryan," Boyle said, his tone condescending.

"And what makes you so sure, Mister Boyle, that in as much as England would become a possession of Germany, might not Ireland fall to the same fate? I'm not as sure as you that Germany would allow Ireland to be a free state either."

Boyle was visibly upset with Ryan's down-to-earth assessment of the situation. The idea that Germany would not acknowledge Ireland's attempt to dislodge England's dominance had never crossed his mind.

"I guess there are no guarantees, all right," Dennis said. "I hope for Ireland's sake you're wrong about German intentions, Ryan."

Mrs. Dunne had outdone herself. Fresh shrimp salad, rack of lamb, new boiled potatoes and a dessert fit for a king. Cold custard, imported berries for dessert, soaked in brandy, topped off with fresh whipped cream. The dinner conversation continued, mostly about the war in Europe. The consensus was that America should try to stay out of the war. Mrs. Dunne served an after-dinner drink, and the men returned to the drawing room to smoke and discuss men's matters.

Dennis poured generous portions of brandy into three glasses. One of the rosewood desk drawers held a box of Havana cigars.

"Have a Havana?" Dennis had removed one of the large cigars and passed the box to Chuck.

"That's clever," he said, passing the cigar under his nose. "Hmmm— what flavor, I love a good cigar."

Ryan said he'd prefer not to smoke, if that was all right.

"Sit, please," Dennis gestured to the plush diamond-tufted chairs. He ceremoniously snipped the end of the cigar, and lit it with a tall table lighter. "Did you enjoy the dinner, Ryan?"

"Yes—very much—thank you." He hesitated, "And I really do appreciate the watch. It was very thoughtful of your son. I feel a little awkward accepting any gifts," he gestured to Chuck. "I know Mr. Boyle understands that it is against Department policy to accept any gratuities—I hope everyone understands that I couldn't hurt the young boy's feelings."

Chuck's question was immediate, in a courtroom manner. "Do you always abide by, ah—Department policy, Ryan?"

Ryan perceived an effort to discredit his sense of duty.

"No, I'm not always so well-behaved and I don't always agree with the policy. I do my job, Mr. Boyle. I don't, however, disagree with the Department's viewpoint on accepting gratuities."

"Don't mind Chuck, Ryan. He's a born cynic. He doesn't believe that honest people exist. The few people like you in this world are an enigma to men like Chuck."

Ryan stood, emptied the brandy glass and put it on the desk. "It's probably best that I be going, Dennis. It's getting late. I have to get up early."

Dennis came around quickly from behind the desk. He took Ryan's arm and solicitously led him back to the chair. "Please—for me, at least, hear what I have to say." Ryan sat down, and Dennis paced, his hands folded behind his back. "You're a good cop, Thornton, and God knows the city can certainly use good cops, so I'm not saying this just because you saved my son from drowning.

"Chuck here is the best District Attorney this city has seen in a long time. He's really quite pleasant, even though there are times when he appears brusque. Anyway, the reason I asked Chuck to be here tonight was to meet you."

Ryan moved uneasily in the chair, opening his mouth to respond.

"Please," Dennis continued, "Please, let me finish. The District Attorney's Office needs honest investigators like yourself." He gestured to Boyle.

"Right, Chuck?"

"Right."

"So Chuck came by to—well, look you over, so to speak." Ryan stood. It was a rebellious posture, hands by his side and leaning forward slightly on the balls of his feet.

"If that's the only reason you invited me, Mr. Noonan, to be looked over—I thought I was here to have dinner and meet the family—and James."

Dennis tugged at his right ear; his left hand vigorously extinguished the cigar in the ashtray.

"God dammit, man—why are you so—so damn stubborn? No one's

on the take here. Chuck isn't here offering you something for nothing! You're going to work your ass off, isn't that right, Chuck?"

"Look, I apologize if I came on a little strong, okay?" Boyle said, extending his hand.

"Okay," Ryan said, reluctantly returning the formality. "I just don't like being used—I happen to take my work seriously, and contrary to what some of my fellow officers might say about the wages, I really do feel adequately compensated."

"That's, oh—all well and good, Ryan, but we might be a little more demanding of your time." He chuckled. "Dennis is right, We'd, ah, work your ass off."

"So—I'm being offered a job."

"A promotion," Dennis said.

"To detective," Boyle added.

"Sounds tempting—as long as it's not just because I..." He didn't finish, rebuked by Dennis Noonan's glare. "Sorry."

"So you'll join us then?" Boyle said.

"If you don't mind, I'd like to think about it," Ryan said, rising from the chair.

Later, after Ryan had thanked Madge for the great dinner, she handed him the note from Kathleen. He was ecstatic and shook her hand vigorously. He skipped down the short path, thanking her, so immersed in his gratitude that he slammed into the wrought-iron gate.

Dennis and Boyle had returned to the drawing room for a nightcap. Both men lit another cigar and sank into the soft chairs.

"Well, what do you think, Chuck?"

"He, ah, certainly seems genuine enough, above-board, moral, conscientious."

Dennis took a deep drag on the cigar he had just lit. "What the hell's gotten into you?"

"Look, it's getting late," he said, glancing at his watch. "I really should be off, Dennis. I'll, ah, do some looking around when I get back to the office, check the family background, stuff like that."

"You said his record is impeccable. There's something else, isn't there? You've already researched his background, haven't you?"

"Well—it's just that—he's a loner. When someone's record is as clean as his, Dennis, you can be, ah, sure of one thing, he's the antithesis of someone else's actions."

"You mean, as in the opposite of a bad older brother? Come on, Chuck you're pushing a little deep."

Chuck eased back in the chair, his eyes raised upwardly in a blank gaze.

"It might be a father. He might have a scoundrel for a father." He blew a white plume of smoke through pursed lips. "You know, Dennis, in my business—particularly on my side of the law, cops on the take are fairly easy to spot. Usually they get too greedy. They live noticeably beyond their means. I'm talking about cases that involve, ah, big corporate scandals, mob stuff, making it worth an investigator's time to rearrange evidence, ah, withhold evidence. In my department, any of my men living beyond their means is a fair, ah, indication that they're on the take."

"But you just said that Thornton's record is impeccable. Wouldn't he make a perfect candidate for…" Dennis hesitated, "you know something, don't you?"

"Dennis, sometimes you're as unwitting as the people you represent."

"That'll be your last drink, Mister Boyle—when you drink, you become impertinent," Dennis said, smirking. "So what's worse than a cop taking money, Sherlock?"

"A cop being blackmailed."

"Interesting," Dennis said. "Is our young friend being blackmailed?"

"No, but there's nothing tougher to deal with." Boyle went on, "See—when a detective is being blackmailed, unlike people on the take, there isn't an exchange of money or goods, rather we're dealing with character assassinations—family peculiarities—deep secrets, disturbing the status quo, if you will. But the price is the same: furnishing privileged information or altering evidence. Complicity doesn't manifest itself in, ah, change in lifestyle."

"I see—and you think that Ryan Thornton has a skeleton or two in his closet?"

"I didn't say that. All I'm, ah, saying, is that he's almost too good to be true. And that, my learned counselor, bears investigating. I'm not sure if he's being totally honest with us. Actually, I didn't have to check all that deep. What we call in the department a surface evaluation. His record with the Department seems to be, well, impeccable—got his high school diploma through night school. He has a married sister in Montana. He lives with his mother. She works. Secretarial type." Boyle faltered.

"Go on," Dennis said.

"His father is a felon."

"Felon?"

"That's right he's, ah, doing time at Walpole, embezzled from his bank. He's doing twenty at Walpole."

"Jury trial?"

"It looks that way, I, didn't go much further than that."

Dennis finished the brandy and put the glass on the desk. He stood up and paced, tugging on his right ear. "Damn," he said quietly.

"He lied," Chuck said. "Oh, he's okay where he is right now, but I don't need a cop that has to hide anything."

"He didn't lie," Dennis said bluntly. "And what do *you* call it when someone withholds the truth? He said that his father wasn't with them anymore."

"That's right," Boyle said. "Because he was doing time. I suppose if the state had hanged him, we would have been told that his father died while attending a public function—when the platform gave way. Think, man, you know as well as I do that people with something to hide make very good blackmail prospects. I don't need that kind of liability."

Dennis slouched back in the wing-chair behind the desk, obviously disappointed. He deliberated a moment, then he poured another drink. He gestured the bottle to Boyle, who waved it away.

"I've had enough. Florence and I should be getting along."

Dennis chugged the raw whiskey. "I guess I can see now what you were looking for at dinner. Looking for a confession, no doubt?" Chuck didn't respond. "How about a favor, Chuck?"

"How come I get the impression that no matter how I feel about this, I'm going to say yes? Ya know, Dennis, one day I'm going to feel that I've paid you in full for saving my hide back in Cuba. This quid-pro-quo stuff has to cease sometime." Dennis pushed the chair back and stood up. He had a broad grin.

"Look, Chuck—hell, you're the one that always brings it up. All I want is a little favor. Hell, I've forgotten about all that war crap."

"Sure, oh sure, then how come I, ah, always end up capitulating? You want me to pull the transcripts, don't you?" Dennis had his arm on Boyle's shoulder.

"You know I'd do it myself, but, well, you have all the talent to research this case."

"Ya know, Noonan, sometimes I, ah, wish to hell you'd left me on that goddamn hill on San Juan. Shit, I might have made it myself."

"No way," Dennis said. "You would have been crabmeat."

"Okay, okay, I'll do it," he said, opening the library door. Before they joined Madge and Florence, Dennis thanked him again.

"Thanks, Chuck. I really like the kid. I'd like to do something for him, you know."

"I know," Boyle said. "He does seem like a nice young man."

"You know, Chuck, you're not really the hardass you'd like people to think you are."

The baby seemed to be coming too soon. There was an unfriendly chill in the January morning when the sound of the car alerted Dennis to the doctor's arrival. His hurried movements suggested an impatient air that normally was out of character with him. He remembered being this testy when Madge was giving birth to James and Anne.

"About time," he muttered, glancing at his watch as he opened the front door. Beneath the flickering street light he could make out the driver. Martin Wilson reached behind the seat for his black bag and exited, sprightly slamming the door. He then walked eagerly toward Dennis, leaving the engine idling. Dennis cupped his hands around his mouth.

"You've left it running!" he bellowed.

Wilson carried the black medical bag in his left hand and held his other hand to his ear. "Running—not at my age—no siree, babies have a habit of coming whether I run or..." Dennis didn't let him ramble.

"I said, you've left *your car* running." Wilson stopped, put the bag down and turned his head with a listening posture.

"Oh my God—I certainly did, didn't I." He moved quickly and shut off the engine. He returned just as fast and shook the younger man's hand. "Couldn't hear a word you were saying. I'd left the engine running, you know."

"Yes, I know," Dennis said, managing a smile.

"Well, how's our little patient doing? I got Madge's message and came as soon as I could."

Dennis closed the front door. "Missus Dunne is with her right now, Martin. I don't know how far along she is. Father Lane is also with her. Just a precaution. Madge wanted to make sure that the baby is baptized, what with being premature and all."

"I understand."

James was confused and curious. He came running in response to the voices in the hall. Dennis put his arm around the boy's shoulder.

"You know how it goes, Martin. Us men are always the last to know anything. Anyway, we don't want to hold you up."

"Yes, well, that's where I gathered she was—up—yes, well then." Wilson gave a perfunctory nod and quickly headed up the staircase. Hesitating part way, he turned back to Dennis, "Since I don't hear any birthing activity up here...whose room is she in? Yours? Or did you expect me to go around knocking on doors?"

Dennis was a little concerned about Wilson's capabilities; he was getting on in years; still, he couldn't help smiling at the doctor's peculiar behavior.

"She's in our room, Martin," he said loudly, clearly enunciating each word.

"You don't have to shout, Dennis," he said, continuing up the stairs.

Martin Wilson had been the Fitzgerald family doctor long before Dennis Noonan married Madge. He was physically fit and agile, conditions which he credited to abstinence from tobacco, alcohol, fatty foods, and, on the other side of the ledger, adherence to a daily exercise routine. Those who knew him were concerned that the better part of his mind had long since abdicated. He began his internship during the latter years of the Civil War, preparing patients for surgery, sterilizing instruments and sometimes having to assist the surgeons. In 1868 he left the Army and continued his medical studies in Boston, where he had practiced ever since. Now, as he reached the landing on the first floor, he didn't look like a man approaching seventy. He was five-foot-ten with a bony angular body and still had all his hair, which was mousy-colored, thick and wavy. He wore wire-rimmed reading spectacles low on his nose. When he wished to see past his reach, he tilted his head downward and peered over the top of the rims.

Madge had also heard the doctor's arrival and was waiting for him by the open bedroom door. She wore a long, black skirt and a white, silk blouse buttoned snuggly about her neck. Her auburn hair was tied in a bun at the back and although faced with the crisis of Kathleen's premature circumstances, she maintained her stately demeanor. The only thing that seemed out of place was a swirl of hair that spiraled down her forehead. She exhibited a relieved look when she greeted him.

"Doctor Wilson! Thank God you've made it. Obviously you got my message," she said, leading him into the room.

"Of course," Wilson said. "Haven't let the family down yet."

Ignoring Father Lane, who was praying by the other side of the bed, he moved quickly past Madge and went directly to Mrs. Dunne, who was just leaving again for more boiling water.

"You know Missus Dunne, Doctor," Madge said. "Oh, and Father Lane."

"Yes, I believe I do." Mrs. Dunne acknowledged his presence with a nod. The priest looked up briefly, simulating a smile, never losing the cadence of the chant.

"Doctor," she said, "excuse me, I have to get some more water."

"Here," Madge said, "why not let me do that, Missus Dunne? You two see to Kathleen."

"How far along is she, Missus Dunne?" Wilson asked. He had removed the tweed jacket and was rolling up his sleeves. Kathleen looked tired and had beads of sweat on her brow. The long, black hair was disheveled about her shoulders and her arms extended behind her, tightly grasping the finials of the brass bedstead. Her body arched in an almost constant pain.

"I'd say anytime now, Doctor. The baby has crowned."

Wilson took his position at the bottom of the bed. Kathleen exerted downward and expelled a loud blast of air through tight lips. "That's it, Kathleen. Push. Push. Anytime now, Kathleen. We're almost there!"

Wilson had his hands cupped around the baby's head, pulling carefully.

"Push. Push." Mrs. Dunne wiped Kathleen's brow. Downstairs, Madge was pouring more boiling water into a large bucket. Anne was sitting at the kitchen table. She was talking to her doll, Mrs. Bee, which she held on the table with her legs apart.

"Now, Missus Bee, let's have a baby. Look, Mother, Missus Bee is having a baby."

"Anne, dolls don't have babies, women have babies."

"You mean like Kathleen?"

"Yes," Madge said impatiently. She kissed Anne on the cheek as she hurried past. "Sorry, dear. I don't mean to be short with you. It's just that I'm busy right now. Kathleen's having a *real* baby. It isn't a game, you know."

Madge passed Dennis and James in the hall.

"How's it goin'?" Dennis asked anxiously.

"Anytime now," she said.

"What are they doin' with all the water, Dad?" James asked. Never having witnessed a birth himself, Dennis had asked the same thing when his own children were born.

"I really can't tell you, son, but it must be important. They did the same thing when you and Anne were born. I guess it's one of the mysteries of childbirth."

CHAPTER THIRTY-TWO

A T EXACTLY THE same moment in London, the pneumatic-tube system to Room 40 had just been activated by a young radio telegrapher. He made note of the time and date in the log: 0955 January 17, 1917. Like an oversized bullet, the projectile whirled toward its destination, making a great sucking sound. It was the first intercept of the day, and the tube lid snapped shut behind the canister as it unceremoniously dropped into the basket. The officer on duty at British Naval Intelligence turned the cap and examined the contents.

The wireless intercept was not naval code, rather it displayed the numerals 13042, which he knew to be the German diplomatic code. He immediately walked it over to the Political Deciphering Department, the most secret room in Whitehall. A tall, thin, middle-aged man with white hair and inquisitive, steel-blue eyes thanked the officer and gently closed the door. The Reverend William Montgomery, a genius when it came to interpreting codes, was on duty with another eccentric civilian named Nigel DeGrey. The message laid out before them was longer than usual and composed of row after row of four- and five-digit numerals. Their eyes immediately focused on the initial five-digit code. They looked at each other casually, displaying no more emotion than sitting through a boring chamber recital or attending a chess tournament. Even the five-digit signature seemed fairly routine.

"It's another message from Zimmerman," DeGrey said mechanically.

"Who's it going to then?" Montgomery asked.

DeGrey's finger traced through the numbers at the top of the page.

"Looks like it's directed to Washington, probably another attempt to keep America as a friend. Yes—here we are, it's to the Ambassador, Count Von Bernstoriff. This should keep us engaged for a while, eh what?"

Montgomery walked briskly to a large, black safe and rotated the dial to the right then to the left, slowing down, stopping, and turning right again. Opening the heavy steel door, he removed a black code book. The book, compiled over the years, opened the door to the majority of the numerical variations of the German code. DeGrey called out the numbers and Montgomery scanned the book for the translations, first in German then in English.

"17214?" DeGrey queried, looking over the rims of the reading glasses.

Montgomery slowly scanned downward, his finger finally stopping. He looked up at DeGrey. "Ganz geheim," he said.

"Well now, this could prove interesting." DeGrey scratched hastily, interpreting as he wrote. "All secret," he said, showing more concern.

"Strictly secret," Montgomery corrected. "Let's have the rest then." 'The rest' consisted of over a thousand groups and would take the better part of the day to decipher completely. Now totally enthralled by what they were seeing, both realized that this telegram could change the course of the war. DeGrey couldn't wait to decode the German into English.

"14963?" Montgomery whispered.

"Eingeschrankt—98092? U-Boot, krieg zu beginnen." DeGrey gasped, writing furiously the English translation.

"My God! Unrestricted U-Boat war to begin—and against the Americans!" He was as happy as a child with a new toy. "If anything provokes the Americans, this surely will."

Other numbers suggested an alliance with Mexico in trade for former territories lost to the United States: Arizona, Texas and New Mexico. The telegram also went on to include a 'beitretung' or 'einladen,' 'joining' or 'invitation' to Japan to help conquer America. Montgomery and DeGrey had no doubt that this information had to reach President Wilson and Congress, but how?

They had to answer this question: *How could they inform the Americans without alarming the Germans that their precious code had been violated?* They would soon conclude that the contents of the telegram could be leaked at the German Embassy in Washington after it was decoded.

All they had to do was deliver it into the right hands.

CHAPTER THIRTY-THREE

I N BOSTON IN the bedroom on the second floor, Kathleen gave an enormous push and delivered a beautiful baby boy. He entered the world screaming, as if to protest abandoning his warm, secure home.

"A little small," Wilson said, "but he's perfect." He examined the baby while Mrs. Dunne attended to Kathleen. Kathleen was elated. At last she had her son, Liam's son. Anxious to see if he resembled his father, she reached out.

"Let me see him."

As she reached, a spasm of pain crossed her face.

"Doctor," Mrs. Dunne exclaimed, "we've another baby here—it's twins!"

Within a few moments, Kathleen had delivered another son. Wilson was ecstatic. Even after all these years he never took the miracle of birth for granted.

"Twins," he said, "perfect identical male twins."

As she held one son and reached for the other, Kathleen was joyous. Her first hope that they resemble their father was not answered. They looked exactly like her father, Mick Barrett. Each had a small dimple in the chin and lots of black, curly hair. She wasn't disappointed.

Wilson was also amazed at the perfect mirror-image twins. It would take an hour or so for Kathleen to see the only visible difference, each having a small but similar birthmark on the inside of the wrist, one on his left hand, the other on the right.

Ryan Thornton was trying to remember the last time he had been in a place where he was happy and unhappy at the same time. He opened again the note from Kathleen. He read:

> *Dear Officer Thornton,*
>
> *Because you saved my life and the life of my baby, I shall be forever in your gratitude. There's nothing I can do or say to repay you but I hope you'll give me the opportunity to thank you personally.*
>
> *Kathleen*

He sat hunched and placed the note back in his inside pocket. Resting his elbows on his knees, he stared at the floor. He thought about his father. His gaze was accompanied by tightened lips. He told himself that what he was feeling was appropriate. After all, it was he who was responsible for the relocation of many misfits of society to the dreary God-forsaken prison in which he now waited. Waited to see a father he hadn't seen in eleven years. Time had erased much of the mercy he had felt in his younger years. Lately he didn't care if his father lived or died. Now he was dying. That is what his mother had told him. He was really there to ease her agony.

The Walpole State Prison didn't spend time considering even the slightest comfort for waiting visitors. He sat on a hard, wooden bench in a room barely nine-feet long by seven-feet wide. There were no windows, just dirty, white walls on which obscenities still showed through the thin paint. Ryan fidgeted nervously, waiting for his mother to return, indicating that it would be his time. He had firmed in his mind exactly how he was going to handle the conversation. He was convinced that it would be easier to let his father do the talking. He would just answer questions. That's the way he finally decided to approach the meeting; even if it became awkwardly quiet, he would wait for his father to break the silence.

The noise of the heavy steel door opening brought the reality of his meeting closer. His mother entered the waiting room and walked slowly toward him, her eyes locked on his. The guard left them. Ryan arose to greet her. She looked tired, and her eyes were red from crying. She placed her hands in his and squeezed tightly.

"He's very anxious to see you, Ryan." She took a deep, composing breath. "I don't know when I've seen him so alive."

Ryan said nothing. He could not look at her. He stared blankly at the concrete floor, suppressing the need to hold her, holding back tears himself. He stood up and vigorously dry-washed his face with his hands. He inhaled deeply.

"Well, here goes nothing," he said, still avoiding her eyes. As he left, she reached for his arm and held it tightly.

"Remember, Ryan, he still loves you very much. I'm not sure…well, I'm not sure he knows that you don't love him."

A guard showed Ryan into a much larger room, the only appointments crude, wooden furniture on a concrete floor. The room was separated into two parts by a solid wainscot about four feet high; above, a tight-wire diamond screen continued to the ceiling. There was room for half a dozen or so visitors on one side and as many inmates on the other, each one given a small amount of privacy by a wingwall partition.

Ryan was gestured mechanically to number-three cubicle by the guard. Before sitting, he could see the outline of his father behind the wire mesh. Slowly he eased himself onto the seat and placed his elbows on the shelf in front of him, and for the first time in eleven years, he saw his father. At least he resembled what was once the man who had taken him fishing, played baseball, and counseled him with a young boy's problems. His face was gaunt and waxen. The dark, curly hair that he remembered was all but gone except for a little gray at the sides. John Thornton was fifty and looked twenty years older. He wore a blue denim shirt buttoned to the top and so loose fitting that it made his neck appear scrawny. Ryan recognized the pale-blue eyes, and, although slightly glazed, they were exactly the same as he remembered them. Bright, smiling eyes. He recalled vivid pictures of times when he had been in trouble. His mother was always the disciplinarian. His father was always more understanding, taking time to explain things to him, why he shouldn't do this or that, why he should always tell the truth. And it was always the insightful blue eyes that gave credence to the words.

"Hello, Ryan," the voice said. John Thornton placed his hand to the screen. Ryan hesitated for a moment then placed his left hand over his father's.

"Hi, Dad—it's…" They both said something together and stopped, waiting for the other.

"It's been a long time," they said in unison again; they smiled.

Ryan continued awkwardly, "It's been a long time—and I really don't have any excuses, I…"

"That's all right, Ryan," John Thornton interrupted him. "Your mother tells me everything—ever since you joined the force we both knew that having a father in prison wouldn't be good for your career. As a matter of fact, it wouldn't be too good for my situation here either. You can imagine how worthless my life would be. Anyway that's not important now. How about you?" He didn't wait for Ryan to answer. "I understood why you couldn't come; besides, your mother has always kept me informed of your work. You don't know how great this is for me to see you—how you've grown, I really…" He took a deep breath, "I really miss the times we should have had."

"So do I," Ryan said. He felt stupid giving the trite response.

"I can't get over how well you look, Ryan."

"It's Mom's cooking," Ryan said.

"Ah, yes, that's something I miss too."

"Mom tells me you're sick."

"Well, you know how mothers are, always making mountains out of molehills."

"She said that you have cancer."

"She did, did she? Is that why you came, Ryan? You shouldn't have risked the Department finding out that you have a jailbird for a father. That wouldn't be smart. Especially for any advancement. Your mother shouldn't have told you."

"She said that you needed to see me."

"Of course *I want to see you*. It doesn't mean I *have to*. You took a big risk." His eyes smiled again. "I'm glad you did though. Thanks."

"There's something, Dad, that I've always—well…" Ryan hesitated.

He was about to ask why his father had stolen from the bank. He had read all of the transcripts and depositions. Some of the money was discovered in an envelope in his inside pocket. There was a responsible witness, an auditor from the bank. He dismissed the idea of pursuing the topic.

"You can ask me anything, Ryan—anything. I owe you that."

"That's okay, Dad. It wasn't that important."

Ryan listened more than he talked while John Thornton described his life at Walpole. For a while his mind wandered to thoughts of Kathleen Riordan. Dennis Noonan had informed him of her giving birth to two beautiful boys, identical twins. He was momentarily jealous, knowing that they would always remind her of their father. He wanted to see her right away; however, he knew that she would need time. Dennis might be willing to make arrangements for him to see her. He had to be sure that it was something that she wanted, too. He decided that the best avenue to take would be to ask Dennis Noonan if he could call on his niece. That was the honest, straight-forward thing to do, he thought. It was a happy decision and made him smile, outwardly content to listen to what his father had to say.

His father's voice imposed on his reveries. He was talking about Deirdre and asking why she hadn't written. Many times he said he understood why Ryan couldn't visit him. The probability of his survival to this point was the result of the well-kept secret that his son was a policeman. Now that he was diagnosed with cancer, it did not seem to matter.

"You got one more minute, Mister Thornton," the guard said loudly.

Ryan was glad that they didn't have to talk about his father's guilt or innocence. The visit hadn't been as traumatic as he'd anticipated. As far as he was concerned, his father was still a felon. Only briefly did he find himself recognizing the man on the other side as his father. For his mother's sake, he had made the effort to lift the barrier between him and his father, but he had no desire to visit again. It was easy to lie. It was easy to say 'yes' when asked if he would return soon, especially if he could avoid the eyes, the lively, blue eyes that replayed images of fonder memories.

CHAPTER THIRTY-FOUR

BLINDS HUNG HALF-WAY to keep out the glare. An inlaid-paneled oak desk had reams of paper stacked high in official, manila-colored folders. Boyle wore a white shirt with a V-cut cardigan. His collar was open and a poor choice of ties knotted loosely was tucked inside the sweater. He was preparing for a hearing and was methodically reviewing depositions when the woman's scratchy voice broke his contemplative mood.

"Mister Boyle, it's Roger Hayes. He's calling from the state prison in Virginia, says it's urgent that he talk to you." Boyle had a tendency to be indelicate when he was interrupted, particularly while he was busy preparing for a case hearing.

"Damn it, Carol! I told you—I don't take calls when I'm, ah, reviewing depositions." He hesitated, then in a calmer tone he asked, "Can you take a message?"

"I don't think so, Mister Boyle, he said it's important. Please hold." A short silence followed. The intercom clicked on again.

"He said he has information on the Thornton case. He says you have the wrong..."

"I'll take the damn thing, Carol. Put him through." Boyle picked up the phone abruptly. "This had better be good, Roger," he said, then he listened. He relaxed, his eyes stared blankly at the windows, and his lower lip dropped away, leaving him gawking. He uttered 'uh huh' a few times and reached into the top drawer for a cigar. He lit the cigar and took a deep drag.

"That's absurd," he whispered. "Preposterous! Why didn't he come forward before? Very good, no, ah, wait, just in case, get him to sign a statement there, you know what I mean? Anything could happen between now and when we might need him—and, ah, Roger, you're a goddamn marvel! Thanks."

He placed the phone on the receiver and pushed a buzzer. The door opened and Carol entered. She was beyond middle age, and her black hair was tied in a bun. Her youthful figure had long since disappeared. The severe face was framed by black-rimmed glasses, and she looked the epitome of order.

"I told him you didn't wish to be interrupted."

"That's all right, Carol. Listen, I want you to pull all the files again on the Thornton case. Then call Wilson and Barnes. Get a hold of Dennis Noonan. Tell him I have to see him right away. Got it?"

"Yes, Mister Boyle," she said, waving away a long stream of smoke.

"Oh, and coffee, we're going to need some coffee."

"It'll be a long evening then, Mister Boyle. Do you wish for me to stay?"

"No, Carol." He turned back to the depositions and waved her away. She was anesthetized to his insensitivity.

"That will be all then?" she asked curtly. He looked at her over the top of the reading glasses and smiled.

"Thanks," he said.

It was past six-thirty when Dennis Noonan arrived at the courthouse. People still milled about carrying paperwork in various forms. Dennis nodded to the guard at the bottom of the staircase.

"Evening, Mister Noonan." Dennis acknowledged the man and continued up the steps. The door at the end of the hall had a dimpled-glass panel with "District Attorney" painted in bold-black. He knocked and entered. Boyle stood from behind the desk.

"Dennis, glad you could make it." He glanced at his watch. "I see you, ah, got right over," he said sarcastically.

"You're lucky I came at all. You really should get a new secretary, you know. She has the personality of a tax collector. No explanations. Just that District Attorney Boyle wants to see you right away." He dropped into the black-leather easy chair. "What's going on, Chuck?"

Boyle came around the front of the desk with a bottle of bourbon and two glasses.

"Oh, it's going to be one of *those* nights is it?" Dennis asked. The glasses looked dirty, but he didn't mind. It had been a long day.

"You're not going to believe this, Dennis," he said, pouring. "You know Roger Hayes." Dennis sipped and nodded. "Well, I, ah, put him on this Thornton thing. Remember, you asked if I'd look into his conviction. I put Hayes on it. He's a goddamn bloodhound. I went over the transcripts myself, thoroughly, I might add. The trial didn't, ah, last long. As a matter of fact, the jury made their decision in a few hours."

"Go on," Dennis said, becoming more interested.

"Well, the thing that put him away was the state's witness. It turns out that the bank auditor was the *only* witness. Ah—a lot of money was missing over a period of time. The main branch was being apprised of the status of the losses by the auditor. They, ah, marked some bills and placed them in the vault. To make it short, the auditor had a search done at the end of the day, and, ah, found the marked bills in Thornton's inside pocket. Thornton claims he had no idea how the money got there."

"He was set up then?"

"Looks that way, Dennis."

"How about the money? If he was doing this over a long period of time, it must have been substantial. It must have been thousands of dollars."

"Not a penny recovered," Chuck said.

"Did anyone bother to check Thornton's style of living? You know, any major acquisitions, bank deposits, anything?"

"Nothing."

"Anything unusual after the conviction? Did the family prosper?"

"No. Ah, as a matter of fact, they lived close to the poverty level."

"Christ, Chuck, didn't anyone continue the investigation? The goddamn money had to end up somewhere."

"It did," Chuck said. He took a sip of the whiskey and lit a cigar. "It ended up with the auditor."

The silence ended with Dennis Noonan. He put his glass on the end table, threw back his head and gave off a great sigh.

"Jesus Christ," he said, almost inaudibly. "He was innocent. All these years just sitting there in Walpole, torn from his family. How come no one caught this, Chuck?"

"Hey, I wasn't around, remember? This wasn't my trial. Hell, we were just, ah, shitnosed attorneys at the time. At least we, ah, finally did something."

"Yeah, only after I begged you," Dennis said, tugging on his ear.

"It's not my responsibility to open every goddamn guilty case, Dennis. I work for the state. Shit, if it wasn't, ah, for me, your nice, safe city would be overwhelmed with hoodlums!"

"You know, Chuck, I'm really glad now that I chose private practice. I'd much rather suffer the consequences for getting one guilty man off than putting an innocent man away." Dennis took a long swig of the whiskey. "How did Hayes get this information?"

"You won't believe this, Dennis—we, ah, naturally thought a good place to start would be with the witnesses, just to see if there wasn't something that the defense missed. Anyway, the, ah, bank auditor wasn't difficult to find. Seems he's been busy living off the state for the past five years."

"I'll be damned," Dennis said. "Jail?"

"Uh-huh," Chuck said, without removing the glass from his mouth.

"What was he in for? Don't tell me it was embezzlement?"

"That too," Chuck said. "Only this time something went wrong. A bank official got wind of the scheme and ended up in the, ah, morgue."

"And no one bothered to do a background check?" Dennis asked.

"All this happened in Virginia. It was cut and dried. He ended up with life. As you can imagine it's, ah, no skin off his back to talk now."

"I guess so. Why didn't he come forward sooner? The bastard knew that another man, at least one that we know of, was doing time for something he didn't do."

"That's basically it," Chuck said, walking back to his seat. He took a note pad from the only clear space on his desk.

"This is what I have in mind. I will work out the statement this evening. It outlines the auditor's actions. It's a confession that has to be signed, but we, ah, don't anticipate any problems. We might have Thornton back to his family within a month. It will require a hearing."

Dennis drained his glass. "No one else knows yet?" he asked.

"You're the first. I will talk to the reporters on the courthouse beat tomorrow. You can tell Ryan and his mother. There could be, ah, remuneration for Ryan's father. Although I, ah, know that nothing can compensate the family for those lost years."

Dennis sighed again and rose from the chair. "I have some news to break to Ryan and his parents, Chuck." They shook hands. "Thanks. You know this means a lot to me."

Chuck wished him good luck and closed the door quietly.

It was a warm day in Boston for March. The Prussian-blue sky was almost totally obscured by white, billowy clouds where a persistent sun found an occasional break. The Requiem Mass at St. Benedict's for John Francis Thornton displayed more than the expected funeral sadness. Everyone in attendance was aware of the circumstances that surrounded the family. There were none of the customary expectations that a life had been fulfilled, none of jubilation for all the good years that mourners resign themselves to. The last eleven years that this family should have had together were taken away by the state.

The real irony was that John Thornton was found blameless before he had the opportunity to experience his freedom. The only consolation for his family was knowing that his name would finally be cleared. Father Rafferty celebrated the Mass and afterwards invited everyone to the cemetery, where he continued the final prayers at the graveside. He spoke about forgiveness and understanding injustices. Man's law was a fallible system that didn't always work in the best interest of those it was meant to serve. He spoke of absolution and the need to make allowances for those involved in Thornton's incarceration.

Ryan Thornton was thinking of the priest's words as he stood between his mother and sister at the parish hall. He was thankful that the reception line was short. He didn't know many of the people paying their respects. Most were his mother's friends from the neighborhood and the factory where she worked. He was happy to see that many of the off-duty officers from his precinct had attended and was elated that Dennis Noonan and his family had come. During the Mass he caught a glimpse of Kathleen. He hadn't seen her since that day at the Public Gardens, months earlier. He had missed seeing her at the Noonan dinner but was happy for her note thanking him for his bravery. He also caught her eye at the graveside ceremony; the winsome smile seemed to say, 'have courage.'

He shook hands mechanically with people paying their respects, his gaze never leaving the entrance, looking for her arrival. *Maybe they went home*, he thought, *after all, they weren't family*. He couldn't even consider them friends. The thought that they might not attend the reception brought a doleful look to his face. His disappointment could be misunderstood as a feeling of bereavement for his father.

The last person through the line was Father Rafferty, a slightly built man in his early thirties. He wore black, horn-rimmed glasses and a big toothy smile. He was genuinely responsive to the family's needs. He laughed loudly when he considered something even the least bit humorous. His body arched and he threw his head back in hysterical convulsions, issuing great belly laughs. He was also fervent, as he was now, capable of such compassion as to shed tears. He shook Ryan's hand vigorously with two hands.

"Remember, Ryan: to forgive is divine," he said in a murmur. Ryan's images of Kathleen Riordan and his disappointment at her absence were eclipsed by the forlorn face of the short priest.

"Oh, yes, yes, I agree," Ryan said, remembering the priest's comment. "I don't hold any grudges, Father. It'll take me a while, I guess, to accept everything that's happened. At least my father knew before he died that he had been found innocent. That really meant everything to him. Things could have been worse; he might have died without ever knowing. No, Mother and I are actually relieved."

"That's an admirable attitude, Ryan, but if you need to talk…"

"I know, Father, and thank you for the Mass. I know Mother was thankful you could make it. Anyway, she's glad now that it's all over."

"Your dad had been sick for a while? Your mother told me you paid him a visit."

"I saw him earlier—yes, a few weeks before he died."

"That's good, Ryan," Father Rafferty said, and excusing himself, left Ryan to his thoughts.

He was happy now that he had seen his father. If it hadn't been for his mother's perseverance he might have had to take Father Rafferty up on his offer of free counseling. He recalled the day Dennis Noonan had stopped by the precinct and told him of his father's innocence. In the beginning he thought it might have been a mistake. It was a confusing day. He had periods of anger turning to moments of bliss. He thought about his mother. She had been right all along.

She had gone alone to see his father the following Saturday. When she returned, she told Ryan that his father broke into tears when she informed him of the investigation that had found him innocent. 'All he could talk about was you, Ryan.' His mother's words echoed over and over in his mind. 'At last you can be proud once again of your father.' The following Saturday was going to be a special day. She was happy when Ryan told her he would be there. The Governor was going to attend and issue a public apology. Charles Boyle was going to be there also. Ryan had never seen her happier.

The first meeting with his father had gone well, certainly better than he had thought it would. He remembered thinking that he had a lot of making up to do. He could apologize for his lack of faith. He could take his dad fishing, he could… His happy reveries were abandoned, replaced by reality. John Francis Thornton had passed away on Thursday, just two days before his exoneration had been made official.

Ryan moved throughout the crowd to the table by the entrance. The long parish table was filled with edibles that people had brought for the reception. Ryan was offered coffee. Startled by the unmistakable Irish accent behind him, he stopped, the cup almost to his mouth.

"Officer Thornton, I'm sorry we missed the reception line."

He turned so quickly that he spilled his coffee. He took Kathleen's extended hand and held it without saying anything, momentarily engaged with her deep-blue eyes, her perceptive smile, her expression easing his sadness. She was stunning. She wore a white-lace shawl over an appropriate black-satin dress. Curly, black hair shone beneath a white hat with a pink rose on the side. Her face bloomed like a fresh peach, and her slender lips smiled, revealing glittering white teeth. Her fragrance sent a rush of blood and foolish feelings through his body. Dennis Noonan broke the silence.

"Are you going to hold that young man's hand all day?" Just a few months earlier, Dennis Noonan's comment would have embarrassed her. Living with her uncle had given her more self-confidence. She moved back slowly, allowing Dennis to take her place. Ryan withdrew his hand as she moved away.

"Mister Noonan, glad you could make it."

"Sorry about your father," Dennis said.

"Thanks, I mean thanks for everything you've done. My mother and I will always be in your debt."

"Actually, it was Chuck Boyle who did all the work," Dennis said.

"Well, if you hadn't pushed him…"

"Ryan, I just wish we could have done something earlier on." Ryan's eyes wandered past Dennis to where Kathleen stood. "You're really smitten, my boy, aren't you?" he asked directly.

Ryan was finally confronted with the question that allowed him to express his feelings. He could make a commitment to someone other than himself about his enchantment with Kathleen Riordan.

"You noticed?" Ryan said.

"Noticed!" Dennis was smiling. "A blind, dimwitted eunuch could feel the carnal indulgence."

"I like your niece, Mister Noonan…and there's nothing carnal about my intentions!"

Dennis placed his hand on Ryan's shoulder and steered him to a more secluded area of the room. "I can see that my attempt at making light of this whole thing isn't working. I've known for a long time about your attraction to my niece, Ryan, and I believe that she likes you, as a friend. I'm surprised you didn't come forward sooner. Both Madge and I think it would be appropriate for you to call on her—if you wish, that is?"

"Wish?" he said quietly, but losing none of his enthusiasm.

"You decide—you and Kathleen, that is. We can't speak for her. You'll have to make that overture yourself."

"I understand, Mister Noonan."

"Really now, Ryan, how many times do I have to ask you to call me Dennis? It seems that when you get that defensive attitude you always call me by my father's title."

"I'm sorry, Dennis. Maybe you could help me? With the meeting, I mean."

"I'll try. What do you have in mind?"

"The park? Does she still go to the park with the children?"

Dennis thought for a moment and rubbed his chin. "No, I don't believe so. I don't believe she's been back there since the accident. Why? Is that where you'd like to meet her?"

"I'd feel more comfortable if I could. It would be more casual that way. My beat takes me there."

"Yes, I see what you mean. 'Course I don't understand why you just don't come right out and ask if you can see her. Whatever makes you feel right."

"Yes, I'd feel better," Ryan said. His voice carried the tone of a plea.

"If it was me," Dennis said, "I'd just go ask her. I'd ask her outright if I could call on her. That's what I'd do."

Ryan nodded in agreement. "You're right, Dennis. I'll ask her myself. After all, what the hell, she can only say no, right?"

"Right," Dennis said.

Kathleen seemed to be having a good visit with Father Rafferty.

"A friend of mine just returned from Cork," he was telling her loudly. "On vacation, visiting a cousin, I believe. The cousin has a small farm, half an acre or so." He spread his arms as if describing a fish he might have caught.

"He's lucky he has a farm," Kathleen said. "He isn't starving, like some of the people that live in the cities. Even half an acre, small as it may seem, could produce vegetables to feed a family."

"Speaking of small, my friend hails from Virginia and happens to own thousands of acres."

"He must be fortunate, owning so much land, Father!"

"Actually, he's a very charitable man. He was telling his cousin all about his livestock and the extent of his land. 'Why, I can get on my horse and go for days, and still not see one end of my property to the other.' 'Dear God,' said his cousin, 'shure, didn't I have a horse like that meself one time.'" Father Rafferty arched his back and laughed loudly.

Kathleen found the priest humorous. She smiled more from his infectious laughter than anything else. Ryan caught her eye and walked toward her.

"I see you've met Missus Riordan, Father," he said.

"Yes, we've just met and I'm awfully sorry that she's not in my parish. Dear God, she has a great sense of humor."

"I haven't had the pleasure of Missus Riordan's company long enough to know that, Father," Ryan said.

"Well, you can trust me, Ryan. Anyone who laughs at my stories is all right in my book. If you two will excuse me I'd like to get into the food line." He arched his back again, patted his stomach and laughed loudly. "It's eat or get a new cassock," he said, ambling off.

Ryan was finally alone with her, and his mind abandoned all communication with his mouth.

"He's a funny priest. Is he your pastor or a friend of the family?"

"Pastor," he said.

"I've met your mother. She seems very nice." Ryan nodded appreciatively, and Kathleen continued, "I'm sorry about your father. You must be very upset about the fact he was innocent all the time."

"Mistakes happen," he said unemotionally.

"I'd be mad if it happened to my father," she said.

"I really don't remember that much about him. I'm not very popular with my mother when I say that, but that's the way I feel. I wish things had turned out differently."

"Nonetheless, it must have been agony for him to know that only two people in the world believed in his innocence."

"Actually, it was just my mother."

"I don't understand. You mean, you believed your father to be..." The implications made her feel uneasy. She thought that pursuing the conversation was bringing back unpleasant memories.

"By the way, I never did get to thank you personally for the flowers," she said, changing the subject. "Thank you—for everything—for saving our lives." She heaved a sigh of relief. "There, I've finally gotten to tell you!"

His face glowed with gratitude. "I'm glad I was there to help." There was a momentary silence as he searched for words. He blurted out, "You look...beautiful." When she appeared embarrassed he could have kicked himself for being so forward. "I'm sorry," he said, "I didn't mean..."

"Please, don't apologize, compliments like that I don't hear every day," she said graciously. "You should see the twins," she said, moving the conversation away from her appearance.

"I'd like that very much."

"Well then, has Dennis invited you to the St. Patrick's Day party? This will be my first year, of course, but I hear everyone has a good time. Dancing, singing..."

"I haven't been invited."

"I'm inviting you...oh, I'm sure he simply forgot."

"That's two weeks away."

"Yes, the seventeenth," she said.

"How about this Saturday?" There, it was finally said, and so enthusiastically he knew she wouldn't say no.

"This Saturday? You mean you'd like to come by and see the twins?" she asked him demurely.

"That, too, Kathleen, but I thought that maybe you might come by the Public Gardens—just to talk."

"It's still a little cold yet to take them." She hesitated, recognizing his immediate disappointment. "Maybe Madge would baby-sit. I'm sure she wouldn't say…"

"That would be great," he said anxiously. "If it would make you feel more comfortable, ask James and Anne along."

"Oh, I know they'd love it," she said.

"It's a date then."

"It's a date," she said.

One baby that looked the very image of her father would by itself have made her extremely happy; now she had two. Because they were so small and vulnerable, the baptisms had taken place immediately. They were named Michael and Lawrence, after her father and uncle. Kathleen knew that she was going to be a good mother. Madge, who was already taken with Kathleen's merits, was even more so now. She credited Kathleen's motherly reactions to her nursing experiences. Kathleen knew how to discern cries that needed attention. She knew when they needed to be left alone. There was a time for holding, a time for developing learning skills, feeding, and playing. Then there was alone time.

There were early indications that Lawrence was left handed. Doctor Wilson had visited a number of times since the birth, always curious and sharing some new piece of information he'd gathered about twins. On his last visit he suggested that they might be known as 'mirror-image twins,' particularly possessing opposing birthmarks. She shared her observations about Lawrence's favoring his left hand. Each crib had a colorful mobile just out of the baby's reach. Lawrence always reached with his left hand. Wilson maintained that it was nothing to be concerned about and told her to avoid being negatively influenced by the rarity of twins born as mirror-images. It wasn't long before she familiarized herself with their unique peculiarities. Michael loved being coddled, especially when she caressed his tiny form and stroked his cheek gently with her fingertips and sang Irish lullabies. Lawrence, on the other hand, became fidgety when held for too long. After he nursed, it was a quick burp and back to the sanctity of the crib.

Kathleen was determined to learn more about twins. One cell splitting gave them a unique alliance, sometimes closer than a mother and child. Each boy would probably develop a language of his own. She would watch for that. She was becoming aware of the mistakes that parents of twins usually make in those formative years, treating them as one child, even to their identical dress. She found that little had been researched regarding mirror-image twins beyond recognition that identical appearance was sometimes the only similarity. She was remembering something that Doctor Wilson had mentioned. Their personalities would be as opposite as night and day. That could be a godsend with twins. It would certainly be convenient to differentiate one from the other.

She also hoped that they would, in some way, remind her of Liam Riordan. It was just an expression, a certain way they looked at her, but there were times when they favored their father. It was hard for her to believe that nearly a year had passed. She had mixed emotions about her feelings. Her recollections of the man she loved for such a short time were waning, and during these reflective moments she tended toward melancholy. The only happy moment of her reveries was of the Hill o'Howth.

She sat in her room, reading until both babies dropped off to sleep. It was Saturday, the third of March, and two days had passed since the funeral. This was the day she was looking forward to and yet there was a touch of apprehension. This was the morning she had agreed to meet Ryan at the Public Gardens. She would feel more at ease taking along James and Anne, and of course, a book. Lately she had an insatiable thirst for reading. Apart from the technical symposiums on medicine, she found relaxation in a good novel, especially works of Dickens. She put *The Tale of Two Cities* in her purse, checked the twins one last time, and tiptoed from the room. Madge sat at the kitchen table with a cup of coffee. Dennis had left already for the office.

"Don't you look lovely this morning," Madge said, standing to get Kathleen a cup. Kathleen sat and for a moment looked disconsolate. Madge poured her a coffee and returned to her seat.

"Is something wrong, Kathleen?" She answered her own question. "I know, it's Ryan Thornton, isn't it? You're not sure about this are you?"

Kathleen welcomed Madge's insights. "I really don't know how I feel, Madge. Oh, I like Ryan, as a friend. I just don't want to give him the wrong impression. Do you know what I mean?"

"Of course, dear. No one ever said you have to fall in love on your first date. That comes later, if it comes at all."

He arrived on time. James saw him first, then Anne, just as excited, jumped up and down.

"Look, look, Kathleen, it's Officer Thornton!" Kathleen looked forward to seeing him. She looked up nonchalantly from Dickens, whose final page she discovered had not registered a single sentence with her. In the distance he wasn't immediately recognizable. She knew it was him by the way he twirled the baton. As he drew closer she also heard his whistling. She kept her gaze on him until the familiar face smiled and he waved in her direction. There were small pleasures these long days and the vision of him was one. She removed the Our Lady of Perpetual Succor prayer card from her purse and used it as a book marker. She waved back at Ryan. James and Anne pushed to greet him, each taking an arm.

"Officer Thornton, you're wearing the watch I gave you, aren't you?"

"James, really," Kathleen scolded him. "You must learn to be more gracious. You don't need to be praised every time you see Officer Thornton."

"That's all right, Kathleen," Ryan said, raising his sleeve to show James the watch. "I'm very proud of this, James—so proud, in fact, I hardly take it off."

With black eyes widening, James said, "Cripes—not even when you bathe?"

Ryan smiled. "Never," he said.

"Would you care to sit down, Ryan?" Kathleen said, making room on the bench. "You must get awfully tired, what with all the walking you do."

He looked around nervously. "It's very tempting, Kathleen; I think the Department would frown on that."

"Shame on your Department!"

"I guess they want us to keep moving. Actually, I don't feel uncomfortable standing."

James was becoming bothersome, asking questions and constantly tugging at his sleeve. "Can I play with the billy-club? Please, please, may I?" There wasn't a lot of time to talk about anything with James around. Kathleen was also a little frustrated with her cousin.

"James, I want you and Anne to go over there and play for a while."

"But, Kathleen."

"*Now*, James," she said, more demanding. Finally they obeyed. James knew when Kathleen was irritated. It was time to leave. Ryan broke the silence that followed.

"You haven't changed," he said.

"Well, now, I'm not sure how to take that, Ryan Thornton. Am I to believe that I'm a grumpy old widow or still as fat as I was when I carried the babies?"

"No, not at all." He was visibly flustered. "No, what I meant was, well, you still look…" He gathered his thoughts. "It's just that you're so beautiful."

She didn't respond, at least not the way he thought she would. She continued to look at him, as if sensing he had more on his mind. He decided that the look on her face was more affectionate than disagreeable and continued.

"I've been on a cloud since I first saw you. I've been thinking a great deal about you."

"On a cloud? That's nice, but not practical."

"I know. When you can't think of anything else…or anyone else, it is a dreamland."

"I see," she said, maturely. "I like you, too, but I don't think I'm ready for anything serious. I wouldn't want to give you the wrong impression. I guess I still love my…husband."

"I wouldn't expect you to begin a new life right away, Kathleen. I'd be happy just calling on you, well, as a friend—if that's okay."

She looked to where the children were playing. Now she seemed uncomfortable to him. *Dammit,* he thought, *now I've done it.* He halfway sat on the bench.

"Look—I'm sorry, Kathleen. I shouldn't have been so forward. I should have given you more time. As a rule I am not this forward." She turned her face to him. This was as close as he'd ever been to her. He could smell her fragrance. She smiled. He thought she was the most beautiful woman he had ever met.

"Dennis told me more about your father, how it all happened," she said, off on another track. "I'm sorry he died before you had a chance to say a proper goodbye. I know what it's like, losing someone."

"I know," he said. "I'm sorry, you're still in mourning and I acted like a…"

"Oh, no," she said, "no, not at all. I'm talking about my own family, my father in particular. I know he's alive, but, well, sometimes I'm certain I shall never see him again."

He eased back on the bench, relaxing, getting a little more comfortable.

"I heard your father was imprisoned by the British. Dennis told me that a priest helped him escape." She stared blankly at her hands.

"Yes—Father Donnelly..." Ryan could tell at that moment her thoughts were of Ireland. "Father Donnelly," she said, reminiscing. "Sometimes I really miss the old sod." Seeing his confusion, she smiled and immediately corrected herself. "I mean Ireland, Ryan. Ireland is the old sod, not Father Donnelly." He smiled.

"And what about the rest of the family?"

"My father, mother, the boys—little Jamie..." Her voice saddened.

"Little Jamie?"

She looked up.

"Yes, my little brother. He was in the house with my ma when the soldiers picked him up, my father. I don't think he'll ever forget that moment. My father was dragged off like some animal, right in front of them."

"You don't like the British, do you? Oh, not that I blame you, Kathleen. I mean, you have good reason."

"I don't mind the English people, Ryan, sure, they're just like you and me. No, it's the government, the damnable soldiers following their duties. That's what raises my ire."

"Soldiers have to follow orders, I guess, otherwise they wouldn't be soldiers."

"Are you saying you agree with what those soldiers are doing in Ireland?" she snapped. It was his first encounter with her indignation. He arose and straightened his uniform.

"I didn't say they were right, Kathleen. What I meant was they were doing what they were trained to do, that's all."

"They were trained to kill Irish men and women! I saw the results of their bloody fine soldiering first hand." The words echoed in the silence that followed. She looked away as if to change the subject. Her eyes steadied on James and Anne playing by a large oak tree.

"I heard from Uncle Dennis last night that they are already calling men for the service. Do you think America will go to war?" she asked, her tone more civil.

"Yes, I do." All he could think of doing now was to answer her questions. He had felt her wrath once after saying the wrong thing.

"I'm sorry," she said.

"I'm sorry we're going to war, too," he said.

"No—I mean, I'm sorry I got mad at you. It's a bad habit of mine."

"It's my fault," he said. "I'll—I'll try to be more understanding. Please forgive me, Kathleen. You're the last person I would want to upset."

"It's not your fault…They say I'm just like my father. I suppose it's just as well that you find out now." What she said dawned on him.

"You mean there's still hope that we can see each other, er, as friends, I mean?" He was elated.

"I never said we couldn't be friends," she smiled. "I have you to thank for a lot of good things in my life. And I don't mean that because I think I have to repay you either."

"Thank you for that," he said. He checked the time. "Look, how about if I call on you Monday, that's my day off. We could take in a flicker and go to dinner, maybe even to a—"

"I'm a mother with new babies, you know. I just can't take leave."

"I'm just not thinking," he interrupted. "What am I thinking about anyway…"

"Well, maybe Madge could…"

"Do you think she would? That would be great!"

"She's taking care of them now. I don't see why she couldn't…Monday, did you say?"

"Yes, it's my day off."

"I'll have to ask Madge," she said. "I mean…if she could. How would I get in touch with you, if it's all right, I mean?" He thought a moment.

"How about Mass tomorrow? You could tell me then."

"You'd have to come up from Roxbury. You wouldn't mind?"

"Mind! Mass it is then," he said. He checked his watch again. "I really have to be getting along, Kathleen. See you tomorrow then," he said, walking back toward Park Street. She hollered after him, "We go to the ten o'clock Mass, Ryan!" He waved the club and went off whistling.

On Saturday the seventeenth of March, the Noonans, like all Boston Irish Catholics, began the holiday by attending Mass. Everyone wore a little patch of shamrock, the men in their lapels and the women a sprig in their hats. Father Lane gave a spirited sermon, becoming even more furious as he approached the close. He drew a parallel with meddling Englishmen contributing to the Troubles and Patrick driving the snakes away over fifteen hundred years ago. He spoke of the continuing prison barbarities and asked the congregation to pray for peace in the world, and especially that they pray for President Wilson, that he might stay on the path of peace.

There were a lot of German parishioners that murmured their approval when he made the announcement. By now most Americans were aware of the recent news reports of Zimmerman's intentions and outraged at the German plot to bring Mexico and Japan into the war against them. Most

Germans still believed that the published telegram was a fraud and an underhanded anglophile deception to press America and Congress into war. Nonetheless, German newspapers from Milwaukee, Cincinnati, and Detroit to St. Louis suggested that if the telegram was truly from Zimmerman, their loyalties were to their adopted country. Theodore Roosevelt was openly infuriated at the President for not taking immediate action. The Irish and the German communities had one thing in common: Their antipathy toward the English manifested itself in the desire for America's continued isolationism.

After Mass, the Noonan family came home to a breakfast feast prepared by Mrs. Dunne that consisted of Virginia ham, homemade sausages, scrambled eggs, potato pancakes, and Irish soda bread fresh from the oven. When breakfast was over, Kathleen shared a letter from home. Things were not going well in Ireland, Annie wrote. Since the rebellion, the British had stepped up their authoritarian rule with more constraints, more restrictions on food, and of course, more troops. Annie said she was lucky to be in the country with Larry, where at least they had plenty to eat. Mick was anxious to get back to the city and the business, but reason always prevailed. To return to Dublin would surely have placed the family in grave danger; besides, Padraig was still running the furniture store and sending them a monthly stipend. Paddy was working in Clonmel as a junior dairy inspector and still courting Cora Jamison. Michael would be graduating this year and Jamie was determined to be a stamp collector. Annie said that so far his whole collection consisted of stamps from Kathleen's letters. Also, Bridget McIntee was engaged to a pioneer who wouldn't come within a mile of the pub. A tee-totaling wedding at the McIntee's would be about as out of place as a monk's vows in a brothel. She mentioned Sean only briefly, saying that he had a great paying post with a Chicago distillery. Annie finished by expressing her unhappiness at not being able to see the babies. Maybe one day, God willing, she wrote. Kathleen sensed her disconsolation.

"It's a shame there's such distance between us," Madge said when she finished the letter.

"Sometimes I feel as though I'll never see them again, Madge," Kathleen said, folding the letter and carefully placing it back in the envelope. "They may as well be in another world. Letters are helpful, but I miss seeing them. I miss touching them. They at least have one another."

"Thanks," Madge said.

"Oh, I'm sorry, Madge, I didn't mean it the way it sounded."

"That's all right, Kathleen, I understand," Madge said. "You'll have fun tonight. Our St. Patrick's parties are unforgettable. Besides, Ryan is coming, right?"

"Yes. I am looking forward to tonight."

"You've been seeing a lot of him lately."

"He's a good friend, Madge, that's all."

Madge smiled knowingly. "Sure," she said. "He attended the last two Sunday Masses and you've seen him as many times at the park."

"I enjoy his company. Oh, I'm sure he'd like things to be a little more serious. I just don't think I'm ready for that yet. It's not something I can explain."

"I understand perfectly well, Kathleen. We all can't experience love at first sight."

"I did, Madge—once."

"I know, dear, and I do believe that you're still in mourning."

They sipped their coffee in silence, which was eventually punctuated by what sounded like two violins trying to tune to one another, first one and then the other. It was the twins' way to announce to Kathleen that it was their time to eat.

Later that same day, darkness had replaced the evening sun, and a March chill filled the air. Mrs. Dunne lit the logs in the fireplace and indoctrinated the bartenders in their duties. The caterers had also arrived early to prepare the dining-room table with an abundance of food. The house was ready for a party. Dennis hired the same Irish Celtic band every year. Actually, it wasn't really a band, including only an accordion player, a fiddler who also played the uilleann pipes, and a piano player who never did much more than vamp.

Dennis left them in the living room, playing a reel. He returned shortly with a large tumbler of draft Guinness, a priming of sorts for the Powers that he would continue through the evening. This was the part of the evening he liked most. He sat in his favorite chair by a roaring log fire listening to live Irish music, sipping on genuine Irish porter. He closed his eyes and allowed his mind to drift to places in Ireland he'd never been, seen only in illustrated books or recollections of places on the map. He stayed in this romantic state until the first revelers arrived.

Silently, he listed those who would arrive first. Of the hundred or so people that would attend this special event, which anxious spirit would be the first to venture in from the cold night? He would know soon. Mrs. Dunne left her kitchen duties to answer the loud knock.

"Good evening, Officer Thornton."

Dennis smiled. He had guessed right.

"In here, Ryan!" he shouted over the band's rendition of *The Maid*

Behind the Bar. Dennis asked him what he wished for a beverage, and Mrs. Dunne graciously brought him a glass of Guinness. They talked a while about nothing important and soon their perfunctory conversation was interrupted by arriving guests.

Ryan was introduced to everyone as Kathleen's friend. Dennis became the busy host and Ryan had to fend for himself. He wasn't good with superficial tete-a-tete. He wished that Kathleen would come down soon. Madge had, but he couldn't wedge his way to her; instead, he was corralled by one of the partners of the firm, a Mr. Reginald Barnes. Barnes was a fat, balding man in his late fifties. He had an enormous hairless round head that reminded Ryan of a streetlight globe. Barnes did most of the talking, first offering condolences over the death of his father, then congratulations on saving the life of his partner's son. Ryan looked past the man's globular head to the attractive woman on the staircase, instantly silencing the bald man's banter.

Kathleen was beautiful. She wore a green, velvet dress with a modestly cut bodice displaying an embellishment of white lace. All who saw her descending the stairs would have to admire her. She was intriguing and desirable, and Ryan knew that one day soon he was going to ask her to marry him. Her blue eyes traversed the foyer, finally resting on him, their eyes transfixed; both were lost in their own world, now smiling. He had no doubt that Kathleen was the most beautiful woman here. She waved modestly and her mouth welcomed him with a silent hello. As abruptly as he had ignored Reginald Barnes, his attention returned to what the bald man was now saying.

"That's why I really do believe that our merchant ships have to be armed. It's the least that we can do for our seamen, don't you agree, Ryan?"

Ryan was glad that all he had to do was agree, and right now he would have agreed to anything to end the chitchat. "I certainly do," he asserted, "and now if you'll excuse me there's someone—"

"I know where your mind's been, son, and there's no need to apologize. I was young once myself, you know."

Ryan was momentarily embarrassed. "I really was paying attention."

"You're a bad liar. Now off with you to see your girl," the portly man said, smiling.

Ryan moved through the people in the foyer, excusing himself, finally greeting Kathleen at the bottom of the staircase. He felt brave and kissed her on the cheek she had graciously offered. He tasted her fragrance. It was the first time he had kissed her. Happy, trancelike, he was captivated by her beauty. Although aware that he had finally kissed her, he was doleful.

It was something he'd thought about doing for so long and now his mind was totally blank. He wanted always to savor this first kiss and now he didn't even remember doing it.

"You seem awfully somber," she said, barely audible over the band and noisy partiers.

"You look beautiful—unbelievably beautiful," he said seriously.

"And that makes you sad?"

"No—so happy I am afraid it cannot last," he said loudly. "Is there somewhere we can talk quietly?"

"The terrace?" She shrugged. "I can't imagine anyone venturing out there, not on a chilly March night."

She was right. He closed the French doors behind them, silencing the noise of the party. He had picked up a Powers and a glass of wine on the way. They were finally alone.

"Ahhh," she sighed, "quiet."

"It's quite a party in there. I recognized people I normally just get to read about," he said.

"Uncle Dennis does have influential friends. Some of them are odd though, like Joe Kennedy. He gives me the creeps. Then there's our side of the family. Rose Kennedy is all right, she's a Fitzgerald, but that Joe is a rake." She sipped on the wine. Normally she didn't drink, but it made her warm and she felt carefree, as if floating. Although warmed by the wine, her body trembled, reminding her that it was still March and sensible people didn't venture into the chilly evening without something warm. He placed his glass on a patio table, removed his jacket and placed it on her shoulders. He closed the coat about her neck and reaching back with both hands, pulled the collar up around her neck. Even in the darkness he focused on her face. He leaned and gently kissed her cheek as he had earlier, this time staying. She didn't move, rather he felt her push toward him. Slowly savoring every touch of her face, her fragrance, he edged to her lips. She opened her soft mouth and allowed him to touch her tongue. They embraced hard, their bodies touching full length. She had yielded, and now she permitted him to finish and pulled back, gasping slightly. She removed the jacket and handed it to him.

"We should probably be getting inside," she said, regaining her composure.

"You're not mad at me, are you?" he asked, putting on the coat.

"Not at all," she said nonchalantly, "and why should I be mad—it, it was just a kiss, wasn't it?"

He smiled inwardly. He knew it meant more than that. The first great leap had been accomplished. There was no doubt in his mind that she had responded favorably to his kiss. He could be patient now, knowing that she wanted his company as he craved hers. They didn't appreciate how cold it was until they stepped over the threshold into the dimly lit anteroom. The small room served as both mudroom and pantry. Kathleen sighed, responding to the warmth. They sat down on the plain wooden bench, their eyes adjusting to ambient light that streamed through the French-paned kitchen door, and they watched the flurry of activity. The pantomimes were reminiscent of a silent-picture show with Madge as heroine, issuing orders to the scullery help. He spoke first.

"I signed up for the Army."

She didn't respond. She couldn't.

He reasoned that his terse announcement sounded more like an ultimatum, blunt and unbelievably immature. His matter-of-fact pronouncement was an effort to test her feelings. In his mind she was supposed to plead with him not to go. For centuries men had proclaimed their obligation to go to war. It was the patriotic thing to do. It was his God-given right. His quest to protect his country from German aggression. Somehow it wasn't working. Now he had some explaining to do.

"I wasn't going to tell you, not for a while anyway. It's just that…well, I'll probably be leaving soon. I want you to know that I've never been happier than in these past few weeks. When I'm not with you I'm…well, desolate. What I'm trying to say, Kathleen, and not doing a very good job is…I love you very much and I think you like me." She was silent. He looked away momentarily, carefully deliberating how to phrase his thoughts. "When we kissed I experienced something much more than…" he said, "you know, people just liking one another. I guess from the way you kissed me back I think it's special for you too."

"I wish you could hear yourself, Ryan," she said derisively. "You're telling me that you love me. That life is miserable when you're not with me, and you really hope that I feel the same way about you. Right?"

"Uh-huh."

"So what do I do while you're off fulfilling this manifest destiny of yours, saving the world from the Germans? Just what do you expect me to do? I'm not a Penelope, willing to sit around weaving a tapestry while you do this…this manly thing."

"So you do care for me?" he said jubilantly.

"Of course I do, you big dummy. I care for you a great deal. I don't make a habit of kissing just anyone, you know."

"I didn't think you would."

"Thanks for giving me credit for that," she said. "Look, Ryan, I've been through all this before."

"I know," he said apologetically.

"You *don't* know. I loved a man dearly who was caught up in this same war that compromised our relationship."

For a hasty moment her heart wanted to tell him everything about Liam Riordan. His involvement in her father's imprisonment, the truth that they weren't married, and what she knew about his death. For her sons' sake that knowledge would have to remain her dark secret.

"I'm sorry you lost your husband, Kathleen, and I really mean that. I don't want to sound like some crusader. As a matter of fact, right now I would like nothing better than for us to be together…married."

"Ryan, I'm not sure…"

"Please, don't say anything just yet," he stopped her. "As far as joining up is concerned…well, I did that weeks ago, just after my father's death and before you and I…I just wanted to get away, if you know what I mean. I knew Mom would be all right with a monetary settlement from the state. I guess I thought that the Army would be a good place to lose myself. I was angry. Kathleen, even at that time I knew I loved you. I just didn't know that you would be willing to be with me the way I wanted you. I don't think I could have handled the rejection."

She took his hand and leaned her head on his shoulder.

"I'm sorry," she whispered. "Why is life so complicated, Ryan?" She answered herself. "It's this damnable war. Politicians and land-hungry bureaucrats can't get along, and ordinary people like you and me can't make a life together."

He could feel her body sigh. He put his arms around her and pulled her close. This time he would remember every enjoyable moment. His hands enveloped her tiny waist. He drew her closer, and turning his face to her forehead, he kissed her gently, then the bridge of her nose, slowly moving downward. She responded, raising her face, parting her lips while he found her mouth. Their hands parted, his moving slowly upward, resting gently on her breast, massaging, every deep breath forcing her heaving bosom to his touch. His mind was alert to every sensation. He left her lips and kissed her cheek at the same moment he yielded to her delicate removal of his hand.

"I love you, Kathleen," he whispered.

"Oh, Ryan…I don't know if I'm ready for…" Instinctively they both pulled apart, their seclusion interrupted by the harsh light. It was Madge looking for something from the pantry.

"Oh, dear…I had no idea you were both here," she said, startled. Gesturing to the switch, she smiled. "Shall I turn it off again?"

Kathleen stood, her face a shade of pink. "That's all right, Madge, we were just…"

"You don't have to explain to me, Kathleen. Really! I'm happy for you both." Casually she reached for a jar of pickles from the pantry. "I just need this," she said, standing on her toes.

"Here, let me," Ryan said, glad for the opportunity for something to do, his face still showing signs of embarrassment, but not as obviously as Kathleen's.

"Thanks," Madge said, sparing no time departing. "Shall I leave the light on?"

"Please do. We'll be along in a moment," Kathleen said.

Madge turned back, smiling, "Oh, and Ryan, be sure to remove the lipstick. I'm not sure how some of our guests feel about men wearing makeup. Don't be long though, Dennis has some people he'd like you to meet." She left them alone.

Dennis quickly introduced Ryan to Tim Fagan, who said hello on a volley of great wheezing sounds.

"Would you two excuse me, Chuck Boyle wants a word with me in the library. No rush now, Tim, but when you're ready, swing by," Dennis said, leaving the men alone. Fagan waved affirmatively without saying anything.

"Are you all right?" Ryan asked, concerned.

"Oh…it's…it's just my asthma. One of these…these days it'll be the death of me." He tried laughing but could only muster another bout of irritable wheezing. Ernest Conway came over.

"Jeez, Fagan, you sound like hell." He looked at Ryan. "Hi, I'm Ernest Conway, accountant for Dennis Noonan, and you're…?"

"Ryan. Ryan Thornton."

"Ah, yes, the young policeman that saved his boy." Conway shook his hand vigorously, "and his niece's babies. You're very special to Dennis. Very special indeed."

"Anyone would have done what I did, Mr. Conway. I just happened to be there, that's all."

"I, he…heard that Chuck is trying to get you into the District Attorney's Office," Fagan wheezed.

"I appreciate that," Ryan said, "but I think the Army is going to have other plans for me."

"Christ, I didn't know they were calling people up yet." Conway was puzzled.

"They're not. I volunteered."

"Enlisted? You gave up a great opportunity, son. 'Course I suppose you'd have had to go in anyway. It's just a matter of time, isn't it?"

"Sure looks that way," Ryan said, his gaze galvanized on the couple dancing. It looked like 'Joe the Terrible' had coerced Kathleen to the dance floor, and as far as he was concerned was holding her much too closely. The lights had been turned down for a slow waltz. Joe Kennedy was powerful, handsome, and a dangerous man whose days of profligacy were going to be numbered if Ryan had anything to do with it. Ryan politely excused himself. Before he reached them he could tell Kathleen was uncomfortable. He didn't wish to create a scene; however, he mentally prepared himself to be firm. Quiet, but to the point. Joe Kennedy's back was to him. She smiled appreciatively as he approached. His hand firmly grasped Kennedy's shoulder.

"Mind if I cut in?" Ryan said passively. Joe Kennedy didn't respond immediately; when he did, he displayed a deceptive, toothy smile.

"Yes, as a matter of fact, I, ah, do mind." This was not the response Ryan Thornton needed. His hand moved from Kennedy's shoulder to the trapezius and with his fingers pushed into the fleshy muscle beneath the jacket.

"I asked politely, now I'm telling…"

"Well, well. I see you two have met." It was Madge whose prudent intervention offset what was about to become a disquieting circumstance. Joe Kennedy was not known to back away from a disagreeable situation. "You've been avoiding me all night, Joe Kennedy. I requested the band to play *Sally Gardens for a Siege of Ennis* and selected you as my partner."

Turning to Dennis, Joe Kennedy said, "I was just enjoying this waltz with your beautiful niece, Kathleen."

"Yes, isn't she! and this is Ryan Thornton, her escort…boyfriend."

Kennedy, completely oblivious to the altercation, the wide grin genuinely amiable now, took Ryan's hand as if nothing had happened. "Nice to meet you, Ryan. You should take better care of this perfect treasure," he said, turning to Kathleen. "You're the luckiest man here."

"I think so," Ryan said curtly. Then he turned to Kathleen.

"I don't know if I'm as good as Joe Kennedy here, but would you care to finish the dance?" he asked.

"There's only one way to find out," she teased.

They talked about a lot of things while they danced, mostly what things might have been like without the war. If it wasn't for the twins, she said, she would most likely have joined the Army hospital corps. She told him that a job had already been offered her at City Hospital.

"Will you take it?"

"As soon as the twins are weaned. I feel that I should be on my own, not that I want to leave Uncle Dennis and Aunt Madge. They've been good to me. I have to make a life for myself, you know."

"I know," he said, pulling her a little closer. "And I'd like to be a part of that." He waited for a response, finally breaking the silence. "I'd like you to be my wife, Kathleen."

The music stopped. The lights came on and a loud Irish dialect announced that the men should take their partners for the *Siege of Ennis*. Ryan and Kathleen moved through the couples lining up for the dance. They passed Madge and Joe Kennedy, whose grin was apparently perpetual. He winked knowingly at Ryan, who nodded back without smiling. They found an unoccupied corner. Everyone was dancing, rows of four moving in and out, feet tapping to the fast reel.

"Well," he said.

"I'm just not sure, Ryan." She took his hand. "I don't want to make any mistakes. If we did get married, you'd probably be shipped off to Europe right away. What kind of a life would that be for me?"

"We don't know that, Kathleen. I may get to stay here. Who knows? The war might be over before I leave."

"Ryan, that's gibberish and you know it. This war is only going to be won if America gets involved by sending troops, and that means you."

"Are you sure the war isn't an excuse not to marry me?"

"If I didn't want to, Ryan, I wouldn't need an excuse to say no."

"Then say yes. Say yes if you love me."

"Ryan, I just feel a little rushed, that's all. I like being with you. I just don't know…" she hesitated, "I'm just getting over the remorse of havin' given myself to someone before. I don't want to lose another husband."

"I understand," he said thoughtfully. She reached up and kissed his cheek.

"You're very special to me, Ryan Thornton. You're the most understanding man I've ever met." Her face beamed. She took his hand. "Come on, I'm going to show you how to do a *Siege of Ennis*."

Dennis was irritated. "What's going on, Chuck? This had better be goddamn important to interrupt my St. Patrick's Day party," he said, tugging on his ear. "This could get you into trouble, you know, the least of which might include grievous bodily damage."

"You haven't heard the news yet, Dennis?"

"What news is that, Chuck?"

Boyle threw the *Literary Digest* on the table.

"It's all there in the headlines.'*Zimmerman united the United States.*'

The published telegram outlines Germany's intention to begin unrestricted, ah, submarine warfare. A proposal to Mexico suggests an alliance on the following basis: Make war together against America. In return, Germany will return all lost territory to Mexico, namely, New Mexico, Arizona, and of all things, Texas, for Christ's sake. Can you believe that shit? This fucking Zimmerman has really gone and, ah, bolixed things up." Dennis snatched the magazine and read silently.

"So!" he said belligerently, tossing the paper back on the table.

"This shit's been going on now for a while. We all knew that Germany was going to subject all neutral shipping to attack. Congress will just have to vote in some kind of protection."

"Ah, that's not all, Dennis," Boyle said vehemently. "I had a visit from some asshole from the State Department. A goddamn skinny runt with an oversized head and no shoulders. He asked about the IRB and my affiliation with the group."

"The Irish Republican Brotherhood?" Dennis said.

"Us! Yes! The group. He knows all about us. He told me that he already set Senator O'Gorman straight. He mentioned sedition."

"Sedition?"

"Sedition!"

"In other words this…this asshole is accusing our organization of anti-American activities. So we just put Constitutional niceties aside to accommodate the Federal Government?" Dennis stepped behind the desk and poured Powers to the top of a tumbler. "This little bastard insults my intelligence."

"He insulted *me*," Boyle said. "Told me that I, of all people, I should know better. 'Being a member of a pro-German organization will see you behind bars,' he said."

"You know, Chuck, this isn't the first time our Constitutional rights have been compromised to accommodate the government, and we're not even at war."

"This little fucker had files on everyone in the group. He referred to us as subversives. As the vice president, he said, I should disassemble the chapter."

Sweeney waved the thick smoke away. "Must be the same man that called my wife," he said.

Dennis snuffed the cigar violently into the ashtray. "Called your wife?"

"Yeah, some guy from the State Department, Bureau of Investigation. Said his name was Hoover, I think."

"Hoover? That's the asshole, Edgar Hoover," Boyle said.

"What a little prick." Dennis took a swig of the Powers. "Let's not get too excited about all this. Frankly, I don't believe that Mr. Hoover has any foundation. We're not at war with Germany yet, anyway. And since we're not at odds with either England or Germany, the government has no reason to interfere with meetings regarding *Ireland's* freedom. We don't have to buy arms from Germany. Hell, we can just as easily buy from our own country. *That's it.* We should talk with Creehan when he gets back, arrange for an American broker."

"Oh, that's another thing, Dennis," Boyle said. "Anthony Creehan won't be coming back."

"What?" Dennis said angrily.

"This guy Hoover said that our Irish friend has been deported. Permanently. I'm telling you, Dennis, war is imminent for this country."

Dennis sat down and lit another cigar. "I suppose we're being lumped into a common threat opposed to America's participation in the war. I guess we wouldn't be very popular at a Flag-Day rally, boys. If we do go to war because of this telegram business—well, I don't see much hope for our organization. I believe then it would be considered…" he hesitated, "traitorous to deal with the enemy. I'm not sure I could expose my family to that."

Conway sat down on the edge of the sofa. "Supposing we were more secretive? We don't have to broadcast where we're meeting. I mean, look at us here. Do you think they know we're having this meeting?"

Boyle snickered. "There's a hundred people just outside this door. Can you, ah, vouch for *all* of them?"

"Chuck's right," Dennis said. "They're not beyond censorship, wire tapping, confiscating property, opening mail, restricting the right to assembly: you name it, shit. I wouldn't even want to be a member of the Harvard Liberal Club right now, let alone the Irish Republican Brotherhood. No, as much as I hate to say this, I think we should use some restraint. We can meet in small parties, two to three, no more."

"That's all great, Dennis, but what can we accomplish without Creehan? What's the use?" Boyle said.

"I agree with Chuck," Conway piped in. "We can't collect money like this. We need a bonafide organization. There's too many risks, Dennis. I worry about my wife and family; after all, I'm the one they contacted. Probably because I'm the group's accountant…I couldn't handle going to jail, Dennis."

Dennis drained the Powers and stared vacantly into the empty glass.

"You're right," he said resolutely. "I'll be in contact with all of you through Chuck here. In the meantime, if you are contacted again by this

Hoover character just go along with him…tell him…" Dennis looked contemplatively at the ceiling, "tell him, that 'in the interest of America's established order, the IRB has been disbanded.'" He stood and stretched. "Let's get back to the party before someone I haven't invited turns us in." They smiled apprehensively and left one at a time to join the party.

Conway, Boyle, Chuck, Dennis, all in the Irish Republican Brotherhood, saw their contingency plans for the organization evaporate when a few days later the United States declared war on Germany. Dennis heard the report first. "Congress has done it," he told Boyle. "It will be in the papers on the street. I will call you back." Before he reached the street-corner newsstand he heard the vendor shouting: "War!" "Read all about it." "Extra, extra… war declared." While he stood on the sidewalk, he read the headlines, built on Germany's threats to America, the plots with Mexico and Japan, Wilson's call for full-scale Army build-up:

Congress declares war on Germany
German subs attack American ships
German Ambassador forms alliance with
Mexico and Japan / America retaliates

Ryan was spending most of his off-duty time these days at the Noonans'. Sometimes Kathleen met him at the Commons, where they shared lunch. Those were more private times in the park, away from the frustration of Anne and James. Ryan wasn't sure when he was going to hear from the Army and worried that Kathleen wouldn't marry him before he left. It would be easier leaving knowing she would be there when he returned. Assurance of sorts. Finally Kathleen was convinced that it was the right thing to do. In weighing her decision she considered the opinions of Dennis and Madge. They thought the world of Ryan.

Kathleen and Ryan were married in May, one month after Woodrow Wilson's declaration of war. Because of Katy Thornton's heritage, the traditional Catholic service, in the small church in Roxbury, was modified to include a Russian Orthodox concelebrant, which reduced some of the older devout Catholics to near mutiny. Dennis stood in for Mick Barrett, proud as a peacock when he answered the priest and handed Kathleen over to Ryan's arm. Father Lane pronounced them husband and wife. The reception at the Noonans' included an unusual combination of Russian and Irish music. There were great quantities of food and a great number of people to eat it.

Kathleen, still in her wedding gown, was the center of attention. She looked more beautiful than ever, almost saintly, with the white veil, just beneath the large, deep eyes. The black hair shone next to the white lace and the perfect mouth, happy, smiling as she shook hands or offered her cheek to those so inclined. Joe Kennedy, having planted a less than respectable kiss on Kathleen's lips, was immediately removed from the reception line by Madge before Ryan had a chance to react. Ryan was furious, particularly when Joe mischievously winked back at him. For all his roguery, Joe had ingratiated himself with Madge, and he had a great deal of respect for her. At times she questioned how her cousin Rose put up with him.

Their honeymoon was short but memorable. Kathleen did not wish to spend much time away from the twins. They stayed three days in Cape Cod, a gift of Dennis and Madge. Within a week they were in their own place, a small rented house in Roxbury. Life seemed perfect for Kathleen. Katy Thornton offered to take care of the twins while Kathleen worked part-time at the hospital. Work agreed with her, and she was happier than she had ever been. Katy Thornton was happy too. She loved her 'new grandsons.' She was retired and well compensated by the state for her husband's misfortune. She was happy for her son, who had finally found a woman who loved him. She was also proud of the way he accepted Kathleen's babies as his own. It was an ill-destined harmony soon fractured by news of Ryan's enlistment orders.

Ryan was having second thoughts about the Army. Leaving Kathleen and the boys wasn't going to be easy. Now he wished he'd taken Chuck Boyle up on his offer. Fighting Germans was the furthest thing from what he really wanted. Kathleen was right. War did nothing more than kill young men needlessly. He adored her more with the passing of every day, wishing the war would end that he might stay with Kathleen, making beautiful babies. It wasn't long before all their fears of disruption came true. He didn't handle the separation as well as Kathleen. She was prepared from the very beginning. From the day they received the notice he had twenty-four hours before departing.

Ryan's perfect record with the police force preceded him. Dennis Noonan still had some contacts and without Ryan's permission arranged for a position that would take him out of harm's way. Ryan was assigned to MID, the Army's Military Intelligence Division. He earned just two leaves of absence in 1917, the first after basic training and the second after language school, where he studied Russian culture and language. Sometimes he embarrassed his instructors with his knowledge. His second leave lasted ten glorious days and nights, every moment cherished. It was fall and the twins were growing. It did not surprise Kathleen that Lawrence was the first to walk. He was always more fidgety and impatient.

In the evenings when they were alone they avoided conversation about the future. Kathleen didn't seem interested in what the Army had in mind for her husband. She realized that her opinion would change nothing. Ryan couldn't question her indifference, since she had foretold what married life would be like while he was in the service. She was the perfect wife for a husband assigned to the intelligence corps. Uninterested.

Eventually Ryan was shipped overseas, attached to the Embassy in Moscow. The Bolshevik Revolution was still in full swing. Everything in Russia was like a whirlwind, events were taking place so fast. Red Russians were still fighting the White Russian minority. Now with the Bolsheviks in command, American intelligence had to determine if Russia was going to stay in the war. The Germans had at least thirty-four crack divisions fighting on the Eastern Front. Some propaganda gleaned from the American Committee on Information had even suggested that Lenin and the Kerensky government were being paid now by the Germans to sign a peace treaty.

Ryan's military chief was a colonel named Ruggles. Ryan didn't see much of Colonel Ruggles. He reported directly to Captain Valeri Agranof, who preferred being called Val. He was stocky with tight-black, curly hair, a round, happy face and spoke very softly, almost inaudibly. Val didn't endorse military protocol. In civilian life Val was a history and sociology professor at the University of Washington. He spoke fluent Russian and Polish. He was personally recruited by MID, as were the majority of the officers. America's attempts to understand events in Russia through intelligence and espionage were incompetent. Ryan and Val agreed that most of the Russian peasants and workers were favoring the Bolshevik movement. They had no doubt that the Bolsheviks were going to prevail. Besides, any political opposition to the revolution was summarily eliminated.

A police network had been formed almost immediately; called CHEKA, it was a fanatical secret police, ruthless in its quest to assure obedience to the new order. Hundreds of thousands, whole families, were executed. If an officer defected to the White Russian side, the family, including children of any age, were eliminated. Earlier, Ryan had made many friends among the Russian people, who now turned on him. Their lives depended on their open denial of friendship with anyone who was not a professed Party member. The reports and concerns of Val Agranof fell on deaf ears. Some American politicians still believed that there was hope for a White-Russian counterattack supported with money, guns, and if need be, American troops. Ryan was sure that America's open support of the anti-Bolsheviks would only force them to withdraw from the war. Without Russia the war would undoubtedly be prolonged.

Up to this time, Ryan was spared the real face of the war, the mangled bodies, the effects of mustard gas and roasted human flesh inhaled in the fiery tongue of a new anti-personnel weapon called a flame thrower. No, Ryan Thornton spent the war being programmed into discerning the difference between a White Russian and a Red, the latter being the consummate enemy. Mail was censored, if he got any at all. Any reference in letters from Kathleen that might give insight to the attitude of the country was blacked out. He was, however, allowed the letter that informed him of Kathleen's pregnancy. Ecstatic, he mentally counted back the days. It would probably be a June baby. He had always wanted a boy, but in June of 1918 he received a long letter from Kathleen informing him that he had fathered a baby girl and expressing hope that he'd be happy with the name she had chosen, Maggie.

Ryan was homesick, anxious to see his new daughter. His concerns about this war ending soon seemed well founded, since the new government of Russia had signed a peace treaty with Germany. Now there was no doubt that all those German divisions would be assigned to the Western Front. The treaty was a slap in the face to England, France, and America. There was even talk at the embassy of American troops being sent into Russia to fight with the White Russians to regain power. Ryan knew that this would be foolhardy and only aid in prolonging the war. His was a voice lost in the roar of a tornado. The war did finally end and the Armistice was signed in November. Ryan was elated to be returning home. Home for Christmas.

Everyone was proud of Ryan; it appeared that it was indeed going to be the best Christmas ever. They had a lot to celebrate. Many young men came home to bands of glory. They had turned the tide of Germany's aggression. They had made the world safe for democracy. The war for Ryan Thornton was fast becoming a bad dream, an event somewhere in the past, a short span of time in another dimension. Sometimes it was hard to believe that it all had really happened.

At Christmas, Ryan vowed that his family was more important than anything else. He vowed never to leave them again. It was a pledge he wouldn't be able to keep.

CHAPTER THIRTY-FIVE
Shevogarsk, Northern Russia

R YAN TOOK A deep breath. He slowly raised his head above the shallow trench. He had cut the finger tips off the army-issue woolen gloves so that he might better sense the trigger on his semi-automatic rifle. All around him the landscape was white, and although it was daytime there was no sun and the temperature was fifty degrees below zero. Through the falling snow he could barely see the grove of trees a hundred yards away. He waited patiently, not breathing; his forefinger had already frozen to the trigger. He forced himself to wait a little longer. Just as he was about to ease himself back down in the trench, a frozen white plume of expelled air appeared and Ryan squeezed off a burst of fire. Before the crack filled the air, a great explosion of red punctuated the white landscape just below the still, frozen breath. Immediately after killing the white-uniformed Communist, he dropped down to the safety of the trench. As he did so, six inches of snow-covered tundra were ripped away by machine-gun fire. He was amazed at how close he had come to dying. It was ironic, he thought, that in this place breathing was hazardous to your health.

"Dat vos gud, yeah." The soldier nudging Ryan was a White Russian fighting against Red Russians to reinstate Nicholas. He was a professional soldier, however, one of those kind that stay corporal all their Army career. Ivan Bishoff was forty or so, Ryan couldn't really tell. Behind the Russian's coal-black vacuous eyes, a small part of his brain still remembered his family, the family he once shared and loved, and which now, because of his alliance with the Czar, had been executed. All that was gone now. Corporal Bishoff didn't have much to live for except to kill Bolsheviks. His eyebrows were almost as bushy as his mustache, now frozen with residue of dribble from his nose. The stubble on his face was two weeks old and he hadn't bathed in as long. What was left of a cigar was stuck in the side of his mouth. Keeping low, he lit it, almost igniting his mustache. The cigar helped kill the stench. For two weeks the trench had been their living quarters. They ate in it, slept in it, and used it as a latrine. Ryan thought if he ever survived this unknown war at Shevogarsk in Northern Russia he would settle down in some place with a warm climate, like Florida or Southern California.

Just a few months earlier the real war had been declared over. After the surrender, Ryan was relieved of his duty in Moscow and arrived home in late November. Even though he hadn't fired a shot during the war, he was treated like a hero. He felt the honor was undeserved. He didn't have much time to regret his non-combatant status. He was fortunate; he was able to spend Christmas at home. Ryan gazed down vacantly at the Enfield. Now he was considering the futility of America's involvement here in this Godforsaken Russian wasteland. At least he didn't feel singled out. Agranoff was in charge of the small force and had been promoted to major. Supposedly, at least as it was outlined to him, some ad hoc committee in Washington decided to send American soldiers to help the vastly out-numbered anti-Communists defeat the Bolsheviks. Now, in the middle of January 1919, he knew this was a hopeless cause. Why didn't Washington? So here he was, a sergeant in Company A of the 339th Infantry. Some of the other Russian allies had already defected. Ryan knew they couldn't hold on much longer, not without back-up artillery.

"Next time—don't kill him, you must wound him. Dat takes another man to take care of him, okay—two less to deal with." Ivan spat the cigar stub without touching it, "Okay?" he nudged Ryan again.

"Okay, Ivan, okay."

"Bolshevik bastards, dat's vot dey are—low-life vermin," he said, reverting to his native Russian. Ryan smiled. He genuinely enjoyed the older Russian's company, especially when he spoke his native language. Ryan found it interesting that Ivan, when communicating in English, wasn't crude, but articulate and insightful.

"You know, Ivan, this is an impossible situation here," he said in Russian. "We've been pushed back about as far as we can go." He didn't want to use the word *retreat*. "The Port of Archangel is the next stop and that's the end of the line."

Ivan looked despondently at the American-made rifle. He rubbed the stock affectionately. "I suppose deep down in my heart I've always known there was no going back—I mean, to the way things used to be. You'll be all right though, my American friend. You'll go back to America, to your family."

Ryan reached for the brass Primus and shook it, making sure it had sufficient fuel. "I hope so, anyway, if I do get out of this mess, you're coming too," Ryan said enthusiastically.

Ivan shook his head. "Thanks, Ryan, but there's no place for me in America. This is my home," he gestured around him. "Mother Russia. I can't imagine being forced into exile never to return. No, my friend, I will die on Russian soil before I'm forced to retreat."

Ryan opened two cans of bully beef and scooped the contents into his mess pan. He pumped the Primus until the fuel pressurized. After the third match, the gas ignited. It took little time to warm the meat, which he shared with his friend. Ivan inhaled the meat and burped.

"Delicious. You Americans really know how to eat." After they had eaten, Ivan reached deep into the pocket of the heavy overcoat and produced a flat flask. He shook it and grinned widely. Then he pulled the cork and took a long swig.

"Ahh, now that's nectar from heaven, Comrade Ryan." He wiped the top with his sleeve. Ryan found the gesture at sterilization ironically humorous. His sleeve was filthy. "Vashe zdorovge," he said, offering Ryan the flask.

"And to your health, Ivan." Ryan shook after gulping down the mouthful of vodka.

In the next weeks they shared more than food. They shared stories of the good times before the war. Ivan was tired of fighting, having been at it since 1914. Ryan talked about his family, his feelings toward his father, the guilt in refusing to believe in his father's innocence. Ivan was understanding, even more so than a priest, Ryan thought. They had become more than friends. Their very survival depended on each other. Ryan couldn't remember feeling this close to anyone before, not even Kathleen.

As the months passed, the weather warmed and the planes came. Russian planes. The Bolsheviks came in great waves; still white-clad, they forced the 339th and its allies to within ten miles of Archangel. Their group was now reduced to fifty or so men. The biplanes came almost daily, dropping leaflets demanding surrender. No prisoners would be taken if the Americans persisted in fighting.

Major Agranoff confronted a crisis. What was left of the heavy artillery backing the small force had been abandoned. Ryan reported to Agranoff every day, given the threat of anniliation. After surviving another attack, Ryan arranged for a burial crew. Five Russian allies and two more American soldiers would go to their eternal resting places in the cold tundra. No one would be paying visits here, Ryan thought as he entered the temporary dug-out they called headquarters, a hole in the earth covered by large timbers. He could feel the tension. The radio operator was frantically trying to reach Archangel. Agranoff was occupied sorting papers. He threw most of them into a fifty-gallon drum that had been set alight.

"Oh, Ryan, do me a favor, will you?" Agranoff asked casually. "Assess our supplies and prepare the company to move out. We'll need sleds for the wounded—and, ah, see if we have enough mules. If not, we'll have to use some of the stronger men to carry the litters."

"We're going home?" Ryan asked. It was difficult not to sound like an excited schoolboy.

"I hope so, Ryan. There's nothing left here. Even the damn Russians we've tried to help have deserted or defected."

"Oh, I think we still have some dedicated comrades left, Val. Anyway, I'll get on it right away. I'll have Corporal Bishoff organize the Russians for the withdrawal." The bunker shook as a shell landed nearby. Ryan waited before leaving.

"Oh, Ryan."

"Yes, Val?" Ryan turned.

"I don't want you to tell the Russians anything. They won't be coming with us, and that's straight from the top. It would not be a good idea to break the news now. We'll tell them when we reach Archangel." Ryan was stunned. He had never questioned an order before. Val Agranoff was more like a friend. During their time together at the embassy in Moscow he never found it necessary to disagree with Agranoff, but this was different. This was wrong. Unjust. They had fought alongside these Russians for months! Washington had forced them into a union, a worthy cause, or so they thought, and now because the mission was failing, just get the hell out? Leave them to a fate you wouldn't wish on a dog? Ryan was furious.

"Excuse me—Val, did I hear you right? We're retreating—as a group that is, us and the Russians, even using them to help us with our wounded?" Ryan hesitated, "And they're not coming with us? To America, I mean?"

"Right—that's the idea, Ryan—carry on."

"I'm not finished yet, Val. You mean we leave them to the Communists at Archangel? Hell, Val, you know as well as I do they'll be slaughtered, for Christ's sake."

"I don't have time right now, Ryan, to argue the morality of the situation. I have my orders and now you have yours." His voice was strained, higher than usual, and his mouth was tight.

"Look, Val, I know how you feel about—"

"That's Major Agranoff, Sergeant Thornton, and I'd greatly appreciate your support here. I don't have time to discuss this. Now be a good soldier and move along." Then he raised his voice. "Before I have your ass court-martialed." He turned back, his face fierce. Ryan froze in the entrance, dumbfounded. "That will be all, Sergeant."

Ryan saluted and left. He knew that this was not Val's choice. His friend, obedient to a higher authority, was blindly following orders—as he himself would have to. It was easy for those who hadn't fought alongside these Russians to make insensitive decisions about their fate. Ryan shook off the visions of Ivan and the others being riddled by Bolshevik killing squads. He thought about the advantage to himself. He would be going home. Archangel would have Navy support. They would have some real fire-power to back them up.

The days passed. The Communist barrages were becoming more frequent. Men and animals were left where they fell; there was no time to bury them, no time to say a short prayer. Many were suffering from frost bite, their bodies dying a little at a time.

Ryan studied the map. Another day and they would reach Archangel. So far they had managed to stay ahead of the Communists. They were being nudged slowly into a retreat rather than extinction, action overcoming hopelessness with wishful thinking.

Soon the Communists were attacking what was left of the 339th. Tacticians could say that a stealthy approach would have been more advantageous, but Ryan knew now the reason for the collective frenzy, the screams as they charged. Sunlight reflected off the hundred or so cold, steel bayonets. Ryan had heard stories of hand-to-hand combat. Others who had been exposed to this kind of warfare said that it helped to scream, to yell like a banshee as if to confirm that you were still alive. His ruminations stopped when he heard someone up the line yell for fixed bayonets. Momentarily confused, Ryan fumbled with the long blade. He had lost all memory of his training. The blade wasn't engaging as it was supposed to, as it did in basic training. He was mad at himself for not being prepared.

The screams were getting closer now, accompanied by automatic fire. At last the jagged blade snapped into place! Ivan was already hunched over the trench beside him, carefully metering every round. Ammunition was scarce; each shot had to stop a man. Ryan took a deep breath, forcing composure. Figures in white loomed ahead. He took his time. It was like shooting ducks at a carnival, each man reeling back with arms and legs flailing, some grabbing at the place where they'd been shot as if to reach inside and retract the bullet. To his right a number of the screaming

Bolsheviks had already swarmed the trench. They came relentlessly, as though dispensed from an assembly line producing white-shrouded mannequins. The rifles were useless at close range.

Bayonets were another story, ripping through the heavy clothing and tearing into the soft flesh. They continued to come, madmen from hell with wild contorted faces, so close now as to almost touch the defenders. He continued to silence their screams. Their fierce faces froze with mouths still agape and great lifeless bulging eyes staring vacantly where they lay, some with eyes that had been plucked out by a bayonet, leaving deep mucous sockets oozing blood. In an instant a huge form was silhouetted against the sun. Ryan rolled and allowed the bayonet to bury itself in the wall of the trench behind him. With just enough room to make the thrust, Ryan plunged the steel, ripping into the man's throat. The man clutched at his neck and Ryan stabbed again, first finding resistance in the man's heavy clothing, finally pushing to the hilt, splattering the white tunic like an abstract painting. It had lasted just moments, yet to Ryan the moments seemed like hours.

He sat in the trench with his legs outstretched, his back supported by the wall. His rifle and blood-stained bayonet lay beyond his reach, as if removing him from the instruments that had caused death around him. It didn't bother him that he sat in a pool of blood contained by the hard clay. His fear gone, he could see the quiet, drawn, white faces, bloodless, some with their eyes open, their fear still there.

"Holy Jesus, will I ever be able to forget this?" he mumbled. Close by, Ivan was wiping his bayonet.

"What did you say, Comrade?" Ryan looked up at Ivan. Just as moments earlier the loud gunfire and screams were deafening, now it was quiet except for an occasional soft moan. "You said something, Comrade—I was just asking what you said," Ivan repeated. Ryan's head dropped back down.

"I—I just don't understand what the hell I'm doing here. I've been pinching myself till it hurts—hoping to wake up from a nightmare. We're just like animals." He looked up at Ivan. "No—not animals. Animals don't do this to one another."

Ivan sat on his haunches. "That's not so, my friend. Animals do kill—for territory, even love. Males protect their sows—yes, and they fight for survival."

"No, Ivan—not like this they don't. They fight with what God gave them. We manufacture insidious weapons, mines and grenades that blow people apart. Bullets that rip through a body, a small insignificant hole, that doesn't come close to reflecting the devastation within." He reached for the rifle beside him, "And this damn thing…" His voice becoming more strained, he unclipped the bayonet. "This goddamn invention with jagged teeth and hooked end—designed by some—some psychopath, slices through clothes and flesh and on retraction pulls intestines back with it." He gestured at the dead Bolshevik. "Hell, in some ways he's better off than we are."

Ivan shook him by the shoulder. "Don't let those thoughts enter your brain, my young friend, or indeed you will end up like this poor soul. Never forget, the whole object here is living."

"You call this living, Ivan?"

"Yes! I call this living." He clutched his chest. He began to feel his body. "Yes, I'm alive, Comrade, and for now at least I live another hour—another day." He grabbed at his crotch. "Even the little things are important." Ryan finally smiled at his overactive friend. "If you live long enough, Ryan, you'll come to have an appreciation for life like no other. Certainly not some civilian in the city working ten hours and coming home to a fat sow of a wife and ten screaming kids. You'll know what it's like to live." He stood, turned his back, and faced the trench wall. Ryan could hear the splash, see the hot stream surrounding his Russian friend, smell the urine. "Ahh," Ivan sighed, "dis is living. You know, Ryan, I wouldn't trade this moment for a million rubles."

They both laughed. "Now clean that bayonet of yours. It works better when it's bright and shiny—see." He held his toward Ryan and rubbed the solid steel proudly. "See—like this."

In the days that followed there were more attacks, always announced by the same early-warning screams. Ryan felt more confident with Ivan close by. The Russian was an indefatigable presence. Ryan had lost track of the days. With each night's passing, the reality of survival and home was becoming a sharper image. Archangel was getting closer and that meant home and Kathleen. It was all right now to reminisce. Sitting back in the trench, he closed his eyes and lifted his head to feel the warm morning sun, and for a brief moment he was back with her. She was in his arms, their lips barely touching, soft, moist, slowly opening to one another, his hands exploring, removing the strap on her satin slip. His palm was slowly rotating, barely touching, priming her sensuality. He left her mouth and gently kissed her neck, her shoulder, his mouth opening to receive her firm breast, then puzzled because she screamed, screamed louder, evoking sounds—of gunfire accompanied by a chorus of piercing shrieks.

Instantly he was upright, dismissing the dream and adapting immediately to the role he was beginning to play so well, that of a perfectly desensitized killing machine. They were coming again and it didn't bother him that he was becoming like Ivan. It was a choice he made willingly to guarantee his survival. Both fired a round simultaneously into the same camouflaged figure and gave each other a thumbs up. As if pushed by someone, Ryan was thrown backwards. He knew he'd been hit, yet he felt no pain. Still aware of his surroundings, he raised himself in time to thrust at other Communists as they entered the trench. He turned to fight another enemy soldier only to find the stock of a rifle smashing his face. Knocked backwards, he lay still. Visions of what heaven must be like streamed into his semiconsciousness. Kathleen was part of his reveries again. Then the twins floated silently like an abstract dream. They moved on, away, as he became fretful, thinking about the daughter he might never know. Hours were passing in seconds. Although aware of the scruffy soldier standing above him, he didn't care. He saw clearly the steel scabbard at the end of the rifle pulling back, ready to thrust into his body. He had no strength to move, no will to live. He closed his eyes and waited, hoping the Russian's aim would be true and find his heart. What hit his head was Ivan's body, landing across him, pushing the intruder to the ground, and dispatching him with a single blow.

"Spacebo," Ryan whispered.

"My pleasure, Comrade," Ivan said, straining to remove the bayonet from the Russian's ribs.

Ivan was sprawled on Ryan, breathing heavy, his breath foul. What had been offensive to Ryan was now acceptable, yes, welcomed. The man smelled like a latrine. Both sat upright, Ryan finding it more difficult. As quickly as it had begun, it was over. It had lasted only moments. Those still alive were exhausted. Agranoff popped his head over the trench.

"You okay, Ryan?"

"I think so."

"Your face looks like it's seen better days."

Ryan put his hand to his cheek and flinched. "You're not going to believe this, but I think I've been shot—no idea where though." Ryan cautiously brushed his fingers through his hair, prepared for the worst. A hole maybe, or some indication of where he might have been hit. His fingers continued to return to the only area where he could feel a small bruise and a little discomfort, insignificant compared to his bloody cheekbone. "I guess it's not as bad as I thought," Ryan said.

Meanwhile Ivan had picked up Ryan's helmet. "Your guardian angel has been good to you today, my comrade." Ivan's lower lip hung involuntarily and the black eyes panned downwardly to the helmet. His animated finger poked through the hole left by the bullet. Ryan took the bruised helmet and placed it back on his head, the hole corresponding to the lump just above his right temple. The men laughed nervously, then went about their business—preparing for their continued retreat.

By the time they reached Archangel, fewer than thirty Americans remained. More of their Russian allies had defected, always after one of the many charges. Ryan feared the hand-to-hand combat more than anything else. Each engagement would be his last. He chalked up his survival to his determination to live, to see Kathleen again, to be with his family. He was vulnerable, a state of mind that made him more careful.

Val was busy trying to hold things together, afraid that one of these times, the whole Russian contingent they had come to aid would revolt against the Americans in a show of good faith before their defection. He had long talks with them in perfect Russian, describing what would become of them if they moved over to the Bolsheviks. Shooting would be too good for them; hanging would be likely, not hanging carried out swiftly, not hanging from a platform, not a drop snapping the vertical vertebrae, issuing instant death. Rather, they would be pulled inches off the ground by ropes tied to their necks, their bodies dangling, some surviving as long as an hour. Val made every effort to keep the White Russians focused on their original intent to suppress the revolution.

Ryan was relieved that Ivan hadn't made it to Archangel. During one of their usual conversations, with no apparent danger from attack, Ivan was killed instantly by a sniper. The bullet entered his forehead, centered between the eyes. Ryan would remember the man responsible for his survival. Ryan would live with the knowledge that he could not help his Russian friend.

There didn't seem to be a great rush to get the Americans on board the converted freighter. It was as if their pursuers wanted them to leave. The Bolsheviks had already won the battle. The Americans and their allies had been beaten. Ryan and Val were the last Americans to leave Russian soil. To avoid a scene, the Russian allies were told that another ship was on the way, coming for them. They were told that they would be going to Finland temporarily, for screening, before continuing on to America. Ryan couldn't believe how naive they were, how easily they accepted the gross fabrication. Val had done a remarkable job of diverting panic. *How they trusted him,* Ryan thought. He felt sorry for Val and knew that he would have to reconcile over and over for the rest of his life this and the bloody action that would follow.

The ship finally pulled slowly away from the dock. Ryan acknowledged the waving soldiers waiting for a ship that would never come. He waved back at the men he had befriended for the past four months, and he cried.

Part Two

Part Two

CHAPTER THIRTY-SIX
Boston, 1933

O N SEEING DR. Joseph Kortner the first time, Kathleen sized him up as another know-it-all. When Kathleen was introduced to him by Dr. Paul Wallace, the head of pediatrics, Kortner seemed to be an arrogant skeptic. He dismissed her as one might a school child or simple hireling. It was, however, her duty as matron to introduce the new orthopedic surgeon from Austria to the young patients in her ward, and she refused to let his superior German attitude bridle her enthusiasm.

Joseph Kortner had studied at the College of Surgeons in Berlin and had learned to speak English while studying at the Royal College of Orthopedic Surgeons in London. He appeared to be in excellent physical condition. He was forty-six, a tall, wiry man with deep-set, penetrating, ice-blue eyes that peered from behind gold-rimmed glasses. His brown hair was combed straight back with no part. He had been in America for just a month, having left Austria with his wife and two children to avoid what he believed inevitable—the annexation of his country to Germany. He was a Jew, and unfortunately, in the wrong place and time if he was to save his family. Friends had written from Germany of the growing hatred there. It wasn't even acceptable for German gentiles to have Jewish friends. Although he thought of himself as Austrian, in the eyes of the new regime his nationality was inconsequential; he was a Jew. It was inconceivable to him how they could think he was an enemy. During the Great War he was decorated for his service in the hospital corps. Yet, to the state, he was a Jew, a Jew alone, not a veteran, not a surgeon, not a husband and father, only an outcast. So he and his wife, Wieslawa, from Warsaw, emigrated to America.

Here he was in a Boston hospital, having left a lucrative and eminent practice, to be introduced to his new patients *by a nurse*. He had expected another doctor, one of his own. He was aware of America's lack of regard for protocol; still, he thought that this inattention to authority and rank would never affect him. Her low expectations of him corresponded with his low expectations of her.

Kathleen was as professional as she could be. She introduced Kortner to every child and reviewed assiduously each medical record. There wasn't a patient over fourteen years old in the ward. All were afflicted with deformities resulting from infantile paralysis. Most were kept immobilized, in casts or splints, which rendered them rigid and unyielding as concrete blocks. They had to be fed, dressed, bathed, and their toilet needs attended to. This treatment for poliomyelitis, which was the policy of most modern physicians, supposedly relieved the painful contractions. Kathleen thought the remedy was unsympathetic and archaic. They came to the last bed in the ward. The little girl had just been admitted and looked fearful as they approached. She was in the early acute stages of the disease. Kortner, who up to this point had made only facial expressions, examined the chart closely.

"How come this child is not in splints, Nurse?"

Kathleen hesitated. Sensing his displeasure with her qualifications, she wasn't sure whether to accept his tone as smugness or as genuine interest. She decided that he was sincerely searching for an explanation.

"I'm not sure, Doctor, what you think of mere nurses taking on—shall we say, 'more advanced duties.'"

"I don't understand, Nurse…" He tried to think of her name.

"Thornton," she said gently. "Kathleen Thornton."

"Yes, I remember the Kathleen—such a beautiful name. Irish, isn't it? I should have recognized the accent; however, I am not very good at that yet since I have one myself." He smiled for the first time since they had met. "I have a daughter named Katia. I think it's the same as Kathleen, no?"

She was totally disarmed by his smile. Maybe it was the way he spoke of his daughter. She considered him to be human after all.

"I would think so," she said.

"And what about the splints, Nurse Thornton? I'm curious why this child is not immobilized." He gestured to some of the younger patients who were also free from their splints. "What about them?"

"They're my patients, Doctor," she said with a smile that most men found difficult to resist.

"Yours? I don't understand. Nurses have patients here in America?"

"No, Doctor, nurses do not have patients here in America—well not normally, anyway. You see, I have a daughter who was stricken with infantile paralysis four years ago."

He interrupted. "I'm terribly sorry, Nurse Thornton, it must have been awful for you."

"Well—yes. Actually it was a nightmare. Maggie, that's her name."

He broke in, "What a nice name."

"Thank you." Kathleen continued, "Maggie was totally paralyzed. She couldn't sit, she couldn't walk. She couldn't draw like other children, and she was in great pain. She was eleven years old and suffered more than most of us will in a lifetime. To look at her now, Doctor, it is hard to believe she is the same little girl. Dr. Wallace was very straightforward and didn't have much hope for her survival."

What Kathleen did not tell Kortner was that despite the painful affliction, Maggie had an enchanting personality. She had a passion for life and had been endowed with all the charm and magnetism of her mother. Maggie's courage affected everyone around her. Happiness for Maggie was a painless hour. It was easy to see how she could influence so many people. Kathleen was the only one who knew of her agony. Often, while massaging Maggie's twisted, aching limbs, Kathleen cried inwardly, knowing that even her attempt to soothe the pain caused more anguish. Sometimes Kathleen tenderly kissed the deformed legs as a mother would a child with a minor abrasion. Many times it was also a way to hide a tear, asking God to take her precious Maggie to Him. Usually it was Maggie who brought her mother back to reality with a smart or humorous comment through gritted teeth. Now her looks were striking. Bountiful curls hung haphazardly over a round face that seemed luminously white.

Kathleen also refrained from telling Kortner the personal shortcomings their marriage endured and Ryan's helplessness in those early years. Not knowing how to solve Maggie's suffering, he turned to drinking. She finally brought Ryan to his senses, admonishing him for placing his faith in the expectations of doctors who, in her opinion, knew little of faith and self-healing. She told him she was not about to take care of him too. To heal their daughter she needed his help.

Ryan, back to his old self, fully embraced the challenge never to give up on Kathleen or Maggie again. Together they went about Maggie's survival with a passion. Although they knew there was no cure, their combined determination to treat the child and instill a sense of worthiness was successful.

It was obvious that Kortner was uncomfortable listening to her describe the hot-soaked towels and her daughter's deformed limbs. He handed her the chart and gently pulled back the sheet covering the child. The girl's right foot was deformed and twisted outward. When he made an effort to straighten it, she flinched.

"This child, in my professional opinion, will suffer greatly, and quite unnecessarily, I might add, unless an orthodox splint is applied." He studied Kathleen's face, hoping for some sign of agreement.

"I didn't say that the treatment I gave my daughter was not without some pain. Naturally there's pain, initially, to get the muscles moving. As you can see, Doctor," she gestured to the little girl, "it takes a great deal of patience to re-educate the muscles."

"Re-educate the muscles?" His head dropped and now he looked at her quizzically over the top of his glasses.

"I can only tell you what has worked for my daughter, Doctor. Yes, I believe that the muscle function can only be restored by massaging and working them and not confining them to some rigid brace."

"And that's what you call re…" he hesitated. "Re-education?"

"That's what I believe takes place, yes." Kathleen realized it was time to hold her tongue. After all, she didn't need his approval for anything. He wasn't the head of the department. She had already been given approval to use physiotherapy. She decided that she would have time to explain her theory to the new skeptic from Austria later.

"I would very much like to meet your daughter. Do you have photos of her before the treatment?"

"Of course, Doctor. You could also talk to Dr. Wallace," she said brusquely. "It was he who treated her in the conventional methods before I grew weary of seeing her paralyzed, strapped to a board. Finally, I brought her home and asked Dr. Wallace if I could try something different. He agreed and within three months she could sit up and eat—using her own hands, I might add."

"Sounds like a miracle to me," he said, "and I mean that as a compliment. Please, do not be offended by my questions. I am truly curious and I sense that you are a little defensive about your treatment—no?"

They both smiled. "I guess I am, Doctor."

He reached into his waistcoat pocket and flicked the cover on the gold watch.

"It's after eleven," he said, "what do you say we discuss this over lunch?"

"I'd like that very much, Doctor." She closed the door behind them.

"I find it interesting that polio is just one among our common enemies, Nurse."

"Oh?" she inquired.

"I am talking about England," he said, changing the subject. "We both have fought the English."

Kathleen smiled, "Yes, Doctor, but we finally won, didn't we."

The summer of 1933 passed quickly for Kathleen. As the end of September drew close, Joseph Kortner was beginning to show a keener interest in her treatment of paralysis, more so than any of the other doctors. He was amazed with Maggie's partial recovery and attributed this not to any miracle but to Kathleen Thornton's perseverance. Every week for three months he examined Maggie's progress. Kathleen convinced him that the muscle spasm that constantly accompanied the pain was the only rational explanation for the neck and upper rigidity. He concluded that with the exception of her leg movements, Maggie could do everything other normal children could. More than anything in the world he wanted to avoid dampening her spirits, but he did caution her not to expect total recovery. Kathleen's enthusiasm never waned. It was she who rested her hand on his arm and exuberantly told him that everything would be all right, that Maggie would one day walk without the aid of braces—and look who's getting personally involved. Kathleen was happier than she'd been in a long time. She had more freedom for hospital work now that the boys were back in school.

Sometimes it bothered her a little that she didn't have more time for Ryan. Usually when these feelings occurred, she dismissed them because he never seemed to complain. After the war he had gone to work for Chuck Boyle, and his schedule was even busier than hers. When they did have time for one another, which was after dinner late in the evening, they talked about each other's events of the day. Their conversations were seldom perfunctory; he spoke of details in a case that might have made earlier headlines, such as a bank robbery or a slanderous account of some Boston blueblood who had cheated on the government—or in this society, even worse, his wife. More often than not, the conversation reverted to Kathleen's pursuits. Even when they discussed politics she managed to find a parallel to polio. He was a strong supporter of Franklin Roosevelt and the New Deal; she believed that the President, who eleven years earlier was paralyzed from the waist down, was an asset to her cause. She didn't wish the disabling disease on anyone; however, she believed that the only way to beat this horrible plague was through the attention given prominent people stricken with it.

"Then and only then will we find a vaccine," she would say.

Many times Kortner would look at her in disbelief and remind her of her Catholicism, which always guaranteed a sign of the cross followed by a quick Confiteor. It was just one of their usual visits, only this time Maggie had complained of a pain above her knee.

"We will have you walking without those contraptions in no time, Maggie," Kortner said, with his back to the girl. When he finished studying the x-ray, he walked to the light switch and in an instant Maggie was rubbing her eyes. He helped her to stand.

"I want you to put as much weight as you can bear on your right leg now, Maggie, okay?" He knelt on one leg and began to place pressure with both hands. Slowly his hands moved from below her knee joint, pressing gently, as he looked for some reaction. Just before he placed his fingers to a point above her right knee, he looked at her with what seemed like fear in his sunken eyes. He knew by the way she tightened her face that he had located the tumor.

"It is all right to cry out if it hurts." He stood and patted her head. "Of course I should know better than to think that with your mother's blood in you I would expect anything but indefatigable bravery, no?"

Her smile was familiar to him. He had grown very fond of her, and judging by the puzzled look on her face, he surmised she hadn't understood a word he had said. "I am so sorry that my English makes it difficult for you to understand me."

Her face registered a sad, apologetic expression. "Oh no, Doctor, really—you're actually very easy to understand. It's my fault that I don't understand. Your English is fine—some of the words I'm not familiar with, that's all."

"Sometimes, Maggie, you give me reason to believe that I have so much to learn about humility. You are always giving me the benefit of the doubt, no? Anyway, I would like it if you would sit here while I go talk with your mother—okay?"

"Okay" she repeated.

He found Kathleen in the children's ward trying to straighten a little boy's leg. One knee was drawn up and tucked under his chin and with every effort she made to draw it away, he screamed in pain. Realizing she wasn't going to have much success, she gently wrapped the leg with a hot towel. She then wiped his tears and held him, rocking back and forth. "There, there, everything's going to be all right." Finally, Dr. Kortner caught her attention. "Doctor! How long have you been standing there?"

"Long enough to witness your pain," he said sympathetically.

"Look at this, will you," she said. Ignoring his empathetic comment, she held the boy's right foot. "This condition is not caused by the paralysis, rather by a spasm. You tie this boy's foot to a board and you alienate the muscle from the brain."

He gave her a faint smile. "You never stop, do you?"

"Not as long as I continue to see progress, Doctor. How's Maggie?" she asked as she covered the boy's leg with the sheet.

"That is what I came to talk to you about."

She turned and looked at him squarely, immediately frightened by his tone. "You examined her—all went well, I assume." Her smile was halfhearted.

"Kathleen." He hesitated. "You know that I am not going to hold anything back from you..."

"No, of course not, Doctor." Her voice was shaky. She stood and felt her legs tremble. She stared blankly at the wall behind him on which hung a reproduction of a Degas. That painting of the little ballerinas would forever remind her of this moment. He didn't have to say more. He would never be this cautious unless there was something radically wrong.

"Please, Kathleen, it is just a preliminary diagnosis. Let's not talk here." He took her arm. "See for yourself. I want to show you the x-rays."

She moved with him through the long corridor and up a flight of stairs, not remembering time or who she might have passed. Before they went into his office, he told her Maggie was still in there and she would have to act as normal as possible, for the child's sake. She had a lot of experience in that role. Maggie was exactly where he had left her, sitting on the edge of the examining table. In that instant, when she entered the room, her demeanor changed. One would never know she had questions that needed answering.

"Hi, Mother—Dr. Kortner wants to show you my progress," she said eagerly, "and I don't have that pain in my knee anymore."

"That's the best word anyone could tell me, Maggie," Kathleen said, beaming. A rush of protectiveness flooded her. She went right to her daughter and gave her a great hug. "Why don't I take you down to the waiting room? You can read a book there. The doctor and I want to review your progress."

He thought Kathleen was remarkable. "Are you going to be all right?" he asked.

Kathleen led her daughter out and looked back. "We'll find our way just fine, Doctor—thank you."

He had turned on the lightbox behind the film by the time she returned. She was maneuvering a little steadier.

"Now, Doctor, what's this preliminary diagnosis of yours?"

He pointed with his pen to a mass just above the right knee. "This is what I am concerned about, Kathleen. Maggie has a great deal of pain when I apply pressure to the mass. I have no doubt that it is a tumor."

"A tumor? Are you sure? You don't think it's malignant, do you?"

"Kathleen, please, it is too early to tell. I need to do a biopsy. Let us not expect the worst."

He gently moved her to the chair. She was completely submissive.

"What if it isn't benign? Can we operate?"

"We will cross that bridge when we come to it, Kathleen."

"She won't..." Kathleen was desperately trying to retain her composure. "Her leg—she won't lose it, will she?"

His silence answered her question and the blood seemed to drain from her face. Her hand traced her quivering mouth as she tried to hold back the need to cry out.

"If you are up to it, Kathleen, I would very much like to do the biopsy tomorrow."

"Yes, yes, of course, Doctor," she murmured. For a moment the room was still. She wiped her eyes. "I'd like to know what the chances are of saving Maggie's leg. You're familiar with this type of cancer? I want you to give me your expert opinion; I need to know."

"I have seen this many times, Kathleen." His voice was strained. "It is probably on the femur—and, well, if connected tissue is involved..." He hung his lower lip. "I mean if it is a sarcoma—yes, we would most likely have to amputate."

"But, Dr. Kortner, what if you just took all the tissue around the..."

"I am trying to be forthright with you, Kathleen. You asked me for that, no?" She nodded in agreement. "In my opinion, there is a thirty-percent chance, maybe, that it is benign. Of the seventy percent or so of sarcomas, I would say that amputation would be required in maybe ninety percent of the cases."

"Ninety percent?" she asked in a loud whisper. "Thank you for your honesty, you've been a good friend." She rose and moved toward him with outstretched arms, and he held her for a while until she was through sobbing.

By the time they left the hospital, the sky had begun to darken and the street was already bustling. What Kathleen needed was a walk—a brisk walk to think things over. **When we get home that's what I'll do,** she thought. On the bus ride home, Maggie did most of the talking, which wasn't unusual. Kathleen heard nearly all of what she had to say, especially questions about the procedure tomorrow, but she had to be reminded when they arrived at their stop.

That evening she phoned Ryan, who was investigating a case that had taken him to Atlanta. Even though she sounded positive and didn't divulge the chances of a sarcoma, he was devastated by the news and arranged to fly back the following morning. Knowing that Ryan was returning gave her some relief; she needed him more than ever. After a sleepless night, Kathleen washed with cold water and awakened Maggie, who seemed to be looking forward to the experience. Before they left the house, Maggie told her the pain had returned.

They arrived at the hospital an hour early. Joseph Kortner was already there to greet them. He introduced Maggie to his assistant, who would prepare her for surgery. Before Maggie left, she hugged her mother tight and whispered into her ear.

"Mother—I love you very much and I don't want you to worry. I really don't mind if God wants me to be an angel, and I wouldn't have any more pain, would I?"

Kathleen didn't have time to respond, not that she could have. Maggie was hurried off with the nurse. In his usual unguileful way, Kortner told Kathleen that she looked just awful and suggested they have a cup of coffee. She was amused and told him that he looked pretty shabby himself. They talked about everything but the surgery, masking the tension with trivial chitchat and silly humor.

The biopsy took less than an hour, but to Kathleen it seemed like forever. She prayed that God would forgive her for the times she had wished for Maggie's suffering to be over, that He might find mercy and take her to Him. Maggie's life meant more to her now than ever before. Even if it was God's will that Maggie lose her leg, Kathleen knew now she could reconcile herself to the inevitable

Joseph Kortner pushed through the double doors from the operatory and tore the mask from his beaming face. Kathleen quickly rose to meet him.

"I believe it is benign! That's never one hundred percent, mind you, but I am almost certain." She couldn't contain her excitement.

"Oh! Thank God—she's going to be all right, she won't lose her leg will she?"

"I don't think that will be the case, no. Still, we must wait to see what pathology has to say," he said reservedly.

"When can I see her?" she asked anxiously.

"Give her fifteen minutes or so. In the meanwhile, because you're so special, I am going to run the sample to pathology myself. If you can wait around—two hours, maybe three, I will be able to say for sure."

This time the wait was easier. Joseph Kortner's diagnosis was accurate. The tumor was benign.

Ryan arrived in Boston just in time to see his daughter tucked in by the night nurse. Maggie was a veritable chatterbox, going on and on about the surgery. Later that week, Kortner removed the rest of the tumor. It took Maggie almost six months to heal properly. In the meantime, Kathleen had become worried again because the wound had ulcerated and was constantly oozing. At one point she was afraid that Maggie might lose the leg after all. Kortner was not only there for her as a doctor but also as a friend, a true confidant. By summer Maggie was back to walking again with the aid of braces. It was still painful and took concentration and great effort to move her legs. There were times when she lost her balance and refused help, determined to do it alone.

Kathleen was ecstatic with her progress. Kortner did not want to give her false hope and often reminded her that Maggie's immune system wasn't as strong as it was in healthy children. That's why it had taken her so long to recuperate from what he considered minor surgery. The circulation in her lower body was not good, and he more than once mentioned the possibility of a recidivous attack. She would immediately direct his attention to the incredible results the children in her ward were experiencing with muscle rejuvenation. He, like most who came to know her, understood when it was time to concede.

It was as though Kathleen was reliving Ireland's troubles. Her mind reawakened to the confusing times, times that included images of Mercer Street Hospital and a beaten people, self-respect and pride suffocated, and a time of love. She was alone in the house when the letter arrived, interrupting preparation of a surprise party for Ryan's fortieth birthday. She strolled from the dining room into the glaring afternoon sunshine of the kitchen. She was unaware of her surroundings, clutching the letter with both hands and shaking slightly. Her lips moved, barely sounding the words. The formally spaced crest at the top of the letterhead identified the source as Father Donnelly's parish in Clontarf. The letter read:

My dearest Kathleen,

Your mother was kind enough to give me your address.

By the way, she is doing fine, as are the rest of the family. Paddy is still not happy with the exclusion of the North in a United Ireland. I have a feeling we haven't seen the end of the I.R.A.

This letter is long overdue and wasn't possible until now. I promised your father, God rest his soul, that I would never speak to anyone, especially you, Kathleen, about particular events surrounding his escape from Kilmainham Prison.

Kathleen's thoughts revisited her mother's letter three weeks earlier with word of her father's death. She suffered all the usual emotions of separation, including guilt by her absence. Her slim body shook as she continued to read Donnelly's letter, describing in detail Hamilton's courageous plan to rescue her father. The letter went on:

I am heartily sorry that I kept this from you all these years. I also feel that I should share with you another piece of truth that was kept from you all these years. I know for a fact that Liam Riordan had nothing to do with the arrest of your father. He did tell me that investigating your father was his assignment; however, he couldn't go through with it. He loved you more than you'll ever know. In fact, the informer was one of our own. There were many rumors floating around Dublin later on but at the time without any certainty. I will send you a folder that has been in my care. It contains all the paperwork surrounding your father's trouble. It also includes a letter from Nora which I asked her to write. I think you'll find her short epistle persuasive testimony.

Anyway, since we've gotten our independence the need for leniency has never been more imperative. It isn't necessary now for any more bloodshed, neither English nor Irish. I'm sure that this information is of little or no importance to you now, Kathleen; however I write this letter for your children. It would be an awful thing for them to learn that their own father was responsible for your father's imprisonment. Knowing how upset you were at Liam Riordan, I sincerely hope that this affirmation of his innocence will bring you some contentment.

The letter, signed *Reverend Michael Donnelly*, had a postscript: *God Bless you and the family*.

Kathleen read the letter again and thought it interesting that the priest never mentioned Liam Riordan's real name. She laid the letter on the table and went upstairs to the bedroom. She went directly to her armoire and opened the bottom drawer. Moving some articles of clothing aside, she lifted the small wooden box and placed it on the vanity table. Inside she studied the old tarnished photo of her and Liam Riordan. It reminded her of times sharp in her memory. Gingerly she put it back and picked up the cigarette case. She thought Donnelly might know his real name and didn't want her to know. She pondered again the inscription inside, **WA.H.** She shrugged her shoulders and put everything away. It was all in the past, like another life. It wasn't as if she still loved him. However, the letter did make her feel better, at least for the twins' sake, as the priest said.

At the same time, she felt weak and needed to sit. Returning downstairs to the dining room, she poured a generous amount of Irish whiskey in a tumbler, sat down and slowly drank, allowing her mind to wander. Her mind seemed to have no order or reason, just spasmodic images of Dublin. She thought of her introduction to love on the Hill o'Howth, and of the ride back on the tram. She recalled his clumsy attempt to tell her about his indiscretions. Very graphic images now entered her reveries: that fateful day of her father's arrest, her denouncement of Liam Riordan, the pregnancy, and the cold-hearted spiteful declaration to her family, particularly her father. Thoughts of her father made her eyes tear again. She quickly finished the whiskey in an unladylike gulp and braced herself stubbornly. It was too late now for redeeming thoughts; eighteen years had passed and she had her immediate family to consider. She took a match from a box on the mantelpiece and lit a corner of the letter. When it was fully aflame she tossed it in the fireplace. She was bound to eternize the veil of secrecy. Raking up the past was futile; she would divulge what was important to the boys when they were older.

She stayed in her drifting frame of mind until the familiar voice of Maggie jogged her to reality. She was still outside saying goodbye to her classmates. At fifteen she was their miracle child. For a couple of weeks now it had become easier to take care of Maggie since the twins had returned to St. Martin's Minor Seminary. It wasn't that she wanted the boys elsewhere, rather it was Michael's wish to become a priest. Actually, it was more like an obsession. She felt that it was her responsibility to give him every chance. The boys were inseparable, so Lawrence went along. She was glad that Lawrence didn't seem to mind the idea because he needed the exposure a great deal more than Michael. She wished and often prayed that Lawrence would become more like his brother, so on their thirteenth birthdays, with the help of the parish priest, they entered the seminary. Lawrence wasn't impressed with things that were holy. He had no desire to study priestly things; he went along to be with Michael. Kathleen prayed that the Benedictines could teach him more than just to stand straight, break the bread before eating, wash his hands, and recite the repetitious cadences of the rosary.

Like all insightful mothers, she was well aware of their differences. They could deceive everyone except her. One simply could not tell them apart by their speech, mannerisms, or behavior. Sometimes one seemed to know what the other was thinking. One might even finish a sentence for the other. Kathleen wasn't always conscious of their differences. She thanked God for the opposing birthmarks, and she was aware that Lawrence wore a Saint Christopher medal, while Michael wore the Blessed Virgin. It frightened her that Lawrence could be so devious. He could lie, even allowing his brother, in his kindness, to take the blame. No, virtue was not a gift handed down to Lawrence.

One of her lamentable discoveries of their obvious differences was on their seventh birthday. Times were meager. It wasn't long after Ryan's discharge. He had an excellent job with great opportunities, but working as an investigator for Chuck Boyle didn't afford many luxuries. Not wealthy in a material sense, they experienced a richness of another kind. Family members recognized that when it came to giving at holidays and birthdays, the giving was much more important than the gift. Lawrence had difficulty with this idea.

It was colder than ever that winter and Kathleen decided to give the boys warm boots for their birthday. She knew Michael's desire for a sled, and yet, when he opened his gift, he gleamed and thanked her with a big hug. He knew his mother was giving him what he needed most. His brother, on the other hand, after accepting the boots, seemingly in the same spirit, stormed outside and angrily kicked at a lamp-post. He continued until the rugged stitching split at the seams. By ruining the boots he was hurting his mother, hurting her for not giving him what he wanted, the model biplane at Switzer's toy store. Often his obstinacy manifested itself in childish tantrums. Michael was more aware than anyone else of these moments of sardonicism and had become accustomed to his brother's fits of anger, especially when Lawrence didn't get what he wanted.

At first Kathleen believed the bizarre excuse. Lawrence's acting career began early, and he had an incredible knack for the art. He convinced her that he and Michael had been playing in the park close by. While dragging his feet on the round-about, some sand had accumulated in his boots. *Walking home*, he said, *had become almost impossible. We sat on the curb, removed the boots and shook out the sand.* She was remembering how believable he was, looking to his brother for support of the lie. Even the idea of the dangerously driven horse-drawn carriage that ran over the boots, almost killing them both might have been reasonable. It was Michael's inability to lie that made her press on for the truth. She knew she could read him like a book—his totally honest eyes not only couldn't lie, but couldn't even support one. Lawrence never knew that his brother caused the relentless interrogation that followed. She had almost given up hope of ever getting at the truth when he finally capitulated. He poured out everything, his anger at not getting the biplane, even the heartbreaking truth about wanting to hurt her. He cried uncontrollably, begging her forgiveness. Kathleen was steadfast in her resolution to teach him never to lie. It was a week before he could sit fully on his buttocks. That wasn't the first time he had lied, and she was afraid it wouldn't be the last. Later, he would even resort to placing blame for other misgivings on the one he really loved most, his brother.

The closing door caught her attention.

"Hi, Mom, I came home early—wanted to help with Dad's surprise party." She hung her coat and leather satchel on the back of the door.

"Mags," Kathleen gave her daughter a firm hug. Maggie could tell Kathleen had been crying.

"What's wrong?" she said, pulling back. Then, observing the embers in the fireplace, she asked, "More bad news from home? Is it gran'ma?"

"No, darlin', gran'ma is just fine, it was a letter from an old friend."

"From Ireland?" Maggie asked quizzically.

"Yes, from Ireland." She wiped the moisture from her cheeks with the back of her hand and her body shuddered as if to shake off the earlier events. "C'mon," she said. "Let's put some real fun into your ol' dad's fortieth."

"Yes, Mother," Maggie said enthusiastically. "Now tell me who's coming again."

"Oh, you know, friends of your father, people he works with, Mr. Boyle. Then of course there's Father Rafferty, and Dr. Joe, and Wieslawa."

"Oh, good, that means Katia?" Maggie interrupted. "And of course gran'ma Thornton?"

"Of course," Kathleen continued, "Dennis, Madge, and, I imagine, Anne and James." At that, Maggie seemed unresponsive. She played with the lace table cloth. "Now why your long face?" Kathleen placed her hand on Maggie's shoulder.

"Oh, Mother, I just wish that Michael and Lars could be here."

"Yes," Kathleen said forlornly. "So do I."

Father Rafferty gave an impatient shrug and glanced at his watch. "What in the world is keeping them anyway?" He wasn't addressing anyone in particular.

Kathleen entered the crowded living room from the kitchen carrying a tray of hors d'ouevres.

"You should know better than asking a question like that, Father," she said. "He's with Chuck Boyle, isn't he."

"They'll be investigating every pub in Boston," Madge said.

She thought that Ryan was more responsible than that and would most probably be walking through the door any moment now, supporting Chuck. Florence Boyle smiled approvingly. Katy Thornton accompanied some of the song-loving revelers. The old upright piano shook with jubilation as they sang George M. Cohan's *It's a Grand Ole Flag*. Father

Rafferty, the only one who knew all the words, took great pleasure in leading the songsters. Maggie and Katia, with their noses against the window and the curtains drawn behind them, served as lookouts. Kathleen was concerned that Ryan and Chuck might be tipped off by the rousing music and suggested that Father Rafferty hold it down. She then asked her daughter if there was any sign of her father.

"Don't worry, Mother, I'll make sure Daddy will be surprised!"

Kathleen sank into a chair next to Dennis Noonan and sighed. He placed his hand affectionately on her knee.

"Relax," he said. "He'll be here soon and believe me, he'll be surprised as hell." She laughed feebly.

"I guess I'm just concerned that—well you know Ryan. He's not exactly a drinking man, is he? What if Chuck gets him, well…"

He stopped her midsentence, "Drunk?"

"Uh huh," she shrugged.

"I know for a fact that he wouldn't allow any harm to come to Ryan, and besides, Ryan has more control than you give him credit."

"James is getting so tall," she said, changing the subject. "It's been so long since I've seen him. He's still in school?"

"Yes, Harvard. He's taking some post-graduate courses before he joins the firm," Dennis said, twirling the empty glass with both hands.

"Straight A's and still manages time for the boxing team."

"So he's still doing that—that manly thing, is he?"

"He's very good, too, Kathleen," he said, "but still not as good as the ole man."

There was a silence. She brushed a stray hair from her forehead.

"Dennis," she said, turning away, averting his eyes, "have you noticed anything different about Ryan? Lately, I mean?"

"Like within the last few weeks?" He was puzzled by her question. He made an exhausted face, searching for something to say. Finally he spoke, "The only contact I've had with Ryan was a lunch." He thought awhile, "It was the week before last—with Chuck. I ran into them purely by accident. We talked business, politics, you know, that sort of stuff. I don't remember anything in particular about Ryan. He's so quiet it's hard to tell. Why, you aren't having problems are you?"

She moved closer, wishing to be more discreet. "No, it's not like that. He just hasn't been himself—like there's something occupying his mind. Ryan is quiet, yes, but he's always been responsive. It seems that lately I'll ask him something, sometimes two or three times, before he realizes anything. I wish I knew what it was."

Dennis smiled, "Christ, Kathleen, he's going deaf." He knew she thought little of his attempt at humor and mustered a more considerate demeanor. "You want to know what's on his mind? Ask him," he said pointedly.

She finally smiled, "Oh, you're so damn practical."

"That's right, and you women always want ordinary situations to be mysterious. Like I said, you ask Ryan, and I'm sure he'll explain in detail why he's being so goddamn aloof." They laughed.

She stood and straightened the front of her skirt. "I think I'll join the songsters for a while. And thanks for the profound advice." She walked away.

"You'll be getting my bill," he said with a smile.

"Katy, how about an Irish song?" Father Rafferty asked, seeing Kathleen approaching. When she came nearer, he genuflected, pleading, "Please, Kathleen, give us a little song, something lively, like *The Rising of the Moon*."

She graciously agreed, taking a sip of Father Rafferty's whiskey.

Katy Thornton adjusted herself on the piano bench and rendered an impressive arpeggio. Kathleen sang the rebel song, and the songsters joined and raised their glasses at every rousing chorus. Kathleen forgot her melancholy drift of the earlier afternoon. Now her thoughts were filled with happier moments of her youth, the parties. Her reveries alternated bittersweet. She thought about what her mother was doing right at that moment. She thought of her brothers and felt sad, never to be home during their transitions to young men. The last verse was for Jamie, and when she was finished, everyone clapped loudly.

"Oh, go on with ye," she said, embarrassed by the attention. Maggie came to life.

"Quick! Quick, someone get the lights! They're here!"

The room immediately went dark and the occupants quietly gathered around the piano. Katy Thornton readied herself, hands poised for her son's entrance. You could hear them coming up the walk, hushing one another. Neither carried a tune well; however, they made a lot of noise trying. As soon as the door opened, Maggie turned on the lights. Everyone yelled, "Surprise!" Kathleen knew Ryan *was* surprised, his gaping mouth wide, then giving the smiling Chuck Boyle a friendly jab.

"Well you sly, deceptive, son-of-a—"

"That's on the record, right? Sure, I'll consider the fact that you've had a little too much of the Irish."

The *Happy Birthday* chorus ended in great applause, and Kathleen moved forward and hugged her husband.

"You're wonderful," he murmured in her ear. "Just wonderful—and I love you more than you'll ever know."

As the evening progressed, those that loved to sing stayed by the piano. The only time the room became hushed was when Katy played Chopin's *Polonaise*, after which they applauded loudly. Kortner gave Wieslawa a reassuring hug. Soon they huddled into smaller groups, pursuing topics that piqued their interests. One could hop from one to the other. Conversations echoed the new era in which they lived. For the moment they put behind them the Great Depression and Roosevelt's promises of a more prosperous future, even talk of Ireland's prospects since its independence in 1922. Dennis, Father, and Joseph Kortner shared their theories on Hitler's rise to power. Kathleen could overhear, now and then, the raised voice of Dennis Noonan showing signs of frustration with Kortner.

"Mark my words, my learned friend, Europe will be at war because what Hitler wants is a united Europe. In its heyday the Roman Empire wasn't so bad. Hell, the world got along just fine."

Kortner smiled and shook his head. "That's probably because they never really occupied Ireland, no? Do you think Herr Hitler will leave your little green island out of his big picture?" Kortner answered his own question. "I think not, my friend."

"Well, if that is the case, we might be better off," Dennis said, becoming more quarrelsome.

Father Rafferty, overhearing, butted in. He was more concerned about the moral question—the treatment of the Jews. "It's very difficult for anyone with Christian morals to discount what Hitler is doing to the Jews, Dennis."

"I believe we have the press to blame for a lot of those stories, Father, and furthermore…"

Kathleen smiled to herself and stepped between them with a tray of crab-stuffed mushrooms. "Something to change the subject gentlemen," she said, emphasizing the word **gentlemen**.

She found them strongly opinionated and questioned how she had come to love them. No one took Dennis seriously, especially her. She felt that some of the things he said were for effect. It was incredible to think that he could believe half of what he uttered. A few moments after the clock chimed midnight, Ryan tapped his glass loudly until the room was quiet. Kathleen thought that his expression was happy, happier than she'd seen him in a long time.

"Thank you," he said. "And I mean that from my heart. I'm blessed to have friends like you." He took a deep breath. He hadn't changed much in fifteen years. The touch of gray in the sideburns gave him a distinguished air. He looked at Kathleen. "And I'm doubly blessed to have such a beautiful, good wife and family. I hear that by the time you reach forty, one should be settled, resigned to a career, if you will. For years Kathleen has been aware of my desire to work for the FBI. Only one other person knew about that dream," he gestured back to Chuck Boyle, "my boss, Chuck. During these last few months I've been taking tests and undergoing evaluation."

Kathleen's eyes brightened; now she knew why he had appeared distant. "I just wish to apologize openly to my wife and family for keeping this a secret. I guess I just wasn't sure I'd make muster—anyway, say hello to the newest recruit to the Federal Bureau of Investigation."

He raised his arms to hush the clapping. "Please, please, I have a few things left—I want to thank two people here who made all this possible." His eyes traversed from Chuck Boyle to Dennis Noonan. "My boss, Chuck, and my wife's uncle—my good friend, Dennis Noonan." While everyone gathered around Ryan, a determined Kathleen sought Dennis and drew him close.

"So," she said, "you had no idea why my husband was acting odd, did you!"

Dennis knew that she wasn't really upset. He had been the object of that Irish temper before. He could tell that deep down her questions had been answered.

"Do you think for one moment," he said in his assertive attorney's voice, "that you women are the only members of the human race endowed with God's gift of secrecy?"

By twelve-thirty everyone had left. Ryan undressed and lay on his back in the bed. The bedroom was softly lit from a lamp on the dresser. Kathleen never allowed a night to go by without visiting Maggie. He could hear her indulgent supplications, always thanking God for sharing their daughter one more day. Soon after, he heard a door close. She stood silhouetted against the hall light.

"Still awake, Ryan?" she whispered expectantly. Although well aware of her dislike of being teased, he answered with a snore.

"Ryan Thornton," she said, more pronounced in her cutting Dublin brogue. She knew he was teasing when he responded with another loud snore. She slipped off her shoes and studied herself in the vanity mirror. He watched as she unbuttoned her dress in the back and let it drop. She sat and raised the champagne-colored silk slip. He thought it inconceivable that he could love her more with every passing day. She was more beautiful than ever. Kathleen knew he was watching and decided it was her turn to tease. With a penetrating sensuality, her delicate hands slowly detached the stockings from the garter belt and removed them as if massaging her thighs. Ryan could hardly contain himself. He knew now she was putting on this act for him and in no way was he about to prematurely interrupt. When she stood and let her dark hair fall about her shoulders, he could smell the perfume with each stroke of the brush. He got up from the bed and stealthily moved behind her. He put his arms around her and kissed the back of her neck. Reaching back, her hands caressed his face. He pulled her to him and knew that this was going to be one of those special times. Her body trembled with anticipation. He gently moved his hands over the silk and cupped her breasts.

"Oh, God, Ryan," she whispered and turned to him. Her mouth opened. "I really do…" Her warm, fragrant breath was hushed by his mouth. He picked her up, their lips never parting, and placed her on the bed.

When they had finished making love, he rolled away, curled up, and was soon asleep. Kathleen lay on her back and stared at the ceiling. She smiled to herself when the silence was broken by the first snort, this time for real. She asked if it was natural to fantasize about Liam Riordan. For a moment she stared past Ryan and thought about the Hill o'Howth, the shrieking seagulls. He really had loved her. She knew that to continue with these reveries would only lead to unhappiness. She was very familiar with guilt and had no desire to blame herself for Liam Riordan's double life. Blaming her indiscretion on Father Donnelly's letter, she rolled on her side and fell into a deep sleep.

CHAPTER THIRTY-SEVEN

I
T WAS ONE of those unusual times when the room was completely occupied and eerily quiet. Other than the sound of a pencil being sharpened or a page being turned, nothing broke the silence. A pungent combination of musk and body odor filled the space. The room was encircled to its center by a dark-stained wood wainscot capped with a massive crown-chair rail. The wall above was painted stark white to the ceiling. A row of windows, floor to ceiling, substituted for one wall. The windows looked down upon a cobblestone courtyard, now alive with rust- and amber-colored leaves twirling about like tiny cyclones in the brisk autumn breeze. According to Father Devine, the cobblestones had been used as ballast aboard ships carrying Irish immigrants to Boston. Now they were an integral part of the courtyard and paths of St. Martin's Seminary.

The courtyard was surrounded on three sides by two-story buildings with steel-framed windows and Spanish-tiled roofs. One building was the school, the other two, dorms and refectory area. The gothic-style church had been purposefully situated away from the other buildings. Above the nave a lofty tower rose another thirty feet or so, housing five large bronze bells orchestrated by Father Sebastian and four brothers for Sunday Mass and vespers. Together the main buildings, church and outer buildings, including a large barn, were located on fifty acres of pristine Boston countryside. Many students at St. Martin's had no intention of entering religious life. The Monastery, besides Christian theology, taught literature, mathematics, Latin, Greek, philosophy, astronomy, and other sciences. Many of the priests' methods of teaching secular subjects, with their disputations on moral issues, raised ecclesiastical eyebrows.

The forty or so boys seated in the orderly rows of plain wooden desks were taking preparatory tests for their admission into the major seminary, where most of them would embrace the priesthood. Father Devine pulled a used, white handkerchief from the sleeve of his black cassock like a sleight-of-hand artist. He wiped his brow and blew his nose, then glanced inquisitively at the white linen before tucking it back in the sleeve. The steely eyes lowered to view the wrist watch.

"Five minutes," he said indifferently.

One of the front-row desks was occupied by a handsome young man with jet-black curly hair and a tawny complexion. His eyes were deep set, strange, yet friendly. They were an unusual shade of blue-gray, light, like those of a timber wolf. He placed his pencil in the routed groove at the top of the desk, closed the folder and folded his arms. It was customary to wait until all had completed the exam. He smiled respectfully at the priest. Father Devine nodded approvingly and found it encouraging that Lawrence Riordan was the first to finish. Both Lawrence and Michael were supposed to be taking this test, but Michael had been given permission to stay in the dorm, having come down with a bout of the flu.

Later the same day, Michael and Lawrence sat on old crates in the basement of the church. No one ever went to the basement, other than to store unused furniture and tools. Their only light was from an oil lamp of an earlier century. It had become their quiet place to share one another's intimate thoughts, dreams, and desires for the future. The open dorm where they slept with twenty other boys allowed no privacy. Even the bathrooms were open, with twenty sinks and as many toilets side by side. Obviously studying for the priesthood didn't encourage an opportunity for a young man to be alone with his foolish thoughts. Their classmates could not tell Michael and Lawrence apart. They enjoyed their uniqueness and weren't about to inform anyone of their only dissimilarity, the birthmarks.

Lawrence lit a cigarette and nervously shook the match, throwing it on the concrete floor. He sucked down the smoke and blew it out his nose.

"Well, how did I do?" he asked.

Michael smiled, enjoying the suspense. He had been taking his brother's place, not only for tests that Lawrence found difficult, but had also on numerous occasions volunteered to receive Lawrence's punishment, taking the blame out of love for his brother. Lawrence, on the other hand, enjoyed manipulating his brother.

"Oh, I don't know exactly, maybe a B." Michael nodded with an assertive expression. "Yep, I'm almost sure I got you a B." He smiled and dodged the semi-friendly swing of his brother. "Hey, a B is a lot better than *you* would have done."

Lawrence produced a flask and offered it to Michael. He declined. Lawrence took a drink himself and shuddered. "No, seriously though, did you really just get me a B, Michael?"

"I think so, Lars."

"Why? You'll get an A for yourself when you take it again—well, won't you?"

"I could have aced it for you, it's just that I'm getting tired of taking your finals, Lars. I'm not really helping you by doing this. Besides, what's going to happen to you when I'm not around anymore?"

"Planning on leaving, Michael?" Lawrence took another swig and placed the flask in the side pocket of his corduroy jacket.

"No, but when I become a priest there are certain vows I'll have to take. Honesty being one of them."

"Honesty! Michael, you're not going to be a priest, that's just Mother talking. She wants a priest in the family and you're obliging her. You won't make a good priest any more than I would—as a matter of fact, you're probably more sinful than I am. You contribute to my—my delinquency. Even legally it's called aiding and abetting."

"I want to be a priest as much as you have desires to be an aviator."

"I still say you're fulfilling Mother's wishes. No one, as far as I know, wants me to be a pilot but me."

"If that's how you feel, Lars, maybe I should start right now correcting that."

That's it!" Michael exclaimed, standing. "Maybe I should go directly to Father Abbott and confess my sins and yours—face to face, tell him I've taken your tests."

Lawrence stopped him, placing a hand on Michael's shoulder.

"Okay, Michael, you win." He stomped on the cigarette butt. "Look, if it makes you feel better, I'll really try—I'll make the effort, okay?"

Michael shrugged and returned to the apple crate.

"Promise," he said.

"I promise to—to try and mend my ways. I'll take at least one of my finals—how about gym class?" he said, smiling.

"See, Lars, that's what I mean. You're never serious. Always joking. I know that there's a religious side to you that you don't let on. Mother calls it your 'divine spark.'"

"My 'divine spark' is extinguished. You, on the other hand, have enough divinity for both of us."

"That's not true, Lars—I…"

Lawrence interrupted, his tone more somber. "I had that dream again, Michael, you know the one where I'm—I'm doing it with…"

"Stop it, Lars!" Michael rose and sat by Lawrence. He put his hand affectionately on his brother's shoulder. "That's just a dream. It doesn't mean anything. People have dreams like that all the time, especially people our age. They call it puberty. It's very normal."

"I'd believe that—if I was dreaming about—well about a gorgeous girl, not a…"

"Look, Lars, your dream is just confused, that's all, an anxiety thing. It's the complete opposite of what you should be dreaming. Not that we should be dreaming about impure things anyway. I just…"

"*I like it*, Michael," Lawrence said, interrupting.

Michael looked puzzled.

"There, you see. I really *do* like it. *Now* what do you think?"

Michael was silent.

Lars stood up and lit another cigarette. He paced. Then he stepped away from the light into the darkness. His back was to his brother. His voice was pleading. "What am I going to become?"

Michael was still silent, thinking of ways to console his brother.

"Am I going to become one of—those—those…" He fumbled over the words, "what Mother calls 'quare fellas'—'fancy boys'? I think it's in the family, you know. Remember when Mother talked about Uncle Larry?—well, I got the impresssion he was a little odd, if you know what I mean."

"Stop it, Lars! You don't know that."

"I know that I like it, Michael, when—this, this man holds my…"

"Don't even say it! That's a disgusting thought—I'm telling you, it's nothing more than anxiety."

"Not when you like it, Michael. Besides, last night's dream we went further."

"Further?"

"Further! We were in the pool—I was alone with Brother David. Yes, and I liked that too."

"I think you should talk to Father Abbott. He probably knows more about those things than anyone." Michael moved into the darkness with his brother.

"Don't worry, Lars. We'll sort this out, and don't worry, I won't let you down on your tests."

He comforted his brother until the wick, starved of fuel, flamed out.

Curfew at Saint Martin's was 9 p.m., after which students had to be in their beds with lights out. To the whole community, talking was strictly forbidden. There may have been exceptions for some of the hierarchy.

Lawrence had been awake for two hours. He lay on his back, hands behind his head, staring at the ceiling. His cold, devious eyes had long adjusted to the darkness of the dorm. Anticipating the night's adventure, he had to be absolutely sure the residents were sleeping. So far the only sounds breaking the silence were the heavy breathing or an occasional snort. One loud endless snort he recognized. It was Whale, a giant, portly boy from Virginia. Nobody gave the Whale a bad time except the teachers.

The majority of the students did have a healthy respect for their superiors, who represented God's authority. The boys always had to show them love and respect, even while being pummeled with the heavy strap.

Lawrence noiselessly shifted his position. Sitting on the edge of his cot, he focused on the boy in the next bed, Felix Peabody, determining if he was awake. He was probably the shortest boy attending St. Martin's. No one called him Felix; he had become known to his friends as Lofty. The distinction wasn't referring to his stature, rather the nickname was a compliment. He had an ability to urinate higher and farther than anyone and held the school record. *It was all in the technique*, he would say, *how you hold it and squeeze it off*. More than once, he held his bladder for hours until he was fit to burst. Finally relieving the contents, his spray would strike the ceiling. He wasn't often challenged, but when he was, the competition drew a large crowd, some placing bets on their favorite whizzer. Lofty always prevailed, his back arched, the eyes closed in deep concentration, both hands squeezing until the pressure built and became too hard to bear. The stream was propelled as if by a bullet. After his spray struck the ceiling he would laugh loudly and finish off in the urinal. Unfortunately, this was Lofty's only claim to fame.

Lawrence reached over and tapped him, "Hey—hey, Lofty," he whispered. Lofty rolled away, pulling the brown wool blanket over his head. Lawrence shook him again. "Up, rise, it's after eleven."

The short boy sat up and vigorously rubbed the sleep from his eyes. "Okay, okay—Jesus, Lars, give me a minute to wake up, will ya?"

"You wake Michael, I'll get the Whale—and don't go back to sleep." He passed the beds between his and the Whale's. He nudged him gently, not wanting to startle the snoring giant. The Whale finally awakened on a string of loud snorts. "It's time to have some fun," Lawrence said quietly. "Are you ready?"

"Yeah, yeah," he said, adjusting to the dark. "Guess I'm as ready as I'll ever be."

"Good," Lawrence said. "And remember, steal someone else's pillow— without waking anyone." Lawrence could hear loud whispering in the direction of Michael's bed. When he got there, Michael appeared to be having second thoughts.

"I just don't think it's all that funny anymore, that's all," he was telling Lofty.

"You guys are going to wake the whole goddamn dorm," Lawrence said, drawing closer. "What's up?"

"I'm not going through with it, that's all, Lars. I don't think that putting pillows on the bell clappers is such a good idea. Not before Sunday Mass— it's a sacrilege." Lawrence placed his hand on Michael's shoulder.

"Aw, for Christ's sake, Michael, it's just a lark. The bells will still ring— they'll just be a little muffled, that's all." He snickered, and the Whale chortled even louder, stopping when Lawrence slapped him on the head. "Shut up or we'll be caught before we even do anything! Well, Michael?"

"I don't know, Lars, what if we're caught? We'd surely be expelled."

Lawrence pleaded with his brother, "I promise you won't get caught. Trust me. Hell, they'll be talking about this prank for years. See, I need you with me on this."

"Well," Michael didn't have a chance to finish his sentence.

"Great," Lawrence said, assuming that was a 'yes.'

The four left the dorm with pillows and twine and headed for the belltower. They had to cross the open courtyard; Lawrence was thankful it was a moonless night. The room below the tower was spacious, with a very high ceiling from which thick ropes suspended through open ports. The ropes, attached to the bells above, came within five feet or so of the floor. Lawrence pointed the flashlight and swept the beam around the room, illuminating a blackboard with a series of numbers. It was a simple code assigning a number to a specific bell. The beam of light continued, stopping at a wood staircase that led to the belfry. The tower was narrow and the stairs seemed endless. The Whale had to stop at every landing."Jesus," he panted, "how much farther?"

"We're almost there," Lawrence said impatiently. Lofty was behind the Whale, who had the urge to break wind. Lofty's face almost touched the heavier boy's buttocks when the Whale decided to let go. It was loud and reverberated through the belfry. The Whale couldn't contain his laughter.

"I think I just broke the grand silence," he said, emitting some minor secondary explosions.

"Aw, shit." Lofty covered his nose. "Did you have to do that?"

By this time the Whale's body was shaking like a large bowl of jelly. Lawrence turned and grabbed him with his free hand.

"Damn it, Whale, you're going to get us caught. You'll ruin everything. No more farting, laughing, *nothing*. All I want to hear from you, 'till this prank is over, is your heavy goddamn breathing, okay?"

At one point, as the foursome neared the top, the banister gave way under the Whale's weight. He pulled back instantly and clung to the wall, almost dropping his pillow.

"For the love of God!" Lawrence was in his face again.

"Sorry, this time it wasn't my fault."

"Okay, just be careful and don't drop that pillow."

Finally they reached the top. None of the boys had been to the top before. It was off limits to the students. The bells were enormous, much bigger than the boys had imagined, some weighing two tons or more. The shafts holding the bells rested on massive steel-pillow blocks. Lawrence pointed out that one of them would have to straddle each shaft in order to tie a pillow to the clappers. It was close to fifty feet to the rafters below. They directed the light into the abyss and struggled to focus where it ended. It was Lofty who volunteered.

"I'm the lightest, why don't I do it." No one argued and Lofty straddled the shaft, working his way gingerly toward the first bell. He positioned a pillow around the clapper of the first bell and secured it with twine. "One done," he said, giving a thumbs up sign.

The Whale's body shook as he attempted to hold back the laughter. He did this every time a bell was sabotaged. The last bell seemed the least precarious.

With little effort, Michael could reach the shorter boy. "Don't worry, Lofty, I've got you." In the darkness, Lofty couldn't see the immense space between him and the distant floor below.

Lawrence produced a bottle from his jacket pocket. He offered it to his brother. "Here," he said, "give this to Lofty, it's just a little something extra, an additional treat for Father Devine and his bell ringers." Michael was curious as Lawrence uncorked the bottle.

"It's just ink," he said, answering his brother's inquisitive expression.

"No, Lawrence, this is going beyond what we agreed to do. Pillows on the bells. That was it."

"Well, my pious brother, let's just say this is my contribution. Besides, nobody's going to get hurt. The most they'll get is," he tittered, "black faced." He wasn't convincing and resorted to the only other means of persuading Michael. "Hell, we're not even talking about a mortal sin here, are we?"

Michael thought for a moment. "That's not the point. Is it a venial sin?" Lofty had finished the last knot securing the pillow. "Okay, okay, quit the arguing and give me the bottle."

"Did you know about the little addition too?" Michael continued, not giving Lofty the opportunity to answer. "So I was the only one not included?" He reached for the bottle, still supporting Lofty with the other hand.

"No," Lawrence pulled the bottle back, "you're not going to ruin our fun—not this time." Lawrence moved quickly, circumventing his brother's reach, stretching precariously over the balustrade.

"Lofty, take it." The shorter boy stared frantically; he hesitated, knowing the prudent thing to do would be to stay where he was.

"Now take it, take it," Lawrence persisted.

Lofty capitulated. His fearful expression should have been a warning of what was about to happen. Lawrence watched, shocked into speechlessness—watched as Lofty lost his balance in an admirable attempt to save the bottle. Michael quickly brought his free hand back, grabbing the falling boy's collar. It was too little, too late. As Lofty slipped, Michael saw his terror-stricken face. There was no sound until they heard the awful thud when Lofty's body hit the rafters below. No one moved. Michael hung over the balustrade, clutching the collar of Lofty's shirt.

Whale, who had been in charge of the flashlight, trained the beam down the deep shaft. His hands shook. Lawrence was first to speak.

"For Christ's sake, hold it steady." The meager light continued to bounce about. "Here, give me the damn thing," Lawrence said, grabbing the flashlight.

Whale wrung his hands. "He's dead, isn't he?"

"Would you shut the hell up!" Lawrence said in a raised voice.

His hand wasn't much steadier, the beam finally focusing on the lifeless form below. Lawrence pulled away from the rail, and for a moment the torch lit their faces, revealing the dumbstruck horror. Michael's speech was anxious and angry.

"We've killed him. Why in God's name didn't you listen to me, Lawrence! If you hadn't brought that bottle of ink, Lofty would…"

"Bullshit! That's just great, blame me. Shit, you're the one that tried to grab it away. If you hadn't…"

Whale pushed his big frame between the brothers.

"Look, you guys, you get any louder and we'll all be in deep shit." He had their attention—clutching each by the shoulder, his voice more dispassionate, he drew their frightened faces closer. "It isn't important now who brought the goddamn ink or who reached for the goddamn ink.

Lofty's probably dead down there and we're dead meat if we're caught."
Lawrence was first to respond.

"The Whale's right. We should pick up anything that might lead them
to us."

Michael jerked himself from the Whale's grasp. "I don't believe you
people," he whispered loudly. "Lofty's down there… for all we know he
might still be alive. What if he's still alive?" he repeated louder.

Whale impatiently grabbed the flashlight from Lawrence and eagerly
descended. "Fuck you two," he said under his breath. "I'm not going to be
here when they come lookin'."

Lawrence followed, then Michael.

"What if Michael's right? What if Lofty isn't—isn't dead?" Whale said.

They moved quickly, skipping every other tread and hesitating
briefly at the last landing. Whale directed the light to Lofty's twisted form
straddling the joists. He held the light long enough to see the white, lifeless
face. A trickle of blood left the open mouth, the only morbid movement a
pulsating steam pumped from the open socket that was once an eye.

"I think he's dead all right," Whale said breathlessly.

Michael blessed himself. "Oh, dear Jesus, oh my God, I'm heartily
sorry for having offended Thee…"

The light shifted to the last flight. Lawrence immediately followed
Whale, pulling Michael. "Leave him be, Michael, for Christ's sake. He's
dead." His voice was authoritative. "There's no time for this Confiteor
shit."

Michael's movements were mechanical, acquiescing to his brother's,
murmuring his frantic supplication.

The following Sunday a Memorial Mass was held for Lofty. The Abbot
presided.

In nomine Patris, et Filii et Spiritus Sancti, Amen. He chanted,
Introibo ad altare Dei, to which the servers replied, *Ad deum que laetificat
juventutem meam.*

After the gospel, La Verdiere gave the sermon and for those who
didn't know Lofty, revealed a side of the boy that moved them from fits of
laughter to moments of sadness. He shared his thoughts as to what took
place.

"An innocent prank with no intention of anyone getting hurt turned
into a nightmare. A nightmare for one boy. And I'm not talking about
the boy whose life we're celebrating today." He went on to say, "No, I'm
referring to the boy who helped in this delinquent prank."

Michael, shifting nervously in the pew, heard little else that was said by the Abbot. Lawrence nudged him.

"Will you relax," he whispered. "They don't know anything—If they did we would have been accused of something before now."

Michael relaxed. He wanted to believe his brother. "Yeah, I guess you're right." For a moment words from the pulpit replaced his concerns.

"...And to that extent the authorities are of the opinion that it was an unfortunate accident. A prank gone awry. The church, however, takes a different view—and I personally intend to root out the other boy," he paused, "or boys—involved." He paused again, his eyes slowly moving through the congregation.

"The sanctity of our order has been compromised by this act. It will go much easier if these perpetrators come forward of their own volition. I know most of you think of me as a reasonable man, but do not confuse charity with complaisance. The confessional is the sanctity of God's forgiveness, and I'm sure that at this moment three persons know who was involved. The penitent, the Father Confessor, that's assuming of course one wished to cleanse his soul," he hesitated, "and Almighty God. By the end of the week I intend to be the fourth."

After lunch the twins found themselves in the church basement. Michael quietly waved away Lawrence's offer of a cigarette. Lawrence struck the match, illuminating his face. In the short duration of the lit match his face had an expression of confidence. He drew the smoke deep into his lungs. Michael spoke first.

"When Mother finds out about all this—God, what will she think if we're expelled?"

"No one is going to be expelled," Lawrence said. "As of this moment the Abbot hasn't accused you or anybody."

"I know he's found my medal—I looked all over and the only place it could have been was in Lofty's hand when he grabbed at my shirt."

There weren't many times when Lawrence was the one dispensing encouragement.

"Look, Michael, if the police had found your medal, don't you think that they would have tracked you down by now? Really, I have all the hope in the world that the Abbot has no idea either."

Michael paced back and forth. He stopped as he said, "Ah, yes, hope. I'm beginning to understand now what Nietzsche meant when he said that hope was the worst of all evils—because it prolongs the torment."

Lawrence flicked the cigarette. "What the hell are you talking about...?"

Michael didn't let him finish, "It's the waiting, the hope, not knowing when you're going to be called. It's like, well, waiting to die or something—that's why it's better to get things out in the open."

Lawrence moved toward his brother and grabbed his shoulders. "Damn it, if you're thinking what I think, you'd better knock that shit off. You're not talking to anyone." He shook him hard. Michael pulled away.

"I went to confession last night."

"And?" Lawrence asked brusquely.

"That's between me and my confessor—I was advised to talk to the Abbott."

"Bullshit," Lawrence said angrily.

"Don't worry, I'm not going to name you or Whale—I'll say it was all my idea. Mine and Felix Peabody's."

"Well, that will be a big relief, won't it," Lawrence said sarcastically. "You think I want to stay in this God-forsaken place? No, if you go I go."

"Don't worry, Lars, Mother wouldn't leave you here if I'm expelled. I'm sure Mother would keep us together."

"That's right," Lawrence said. "We know how everyone likes you, and I wouldn't have to admit any wrong-doing, would I?"

"No, Lars, you wouldn't have to take any blame; it was my medal they found."

"We still don't know, Michael—I mean—that anyone knows about the medal."

"I've made up my mind, Lars. I'm going to confess openly to the Abbot." He placed an arm around his brother. He was resigned to even the worst fate: Not being able to become a priest. They walked toward the door.

"Look, before you do anything," Lawrence asked, "give me a little more time to think things over." Michael nodded.

"You know, in all the commotion, I've only been thinking about myself, Lars. How are those horrible dreams of yours?"

Lawrence opened the door and rubbed his eyes. He smiled wryly. "Oh, they're not so bad."

"Oh, that's great, Lars. You mean they're not so frequent?"

"No, Michael—I mean I'm starting to like them."

Jean Pierre La Verdier had been a Benedictine Monk for fifty years and Abbot of St. Martin's for the past ten. He was a strong leader, particularly when it came to adhering to the rules. In his opinion, the church had survived because of its inflexibility, strengthened by its dogma. He believed that the stability of his community depended on him. He was their father, their father confessor, mediator, judge, and executioner. When it came to wrongdoing he was known to render severe penances, never, however, without absolute incontrovertible evidence. Now he was engrossed with the death of one Felix Peabody; at least he was sure the boy's death was accidental. He was also certain that one other *was* or two or three more boys *were* involved. He suspected Michael Riordan, as incredible as he found that notion. With his elbows resting on the desk, he leaned forward in the chair and wrung his hands. He then picked up the blood-stained medal and held it between his forefinger and thumb. He stared at the medallion as if to solicit a sign, something that might lend even more credence to his theory. After all, medals of Our Blessed Mother were not a rarity in a Catholic school.

In a moment he allowed his thought to relive the drama of the past week. Father Devine was first to arrive at the bell tower that Sunday morning, having been the first informed. He remembered scurrying back to the tower with Father Devine, who had babbled incoherently.

"Dear Mother of God, Father Abbot, he's dead—the boy's dead," he said, blessing himself over and over. LaVerdiere was still content with his decision not to turn over the medal he had removed from the boy's bloody fist. He had convinced the police that an immature prank, an individual act of mischief, had resulted in the accidental death of Felix Peabody. He believed that by placing the medal in his pocket he had saved the monastery an embarrassing investigation. He knew the answer to the question of the guilty party.

Kathleen Thornton knew how important it was that Father Abbot be aware of the boys' only apparent physical differences. She had explained their basic distinctions and their oneness. She had emphasized their uncanny ability to exchange personalities. It was the medals, she told him, that would mark their differences, and if one wasn't sure, the opposing birthmarks would absolutely distinguish Michael from Lawrence. Apart from Kathleen Thornton's accounting of the twins, LaVerdiere's intuition had also led him to be suspicious of Lawrence Riordan. He knew there was something about the boy, a sinister side. More often than not, Lawrence appeared too virtuous to be true; this led the Abbot to believe that the boy was covering up his real character. Even Father Devine had come to him with accusations—unsubstantiated—of cheating on his exams. LaVerdiere was convinced of Lawrence's lack of moral fiber, yet he believed the medal he studied in his hand was Michael's. He also knew that the possibility of other students wearing a medal of the Blessed Virgin was very high. Soon after he placed the medal safely in the desk drawer, he clasped his hands behind his head and eased back in the chair. He imagined the lifeless form of young Peabody, one eye staring at him blankly, the other resting on his cheek, torn out by a nail extending through the lath and plaster ceiling. His body trembled; tasting the evening supper in the back of his mouth, he made a retching sound.

After knocking twice, Brother Sebastion entered the Abbot's office. He was astonished to find the abbot bent over the wastebasket. LaVerdiere wiped his mouth and tucked the handkerchief up his sleeve.

"Excuse me for the interruption, Father Abbott—are you all right?"

"Father Sebastion, come in, come in. Of course I'm all right. Just a little piece of meat from dinner, not completely digested, that's all. We'll have to do something about Father Basil's cooking. I believe cremation, man or animal, is not something we sanction. Now what can I do for you?"

Father Sebastion extended his hand out of the Abbot's view. "Come, Michael," he said gently. "I'm sure the Abbot would like to hear from you."

The boy came closer to Father Sebastion and trembled at the sight of the Abbot. Although he showed no signs, LaVerdiere was overwhelmed with excitement. His voice revealed no surprise.

"Well, if it isn't young Michael Riordan," he said, rising from his chair. He walked to the front of the desk and extended his hand. "Come my boy. Here, sit," he gestured to the chair in front of the desk. "I've been expecting you, Michael," he said.

LaVerdiere wasn't going to let this opportunity get away. He would know the truth by the time this boy had left the room. Michael Riordan was no match for him. He expected the boy to protect his brother, Lawrence, who, he was sure, had to be involved in some way. He was an expert when it came to extracting information and looked forward to this game of cat and mouse. Slowly he maneuvered Michael to the chair.

"That will be all, Father—thank you." LaVerdiere remained standing as the door shut. He rested his buttocks on the edge of the desk and folded his arms.

"Father Abbot, I..." He cleared his throat, "I couldn't go on without telling someone about, about..." He took a deep breath and wrung his hands nervously.

"That's all right, Michael. I know why you've come. It's about Felix Peabody, isn't it?"

"Uh huh," the boy said, his eyes fixed on his lap.

"Look at me, Michael." LaVerdiere reached and raised the boy's head gently. "You were his friend, weren't you?"

"Yes, Father."

"And you cared for him?"

"Uh huh."

"You know he would want you to tell me, I mean, if you knew something, isn't that right?"

"I believe so, Father Abbot."

"Well then, Michael, why don't you tell me exactly what took place in the belltower that night."

"Well, to begin with, it was Lofty's—I mean Felix's idea. That's why he fell."

LaVerdiere stroked his chin. "I see, so Felix came to the rest of you and…"

"Oh, no, Father!" he exclaimed, "he just came to me with the idea to—well, you know, to put pillows on the bells."

"And the ink?" LaVerdiere asked, referring to the spent bottle of ink on Peabody's shirt. "Whose idea was that?"

"The ink? Yes, well that was something Felix wanted to tie to the pillows at the last minute."

For a moment the room was silent. LaVerdiere moved slowly to his chair and sat with a great sigh.

Riordan looked him straight in the eye. The blue-gray eyes welled. "Father, I know it sounds like I'm placing blame on someone who can't—can't tell you his version of what happened. You have to believe as if this was my private confession," he lied. "I mean, I just…" He bent over, his hands clutching his face.

La Verdiere broke in. "Is this your true confession, Michael?"

"It is, Father," he lied again. His expression pleaded for a positive response. "I know that I did wrong also, Father—somehow at the time it seemed like a—like a harmless thing to do. He said, I mean Felix, that all we'd be doing would be making the bells silent. I'm heartily sorry for what happened."

La Verdiere was beginning to feel sorry for the boy. A stream of tears was wiped away by the boy's sleeve. The Abbot reached for his handkerchief and thought better of it. He shook his head, telegraphing his indication for the lad to continue.

"By the time we reached the bells I began to have second thoughts. I tried to convince Felix to—to forget the whole thing and return to the dorm. He told me that I could go back if I wanted. I just thought he might need my help, if he should fall."

"He did fall, Michael. It didn't help much that you were there, did it?"

Michael looked more despondent than ever. "Now I wish it had been me, Father."

LaVerdiere opened the desk drawer. "Did you try to save him?" he asked, hoping the boy would respond favorably.

"It was when he reached in his pocket for the ink. I guess that's when I realized the prank had gone too far. I pleaded with him to give me the jar. It was when I reached for it that he pulled back…" His voice trailed. "That's when he lost his balance."

The lad placed his hands on his face again and wept openly. "It was my fault that he fell, Father. If only I hadn't reached!"

LaVerdiere went to the boy and put a fatherly hand on his shoulder. "Is this your medal, Michael?" The blood-stained oval medal with the image of the Virgin Mary rested in his open palm.

"Yes, Father."

"And you're telling the absolute truth, that no one accompanied you and Felix Peabody?"

"That's right, Father."

"I know how much you love your brother Lawrence. Are you sure he wasn't with you?"

"Father, I know that my brother has not been, well, the best student. It's been very difficult for Lawrence. He's always been compared to me. I've been the fortunate one."

"How so, Michael? I don't happen to find your situation right now the least bit fortunate."

"I don't mean to make light of what happened. I know God will forgive me. I believe that, Father. I also believe that whatever happens, another school will accept me. I will one day take my vows to the priesthood. I dearly love God. My studies and grades reflect this desire. On the other hand, my brother has no intention of becoming a priest and his grades are not as good as mine, so I know that people would naturally think that this is something that Lawrence would do. To answer your question, Father, no, Lawrence was not with me."

Abbot LaVerdiere could find no fault with Michael's explanation. Michael had revealed a poignant compassion for the boy's death. The Abbot appreciated the young man's honesty and his acceptance of guilt, part and parcel of being a good Catholic and, in time, a priest. Still, he found it hard to believe that Lawrence Riordan was not involved.

LaVerdiere reached into his cassock and produced the medal, then handed it to the boy.

"Mother must have told you."

For a moment LaVerdiere looked puzzled. "Oh!" he exclaimed. "The medal. Yes, she did say there would be times when it might be necessary to tell you apart."

LaVerdiere signaled to the boy's neck. "I have to make sure." He felt awkward but he had to know. If he didn't see a St. Christopher medal he could give absolution, a severe penance perhaps, but no dismissal. He believed the lad to be telling the truth. With his left hand the boy fidgeted with the top two buttons of his shirt and pulled back the shirt triumphantly, exposing a bare neck.

"You see, Father, the medal is mine."

LaVerdiere sighed. He assumed that the boy couldn't have known about his knowledge of the medals. That was his secret with their mother. He returned to the chair behind the desk, his chest swelled with satisfaction. He could with good conscience keep this whole mess quiet. He was convinced of Michael's remorse, his genuine spirituality. "I want you to kneel and say an Act of Contrition, my son."

"Yes, Father Abbot," he said, bringing the medal over his head. "Oh my God, I am heartily sorry for having offended Thee."

When the ceremony was over, they stood. The boy was ebullient. He had been forgiven, they could stay at St. Martin's, and Mother would never have to know they were even involved.

"Thank you for your understanding, Father Abbott," he said, and eagerly extended his right hand.Father Abbott grasped the boy's hand with two hands.

The boy was delirious with his redemption and returned the gesture, placing his left hand over the Abbot's right. It was as if they were part of some secret organization and the younger man was being initiated with a special handshake.

La Verdiere felt vindicated in his method of handling this difficult case. He shook Michael's hands vigorously, and as he did, his broad grin turned to a slit that took a downward turn. He focused on the birthmark on the boy's left wrist. He hated himself for wanting to strike the lying little bastard.

The medal belonged to Michael. But the birthmark belonged to Lawrence.

CHAPTER THIRTY-EIGHT

Chicago, 1933

T HE GARRYOWEN WAS the most popular dancehall in the Irish section of Chicago. At the entrance, one whole wall was devoted to the bar. The far end of the hall had a seating area where one could drink and talk between sets. It was no secret that another area of the club, upstairs, was set aside for gambling and prostitution. To off-duty cops, the booze was free. They ran tabs that were never paid. Chicago's Best on the take made it a safe place for the ladies. Women knew that if they didn't care for the annoying advances of an overbearing drunk, the police were always there. It was good business; more women attracted to the club meant more men. It was the men who drank, gambled, and paid the high price of a prostitute.

On paper, the club was owned by an Irishman, Matt Reilly. He had left his home in Ireland in 1927 and ventured to Chicago with his wife, Maeve, and two children. Reilly had been a pub owner in Dublin and a good friend of Nora McIntee. When Reilly decided to emigrate, Nora wrote to her son, Sean, and made all the travel arrangements for the trip. McIntee took special care of his new guests from Dublin, and it wasn't long before Reilly became his employee. Matt Reilly was a fast learner, and after a few months of orientation, McIntee made him an attractive offer to run one of his dancehalls. It was a dream come true for anyone just arriving in America. Some months later, McIntee drove to where Reilly was living and took the family for a tour of the city. When they returned, he handed an astonished Reilly the keys and told him the new automobile was his. Reilly and his wife were excited. They couldn't believe their good fortune. Things were happening so fast. They met new friends in their parish and had come to know the pastor personally, even having him to dinner. Before the year ended, McIntee offered to buy Reilly a two-story house. Reilly didn't know it, but he was slowly being purchased, drawn into the world of crime.

By the end of 1928, after little more than a year in America, he would sign a piece of paper making him the proud owner of the Garryowen. He had gained the respect of the community, exactly what McIntee needed to oversee the seedy side of his holdings. He was the good-hearted front man and was guaranteed that he wouldn't have much to do with the nefarious side of the business. Reilly had power, which he had come to enjoy, and plenty of help, all of Irish descent, to run the club. McIntee employed other people to run the slots and to supervise the prostitution, a madam he had come to like who wasn't anything like the drunken slatterns she employed. Reilly was trusted with the books, separating the legal tender, which mostly involved an admission fee, from the gambling, booze, and prostitution. He was a most precise bookkeeper, adhering to his work with a diligence which would later come back to haunt his boss. All of the proceeds from the gambling and prostitution, in the early days of illegal booze, he placed in a metal box and delivered to a bank on Fifth Avenue, where he routinely transferred the contents to a safe-deposit box. For this he received twenty-five percent of the liquor sales, enough to keep a family happy in an upper-class neighborhood and send his children to a private school. All McIntee asked in return was silence and loyalty.

It wasn't long before Matt Reilly began to have feelings of guilt. More and more the club was taking time away from his marriage. Maeve told him that their children were going to grow up not knowing their father. And she had heard stories about the Garryowen. Her feelings were not cushioned to withstand the haughty stares, the silent accusations directed at her and the children when they attended Mass. She even refrained from enjoying the friendship of coffee and cookies after the Mass for fear of being snubbed. Father Potocsnak had begun to ask about her husband and why he didn't see him after services. She confronted her husband, telling him that his occupation was putting a strain on their marriage and that she was not going to play the wife of *'the whoremaster who runs that vile house of prostitution.'*

The Depression had also strained their marriage. He wasn't bringing home as much as he used to, and what he brought didn't go as far. McIntee was demanding more of his time and sought other favors, none of which could be denied. Reilly was becoming privy to events not originally outlined in his job description, such as the time McIntee came by just before closing. McIntee had stopped the Packard at the curb, waiting for Reilly to get in the car. As Reilly walked behind the rear bumper, he started counting the wire spokes in the wheel of the coupe on the opposite side of the street. He had counted 20 when he reached the passenger door. "Crissake, hurry up," McIntee said. Reilly kept his head down as he opened the door and put his hand on the seatback. "Look at me," McIntee said. "You're driving. Other side."

On this mission to a McIntee club in a nearby district, Reilly would learn a lesson in vice administration. The Depression had hurt McIntee's enterprises. The percentage for the puppet operators like Reilly had dropped to ten percent and some found it necessary to skim off the top. He was about to see McIntee deal with one of the skimmers.

They arrived just after closing and waited in the unlit alley. "I don't like the sound of this business," Reilly said.

"It'll grow on you," McIntee told him.

Reilly looked through the windshield at the black letters in the lighted sign over the building at the cross street half a block away. He could make out the word HOTEL, and the smaller lettering at the edge of the sign: "75 cents." He tried to keep himself distracted.

It took close to half an hour before a man in a raincoat opened the back door and stepped into the darkness. Reilly recognized him as the owner, Brendan Sheridan, another Irishman who had been with the company almost as long as he had. Sheridan had the familiar metal box under his arm and looked around furtively, not realizing how truly exposed he was. McIntee extinguished the cigarette and told Reilly to stay in the car and leave the engine running.

He could see them through the windshield of the big Packard and could tell by their gestures that the verbal exchange was not cordial. McIntee's voice was almost audible over the noise of the engine. He produced a length of pipe from inside his overcoat and struck viciously at Sheridan's head. It all happened fast, but Reilly thought he counted four or five blows before the owner dropped the box and made an effort to protect his head. McIntee drove the pipe end-first into the man's exposed chest. Sheridan immediately slumped to the pavement. He must have been told to empty his pockets because he put the contents into the box with tremendous effort while crumpled beside the door. McIntee hit Sheridan once more. This time he stayed still. Reilly could see the stream of blood form a small rivulet as it made its way to the gutter. McIntee returned to the car and both went for a drink. He told Reilly that these were times that tested men's loyalties.

When McIntee wanted more of Reilly's time, he made it hard to refuse. As the months passed, McIntee ordered Reilly to take on more responsibility. He was promised an increase in income, a little something to make up for the drop in pay because of the hard times, so to speak. Matt Reilly was coming to regret the day he ever saw McIntee. Becoming more and more indebted, Reilly was pressured to join McIntee in increasingly viscious reprisals, assisting one of McIntee's gorillas, disciplining some overzealous fool who thought he could take cash without detection.

By the summer of 1934, McIntee was putting an end to a short-lived marriage, a few months shy of two years. His wife was the daughter of Irish immigrants, hard-working, law-abiding Catholics who wanted better for their daughter. Bridie McSweeny was barely twenty when she married McIntee after a short courtship against her father's wishes. She was infatuated with his wealth and power and soon became ingratiating to his every command. After the honeymoon he treated her like the whores he employed. Her need to please was seen as a weakness he came to despise. He beat her brutally at provocations he staged. At first McIntee thought she might be useful because of her innocence, her ignorance, and her loyalty. He could place some of his ventures in her name, a consideration that could be lucrative, he soon realized. She didn't have to ask for a divorce. One Sunday afternoon she returned from the High Mass at Immaculate Conception, which she attended with her parents, and found a suitcase on the lawn of their expensive house. The valise contained just the clothes with which she had come into the marriage, none of the jewelry that had been purchased since. McIntee never heard from her again.

He still needed, however, to find a more secure place for the fortune he had procured. He abhorred the U.S. State Department and was paranoid about its desire to deport him and confiscate his fortune. He concocted a plan that would protect himself against that inevitability. He bought a new identity, birth certificate, passport, even a phony marriage license to a woman who had since died. He had the gall to pay a visit to her grave at the Holy Sepulcher Cemetery. Her married name was Kenny; after her death, her husband had returned to Ireland. There were no known relatives in America. So McIntee's new name was Kenny, David Kenny. With the help of The Chicago Trading and Trust, he bought blue-chip stocks in various companies in the amount of ten million dollars. The certificates were eventually transferred to the reputable firm of Windleton, Cauthorn and Barrows in Manhattan, where they were kept in a vault. His identification papers were sent to his sister, Bridget, in London, with instructions to keep them in a safety-deposit box in a Waterloo Bank. Bridget was informed of his new name; it was her job to see that the income taxes were paid on the annual dividends. McIntee felt more at ease with his new insurance policy.

Something else nagged at him. He had become well aware of Reilly's displeasure with his new duties. McIntee blamed Reilly's wife. She was a meddling agitator, in his opinion, a nag of a woman, and he hoped Reilly was smart enough not to tell her more than she needed to know. During one of his more vulnerable moments, Reilly had told McIntee that he was being pestered by his wife to return to Ireland and that she wanted a more peaceful life for herself and the children. McIntee couldn't afford to have his good soldier disillusioned and had to involve him in something that would keep him on the payroll. The opportunity soon presented itself. McIntee needed to take care of some business across town.

It was a wet, blustery evening when the car with McIntee, a big man named Condon, and a driver picked Reilly up at the club. Reilly didn't know much about Condon other than that he didn't care much for him. Rumor had it that he took care of those that committed grievous sins against the management. McIntee sat with Reilly in the back seat, and Condon sat up front with the driver. Reilly didn't ask where they were going, and McIntee didn't offer. McIntee lit a cigarette, inhaled, and spoke on a cloud of smoke.

"Show Matt the fukken piece, Nick."

Condon turned and pushed a thirty-eight revolver into Reilly's hands. Thinking that the man was going to shoot him, Reilly froze, speechless. In a moment he realized the weapon was not going to be used on him but rather was for him to use. Confused, he threw the gun on McIntee's lap.

"Be Jasus, Sean, I'll be havin' nuttin to do wit dat. I told ya before I'll not be shootin' anyone." He was adamant. "Absolutely not!" he told McIntee indignantly. Finally the car stopped by a dilapidated building on the pier. Reilly went on furiously about his loyalty *but not this*. McIntee finally calmed him down, something he had to do more than he liked lately.

"No one was goin' to get bleedin' killed," McIntee informed him. "We're just goin' to scare the shit out of someone, that's all. Honest, Matt, shure, if I wanted someone snuffed, wouldn't I be usin' Condon here to do that?"

Before long he was believing his boss's pretense. McIntee told him that all his soldiers weren't loyal like him; some were dishonest in the ranks, taking more than their shares off the top. More stringent measures had to be taken.

"That's where good soldiers like you come in. We don't want to kill those that are cheatin', just teach them a lesson." McIntee told Reilly they reminded him of the prodigal son except instead of throwing them a party they needed a little whackin'. He explained that all Reilly had to do was hold the gun to the man's head while McIntee talked to him.

"Put the fear of God in him—so to speak. We wait till the thievin' bastard begs for mercy. He prays to God and begs my mercy too. That's when you pull the trigger." McIntee concluded that Reilly wasn't convinced yet.

"Look—he hears this click, see—then he realizes there's no bullets in the gun." McIntee held up the gun and unlocked the chamber. "Look—no bullets, nada, zero." He took another deep drag on the cigarette.

"For Christ sake, Matt, the man is still alive—his pleas have been heard, and who d'ya think the poor bastard gives thanks to?" McIntee told him. "No, not God, me boyo—that's right, Matt, me darlin'—me an' yerself, that's who."

McIntee told him they would have a friend for life—and more importantly, an honest employee. Reilly was still hesitant but agreed to act out the mock execution. Condon took the gun and said that Reilly was supposed to demand it from him. He was told he could make that decision when he felt ready. They walked from the car to some large crates where two men were already waiting. One was taller and better dressed. Reilly recognized him as the owner of the Firelight Club, another of McIntee's side businesses that wasn't showing a profit. The tall, well-dressed man moved nervously and spoke softly and apologetically. McIntee was always calm, enjoying the other's fear, and spoke of trust and friendship. Condon was the loud one, demanding compensation. He winked at Reilly, who took it as a sign to join the verbal punishment. He stood, mute. As much as he tried, nothing came to his mind to enhance the charade. McIntee mumbled something that Reilly didn't hear, and soon the tall man was kneeling. McIntee beckoned to Reilly, who obediently moved closer to them. In that instant he felt more powerful than he had ever felt before. He felt empowered to say something.

"Yer a fukken louse—a thievin' prick that doesn't deserve ta live." It was a short tirade that McIntee found so incongruous that it made him snicker. He watched as Reilly commanded: "Gimme the fukken gun, Nick."

Condon, who by now was also smirking, handed it to him. Reilly was sure that the kneeling man's agony would last only a moment. He found consolation in knowing that the gun wasn't loaded. The sinister side of him enjoyed the act. He placed the gun to the man's quivering head. From the doomed man's eyes tears streamed as he begged for his life. Now Reilly felt sorry for him. He noticed the man had soiled himself. He pleaded with Reilly.

"Would ya gimme some time to say a prayer? I need to make an Act of Contrition."

Reilly nodded, unable to say anything. He couldn't endure the man's pain anymore and before he finished blessing himself, Reilly shut his eyes tight and pulled the trigger. The man's final confession was drowned by the explosion. The salvo had removed the side of the man's head. McIntee had switched revolvers.

Potocsnak listened to the man's confession. He knew the man on the other side of the screen and silently thanked God for bringing Matt Reilly to his senses. The priest didn't care that the confession lasted so long; he was, however, concerned that Reilly would return to his dancehall and be forced once again to engage in illicit activities. He would forgive him for a killing where there was no intent, but strongly recommended that he contact the authorities and explain the circumstances that led to the man's death. Potocsnak sensed that Reilly was not altogether convinced that this was a good approach. Under normal circumstances he would never have admitted that he recognized a penitent; however, he needed to convince Matt Reilly that he could be of more help beyond the confessional. He opted for the forthright approach, declared he already knew the identity of the person speaking, and suggested that when he was finished with the waiting sinners, they meet at the parish house. Reilly, who didn't seem surprised by the priest's observance, consented.

Away from the confines of the confessional, Reilly, even more communicative, disclosed other information about McIntee that astounded the priest. Their conversation lasted long into the night. Matt Reilly was emphatic about not going to the Chicago Police. Most were Irish, he said, and too many were on McIntee's payroll. Potocsnak agreed and promised that no harm would come to him or his family. He would contact the FBI, someone with authority.

"I have no doubt that these people would really like to see McIntee behind bars," he said confidently.

After he left, Potocsnak prayed to God that he could deliver on his promises of protection.

CHAPTER THIRTY-NINE

C HICAGO'S GANGS AND bootlegging flourished in the 1930s. For the big names in the streets, risks were high. Alfonse Capone, who had taken over for Johnny Torrio, was tried on income-tax evasion, and his new residence was Alcatraz. Dion O'Bannion had been shot to death in his flower shop. Hymie Weiss managed to botch an attempt on Capone's life. His funeral wasn't nearly as spectacular as O'Bannion's, who went to his rest with a parade of flowers the likes of which had never before been seen in Chicago. The Italians who shot him paid their respects with dozens of extravagant bouquets, to the point of effrontery. A gangster in the '30s had to initiate different tactics to evade authorities.

The public demanded action. J. Edgar Hoover was attracting idealistic men and women to the Federal Bureau, a force in establishing law and order.

One of these up-and-coming paragons of the law was William Armstrong Hamilton. The boyish looks had long since disappeared. Now in his thirties, passing years left an aging line on his chiseled face. His blond hair had darkened a little. His shoulders broadened and he had added twenty or so pounds to his six-foot frame. Occasionally he had to sit and rest the wounded leg over the sounder leg. He had given up smoking and adhered to a healthy diet and daily exercise. He carried a heavy German-made Luger in a belt holster, preferring it to the government issue.

After the war, a war in which his family and friends assumed he was dead, Hamilton returned to America. It wasn't the homecoming he had expected. The elegant home was someone else's. The previous occupants had moved, or rather his father had moved after his mother had died. When Hamilton did finally locate his father, he was working for a chemical company and living with another woman. They were planning on marriage, his father told him. Initially on meeting his son, the older man was surprised and civil. Soon their conversation centered around his mother's death. Civility turned to anger. *She would still be alive had you taken the time to let us know of your survival. You had no goddamn right to put us through that kind of hell. It was England's war.* Hamilton left and did not see his father again. For a while he wrote but gave up after his letters were returned.

Those first years after the war were the most difficult. The feelings of guilt over his mother's death plagued him. Jobs were scarce, especially in his profession. During those years following the armistice, he was still very much in love with Kathleen. One time he even found himself at the Cunard ticket counter to purchase a trip on a steamer to Cork. Better judgment brought a change of heart, and he returned to his apartment. He believed that she had probably married that lanky pimple-faced friend of hers, Sean McIntee. In desperation he wrote a letter to his old boss and good friend, Colonel Lynch.

There is so much privileged information that can not be part of my resume, he wrote Lynch, *that my war record seems insignificant, of no consequence one way or the other.* The Colonel never responded or if he did, Hamilton never received the letter. Instead, he did get a hand-delivered envelope from the Justice Department. He was told to contact a J. Edgar Hoover, the director of the General Intelligence Division, which was to become known as the GID. The note mentioned Colonel Lynch. Hamilton concluded that it wouldn't have been unusual for these men to know one another, even to have exchanged information. Whatever their relationship, Hoover was aware of Hamilton's war record. After the meeting, Hamilton was on his way to becoming an agent. When he mentioned to Hoover that he had previously been denied similar appointments because of physical disabilities, Hoover smiled.

"Maybe it's time we changed some of those rules. Organized crime and Communism will be won over with brains, Mr. Hamilton, not muscles."

It was primarily a research operation, and Hamilton spent most of the time in the field. He didn't get his own office until 1924, when Hoover was appointed head of the Bureau of Investigation. He took several of his favorite investigators with him, including Hamilton. By law they were not allowed to carry firearms. In the mid-to-late twenties, agents were no match for the gangsters, who were well armed and seemed to be winning the war. Hoover, outraged, fought fiercely for his agents' authority to carry guns. At last, with the help of Congress, he won the fight and changed the course of history. By 1929 Hamilton had risen to head the field office in Chicago. Things were improving; he had an office of his own.

Hamilton wrote some final comments on a report he was preparing for the Director and other Bureau brass. Carefully he screwed the cap on the fountain pen and slipped the pen into his pocket. Closing the folder mechanically, he took a sip of coffee and slumped back in the chair, resting the bad leg over the good. His gaze fixed on the wall beside him, covered with black-and-white photos and newspaper clippings, a visual tribute to his accomplishments. It was a rogues' gallery of sorts, depicting good over evil. Earlier photos illustrated a much younger zealous agent standing by the riddled remains of racketeers, bank robbers, and other misfits who thought they could beat the system. One clipping showed him and other agents smiling amid the human carnage of the Valentine's Day Massacre. They seemed as proud as if they had shot Chicago's North End mob members themselves. Some arrests were made but no one was legally charged. It was thought that Torrio and Capone's lieutenants were behind the mass killing, dressing as Chicago's Finest and in more ways than one, disarming the Irish gang. For whatever reason, Hymie Weiss and Sean McIntee were not with the others. Since then, most of the mobs were trying to manage legitimate businesses, and although they appeared to be operating lawful enterprises, secretly they still controlled the brothels, illegal liquor, drugs, and the numbers racket. Mobsters who survived into the thirties, much smarter, weren't apt to do their own killing. They hired professional assassins and continued to buy off public officials.

Hamilton's eyes settled on the most recent editions on the wall. The newspaper headline read, "Local community leader and business man donates two hundred thousand dollars to Catholic orphanage." The black, bold text was accompanied by a photo of Sean Mcintee and Monsignor Mooney with shovels in hand breaking ground for the new facility. Hamilton doubted that the Monsignor could be that gullible. He had to be aware of McIntee's pernicious past. Maybe the Monsignor had forgiven all McIntee's sins. This endowment might be a kind of payoff for the remission of sins. What an opportune arrangement. Hamilton smiled inwardly and bet the judges wished they had that kind of coverage. Studying the Irishman holding the shovel, Hamilton thought it ironic. He thought about the many poor bastards he'd buried.

The brass at the Bureau were convinced that because of his experience, Hamilton was the right man for the case. Even though he didn't remember much about McIntee other than his relationship with the Barrett family, every little scrap of information was important. McIntee had been

Kathleen's boyfriend, or so he figured. It wasn't easy for Hamilton to avoid thoughts of Kathleen. Over the years, the bitterness he felt by her absence had faded. Still it was difficult for him to think of other women. He had dated, but every time things became serious he found ways to end the relationship. He was astounded that of all places he should run into his past, it would be Chicago, hunting criminals. He opened a manila envelope and scattered the glossy prints on the desk. In fifteen years, this Irish immigrant had elevated himself from a so-called flower-delivery boy to the owner of one of the most lucrative construction firms in the city. He also owned a cement company and controlled the Irish union bosses. Hamilton thought that McIntee was even more ruthless than his previous boss, Dion O'Bannion. He had come to loath McIntee and scum like him, who acted like consummate do-gooders and genuine benefactors of the poor, veritable Robin Hoods. The Bureau had unsubstantiated information implicating McIntee in the deaths of two agents, unarmed, shot down while escorting a witness to the federal building.

McIntee's cement company was a subcontractor for work on a new Post Office located on the outskirts of town. A foreman of McIntee's was charged with the death of one of his carpenters. The carpenter had refused to perform a duty that was in the jurisdiction of another trade. What should have become an issue for the union to resolve was handled the way most disagreements were, with a beating. The carpenter died from his injuries and the foreman was indicted for murder. Some men admitted to hearing them argue, but only one man, a witness to the crime, agreed to testify. He never made it to the courtroom, nor did the two agents escorting him. Maybe their file would forever describe the assailant as an unknown subject, but the Bureau would obstinately pursue McIntee with consummate vengeance.

Hamilton believed that McIntee was close to his demise. McIntee's secret activities depended on the loyalty of too many people. Those required to keep secrets needed to be kept happy.

Hamilton was elated with Father Potocsnak's visit. The priest was a priceless source of information. Hamilton respected his office and his need to protect his penitent even more than a doctor might a patient or a reporter his source. Before he left, Hamilton gave the priest directions, which if successful would probably put McIntee behind bars for a long time. Sooner or later, he was going to have to meet this secret witness. He was encouraged by the priest's visit. It looked like he was going to get his witness. Now all he needed was an honest judge and an untampered jury. Not an easy task in Chicago in 1934, but getting better.

When he entered the building on Pennsylvania Avenue, it was exactly ten a.m. The elevator doors opened to a large room and a matronly woman with a stern face looking at him from behind a large desk.

"Good morning, Mr. Hamilton," she said, turning her attention to the clock on the wall. "How was the flight?"

"Long—ran into a little weather."

"The Director's expecting you, and you know how he hates to be kept waiting." Hamilton smiled as he walked past the desk.

"Is he in a good mood?"

"There were two other short meetings this morning…"

"And?" he said impatiently.

She didn't look at him, rather she continued to sort the morning mail mechanically. "Looked like they'd been dragged through the ringer."

He mumbled a sarcastic, "Thanks," and opened the door.

The room was large, windowless, stuffy, dimly lit, and smelled of tobacco. Its furniture consisted primarily of a long conference table with twelve or so chairs. The flag hung in front of a picture of Roosevelt. Most of the light came from incandescent pendants that focused on the table-top. One wall had a retractable screen. Behind it was an enormous map of the world. Longitudinal lines demarcated time zones. Clocks showed the current time in each zone.

A man sat on either side of Hoover, who appeared taller. Everyone at the Bureau attending these meetings knew that Hoover had the base swivel of his chair fully extended, putting him as much as a head taller than anyone else at the table.

Hamilton had worked with the other two men. One, Mark Gerlitz, with the Bureau since its formation, was now in charge of all field offices. He was in his late fifties, but didn't look it. His record was impeccable, as were his family affairs. According to Hoover, Gerlitz was an example of what an agent should be. The man on the director's right was his assistant, deputy director, mentor, and close friend, Craig Tolsen. They exchanged "good mornings," and Hamilton expressed regret for his tardiness. Hoover waved off the apology.

"Please," he said, gesturing to the chair next to Gerlitz. Hamilton sat and laid the envelope on the table. "Coffee?" Hoover pushed a tray with a pot and cups in his direction.

"Thanks, I always have room for more." He poured the coffee into a porcelain cup.

"How was the trip?"

"Fine," he said, "touched down a little later than scheduled."

"That's not unusual—civilians," Hoover muttered.

Gerlitz lit a cigarette while Hamilton nervously opened the envelope. Hoover turned over a page of his morning agenda.

"If you don't mind, Agent Hamilton, I would like to bring Mr. Gerlitz and Mr. Tolsen up to date on what you're going to be presenting this morning."

"It would probably help, Mr. Hoover," Hamilton agreed after taking a sip of hot coffee.

"I have assigned agent Hamilton," Hoover went on, "to the case of one Sean, no middle name, McIntee, an Irish immigrant who came here eighteen years ago from Dublin. That's where Hamilton, here, came to know the man while he worked with British Intelligence." He nodded approvingly. "Now we—or rather Hamilton, suspected that McIntee, who at that time was just seventeen or so, was a member of the Irish Republican Army. We have hard evidence that there are others in this country—members of this I.R.A. organization—who also happen to be hard-line communists." He cleared his throat. "In my mind, this would be reason enough to deport this individual, but the case gets stronger. We also believe that he is responsible for the cold-blooded murder of two of our agents, which might never have happened had we been allowed to protect ourselves. Until now we have never been able to indict the scum.

"Before McIntee can qualify to the status of public enemy number one, we have to prove it."

"Excuse me, sir, but couldn't we just deport him?" Gerlitz asked matter of factly.

"I said, 'in my mind,' Mr. Gerlitz, which as I understand, is still not quite sufficient evidence to deport the bastard." He sighed. "Much to my dismay. Anyway we have reason to believe that he has stopped at nothing to build an empire equal to that of Capone and Lucianno, the difference here being that on the surface everything appears legal. Agent Hamilton has new information, which I hope will change his status. As I understand it, there are some delicate issues to do with the Catholic Church. A man of the cloth supposedly on the take. I for one, would not want to besmirch the whole Church because of one bad priest, but I will if it justifies the ends. Keep in mind it's McIntee we want." He nodded to Hamilton, folded his hands and sat back.

Hamilton broke the silence. He thanked Hoover and spread the contents of the envelope on the table. "Two weeks ago I received a call from a priest. He identified himself as Potocsnak and knew McIntee since his arrival in Chicago. He remembered McIntee's enlistment in Dion O'Bannion's gang and his inseparable friendship with Hymie Weiss. For a man of God, it didn't appear to me that he had any love for either of them."

He passed around surveillance photos of McIntee and Weiss. He also displayed a photo of Potocsnack taken outside the church after Sunday mass. "There were two totally unrelated circumstances that the priest wished to discuss with me. One involved a man who had come to him in the confessional. He didn't say much other than that he gave the man absolution; however, the penance had an interesting clause attached."

Gerlitz interrupted. "I don't understand. I thought a priest wasn't at liberty to…"

Hoover interrupted. "I'd like to hear everything agent Hamilton has to say. Then we will discuss our options." He gestured for Hamilton to continue.

"Potocsnak didn't betray anything the man mentioned in the confessional. Apparently because of the gravity of the man's sin, his penance was to make restitution to society."

"That doesn't sound right to me. I don't think priests can…" Gerlitz stopped mid-sentence; this time it was just a look from the Director.

Hamilton continued. "Frankly, I didn't think priests could make those demands either, Mr. Gerlitz, but after I talked to Father Potocsnak, I began to understand his reasoning. The priest, knowing McIntee and based on what the man told him, felt that he was in danger; worse yet, his immortal soul was in danger. He asked the man if he would be willing to see him at the parish house after he was through with confessions, to which he agreed. As you can understand, he couldn't give the man's name. He has agreed to meet with me if Father Potocsnack is present. I'm looking forward to this when I get back. I believe that what the priest calls 'grave' alludes to murder.

"Later I received a second call. This time the priest said he wanted to meet, but not at the parish house. We decided on my office. We got to know one another. That's when I asked him about this absolution situation—consistent with your concerns, Mr. Gerlitz. He could mention certain aspects of the conversation he had with the man outside of the confessional and enlighten me about a few things. For example, the penitent has to be truly sorry for his sins and make every effort not to commit them again."

He smiled. "Sounds familiar, like intent has a lot to do with the problem, and the penitent can't be a repeat offender. I concluded from this that the man was so involved with dirty tricks he was bound to repeat the crimes to which he was confessing. Nothing, as much as I tried, would induce the priest to reveal any more information.

"The second issue he wished to convey was even more incredible and extremely delicate. He had information that would make the Teapot Dome scandal look trivial if it ever leaked and wanted my word that I would do my utmost to handle the matter discreetly, to which I agreed. It appeared that McIntee had found a way to launder his massive amounts of illegal money through the Church. It was really very simple. All he needed was one bad priest, which he found in Monsignor Mooney, who was in charge of the Chicago Archdiocesan building fund. He was responsible for evaluating the bid process, whether it be for a new church, school, or ancillary building, such as a gym or orphanage.

"McIntee's bid was always higher than the others, sometimes almost twice as high, yet he always got the work. The Monsignor was totally autonomous in selecting the contractor. In return, McIntee donated back, as a gift, the difference between his and the low bid with a little extra for good measure. This gave him tremendous amounts of legal revenue and he made the payback with his illegal tender. And, of course, the good Monsignor feathers his nest with a little retirement fund.

"Potocsnak discovered this after he was assigned by the Archbishop to assist the building committee with the construction of an orphanage in his Parish. He told me the Monsignor keeps impeccable books. So far I haven't had the opportunity to meet the man or the Monsignor. I am waiting to hear how the Bureau wants me to proceed. We have two totally unrelated situations that could bring McIntee to his knees."

He could tell by their looks that he had done well. For the next fifteen minutes or so, Hoover allowed Gerlitz to field most of the questions. Finally the director broke in.

"In your opinion, Hamilton, what sin might a man commit for a priest to deny…" He searched for the term.

"Absolution, sir." Hamilton said, "and he wasn't denied absolution, Mr. Hoover. Potocsnak just imposed some sanctions. To answer your question, I imagine the transgression would have to be extreme."

"Like murder?" Tolsen said.

"Yes, I think that would be the case."

Hoover thought for a moment, biting his lip.

"I guess we're at the mercy of the man's conscience. What I mean is—our hook is only good if he abides by the priest's sanctions. For instance, could he go to another priest? Because if he could, there goes our ecclesiastical edge."

"I suppose he could do that," Hamilton said, "but it's my understanding that he would have to lie to the second priest about the first, which isn't likely."

Hoover shook his head, "It all sounds a little confusing to me. Obviously the first priority when you get back is to set up a meeting through the priest and see what this guy has to say. I'd lay my bet on the other issue—talk to the Monsignor, see what he has to say for himself."

The meeting continued for another hour. Hamilton left with their blessing to proceed. As Hamilton was leaving, Hoover said, "Proceed with great caution. I certainly don't want to incur the wrath of the Pope—do I?" He smiled broadly.

Hamilton met with Potocsnak for the second time at his office on Clark street. Potocsnak provided more information, this time with Matt Reilly's approval. He told Hamilton that there were episodes of Reilly's past that he was still not at liberty to discuss. "We're leaving the handling of everything in your hands," he said.

Hamilton was emphatic about his need to meet with Reilly, suggesting the time and place.

They elected to meet at the Garryowen on a night when it was at its busiest, and this Saturday night was unexceptional. Hamilton, no newcomer to the art of surveillance, was confident that if Matt Reilly's movements were being observed, it would take place after he left the club or his house. He felt comfortable with the plan only as long as Potocsnak didn't come dressed as a priest. He glanced at his watch and figured the priest must have had a busy schedule with his sinners tonight. He thought it interesting, even amusing, that this was the second time in his life he was relying on the assistance of a priest. This one seemed to know his way around and was accustomed to dealing with vermin like Sean McIntee. Now he was also willing to take on the Chicago Archdiocese almost single handedly.

He motioned to a lanky, sullen-faced waiter with slicked-back, greasy hair, and ordered a ginger ale. He propped the bad leg on the extra chair and watched the dancers, allowing himself to reminisce. The large hall was smoke-filled, underlit, and reeked of stale smoke, porter, and body odor. A ceili band screamed, and so did the dancers. One reel after the other rocked the hall and couples twirled to the music. When the band stopped abruptly, the dancers separated, the men going to one side of the oak-veneered floor and the women to the other. Standing against one wall, women whispered and laughed, while men, standing against the opposite wall, boldly sized up the woman they might take home, the women skittishly making eye contact in hopes of being chosen for the next dance.

At first Hamilton did not recognize the man walking toward him through the crowd of dancers. He wore a well-used corduroy jacket and a cheese-cutter cap. He dragged back a chair as if he owned the place and sat across from Hamilton, who had begun to snicker.

"I like the mustache—is it real?" The priest moved his fingers to the black bush above his upper lip. He returned the sarcasm.

"If you're so smart, William, you tell me."

Hamilton raised his hands in surrender. "You got me fooled—really, the Irish cap." He pursed his lips. "A great touch."

The waiter returned with the ginger ale and Potocsnak ordered a whiskey. He shrugged when the waiter left. "One of us has to fit in around here," he said, leaning on the table and lowering his voice. "Are you sure this is the safest place to talk with Matt?"

"Look around you, Jim, the place is like a hornet's nest. This is where Reilly meets booze vendors and probably interviews whores. What do you think?"

"I guess you're right. This is your expertise."

They sat back when the waiter returned. He put the whiskey down and left.

"Are you going to be all right with that?" Hamilton asked.

"Don't worry, William. The only difference between this and what I'm used to is that mine is usually consecrated."

Potocsnak recounted his conversation with Matt Reilly. Hamilton didn't take notes. Instead, he listened, totally engrossed with every explicit detail, without interrupting until he was certain the priest had no more to say. He rubbed his chin and gazed with disbelief at the priest.

"This is incredible. After all these years, we have a witness to a murder." He thought for a moment, his enthusiastic expression waning.

"The problem is the murderer, Matt Reilly, also happens to be the witness."

"But McIntee planted the gun, William."

"Yes, Jim, you and I know that, but it may not be as easy to convince a jury. This thing could blow up in our faces, with your penitent doing time for the murder and that bastard McIntee still on the loose."

"Now, wait a minute, William. I won't allow Matt Reilly to take all the blame. I'll admit to his involvement." Potocsnak stammered. "Yes, and I agree he even pulled the trigger."

"I'm just saying," Hamilton interrupted, "it could be an uphill battle to convince a jury, that's all."

"And I'm saying this man told me in the sanctity of the confessional."

"Yeah, we know how far that bit of confidentiality is going to go."

Hamilton couldn't hold back the bitingly spiteful comment. He immediately apologized.

"Look, Jim, from what you've told me, this guy Reilly obviously wants to make restitution; however, our friend McIntee may have his Irish derriere more protected than we think."

"What exactly do you mean?"

"Did Reilly mention what became of the gun?"

Potocsnak thought for a moment: "I don't remember."

"And I'll bet that Reilly doesn't remember either," Hamilton said soberly.

"I don't understand."

"McIntee has the gun, with Reilly's prints all over it."

"Oh, my God!"

Hamilton drained the last of the ginger ale. They sat in silence, Potocsnak waiting for Hamilton to make everything right. Hamilton nodded. "That's it." He leaned forward. "You said he kept a record of cash he delivered to the bank?"

"That's what he said."

"Good. Let's meet with your friend Reilly. If he's willing to give us information on all the transactions, hell, we just might put this guy away for a decade. Maybe not as much as we would with a murder rap, but I'll settle for the same as we gave Capone."

"What about Reilly? Will he be protected?"

Hamilton smiled, reached over and placed his hand on the priest's shoulder.

"I promise," he said, "Now let's meet this friend of yours."

CHAPTER FORTY

MAEVE REILLY WAS in her thirties. She was a striking woman with long red hair and flawless skin, white as alabaster. She employed a special composure that made men maintain a disposition of civility. Her first passion in life was for her husband and children, and when it came to their welfare she displayed an uncompromising commitment. She enjoyed preparing breakfast and getting the girls off to school. Routinely, later, after Matt had left for work, she took her bath. This week was almost over and she felt encouraged. For the first time in years Matt had confided in her. She found that she loved him even more for telling her his troubles. He told her how much he hated Sean McIntee for everything he represented. He hated the gangsters, the cops on the take. He had come to hate himself for his actions that almost wrecked their marriage. She was a compassionate listener, though it was hard to be sympathetic when he gave accounts of corrupt acts. It was especially difficult to listen to his account of the killing. She told him that they were in this together and would see it through. They also decided that when all this was over they would return to Ireland. It wasn't like they were alone. It was a great comfort to Maeve knowing that Father Potocsnak was by their side.

She stood in the bath and reached for the towel on the chair. After drying herself, she stepped into her slip and in one swift gyration pulled it upwards over her naked body. She moved gracefully into the bedroom and sat. She took panties from a drawer in the dresser. She put them on in a mechanical manner as she regarded herself in the triptych mirror. She then drew her hair back and held it in place with a mother-of-pearl comb. *Still good looking,* she thought. She raised her breasts in an upward motion and smiled wishfully. *Well, some parts need a little help,* she thought. She began to put on her makeup, first her lips, then she traced her eyebrows with a pencil. She was oblivious to the first knock. The next was louder and impetuous. Putting on her robe, she quickly moved down the stairs. Through the diffused glass Maeve could tell it was the figure of a man, but not her husband. She opened the door to a tall, well-dressed man who doffed his hat.

"Mornin', Maeve," he said, with an insincere smile.

"Sean, it's good to see you," she said, masking her real feelings. Then her thoughts were immediately of her husband. "Is Matt all right?"

"Why?" He answered with a sarcastic smile, "Shouldn't he be?"

"Yes, yes, of course, it's just that, well, you never come by like this."

He stopped her politely. "Maeve, Matt is fine." His smile was more affable. "At least he was in good spirits last time I saw him. Now, d'ya mind if I come in, Maeve. There's a few things I'd like to clear up with you."

She hesitated.

"These are matters that only you can solve," he said more seriously.

She opened the door wider and motioned for him to come in. When she closed the door, her hand came up, pulling the robe tightly around her neck.

"Please, Sean, sit down. I'll make a cup of tea."

"No thanks, I wouldn't want to be puttin' you to any trouble." He removed his hat and sat upright on the edge of the couch. "I wanted to see if you knew what's bothering Matt. He seems nervous, not himself, if you know what I mean."

She was very uncomfortable and had to keep moving. "I hadn't noticed anything unusual." She went into the kitchen. "I think I could use a spot of tea." It was easier to talk if she didn't have to look at him. "Now, what is it that only I can help you with?" Her hand shook nervously as she filled the kettle. His voice came from behind her.

"I'm worried about Matt, Maeve. You're the only one who can talk some sense into him." Without looking around, she moved over to the stove. "I don't know what you mean, Sean. You know I haven't involved myself in my husband's business." She was performing again, confident she could convince him that everything was all right. She knew that to appear nervous would be an admission of guilt. She opened drawers, looking for a match to light the stove. "Can I help?" he said, producing a lighter.

"Oh, I know I have a box of matches here somewhere. I can never find them when I need them." She began to reach in the top cupboards.

"Sometimes Matt uses them to light his pipe," she said breathlessly. On her toes she could barely touch the box and silently cursed her husband for throwing them back there. She froze. Her eyes closed tightly and she prayed silently that this was just a bad dream, no, a horrible nightmare. His hands, his long wiry fingers, felt foreign on her hips.

The horrible dream became a reality when his voice broke the silence. "Here, Maeve, let me help you."

His hands were on her waist; long bony fingers touched her stomach. He raised her until she was almost off the ground, and when she said that it was all right, she had the matches, he slowly let her down. His hands moved upwards until the bony fingers touched the underneath of her breasts. She tried to stay on her toes but his left hand found the opening in the robe, and sliding beneath the loose-fitting slip, encompassed her bare right breast.

"You're a good lookin' woman, Maeve," he whispered, lips barely touching her neck. She could feel both hands now, pushing and pulling at her like one might knead dough. She bravely pushed his hands away and lit the stove with a shaking hand. Her eyes welled up. She turned to face him, pulling the robe back around her neck.

"I hope this isn't what you came here for, Sean McIntee. If you think for a moment that I'm going to play parlor games with you, you're very mistaken," she burst out.

His eyes were first to convey his anger, squinting with a frightening glare. His mouth became a fierce slit and through it punctuated the silence.

"You fukken Dublin whore." He grabbed her robe and pulled her tightly to him. Maeve turned her head and felt his warm breath on her cheek. "You're a lying little fuck, Maeve, and you know it. That cock-sucken' husband of yours is talkin' to that Polack prick they call a priest."

"No, Sean, it's not true." Her mind spinning, she desperately hoping for something to say that would make sense.

"And what's wrong with a man seeing a priest, Sean? Sure you wouldn't begrudge a man going to confession? Would you, Sean?" She could feel the back of his hands through the robe. He massaged her slowly. The anger left his voice, replaced by a trace of civility. She could feel the hardness of his body pushing her into the counter. "Sean, please," she pleaded. "Let's not do this. You don't want…" Her words were muffled by his open mouth. Her eyes closed tight, and she thought about her husband. If it would take this to protect him… She dismissed the thought and struggled to bring her hands up and made a gallant effort to push him away. She stopped when she felt the cold steel at the back of her neck.

"It wouldn't be healthy to move a lot, Maeve, darlin'. Besides all I'm trying to do is convince you to talk to Matt, that's all." He spoke into her mouth and his right hand pulled the knife, forcing her to touch him. She didn't move and allowed his left hand to open the robe.

She cringed as he fondled, first her breasts then slowly moving to her left hip. What he thought might be teasing was revolting to her. He gathered the slip to the waist band of her panties and slid his hand inside, down her bare thigh. She felt his thumb and flinched, this time feeling the knife sting the back of her neck, then the warm liquid streamed down her back. She winced.

"You're doin' it to yourself, bitch." He was becoming more impatient. She felt him ripping at the buttons on his trousers. "Face it. You're goin' to get fucked and if you fuck me back we might be able to work somethin' out with your auld fella."

Maeve prayed that she would pass out. She prayed out loud. "Hail Mary, full of grace…"

"Shut the fuck up, bitch!"

"Blessed art though among women…" His thrusting was becoming unbearable. The room seemed to rotate above her as if she were trapped on a merry-go-round. She cried out, "Jesus, Mary and Joseph help me."

The front door opened with a loud bang. It was hard to tell which of them was more astounded. The voices were hysterical. Everyone seemed to be hollering at once. Hamilton was flanked by two agents with guns drawn. His left hand displayed the silver emblem of the Bureau.

"FBI, McIntee. Drop the knife, now!" Immediately McIntee raised the knife and forced it to her throat. Maeve tried to wrench herself free but he pushed the knife harder, drawing blood.

"Stay back," he yelled, "or I'll cut the fukken whore's head off. Now back off!"

Hamilton and the two agents halted just inside the small kitchen. He didn't raise his gun to the ceiling, rather he kept it pointed at McIntee's head. His hand was steady as a rock and his voice was firm. "Put the knife down, McIntee, and step aside. Do it now!"

"You can't shoot me. Not for this." His voice was shaky. "Hell, we're auld friends. Tell him, Maeve, aren't we friends?" He squeezed her neck. "Isn't that right, Maeve?" She tried to say something; it came out as a whimper.

Hamilton was unequivocating. "I'm going to count to three, asshole, then I'm going to save the tax-payers of this city a bundle." He was only a few feet from McIntee and pointed the Luger squarely at his head.

The blood drained from McIntee's face. "Now wait just a min…"

"One."

"Go ahead—shoot, an' she comes with me," His voice was jittery and unconvincing.

"Two…"

McIntee waited, then dropped the knife and raised his hands. For a moment the tension was neutralized by the vision of McIntee's pathetic disarray. Now he pleaded for mercy. His trousers hung around his ankles. He began to mutter about his innocence. Hamilton told him to pull up his pants. McIntee was submissive while one of the agents placed him in handcuffs. Hamilton wrapped the robe around Maeve while the other agent, a very tall man, found a towel, wet it, and handed it to him.

"Is she all right?" he asked. Hamilton first wiped the small cut on her throat, then examined the wound in the back of her neck.

"I think she'll live." He grinned at her and she managed to force a meager smile.

"Thanks, you're Hamilton, aren't you? William Hamilton. Matt told me about you. He said you were going to help us." Her voice was weak.

"Don't talk now, missus Reilly." He passed her to one of the other agents. "Take care of her," he said, then he turned back to McIntee.

"You're under arrest, McIntee, for assaulting a federal witness."

"What the hell are you talkin' about? Federal witness, shit, her goddamn husband works for me. She's…"

Hamilton ignored his babbling. "Other charges include receiving funds from gambling, prostitution, conspiracy—oh, and let's not rule out battery and rape. So far that's all that comes to mind. When I think of something else I'll let you know." McIntee's jaw dropped.

"Fuck you, Hamilton."

His gaze became more intense; it irritated Hamilton.

"Get him out of here!" They moved toward the door. McIntee pulled back from the agent's grasp, his head turned around, and he stared at Hamilton.

"Have we met somewhere?" It was a quizzical demand.

"I doubt it." Hamilton looked past him to the agent. "Take him away!"

So what if McIntee recognized him. He had no reason to fear McIntee's recall. Hamilton reconciled himself to the idea that to be recognized by McIntee would in no way affect the case. He still held the bloody towel, folding it subconsciously.

"It is you," McIntee was emphatic. "Well, I'll be damned—if it isn't the fukken missin' reporter." He put his head down, covering the wicked smirk as the tall agent named Jack pulled him away. He stopped in the doorway. "Riordan. That's who you are, isn't it? You can talk about rape.

You're the fukken cool one, aren't ya. You fukked her and walked, didn't ya?"

Hamilton lost his composure.

"What the hell are you talking about?"

"I'm talkin' about Kathleen Barrett. You fucked her."

Hamilton's past began to unfold before him. What did this man know of their love? She wouldn't have told anyone, especially not him. What he said next struck Hamilton like a bolt of lightning.

"Everyone thought you were dead. Nice goin', leavin' her with two bastard babies."

His comments trailed as he was dragged to the waiting car. Hamilton restrained an urge to kill him. Surely he was lying. But what if he wasn't? Was he a father? Questions without answers filled his mind. He was conscious of being tugged by the other agent. Hamilton faced the reality of the present.

"Yes, what is it?" he said bitterly.

"William, are you okay? What was all that about?" Hamilton ignored the question and looked past the man to Maeve Reilly, who sat on the edge of the couch, a dazed expression on her face.

"Get her to a hospital, will you," he said, in a soft monotone.

"Sure thing." The agent nodded and left. In a moment Hamilton was alone in the house. It was quiet. He sat, his gaze fixated on the bloody towel. He dropped it to the floor and placed his head in his hands. He was alone with his own indiscretions.

CHAPTER FORTY-ONE

AT TEN-TWENTY, HAMILTON was informed that the jury had reached a verdict. He left his office on Clark street and despite his leg injuries walked briskly to the courthouse. In the middle of January, Chicago weather was living up to its reputation. He pulled the raincoat tightly about his neck. The seven-week trial was over. Hamilton felt confident that the presentation of the evidence was going to bring a finding of guilty, assuming the jurors hadn't been bribed. He dismissed the thought. If McIntee had managed to fix the jury, he went to an awful lot of trouble at the last minute to sabotage the credibility of the prime witness.

Days before the trial, the Chicago Globe featured a story on the murder of the owner of a local dance club. Where the police found the weapon in this gangland slaying was not reported. Prints taken from the gun had to be analyzed and a duplicate tested by the Bureau of Identification.

What the Chicago Police didn't know was that months earlier, the Bureau of Identification had combined with other Justice Department agencies and was now under the jurisdiction of the FBI. Hamilton made sure that the Chicago Police received a comprehensive report. It included details of the thorough search for a match of the prints found on the gun with every gangster and petty hoodlum who had a record. He ended with an apology, stating that all avenues of research were inconclusive.

Hamilton considered another unusual development occurring just before the trial: Mooney suffered a fatal heart attack. Without the Monsignor, the District Attorney found it impossible to pursue the source of the money laundering. With the death of the Monsignor, it would be difficult to prove that illegal money had been moved through legal channels; besides, there was sufficient evidence to put McIntee away without besmirching the Catholic Church. Hamilton smiled to himself and pondered the odds of a key witness and possible accomplice having a heart attack hours before being deposed.

It was Maeve Reilly's testimony that probably proved the most damaging. She was elegant and believable. She broke down so many times during cross-examination the judge set a record for taking recesses. That was the turning point; no man could have possibly dismissed the overwhelming credibility of her character.

Hamilton daydreamed during much of the trial. Sean McIntee's comments about Kathleen and her babies overshadowed the courtroom testimony. More than once he was tempted to approach McIntee and exact the truth, by force if needed. Hamilton considered taking a trip back to Ireland after the trial to reach the right decision in fulfilling responsibilities to Kathleen. Three weeks ago he had written a letter to Father Donnelly reviewing his assignment in England and noting that secrecy of the mission then demanded that he be remembered as dead. Many times he wanted to write to Kathleen, he said, but guessed she would likely be married. He ended the letter with descriptions of events leading to McIntee's arrest. It was uncanny, he wrote, that of all people to become a public enemy, it would be someone he had met in Ireland during those troubled times, and what were the chances of that happening?

By the time he reached the courthouse, the rain had stopped. He took the stairs. When he opened the door, he was relieved to see the district attorney hadn't arrived yet. Quietly he moved to the second row and sat next to other agents who had also been witnesses.

"How's it goin', Jack," he whispered.

"Just waiting for the jury. I hear they've made a decision."

"Yeah," Hamilton said. "Let's hope it's the right one."

Jack folded his arms and talked out of the side of his mouth.

"The fact they've been sequestered for over a week is a good sign—I guess."

McIntee sat just a few feet in front of them. His feet were shackled and it looked like the prison barber had been an apprentice. He turned his evil white face and glared at Hamilton.

The wicked slit mouthed something. Hamilton interpreted the curse as, "I'll get you, cocksucker."

The district attorney arrived quick footed and looking distraught; his assistant was close behind. The D.A. dropped onto the bentwood chair and broke the quiet of the courtroom by abruptly tossing his briefcase on the table. He shuffled through it, eventually finding a pad and pencil. The judge entered. The bailiff announced that court was now in session. The judge instructed the bailiff to bring the jurors into the courtroom. They took their places.

"Has the jury made a decision?" the judge asked.

The juror nearest him, in seat one, stood and answered.

"We have, your honor." The judge then turned his attention to McIntee.

"Will the defendant please rise," he said with authority. McIntee didn't stand right away; rather, his attorney, who had obeyed the order, pulled him to his feet. The judge observed McIntee's defiant resistance.

"Mister McIntee," he said in a stern voice, "this trial is still in progress and I am still the man in charge. I would proceed with great caution if I were you, sir. You have been in contempt of this court from the outset of this trial. It certainly hasn't been prudent to evoke the wrath of this court. If this jury finds you guilty, you'll be at the mercy of this court. I know you're incorrigible and a poor excuse for a human being. It would be, however, a conclusion of inconceivable stupidity to assume that I wouldn't administer the full extent of punishment afforded me by the law. Do you understand me, Mister McIntee?"

McIntee kept his head down and mumbled something.

"I can't hear you, sir."

"He said he is sorry, your honor, and he completely understands," his lawyer said. The fabrication allowed the judge to proceed.

He turned back to the jury foreman. There was an eerie silence. The man's voice was resonant, punctuating every word.

"We the jury…find the defendant, Sean McIntee," he hesitated as if he had studied how he would dramatize the moment and looked directly at McIntee…"guilty on all counts."

There was a loud outcry from friends of the Reillys.

Hamilton sighed. He was relieved that it was finally over.

McIntee subsequently was sentenced to twenty years.

Later the same day, Hamilton attended meetings to wrap up the extradition of Matt Reilly and his family to Ireland. He didn't let Reilly leave without a scathing lecture. It was his greed that placed his family in harm's way; after all, he wasn't a stupid man and had to know about the gambling and prostitution early enough to have given up his ties to McIntee.

"Had you not come forward when you did, you would have accompanied your boss to Alcatraz," Hamilton said. "You will have to live with humiliation. You will have to live with the guilt you must feel because you shot and killed a man."

Hamilton didn't often let his anger boil. Reilly needed to know that his testimony, as necessary as it was, in no way justified his own criminal behavior. Hamilton wished Maeve Reilly well. He left the office around four-thirty.

His apartment was a half hour drive from the office. Rain began as he parked and entered through the back door. He turned on the light to a roomy kitchen, the only furniture a chrome-legged table with an imitation-marble top and four matching chairs. It was clean and did not look at all like what one might expect of a bachelor. He removed his raincoat and jacket and hung them on the back of the door. He opened the refrigerator and drew a package of meat to his nose. He sniffed it scrupulously, made a face, then ceremoniously tossed the meat in the garbage. He did the same to a half-empty bottle of milk and some leftovers. Obviously he hadn't spent much time at home lately.

Content with a bottle of ginger ale, he located a bottle opener from one of the drawers and popped the top. He moved into the sitting room through an arched doorway and plunged into an easy chair. The room expressed a quiet affluence. A large, white-marble fireplace centered on one wall surrounded by ceiling-high shelves filled with books. He turned a knob on the floor-model gramophone and decided on a John McCormack song: "Memories." Taking a long swig on the ginger ale, he pulled the bottle from his mouth and burped; his gaze slowly traversed the ceiling, down the front door to the floor to where the mail lay strewn haphazzardly. Despite his relaxed position, he felt compelled to pick up the letters. Quickly he glanced at the envelopes, placing each one in turn behind the others until he recognized the one he'd been waiting for. He ripped open Father Donnelly's envelope and sat on the edge of the chair. Music filled the silence. As he read the letter, the lyrics of John McCormack suggested a parallel to his own circumstances:

Memories, memories—songs of love so true.
O'er my sea of memories, my dreams drift back to.you.

> *Dear William, I was indeed surprised to hear from you and I might add somewhat elated. Elated that you are alive and well. The newspapers were very specific about the ship's tragic sinking. Everyone was lost, they said. I can see now, based on your letter, the advantage to you in keeping your survival from becoming known. I find it an amazing coincidence you remember of course that many thought you were*

responsible for the arrest of Kathleen's father. Well, some people here believe that Sean McIntee might have been involved.

Hamilton whispered under his breath: 'That conniving little prick.'

Anyway, William, you must be more anxious about news of Kathleen. After you left and were assumed dead, Kathleen told me that she was pregnant and you were the father. I found it meaningful that she still wanted to give the baby your name, at least what she thought was your name. Her parents sent her to America and it was there she delivered twin boys.

Hamilton's eyes stared beyond the page. For an instant he felt like any proud father, wishing he could hold them, his boys, his twins. God, I'm the father of teenagers, he thought. He returned from his silent musings to the letter.

She married after she had the babies. Talking to her mother, it appears that Kathleen is very happy and I would strongly advise against you trying to contact her or the boys. They believe you to be dead, William. Interfering in their lives would be a grave mistake and it's for this reason I'm not disclosing their whereabouts. Besides, you're already in the business of locating people and will do what you must. I imagine you've adjusted well to the past eighteen years. I know you possess respect for justice and doing what's right and I'll pray that God will show you the way to make the right decision. There's not much I can add to this epistle, William. If I don't hear from you, I'll know you've made the right choice.

Yours in Christ, Father Michael P. Donnelly

Hamilton placed the letter on the side table and eased back in the chair. He locked his hands behind his head and stared blankly at the ceiling. The priest said that he had...how did he put it, *adjusted* to the past eighteen years. Adjusted, he thought, oh, he had adjusted all right. Every waking moment was dedicated to serving the Bureau. He never married because he envisioned Kathleen in every woman he dated. Adjusted? He never stopped loving her. Now he would have to adjust to a new dilemma: abandonment of his children. It was some consolation to know they were happy. As the priest said, it was up to him now to get on with his life, adjust. He smiled, a self-willed smile, and knew he wouldn't be responding to the priest. He closed his eyes and listened to the end of the song. *You left me alone, but now you're my own, in my beautiful memories.*

CHAPTER FORTY-TWO

THE HIGH MASS at Saint Matthew's lasted longer than usual. Ryan and Lawrence moved with exaggerated speed to the car. Kathleen followed closely behind with Maggie. Madge Noonan had invited the family to a Sunday brunch, and Kathleen didn't want to keep her waiting. The car drove away before Lawrence had a chance to close the door.

"Jeez, at least give me a moment to shut the door." Lawrence spoke with a melodramatic tone. "We're not chasing some bank robber, are we?"

Ryan looked at him through the rear-view mirror.

"No, but then again I'd rather chase a bank robber than be late to one of your Aunt Madge's brunches. Besides who gave…"

"Gave you the right to use that kind of language," Kathleen interjected apprehensively. "I'm sure it's not something you learned at the monastery."

"All I said was *Jeez*. Everyone says it, Mother. Even songs have words that…"

"Not the songs I listen to, Lawrence Riordan. When will you begin to act responsibly? The word *Jeez* is just a modern-day slang word for our Almighty God, and I'll thank you not to use it again. It's one of the ten commandments. You did learn that at the monastery, didn't you?" Her tone was inflexible and when she had finished, the car was quiet except for the noise of the engine.

"Mother," Maggie said, "I think you've been acting—well, grudgeful, toward Lawrence since he left the monastery."

"Had to leave, Maggie, had to leave the monastery," Kathleen repeated without turning around. "Expelled, and besides, this has nothing to do with you. You don't know the whole story, Maggie."

"I do know, Mother. Lawrence told me everything, all about that poor boy falling to his death. You act as though Lawrence was responsible." Kathleen ignored the accusation.

"Speaking of responsible, Maggie, what in the world got into you two during the sermon? You shook the pew with your snickers. I've never been so embarrassed."

"Didn't you hear, Mother?" Lawrence said, half laughing.

"Missus Beardsley let a huge fart, then she coughed to cover it up." Maggie laughed. "I think it was the smell that really gave her away." Kathleen wasn't amused. "Since you've come home, Lawrence, all you've done is set a bad example for your sister. Maggie has always acted properly. I was praying that she would influence you, instead it's been the opposite."

"Is this family going to display some politeness toward one another?" Ryan asked. "Kathleen, I think I've heard enough about the problems at the monastery. You've done nothing but ride the boy these past few months. We know what happened. Abbot La Verdiere explained everything. The real tragedy was Lawrence's efforts to place all the blame on Michael. That was inexcusable behavior, but it's all in the past. Now, once and for all, I would appreciate not hearing another word, unless it's to change the subject, okay?"

Although she wanted to, Kathleen knew this wasn't the time or place to respond. The rest of the drive was silent.

Actually, since his return, Kathleen had made an effort to display some respect for her son, but it was with great difficulty. She couldn't get the dead boy's mother out of her thoughts. How sick she must have felt at the death of her son. It was hard for Kathleen to forgive Lawrence; after all, it was his mischievous deeds that caused the accident. The Abbot had pointed out a myriad of lies her son had told. Sometimes she prioritized his acts of misconduct, and always it was the lies that were most bothersome. Knowing that Michael would receive a lesser penalty, Lawrence had concocted a conspiracy to hold his brother responsible for the tragic prank. It was inconceivable to her that he could do this to his brother, who loved him as much as she did. Lawrence had hurt her again. Forgiveness this time was going to take longer.

The car stopped. "We're here," Ryan said, forcing the joviality. "Let's make this a happy occasion, shall we?"

Madge and Dennis immediately answered the door. The reception was loud and cheerful, with huge embraces and the question, why had it taken so long to get together? All the earlier traces of incivility were replaced with what seemed to be a genuine show of good spirits. Missus Dunne directed everyone to the living room; from the kitchen, an appetizing aroma of bacon and black pudding filled the air. Ryan immediately moved to the blazing fire, first drywashing his hands and holding them to the heat, then turning to warm his posterior. Irish music from the wind-up gramophone created the background for their conversation. Lawrence and Maggie sat quietly bored while the grown-ups chronicled the latest minutiae in their lives. The foyer was alive with chatter. Anne and James had arrived. Missus Dunne took their coats and returned to the kitchen. With open arms, James approached Kathleen, who arose to receive the bear hug.

"How's my favorite cousin?"

"James, James," she managed breathlessly. "If you want me to stay your favorite cousin you'll treat me more gently—and you can be thankful I haven't eaten yet."

He kissed her cheek. "You're still as beautiful as ever," he whispered. Then he moved over to Ryan, who hadn't left his position by the fire, and shook his hand vigorously. Kathleen held Anne at arm's length and studied her. "Anne, you're the one who holds the beauty, or should I say Sister Anne?" She hesitated. "That is, if you're still going by your birth name."

"I have taken the name Augustine, Sister Augustine. I guess Mother didn't get around to telling you, did she?"

"I'm sure she'd have gotten around to it sooner or later," Kathleen said sarcastically, throwing Madge a glance. "Anyway, you make a beautiful nun, Anne." Anne looked down piously, ignoring the compliment. "James just picked me up at the station. I'll be home for a few days. I'd love it if we could get together."

Madge, busy with James, overheard the comment. "Few *days*—I thought they'd at least give you a few weeks before you leave," she said.

"Where are you going?" Kathleen asked.

"Africa. Well, actually, I will spend some months in Antwerp, studying at the School of Tropical Medicine; I'm going to be working at a missionary hospital. Mother didn't really tell you a thing, did she? I do have you to thank, you know."

"Me?" Kathleen said, confused. "I was your inspiration to become a nun?"

"No, silly, to be a nurse. I remember when you first came. I was so impressed with your stories of Ireland and how you helped take care of all those poor souls of the Easter Rebellion." Kathleen kissed her cheek.

"You're a darling, Anne." Dennis put his arm around his daughter.

"You can't do this to just any nun." He smiled and pulled her close.

"Just a few days, eh? Well, we're going to fill those few days," he said proudly.

James playfully nudged Ryan aside to get his share of the heat.

"How's the Bureau treating you, Ryan? I'd sure like to join myself, but you know how Dad feels about me working with him at the firm."

"Hoover's looking for lawyers, James. He's convinced that the law is a great foundation for field agents."

"He's probably right," James acknowledged.

"Right, my ass," Dennis said vehemently, overhearing their conversation.

"Dennis Noonan. Watch your language. I'm surprised at you! And your own daughter, a nun."

"I'm sorry for that sordid display of indelicacy," he bowed to his daughter, who smiled and curtseyed. "No offense taken, sir."

"Well I don't think it's so funny," Madge said, with an annoyed tone. Dennis moved closer to the fire.

"That giant-headed pompous midget isn't going to get his supercilious little hands on this lad." He pulled James close. "Right, James?"

"I suppose so, Dad," he said, winking at Ryan. "Ryan will just have to keep me updated on the Bureau. Speaking of which, have you caught any bank robbers or public enemies lately?"

Ryan caught Lawrence's eye and smiled; memory of the annoying car ride vanished. "As a matter of fact, I was accused of chasing one this morning."

"You're kidding?"

"Afraid so, James. Besides, the Chicago office seems to get the lion's share of public enemies."

Dennis, deep in thought, stroked his chin and offered Ryan a cigarette. "Smoke?" Ryan passed.

"Still pure of lung, eh," Dennis said, offering one to James. He accepted it.

"I was reading something just the other day about your Bureau," Dennis continued, lighting James's cigarette. "What was that? Oh, yes, you boys caught another big mobster, put him away on rape charges. Couldn't get him on all the usual felonies, like racketeering and murder, rape, of all things. Now there's an easy trap to set up. What was it you boys drummed up on Capone. Tax evasion, wasn't it?"

"True, and this wasn't a set up, Dennis," Ryan said. "He actually was caught in the act of raping the wife of the prime witness."

"Wasn't he Irish? What was his name?" Dennis asked.

"McIntee, Sean McIntee," Ryan said casually. Kathleen, who had been immersed in Anne's impassioned account of her duties in Africa, looked stunned. She suppressed the urge to cry out that she knew him in Dublin. Instead, she tuned into Ryan's narrative: "Dublin eighteen years ago and made a name for himself in the Dion O'Bannion gang…"

"Doesn't make one proud to be Irish, does it?" James remarked.

Why wasn't she capable of saying that she knew him? Images of their childhood flashed before her. Visions of Sean and Bridget, school days, swimming at Dollymount, and stealing apples from Tom Murphy's orchard crossed her mind. She couldn't say anything because what really occupied her thoughts was Liam Riordan—and Sean McIntee knew Liam Riordan. She smiled inwardly and considered for a moment her paranoia, now magnified. Anne touched her arm.

"Kathleen, Kathleen, are you all right?"

"I'm just fine, really," she said. "It's just that I believe I know the man Ryan and your father are talking about."

Ryan overheard her and moved to her side.

"Are you all right, darling?" he asked, placing a comforting arm around her. "You're white as a sheet." James rushed to get her a chair.

"I'll be all right," she said. "What's all the fuss about? All I said was that I thought I knew the man you were all talking about, Sean McIntee. I knew him in Dublin, went to school with him. It was just a shock, that's all, I mean for him to have done those horrible things. Please, I'll be just fine when I get something to eat." She managed a smile. "Where is all this great food you cooked, Madge?"

In timely fashion, Missus Dunne announced that brunch was on the table. As they moved to the dining room, James muttered that she looked as though she'd seen a ghost.

Kathleen was remote during brunch. Sean McIntee's name evoked a sense of incrimination, which she reasoned was consistent with earlier news of Liam Riordan. She was vaguely aware of the conversation around her and occasionally nodded with an indulgent smile. When brunch was over, they celebrated with a glass of port for Anne's final vows and departure for Africa. Ryan and Dennis retired to the library for a cigar, and James asked Lawrence to join him to look in on his old boxing gym. Kathleen, Madge, and Anne helped Missus Dunne put things away. Of all the rooms in the big house, it was the kitchen where families really gathered to talk.

Anne mechanically dried a saucer as she looked out the kitchen window to where Maggie sat alone in the garden feeding the birds.

Without turning, she asked, "How is Maggie these days, Kathleen? She's not your typical sixteen-year old, is she?"

"No." Kathleen sighed. "There's not much that's typical about Maggie at all."

"I've always remembered Maggie as, well, happy-go-lucky, I guess," Madge said. "Lately I sense that she seems a little withdrawn. It's not like her."

"I don't want to appear forward, Kathleen. Is she still in pain?" Anne asked. "I thought I saw her wince getting up from the table."

"Probably Missus Dunne's black pudding," Madge said, trying to add a little levity.

"Maggie's had to deal with pain all her life. I sometimes wish..." Kathleen's eyes filled with tears, "wish God would take her. I'm not sure I can keep up the facade."

"There, there, Kathleen." Madge helped her to the kitchen table and gently eased her into a chair. "Maggie will survive all this, you'll see. She's a trooper if I ever saw one."

Kathleen sobbed, all the strong-willed conservative armor dispelled. It was as if flood gates had opened, releasing all the anguish. In an instant the indomitable spirit vanished. She wanted to tell Madge about nights of comforting her daughter, massaging her distorted limbs, trying to rub away the pain. How many times had she rationalized her misfortune, telling herself that God surely had a reason to misshape her this way. Then there was Lawrence with all his problems. She wanted to announce loudly that Sean McIntee had been a childhood friend. She wanted to tell her aunt the truth. Living a lie hurt. Instead she cried, and when she finished, she wiped her moist face with a napkin. Sitting more erect, she had once again prevailed, keeping her secrets.

"I'm so sorry, Madge." She managed a smile. "I don't intend to spoil this day for you and Anne. I think what really got to me was Maggie's comment the other night. It seems all right for me to have thoughts about...well, God, taking her. It really hit home when she said, *Mother, sometimes I wish I would just not wake up*. Now it's different, Madge. She's the one wishing it would all end."

"There now, darlin', all that sounds fairly normal to me. How many times have we said the same thing, Kathleen, sometimes wishing tomorrow would never come."

"It wasn't like that, Madge."

Madge touched her hand. "Remember, you're never alone as long as I'm here."

"Thanks." Kathleen caressed her, and after a short silence Anne came over and drew a chair to the table. Her expression looked awkward as she searched her mind to pose the sensitive question.

"What about all the operations, Kathleen? Don't the doctors give you hope for recovery? What's their prognosis?"

"Oh, you know doctors as well as I do, Anne. Sometimes I feel that they're just as surprised as I am that Maggie has survived this long. No, lately, I'm afraid I haven't been given much hope."

"Would you mind very much if I talked to her?"

Kathleen quickened. "Oh, Anne, I'd love that. You're closer to God than anyone. She really adores you—if there's anyone who can make her happy, I'm sure it would be you."

Anne pushed her chair back and stood.

"I don't believe I'm any closer to God than either you or Mother. On the contrary, it's just possible that the one closest to God is Maggie. I'll see what I can do," she said affectionately as she left to join Maggie in the garden.

Rain through the night had left the grass damp. Although the sky was bright and cloudless, a chill was felt in the air. Maggie sat on a wrought-iron bench and broadcast small pieces of bread to the hungry starlings, which flew to a nearby tree when Anne approached.

"Saint Francis would be proud to see that someone is taking care of God's creatures. Mind if I join you?" Anne said, sitting beside her.

"I'd like that," Maggie said cheerfully, making more room on the bench.

"I'm sorry I frightened them off."

"They always come back, Anne," Maggie stammered, "I mean, Sister Anne." She shook her head and drew a sigh of relief. "Augustine, Sister Augustine. Now that you're a full-fledged nun, I don't quite know what to call you."

"Why don't you just call me Anne. That's what the rest of the family calls me."

Maggie looked grateful. "Very good. It's Anne then," she said, and scattered more crumbs. "What's it like being a nun? I mean now that you've made your final vows an' all."

"I've been so busy I haven't really given that much thought."

"Won't you miss your family? I always thought that nuns were isolated. What do they call it? Clust...clois..."

"Cloistered. You're thinking of a particular order of nuns, Maggie, that devote themselves to prayer. The order that I belong to administers to the sick. You are right, though, I certainly won't be spending as much time with my family. It doesn't mean that I won't see them again. I know they're always there for me. Look at your mother. She left her home in Ireland to make a new life here in America and hasn't seen her family in eighteen years. It doesn't mean she's been abandoned, does it? Being a nun, Maggie, is just like any other occupation."

"But you can't ever marry, can you?"

"No, I'm married to God."

"That's what I want...'course, fat chance I'll have of marrying anyone else but God, not with this body." Maggie smiled sarcastically.

"If you want to be a nun, Maggie, you do so because you want to, not because you have to."

Maggie thought for a moment. "You were a nurse before you became a nun?"

"Yes," Anne said, taking a handful of crumbs. "Mind if I help?"

Maggie shrugged. "Were you happy being a nurse?"

"I was very happy, it's just that I wanted to help sick people in Africa. I am particularly interested in tropical diseases. I knew the only help these poor people were getting was coming from missionaries. Somehow I knew that if given the opportunity, I could contribute something." She smiled awkwardly, knowing that she was embarking on the sin of pride. God will surely get me for that little touch of pride, she thought. "Also, I've always wanted to be a nun." She paused. "Enough about me, Maggie, what about you? What do you want to be?"

Maggie's face lit up. "It's funny, but I've always wanted to be a nun too."

Anne looked surprised. "Really I do, just like you."

"That's beautiful, Maggie. I'd like to help you—if that's all right."

Maggie's smile faded. "But you won't be here. You'll be in Africa, won't you?"

"Well, yes, but we can write. I promise I'll write you as often as I can."

Maggie said, "It's nice of you to say that, Anne." Her tone was languid. "It really doesn't make any difference. We both know that no matter what I wish to become, it is very unlikely, isn't it?"

"That's not true, Maggie, you can become whatever you set your mind to. You have to keep thinking that you will succeed."

Maggie placed her head to the side, looking impish, and without enthusiasm she said, "I don't think I'd make a very good ballroom dancer, do you?"

"I believe that with hope and prayer you can accomplish anything. I know your days are filled with pain, and I'm well aware that pain isn't always physical. Some people hurt your feelings with what they say, but you have courage, more courage than anyone I know. It won't go unrewarded." Anne took her hand. "Many rewards are all around you. You're an inspiration to everyone you touch, Maggie, including me."

"You, Anne? Really? I didn't know I affected anyone. I mean, I know Mother loves me, and Father—and of course, Lars and Michael. I know that, but…"

"Don't you see, Maggie, that's what courage is all about. You're the strong one. Your kind of bravery needs no witness. Most of us are sorely lacking in that kind of humility. We want people to see we're suffering. We want them to be aware of our pain so they can see how well we suffer. How I prayed for you, Maggie, when your mother called and told us about your leg. She said it was you that gave her faith. So yes, indeed, you most certainly do affect everyone you touch."

"That's all fine, Anne, but nobody likes to touch me, or so it seems."

"I don't believe that, Maggie. You're a beautiful…"

"That's just it," Maggie interrupted, "I'm not beautiful. Most of the other kids think that I'm a hideous monster."

"I find that very hard to believe…"

"They do, Anne. God, I know how Richard the Third felt. I also seem to attract dogs that bark at me as I walk by them."

"Dogs bark at everyone. Believe me, you're not anything like Richard, Maggie; you're very beautiful and of course, inside…"

"Inside? Who sees your inside? All most people see when they look at me, Anne, is a piteous cripple. Some find it so awful they don't dare look," Maggie said bitterly, her eyes filling with tears. "People can be cruel, especially children."

"I really don't believe it's intentional."

"It hurts, just the same. It's just a different kind of hurt."

Anne wiped Maggie's tears away, and not wanting her to see that she too was beginning to weep, pulled Maggie to her. "One day you'll be truly recognized for what you are, Maggie, I just know that."

Maggie blushed. "Oh, Anne, you make me sound like some kind of saint."

The birds returned, curious at first, eventually trusting the couple on the bench.

CHAPTER FORTY-THREE

L AWRENCE BELIEVED THAT it was fate and not God that issued this strange existence. He knew he was destined to become what he had despised, what his mother called dandy boys and quare fellas. Despite the tremendous inner struggle and stigma of being expelled, he managed to conduct himself judiciously, at least in the purview of his teachers, and graduated from high school in June of 1936. His grades were less than average; he did, however, excel in sports. He took to football so well that he became the team quarterback and during the short time he was there, led his team to a state title. He pushed himself in a direction that would lead most to believe he was the All-American young man, when what he felt he could not say. Sometimes his feelings of guilt were unbearable, an agony he prayed would one day lead him to another with the same needs and desires. He had talked about his ambiguity with Michael, but that was like going to confession; his brother could not understand his fantasies. Their separation had a uniquely different effect on the two brothers. Michael missed his brother's companionship, his fallibility, even his indecorus behavior in his relations with the Church. Lawrence missed only what his brother could do for him, his collaboration. One of Michael's only free days was requisitioned for a task that Lawrence found impossible to fulfill. Some of his football friends had set him up with one of the cheerleaders. She was the school floozy and wanted the new quarterback on her long list of supplicants. She thought that Lawrence Riordan was absolutely adorable. Not wanting to appear uninterested, he arranged to meet her on one of his brother's free days.

Michael was furious with the idea of taking his brother's place. After listening to a great deal of pleading, he consented. The first part of the evening was enjoyable. They went to a movie and afterwards stopped for a soda. Her honesty impressed him favorably. He found her a little crude but not dimwitted, as his brother had indicated. Often she made reference to events unknown to him; he nodded in agreement or sipped on the soft drink. As the night grew dark, she suggested they walk to the park. She assumed he knew what went on in the park, since this idea excited him. It was an evening he would remember. What he saw as nymphomania another boy would welcome as passion. It was the first and last time he would touch a young woman's breast and feel a woman's tongue inside his mouth.

He succeeded in warding off her advances by telling her that he had contracted some kind of horrible rash in his groin area. He convinced her that doctors surmised it might have something to do with the toilet seats at school. He was deeply moved by her sympathy. With mixed feelings, he later told his brother that he could walk with his head high, proud to be seen as a heterosexual. His school chums did not doubt that Lawrence, who had survived an evening with Sheila, "the vix," Delaney, was all man. Apart from this, nothing could help Lawrence with his true feelings. So many times he wished they had been born brother and sister. There were times when he found himself alone in the house and didn't have to hide his homosexuality. Times when he found himself in his mother's bedroom, dressed in her clothes, gazing in the armoire mirror, his face crudely painted in an effort to look feminine. He hated his masculinity and yet it was in his masculine endeavors he was most praised. The Lawrence that everyone encountered was a dare-devil, a fierce competitor, far from the image in the mirror. It was this overly compensated drive that turned him to try his hand at flying. That summer, with the help of Dennis Noonan, he found work as a hod carrier for a construction firm. In two months he saved enough to pay for his first flying lesson, and with Kathleen's permission, soon found himself in the front seat of the Stearman trainer.

When it came to flying, Lawrence was a fast learner. He seemed born to violate Isaac's law of inertia, the idea that things at rest want to stay at rest; within eight weeks he was ready for his solo flight. What Kathleen assumed was just another of Lawrence's whimsical endeavors had become for him an obsession. Ryan thought it ironic that the boy who was not allowed to drive the family car was on his way to being an aviator. His flight instructor was so impressed with Lawrence's progress that he invited the family to participate in their son's first flight. Lawrence was intoxicated with everything associated with airplanes. He couldn't have wished for more that cold September morning. Dennis and Madge, James, and even Father Rafferty, as well as his own immediate family, came to cheer him on. Though he missed Michael, deep down in his heart he luxuriated in the personal attention. Finally it was he and not his brother, the want-to-be priest, who was getting long overdue recognition.

Inside the terminal, Lawrence zipped the fur-lined parka about his neck.

"Well, I guess it's time for my first flight alone," he said matter of factly. He didn't seem the least bit nervous; rather, he was imbued with an air of assurance. Kathleen, openly disturbed, held Ryan's hand for support. Lawrence and his flight instructor, an aviator named Max Deering, veteran of the war, left the warmth of the building. Kathleen hurried after them. "Wait. Wait up, Lawrence." She caught up with them on the runway a few feet from the waiting Stearman. Lawrence turned to see his mother, who was removing the scarf from around her neck.

"Here, darlin', take this to keep you warm." He allowed her to wrap the scarf around his shoulder and tuck it into the parka.

"Thanks, Mother; apart from keeping me warm, I'm sure it will bring me luck."

"Be careful. And nothing stupid like showing off."

She wiped the tear from her eyes, which she blamed on the cold, and reached to kiss his cheek. "Right now I'm very proud of you, son"

"I'm finally doing something I love to do, Mother. I promise, nothing stupid." Ryan also left the building and joined her on the flight line. He put his arm around her and watched Lawrence climb into the pilot's seat. After a few pulls on the crank, the flywheel screamed. Deering yanked the crank from the coupling and pulled the chocks. Lawrence yelled over the high-pitched whine:

"Clear."

Soon the irritating high pitch lowered to a throaty growl as the clutch engaged the engine and the propeller turned over with syncopated jerks. As soon as the fuel and air mixture reached the cylinders, they fired one at a time in great puffs of smoke. The big radial engine coughed and eventually the spurts blended into one great harmonious roar. Lawrence could feel his heart beating, synchronized with the engine.

The tail wheel sat on the ground, making visibility virtually nonexistent. The only way he could find the runway was to taxi in a series of "S" turns. Although he couldn't see ahead, he knew he was properly lined up for take off by his relationship to the edges of the asphalt. He could smell the heat from the engine as he revved the tachometer to 1500 rpm. Some specks of hot oil dotted his face, and he pulled the goggles to cover his eyes. He gave a high sign to the spectators as the Stearman rumbled down the runway. He held the pedals steady while both hands clutched the stick. The wind played against his face, and his whole body tingled with excitement. It was only by his power that the plane moved. He was sensitive to the controls of the very complicated piece of machinery, and for the first time in his life he felt responsible.

When the speed reached fifty miles an hour, he eased back on the stick and felt the change as the plane left the ground. No more buffets from the wheels on the runway. He felt his head being forced back against the headrest as he climbed and experienced a sensation of weightlessness when the plane leveled out at 1200 feet. The rushing cold air pierced the exposed areas of his face, but he didn't care. He held his air speed at 110 miles an hour and studied his surroundings. He believed that if he had died right then, these past few moments would have been well worth it. For the first time in his life, he was totally alone, flying like a bird. He could drop the left wing, and using the pedals and stick, put the plane into a dive. He pumped the rudder, banking from one side to the other. Every part of his being told him to throw caution to the wind. His movements were the plane's movements.

He could see the small terminal below. All had left the building now and were waving to him. They looked so small. They reminded him of the little people in his mother's stories. It was time to show them what he could do. Reducing his altitude to 600 feet, he screamed past them and slowly rolled the plane, then, leveling off, pulled into a steep climb. He felt the plane struggle to gain altitude. The radial engine roared as he pushed more and more to defy gravity. He took time to check the instruments. The altimeter said he was at 3,000 feet. When the plane stalled and dropped into a downward spin, he was not frightened. He screamed with excitement and made every possible effort to pull the Stearman back, barely 200 feet from a stand of trees. He nourished the rush of frightful moments and decided that before he tried this stunt again, he would make sure he had a little more altitude.

When he made his next pass, he could see by Deering's antics that he was upset. He was being waved down by his instructor, whose attention he was going to ignore. He was having too much fun and wasn't about to come down, not before he would attempt additional maneuvers. He decided there would be ample time for pushing his luck and testing the patience of Max Deering. For the next fifteen minutes he put the plane through the simple tasks outlined by his instructor. Finally he set his sights on the runway and slowly reduced power. Close to the ground the wind left the wings and the Stearman settled on the runway. The landing was perfect.

For the next four weeks, Lawrence was grounded. If it hadn't been for Ryan, it would have been permanent. Ryan thought that for the first time in the boy's life he seemed genuinely happy. He agreed with Max Deering that the boy was born to be an aviator. Kathleen wasn't as impressed. She remembered the plane diving toward the ground, the scream of the engine laboring to right itself, closing her eyes tightly, praying to make the screaming stop. It was easy for Ryan to speak of forgiveness, easy to suggest a short-term punishment, easy to say the boy should continue to fly, easy, she thought, because Lawrence wasn't his son. Their pertinacious pleadings prevailed and she acquiesced, agreeing to let him continue to fly after the four weeks with no flying privileges. "If he's so determined to kill himself, then go ahead," she told Ryan angrily. "You can be responsible."

Four weeks passed quickly. Lawrence was back to flying on weekends. During the week he assisted the bricklayers and in the evening attended technical school. At last he was doing something he wanted to do. He wanted to learn all he could about the principles of flight and showed a keen interest in engine mechanics. Deep down, Kathleen was happy that Lawrence had found interest in flying, even if it did seem dangerous, and she was cheered by Maggie, who was showing signs of improvement. She was not as content with the effect the children's problems seemed to be having on her marriage. Ryan's new job was taking him away more and more, and she observed that he was taking too much pleasure in his departures.

CHAPTER FORTY-FOUR

R YAN HAILED A cab at the terminal and told the driver to take him to Pennsylvania Avenue. The cab moved ponderously through the snow.

"In town on business?" the cabbie asked, sizing up his fare through the rear mirror.

"Just visiting," Ryan answered to the point.

"This has been one of the worst Januarys I've seen in years. You sure did choose a bad time to visit D.C., mister."

Hoping the driver would just drive, Ryan did not respond. On one other occasion Ryan had been to the capital. At that time he had come to listen to a lecture by the Director. Now he was here at the request of a Mark Gerlitz, who, according to agents he knew in Boston, was in charge of special assignments. The orders conveyed nothing other than word that he was going to attend a special briefing and be reassigned. He prayed that he would be sent to a field office for a long term for his family's sake.

"Which building, mister?"

Ryan had been deep in thought. He hoped that Kathleen understood why she and the children couldn't join him during this training period.

He knew the cabbie had said something. "Excuse me?"

"This is Pennsylvania Avenue, mister, where do you want to be dropped off?"

"Oh! Right, on the corner of Ninth, the Federal Bureau Building will be fine," Ryan said, reaching in his overcoat pocket for change.

Inside the building, two shadowy looking men introduced themselves and escorted him to the elevator, which they took to the second floor. They moved briskly past busy people in short-partitioned cubicles. Everyone looked extremely efficient. Some were lawyers, technicians, accountants, while others were clerks and researchers. It was a long walk through the tight companionway before the three stopped at a dimpled glass door. One of the men knocked in a code.

"Come in," the voice from inside the room said. Gerlitz came around from behind the desk with an outstretched hand.

"You must be Thornton." They shook hands. Gerlitz dragged a chair over for Ryan and took his overcoat. He nodded to the escorts, who immediately left. Ryan wasn't sure how to judge the preferential treatment. Gerlitz sat on the edge of the desk, one leg propped off the floor. They chatted about the trip from Boston, then Gerlitz said, "Your records indicate that you have a knowledge of Russian and Polish."

"I speak and write Russian fluently, I understand some Polish, enough to get by."

"Excellent, you learned mostly from your family, then?"

"My mother was Russian, Russian Orthodox."

"I gather you also studied Russian while you were with Intelligence during the great war?"

"Yes, sir, I was assigned to Moscow."

"We're going to need more agents with your experience, especially with the growing communist threat in this country. I know you're anxious to hear about this new assignment. I'll give you a brief overview now, and later we'll bring you up to date on the rest, okay?"

"Whatever you say, sir," Ryan answered, his tone composed.

Gerlitz returned to the chair behind the desk and sat.

"Are you a Democrat, Thornton?"

Ryan thought for a moment. "I voted for Roosevelt—so I guess you could say that."

"That's good, because we're going to be discussing certain Republicans whose conduct, however well intentioned, does not appear to be on the right side of the European issues. I'm sure you're aware that Europe is headed for war again?"

"Yes sir, it looks that way."

"Our intelligence informs us that the Socialist Democratic Party in Germany is going to form an alliance with the Soviets. Do you know how many German-Hitler sympathizers, I.R.A. terrorists, and communists we have residing in America, Thornton?"

"Not off-hand, sir—I imagine a great many."

"A great many is right, Thornton, most of them American citizens and all of them well intentioned but tremendously misguided. All are naturally against America getting involved with England and France, which is something Mr. Roosevelt will definitely do if England is threatened by Germany. He's a very good friend of Churchill, you know. If Germany and England do go to war, Hitler will avoid doing anything that would stimulate American aid to Britain."

"Or having America declare war against Germany," Ryan interrupted.

"Yes, Hitler would want that declaration stopped at all costs."

During the short silence that followed, Ryan's stomach gave off a deep, empty grumbling, for which he apologized.

"God, how thoughtless of me. Here I am jumping right into business and I haven't even asked if you'd eaten yet."

"Really, Mr. Gerlitz, I'm not that hungry. Maybe a cup of coffee."

Gerlitz pushed a button on **the intercom.**

"Yes, Mr. Gerlitz," the woman's voice said.

"Miss Hall, could you muster up a pot of coffee and some..." He hesitated and glanced at his watch. "My god, it's almost eleven-thirty. How about some sandwiches?" He turned to Ryan. "Is ham okay with you?" Ryan nodded.

"Ham and cheese?" He sought another affirmation from Ryan, who continued to nod in agreement.

"Thanks, Miss Hall," he said, flipping the button. "Now, where were we? If war looks imminent between Germany and England or France, the last thing Hitler wants is that America should aid the Allies."

"Yes," Ryan broke in, "and he would have every reason to be concerned, based on the last war. Thank God we intercepted Zimmerman's notes."

"And that brings me to my point," Gerlitz went on. "Our Intelligence is concerned with fifty or so Republican Congressmen who are going to meet in Boston next month for a convention, and you're familiar with the man hosting this."

Ryan looked confused. "I'm not sure I understand, sir. What's so important about a Republican Party convention? I mean, they are allowed..."

"The problem we see is in their agenda," Gerlitz interrupted.

"They are in favor of an isolationist foreign policy. They're foolhardy if they think for a moment that this country will not be affected adversely if Hitler rules Europe. I do find it interesting that the majority of them are of German and Irish descent. A small ad hoc committee is running the thing, with German funds. I understand the German Abwehr has given substantial contributions, up to eighty-thousand dollars, for these campaigns. They plan to run full-page advertisements in all the major papers with slogans to keep America out of an alliance with England in the event of war."

"Doesn't the constitution allow them that right, sir?"

"I'm sure it all boils down to…" He searched for the right word. "Well, ignorance on the part of these Republicans. What we're really concerned about is the group behind the funds and their ulterior motives. The money comes from Berlin. We know that pro-Nazi sympathizers and Irish-Americans, all members of the I.R.A., spend the money on ads to influence people to vote Republican. It's un-American. We also suspect them of sabotaging British shipping right here in American ports.

"Last month we arrested a former chief of the I.R.A in New York, a Sean Russell. He had among his belongings a German Enigma enciphering machine. We haven't broken the code yet. We have asked Naval Intelligence for support, but so far we've accomplished nothing. We have, however, recovered memos which we have deciphered. The messages, in a simple code, were sent from a Boston source to Russell suggesting a plan to sink British sea traffic carrying munitions and other valuable cargo, such as aircraft parts, mostly new technology. Warehouses holding war supplies consigned for Britain were to be sabotaged. I believe that the majority of these reports, resplendent as they are with vivid descriptions of exploding ships, are the result of overactive Irish imaginations and a great way to coax pocket money from the Germans. However, we can't take anything for granted. Many are Irish longshoremen and I.R.A. types who also control an important faction of our politics and trade unions. We need to nab the man behind this ring in Boston."

"It sounds like an important assignment. I'm relatively new at this, as you know, sir. I'll do my best, but you must understand that I have questions. I know there are more qualified agents. Did this Russell mention the name of the man we're after?"

The knock on the door was followed by the entrance of Miss Hall with the sandwiches and coffee. The room was silent as she placed the tray on the edge of the desk. When the door closed, Gerlitz handed Ryan a sandwich and poured the coffee. He took a bite and followed it with a sip from the cup.

"To answer your question," Gerlitz said, chewing, "we believe the man we want is your wife's uncle, Dennis Noonan."

Ryan almost choked on the bite he had just taken. His eyes widened. He swallowed and shook his head in disbelief. "But you understand, sir, that Dennis Noonan is…is like my family. If it wasn't for him, why I'd still be a cop on the beat. I'd never have met my wife." His voice pleaded.

"There must be some mistake, Mr. Gerlitz. He's a solid American, sir. I know for a fact…"

"Look, Thornton," Gerlitz declared, "I know this comes as a shock. Believe me, we wouldn't be doing this if we didn't have sufficient evidence." He continued on. Ryan stared dumbfounded at the floor, hearing only pieces of what Gerlitz was saying.

"All the code information taken from Russell's office in New York was brought here to our document lab. All the documents were typed on the same grade of paper with the same typewriter. We need the typewriter to make a conviction. Somewhere in your…uncle's…Dennis Noonan's home, not office, you'll find the typewriter. He's a very smart lawyer; that's why you are so important to this case, Thornton. He trusts you."

"I could show someone else, sir, I'd even help them with the layout of the house. I know I could train…"

"I'm sorry, Thornton, if it were up to me—I understand the relationship you have with the man. Don't think that this decision was spur-of-the moment." He snapped his fingers.

"Just like that! This was debated at the top. The Director has been keeping files on Noonan for years. He's a kingpin. We weren't sure you were trained well enough to handle the case, but you could search his office with impunity. Believe me, we considered your feelings. We knew it was going to be—well, probably the most difficult task a man could ever be asked to perform."

"My family will never forgive me," Ryan muttered. "My wife, Kathleen, she'll divorce me for sure. She's Irish, you know. Of course you know."

"Maybe your wife won't have to know. We might be able to formulate a plan that keeps you…clean, shall we say. Would you feel better with that idea?"

"I'm just finding it hard to believe that Dennis would involve himself in sabotaging a ship. He's a good American, a war hero." Ryan rubbed his face vigorously, then nervously wrung his hands. "Right now, I wish I'd never joined the Bureau," he said, staring at the floor.

"That's a normal reaction. I understand, eat up, and I'll show you the other offices, the cook's tour. Then we'll get you to some good sleeping quarters. Tonight we'll have dinner with my family. Believe me, everything's going to turn out all right."

CHAPTER FORTY-FIVE

M ARCH 15, 1937, just two days before the Noonans would celebrate their most cherished holiday, Dennis Noonan retired to his study, loaded his service revolver and blew his head off. He had just turned 58. He left no suicide note. He did not take time for a parting word with his son or hug his daughter or kiss his wife. The FBI found one last logged call on his office phone to the district attorney, Charles Boyle. There was nothing they found, other than the typewriter and memo pad, that could have incriminated him.

Two weeks earlier, Ryan and Kathleen had dropped by for a visit. It was during the day and Ryan made sure that Dennis was working. They sat in the drawing room and talked, mostly about the upcoming party. Ryan asked Madge if he could check on a book that he thought Dennis might have in his office. She let him in, using a spare key. He closed the door behind him and searched for a second typewriter, thinking the one on the desk would be too obvious. Not finding a second, he took a sheet of paper from a pad on the desk and typed the same coded message that was sent to Russell.

When he was through, he joined Madge and Kathleen in the drawing room. Madge asked if he had found what he was looking for. He answered, "I think so."

As police work, it wasn't hard. The misery of doubt he would have to live with while waiting for the analysis of the typewriter copy. He hoped nothing would happen before St. Patrick's Day that would create self-abasement and remorse. He received word from headquarters March 13. The type was a perfect match. Ryan was devastated.

Gerlitz arrived at the field office March 14 and briefed two other agents on how they were going to handle the arrest. Ryan would stay home that day, supposedly not privy to the plan. An agent would call Mrs. Noonan just before her husband arrived home. Dennis was as predictable as clockwork. When he entered, they would arrest him. Gerlitz assured Ryan it would be a clean action. They made one mistake. After confronting Dennis with the evidence, including Sean Russell's testimony, and he saw that they already had the typewriter, Dennis asked if he could be allowed some personal things from his office. They didn't know about the revolver in the closet.

They had found no records of associates or meetings. They had lied about Sean Russell's willingness to tell the Bureau anything they wanted to know. That was a scare tactic. What the Bureau had was the typewriter and a memo pad, which together looked like damning evidence.

When Ryan discovered what had taken place, he was furious. The following weeks gave him plenty of time to think. He felt sure that Dennis could have fought this accusation of conspiracy. Even Chuck Boyle, who had to be careful now, suggested to Ryan that the two items may not have been sufficient evidence to get a conviction. Ryan called Gerlitz, who was extremely disappointed in the whole operation but did compliment him for his participation. He told Ryan he was one of their most conscientious agents and not to be ashamed of his actions because his uncle had become confused and allowed the misguided ideals of the I.R.A. and their association with Nazi Americans to jeopardize his family. Finally, he told Ryan that Dennis would not have taken his life if he had been innocent. After he hung up the phone, Ryan felt a little better. He concluded that Dennis Noonan killed himself because he wasn't the kind of man who could face up to the humiliation. Chuck Boyle spoke to reporters. The papers ran a front-page story that suggested the lawyer was under great stress and may have been suffering from an incurable disease. The family knew better. Ryan had to keep a terrible secret from Kathleen, one that he would have to carry to his grave.

CHAPTER FORTY-SIX

AFTER AMERICA ENTERED the war, Ryan was sent to Maryland. This time he was allowed to take the family. The move was difficult for Kathleen, who had to leave her work and friends. She was also concerned for Maggie, who lately was beginning to experience a recurrence of pain in her leg, sometimes extending to her lower spine. Joseph Kortner had recommended a surgeon in Maryland and suggested she take Maggie at the earliest convenience. Maggie was a beautiful young woman in her early twenties but still needed Kathleen's support. After graduating from high school, she had decided to stay home; her earlier ambitions to become a nun had long since vanished. Walking with the uncomfortable braces required great effort. For all her grace and beauty, she was conscious of her clumsiness. Motivation to write partly compensated for her physical inadequacy. Her poetry was beautiful, impressively honest, expressing quiet, stoic patience. Many times Kathleen wanted to approach a publisher with some of her stories, but Maggie was adamant about her privacy. She was not at ease with the idea of making public her innermost thoughts.

Immediately after the bombing of Pearl Harbor, Lawrence enlisted in the Army Air Force and continuing flight training. Kathleen hadn't heard a word from him, other than a note with an address in the event someone wished to write. Michael, on the other hand, in his last year of theology, wrote regularly, twice a month.

On his arrival, Ryan was given two days to settle his family matters, after which he reported to the Army's Chemical Warfare Center in Bel Air. The center was a subject of concern. Many of the chemical agents being researched produced botulism, plague, and hoof-and-mouth disease. Through genetic engineering, various strains of bacteria were being produced, some effective when disseminated by a dust cloud, causing the destruction of whole cities.

The cab, not being allowed past the entry gate, dropped him off. He flashed his badge to the military policeman and told him he was to meet a Captain Sandell, who was head of security. The M.P. made a quick call and within minutes Ryan stepped into an Army Jeep and was taken to a dreary-looking, one-story, concrete building with no windows or signs. He thanked the Army driver and stood for a moment looking at the steel door, thinking about the building's significance. He pushed on the bell, and soon the door was opened by a tense staff sergeant.

"Agent Thornton?"

"Yes," Ryan said. The soldier opened the door wider. "They just called from the main gate," he said.

"I'm here to see Captain Sandell."

He stepped into a noisy, brightly lit room and was ushered through a gauntlet of military officers and civilians. They were bending over tables, dispersing data that seemed to be headed to a table in the back of the room, where it was scrutinized by two men, one uniformed. The other he recognized as Mark Gerlitz.

"Ryan, over here," he said. He moved from behind the desk and shook Ryan's hand vigorously.

"It's been a while."

"Yes, it has—a few years anyway," Ryan said, remembering Dennis Noonan's suicide.

"Nonetheless, I've been staying abreast of your career. How's your beautiful wife, Kathleen?"

"Fine, sir, she's fine."

"That's great…and the family? All settled in?"

"Everyone's just fine, sir."

"I'd like you to meet Captain Sandell." The men exchanged greetings. To Ryan, Sandell looked to be in his late forties and not at all like a military man. He was balding and on the pudgy side. Ryan disregarded the soft handshake.

"Captain Sandell is supplying us with names of people who have visited, or should I say reconnoitered, the center in the past five years. Searching for possible saboteurs, enemy aliens." He held the long roll of paper, which almost reached the ground.

"As you can see, the list is lengthy. By the time we've recorded everyone, we expect over 10,000 entries and that's just visitors to this facility. We have data on file of over 100,000 total enemy aliens in the country at large, maybe more. What we're looking for are any inconsistencies, companies that don't exist, German names—the Jap names are obvious. It's going to take some time, as you can see."

"What about the Bureau's file? Wouldn't it be easier to connect with these possible saboteurs using our list?"

"That's what we're doing." He swept his arm around the room. "Everyone you see here has top-secret clearance. They're combing our list of suspects with those who've had access to this facility."

"I don't wish to appear naive, but didn't the League of Nations disallow chemical weapons?" Ryan asked.

"Tell that to the Japs. They've been using new virulent strains on the Chinese since 1939," Sandell said.

"Besides," Gerlitz broke in, "we never signed the ban. We encouraged it, didn't sign it."

"Bingo!" Sandell said abruptly. "This one looks interesting."

Gerlitz looked over Sandell's shoulder and muttered. "Simon Emil Kraemer." He gestured to Ryan. "This is exactly what we're looking for, Ryan. See?" He mumbled the notes: "Born in Wuerzburg, arrived in this country in 1908. He became an American citizen and joined the Army, serving in the war, attaining the grand rank of corporal. Now this is interesting. He is also a member of the A.O.A." He whistled through his teeth.

"The A.O.A?" Ryan asked curiously.

"American Ordnance Association," Sandell said, shaking his head.

"He may as well have access to our War Department's ordnance."

"I'll be a son of a bitch," Gerlitz exclaimed. "Queens Long Island Army's motion picture establishment. Shows here he procured classified training films. Can you believe that? His application was approved by L.A. Codd. Says here he's a chemical engineer and big-time stockholder in the Sperry Gyroscope and Curtiss Wright Defense Industries. I'll bet this bastard has other contacts!"

Sandell reviewed another document in the man's dossier. "Looks like we've hit pay dirt on this one. You folks are going to be busy," he said, handing the paper to Gerlitz.

"Yep, this one's been working everyone he knows, all right." After Gerlitz scanned the list of names, he handed it to Ryan.

"Christ. I don't believe this. It's a who's who of politics," Ryan whispered.

"Yes, it's quite a network, all right," Gerlitz said. "I'm sure, though, that names such as Charles Lindbergh are here because they've spoken out about America's involvement in the war. Isolationists, same I'm sure, with the Republican Congressmen on the list. Sucked in by the enemy because of their isolationist views, goddamn pacifists and America-firsters. What's interesting though is the number of German names on the list." Gerlitz took the paper and placed it in his briefcase. "We have plenty to keep us busy," he said, checking his watch.

"What d'ya say to a little military grub?" Sandell said he'd pass. Ryan and Gerlitz left the building through a back door and drove to the mess hall in a borrowed staff car.

"Well, Ryan, looks like the Bureau is going to be very busy for the next few years," Gerlitz said, grinding the gears. "Damn piece of military junk."

"You think this is going to be a long war then?" Ryan asked.

"Don't you? I think we're about as prepared as a chef without a goddamn pan."

"I've already been in one war, sir. I saw a little action in Russia, not something I'm proud of. It's going to be some round-up, sir. I'm kind of looking forward to seeing some action."

"You're not going to see any action, Ryan," Gerlitz said, coming to an abrupt stop, almost hitting the parked car ahead of him. "Damned piece of military junk has no brakes. Probably just like the rest of our arsenal."

"I don't understand, sir," Ryan said, ignoring the cynicism. "I thought because of all the information you and Captain Sandell…"

"That was just to give you some idea of what we're up against," Gerlitz jumped in. "You're too smart to just be on the arresting end of things. Remember a few years back I mentioned to you about the Enigma machines?"

"Yes, sir."

"The extent of espionage in this country is overwhelming. All of the information we encounter is in code, which the Germans, Japanese, even the goddamn Commies, change almost daily. We have a small group dedicated to breaking those codes, working in conjunction with the State Department's Division of Communications and Records."

"I hope you folks know what you're doing, because my knowledge of ciphers and codes is very limited. What I mean is I hope I can live up to your expectations, sir. I just see myself as an old-fashioned policeman."

"You speak Russian and Polish, right?"

"Yes, but it's been a while."

"Your records show a high level of mathematical skills."

"I guess from the time I was a youngster I was always interested in math. It came naturally."

"We need linguists, Ryan. Besides you'll have an excellent teacher to help you with those areas of decypherment, a man we…" he paused… "particularly the Director, have a great deal of faith in. An American who worked for British Intelligence during the first war. You'll like him. I believe he speaks and writes four languages fluently, not to mention Latin."

"If you think I can make the grade, sir, then I'll give it everything I've got. It sounds interesting. When do I begin working for him?"

"As soon as possible. I'll give you the information over lunch. Maybe you've heard his name throughout the Bureau circles." Gerlitz opened the door and turned to Ryan. "Hamilton, William Hamilton."

"I don't believe I have, sir," Ryan said as they entered the cafeteria.

Within two days, Ryan was back on active duty, having been directed to the second floor of the old rococo State, War, and Navy Building on Pennsylvania Avenue. Up to this time, United States Intelligence had been sorely wanting in cryptographic security. Secretary Cordell Hull called on his friend J. Edgar Hoover to locate the most reliable persons with high-level clearances and linguistic capabilities to help work on deciphering enemy chatter.

At the time, unlike in Germany, America had no agents in Japan, no spy network whatsoever. It was up to a few men and women armed with the brains to decipher enemy intelligence to help change the course of the war. That was not to say that these intelligence gatherers would win the war single-handedly. That would be a gross oversimplification. Their duties would also include the spreading of misinformation. Ryan had no idea what to expect when he entered the building. He was directed by a military policeman to take the stairs to the second floor. Before he was allowed through the double-hung doors, two more M.P.'s checked his I.D. and searched him thoroughly. Ryan was content that nothing was getting past these guys.

Inside, he was greeted by an enormous man in a naval uniform. He wore a 45 strapped to his side and looked more than willing to use it. He ushered Ryan to a small, empty office with no windows. The man said nothing more than to ask him to take a seat and promptly left, closing the door. The quiet was extraordinary, a condition he attributed to soundproofing. The only other furniture in the room was a desk and chair. Ryan thought it odd that the desk-top was completely bare. It was as though he were part of a surrealist painting.

For a moment he allowed his thoughts to drift to Maggie. He pulled the sleeve of the gray-serge jacket to check the time. In the next hour or so, Kathleen would be taking her to the new doctor recommended by

Kortner. This morning she seemed more uncomfortable than ever with the pain in her lower back. He said a silent prayer that she would be all right, then he dismissed the images of Maggie going through painful surgery. He couldn't face the possibility that she might lose her leg. He wasn't the fortress Kathleen was regarding the children's health. He could handle the violence, the accidents and even death related to his work, but the least sign of indignity or injury to his family and he fell apart. His quiet speculations were interrupted when the door opened. The man looked unkempt and not at all like agents he was used to working with.

"Sorry to keep you." The taller man extended his hand, "William Hamilton. You're Thornton then!" Ryan stood and shook his hand.

"That's right. Ryan Thornton, sir."

"Please, sit. Call me William and I'll call you Ryan, if that's okay. We don't have time to stand on ceremony around here."

"That wasn't my first impression," Ryan said.

"Oh, that," Hamilton said, gesturing toward the door. "I see you've met our duty officer. The security around here is all military. We're working closely with all the departments. They've been a great service to the Bureau, helping us identify enemy agents, so we have to go along with their security measures. Actually, they're not a bad lot. We're all on a first-name basis. I'm sure in the coming months we may even become friends, but we don't take security for granted. Screw up in that area and we may have to have you shot."

He smiled and sat down behind the desk. "Since that's not our objective, we'll help you stay clean, ergo the unprecedented security policy. By the way, not all our personnel arrive here pre-screened by Mark Gerlitz. I'm impressed. He must have a great deal of faith in you, Ryan."

Ryan didn't know how to comment. He felt awkward. Clearing his throat, he adjusted his position in the chair. Hamilton opened a drawer in the desk and produced a thick file folder. He read silently, nodding occasionally. He skipped through the file, stopping briefly to read something that appeared to stimulate him.

"These are all the cases you've worked on," Hamilton said, closing the file and placing it back in the drawer.

Ryan nodded, "I guess so. I wasn't aware I'd manufactured so much paperwork."

"It's very impressive," Hamilton said. "There was no mention anywhere if you smoke."

"Never touch the stuff," Ryan said.

"Good, gave it up myself a long time ago. Smokers could be a problem around here. No matches, lighters or the like. We wouldn't want a fire."

"I can appreciate the policy," Ryan said.

"By the way, how do you like D.C. so far?" Hamilton asked in an off-handed aside.

"We're living in Maryland, nice little town called Morningside about five miles from here. I think the family will get used to it. How about you, William? Married?"

"Not on your life, Ryan." He thought a moment, then he smiled broadly. "To the Bureau, maybe. Gerlitz mentioned that your wife was born in Ireland. Not an I.R.A. type, I hope," he said in joking tones.

"If she is, she's covering it up very well," Ryan said, joking back. Hamilton's face turned serious.

"I heard about your wife's uncle, a terrible thing to have to deal with. Believe me, I know from personal experience what it's like to expose someone you really care about. You handled the situation better than I did, I might add."

"Thank you, sir. I appreciate that."

"William," Hamilton said, "No more *sirs*, okay?"

"Okay," Ryan said. Hamilton opened another drawer and took out a pencil and paper. He quickly wrote something in Russian and pushed it toward Ryan. "Gerlitz tells me you're fluent in Russian."

"You want me to read it in Russian or English?"

"Both, if you wish."

Ryan read the note, first in Russian, then in English. "It is imperative to understand our enemy's intelligence, his strength, his weakness, his mind."

"Excellent, that was perfect. And you also speak Polish?"

"I get by," Ryan said.

"Und sprechen sie auch ein bissen Deutch feleicht?"

"Ich radebrechte…sehr bissen," Ryan replied.

"That's okay, Ryan. Between you, me, and the four other people you're going to meet, we speak thirty or so languages. Let's get started."

By the time Ryan got home, it was long after dinner and closer to bed time. Kathleen heard him fidgeting with the lock and let him in. She hadn't seen him so fatigued before and hugged him. "You look jaded," she said. "What have you been up to all day?" She thought better of her words and quickly said, "I should know not to ask silly questions to which I'll receive obscure answers."

He smiled and flopped into the easy chair with a great sigh.

"How's Maggie?"

"Sleeping. She's fine. How about you? You look fagged."

"I think this is going to be a busy assignment, Kathleen. You wouldn't believe the sense of..." He searched for the appropriate word: "awesome responsibility connected with this job. I'm not sure, but I think my boss let me go early tonight." She sat on the edge of the chair and ran her hand through his hair.

"You're right," she said, laughing. "I see a whole bunch of new gray hairs that you didn't have this morning when you left."

"Speaking of when I left, how did Maggie's appointment go—does he look like a good doctor? If anyone would know, you would."

"Hold on there, one question at a time. He seems like a very nice man. I think he's German."

Ryan smiled wryly. "Tell me his name, I probably know him."

"You would?" Kathleen asked innocently.

"Go ahead, honey. I'm just having some fun. What did he say?"

"He needs to do a series of tests," she said. Ryan looked worried.

"Don't you go getting that desperation look. This is a normal procedure, darlin'. Believe you me, if there was something radically wrong, I'd tell you." She was convincing, but deep down Kathleen was troubled that the tumor had returned and was diagnosed as malignant.

"Are you hungry?"

"Not really, Kathleen. I'm just beat."

"How about a nice cuppa tea?" she said, changing the subject.

"Sounds great," he said.

She left him to go to the kitchen, and by the time she returned, he was sleeping soundly.

In the weeks that followed, Ryan saw very little of Kathleen; sometimes he did not get home for days at a time and then found only a few minutes to eat something and speak a few words before drifting into sleep. As soon as he awakened, he could hardly wait to get back to his duties. He was part of a team of six that decoded radio transmissions and telegrams, some from sources they couldn't always identify. One member of the team, Anna Witkiewicz, had worked for Polish Intelligence. She took to her work with a passion, and with others on his team applied every last ounce of effort to entangle the codes.

On their breaks, she liked to beat Ryan at chess. She avoided any conversation that inquired into her life in Poland. She held a hatred for Germans, a hatred that Ryan had never encountered in anyone else. She had a long, deep scar running from her left temple, disappearing behind her ear, yet she exuded a strange beauty. Not soft and feminine or smiling and blissful, rather mysterious and puzzling. Ryan sometimes smiled to himself with the idea that she personified an enigma more than the machine.

Later Hamilton gave him a little insight into her background. She studied cryptography and advanced mathematics at the University of Poznan. As a student, she knew how to read, write, and speak Russian, French, German, Rumanian, and English fluently. After graduation, she went to work for an elite intelligence group on the outskirts of Warsaw. They had broken the German Enigma code. Whether or not the Germans were aware of this, their blitzkrieg of Poland was a complete surprise because they had maintained radio silence. After the Polish defeat, a number of her colleagues escaped to Rumania. She was one of five who didn't make it. All were tortured unmercifully by the S.S., but not one gave information about Enigma. All were shot and buried in a shallow grave. The bullet had just grazed her but she managed to stay still, allowing herself to be buried alive. After hours of staying buried and praying that all was clear, she dug herself out and made it to Rumania. Eventually she joined colleagues at a house outside of London, where American Intelligence was lucky enough to recruit her.

To Ryan, many dispatches looked innocuous, describing nothing more than a division emblem on the uniform of an infantryman who might have been headed for overseas. Hamilton pointed out the significance of every piece of information, no matter how harmless it appeared. He showed Ryan an example of an intercepted telegram to Berlin from a German agent in London. It was sent during Hitler's attempt to bring Britain to her knees with the blitzkrieg. The message was sent to President Roosevelt from Ambassador Joseph Kennedy. It was concise and devastating in that it probably gave the enemy the impetus to intensify the bombing. It read, "England is completely through."

"Well, can you believe this guy," Ryan said eagerly, "so that's what Joe Kennedy is doing these days."

"I know," Hamilton shook his head, "the Director has been trying to nail that son-of-a-bitch for bootlegging all those years, now he's legit."

"I wasn't making reference to that exactly. You see, my wife is related to his wife. She's a Fitzgerald."

"That's a coincidence all right," Hamilton said.

"He was even at our wedding. I never liked him, always seemed to have his damned hands all over my wife's ass."

Ryan was a fast learner. He questioned every detail, no matter how insignificant the text. Once messages were verified and known to be sent by enemy agents, Ryan was the liaison to the Bureau. Arrests were made immediately. Some spies got by with deportation, the FBI lacking sufficient evidence to indict. Ryan learned that Japanese ciphers had also been broken, giving America unlimited access to their entire diplomatic correspondence. He came to have a great deal of respect for William Hamilton. Although Ryan tried, it didn't seem possible that he would ever match his talents or stamina. He rarely saw the man rest. There were some moments when they managed to talk about other things besides the code room. Ryan also learned that Hamilton was a very private man and found that the only way to learn more about his boss was to ask questions. Hamilton didn't mind revealing details about his years in Chicago. He even related his participation in the McIntee case. It was the closest their conversation came to involving Kathleen. Ryan said that he remembered the case well and for whatever reason failed to mention that his wife knew the accused. Ryan's question about Hamilton's involvement with the British during World War I was met with silence and a change of subject.

CHAPTER FORTY-SEVEN

WITH EXAGGERATED INDOLENCE, Kathleen left the bedroom to answer the door. On the way, she turned on a light and looked at the clock on the mantel. She stood by the door waiting again for the quiet knock.

"Ryan?" she said. "Is that you?"

"Kathleen," the voice said, and immediately she opened the door.

"Jesus, Ryan, it's three in the morning," she said in a loud whisper so as not to wake Maggie. "You look terrible. Are you all right?"

"Is it that late?" he said, dropping into the chair. "Hamilton sent me home. Said to take a couple of days off."

"Well, I'd say it was about time. This job'll be the death of you. I'll put the kettle on." He could hear the water fill, stop, and the gas ignite. He looked at her through the doorway. "God, I've been so busy I forgot to ask if Maggie had her tests yet."

Kathleen came in and sat by him. "That was last week, Ryan," she said compassionately. "You're so tired lately, Ryan, shure, you don't know what's up or down."

"I'll be fine with a few days' rest; now, about Maggie's tests? You took her to…"

"Kreuger, Walter Kreuger, and yes," she said protectively, "he's a German, but he's not a Nazi."

"You're absolutely sure, are you?" he said, pretending to be serious.

"Don't you go worrying about Maggie, that's my job. Believe me I'll tell you if they find anything that needs special attention."

"So the tests showed nothing wrong then?"

"Well…" She seemed to be delaying. "There are still a few procedures left. I don't want you getting stressful over things that may not happen, that's all."

"Now I'm concerned, Kathleen. I know you when you get that protective air about you. This doctor…," he stammered.

"Kreuger, Walter," she said.

"Yes, Kreuger. He did the tests and wasn't satisfied. Is that it?"

"Ryan, we just don't have any sure answers as to why she has these pains. Medical prognosis isn't always confined to one procedure."

"Just be direct," he said louder, becoming irritated with her ambiguity. "Is there a possibility she may lose her leg?"

She hushed him. "If you wake her with your outbursts, I'll never forgive you," she whispered loudly. "You're not the only one with crosses to bear, you know."

He noticed that when she was angry, the Dublin accent returned more incisive than ever. He knew when it was time to back off.

"I'm sorry. You know the last thing in the world I want to do is hurt you or Maggie. I just need to know. I have to bear the hurt too." He placed his hand on hers.

"She's going in for a biopsy tomorrow," Kathleen said. She could sense his freezing. "We really won't know anything 'till we get the results." The room was quiet for a moment except for the sound of the clock.

Ryan spoke. "Does Kreuger suspect that the tumor may be cancerous?"

"He wouldn't say either way, darlin'." The kettle whistled and she sat upright. "And that's why I don't want you worrying about it either. We'll face whatever comes. Now let's have that cuppa and get you to bed."

Kathleen was first to awaken. Soon after, Maggie joined her in the kitchen. "Mornin'," she yawned. "Smells good. I thought I heard Dad's voice last night."

"You did, he came home late. He's been allowed a few days off. Nice of them isn't it?" she said, turning the bacon. "How are you feeling this morning?"

"I probably still have that cold in my chest." She took a deep breath. "I still can't seem to fill my lungs…like there's fluid there or something."

"And your back," Kathleen asked. "Still bothering you?"

"Just an ache," she said, reaching for a piece of toast. Kathleen slapped her hand. "There's a good girl. Wake up your father and tell him to hurry. It'll be on the table in five minutes."

The conversation at breakfast was about everything but Maggie's hospital appointment. Kathleen showed Ryan a letter, more like a note, from Lawrence. He had been transferred from Gowan field and been reassigned to the 384th Bombardment Group at Wendover Army Air Base. He said the weather was viciously cold; however, he still had his mother's scarf to keep him warm. Ryan thought it odd that the censors admitted the part about working with a new crew and awaiting the arrival of their first B-17. He handed the note back to Kathleen.

"Doesn't say much, does he? What surprises me though is that the little he does say seems like a breach of security."

"Oh you and your security," Kathleen said, clearing the table. "Isn't it good enough that we hear something at all from the boy?"

"I suppose you're right," he said, checking the clock. "What time do we have to be at the hospital?"

"We should have her there by ten o'clock. Since you've brought the car home, we can leave at nine-thirty," she said.

They arrived at the hospital with minutes to spare. Kathleen introduced Ryan to Walter Kreuger. He was in his middle sixties, short and stout, with great shocks of white hair at the sides of his head and completely bald on top, reminding Ryan of a circus clown. While Maggie was being prepped for the biopsy, Kreuger asked them to come to his office, where they could speak in private. Kreuger closed the door and offered them a seat. Ryan sat nervously on the edge of the black-leather couch, and Kathleen sat beside him. He noticed all the diplomas arranged haphazardly with photos of what looked like his family. Kreuger picked up a large manila envelope from the desk and withdrew the contents.

"Zese are Maggie's last x-rays," he said with a thick German accent. "I show'd zem to your vife last veek. Since dat time ve have had ze time to review mit my colleagues und ve have come to ze same conclusions about her pain. I must apologize for my poor English."

"That's okay, Doctor," Ryan said. "What about Maggie?"

Kreuger ambled to a light-box on one of the walls, clipped the negative over the white Plexiglas, and turned on the inside light.

"Dis is a picture of your daughter's lungs."

"This is what we talked about last week, Doctor," Kathleen said. "You said it might be a good idea to do a biopsy."

"Dat's right, und dat's exactly what we are doing—I just vant to prepare you for ze outcome."

"What outcome?" Ryan said, standing. He looked at Kathleen. "Do you know what he's talking about?"

Kathleen stood and walked to where Kreuger was standing.

"I get the impression that there's something else to be concerned about, is that right?"

"I talked to my colleagues und..."

"Yes, yes, you already said that," Ryan interrupted. Kathleen grabbed Ryan's hand. "Ryan, please let Doctor Kreuger finish."

"Tsank you, Missus Thornton. As I vas saying, ve are very concerned about dis mass." He pointed to a dark area on the negative. "Dis could very vell be ze reason for ze back pain. Maggie alzo mentioned a shortness of breath. Ve believe ze sarcoma may have returned, only dis time it has metastasized to ze lungs."

Ryan could feel Kathleen's hand relax and fall away.

"What does all this mean, Doctor? Maggie's not going to...?" He couldn't say the word. He held Kathleen, whose face had drained of its blood, and walked her to the couch. They sat for a while, not saying anything. Kreuger pulled a chair closer and sat with them.

"Dis is never a hundred percent conclusive until ve do ze biopsy. I'm very sorry, you must understand dat I just vanted to prepare you for ze vurst possible outcome."

"And what if it is the worst?" Ryan said in a low voice. "What if it is the cancer that's returned to her lungs? Is it operable?"

"I'm afraid ve have no solutions for dat kind of zituation."

Kathleen broke in, "I'm getting the impression, Doctor Kreuger, that the biopsy is just a formality." Her fear seemed to have been transformed into resignation. Only by accepting the possibility of Maggie's death could she acquire a capacity to deal with adversity.

"If you and your colleagues are right, and this sarcoma has metastasized to her lungs, how much time do we have?"

"If that is ze case, I vould tsink maybe...tsree, four months."

Ryan, speechless, stared at the floor. Nothing was important anymore, his work, Enigma machines, the war, nothing. Kathleen asked all the questions now, details she would have to know to prepare the fight. Nothing was going to take her Maggie, not without a fight.

The results came back as Kreuger had expected. In his opinion, Maggie had just a few months to live. Kathleen asked that the x-rays, lab findings, and any written information regarding the prognosis be sent to Doctor Kortner for a second opinion. In her estimation, the war wasn't over. Ryan admired her stamina and secretly wished that he was as strong as she was. Kathleen convinced Ryan that it would be best if they told no one, not the boys, and especially not Maggie. If she was to help their daughter it would be better if she didn't know the truth. Ryan wanted desperately for her to be right. After all, she had proved the doctors wrong before; he prayed she would do it again. This was her professional field, and he promised to help her in whatever she asked. A week later they received word from Kortner concurring with Kreuger's diagnosis. It was a low point in medical reports, but Kathleen did not despair.

For the next couple of weeks, Ryan totally absorbed himself in his work. He had confided only in William Hamilton, who forced Ryan to leave the office each day at a reasonable hour. After dinner, they usually spent what Kathleen called family time together. There were moments when Maggie was jubilant. Those were the occasions when thoughts of her death were suppressed. She never seemed happier than during the evening when they planned a trip to Grandma Barrett in Dublin. Ryan believed Kathleen at first. The idea of a trip to Ireland with Kathleen and Maggie excited him, until she reminded him that these were just some of the positive notions devised to give Maggie a will to live. As the months passed, Ryan noticed that Maggie's breathing was more labored. Kathleen agreed, but thought it was just a slight setback. As soon as the weather gets better, she would tell Ryan, when the sun comes out, just you wait and see, Maggie will feel much better.

It was the middle of August in 1942 when Lawrence arrived home. He was given a 10-day leave before going to England. Kathleen thought he looked "smashing" in his Army Air Force uniform and was especially impressed with his shiny new wings. Ryan was so proud he took him to meet some of his co-workers. Hamilton wasn't there; Anna said he had been ordered to an impromptu meeting at the main office. Ryan was sorry that Hamilton didn't have an opportunity to meet his son.

It was a humid Saturday afternoon when Michael showed up. He was determined to see his brother before he went overseas. He arrived with a friend from the seminary who was going to stay a short time before continuing on to his home in Virginia, and was introduced to Kathleen as Billy Morrison. She extended her hand and thought that he was the largest man she had ever seen.

On seeing the visitor, Lawrence, who was at the kitchen table talking with Maggie, jumped up and yelled, "Whale! Well, I'll be a monkey's uncle."

He stood in the doorway between the kitchen and the living room for a moment to look at them. "If you two don't look like goddamn priests,

I don't know who does." Kathleen told him to watch his language, but Lawrence was too busy hugging the Whale, who had grown another three inches and added extra pounds. He stood back and looked at his brother for a moment.

"I really do miss you sometimes," Lawrence said seriously. Then he laughed. "Like when I needed to pass some of those math tests." He brushed Michael's cassock with the back of his hand. "That black robe, it's really you, Michael," he said, teasing. As they hugged, Michael looked over his brother's shoulder and saw Maggie standing in the doorway. Lawrence could feel the change in his brother's body. He knew he had to be looking at Maggie and had seen how pale and drawn she'd become.

"Stay where you are, you look beautiful," he said. He hugged her and felt her skin move under her cotton dress. He was feeling bones where he knew there was supposed to be muscle. He held her frail body as gently as he could and held back the tears. For a moment he was upset with his mother for not telling him about her condition.

That evening, when the Whale left and Maggie and Ryan had retired to bed, Michael, Lawrence, and Kathleen sat around the kitchen table. The boys talked about some of the mischief they had been involved in when they were young, before their departure for the seminary. They were surprised to learn that there wasn't much Kathleen didn't know. Michael noticed that his mother was quiet when they mentioned Maggie. He was unrelenting and persisted in asking what caused Maggie to look so ill.

Kathleen evaded Lawrence's questions until he said he would be going to England for God knows how long. It wouldn't be fair to let him go without knowing that there was a problem. Quietly, she revealed everything. She seemed resigned to her daughter's eventual death. Maggie must never know, Kathleen said, never. It was past midnight when Michael suggested they say a rosary for their sister. They then stood to walk to bed.

Michael showed his emotions more than anyone else, knowing that this could be the last time he might see his brother. Lawrence, on the other hand, concealed his feelings with spirited talk. "Don't worry about me, Michael. Remember, only the good die young." After he made the comment, he thought about Maggie and quietly apologized to his mother. Michael was the first to leave the room.

Kathleen knew the offhand remark was unintended. She felt sorry for Lawrence's obvious pain and smiled, kissing him on the cheek. She didn't believe the Army Air Force would feed him well enough, so the day before he left, she served a dinner of ham, cabbage, and potatoes, followed by his favorite dessert, jelly trifle. At the table, the conversation was a seesaw of emotions. All tried to avoid talk of war or illness. The following day, when Michael left, everyone seemed dispirited. Although the sun had set, the still, warm air was confined in a fine haze. Even with all the windows open, they could feel only a slight breeze. Maggie wanted to go for a walk and asked if Lawrence could accompany her. As they left, Kathleen suggested that if Maggie became short of breath, Lawrence was to bring her right home.

He walked at her pace and she held his arm tightly. They had walked a few blocks, talking about unimportant things. "Has Mother ever talked to you about your father?" He thought it an odd question.

"Not really, besides you know how closed-mouthed Mother is. I know just what you know, that he was an American working for the British during the first world war and was killed when the ship he was on was torpedoed. Why, have you learned anything different?"

"Not really, but you know it's always bothered me that you had a different last name than me, especially when we were in grade school."

"Why on earth should that have bothered you, Mags?"

"Well, for one thing, nobody believed that you were my brother 'cause we had different names. I was so proud of you."

Lawrence didn't know what to say. "Sometimes you can be silly, you know that. What in the world possessed you to think about something like that?" He chortled.

"I'm being serious, Lawrence, and all you do is make fun of me. I'm telling you, that really bothered me and I thought it was something you should know—that's all."

He apologized, and they walked for a while saying nothing.

"Lawrence, I'm really awfully worried about you flying those bombers," she said out of the blue. "I hear they make great targets for the German fighters."

"Not so, Maggie. You haven't seen what the B-17 can do. Why, it's a veritable pill box. You wouldn't believe it, guns everywhere. The Jerries are gonna get a real lickin' when our outfit gets there."

She squeezed his arm tightly. "Promise you won't take unnecessary chances." He smiled and squeezed back.

"Sure," he said nonchalantly.

"I mean it," she said seriously. "I know Mother's really worried about you, too…" She took a deep breath, which in his estimation fell short of filling her lungs. Then she finished the sentence. "Although she doesn't show it."

"How about you, Maggie?" he asked. "Are you all right? The thought of you being in pain…"

"I'm not in any pain, Lawrence. I get backaches, that's all. I did have an ulterior motive, though, when I asked if we could go for a walk," she said.

"Well you sly little devil. You're just looking for trade secrets, aren't you? If I didn't know better I'd say you were working with the enemy," he joked.

"Lawrence, I'm dying," she said indifferently.

That's what he expected her to say, but still he was unprepared, shocked. "Now what gives you that impression," he said, making every effort to appear confident. "That's a bunch of poppycock. You're doing nothing of the sort, why just last night we talked with…"

"Lawrence. It's okay, I've known for a long time. I don't mind, really. I know that Mother and Father don't want me to know. Please, you won't say anything."

He couldn't look at her. He wasn't sure he could say anything, and when she asked again for his confidentiality, he choked, "Sure." It was all he could say without holding her and breaking down.

She was aware of his embarrassment. "Please don't be afraid for me, Lawrence. Believe me, in some ways I'm really looking forward to it. I'm afraid God hasn't given me much of a body in this life…" She took a breath. "Maybe he'll make me look more like Betty Grable in the next."

Now it was her turn to make light of the seriousness of the subject. She knew this would put him more at ease.

"Com'on, it's okay to talk about it. I mean, look at you. You'll be facing danger every day, won't you?" She thought she had justified her forthright remarks.

"I suppose so, Maggie, but I don't look at it that way."

"Well, neither do I," she said adamantly.

They talked for at least an hour about life, death, and their most personal feelings. He expressed his thoughts about his homosexuality. He loved her openness, her sensitivity, and her understanding. She recommended that he tell their mother.

"One day, maybe," he replied. The warm haze had dissipated, replaced by the chill of the evening, and he suggested that maybe they should be getting back. He opened the garden gate for her and she whispered. "I love you, Lawrence." She said it unexpectedly, catching him unawares. He could never remember saying the words to anyone, ever, but these circumstances were different. He looked right into her blue eyes and kissed her forehead. It would be the last time he would tell her that he loved her. "Very, very much," he had said.

CHAPTER FORTY-EIGHT

L AWRENCE ARRIVED AT Prestwick Airfield, Scotland, the last day of
August, 1942. His was the first of twelve crews assigned to the 97th
bomb group. It was their job to take the war to the enemy. Their
grand plan was to reciprocate for what the Germans had done to London.
Lawrence was never happier. Other bombers had names like Baby Doll,
Peggy Dee and Yankee Gal, names of girls the pilots knew back home.
He had the name "Maggie" painted on his for good luck. Other fortresses
began to arrive, stopping briefly at Prestwick before continuing to their
home bases in England. They followed a rhumb line across Canada and
Iceland to Scotland, ultimately to devastate Hitler's Germany. Lawrence
knew he was flying the best war machine ever built. Separated from its
inhabitants, it was just another elaborate piece of machinery. The crew
together with the plane made a living entity, an awesome force.

The B-17 was a maze of wires, tubes and hydraulic lines, some joining
the men to the machine like umbilical lifelines, administering oxygen,
communication and body heat. It may have been scientifically designed
but it wasn't built for comfort. Lawrence surmised that quite possibly the
designers knew what they were doing by making it noisy, with guns poking
from open hatches, permitting screaming cold air to freeze the occupants
within; something to keep the crews awake, he guessed. After they leveled
off, reaching their desired altitudes, and the propellers synchronized, the
big plane rattled and vibrated. Lawrence became accustomed to one noise,
a culmination of the variety of sounds the plane made. Any change in the
sound was immediately obvious and became a concern. At 24,000 feet the

temperatures descended to fifty degrees below zero. The metal parts of a gun, particularly for the waist gunners, became hazardous to the touch at those altitudes. If it wasn't for the fur-lined gloves, a crew member would find his hands permanently attached to the gun.

Lawrence's copilot, John Harvey, was from Walla Walla, a town in Washington. He was the only man, besides Lawrence, who sat during a bombing raid. The other eight were busy standing or kneeling, fighting off enemy fighters or, as was the case with the navigator and bombardier, crouching in the transparent nose like monkeys.

Lawrence was beginning to get a reputation for daring. To his crew, he was their fearless leader, taking them to the target and getting them back safe. He was an exceptional pilot. The men driving these machines were surrounded in the cockpit by more than a hundred and fifty switches, knobs, and gauges that controlled the myriad of operational attitudes of the plane. Whenever one or more of these indicators flashed, buzzed, or oscillated like a siren, Lawrence moved with the skill of a cheetah honing in on the kill.

He wrote home every chance he got and enjoyed more than anything the letters he received from Maggie. The American sorties took place in the daylight hours, and it wasn't unusual to be awake at five a.m. Lawrence was already awake and writing a short letter to Maggie when the orderly entered the quonset hut.

"They want you at H.Q. right away, sir," he said briefly and left.

Lawrence dressed quickly and was soon joined by John Harvey, Mitch Cassidy, his navigator, and Pat Cummins, his bombardier. They were given the exact location of their target, a factory where Messerchmitt fighters were being assembled. Within minutes they were signaled to take off, leading the Vee formation. As they crossed into Germany, Lawrence was startled by the call on his headphones.

"Lieutenant. Lieutenant: bogies, three o'clock low."

"Can you make them out, Harvey?" Lawrence said casually.

"Got'em, Lars, just below and to the right."

"Stay in formation, stay in formation," Lawrence said into his interphone. "Keep it tight, you guys." It looked like two whole squadrons of Me109's and a dozen FW190's were coming in for the kill. Some of the fighters stayed out of reach of the bombers, radioing ahead their position for the ground ordnance. Harvey spotted two Me109's at twelve o' clock.

"Got 'em, Pat?"

Pat Cummins also manned the nose armament of the bomber, a single 30-caliber machine gun grossly underpowered, as these crews would soon find out. The German pilots knew where the B-17's were most vulnerable.

"Got 'em, John," he said.

The Me109's sped past them to the right. They soon made a wide U and came straight at the B-17 with their mesmerizing yellow noses, emitting a storm of bullets that raged toward them. Lawrence could hear the loud staccato noise of the top turret gun just behind him. The young man firing the gun, Jake Bergman, was from Brooklyn. He was also the flight engineer. He commanded a perfect 360-degree view from the Plexiglas dome on top of the plane. The two 50-caliber guns were installed with an interrupter mechanism so that he couldn't blow his tail off. Almost everyone but the pilot had a second job. Lawrence wished he had a 50-caliber right now and wasn't just the driver. Not having a weapon, he felt an urge to ram the Me109's but knew better than to follow momentary urges. To his left he saw a B-17 completely disappear in a blinding flash. He thought they must have hit the fuel tanks; any sign of chutes would have been a miracle. The fortresses continued on, never leaving sight of their target. The frontal attacks weren't over yet. It looked to him like the same two planes coming at them again and with the same fury. This time Bergman made the hit, blasting the yellow nose to pieces; engine parts, the cockpit, part of the tailplane, and a piece of the wing flew past them in the slipstream. Lawrence saw a dark bundle coming toward him at one o'clock. It was the pilot of the Me109. In an instant, he hit the right-inside propeller, spattering the Plexiglas window with thick, red pieces of flesh that were seconds earlier a human being.

"Feather number three," Lawrence said casually, adjusting the plane's attitude. Harvey almost threw up. Lawrence laughed.

"Glad it's on your side, John—I have to land this son-of-a-bitch. That's after we give these bastards a taste of what they gave London." The plane began to yaw, pulling the B-17 to the right. Lawrence gave number-four engine more power. His preoccupation with steadying the plane was interrupted by the excited voice of Bergman.

"Lieutenant, you got bandits at 12 o' clock." It was a Focke-Wulf coming straight at them, trying to make the bomber veer off, breaking formation. The fighters liked to isolate a B-17 if they could, as a lion concentrates on a single wildebeest to separate him from the herd. The planes approached at a combined speed of almost 600 miles an hour. Lawrence didn't flinch. He could feel the tension as tracers ripped through the cockpit. The FW came so close that Lawrence could see the pilot clearly as he dove under the B-17.

"Christ! That's about as close as I ever want to come to those bastards," Bergman said, wiping his brow. Lawrence smiled.

"At least now the Hun knows he's not dealing with a chicken."

"I'm just glad he wasn't a Jap, Lars," Harvey said. "I have a buddy flying forts in the Pacific who says that they have a destiny with death or somethin', like it's okay to die, an honor to do it for your country." The bomber shook again as Bergman and the port-waist gunner blasted another Me109.

"Ain't ever heard of anyone believing that death was some kind of privilege," Bergman said, picking up where they'd left off.

"You haven't met any Catholics then, have you?" Lawrence said, shaking his head in disbelief, "Or read a Baltimore Catechism."

Bergman laughed out loud.

"I think I know what you mean, sir," he said.

German pilots seemed to know exactly where the bombers were headed and displayed a fanatical determination to stop them. Over the target they were buffeted by heavy flak while Cummins synchronized the Norden bombsight on the factories below. When the bombs were away, the fortress lifted itself automatically and the red light shut off. It was time to go home.

"Bingo, you son-of-a-bitch," Cummins yelled over the intercom as the ordnance found its mark. Lawrence felt good that the mission was a success. They had pummeled the target.

"How about a little more power on number four, John?"

"You got it," Harvey said, pushing the throttle forward. The engine sputtered. "Rally, you son-of-a-bitch," he said. "Don't cut out now. Jeez, I hope we didn't pick up some of that Me109 in the engine." He babied the throttle and it continued to lose power.

"Oil's dropping," Lawrence said. "Shut 'er down, John."

"Are you crazy? We'll never get this bird back on two port engines, Lars. I know you're good, but you're not that good."

"Just do what I say, damn it." Seeing Lawrence antagonized for the first time, John Harvey immediately shut the engine down. The big bomber pulled and dropped to the right. Lawrence asked Harvey for climb power and turned the yoke to the left, dropping the left wing and raising the right. At the same time, he gingerly applied the pedals for left rudder. He asked Mitch Cassidy for a heading to the coast and nursed the crippled plane back to Prestwick. On their approach, he had to slow the plane down, causing the right wing to lose lift. He then asked Harvey to start number four. After a couple of attempts, the engine fired and gave them just enough power to keep the plane straight. He asked Harvey for full flaps. Finally the wheels touched down, and in seconds the tail rested gently on the runway. They had made a perfect landing. On the ground, Harvey gave a deep sigh. He realized why Lawrence was the captain. Lawrence never mentioned his disobedience, and Harvey vowed never to question him again.

After a debriefing, Lawrence picked up his mail and returned to the quonset hut for a nap. He shuffled through some military correspondence and opened the letter from home, V-mail from his mother:

Dear Lawrence, there isn't a day that goes by that I don't pray for your safety. I don't want you to feel sad with what I'm about to tell you. Maggie's suffering is over. I'll miss her more than anyone, not only as a daughter but also she had become my very best friend. In some ways I'm happy for her, she wanted to die, she was prepared to go to a better place. We could all learn from her great faith. More than anything, she wanted you to be safe, even suggesting that she would have more power in death to protect you from harm. Believe me, son, she was happier than I had ever seen her the night before she died. Michael has been a great source of courage for all of us and was with her constantly. By the way, he takes his vows next month.

I wish there was some way you could make it home but I know I'm asking the impossible. Father Rafferty is coming over to say the Funeral Mass. Of course with the time difference and all everything will be past by the time you get this letter. Please stay well,Lawrence, somehow I believe that Maggie will always be with you, as will I.

Love, Mom

Lawrence placed the letter on the night table. He lit a cigarette, lay back on the bunk, and thought about Maggie. Visions of their childhood emerged. He remembered getting into fights when someone made the slightest comment about her deformity. He thought about the time they left for the seminary and how lonely he knew she'd be. He thought about the last time they talked, how contented she seemed. He extinguished the cigarette and continued to indulge in reveries until they dissolved into the darkness of sleep.

Time moved fast for Lawrence. Within two weeks of Maggie's death he had flown seven missions and lost John Harvey. He was no sooner assigned a new copilot then Pat Cummins and Mitch Cassidy, his bombardier, disappeared over the target. The nose of the B-17 was completely blown away by a 20-millimeter shell. Initially, the crew believed that Lawrence was fearless and, more importantly, invincible. Now with every mission they returned with a crippled airplane and at least one of the crew dead or wounded. Command wasn't sure that the number of enemy planes to their credit and bombing accuracy was an equitable trade for men's lives. The crew was beginning to believe that Lawrence purposefully went out of his way to attract fighters and enjoyed more time over the target than was necessary. Once when they reached the channel and the fighters were ready to break off the fight, he turned to follow two fighters who were probably the most surprised pilots in the whole Luftwaffe. Lawrence was transferred to the 486th bomb group at Sudbury, England, and was ordered to take a three-day pass before reporting for duty. His C.O. recommended London.

"Find a gal, have some fun, live it up," he said.

Lawrence packed and shipped his belongings on to Sudbury, keeping an awol bag for his trip. He left by train and arrived at Euston Station the next morning. He took a bus to Oxford Street near Piccadilly Circus and found a place to stay close by. A cockney lady showed him up three flights of stairs to his small room, which looked over a green square with beautiful tall oak and elm trees. She then took him down to a small room with a bathtub and toilet on the second floor and told him he would have to share the bath with the other tenants. This, she said in her cockney accent, would cost him another tanner. After he put away the few clothes and toilet articles, he walked around the area. He couldn't believe the devastation. It was the first time he saw on the ground the damage caused by carpet bombing. He passed the Palladium and stood awhile looking at a billboard. Someone named Tommy Trinder, the host, he surmised, was introducing an American comedy group. The show was to begin at seven o'clock; since he had no intentions of following the C.O.'s orders regarding female company, he thought this would be a good way to pass some time.

That afternoon he gave the landlady a sixpence and took a bath. The porcelain tub was small, chipped, and the water lukewarm. He put on a clean shirt and buttoned the uniform jacket. A few ribbons under the shiny pilot wings added some color. He pulled the cap at the sides, enhancing the fifty-mission crush, and placed it on his head in a cocked fashion. Happy with the way he looked, he left to get something to eat before the show.

The sun disappeared behind an ominous black, low-stratus cloud. He didn't realize that in England one didn't walk into a theater without standing in a line or *queue,* as they referred to it. He stepped in behind a long line of Londoners who looked at him curiously and whispered among themselves. At the first sprinkle, umbrellas began to pop up all around him. Soon the sprinkle turned to a downpour and he was getting soaked.

"May I?" a voice from behind said. He turned to find a strikingly beautiful woman, tall, he guessed to be about five seven without the heels and in her late twenties. She raised her umbrella, partially covering his head.

"I hope you don't think me forward. Would you like to share my umbrella?" she said in a deep, velvet voice.

"I don't mind a bit," he said appreciatively. "This weather of yours sure comes on fast." They huddled close as rain poured off the edges of the umbrella; her long, blond hair touched his chin and he loved the fragrance of her perfume.

"Are you on leave then?" she asked.

"Just three days, then I have to report back to my base."

"And where's that?" Without waiting for an answer, she apologized.

"Sorry," she said. "I don't mean to sound inquisitive, it just came out, spur of the moment."

He smiled. "That's okay. How about you, is your life so secret you can't tell me what you do?"

"No such luck," she said. "I'm in the entertainment business."

"Oh," he said, his eyes widening.

She looked embarrassed. "Not what you're thinking—I'm in show business." She smiled up at him, showing perfect white teeth. "Off Piccadilly."

He looked confused.

"Off Piccadilly. It's a little like your Off Broadway."

"Oh," he nodded. He was content to let her take the conversation wherever she wished. It was a pleasure just talking to someone about other things besides military matters. Fifteen minutes passed and all signs of daylight were completely overshadowed by lowering, black, gloomy clouds. The rain turned to needles of ice and a bright flash was followed instantly by a loud, rolling clash.

"Welcome to England's nice weather," she shouted up at him over the hail. "If it's not this," she indicated with her hand, "it's bloody doodlebombs." He took no notice of her body pushing closer to him.

"I hear it's an excellent show, if we get in, that is," she said excitedly.

"An American family, Bebe Daniels and Ben Lyon, I hear they're very funny, ever heard of them?"

"Can't say I have. I could use a good laugh, though."

A man's voice was hollering something to the people in the queue, becoming more discernible as he came closer.

"Standing room only folks, standing room only."

People were becoming restless. A low grumble came from the crowd muttering their discontent. Many began to leave, shortening the line.

"That's too bad," she said, "and after waiting this bloomin' long."

"I think I'll just mosey on and find something else to do," he said, stepping out from under the umbrella. He put out his hand.

"It's been nice."

"Me too." Her voice was soft, coquettish, and she held his hand longer than he thought customary.

"I don't even know your name," she said.

"Lawrence Riordan."

"Mine's Terzina Sinclair. Actually that's my stage name. My real name is Terry, Terry McCabe." She finally released his hand.

"You're Irish?" he inquired.

"On my father's side. Mum's English."

Lawrence had nothing more on his mind than a drink and friendly conversation. When he asked if she'd like to go somewhere, he was happy when she agreed. They stood by the curb huddled under the umbrella. The street looked like a pond. When the red double-decker bus passed, they failed to move fast enough and were sprayed with water. Lawrence got the worst trying to protect her.

"I took one bath today that cost me sixpence," he laughed. "This one was free." Within moments he hailed down a cab.

"Where to, guv."

"Albion and Edgeware Road," she answered and turned to Lawrence.

"We're going to get you dried off before we go anywhere."

They drove up Oxford Street past Marble Arch. The hail persisted, pounding the windshield, merging into a sheet of ice; wipers laboriously swabbed to create a field of vision. It was a short drive, but she pointed out many sights.

"That's Speaker's Corner. You can say anything there that's on your mind, and no one will take you away."

"Anything?" he said.

"I believe so."

"That's what I call free speech," he said.

The cab turned down Bayswater road and turned right on Albion. It came to a stop at the corner of Edgeware Road.

"One and thruppence, mate," the cabbie said. Lawrence gave him half a crown and they got out.

"You Americans are going to ruin our cabbies with your big tips. This is where I live," she said, pointing up to the second story above an electrical appliance shop. They entered through a side door, and she led him up a narrow staircase. She fumbled about in her purse until she found the key. The door opened to a spacious room with a gas fireplace at one end. He saw three additional doors. One was open, leading to the kitchenette, the other two, he assumed, led to a bedroom and bathroom.

"That's the bathroom," she said, pointing to one of the closed doors.

"Take off those wet things. You'll find a bathrobe hanging on the back of the door."

He hesitated. "Look, if this is putting you out…"

"Go," she ordered, "while I mix us a drink."

"Yes, ma'am," he said, joking, giving her a salute. He turned toward the door.

"Will Scotch be all right then?" she asked tentatively.

"That will do just fine," he said, closing the door.

When he came back into the room, he saw flames in the fireplace, and she had put a record on the gramophone. Vera Lynn was singing "We'll Meet Again." She had removed the wet dress and wore a white slip, through which he could see her shapely legs. She held a glass in each hand and for a moment he wished he were heterosexual. She held the glass to him.

"I hope you like it without ice."

"As long as it's alcohol."

"Here's to a short war and long friends," she said.

"Cheers!" Their glasses clinked and he chugged the warm Scotch. It warmed deep into his chest. She replenished his glass right away and he dropped into the easy chair by the fire. When she finished her drink, she went to the bathroom and returned with his wet uniform. She carefully hung the pants, jacket, and shirt by the fire. She sat on the floor by his feet and they listened to the music. He talked mostly about his family, his brother, Michael, and Maggie. The whiskey was beginning to make him maudlin, and he was soon apologizing for his gloomy attitude. She shot up.

"Up," she said, taking his hand," let's dance." He drew his hand back.

"Oh, no, no, that's something I don't do, can't do."

"Oh, yes, I'll teach you, it's easy, there's nothing to it." He acquiesced and stood.

"You're going to be very disappointed in me," he said, almost prepared to tell her about his predilections. She took his right arm and placed it about her waist and held his left hand with her right. They waltzed slowly to the music. She pulled him close and she slipped her left hand around his neck. He knew she was going to kiss him. He felt awkward. She had been so kind to him; the last thing he wanted to do was hurt her feelings. He allowed her to find his mouth. She had soft lips and he could taste the lipstick. Her tongue gently eased inside, moving against his. It was the first time he ever kissed anyone like that. He thought of his days in the seminary. How he wished for that from Brother David. He pulled back abruptly.

"Look, Terry, there's something -"

She hushed his words with her fingers.

"Don't say anything, please, I have a surprise for you." She sat him back down. "I'd like very much to show you my act." She poured him another drink. It was a double and straight. He took a great gulp.

"Your act?" he said curiously.

"Yes, Lawrence, I'm going to give you a private showing of what I do. Would you like that?"

"Yes. Yes, that would be great," he said, willing to sit through anything rather than dance. She put on another record, a jazz number, and went in to what he assumed was the bedroom. When she closed the door he had an urge to get dressed and leave. He decided that would be rude and relaxed into the chair, taking another gulp. In a moment, the door opened and she entered the room. Her hair was shimmering, black, and hung about her shoulders. She wore a black-satin, tight-fitting dress with a long slit exposing shapely legs. He admired her beauty and knew that the guys at the base would give plenty to see this. She danced exotically, sometimes falling to the floor, moving to him and massaging his legs with her breasts. She returned each time from the bedroom displaying new costumes and wearing wigs of different colors and styles. Lawrence fixed a number of drinks between acts and was beginning to feel more relaxed. He smiled to himself, asking what she would say when he told her that he preferred men. For her last dance, she donned the white slip and was back to her blond hair. She danced over to where he sat comfortably and pulled him to her.

"This is where I grab someone from the audience and make him dance with me," she said seductively. He went along with her passionate display and grinned. She kissed him again. This time he was going to kiss her. He was about to kiss her hard and proclaim his homosexuality. He held her head with both hands and noticed her hair seemed to move. Surprised, he pulled back, the blond wig fell away with his hand, exposing short, black, curly hair. He was astonished. "My God, you're—you're a man!"

he exclaimed. "I don't believe it!" He stood for a while with the wig in his hand.

"Lawrence, I'm a female impersonator. I'm so sorry, deari—I thought you might have guessed. Are you mad?"

Lawrence hesitated briefly.

"Mad! God no, a little embarrassed. No, surprised, Terry, I'm surprised, that's all, and I'm not the least bit mad."

"Look, let's start all over again," Lawrence said excitedly.

Lawrence permitted Terry to slide his soft hands inside the robe and over his shoulders, allowing it to drop to the floor.

"You're not offended, are you?"

"Not in the least," Lawrence said, kissing the painted forehead. Lawrence trembled, feeling the half open mouth kissing his chest, slowly tracing downward. He raised his head to the ceiling, closed his eyes, savoring the moment, intoxicated so much by the passionate display that his whole body shuddered, then stiffened, aroused to the touch. He asked if this is really what heaven was all about, the gates of paradise. On second thought he mused, more like the gates of hell.

CHAPTER FORTY-NINE

ICHAEL PUSHED HIS face into the plush wine-colored carpet and wasn't about to let the musty odor spoil the magnificence of the event. His body procumbent, arms extended, emulating the cross, Michael was finally fulfilling his destiny to become a priest. The great Cathedral was packed with priests, deacons, friends, and relatives of the ten young men receiving their final vows. The sweet odor of incense filled the church. The altar was decorated with a profusion of roses, calla lily, and jasmine. The sanctuary and great pillars were entwined with wreaths and brilliantly illuminated with wax tapers. Michael pondered on his insignificance, on the knowledge that all God's creatures are needy because each one in and of itself is imperfect and dependent; animals need food, the earth needs rain and sun. The greater God's creatures, the poorer they are, because their needs are more demanding, more numerous. For this reason, he was the poorest. He prayed to God for material and spiritual strength to love, honor, and obey God for all his blessings. He prayed for Maggie's soul and was content with knowing she would have no more earthly suffering and that she would finally find peace with God's angels. He prayed for his family and asked God to keep his brother safe and bring peace to his troubled mind. As Michael prayed, the Archbishop of Boston faced the altar and raised his arms. He prayed, surrounded by priests from the various parishes in the Archdioceses, among them Father Rafferty.

Tibi populoque Papa benedicit, he said. It was a blessing from the Pope. The music of the ordination received special attention. The Cathedral choir of fifty voices chanted gloriously and a double quartet was accompanied by the massive pipe organ.

Ve-ni Cre-a-tor Spi-ri-tus,
Men-tes tu-o-rum Vi-si-ta;
Im-ple su-per-na gra-ti-a,
Quae tu cre-a-sti, pe-cto ra.

The Gregorian chant undulated, resonating, its great crescendos and diminuendos complementing the solemnity of the occasion. Ryan, Kathleen, and their families sat in the first pew. She wore a white skirt and jacket with a lilac-colored corsage and a simple, black, turtle-necked silk blouse. Around her neck, a single strand of gold supported an emerald in a heart setting with earrings to match. On her head, a white hat with a broad brim contrasted with her shimmering black hair. She looked exquisite. It was the first time since Maggie's death that she had worn anything but all black. This was a joyful occasion, this was Michael's marriage to the church, and she was determined to at least appear blissful. She had succeeded in looking radiant. Ryan wore his usual black suit with a red-and-black diagonal-striped tie. Madge Noonan, James, and Katy Thornton represented the entire family. Chuck and Florence Boyle also occupied the first pew. Ryan looked around, scanning the congregation, looking for William Hamilton. He had been out of town for Maggie's funeral and promised Ryan that he would definitely try to be there for Michael's ordination. Hamilton had insisted that he needed to discuss some things with the Boston field office. Not seeing Hamilton, Ryan, disappointed, returned his attention to the Mass. He reasoned that maybe Hamilton stopped by the field office first and was detained.

Outside the Cathedral, Hamilton was driving around looking for a place to park. He checked the time and swore. He found a vacant lot about two blocks from the church. His leg was aching more than usual and he cursed because he had to walk so far. By the time he reached the church, people emptied out to the street. A large black sedan hurried past him, and he thought he recognized Ryan in the back seat. Other cars were following in a procession. Hamilton asked an older couple if the service was over. The man, who appeared to be in his seventies, stepped forward tentatively as if to protect his wife.

"What's that you say, young man?"

"I asked if the service is over," Hamilton said, louder. "I was supposed to attend the ceremony, but I was delayed. I'm a good friend of one of the family whose son was being ordained."

"Well you missed it, didn't you."

"I guess so. Do you happen to know where everyone is going? Is there a reception where families are meeting?" Hamilton asked. The old man removed his hat and began to scratch his bald head. The woman, who, Hamilton assumed, was his wife, answered.

"I believe each family is having its own reception. That's what I think. What's your family's name, that might help?"

"Thornton, Ryan Thornton, his wife's name is Kathleen, I believe."

James Noonan, walking to his car with a friend, overheard Kathleen's name. "Excuse me," he said, "I couldn't help overhearing. Are you looking for Ryan and Kathleen Thornton?"

"Yes, my name's Hamilton; I work with Ryan in D.C." He turned back to the old couple and thanked them for their help. They left mumbling, saying people should be better informed about where they were going. Hamilton smiled at James.

"They're right, you know," he said. James smiled back and extended his hand.

"I'm James Noonan and this is Carol Hartung." Hamilton shook his hand and waited for the young woman to offer hers. He took her gloved hand and held it sensitively. "Pleased to meet you—Miss?"

"Yes, Miss," she said. "Miss Hartung." Hamilton bowed his head politely.

"The reception for Michael—that would be Father Michael now, is at my mother's house," James said eagerly. "Why don't you drive with us?"

"I have my own car." Hamilton pointed up the street. "It's only a few blocks that way. I appreciate the offer, but I think I'll follow you—if that's okay."

"Certainly," James said, and the three left for the reception.

Hamilton followed their car and soon found himself outside the beautiful red-brick house on Louisberg Square. Missus Dunne, now in her seventies and familiar figure in the household, answered the door. The three stepped into the crowded foyer. It had been a long time since Hamilton had seen so many people packed into one place. James introduced him to a few guests and offered to get him a drink. It was a while before he returned with the ginger ale. Hamilton thanked him and said not to worry, he'd find Ryan himself.

The foyer was becoming even more cramped; he found the larger living room offered some mobility. His eyes caught the back of a woman in a white skirt and black chemise. She was conversing with a priest and another woman. Aware that his staring was conspicuous, he glanced away. He took a sip on the ginger ale. His peripheral vision, although blurred, showed that she had turned around. He was aware of someone staring at him. It seemed incredible that even with all the other people in the room, he knew she was looking at him. He reasoned that it must have had something to do with Dennis Noonan. Remote as it seemed, she was a Noonan and recognized him as FBI, what with the Bureau being responsible for a death in her family.

He was beginning to feel uncomfortable and stilled an urge to move back to the foyer. Before walking way, his curiosity suggested he look quickly in her direction. He took another swig, and his eyes checked over to where she was standing. Believing her to be an apparition, his eyes playing some kind of heartless joke, he blinked. She was still there looking back at him, seemingly transfixed. God, how he wanted to cry out, *Kathleen, it is you!* He wanted to take her in his arms. His eyes focused on her, stayed on her. She looked ravishing, the embodiment of beauty, as beautiful as when he last saw her. If it was a dream, he didn't want it to vanish. Each stood for a long time, about ten feet apart, just staring. They stayed that way until another person in the room passed between them, breaking the spell. She was still there. His smile was tender. Without taking his eyes from hers, he attempted to move with legs he couldn't feel. He wanted to close his eyes and concentrate, regain his composure. He was terrified that if he blinked she would dissolve to someone unfamiliar, a resemblance only. He slowly approached her and stopped close enough to embrace her fragrance. He knew she recognized him, yet she never smiled.

"God in heaven—it is you, isn't it?" she said in a loud whisper. He couldn't believe that he was hearing her voice again.

"Liam Riordan, I thought you were dead—they told me you were dead," she stammered.

Speechless, anchored in place, he stood still, looking at her.

"It is you, isn't it?" she asked dubiously. He had trouble moving his mouth, afraid that anything he might attempt to say would sound abysmally stupid. He managed to say her name.

"Kathleen."

Her mouth trembled, color moved from her face; blue eyes at first curious, almost beaming, now disappeared upward and eventually closed as she dropped. He caught her before she hit the floor. In a moment, he was surrounded by Father Rafferty, James, Michael, others who thought they might be of help, all talking at once.

"Give her some air."

"Someone call a doctor."

Other voices outside the circle asking, "What's happened?"

And answers, "I think somebody's fainted."

Ryan broke through the crowd. "Oh, my God! Is she all right?" he said, asking anyone, everyone.

"I think she just fainted, Ryan," Father answered. "Let's get her to somewhere quiet."

Madge, who had stepped in quickly, said that Kathleen would be better off in the library. "There's a comfortable couch there; we can lay her down."

Hamilton was still holding her, waiting for someone else to carry her, but every indication suggested that he was the one. He reached behind and raised her legs. Holding her close, he could feel her soft face just beneath his chin as Madge cleared a path to the library. She told James to find Joseph Kortner, who was somewhere in the house. Hamilton laid her down on the leather couch and stepped back, making way for an older man he assumed to be the doctor. Kortner took her pulse, touched her forehead with the back of his hand, then raised her eyelids. "For no apparent reason, she has fainted," he said.

Ryan was relieved to hear that her condition was presumably mild.

"She's been under a lot of strain lately, what with Maggie's..." He couldn't admit to himself that Maggie was dead. "She's been worried about Lawrence and the ordination; it's all been too much for her." Kortner nodded and produced a small vial of smelling salts from his pocket. He broke it and released the pungent contents under her nose. In a moment her head drew back. She wasn't coherent until she saw Ryan.

"You're going to be fine, honey, you need something to eat, that's all," he said enthusiastically. She made an effort with her mouth, only to produce a capricious smile. She was remembering why she fainted when Ryan moved aside, permitting her to see Hamilton.

"If it hadn't been for William here you might have hit a chair," Father Rafferty said. "He's the one that caught you."

She looked past him to Hamilton, who appeared worried. "William?" she said curiously.

"Yes," Ryan said, "William Hamilton."

Past the initial shock, she could look at him now and observe the changes in his face. Other than a few wrinkles, he looked the same. It was the eyes, she thought, that hadn't changed.

"So you're William Hamilton," she said, emphasizing his name, "Ryan's boss, the man who's been making him work those ungodly hours."

He wasn't sure how to take the remark. She offered him her hand, which he took with both his hands. "I'm afraid so," he said, "and I certainly am very glad to see you're all right."

She made an effort to sit upright, with Ryan's help. Madge sighed with relief, seeing Kathleen with the color back in her face. Michael looked concerned for his mother.

"You two are to go back in there," Kathleen told them, "and give the party some life—get Katy to play a lively song." Kortner told her not to try to get up too fast. He checked her pulse again and excused himself.

"If you need me, I shall be by the piano."

"Thanks, Doctor Joe," she said. Her voice still quivered.

Ryan held her hand. "Can I get you a little something to drink? A little brandy might do some good," he said.

She held up her hand, thumb and middle finger, almost touching. "Just a wee dram, maybe."

Ryan asked Hamilton if he would stay with her; he left, not waiting for an answer. He closed the door gently, leaving them alone. They looked at each other. When they decided to say something, they spoke in tandem, stopped, more silence, apologies, silence. Finally he said without punctuation, "You go first."

"How come you're not dead?" she asked. "Answer that first."

"That's a long story. From what I could tell, you wanted me dead. Do you still believe I was responsible for your father's arrest?"

"No, I've since learned it wasn't you, but you can't deny that you lived a lie—you weren't who you said you were." Color was returning fast to her face.

Hamilton was remembering her seesaw personality and knew better than to upset her. All he could muster was trite.

"Sorry—really," he said. "I was going to explain everything." As if his being there wasn't surprise enough, the next comment left her awe-struck. "I had no idea about the babies."

She couldn't respond immediately. Everything was happening too fast. She needed more time to assimilate this unanticipated statement in an unanticipated event. "What about the babies?" she said fiercely. "I hope that you don't think that for one moment…"

Ryan opened the door, instantly stopping her tirade. "How are you two getting along?"

"Oh," she cleared her throat, "we're getting along fine," she said in her most sincere voice.

"That's right," Hamilton concurred, "like old friends." He could feel her looking through him, the unkind scrutiny.

"The color's even returned to your face, you look great," Ryan said, turning to Hamilton. "Doesn't she, William?"

Hamilton shrugged. "An amazing recovery," he said.

Ryan handed her a short brandy. "Take this anyway, it won't hurt."

She finished the liquor in two sips, shuddered, and made an effort to stand. Ryan immediately took her arm.

"Oh stop fussin'," she said, an order Ryan ignored.

"I don't want you taking another spill," he said. "William, would you mind taking her other arm?"

"I'd be happy to," he said.

When they reached the door, she broke away. "I'd as soon rejoin the party not lookin' like an invalid, if you don't mind," she said tempestuously, with a judicious smile.

Hamilton was soon in control of another ginger ale and moving about, enjoying the brief encounters with Ryan and Kathleen's friends. By far the most momentous and apprehensive time occurred when Hamilton met his son. It was Kathleen who introduced them. She was composed, even casual. He was amazed by her self-control.

"Michael, this is your father's boss at the Bureau."

For a moment, he thought she was going to say *father*. She hesitated with his name. He broke in and together they said, "William, William Hamilton." He continued, shaking his son's hand vigorously. "I'm sure your mother is very proud of you, Michael, I mean Father Michael."

"If Mother had her way they'd be making me a Cardinal instead of a priest." He laughed and placed an arm around Kathleen. "Isn't that so, Mother?"

They talked a long time, mostly about Michael's future, and it was becoming obvious to Hamilton that she was not about to leave him alone with their son for a minute. He sensed her distress and obliged her by dismissing himself.

"Well, I should be getting along." He shook Michael's hand.

"It's been a pleasure meeting you, Mr. Hamilton. I hope we can get together again sometime."

Hamilton could feel her cringe. He found Ryan in the kitchen and said he had to leave. He told him to take a few days off and said he'd see him back at the office. The reception had lasted only a few hours, but to him it seemed like days. Kathleen was busy talking with her aunt and a priest he hadn't met. He was going to depart without her knowing; however, she caught his eye and followed him to the door. She didn't offer her hand. He could see that she continued to be upset at his emergence.

"I really am sorry to have caused you so much pain, Kathleen. Had I known…"

She stopped him.

"I'm sorry I treated you so badly. I've had a little time to think. I know you were probably as shocked to see me as I was you. I hope you can understand the concern for my sons."

"Completely, Kathleen," he said. "I won't be bothering you again."

CHAPTER FIFTY

W HEN SHE WAS alone and yearned for Maggie, Kathleen accomplished little. At other times, she engaged herself in productive work. She busied herself at the hospital. And with the help of her Boston employers who furnished affidavits of her successful treatment of infantile paralysis, she found herself working in pediatrics. She knew it was going to take time to establish her credibility, that it would take patience. It was a new challenge, one that made her more determined than ever to continue her research.

Her life was returning to normal, never quite like the past but nonetheless becoming perfectly arranged. William Hamilton shared a good part of her thoughts. She was surprised that he made no attempt to call. He was honorable in keeping that pledge, she thought.

There were moments when she considered his disregard a discourtesy. She attributed these thoughts to his apparent lack of interest. So many questions hadn't been answered. He hadn't died and had not lost his memory, so why did he not try to contact her years ago? Did he know she was pregnant, and that's why he left? What in the world did the "A" stand for in his middle name? And why was she thinking the name important? She had questions about her father's escape from Kilmainham prison. *If it wasn't he who was responsible, then who was?* She needed answers; however, the thought of meeting him secretly, to which he would no doubt agree, frightened her to death. Was she afraid they would be caught and people would not understand? Could she really trust herself, trust her feelings? Was there a need to bring a clear end to their relationship, on her terms? Did she still love him? That thought frightened her most.

Three days before Christmas of 1942, Kathleen decided she would ask Ryan to invite his boss to Christmas Eve dinner. Lawrence was coming home on furlough, and Michael, who was now serving as assistant pastor in a New York parish, would also be home. She was feeling the holiday spirit and wanted William Hamilton to see his sons. He had been gracious enough to stay away. She would allow a visit on her terms, a reward for his promise kept. Ryan told her of the little he had learned about Hamilton: He'd never married, he had no living relatives. Ryan thought Hamilton mentioned a sister somewhere but wasn't sure. He also wasn't sure if Hamilton would accept the invitation, given his policy on socializing in or outside the department. He promised her he would ask and mentioned that since she was the one asking, Hamilton would consider the invitation more favorably.

She spent the day preparing the meal. Lawrence helped, peeling potatoes and cleaning carrots. In these times when they were alone, he came close to telling her about who he really was, close to saying that there was a serious side, screaming to be heard. He yearned to mention his lover in England, to tell her about the happiness they had together. The subject had become as elusive as trying to convey what it was like to sit in a hollow tube with windows, freezing temperatures, at 25,000 feet, which was bad enough. Now add that you're a target for hundreds of massive guns trying to blast you out of the air. He mused: the bombing missions would be easier to explain than his relations with a burlesque entertainer. How in God's name would he ever explain Terrance? She asked if he wouldn't mind putting on a fire. That simple request spoiled the moment.

She recognized a change in Lawrence. He seemed more content. There was no more pretense; the schoolboy naiveté was gone. He never talked about the war, but Kathleen knew he must have endured terrifying experiences. Ryan had explained the importance of the medals on his uniform, among them the Air Medal for completing ten missions, and the Purple Heart. Ryan tried to reduce her anxieties by saying that Lawrence assured him the wound that the medal represented was not much to write home about. "He is as good as new, Lawrence told me." They decided that they wouldn't talk about the war unless Lawrence brought it up.

"What's the time, Lawrence?" she asked, setting the table with her finest china and silverware, reserved only for holidays and special events. "Almost six-thirty, Mother."

"God, I'd better get this dinner moving," she said, moving quickly to the kitchen to check the Yorkshire pudding.

"Is there something I can do to help?" he said, placing the book he was reading on the side table.

"No, you relax," she said, closing the oven door. She brought him a sliver of meat cut from the standing rib roast, flavored with garlic and rosemary.

"It's hot," she said, "don't burn your tongue; you'll ruin your dinner."

He chewed slowly, smiling, savoring the flavor, his eyes closed. Although she knew he liked it, she waited impatiently for his response.

"Well?"

"At last," he said, still chewing. "I know now why I'm over there fighting: so those goddamn Nazis don't steal your recipes."

"Oh, go on with ye." The Dublin brogue returned whenever it wished.

"You're never serious—just like yer auld gran'dad, and you can stop that swearing any time you want," she said, losing the accent.

Hearing the latch key, they turned their attention to the door. Ryan gestured for Hamilton to step through first. He removed his hat.

"Merry Christmas, Missus Thornton," Hamilton said.

"If you call me Kathleen, I won't call you Mister Hamilton." She extended her hand. "Merry Christmas," she said.

Ryan stepped past him and kissed her cheek. "Dinner smells great," he said, and went into the kitchen.

Lawrence stood, waiting to be introduced.

"This is my other son, Lawrence," she said. "Michael is out with a friend he'd known at the seminary. Lawrence is in the Army Air Force. This is William Hamilton. He works with your father."

"My pleasure," Hamilton said. "You certainly are a ringer for your brother."

"We're one and the same," Lawrence said. "The only real difference is what we do for a living."

"You're a military man, and he's a priest?" Hamilton asked.

"Also the fact that I kill souls—and he saves them."

Kathleen was horrified. "Lawrence Riordan," she said, in her admonishing tone. Hamilton was speechless. He put his finger tips on his forehead. His bewildered expression stopped Kathleen for a moment. *How could he have known?* She had taken for granted that he would have learned her widowed name. Just something more that needed sorting out. She gave him a look as if to say *please, don't ask*. Hamilton, on the other hand, was flattered. He smiled.

"Ryan," he said, making a conscious decision not to say *your father,* "tells me that you fly B-17's. You young men are really making a difference over there. So now that you've been awarded the Air Medal and completed additional missions, are you coming home for good?"

Kathleen excused herself.

"Got to get in there," she said, "before Ryan eats all the gravy."

"I'm here to get a little more information on some new engines ... to give us a little extra speed to get to the target," Lawrence said. "You can understand the reason I can't say much more."

"I appreciate it," Hamilton said proudly. The door opened. It was Michael.

"Mister Hamilton," he said enthusiastically, "Merry Christmas."

They shook hands, and the three talked for a while before being motioned to the table by Kathleen and Ryan, who came from the kitchen carrying the aromatic dishes. They sat, and Michael was asked to say the grace. It was their first Christmas without Maggie.

"We thank you, Lord, for this food which we are about to eat and for friends with whom we wish to share. We pray for those who are without sustenance on this holy night and that this war will soon be over ...and thank you, Lord, for bringing Lawrence home safely." He hesitated. "We know that in Your infinite love You have taken Maggie to be with You and by doing so, You took away her suffering ... and it is through Your love that she is always here with us...Amen."

They said Amen in unison. Kathleen wiped the tear forming on her lower eyelid. "Let's eat," she said jovially, "before it gets cold."

"You should have known better," Lawrence said, joking, "than to let a priest say grace." They passed the plates, silver utensils clanking against china, talked while Harry James's Christmas Carols played on the radio. They found humor in tragedies past. Hamilton wanted to hear more about the boys when they were young. Kathleen knew his requests were more than patronizing curiosity and tried to be accommodating. They poured wine and Hamilton stopped at two glasses.

"Any more than that," he said, "and I'm ready to hit the sack."

After dinner and dessert, Kathleen retired to the kitchen, allowing Hamilton time to get to know the boys. She was content that he no longer posed a threat to her secret. Ryan joined her and commenced drying plates she'd already washed.

"Well, what do you think?" he said offhandedly.

"Think?" she asked. "Think of what?"

"William," he said. "He's quite a guy, isn't he?"

"He seems to be. He doesn't talk much about himself. Has he said anything to you about his past?"

"Not a lot. I guess he did spend some time in Ireland during the first war." He thought for a moment. "Dublin, I believe—I'll ask him."

She held his arm. "No, not now, it's not that important."

The evening drew to a close when Michael stood, excusing himself.

"I'm sorry to be an old party pooper, but I have to prepare for tomorrow's mass."

"Michael is assisting the Archbishop at the Cathedral in D.C.," Ryan said proudly.

"Maybe you'd care to join us, Mister Hamilton?" Michael said.

Hamilton was immediately prepared to say no. He stood and looked at Kathleen, whose expression said it was okay. This was his son's first big event. He thought of all the pageants he'd missed. He looked at Ryan's proud expression and recognized that this was his real father. He shook Michael's hand. "It's honor enough that you asked me, Michael … maybe some other time."

"I wish I could decline as eloquently as William," Lawrence said, smiling.

Kathleen gave him a friendly swat. Hamilton thought it was time to leave, and Ryan disappeared to find his coat.

"This has been one of the happiest evenings I can remember." He looked into her blue eyes and wished they could have been alone just for a moment. He held her hand again. She didn't pull back, permitting him more time to feel her acceptance.

"You'll have to come and see us again," she said. He said goodnight to Lawrence, and Ryan returned with his coat and hat and said he'd walk him to the car. It was a starry night. Their steps crunched in the fresh snow.

"Hope you had a good time," Ryan said, "that's an awful lot of family stuff for a single guy." Hamilton got in the car and started the engine. He rolled down the window.

"You're fortunate, Ryan; I think they're great."

"Guess I'll just have to keep them, eh," he said, as Hamilton drove away.

CHAPTER FIFTY-ONE

I T WAS LATE spring before Hamilton heard again from Kathleen. He had
determined to wait until she made the first overture. He had declined
a dinner invitation, her way of apologizing for her actions with him
in the library.

Ryan, on assignment, wasn't due back for two days. Hamilton was in
his office reviewing a code when the phone rang.

"It's Missus Thornton," the voice said.

"Did you tell her that Ryan's not here?"

"I told her that, sir."

"Well?"

"She wishes to speak with you, sir."

Hamilton thought a moment before accepting the call.

"I'll take it." He waited for the transfer.

"Hello." Her voice sounded good.

"Kathleen—it's been a while. Is everything all right?"

"Oh, yes. Nothing's wrong. I just thought it was time that we should
talk," she said confidently. "I thought you were very good with the boys,
and I appreciate your …"

"Tell you what," he interrupted, knowing that all conversations
were taped. "Why don't I call you. Things are a little busy right now."
He despised himself for having to cut her off. He waited. No response,
"Kathleen?"

"I'm here." Her tone was terse. Christ, he couldn't do anything right
with her, he thought.

"Kathleen—I'll call you shortly, okay?"

"Okay," she said and hung up.

Later he left the office and called her from a pay phone. He apologized and explained the reason for his hastiness. Content with his explanation, she chided herself for being thoughtless. They agreed to meet at a small cafeteria in Morningside at noon. He arrived first and ordered a cup of coffee. He checked the time. The clock on the wall concurred with his wrist watch, eleven fifty-five. He felt like a love-stricken schoolboy.

At exactly noon she walked in wearing a green coat and white scarf. Her cheeks glowed pink from the chilly March air. *Beautiful,* he thought, *she is beautiful*. He stood and drew the chair back. She sat and placed her hands on the table. They spoke at first of trivialities.

After a few moments, she said, "There are many things that I have to ask you...you'll probably laugh at something that's been driving me absolutely mad."

He smiled. "I'll tell you anything, Kathleen, as long as it's not classified."

"Your middle name," she asked curiously, "what does the 'A' stand for?"

He laughed loudly. "Why in the world..."

"I wouldn't laugh too loud. If I wasn't a lady, I'd tell you what I thought it should stand for. I'm talking about your cigarette case," she said. "You don't remember? I kept it."

There was nothing wrong with his memory. "I remember as if it was yesterday, Kathleen," he said quietly. "So you kept it?"

Her thoughts were immediately synchronized with his. The rose in her cheeks turned red.

"Anyway," she said, breaking into their recollections, "I was just curious about the W.A.H. and what the 'A' stood for."

"Armstrong," he said, "it was my mother's maiden name."

"Armstrong ... it suits you." A portly waiter appeared, asking them if they had decided. He awakened them to their closeness and they withdrew, removing their arms from the table. Hamilton said they hadn't decided and the server left in a huff.

"Speaking of names," he said, "the boys ... their name is Riordan?" She knew that her answer would disappoint him. But he understood. At the time, it wasn't love but out of necessity that she chose the name.

She talked about the realization of her pregnancy and her parents' determination to send her to Boston, and recounted her visit to Dublin seeking the confidence of her friend Bridget McIntee. As she related the story, it became apparent to her how Sean McIntee knew about the twins. She told Hamilton about Father Donnelly's involvement. He was listening intently, hanging on her every word: the decision to leave Ireland for Boston, Ryan's rescue, birth of the twins, and her eventual marriage. Within half an hour she had completely updated him on her past and his lost dreams. She talked about Maggie, who, he learned, had been the real love and joy in her life.

"So, Mick never told you about Kilmainham?" he asked.

"No, nor did Father Donnelly. I believe my father made him swear not to tell a soul. After he died, Father Donnelly wrote me." She thought a moment. "That was about eight years ago."

"And you never knew of my attempts to tell you that I was being shipped out?"

"Nothing," she said, shaking her head.

He reached over and placed his hand on hers. "I would have married you, Kathleen ... given up everything, I loved you so ..."

"Please don't," she said, pleading. "Don't ruin what friendship we have left ..."

"But, Kathleen ... I know you still care for me and ..."

"Stop it, now." Her voice carried across the room and people were staring. "We can't go back, William," her voice hushed. A wry smile crossed her face. "Did you have any idea that William is the English for Liam?" she said, changing the subject.

"I found out the hard way," he said, smiling.

"Some bloody spy you were."

"I guess I botched just about everything I touched."

"Look, William," she said in a more serious tone. "We can never go back. We've changed. I wouldn't hurt Ryan for the world. I would rather die, William ... I mean that."

"So our meeting today was just to ... catch up on the past, fill the gaps in your life?" It was his turn to be terse.

"That's not true and you know it. I am risking my marriage to see you alone, tell you about your sons, yes, and to learn answers to questions about lost years ... our lost years."

"You still care for me then?" She was silent.

"You loved me then, didn't you, Kathleen?" More silence. "Didn't you?" He persevered. Her eyes were beginning to tear. "You loved me, say it!"

"Yes, yes, I loved you," she whispered loudly.

"And now, Kathleen?"

There was a long silence. Then she said, "At first ... when I saw you at the reception, I wasn't sure. Later I thought about you more than I should. I prayed that Ryan would be reassigned somewhere far away from you. I had to see you again, thinking that if I could see you face to face, maybe, just maybe, I could come to grips with this awful dilemma, and that's …"

"That's when you asked Ryan to ask me to Christmas dinner," he said.

"Yes, that's right."

"And what happened to this awful dilemma?" he asked, emphasizing the last two words. "Did it work?" He intended to wait as long as it would take for her to answer. She broke the silence.

"No," she said softly. "It didn't."

He was devastated by her obvious hurt and confusion. He knew that it was she and not he who had everything to lose. He would do anything to make her happy. It seemed enough that she still loved him.

"What can I do for you, Kathleen? Anything? You have to know that for the past twenty-five years, I've never stopped loving you. I will put in for a transfer … if that's what you want. Kathleen, talk to me, please. What do you want of me?"

"Friendship … I know it's asking an awful lot, but that's what I want. I want you to be my friend."

CHAPTER FIFTY-TWO

IT WAS A beautiful summer morning when the boat train from Wales pulled into Euston station. Lawrence stood by the door, looking up at the arched glass ceiling, its dirt and soot diffusing the morning sun. The metal against metal screeched, and clouds of hot steam from the giant pistons gushed and hissed. Finally it jarred to a stop. Lawrence stepped down to the platform and looked for Terry in the crowd behind the wire barrier.

"Lawrence." He heard his name again. "Lawrence, over here." It was Terry. Lawrence thought he looked like a Wimbledon tennis player, wearing white trousers, saddle shoes, and a diamond-patterned cardigan. Lawrence handed his ticket stub to the uniformed man at the gate and made his way through the few waiting people. Both wanted to embrace. Their better judgment suggested that they settle with a handshake.

"Well, how's the ol' sod?"

"Great—it was good to visit my roots. At first I wasn't sure. I'm glad now that I took Mother's advice."

"I'm happy that you got to see your grandmother," Terry said, leading the way. I'm really glad to see you, though—it's been a while."

"Eleven days," Lawrence said, smiling, "but who's counting?"

Outside the dreary station that smelled of hot steam and burning coal, the morning sun returned. Terry walked them to where a new shiny Vauxhall stood by the curb and opened the door. He wore a proud smile. "Get in," he said, holding the door.

"Where in the world did you get this? It's gorgeous," Lawrence said, climbing in the front seat.

"It's mine—ours," he corrected, "I bought it from a friend who moved up to better things. I have another surprise." Terry moved into the driver's seat. He started the engine, put it in gear and headed for Baker street. "I'm not living on Edgeware road anymore."

"Is that so?" Lawrence said inquisitively. "So where are we headed? I sure hope it's not too far 'cause I'm dead on my ass."

"It is a long trip," Terry said, "Ireland, I mean."

"Twelve, thirteen goddamn hours." Terry opened the glove compartment and handed the newspaper to Lawrence.

"What am I supposed to be looking for?"

"Open to the variety page."

Lawrence fussed with the pages, finally folding the paper. The headline over the review was impressive. The bold type proclaimed that Terzina Sinclair's female impressionist performance was one of the zaniest acts in London cabaret. Photos showed Terry as a man and Terry as the beautiful Miss Terzina Sinclair. The article predicted that the witty Miss Sinclair was going places and expressed hope that there was room for her alter image, Terrance McCabe.

"Congratulations—I can see I'm in the company of a real celebrity."

Terry smiled. "You can keep it," he said.

The car drove past the old flat on the corner of Albion street and made its way around Marble Arch and headed toward Knightsbridge. Lawrence was impressed. Knightsbridge, across from the park, was an exclusive area. Terry stopped the car outside a two-story, red-brick house. The decorative wrought-iron railing was separated from the house by a narrow, grass lawn.

"Walla!" Terry said excitedly. "Well, how do you like it?"

"Like it, hell, I love it," Lawrence said, getting out of the car.

Inside the house, Terry moved gracefully, explaining this room and that room.

Lawrence did not take much notice of where everything was. All he wanted was sleep.

"Yeah, yeah," Lawrence said facetiously, "where's the goddamn bedroom?" Terry gave him a playful smile. "Oh, you devil."

The following morning, Lawrence arose, took a bath, and packed his awol bag. The aroma of bacon wafted from the kitchen. He moved quickly down the stairs and dropped his bag by the front door, then he sauntered into the kitchen.

"You're up early. Why didn't you take advantage of the chance to sleep a little more? I would have … knocked you up," Terry said, mockingly.

Lawrence pulled a chair and sat at the table.

"You like those double meanings, don't you?" he smiled. "Look, I have to get going. I just allowed for a stopover … have to report in by eighteen hundred … six o' clock."

Terry looked disappointed. "Darn," he said, "here I was looking forward to you seeing my new act tonight."

"Sorry," Lawrence mumbled, biting a piece of toast.

"Do you know where Holgate is, Terry?"

"Yes." Terry shoved the bacon, eggs and fried tomatoes from the pan onto his plate. "Why do you need to know?" Lawrence ignored the sullen disposition.

"Gran'ma Barrett asked me to look someone up … for my mother. She's an old friend of the family. Her name's Bridget, Bridget McIntee. I have the address here," he said, shuffling through his pocket. He handed the crumpled paper to Terry.

"I can take you there, it's not that far, half hour, maybe," Terry said, reading the paper, "but I see a Bridget Carlson here, not McIntee."

"I think McIntee was her maiden name. She was my mother's closest friend back in Ireland."

"Do you want me to take you after breakfast?"

"If you wouldn't mind?" he said, munching on a piece of bacon.

Terry's time-distance tables proved to be accurate. Half an hour exactly. He parked the car outside a three-story, tan, stucco building that in earlier times was occupied by one owner. Now each floor housed a single family. They located the Carlsons on a directory by the entry door. On the second floor they rang the door bell and waited. A middle-aged woman answered the door. She looked to Lawrence to be about ten years older than his mother. After Lawrence introduced himself, she became excited. Impassioned, she greeted the pair like family. They were no sooner inside when she motioned them to sit and rushed to put on the kettle for tea. Lawrence met her daughter, Maureen, a hard-looking woman who, he guessed, was a little younger than he. She cradled a two-year-old boy whose father, she told them, was fighting in Africa. Bridget talked incessantly, mostly about Kathleen and their times together back in Ireland. They were inseparable, she told Lawrence. Of course that was before she married and had to leave for Boston. Lawrence hadn't considered the possibility that she had known his father. He became interested in Bridget's ramblings. He reached in his pocket for the pack of cigarettes.

"Do you mind?" he said.

"I'd love to," she said excitedly, "American, great."

Maureen and Terry also accepted his offer and in a moment they conversed through a thick blanket of smoke.

"So you knew my father?" he said, leaning forward in the seat.

"I met him, yes," she said, her head tilting back, her face thoughtful, expressive, her lips blowing a stream of smoke. She was also reminded of her promise to Kathleen, the secret they shared.

"He was gorgeous, with black-hair," she turned to him, "like you that way…but you look more like your grandfather, God rest his soul."

"You knew my father then … to talk to?"

"Actually, not that well. Kathleen, your mammy, was very protective, you know. Shure, we all thought he was a bloody spy," she tittered. "It was just the opinion of a few."

"A spy?" Lawrence asked. "And who did … did these few people think he was spying for?"

"He was an American. I believe there was talk of him spying for the British. They weren't good times, Lawrence, remember, a British spy in Dublin in those days …" She clicked her fingers. "His life wouldn't be worth that."

"Are you saying that my father may have been … murdered?"

"I'm not saying any such thing. I believe what your mammy told me."

"What did my mother tell you, Missus Carlson?"

"That your father, God rest his soul, died at sea. Oh, there were the few as I said, that believed your father was responsible for your grandfather's imprisonment," she said nonchalantly.

Lawrence looked startled. "What?" he said, "My father was responsible?"

She broke in. "I said that's what some thought."

Lawrence placed his hands on his head; he could hardly believe what he was hearing.

"Well, ole' boy," Terry said, flicking the ash, "that's some heritage you have there." Any further intention to be humorous was silenced by Lawrence's severe gaze.

"Well, that's a helluva how do you do," Lawrence said. "My father the spy."

"I never believed a word of it myself," she said casually. "Have another cuppa."

"You're absolutely sure there's nothing more I should know? Like maybe my grandfather was incarcerated because he was an ax murderer?" he asked sarcastically.

"Oh, dear God, no," she said seriously, "not at all. Shure, we'd have known that." She said she couldn't think of anything else about his father and thought that was the extent of her knowledge of the man. She had a few more tales about his mother, all fun, harmless things that children are prone to do.

As Bridget talked, Lawrence was beginning to feel uncomfortable about Maureen's preoccupation with Terry. One wouldn't need the experience of Sherlock Holmes to recognize Terry's homosexuality. Lawrence knew that she could see his preference. He imagined Bridget Carlson writing his mother. God knows how she'd describe his visit and friend. He could imagine her saying, "Now, I'm not saying he is a fairy and I'm not saying he isn't, but …"

He wished he'd never brought Terry along. He asked why Terry hadn't hidden his homosexuality here. Damn it, why couldn't Terry be more like him? He also thought it might have made a difference if he'd worn his uniform instead of the white-knit shirt and slacks. He had promised himself to keep the alliance top secret. The Army Air Force would ground him for sure. If their homosexual association wasn't enough, Terry's radical politics would lead to attacks in the press and investigation.

The real test of his disconcerting thoughts occurred just before they got up to leave. That was when Bridget asked her daughter to get the box camera. She was adamant about getting Lawrence's picture before he left. He couldn't think of anything that would sway Bridget's photographic endeavors. One photo wasn't enough. Soon she organized the group shots. When she wanted a picture of just him and Terry, Lawrence insisted that Maureen join them. He bordered on being rude to no avail. Lawrence promised himself that he would never put himself in that position again. After they left, Bridget cleared the table.

"Nice young boys," she sighed, "hard to believe … Kathleen's boy, all grown up."

"And bent like a bloody twig," Maureen said.

"Bent?"

"Bent, Mammy, queer, bum-boy, you know, they're both flaming homos."

"Do you think so?" Bridget said in a sing-song voice.

CHAPTER FIFTY-THREE

L AWRENCE HIT THE chow hall at 1400. He noticed some of his crew
missing and assumed they had decided to get extra sleep. Some
crewmen were too tense to eat just before a mission. Lawrence was
beginning to react to mission assignments mechanically. In the last three
months forty-five bombers didn't make it home. Simple math told him they
were losing one out of every ten planes. He knew he was on borrowed time.
He had flown so many missions he had lost count. He could have applied
for reassignment, a safe position back home teaching green airmen how
to fly the big bombers, but he wasn't ready to leave.

Besides, he couldn't bring himself to leave Terry. After the briefing,
the crews manned the "Maggie" and prepared for take-off. Their target, an
enemy base in Brussels, fuel-storage facilities. A green flare was their signal
to gun the engine. Each bomber took its turn, engines revved, cumbersome
at first, aching with maximum bomb loads to lift-off speeds. Soon they
eased off the runway, wheels up, the ponderous look replaced with grace
and beauty. Lawrence was the lead of forty-five planes. He cut through the
thick fog and within moments found blue sky. At twelve-hundred feet,
Lawrence made a great circle, waiting for the bombers to assemble the
formation that they would hold to the target. They left Dover far behind
and saw no sign of fighter escort. Lawrence shook his head. "Guess we're
on our own," he said into the intercom. "Looks like our guardian angels
decided to sleep in." With no fighter escort it was up to the leader to make
the decision to turn back or go on to the target. A conscientious leader
would have returned to the base, saving his men and planes to live and

fight another day. He continued on an easterly bearing. The eighty-mile journey was quiet with anticipation.

The windshield shattered. Lawrence wasn't immediately sure how much damage the cannon shell had done. Everything happened fast, first the impact, then the ear-shattering explosion behind him. What was left of the turret gunner slumped between him and the copilot? Lawrence looked to where his head had been and tried to recall the boy's face. He was a rookie. Lawrence didn't remember his name.

The plane continued through the field of flak to the target and dropped the thousand-pound bombs, then he turned the slow-to-respond bomber to the west. He was having problems keeping the plane on course. With the top turret blown away, it was difficult to assess the damage to the tail. His suspicions were affirmed when the waist-gunner informed him the tail gunner was gone. Over the base, he struggled to align the plane with the runway. He could hold the glide path for only seconds. The plane strayed to the right. Response was slow. He seemed to over correct and the plane pulled to the left past the runway. He continued this right-then-left attitude, finally touching down. They missed the runway by ten feet or so. The B-17 buckled on impact, the tail separated from the fuselage, and what was left of "The Maggie" skidded to a stop by the fire trucks that had come out to meet it.

Of the forty-five planes, twenty-four returned. During the debriefing, Lawrence realized he was chewing his nails. He was aware that he hadn't listened to a word about effectiveness over the target. Nor was he concerned about the loss of his radio operator and tail gunner. Instead, his thoughts focused on himself. He had become paranoid and was terrified with every request to see the squadron commander. He envisioned all the additional brass, the Adjutant General's staff officers not involved in flying tactics, asking questions regarding his affiliation with one Terrance McCabe. As long as someone had a picture of them together, the photographic evidence would be disastrous. On the other hand, there was no reason to believe that Bridget would do anything to hurt him. After all, she was his mother's best friend. This was the longest he and Terry had been apart. He appreciated Terry more and more for his discretion, not trying to make contact. He missed their conversations, missed being with him. He was sure that this was what love was all about, wanting to be with someone, feeling a great void when parted.

He checked with weather and was informed that the next couple of days were going to be socked in. "The barometer's really dropped, Captain," the lieutenant in charge of meteorology told him. He went back to the quonset hut, cleaned up, and packed a bag. He arrived in London a little after six p.m. He hailed a cab and gave the cabbie the address in Knightsbridge. At the bottom of Bayswater road, he saw a young girl selling flowers and impulsively asked the driver to stop. He gave her two shillings and took the lot, roses, carnations and bluebells.

"Nice batch o' flowers for the little laidy?" the cockney cabbie asked.

"I guess you could say that," Lawrence answered with a broad grin.

"She must be very special, mate."

"Yes, he is," Lawrence said in a hushed voice.

"Beg you pardon, sir?"

"I said—yes—she certainly is."

During the rest of the journey they talked about insignificant things. Lawrence was anxious to see Terry. Maybe this time Terry would admit what their friendship really meant. Lawrence was smiling at something the cabbie said. The smile soon turned to a grimace.

"'Ere we are mate," the cabbie said, thinking it might have been the only house standing on the block. Lawrence sat dumbfounded. The cab had stopped by a house all right, but it wasn't where Terry lived. The bombed-out heap of bricks beside it, that was where Terry lived. Lawrence got out and stood in the ruin with his back to the cab. The cabbie watched him for the longest time. He stood, his head arched to the gray sky, and in a moment his hand released the flowers. The cabbie saw he was crying and waited to take him to the closest bar.

The following morning, he returned to the base. There was a note on his bunk. It was succinct: Please report to the base commander's office asap. He didn't bother to shave. The way his luck was going a shave wasn't going to make much difference. He stayed in the quonset hut long enough to make a cup of instant coffee on the pot-bellied stove. He lit a cigarette and thought about Terry. The neighbors told him he must have gone fast. Some consolation. He ground the butt into the floor and headed to face his destiny. He walked up the wooden stairs of the H.Q. building. Inside he was ushered to the Base Commander's office by a burly staff sergeant, who closed the door behind him. At least he was right about the brass and prepared himself, standing at attention.

"Captain Riordan, you look disgraceful." Commander McGee held the rank of Brigadier General. He was a tall man in his early forties, with bushy hair and eyebrows and had a slight paunch. In his hand he held what looked like photos. He spoke to Lawrence again.

"You're an enigma, Riordan," he said, taking time to light a cigar.

"Prestwick sent you to us thinking there might be something we could do to straighten you out." Lawrence was sure the photos were of him and Terry. He tensed waiting for the accusation.

"It's difficult to chastise a man who has earned so many honors, the Air Medal and D.F.C. That's all well and good, but you have this devil-may-care attitude regarding your own safety and that of your crew." He hesitated, drawing in a great volume of smoke, then continued. "Well, what it boils down to is that every man under your command has requested a transfer." More smoke exhaled from somewhere deep in his lungs, "and based on what I've read, I can't blame them. You're either the bravest man I've ever known or a goddamn fool."

Lawrence was relieved; his previous concerns were minimized. McGee tapped the ash and turned to look out the window.

"How many missions have you flown, Riordan?"

"Twenty-five—maybe twenty-six, sir."

"You're not sure, are you? You don't even know how many missions you've flown. Everyone keeps track of the missions they fly, Riordan, that's what's so damned weird about you. Would you believe thirty-one!"

"Sorry sir … I guess that didn't interest me … I mean keeping track."

"Captain Riordan, or should I say Major Riordan." He turned and cast the photos on the table. Lawrence looked shocked. "Your mission over the target today was one hundred percent successful. Your decision to proceed without cover was hasty but admirable. By eliminating those fuel depots, you are responsible for saving the lives of God knows how many foot soldiers. It could be in the thousands, to say nothing of shortening the war. Now I know you had your casualties and they were pretty damned high, but you did the right thing. I'll sum it up by describing it as … as an awful triumph." Lawrence was speechless. He swallowed hard. "Yes sir," was all he could muster.

"Colonel Travis here, who you already know…"

"Yes, sir," Lawrence gave a perfunctory nod in the direction of the second in command.

McGee continued, "… has suggested that we recommend you for the Medal of Honor. What do you think of that?"

Lawrence was slow to answer. "Sir … you mean me, the Medal of Honor? But, sir, all I did was … well, follow orders. Really, sir, I don't think I deserve the honor."

"First thing you're going to learn, Major, is how to take orders. It's a done deal, Airman, the recommendation that is. We still have to get approval. That comes from Washington."

"Yes, sir. I imagine that means I'll be going home, sir?"

"If everything works out, you'll finish this war selling war bonds," Travis said.

"But what about my flying, sir?" Lawrence pleaded. "Wouldn't I be of better use, at least teaching others how to fly? This is a tricky war, sir, it's not just knowing how to fly, you have to know how to fight, how to stay alive." He was becoming agitated. "I think that's important too, sir, don't you?"

"I'm afraid it's not important what you think, or I, for that matter. We do what we're told and right now I'm telling you to get yourself packed ... You're going home."

Part Three

CHAPTER FIFTY-FOUR
London, 1954

T HE SUPER CONSTELLATION made a slow right turn and came to a stop
near the terminal. The flightline specialist waved the torches to
his sides, and the pilot cut the engines, which soon whirred to
a standstill. In perfect English, a female voice announced the arrival of
T.W.A. flight 193 from La Guardia, New York. While the message was
repeated, Bridget, who waited outside the customs area, stood and brushed
the wrinkles from the green, pleated skirt. She hurriedly rooted through
her purse, finally locating the compact. Quickly she snapped the mirror
open, rotating one side then the other, vainly studying her face. She used
her little finger to wipe away a smudge of lipstick from her lower lip and
primped the new hairdo with the back of her hand. Satisfied with the way
she looked, Bridget closed the compact and returned it to her purse. Her
body trembled with anxiety. Soon her brother would be walking through
the gate. She prayed that she would recognize him. Since his imprisonment
there had been no pictures. In twenty years there had been few letters,
those few usually giving instructions regarding his estate, concentrated in
the safety deposit box at Waterloo. He never mentioned, nor did she ever
question, the contents of the envelope he sent her. When she wrote of their
mother's death, he took months to respond, and when he did, the letter
showed little emotion.

What did concern her had more to do with remembering him, how he
was, hoping for a glimmer of his boyhood looks. She questioned whether
they would have anything in common; so much time had passed. Memories
of their childhood had become vague, contrived, and so embellished she

questioned whether there was an ounce of true reverie. She did remember saying goodbye. At the time, Nora felt it was better if they didn't accompany him to Cork. She hugged him on the Kingsbridge railway platform near the Guinness Brewery in Dublin. She was remembering how frightened he looked, alone, going to a strange land with no friends. It wasn't until her mother lay dying that she would learn more details of her brother's treason and why it became necessary for him to leave. She justified his betrayal as a reaction to spurned love and adolescent stupidity and for a while even blamed Kathleen Barrett. All that was past, and in moments they would be embracing again.

People began to walk past now, looking tired after the fourteen-hour flight. She strained to recognize him among the tall, older, unaccompanied men who passed.

On the surface, the years had been good to McIntee. He had a sophisticated manner. His frame was still wiry, as one might expect of a runner. His face was tawny, drawn with aging lines resembling a road map. The trimmed, gray mustache and rimless spectacles contributed to his businesslike demeanor. He looked more like a professor than an ex-con, a realistic perception, given the time he was allowed to read and study. His first years of incarceration were the worst, a common feeling among those whose most fundamental of all rights, freedom, had been removed. He realized that to maintain his sanity he needed to pursue an objective, a hobby, anything, just to be motivated so that every tomorrow was desired. He found comfort in talking about schemes, heists, murders, with other inmates. Listeners were quietly impressed as he chronicled a mystery that made the headlines. Skeptics among them remembered their own stories.

"So dat was you … I remember dat caper." Comments such as this inspired him to expand his story-telling beyond his brutal crimes. He embellished an uneventful misdemeanor or took credit for one he didn't commit. He was on the honor role of crime. It wasn't always one sided. He found there was much to learn by listening. His criminal education was broadened by prisoners, some of whom he found brilliant. They didn't have ridiculous names like Jimmy the Rat or Cracker Jack Dolan, rather they were most likely referred to as Robert Ginsburg, a corporate executive type, and Augustin Flemming, who soon answered to the name of Gus. In better times, Flemming owned one of the largest print houses in New York and had manufactured some of the most sophisticated bills ever distributed, or so the FBI proclaimed.

Sometimes respect could be measured when a man was addressed by two Christian names, such as Peter Michael Carpenter, whose previous occupation was principal in a very respectable brokerage firm in San Francisco. Many had formulated the almost perfect corporate conspiracy, held the perfect bank robbery, and some were sure they had concocted a plan for the perfect murder. It was interesting that not one gave credit to authorities for being a step ahead of them. Rather, their apprehension was made possible by a small error on their part, like a bribe, payoff, or a fix gone wrong. Others were top-of-the-line forgers, who, but for one small breach of judgment, epitomized perfection.

The concentrated curriculum afforded the residents the equivalent of a degree in a college or university graduate program in criminal justice from the criminal's point of view. McIntee expanded his knowledge of white-collar crime involving skills in banking, investing in the stock market, printing, engraving, and extortion. He had nothing but time, and by the tenth year of his incarceration, he had found a purpose in a scheme to get revenge on William Hamilton. What began as fantasy emerged as a reality. When he got out, he would spend every waking hour making Hamilton's life miserable. McIntee was driven by hate, and it was hate that kept him alive. His dominating characteristic was patience. By the time of his release, he had concocted a plan to destroy Hamilton. He prayed that Hamilton would be happily married; the idea that Hamilton had a happy little family conjured up a devious smile.

His revenge would begin with Hamilton's bastard twin sons. His plan would ultimately bring dishonor to the whole family. He hadn't considered yet if his vendetta would include Kathleen Barrett. At all costs, he would manage the plot over an extended period, prolonging the pain. In his mind, nothing short of eventual death would give him equitable retribution. If the twins were dead and Hamilton hadn't married, his alternate plan was simple. He would have Hamilton killed. The alternate was less satisfying; it didn't appeal to his cat-and-mouse objective.

He wore a gray fedora and a dark-gray pinstripe suit; over his right arm a black wool overcoat partially covered a briefcase. His left hand clutched a medium-sized valise. He saw her first and called her name. She couldn't contain the tears. They embraced, then he held her at arm's length. They talked over one another, small talk, how was the trip? How they looked. It took a while to settle down.

"Follow me, Sean," she said, finally moving, "Wally's out in the parking lot. Here, let me take that." He told her to point the way, he could handle the baggage. He met Bridget's husband for the first time. Wally was more impressed with his brother-in-law than McIntee was with him. Wally placed the baggage in the back seat, leaving room for Bridget.

"You can ride up front with me, Sean." McIntee was curious how they were going to fit into the Morris Minor. He hunkered in the front seat; Wally, who was about five-seven and weighed about sixteen stone, squeezed into the driver's seat on a series of huffs and sighs. When he finally closed the door, his right shoulder and arm hung from the open window to make room for the rest of his obese body. The wheel was in his chest, yet the man managed to light a cigarette.

"Fag, Sean?" he said, looking in the rear-view mirror, simultaneously merging into traffic.

"Thanks, I think I'll pass," McIntee said.

It was a long drive to Hammersmith, where Wally and Bridget owned a large red-brick Tudor home. She had been well rewarded for her loyal custodianship of his affairs. Every year she diligently paid taxes on his investment dividends. She couldn't wait to give him the good news. His one-million dollars of stock bought during the reconstruction years of the depression were now worth over twenty-five million dollars. Stocks of Chase Manhattan, A.T&T, General Motors, Mellon Bank, General Electric, all had split over the years, multiplying so much she couldn't keep count. Mr. David Kenny was a rich man indeed. By the end of the week, McIntee had filled his sister in with everything he wanted her to know, most of it lies. He showed much more interest in Bridget's account of events regarding Kathleen Barrett and especially Lawrence Riordan's visit during the war. She showed him old photos and newspaper clippings from the cabaret page. He smiled perversely when he read the obituary portion that mentioned an American Airman and alluded to a homosexual relationship. Bridget said that Maureen had them pegged right off.

McIntee had good reasons for avoiding Ireland and had kept his presence in London quiet. Together they visited the Bank in Waterloo and retrieved the envelope, which he opened in the privacy of his room. Everything was there in perfect condition, the birth certificate, marriage license, and Mrs. Kenny's death certificate. It took him six weeks to renew the passport, and within three months he had acquired re-entry to the United States as David Kenny, whose long-lost wife was still buried in the Holy Sepulcher Cemetery in Chicago. He thanked Bridget and Wally for their hospitality and promised to send something to show his appreciation. He decided on the services of a taxi and left for the airport.

Within sixteen hours he was stepping off the plane at La Guardia and passing through customs. He left the terminal, opening the door to an early-morning haze and a cacophony of busy street sounds. He took a cigarette from the pack of Players, lit it and inhaled deeply. Then he blew a stream out the side of a crooked, smiling mouth. At last, he was in New York. By tomorrow he, a multi-millionaire, would be making use of his fortune, taking the first steps in the preparation of a long-awaited vendetta against William Hamilton, his bastard twins, and, although he hadn't made up his mind, Kathleen Barrett.

CHAPTER FIFTY-FIVE

ATHER MICHAEL RIORDAN began his priestly career at St. Peter's Parish on Staten Island. The year was 1943. Actually he was more on loan from the Boston Archdiocese while he pursued his Doctor of Letters from St. Francis College, Brooklyn. In what spare time he could muster, he performed the duties of assistant pastor at St. Peters. They were extremely difficult years for Michael because of the war. He was attending school at twenty-six while most men his age and younger were serving in the military, signing up, or being drafted. They were going off to war, fighting or training to fight in the Pacific, the Atlantic, North Africa, and Europe, while he went off to school across Manhattan.

These times truly mandated an examination of conscience for any man entering the priesthood. Sometimes he thought he saw questions in the faces of his parishioners. Wasn't he the lucky one, choosing to be a priest, and how come he got off staying home, advocating prayers of gratitude for the men overseas fighting for his freedom? He didn't for one moment believe that he chose to be a cleric so that he might avoid the war; however, ministering to a parish of women, children, middle-aged and old men made him feel guilty. It bothered him so much that he requested a meeting with Archbishop Spellman. He knew exactly how he was going to broach the subject to Spellman, a Massachusetts man at heart. Michael thought it would break the ice if he mentioned that during the first world war, his mother was a parishioner at Roxbury when he was assistant pastor. He also believed that the Archbishop would be understanding because at the beginning of the war he was nominated Apostolic Vicar to the U.S. Armed

Forces and had been known to travel abroad to visit personnel. Michael, knowing the need for chaplains, believed in the American mission and was convinced that he could be inspiring to the troops.

It was in this positive frame of mind that he approached the Archbishop, explaining his decision to give up his studies and go to war as a chaplain. Spellman seemed gracious at first and listened attentively until Michael had finished. The Archbishop's comments were succinct. He was adamant about the need for priests at the chancery and parish level, especially those endowed with natural talents for business. Michael told him that his studies were becoming uninteresting and his parochial vitality was at such a low that he couldn't lift the spirits of a fallen evangelist. Spellman suggested that his statement was most unfortunate because what the men at the front needed was someone who could lift the spirits of just that, a fallen evangelist.

The argument for his becoming a chaplain wasn't going well. He rejected the Archbishop's intimation that being a business administrator was as important as ministering to men in the service. His reasoning was cut short by the Archbishop. He was told that the Church needed enthusiastic young men with vigor, men who could continue to build the Church, lawyers, educators and construction professionals. He was informed that he had been hand selected for such a role, and with all due respect, he could find domestic prelates anytime, including chaplains. Priests with his capabilities were another story. Spellman summed up the meeting: it was good that he had feelings of guilt; self-scrutiny was a normal emotion. It reflected his humility. He said he was glad that Michael had come to see him with these concerns. In summation, he blessed Michael and extended his hand. The younger priest knelt and kissed the ring. He left disappointed, vowing that if he ever had a disagreement with Spellman again, he would think twice before airing it face to face.

When Lawrence was shipped home, Michael took time off to see him in New Jersey. Ryan and Kathleen joined them from D.C., and they enjoyed a great week. All were proud of Lawrence's war record, none more than his brother. Everywhere they went, they were hounded by reporters. Photographers posed the twins together; their likeness was incredible. They liked to play on the idea that here were two brothers, identical in every way except that one saved souls while the other, apologetically, for the country's sake, eliminated them. By the end of the week, Hamilton stopped by, saying he had some business in New Jersey. Kathleen knew otherwise.

Lawrence didn't care much for living conditions on the post. Within a few weeks, he found a small apartment off base. Michael saved every newspaper article describing his brother's busy agenda, which turned out to be busier than Lawrence had anticipated. He spoke at universities to recruit men and women for the Armed Forces. He attended political assemblies, private associations, and service clubs to promote the sale of war bonds. Lawrence was becoming a celebrity, and Michael was proud.

When the war ended, Michael convinced his brother to take advantage of the G.I bill. After a good deal of badgering, Lawrence, because of his war record, was accepted at Harvard, where he studied political science and went on to law school. After returning to New York, he joined the respected law firm of Bickford, Maher and Clark, where he would intern for two years before passing the bar. Michael also got his wish. He became chaplain of a union. While he was enrolled at Fordham University, he was asked to minister to the Association of Catholic Trade Unionists, many of whom were members of the Brotherhood of Teamsters.

Michael, fast becoming recognized as a scholar and social-justice activist, found time to write columns for professional journals. He became the sounding board for social justice and related economic, ethical, and religious issues. He also found time to fill in as assistant at St. Peters. His contribution showed fast results, increasing the parish income by more than $1,000 a month. His presence energized the pastor, for whom he wrote sermons that always included appeals for funds to improve the appearance of their house of worship. Michael's contribution to the business standing of the parish was successful, so successful that he was reassigned to a parish in Hell's Kitchen. Coincidentally, the name of the parish was St. Michael's.

Father John J. Kiernan was a New Yorker whose priesthood was spent almost entirely on the west side. He was a tough administrator who, Michael later found, had joined the Army in the first world war as chaplain, something Michael had wished for. Michael asked whether Father Kiernan would have been dissuaded if he had encountered a man like Spellman. After he got to know the priest, he concluded that Spellman would have lost to Father Kiernan.

The Church, founded in 1857, was architecturally typical of that time, Romanesque with a gable said to be five feet or so higher than the closest Protestant church. Steps, almost the width of the main facade, led the parishioner through three great stone arches into the main sanctuary. The lofted ceiling was sixty feet high. Rounded windows of rich-colored stained glass were designed and manufactured in Munich. They were brilliant when illuminated by the sun, which enhanced portions of the ivory walls with diffused images.

Michael's strongest first impression was formed by the great mural over the main altar. It represented Christ at the moment of death. Three figures were illustrated below the cross: Mary, his mother, Mary Magdalen, and John. They were surrounded by a choir of angels. He found it magnificent when it was lighted. Lighting the mural was reserved for special occasions, including Christmas, Easter, and holy days of obligation.

The parish, on the other hand, was a contrast to the church. Hell's Kitchen was made up mostly of poor immigrant Irish, Poles, and Italians living in cold-water flats. A room was attached to the buildings like some after-thought, with one toilet and sink accommodating four to five families. These poor slums with no hot water, with sanitary conditions unfit for humans, were a breeding ground for pneumonia, consumption, scarlet fever, and a host of infectious diseases with unpronounceable names. Epidemics swept through the area. Those in the upper class said they were a necessary instrument of purging.

Poor of pocket, the parishioners could never be accused of being poor of spirit. The one thing all these people had in common was the church. No matter what their native language, all understood the custom and language of the mass, Latin. There was also the seedy side, and an occasional gun battle wasn't unusual. The school was run by the assistant priests and sisters. Discipline was stern, but when school was over, dismissed youngsters returned to the turbulent streets. Michael sought to help every young boy and girl know Christ. Sunday service for many of these youngsters was a cultural event, something they practiced because they were forced to by teachers and parents. Hell's Kitchen became Michael's mission. He was the one they wanted as arbiter when they were accused of stealing, or worse, according to the sisters, cheating. He became dedicated to keeping his flock out of jail by finding them honest work after school, sponsoring them, and even pledging their honesty.

Sometimes he had to make apologies, expressing his regret for some youngster not showing for work or robbing the till. He influenced many to go on to higher education, others he inspired to feel proud of electing a trade or joining the service; some even turned to Holy Orders. Michael wasn't one hundred percent successful, but his work didn't go unnoticed. Because of him, many were saved from residency at Attica and Sing Sing. When the time came for Michael to leave, parents were sad to see him go, and he, too, was sad.

In June of 1955, Michael graduated from Fordham with a master's degree in business. He was the most quoted thirty-eight-year old priest in the New York dioceses, his school of thought welcomed in the new-age parish. For all his modern ideas, he never lost sight of his Christian humanitas.

He was ministering unofficially to the parishioners, and although the idea of acting pastor was challenging, he remained unfulfilled.

As September approached, Cardinal Spellman summoned him to chancery. Michael arrived early and sat in the stuffy foyer. He picked up the *Life* magazine and studied the table of contents. He was shocked to see his brother's name in a heading. Quickly he flipped through the pages until he came to a photo of Lawrence. Michael found the picture impressive. Lawrence sat on the edge of a desk stacked with papers. His arms were folded across his chest and the top button of his white shirt was open, showing the old school tie. Michael smiled.

The headline was even more surprising. It read, *War Hero Enters Democratic Senate Race /New York Approves of Outsider.* Michael had just begun to read the text when the secretary left her desk to give him the word:

"Father Riordan, Cardinal Spellman will see you now."

Michael remembered the last time he was in Spellman's domain. The Cardinal came from behind the desk, his hand extended.

"Michael, I'm so glad you could find time to see me at such short notice." Michael recognized an obsequious tone in Spellman's voice and knew he was going to be asked a favor. Spellman was a master at getting things done. Father Kiernan told Michael during one of their chats in the rectory that the Archbishop could inveigle a starving lion to relinquish a water buffalo's arse. His authority alone was sufficient, a simple demand or requisition, but that wasn't his way. He wanted those subservient to believe they were part of the solution, thus the ingratiating demeanor.

"Your Eminence," Michael said, kissing the ring.

"Here, come sit," Spellman said, pushing the plush, red-velvet, Louis-the-Fifteenth chair in his direction. The Cardinal sat across from him in a matching chair. "Some of the staff are of the opinion that you are not busy enough and have to occupy your spare time running the affairs of St. Michael's from the Senate," he smiled, making reference to the open article on the table. "A remarkable likeness."

"Yes, we're identical … in looks, anyway."

"I studied the descriptions of your brother carefully. As I read between the lines, I recognized some remarkable similarities."

"That's interesting, Your Eminence. I'd be honored to have some of my brother's attributes."

Spellman placed his hand on his forehead. "Sometimes, Michael, I find that your humility, although well intentioned, is not in keeping with your desire for power."

Michael looked surprised, an expression turning to one of umbrage. Spellman spoke before Michael could respond.

"I can see that my comment has disturbed you," he said seriously. "You're assuming that a desire for power is a bad thing. Believe me, before long you'll come to realize that there's not a lot of difference between what you and your brother are trying to achieve. Politics and religion make interesting bed fellows." He moved forward in the chair.

"Let's have this conversation at some later date. Tell me, Michael, what have you been up to?"

"I'm sure Your Eminence is familiar with everything that I do," Michael said cautiously. "I suppose my being here may have something to do with my requisitions for more gym equipment." He smiled. "'Course, then again it may be that some of the parishioners are complaining about the harsh penances I've been dealing."

"How's your Spanish?" Spellman said out of the blue.

"My Spanish?" Michael thought for a moment. "It's all right, I guess—I mean, I manage. Sometimes the confessionals take a little longer."

"You've obviously noticed the sociological changes taking place, especially in our poorer parishes, like St. Michael's. We're receiving more and more Puerto Ricans on Manhattan Island. It's like the Irish immigration all over again."

"Except, Your Eminence, these Puerto Ricans are American citizens. They just happen to speak a different language."

"No need to get upset, Michael. I'm not making judgments on these people." Spellman waved his hand, "No, God forbid I would say anything bad against these God-loving people. I'm just stating some facts right now." He leaned forward. "I'm more concerned about their treatment by the Irish and the Italians. I'm of the opinion that they are suffering under the usual conditions." He sat back. "You know, they're the newcomers, they don't speak English, and they're a very poor people."

"That's because they have to take the menial jobs," Michael said. "The women work as domestics, they take in washing and…"

Spellman interrupted him. "I understand all the reasons, Michael. I suppose I should come straight out with the reason you're here."

Michael nodded in agreement. "Yes, Your Eminence." He wanted to say "that would be nice," but thought better of it.

"I don't like hearing about dissension in any parish of the archdioceses. Any time you have a language problem, a failure in listening, a failure in speaking, you open the door to misunderstandings, which invariably lead to murmuring. I don't like murmuring, Michael." He rang a small brass bell on the table by his chair. "Would you like some tea, Michael?" he said, interrupting himself. The secretary opened the door and Spellman asked her to please bring a pot of tea. "Oh, and some biscuits—those good ones with the cream inside." He turned to Michael. "You have to taste these, Michael, they're absolutely sumptuous—sinful, I might add." Michael said that would be grand and waited for the Archbishop to continue.

"Let's see now, where were we?" Before Michael had an opportunity to prompt him, he went on. "Yes," he said, "a language dissimilarity creates a real barrier. It creates suspicions, if you know what I mean."

Michael nodded in agreement. "I do indeed, Your Eminence."

"Therefore, I have selected a couple of parishes, including St. Michael's, to have the schools teach English to these families, in the evening. I know the children are learning English in school, the problem is when they get home they have to revert to Spanish because the parents don't speak English. What do you think?"

"I think it's a great idea but it's going to take new teachers." Michael stroked his chin. "I'd like to think we could get volunteers—it would take money. We'd need books, visual aids, teachers—we may have to pay teachers. We are talking about a free school, is that right?"

"Free to the families, of course. That's the problem," Spellman mused, "the money. These parishes I'm talking about are already on the brink of collapse. Irish, Polish, and Italian families that were the bulwark of the parish are moving out. Just last month ten Irish families moved into Corpus Christi. The chancery can't afford to keep pumping money into the Middle West Side. You can see the dilemma, Michael, can't you? It's like the early days again, when we had to operate on a shoe string. The difference now is, we don't have the good sisters anymore—not in the same numbers, nor do we have the priests. Dear God, Michael, I can remember the days when we had as many as five assistants for every parish."

He sat back and focused on the ceiling. The secretary returned with a tray. She placed it on an end table and poured from a silver tea pot. She sugared and creamed the Cardinal's tea and asked Michael if he wanted some. He said he preferred it black, and she left. Spellman took the saucer in his left hand and held it close to his face. His right hand delicately raised the cup to his lips. He sipped.

"Michael, you're a bright young man and I trust your judgment, more so, I might add, than my own."

"I'm honored, Your Eminence. I'll do whatever I can to help." Michael was hesitant. Spellman did not often reveal himself, especially to priests, who seemed to him perpetual students.

"I imagine we could sell some land, Your Eminence," Michael said enthusiastically. "It wouldn't be the first time. I remember reading somewhere that we sold a piece of land belonging to St. Michael's." He probed his mind for the circumstances. "Wasn't it to the railroad? To build the elevated railway, I believe."

"Not this time, Michael. We're not selling any land. On the contrary, we need all the land we have—and more. I have something else on my mind. What we need is for the church to make some rewarding investments. I could place somewhere in the area of one million dollars at your disposal."

Michael choked on a piece of biscuit. It took a moment, and he excused himself. "I'm not sure I understand, Your Eminence. Are you telling me to take one million dollars and invest it in the market—pick the stocks that will return the best investments?"

"I'm saying even more than that, Michael. I'm saying that it's time all this education paid off. You should take educated risks." He laughed loudly. "I'm not giving you permission to go to Las Vegas; on the other hand, I'm not limiting you to blue-chip stocks with no-risk return. I want you to use the brain God gave you, and we paid for, to turn things around in these poor parishes. You're absolutely right when you said it will take money. I'm praying that you have some answers."

"You know I'll do my best, Your Eminence."

Spellman stood and glanced at his watch. "I want you to report to Manzini on this. I only wish to be consulted when the news is extraordinarily positive."

Michael's concern must have shown on his face. Spellman disarmed the younger man. "I know the market enough, Michael, to recognize its fluctuations. Although I don't want to dwell on a negative market, you may also contact me if things take a turn for the worse. Does that make you feel better?"

"That sounds most reasonable, Your Eminence," Michael said.

Spellman showed him out. "Look, why don't you think on it," he said, extending his hand, "and I'll call you next week. Take some time and study the market—maybe that isn't the way to go, I don't know. Anyway, you take a look at the situation."

Michael left the chancery on a cloud. Of all the priests and Monsignors, Spellman had chosen him. The responsibility was imposing. He could not wait to tell Lawrence.

CHAPTER FIFTY-SIX

MCINTEE SAT ACROSS from a frail, middle-aged man with a long, bony nose under horn-rimmed glasses. He sported a bow tie that announced a boring person who specialized in details of interest to no one but himself. His lips were almost non-existent; when they moved, the accent was southern.

"Well, now, Mr. Kenny, it appears that everything is in order, and you, as a...shall we say significant stockholder in the Chase Manhattan bank, can be assured that I, that is, we, will be more than happy to handle your affairs.

"I've informed the brokerage firm to contact the D.T.C. and have all the stock transferred to you."

McIntee said laconically, "As soon as you make a record of everything, I want you to send me the certificates. I'll be keeping them in my own safe."

"I'll attend to that immediately, Mr. Kenny. Now, if you don't mind, I need a signature." He rotated the paper on the desk top, suggested McIntee read the circled areas, initial and sign. After writing his name on the form making him a most-coveted customer, McIntee shook hands with the man and left.

Later that evening, he dined at the Ritz and returned to his penthouse suite, where he browsed every borough looking for Augustin Flemming. McIntee, if nothing else, had learned to be patient. Three times he repeated the search and found no Augustin Flemming. He dropped the directory on the floor, arose slowly from the chair, and walked to the cocktail cabinet, where he poured brandy into a glass. He swirled the contents and relived some of their conversations. He wanted Flemming to be part of his plan. However, not having him wouldn't dissuade him from his obsession. He returned to the chair, lit a cigar, inhaled, and took a sip of brandy. He took a relaxed position and blew a stream of smoke. If only he could remember where Flemming said he was from in New York City. Hell, he had to have relatives.

His face lit. "The Bronx," he said out loud, "the goddamn Bronx, that's where he said he was from." He grabbed the directory from the floor and looked up all the Flemmings in the Bronx. He traced with his finger. There weren't that many. After the fifth try he hit pay dirt. A Ron Flemming answered and asked McIntee why he wished to contact his father. McIntee was satisfied, even though the son obviously had no intention of giving him any information about Flemming's whereabouts. McIntee gave the son his phone number and suggested he contact his father.

"Tell your father Sean McIntee wants to see him. Tell him I have a very high-paying consulting position to offer."

The son was brusk. He seemed put out. McIntee was persuasive. Ron Flemming agreed to call his father. He hung up the phone and poured another brandy. Things were beginning to fall into place. It was after ten when Augustin Flemming called from upstate New York, where he had settled down with a spinster sister.

McIntee said he didn't want to say much on the phone. They arranged to meet the following day at a restaurant in the village on the corner of West Tenth and Ninth.

McIntee arrived late. He told a lanky waiter with a crew cut he was supposed to meet someone, a short, older man. The waiter nodded and directed him to a corner table, where Augustin Flemming stood to meet his old companion. Flemming had been released six years before him. McIntee thought his prison friend hadn't changed much, a little heavier maybe. Augustin Flemming was in his early sixties, short, pudgy with a globular red face. His hair was pure white, long at the sides and back, his head bald as a billiard ball on top. They shook hands and patted each other's back. Flemming sat first.

"This is a surprise, Sean. You're one of the last people I thought I'd ever see again. When did you get out?"

"A few months back. By the way, I'd appreciate it if you'd call me David, David Kenny."

Flemming's mouth pursed. "I like it," he said, "David—yes, it suits you." They talked about old times and acquaintances and ordered lunch. After the meal, McIntee, taking the direct approach, asked Flemming if he would be interested in making half a million dollars, maybe more if things went as well as expected.

There wasn't a hint of hesitation. "I would most certainly give your offer consideration," he said, smiling. McIntee waited.

"My God! You're serious, aren't you."

"Very," McIntee said, "I need your talents and I'm willing to set you up in business. Legit!"

"What kind of business?"

"Something you're very familiar with—printing."

Flemming sat back in the chair and locked his hands behind his head.

"Let me see if I understand this. You're going to let me run a printing..."

McIntee stopped him. "Own a printing shop, at least for a while. After my needs have been fulfilled, you'll have to sell—and keep the profits, of course. If you have any objections about leaving the U.S., you'd better say so now—that's critical."

Flemming looked bewildered. "I guess I don't have a whole lot of reasons to stick around here since my family disowned me. Running a printing shop, eh?" He pondered.

"That's right—and on top of that, I'm going to give you half a mill."

"What do I have to do in return?" Flemming asked quietly, "kill someone?"

McIntee ignored his sarcasm. "Among other things, print some stock certificates," he said.

"I see," Flemming said. "So you've found a new interest. By the way, where are you getting the money to back this venture?"

"That, my short friend, is none of your business, but I don't mind telling you—I happen to be worth over twenty-five million, all legal. I invested wisely before I went to the pen." He glanced at his watch. "Hell, every hour goes by I'm probably worth another couple o' grand."

"I don't understand," Flemming said, looking confused, "you have all the money in the world. What the hell do you want with counterfeit stocks? Hell, you'd be taking a big chance duplicating registered stocks, even having them fenced they wouldn't be worth twenty-percent of face value. Why take a chance? You have all the legal money any man could want."

"I want you to duplicate twenty-million dollars of my stocks."

Flemming tried to break in. McIntee raised his hand.

"You'll have the real McCoy to go by. That should make your job easy. I should have the certificates in two, three weeks. I want you to find paper stock that on the surface looks perfect, so good it would need to be scrutinized in a lab to tell the difference from the authentic."

"That will be hard but possible," Flemming butted in. "Finding the right paper is usually our biggest problem. The stock certificates that I replicate will be perfect to the naked eye, but they would never stand the analysis of the lab technician."

"Good," McIntee said, "now I'm going to demand that if you take the offer, you ask no questions as to my reasons. Fair? Oh, you also have to learn how to duplicate my signature."

"Your new one, David Kenny?"

"That's right."

"Sounds crazy to me, but you're the boss. By the way, why do I have to leave town?" He looked troubled. "I'm not into killing anyone, not for any money ... I couldn't..."

McIntee broke in, "Don't worry." He gave a wry smile. "If you do your job you shouldn't have to snuff anyone. I need a patsy to take the hit for the counterfeit stocks, that's all. You'll have to live out your days on a beach in South America. Now I ask ya, does that sound half bad?"

"As long as you give me plenty of time to make the break, it sounds okay to me."

"You'll do it then, you'll make the plates?"

"Count me in, Mr. Kenny." They shook hands. McIntee reached into his inside pocket and unfolded the page from the classified section of the *Times*. He had circled an advertisement of a print shop he wanted to purchase. He also left it for Flemming to line up any extra equipment he would need and gave him an envelope containing fifty thousand dollars.

Flemming immediately opened a bank account and told his sister he found new employment. He told her that their life was going to improve, things would be better. He also mentioned that he might have to do some traveling. In the months that followed, Augustin Flemming became a rich and happy man.

His wife had died while he was doing time and his only relative other than his sister was his son, who hated him so much for what he had done to him and his mother that he refused any contact other than a perfunctory interaction. Ron Flemming was just ten when his father was taken by the authorities. Up to that point Flemming had been living the high life on counterfeit twenties and fifties manufactured in his print shop. Ron remembered seeing him at the trial. He attended at the request of his father's attorney to gain sympathy from the jury. It was too little, too late. Augustin Flemming got the maximum of twenty years. Ron was now married and had two children. When they were old enough to ask questions about their grandfather, he told them that he had died.

After Flemming's release from prison, he tried many times to approach his son, without success. Now, thanks to Sean McIntee, he had enough money to salve his conscience by setting up trust funds for the grandchildren. McIntee opened a separate business account in Flemming's name so that he could make the purchases, beginning with the print shop in the Bronx. Flemming did the negotiating. The business had good accounts and equipment to produce the work. It had been poorly managed, and Flemming bargained a cash sale that made everyone happy. He had more equipment than he needed to satisfy McIntee's requirements. With his experience, he could fulfill his desire to run the business in the black. He was the proud owner of three Heidelberg two-color presses, a three-color press and a Linotype machine. There was also a camera room and art department, complete with operators, strippers, an artist, and one salesman.

In the weeks that followed, McIntee didn't press him. Flemming took the opportunity to concentrate on the business. He was a taskmaster, logging twelve- and sometimes fifteen-hour days. He was an example to his employees, so much so that they too worked overtime to help turn the business around. He couldn't wait to show his boss the books, couldn't wait to point out the healthy profit.

McIntee didn't show much interest in Flemming's flow sheets; he had his own agenda and would soon be utilizing Flemming's special talents. He spent most of his time pursuing three men whose lives and characters he had determined to ruin. The pursuit would be the beginning of a series of events that would ultimately destroy William Hamilton.

Michael was the easier of the twins to track. McIntee never missed the eight o'clock Sunday mass at St. Michael's. He usually sat unobserved in the back of the church and paid more attention to the sermon than many of the regulars. He rejoiced, not in the Lord, rather in hearing Michael's supplications for additional pledges. His plot was being fulfilled beyond his expectations. It hinged on the understanding that the church would never turn down a wealthy benefactor, but this was even more than he hoped. Every Sunday the pleas continued: the church was badly in need of an infusion of money, and he was about to oblige. He believed that Father Riordan and the church he represented would undergo a scandal so great that he would be defrocked. They would perish through their greed, and prayers for its resurrection would be like raising the dead. And he was in no hurry.

Lawrence, on the other hand, was more difficult to observe. Once

McIntee had the good luck to attend a case Lawrence was hearing at the New York State Supreme Court. McIntee was amazed at how well he concealed his homosexuality and trusted that Bridget's assessment of him was correct. Everything hinged on her call. When McIntee returned to the penthouse suite on Park Avenue, he studied the photo again and decided Bridget was probably right. Lawrence was getting a lot of press running for the Senate. McIntee, like a dogged fan, saved every article no matter how insignificant.

McIntee and Flemming never met at the same place twice. This meeting was conducted in an obscure workman's cafe on the waterfront by the south ferry. McIntee planned the time around mid-morning. He walked over to Third, hailed a cab, and told the driver to take him to Water Street. Flemming was standing outside the restaurant. McIntee gave the cabbie a big tip, motioned to Flemming to follow him through the doors, walked to a booth at the rear, away from the noisy regulars, and ordered coffee. Flemming ordered ham and eggs. McIntee opened a briefcase and selected a file folder, which he laid on the table.

"How's the print shop doing?"

"Let me show you the latest numbers. I think you're going to be excited, Sean," Flemming said, producing a folded paper from his inside pocket.

"Do me a favor. It doesn't make any difference where we are, even if we were on the goddamn desert with no one for miles. Ya gotta get used to callin' me David. Remember, Sean McIntee is in Ireland, gone, forget he even existed."

His voice, although calm, frightened the older man. McIntee was declaring an ultimatum. Flemming apologized and vowed never to make the mistake again.

"I have two jobs that require your expertise," McIntee said calmly, "and I want you to hire the best in the business. Loyalty is of the utmost importance."

Flemming moved forward, his voice compliant. "I've been waiting for this moment. I'm still the best. You can trust me. If it has anything to do with printing, I can duplicate it."

"Good, here's what I want you to do first." McIntee arranged the photo of Lawrence, Terrance McCabe, and the double truck of the cabaret section of the London newspaper. The fragile paper had yellowed with age and McIntee handled it carefully.

"I want this photo," he directed Flemming's attention to the picture of Lawrence and McCabe, "inserted here, replacing this column. We're going to have to do some typesetting so I want you to find the exact same font."

Flemming made a groaning sound and stroked his chin. "That could be a tough one ... How long has it been, twenty-odd years?"

"I don't care if you have to go to bloody England, I want the same type." McIntee lowered his voice. "Look, Gus, money is not an issue here. I'm buying perfection, okay?"

"I understand ... David, don't worry, I'll find the type."

"Good. Now I'll give you the text of what I need you to print. I want you to find the exact newsprint paper," he thought a moment, "or even if we have to age the paper, I don't care how you do it. I want a perfect reproduction of this paper, with the photo and article inserted."

"Consider it done." They stayed silent while the waitress put the plate of ham and eggs on the table.

"That's it for now," McIntee said. "Next week I'll bring you the second project, probably more complicated."

"The stocks?" Flemming said, with a full mouth.

"That's right, the stocks." They talked for a while about masters of forgery they'd known in prison. McIntee said he would also need a notary. Flemming mentioned some new equipment he would have to buy, such as a sequential numbering machine. McIntee told him to make a list and once again insisted on nothing less than perfection, always with the same stipulation: When the certificates are examined, they will look authentic; when they are tested, they will be seen as fraudulent.

"Remember, Gus, I'm dealing with a lawyer and a priest, and as much as I despise them, I know that they're not stupid."

When Flemming was through eating, they left, each going in a different direction.

It took Flemming only six weeks to complete the project. McIntee picked up stock at the Chase Manhattan, detouring from the usual route to the print shop in the Bronx. He waited ten days and called the bank, saying that the stocks had not arrived. He was told to give the mail another week and call the officials back. If he hadn't received the certificates by then, he was to call the officials and they would conduct a search. McIntee wrote the bank, putting on record his report of the loss of the stock. The letter would support the finding of bogus stock certificates.

As the search for the lost stock was initiated, McIntee called the bank to give notice that the certificates had arrived. The master engraver, working with the certificates, made copies so like the originals that Flemming couldn't tell them apart. He then located an old acquaintance, a respected forger named Karl Lerner. Lerner copied every signature on the blank certificates to perfection. After the numbers were duplicated, the only thing left was the notary seal.

McIntee arrived at the shop at the arranged time of nine-thirty. The weather was ugly. He asked the cabbie to turn off the headlights and wait awhile, wanting to make sure all the employees had left. They waited in the dark with the meter and engine running and windshield wipers on high. Ten minutes passed before a man left the shop bundled in an overcoat, huddled to face the rain. Flemming appeared in the doorway and said goodnight. When he was sure all was clear, Flemming waved McIntee inside.

The cabbie flipped the handle on the meter. "Dat'll be four-thoity," he said. McIntee gave him a ten and told him to keep the change.

Flemming closed and locked the door behind them and pulled the shade. When McIntee saw the results, he was astonished. "Here," Flemming said, "put these on. We don't want your fingerprints anywhere on the phony stock, do we?"

"Goddamn fantastic, Gus." McIntee laid them side by side on the light table and lit a cigarette. He was comparing the two documents. "Christ, I can't tell the difference—I hope you know which is the original." His voice showed concern.

"Actually, I was worried about that myself." He smiled and turned them over. "See, I had to make sure myself. I numbered the back."

McIntee laughed out loud. "You're a goddamn genius, Gus—a goddamn genius."

"Now, you do understand that the watermark is not perfect, but that would only be found in a lab by experts," Flemming said.

"That's the way I want it," McIntee muttered.

"Wait till you see what else I have to show you." Flemming opened the wall safe and removed a large manila envelope. He prolonged the anticipation. Unwinding the string tab, he slowly removed the contents. He unfolded the newsprint and displayed both sides. Once again the duplicated looked exactly like the original.

"Well! What do you think?" Flemming said, proud of his endeavor. McIntee turned the paper, examining one side, then the other.

"Fantastic. I'd be fooled."

"Even if someone took a glass to the paper, they wouldn't know the difference. I matched the dots per square inch with the other photos. No one, and I mean no one, could tell that this photo wasn't printed with the original paper."

"I'm impressed," McIntee said. "Now I have a real favor." His tone was somber. "I need you to do an acting job."

"Acting?"

"That's right, I want you to become a parishioner at St. Michael's. I want you to donate some money to the Catholic Church ... for a small fee, of course."

"I'm afraid I don't get you ... you want me to unload the stock?"

"That's right, Gus. You're going to give the Catholic Church twenty million dollars ... no strings."

Flemming looked concerned. "They'll be suspicious. For chrissake, I'm not even a Catholic ... I'm a goddamn Presbyterian. Nobody gives away that kind of money." He walked away from McIntee.

"You do if you're dying and have no one to leave it to. You're buying your way into heaven, goddamn it. They understand that logic, believe me."

Flemming turned around, rubbing his hands vigorously. There were so many questions he didn't know where to begin.

"I really would like it if you could find someone else ... I don't think I could pull it off ... I know shit about Catholicism."

"First, I don't want anyone else in the know," McIntee said, growing tired of the ponderous man's disobliging attitude, "and secondly, I personally will take you on as a student in the ways of the Catholic Church. Believe me, by the time we're through, no one will know you're a goddamn heathen." Flemming continued to pace nervously.

"You're goin' to impersonate me. You'll be David Kenny. You realize you don't have much time left and have returned to the Church. I want you to befriend a particular priest and give him the money. Afterwards you leave town ... It's that simple. After they've placed the stock in their bank and have, shall we say, borrowed on the stocks to capitalize their very worthwhile ventures ... well, that's when I show up, the injured party."

"Christ ... I don't know. Sure, it all sounds simple when you tell it." Flemming looked distraught. Why this parish anyway? I mean, won't it look odd? Hell, they'll know I wasn't a member."

"You're not giving it to a parish ... You'll be donating to the Archdiocese of New York." McIntee smiled. "Trust me, they'll love you all to hell."

"That's exactly what I'm afraid of," Flemming said.

CHAPTER FIFTY-SEVEN

A FTER MAGGIE'S DEATH, Kathleen and Ryan moved to another house in Maryland. Maggie had been such an important part of their lives, her absence made it difficult to concentrate on the every-day duties. Normal chores were interrupted by thoughts of her voice, her laughter, the bedroom where Kathleen held her hand as Maggie passed away. She tried to convince herself that Maggie's passing was a blessing, a relief. It was a logic overwhelmed by sadness and a monumental sense of loss. They were also difficult times for Ryan, though his job was a distraction from his despondency. Kathleen came to realize that her indifference to keeping up the house, preparing meals and her self-abnegation, her inability to move ahead, were wearing on Ryan's patience. He knew better than to confront Kathleen while he was in an antagonistic mood. For almost a year after Maggie's death they talked only of trivial things.

It was Madge and Anne's visit that changed Kathleen's attitude and saved what many friends had come to believe was a marriage of convenience. Anne and Maggie held memories in common. They had been close in a spiritual way known only to them. Through Anne, Maggie had lived out her desires and dreams. Anne believed that Maggie's time on earth, brief as it was, affected everyone she touched, including her, in a positive, spiritual way. Anne's faith was contagious. Ryan noticed the change in Kathleen during their stay.

In the months that followed, it was Kathleen who broached Ryan with the idea of moving. They chose a house in Suitland, Maryland, to begin a new life. Hamilton was never far away. He had become a close friend to Ryan and was a regular for dinner. Many times the three went out to restaurants. It was an interesting trio, Ryan playing at matchmaker, trying to set Hamilton up with a single or divorced friend. Kathleen was comfortable with them both, as they were, telling Ryan to mind his own business and leave the poor man alone.

Hamilton, happy to see her from time to time, was never completely gratified. He fantasized, his abstract notions always ending in stalemate. He couldn't degrade his relationship with Ryan. To the twins, Hamilton had become a third party, sometimes taking time to visit them. They enjoyed his company. He opened up more with them than with anyone else. That relationship gave meaning to his otherwise isolated life.

He became their mentor and often asked himself if he would have had the same rapport had they known he was their father. Why was it that the father was so many times remembered only as the man in the wedding picture with the mother? The man who was the bread earner, the disciplinarian, someone who was always there when you needed him, though seldom a confidant? Hamilton knew what the boys thought of Ryan. They loved and respected him; however, he preferred his own relationship. He was the blood that flowed through their bodies; he was their revered confidant.

By 1955 Hamilton received an offer to head the New York field office. Taking the post was entirely his decision, his tough decision. Moving to New York would mean leaving Kathleen. Even though he didn't see her often, he cherished the idea that he was closer to her in Washington. In his imaginary attachment, he could see her any time he wished. That had not been enough. The dream was going nowhere; he could never be with her in a husband-and-wife relationship. Moving to New York was logical. Knowing he would be seeing Michael and Lawrence more often was a consolation. His self-analysis told him that the older he became the closer he needed to be to his sons. Even if Ryan were out of the picture, what love Hamilton and Kathleen once had was gone forever. Theirs was a friendship both satisfying and disappointing.

Although he hated to leave Kathleen, he took the position. Before he left, he was determined to see her alone, a thought he had never entertained before, fearing an ugly scandal. If she was willing, one time wouldn't hurt anyone, particularly if Ryan was out of town. He hated himself for orchestrating a plan to make sure that they could have time alone, uninterrupted. That was the easier part. His greater concern was in asking for Kathleen's agreement to meet him alone. As time for his departure approached, Ryan told him that he and Kathleen would like to prepare a going-away dinner. Nothing big, just the three of them. As far as Hamilton was concerned, this would be an ingenuous opportunity, an uncontrived way to feel the overtone of his departure. During dinner they drank more wine than usual. Ryan raised his glass excessively with toasts to old friends. Kathleen, looking directly at Hamilton, added, "Yes, and very dear memories."

After dessert, they moved to the living room. Kathleen joined them, leaving dishes on the table. Hamilton noted that of all the times he had attended dinner at the Thorntons, this was the first occasion when she didn't clear the table. Ryan and Hamilton smoked cigars while Kathleen opened a bottle of Five Star Powers. During the camaraderie that followed, Ryan, whom Hamilton had never seen out of control, was becoming inebriated. Hamilton became singularly attuned to Kathleen's disposition and concluded that she seemed genuinely sorry that he was moving.

When it came time to leave, she helped him on with his coat. For the first time since Dublin, he held her close. She hugged him, kissed him tenderly on the mouth, and said she would miss him very much. He was embarrassed until he noticed that Ryan displayed an inane smile that appeared to suggest acceptance. There was no doubt that he favored his wife's show of affection.

A perfect morning for a drive: the sky was cloudless, giving Hamilton the feeling that this was going to become one of those muggy *last days of summer*. He drove southeast from his office in D.C. on the Suitland road to the Thorntons. More than once in the ten miles, unsure what to expect, he felt like turning the car around. Three days ago, he asked Ryan to go to Louisville, Kentucky, to investigate actions involving transportation of illegal liquor, a matter that Hamilton hoped would take at least a week to solve. He waited until the day after Ryan's departure to call Kathleen. His excuse for calling sounded sophomoric and fabricated. Like a schoolboy trying to arrange a first date, he stammered through transparent suggestions. Maybe there was something she'd like him to take to the boys. By the way, I have a little something I want you and Ryan to have. I have bought a silver serving tray for your coming anniversary.

He found her gracious on the phone, saying that she thought it would be just grand if he stopped. He didn't need the excuses. He hung up, feeling stupid.

He stopped the car in the Thornton driveway, stepped out, and took the wrapped gift from the back seat. As he shut the door, he looked around as though he were casing a suspect. Kathleen opened the front door. Hamilton stared for a moment. She looked beautiful. She was still the same little Dublin girl, especially when she tilted her head and allowed the black shoulder-length hair to undulate, sometimes partially covering her face, mysteriously teasing. The white-knit dress was a perfect choice, a finishing touch to her attractive, tanned complexion. He felt successful. For no reason would a woman look this good at ten in the morning except to please someone other than herself, and certainly not simply to bring an amorous form to a mirror.

"William, somehow I knew we hadn't seen the last of you," she said, smiling, showing perfect white teeth. "I have a pot of tea brewing."

She had used the plural, adding a sense of respect to their meeting. "Sounds good to me," he said, handing her the package. She allowed him to kiss her cheek, which he did, slowly relishing her fragrance. He followed her to the kitchen, where she hurriedly put the gift on the table and removed the whistling kettle.

"Pass me that pot, will you, William, please." She pointed to a blue and white teapot in the open hutch.

"Any news from Ryan yet," he asked, handing her the pot.

"He just left yesterday, or didn't you know? It's still a little early. He'll probably call tonight. How about you? When are you leaving?"

"This weekend," he said, "probably Sunday."

She warmed the teapot with boiling water, dumped it, poured the rest of the boiling water into the pot, and added three heaping tablespoons of tea leaves. What followed was a game of pretending. They sat at the kitchen table pretending to be interested in the conversation. Embarrassing silence followed each hesitant mention of an unimportant topic. During one of the quiet moments she opened the gift-wrapped package. Exclamations of gratitude became a diversion.

"Would you rather have a drink, William? Something stronger than tea, I mean. I have a bottle of brandy." Before he could answer, she took his cup. "Here, let me sweeten that up for you."

"I'm afraid I'm not much of a drinker these days," he said, stopping her.

"I'm having a drop myself," she added, as though conspiring.

"Oh, what the hell," he said, "in that case I'll join you."

She poured a generous amount of brandy into each cup and returned to the table. Conversation settled on the twins. Her recounting of events in their early lives was bitter sweet, embracing moments of earnestness, from Lawrence's expulsion from the seminary to strafing the airfield on his first solo flight. There wasn't a lot about Michael that aroused the same passion. Kathleen refilled the cups and found no dispute this time as she poured the brandy.

"Have you heard from them lately?" he asked.

"Not as much as I should."

"Do you think they'll one day give you grandchildren? Obviously I'm referring to Lawrence," he said into the cup.

"Let's hope he gets married first." Her face immediately flushed as she remembered her own predicament. "I don't think that will ever happen though," she continued.

"I think you're right. From what time I've spent with Lawrence, he didn't appear to be the marrying type. He's very private about his love life, isn't he?" He sipped on the tea and brandy and studied her over the rim of the cup.

"I don't know how to put this, William, I mean I'm really surprised you hadn't noticed."

"Noticed?"

"Lawrence is a homosexual, William," she said forthrightly. The short silence was broken when he placed the cup on the saucer.

"And I thought he was just, well, shy," he said, staring at the table.

"God. I had no idea."

"Don't blame yourself, William. It's probably some stray gene from my side of the family," she said facetiously, "I had an uncle —"

"I wasn't blaming anyone, Kathleen. As a matter of fact, I was feeling bad for Lawrence. He's covered it rather well. Christ, he's a war hero." He looked into her blue eyes. "Are you sure?"

"For what it's worth, you're taking this a lot better than Ryan. He felt responsible and he wasn't even his biological father," she shrugged. "And yes, I'm sure. Maggie told me. He confided in her. Interesting, isn't it? He could tell her but not me."

"Kathleen, I don't think I would have shared that with my mother either."

She looked distant. "I suppose I suspected it for a long time."

As the minutes passed, they laughed and shared stories of the lost years. He felt the liquor warm his throat and relax the earlier tension. He studied her, listening intently when she laughed and threw her head back. It was while she was laughing that he posed the question that would finally demand answers to the deeper feelings, the years of silence.

"You have no idea how much this means to me, Kathleen," he said, fixing on her eyes. "I've only imagined moments like this with you." He shook his head. "Ordinary moments, just to sit and talk. I'm curious to know …," he hesitated, "if you still care for me the way I do you." She looked down, staring at the cup, running her finger nervously around its rim, and didn't respond.

"For almost ten years I've been just a few miles away," he continued, "it may as well have been a thousand."

She raised her head. "It's been a fine ten years," she stammered, "at least I thought we've all had a good time. You were always included in our evenings out, William. Even Lawrence and Michael have probably seen more of you than they have Ryan or myself."

He waited, thinking of something to say.

"We're an interesting species, aren't we? What I mean is, I don't believe there's another animal that doesn't respond to its instincts. Humans on the other hand are governed by all kinds of rules to suppress their feelings. Take us, for example."

"I'm not sure I follow you."

"How long has it been, Kathleen—since Ireland? All the years in between have been ... have been," he hesitated, "well, it's kind of sad in a way that we, that is, some of us, have to spend all our lives living with a few memories out of the past."

Kathleen began to clear the table. She stood, removed the cups and took them to the sink, where she stared blankly out the window. A sprinkle of rain struck the panes, diffusing her view. "I try not to think about those days," she said.

"That's what I'm talking about," he said. "We have avoided talking about times ... times and feelings." He stood and slowly moved behind her. He gently placed his hands on her shoulders. She made a feeble effort to twist from his touch.

"Please," he said, "please allow me this small gratification."

She didn't move, instead she placed her hands over his, patting indulgently.

"It's the brandy talking, William. You know as well as I do that this is wrong."

"That's exactly what I'm talking about. Is it really wrong to ... to need to be with the one you love? What's so wrong about that? We've lived our lives by rules, abiding by society's sense of justice." He sighed.

"Sometimes I wish the Christian ethic hadn't been the basis for our every-day standards. Thou shalt not kill or steal, I understand that, but coveting your neighbor's wife ... especially when both parties are in love. Condemning natural feelings just doesn't seem fair. They've handed us some punishment, haven't they?"

"We have to be able to live with ourselves, don't we," she said. "And what would happen to Ryan? Do we just discard those whom we've made a vow to love, cherish, 'til death do us part?" She drew away and turned to face him. "I'm not sure what I am to you, William. Do we really know one another? I mean other than the pleasure of love-making forty years ago in Dublin. As I see it, we've developed a great friendship over the years. I'd hate to ruin that, wouldn't you?"

Hamilton moved away and sat with his elbows on the table. He placed his hands under his chin. "You know how I feel about Ryan," he declared apprehensively. "He's become one of my closest friends, and yet I have been deceiving him… That's how much I still love you."

"You haven't been deceiving Ryan because you haven't done anything wrong."

"Wanting you isn't wrong? I've been working with your husband for thirteen years or so, some assignments risking our lives, and all the time he believes my bachelor status to be just a little eccentric. He tells me constantly that I just haven't found the right woman. Christ, little does he know I'm in love with his wife, always have been. His sons are not really his but mine, and you don't believe that I've done anything wrong, Kathleen? Hell, a big part of my life has been lost on a woman I could never be with."

She walked behind him, and this time she placed her hands on his shoulders. "I'm really sorry, William. I thought that all these years you had come to enjoy our friendship. I saw us as an inseparable threesome. I guess I didn't know that you still loved me that way. At least I was hoping that you had come to accept me as a good friend."

"It has been a little easier for you, Kathleen, because you had a husband. You had a husband and in a vicarious way, an admirer, a lover. You had to know I worshipped the ground you stood on." He rotated the chair and she allowed him to put his arm around her waist.

"I have a confession," he said, looking up at her. "Ryan didn't have to go to St. Louis."

She stopped him. "I know."

"You knew I sent him?"

"I wasn't born yesterday, William. I realized that after you called and wanted to come by. First, you offered to take something to the twins, then you used the gift as an excuse." She smiled down at him. "You know, for a spy, you're quite predictable."

"And you allowed me to make a fool of myself."

"That's something you've never done." She smiled and pulled herself away, "at least not yet anyway." He stood and moved close enough to feel her breath.

"He doesn't suspect anything, does he?"

"Ryan?" she shook her head," I don't believe it's ever occurred to Ryan that anyone would look at me twice."

"Then," he said, "and I hate to say this about a good friend, but if he thinks that way, he's an idiot. I'm assuming that since you knew about my little charade," he hesitated, "you were also a willing participant."

"Guilty as charged," she said, looking up into his steel-blue eyes. "I have to admit I did want to see you alone… I don't know who I'm trying to convince."

"Convince of what?"

"That I didn't really love you, I guess."

"And?"

"I'm confused."

He lowered his face to hers. Her voice trailed as their lips slowly joined. He made an effort to control the trembling. Her arms raised, hands combed his hair, pulling down. He fumbled nervously, his hands finding her breasts, pressing his body to hers. He felt her respond, undulating her hips. He could taste the brandy in the mouth that was once a temple only to be revered at a distance. Now he could more than speculate; after all the dreams and craving, this was the most wondrous dream of all, set apart from the others. He explored the warm, soft interior of her mouth with his tongue. He was careful to be gentle undoing the buttons on the dress. With his fingers he touched the bare skin just above the brassiere. He slid the straps aside and massaged her warm, soft breasts. He prayed that he wasn't moving too fast. The last thing he wanted now was a sudden eruption of conscience. She pushed harder on his mouth, pressing with her tongue as his right hand moved down between their bodies. Their lips parted.

"God, I love you, Kathleen, more than when we first met, more than I could dream possible for a man to love a woman."

"I love you, too, William. All these years I've tried to convince myself moments like this didn't matter." He raised the knit dress and could feel the silk slip. Past the top of the nylons his hand found the softness of the inside of her thighs. She tried to push him away.

"I can't," she said breathlessly, "I can't do this, William."

He pulled her to him, his voice gentle, pleading.

"Don't pull away, Kathleen. Please, just let me hold you. I promise, all I want to do is hold you." His whispered pleadings continued in her ear.

"Please." He caressed her head and soon her body responded. They stayed that way for a while, holding each other in silence until their breathing returned to normal. He held her at arm's length, then touching her chin, he tilted her head.

"I shouldn't have done that," he said sincerely. "You have to believe me when I tell you that my coming here was really just to talk, to see you

one more time alone before I left. I had no intention of acting this way."
Her eyes were teary as she fumbled to button her dress. He turned away,
feeling ugly. She was the vulnerable one, torn from her convictions to
become adulterous, and for all his desires, it wasn't the way he wanted her.
He returned and slumped into the chair in silence. Finally she spoke.

"What just happened wasn't all your fault, William. I suppose we've
both been … well, like time bombs waiting to go off. My life has also
been missing a fullness since Maggie's death. A good deal of me died with
her. My marriage was never the same. Both Ryan and I lost the one thing
that held us together. We should have talked about these things after she
died, but time erased any opportunity we might have had. I'm telling you
this because I believe you feel the same about me. Something very special
happened to us years ago. We were madly in love, we even have two
children to prove it. Sadly, though, we may as well have died, William."
She took a deep breath, then sighed.

"Which reminds me," she said, leaving the room, "I have something
to give you."

"Sounds like I've been forgiven then," he said.

She turned her head. "I hope we've both been forgiven." Her tone was
skeptical. She returned with the small jewelry chest and sat across from
him, her hands placed over the lid. "Before I open this, I want you to know
that—that I know now I still love you very much." He was astounded by
her matter-of-fact honesty. She opened the chest and handed him first the
tarnished cigarette case.

"Oh my God!" he said, opening the case. Five Players were still held
in place by the elastic strap. His thoughts instantly returned to the Hill
o' Howth. "I don't know what to say," he stammered, shaking his head.
"W.A.H.," he said disconsolately, "those initials must have driven you up
the wall."

"Uh huh," she said, smiling.

"My father gave it to me when I graduated." His voice choked. "I really
would like you to keep it."

"I want you to have this back, because as long as I have it I'll always
feel guilty. I don't need a cigarette case to remind me that I love you and
probably always will." He placed the case in his inside pocket. Then she
asked him to open his hand. He had no idea what she dropped into his
palm until his eyes focused on the bairin breac ring. For a moment he
just stared at the brass ring, remembering their dinner at the Elliots' in
Dublin. He wanted to say something and, on the verge of tears, found it
impossible. He managed to clear his throat. Seeing his sorrow, she held his
hand in hers and cried for them both.

"I think this last thing I want to show will at least make you smile," she said, wiping her eyes with the back of her hand. She held the tarnished photo. "Now there's a pair," she said.

He drew the photo closer. "Jeez, after all these years. I remember the day this was taken." He looked away for a moment, searching his memories.

"It was by that park…"

"Stephens Green," she said.

He whispered the words again, "Christ, look how young we were."

He went to slip the photo into his shirt pocket.

"Not that, William Hamilton. That one I get to keep."

He was happy that she decided to keep something of their reveries. He looked at his watch. "Can you believe I've been here for over four hours?" He stood.

"I suppose I should be getting along, … unless …" He stopped, "No, I guess not."

"Not what?" she asked.

"Oh, nothing," he said, "it was just a stupid thought."

"No, tell me what you were thinking."

"Well, I thought it was getting so close to dinner time that you might…"

"Might be hungry enough to join you?" she asked

"I realized it wouldn't look good to the neighbors to see you hanging out with a strange man."

"Oh, to hell with the neighbors," she said triumphantly, "Let's eat out."

"Great," he said, "I'd love that. Hell, I'm so hungry I could eat a horse."

She laughed loudly. "Just give me a moment to clean up," she said.

"What's so funny?" he asked. She threw her head back. "Remind me to tell you over dinner … about eating a horse."

CHAPTER FIFTY-EIGHT

THE FIRST TIME Lawrence realized he was being used was after the Democratic convention in Chicago. He was one of the many speakers and had received rousing applause. It was the first time he had met Jack Kennedy, who told him that the Party needed the Catholic vote but wasn't quite ready for their Catholic candidate, at least not for President or Vice President. They talked for a while and Lawrence reminded him that back in 1918 they had shared a crib together at one of Dennis Noonan's memorable St. Patrick's Day parties. He mentioned that his grandmother's maiden name was Fitzgerald and she was related to Jack's mother, Rose. Joe and Rose were also present at his mother's wedding. When Kennedy found out they were shirt-tail relatives, nothing was too good or too much for the new Senator from the State of New York. Kennedy joked about the difficulty of getting one Catholic into the system, let alone two.

Although Kennedy's hopes of winning the Vice Presidential nomination were not realized, Lawrence thought that Kennedy's graceful acceptance of defeat won great favor and insured him a place of prominence in the future. Lawrence believed that there were no regrets for Kennedy. Lawrence could see the delegates switching to Kennedy had they known how close he had come to winning. He was short by a few dozen votes, but no one at the convention could know this because the electric tote board had been dismantled the night before.

The convention ended on a note of brotherly harmony. Mahalia Jackson sang the Lord's Prayer. During the chatter that followed, Lawrence was handed a note by a well-dressed, robust, swarthy man with deep-set, dark eyes. "I'd like for you to read the note, Mr.Riordan. There's someone wants to meet you who could make a difference in your career." Before Lawrence could say anything, the man disappeared into the crowd. When the song ended, everyone cheered. Adlai Stevenson and Estes Kefauver were the choices of the Democratic Party to take on the Eisenhower/Nixon ticket.

Later that evening, he had a drink with Kennedy at the Stockyard Inn. Each ordered a Chevis.

"Disappointed?" Lawrence asked.

Kennedy thought for a moment, then shrugged, "I've always observed that what is good for the party is most important. That's paramount. I'm just not convinced that Stevenson is the man to beat Eisenhower—and I don't underestimate Dick Nixon, either."

"You would have been a much better choice of Vice President for the party, Jack."

"I really appreciate your vote of confidence, Lawrence, but my name on that ticket wouldn't make any difference. Actually, the more I think about it, the better I feel about the whole thing." He rubbed his chin with his thumb and forefinger. "If I'm going to concentrate on the '60 nomination, I sure wouldn't want to be associated with a losing ticket." He changed the subject. "By the way, what do your friends call you? You're not always Lawrence, are you? Someone must call you Larry. Hell, even Lawrence Olivier is Larry to his friends."

"My family calls me Lars."

"Lars," Kennedy said thoughtfully, "I like that. Lars it is then," he said, raising his drink. "God, I needed this." Their glasses clinked and both took a healthy swig of the Scotch.

"Do you think," Lawrence said, "that had the tote board worked, it might have shown the delegates that the race was closer than they thought?"

"I wouldn't begin to second guess that," he said. "You know, Lars, I have no time for people who say one thing and do another." He rotated the glass on the table.

"I don't understand."

"Gore's a quizzling son-of-a-bitch. He told me that he would like to see me on the Democratic ticket—first or second place he told me—then what does the bastard do?" Lawrence butted in, "He released his Tennessee delegates to Kefauver."

Lawrence looked around as if they were being surveilled, then whispered loudly. "You mean he switched at the last moment?"

"Oh, what the hell, Lars," he waved his arm, "it's all part of the game.

That's what makes the damn process interesting—you never know what tomorrow brings." Another drink was ordered and the conversation centered around family. They soon grew tired, and Lawrence excused himself, shook Kennedy's hand, and returned to his room.

He removed his jacket, hung it in the closet, and walked back to the bedside, where he threw the contents of his trousers pockets on the night table. He reclined on the bed, stared at the ceiling, and thought about the outcome of the evening. He reflected on Kennedy's remarks about Gore's switch in delegate votes. Earlier in the day, he had watched little Al Gore come bounding down the steps. Kennedy had hailed the boy, picked him up, patted his head, put him down, patted him on the back, and said, "There's a kid that's going to make us forget his dad."

Lawrence thought that his own speech had been good. He had addressed the issues affecting working-class families and supported policies that would improve their lives. He related his life to theirs and touched on his time in the service in a humble way. He had spoken of a need to stamp out crime and said that the need for social justice was now, not sometime, but now; this he had emphasized, and he had to wait for the applause to subside. He should have been feeling qualms for insincerity. He sounded more like his brother, who would have meant what he said. Why, he thought, am I not really deeply interested in the plight of the poor?

He did, however, have genuine feelings of concern when it came to civil rights. He was sure, beyond doubt, that no one, including his close friends, believed him to be a homosexual, otherwise he might not have been accepted as a member of the group expected to laugh at repetitious off-color jokes centering on homos, queers, bum boys, freaks and faggots. He had to be careful in his speech to avoid any appearance of empathy with homosexuals. His party leaders made it clear that he was not to include references to homosexuality in the civil-rights speech. In all, he had been schooled well by the members of the committee working to elect him. They recommended the issues in which he should show interest, and it was his obligation to conform to the Democratic platform.

He wasn't sure if he was being completely honest with his benefactors. Deep down, he didn't feel the call to be a crusader for any cause and had little interest in crime as a national issue; still, the idea of becoming a Senator was more appealing than continuing to work out of an attorney's office. He could espouse issues for which he had little concern as long as they fit within his broad political ideology. The local unions had given him a strong endorsement. It certainly made Michael happy that his brother was doing something good for the working man. When he turned to extinguish the lamp, he noticed the crumpled paper on the table. Curious, he unfolded the note, crude block letters written on hotel stationery: *Please call me when you get back to your hotel. Our company needs your services.* Lawrence checked his watch and decided that whatever it was it could wait till morning.

He was awakened by the phone ringing. He picked it up slowly. "This is Lawrence Riordan," he said in a gravelly voice.

"Mr. Riordan, this is Giovanni Lugano."

Lawrence recognized the name. Lugano was one of New York's big crime bosses. He sat up in the bed and cleared his throat.

"What can I do for you, Mr. Lugano?"

"I'm assuming you got my message?" Lugano said, with a diction you could cut with a knife and not the heavy Italian accent he expected.

"You'll have to forgive me, Mr. Lugano, the note made no mention of your name. What can I do for you?"

"Not on the phone, Mr. Riordan," he said. "How about breakfast—in my suite—I'd be in your debt." Lawrence thought that was amusing. The man was smooth. "Give me a chance to clean up and I'll be right there."

"I'll expect you in—shall we say an hour?"

"Half hour," Lawrence said. While he showered, he thought about Lugano's note. He dismissed the notion that Lugano had been offended at his speech about the need to repress crime. This man was much too powerful a boss to concern himself with nominal campaign speeches by a shavetail Senator; besides, despite all of Lugano's arrests, he never spent more than a few hours in jail. Sometimes the evidence had been overwhelming, yet he managed to have all charges dismissed. Lawrence put on the gabardine jacket and headed for the penthouse suite. Before he was allowed to enter, he was searched by the same man who had handed him the note at the convention. Finding no weapon, the man apologized. Lawrence considered the apology humorous, assuming that the big gorilla didn't apologize very often for what he did. He opened the door and indicated that Lawrence was to precede him.

Lugano was seated behind a table set for two. A man in a white jacket, who, Lawrence assumed, was a waiter, stood beside Lugano. He wore a colorful silk dressing gown with a black-velvet, Edwardian collar. Lawrence had seen photos of Lugano in magazines and newspapers. He looked to be in his mid-sixties, friendlier than the press had portrayed him. He was a big man with a round, tanned face, accented by the shock of voluminous white hair. Even more distinctive were the black eyebrows. He bore a wide, toothy grin as he motioned for Lawrence to join him.

"Welcome, welcome, Lawrence. Do you mind if I call you Lawrence?"

"Not at all Mr. Lugano." They shook hands. Lawrence sat and unfolded the napkin and placed it on his lap.

"I heard you gave a great speech last night."

"News certainly travels."

"I make it my business to know what's going on in politics, Lawrence," he said, lifting the silver dome, releasing the aroma of boiled fish. "Do you like poached mackerel?"

"I guess there's a first time for everything."

"My sentiments exactly," Lugano said, gesturing for the man in the white jacket to serve. Lawrence thanked the server and cut a piece of the fish with his fork. Lugano waited for a sign of approval as Lawrence chewed for a while, exploring the taste. Soon he broke into an appreciative smile.

"It's delicious—an excellent flavor. It's not what I expected."

Lugano poured champagne into two tall-stemmed glasses and handed one to Lawrence. "How many times do we come across food—or a man, for that matter, that does not conform to our expectations?" he said. "Salute."

"Here's to the Democratic Party. The Party of the little man, the downtrodden. To us, Lawrence."

"To the Democratic Party. To us," Lawrence repeated.

"Which brings me to the reason I wanted to talk with you," Lugano said, chewing. "You're familiar with a case about to go to trial in New York, the Nick Di Angelo case?" Lawrence remembered reading about the horrendous murder and Michael telling him about the case, which involved a member of his parish.

"He's accused of murdering a Puerto Rican truck driver, isn't he?" Lawrence said, wiping his mouth with the napkin.

"Nick is like my brother. All my life we've been like that," Lugano said, crossing his pudgy fingers. "I believe he is innocent and I intend to see that he doesn't serve any time. That's why you're here, Lawrence. I want to hire you to represent him."

Lawrence swallowed. "Me? I don't understand, you have one of the…" Lawrence thought before choosing the right word to describe Lugano's slick-talking attorney, "most effective lawyers in New York, and you want me? Why?"

"I happen to know that my usual legal counsel is going to be issued a court mandate that will prevent him from representing Nick. Myself, I don't understand how the state can do this."

"There is a situation, Mr. Lugano, where counsel would be dismissed from the case if he was going to be called as a witness in that case. It's most unusual. They'd have to have film or audio tapes, such as wire tap, showing some conspiracy on the part of your attorney. Do you think that's the case?"

"I believe that's what is happening here, Lawrence. That's why we've chosen you—to handle the case for us."

"I still don't understand, Mr. Lugano. First, I'm Irish. Let's be honest, okay? How many other Italian…" Lawrence hesitated, "businessmen have an Irish consigliere? I'm sure I'm missing something here."

"Sure, you're Irish, Catholic, you're also a damned good attorney. You're a respected war hero and soon to be Senator of the greatest state in the Union. You want me to keep going?"

"No, that's okay, I think I get the picture."

"I won't lie to you, Lawrence. Your brother—don't get me wrong, he's a fine priest. I happen to have a great deal of respect for priests. It's just that—well, your brother, Michael, isn't it?"

"That's right," Lawrence said, alarmed.

"Your brother, Michael, is in charge of a union newsletter that espouses civil liberties for the little guy, and, of course, represents the Catholic vote. Their newsletter questions too much. Not that that's a bad thing, mind you." Lawrence wished he'd press on.

"Your brother and this Puerto Rican stirred up a lot of—shall we say *anxiety*, for those of us who have a real interest in the success of the union. For example, we help by wisely investing savings, dues, and pension funds in profit-producing businesses. Your brother, Michael, seems to be misinformed. He fostered this Puerto Rican's views, both of them writing out against those same people who are trying to help them. This man and his family, who was—shall we say, hurt." Lawrence was beginning to realize why this man was feared and treated with deference. He employed understatement with implied threat.

"The man died from his injuries, Mr. Lugano."

"That was unfortunate. I'm sure it wasn't anyone's intention to kill him—whoever it was." Lugano picked a piece of food from his mouth and wiped it on his napkin. "Anyway, Nick Di Angelo, my good friend and business associate, was nowhere near the place where the accident occurred. These articles that your brother continues to write are coloring public opinion about the case. It's going to be difficult to find a jury that isn't prejudiced."

Lawrence wanted to laugh. He doubted that Lugano really believed he was that stupid. "Are you asking me to take the case so that I might shut up my brother," he said firmly, "or is it as you said earlier, because you think I'm a good attorney?"

"Both," Lugano said disingenuously. "You see, Lawrence, I'm a man who believes in covering all his bases."

"Does it concern you at all, Mr. Lugano, that my speech last night called for action to reduce crime? Do you think that my representing Nick Di Angelo will do anything to help my Senatorial race?" Lawrence answered his own questions. "I don't think so."

"I think you're being naive, Lawrence, if you think that principles get you elected, and besides, you have me confused with car thieves, muggers, bank robbers, crime on the streets, and murderers. I do none of those things, Lawrence. I'm a respectable businessman."

Lawrence stood. "Mr. Lugano—I want you to know I'm honored by your proposal."

Lugano raised himself from his chair and stepped around the table. He placed his arm around Lawrence's shoulder. "Please, Lawrence, don't say no yet, not until you have a chance to examine the evidence against my friend—or hear the fee." Lawrence moved toward the door. From what he understood of the case and what he was told by Michael, the evidence against Nick Di Angelo was overwhelming. There were eye witnesses.

"I promise to look at the case, Mr. Lugano. That's all I can say right now. I can't guarantee anything else until I read the state's case, okay?"

"That sounds fair enough to me," Lugano said, smiling and offering his hand.

"By the way, about the fee…How does fifty grand strike you?" Lawrence shook his hand and tried not to appear dumbfounded.

"That strikes me as generous. I'll contact you when I get back to New York."

"I look forward to it, Lawrence."

Lawrence closed the door behind him and whistled. In his room he found a note from Kennedy, thanking him for the conversation and updating him on the other Fitzgeralds in the family.

When Lawrence returned to New York, he called Michael and told him about his meeting with Jack Kennedy. He wanted to talk about Lugano's offer but not on the phone. Michael agreed to meet him the next day, a Saturday, for lunch in a workman's cafeteria near St. Patrick's. On Saturday morning, Lawrence checked into the office for a few hours to catch up on his phone messages. It was almost noon when he stepped out into the windless, muggy, midday sun and flagged down a cab. After a five-minute ride, the taxi driver dropped him off at Kell's Cafe on the corner of West End and Forty-Second. Michael, seated outside under a sun umbrella, smiled broadly when Lawrence stepped from the cab just a few feet away.

"Do you ask what the poor people are up to these days?" Michael said, standing, approaching his brother with open arms.

"I don't know if you have heard yet, my pious friend, but cabs are a thing of the future. It's amazing, for just a few bucks they drop you off right at your destination," Lawrence said, seating himself at the table.

"So you had a good trip then?" Michael said. "Oh, by the way, William said he might try to make it over to Chicago to the convention. Did he catch up with you?"

"I didn't see him," Lawrence answered. "As I mentioned on the phone, I did see Jack Kennedy though. God, I wish you'd been there, Michael. We had a grand ol' time talking about Mother's side of the family. I know you're interested in that, much more than I am."

"Maybe next time you have an opportunity to see him you'll give me a call."

"I promise," Lawrence said.

A young woman with a Bronx accent interrupted them.

"Well, what'll it be, gents?" When her eyes saw that Michael was wearing a collar, she said, "Oh sorry, about that, Faddah—I didn't catch the collar right away."

"That's okay, I've been called everything from a reverend, minister, parson, rabbi, and some words I can't repeat," Michael said, smiling. "Gent isn't bad." They both ordered pastrami and Havarti sandwiches and iced teas. After she left, Michael spoke first.

"Well, what's on your mind, Lars? I know you didn't just call me to break bread, did you?"

"Now that's not fair," Lawrence said firmly, "Why wouldn't I want to spend a little time with my brother?"

"I would hope you would want to see me because I'm your brother and share your thoughts about your desires to become a Senator. I should also hope that you might be a little interested in what I've been up to—I happen to have this feeling deep down that you need my opinion on something or other."

Lawrence was quiet for a moment. He leaned back, locked his hands behind his head, and beamed. "You've always known about my intentions, haven't you? I mean, more than I've known about yours." He leaned forward. "You're right." He looked around to see if anyone nearby was paying attention to his conversation. His voice lowered. "I'll come right to the point."

Michael thought he was being overly dramatic and mimicked his brother, to which Lawrence immediately responded.

"I'm serious, Michael. While I was in Chicago I was approached by one of Giovanni Lugano's henchmen and ended up being invited to breakfast in Lugano's suite." Michael's face became tense.

"What did he want with you?"

"What do you know about the Puerto Rican murder?"

Michael was going to remind him that they had discussed the case earlier, but Lawrence continued.

"Oh, I know you filled me in a few weeks ago, but I wasn't that interested at the time. Now I am." The waitress returned and rudely dropped the plates on the table, almost displacing the sandwiches. She took a step, turned abruptly, tossing on the table napkins she produced from her apron pocket.

"You'll be needin' dese—I'll be back wit de drinks," she said and left. They laughed. Michael repositioned the sandwich on the plate. She returned promptly with the glasses filled to the brim, placed them loudly on the table and walked away, not saying a word.

"What we won't endure for a good meal," he said, biting into the thick sandwich. Lawrence sugared the iced tea and continued.

"Lugano offered me fifty thousand to represent Di Angelo."

Michael put the sandwich down and wiped the mayonnaise from his mouth. It was his turn to lean forward.

"You can't take it, Lars." He took time to swallow. "It's money earned at poor people's expense; it hasn't been earned honestly. You'll be paid for your services with dollars earned through prostitution and gambling." He hesitated. "You're not considering this?"

Lawrence's silence was enough to suggest that he hadn't made up his mind.

Michael leaned back and waved his hands.

"You're really considering this, aren't you?"

"That's why I'm here. I haven't said yes, Michael. I did promise I'd call him when I got back."

"You should have told him no," Michael said, infuriated. "That should be a given. You shouldn't need my approval to make that kind of decision. I'm very disappointed in you." He pushed the plate aside as if to dismiss the conversation.

"What do you know about the man who was murdered?" Lawrence asked, dissociating himself from his brother's frustration.

Michael shook his head. "I don't believe we're having this conversation."

Lawrence decided it would not solve anything to become upset with Michael. He would have to reason with his brother.

"I would hope that you, more than anyone else, would understand that my job as a defense attorney is to offer a defense to those accused of a crime. Without this process we may as well find all people accused of a crime guilty and put them away—or kill them. All I want to know, Michael, is what you know about the case. I haven't taken the money—and I won't until I hear your side of what happened."

Michael returned to the sandwich. "The man had a family," he said, examining where to take his next bite.

"Go on," Lawrence said.

"He was a good friend and a good Catholic. He worked with me on the union trade journal. He wrote a column in Spanish. He was intelligent. I believe he had a degree in accounting. He was a diligent worker. He moved fast up the ladder, from truck driver to assisting the secretary/treasurer of the union." He took a bite and followed it with a drink. "After I'd gotten to know him, he confided in me that he was aware of funds being misappropriated—used for loans to syndicate bosses, interest free," he motioned with his hand, "like your friend, Lugano."

"Now you're being facetious—he's not my friend, Michael."

"Sorry. It just makes me furious to think that you are even thinking about taking part in action to let this man Di Angelo go free."

"You think that Di Angelo murdered your friend—what was his name?"

"Martinez, Julio Martinez, and yes, I believe Di Angelo beat him to death with a baseball bat. Maybe you should be talking to his widow."

"How do you know it was Di Angelo? You sound so sure."

"I believe the men who were with him when it happened were friends. They were leaving a union meeting when this man Di Angelo and his cronies approached Julio."

"You mean he killed him right there?" Lawrence looked astonished. "In front of everyone—there are witnesses?"

"I don't know if you've noticed, Lars, but with these mob slayings, witnesses have a habit of not remembering anything—I don't blame them for not wanting to testify. If they do, they end up on the list of missing persons." Lawrence finished the iced tea, and the waitress poured him some more, overfilling the glass. When she left, Lawrence stroked his chin.

"I suppose—unless Di Angelo was trying to protect himself, it doesn't look good—I mean, based on what you believe happened."

"I know he's guilty, Lars. I also know that if there are no witnesses he'll get off. I just don't think that you should be the one to do it. You have too much to forfeit, your reputation, your war record, not everyone got a D.F.C and a Medal of Honor."

Lawrence leaned back and gave his brother an understanding nod of gratitude.

"You know, Michael, I don't give a good crap about that war hero shit—sometimes I get tired of hearing about it." He leaned forward, his voice lowered. "Every time I hear that stuff I see the faces of crew members that never returned, all because I wanted to die."

Michael looked puzzled. "I don't believe you." He searched his mind for something intelligent to say. "Any combat soldier would probably assess the war in the same way; there's always that wish to end it all."

"Is that what you've learned in the confessional, Michael?" Lawrence's tone was sarcastic. For a while both were silent.

Michael apologized first. "I'm sorry, I know you've experienced more hurt than I'll ever begin to know. I didn't mean to sound patronizing, it's just that I really can't imagine wanting to die. Then again, given the conditions you experienced—all I know is what I've seen in movies." He laughed. Soon Lawrence joined until the laughter died into silence. He rotated the empty glass.

"You wouldn't find my reasons for dying in the movies, Michael; it wouldn't make good cinematography." Michael's face took on a look of curiosity. Lawrence continued, "I wanted to die, Michael, because of what I'd become. It was a long time before I realized that I wanted to live—that I had something to live for." He swallowed the remains of the iced tea. "I met someone in London that made my life worth living. He loved me for what I really was—and I guess I loved him." He could see that his recollections were bothering Michael. "He was killed in a German bombing raid. Soon afterwards, I was shipped home. Funny, isn't it?"

Michael's inquiring look asked the question.

Lawrence went on. "What I find ironic is that I can have women and don't want them, and you—you probably want them and can't have them."

Michael did not respond at once. He sensed it was Lawrence's way of putting off discussion of the topic they had side-stepped again and again.

"Maybe it's time you came to confession. Sounds to me like you could do with a good conscience cleansing," Michael said, breaking the silence.

The sun's rays had dropped below the umbrella and reached Lawrence's face. He pulled sun glasses from his top pocket and placed them over his eyes with both hands.

"That's one thing I hope I never become: hypocritical. When you see me in the confessional, Michael…" He smiled winsomely, "I'd probably be the priest and that, my friend, won't happen."

"That's something I'll remember to pray for, Lars."

"Speaking of which," Lawrence said, "this Di Angelo situation—your self-confidence would lead me to believe that since you weren't there at the crime scene, you no doubt heard all the accounts of the murder in the confessional."

Michael's downcast glance suggested Lawrence was right.

"Do you believe that what you're told in the confessional is always true?"

Michael made an attempt to answer, but Lawrence continued. "Hell, even if you could speak up it wouldn't rule out that you hadn't been lied to."

"I don't believe that," Michael said.

"Well, I guess it really doesn't matter, does it, Michael? Because you're not going to tell another soul anyway." Michael was becoming angry.

"I know that Di Angelo is guilty and it upsets me that you might be representing him. It upsets me that you can't see that you're being used, which leads me to believe something else."

"What's that?"

"Why you? It sounds to me that any Italian lawyer could get this guy off, especially the way they fix juries, and I wouldn't doubt for a moment that they have the judge in their employ also. So I ask, why you?"

"I don't know, Michael. I'd like to think it was because I am a damn good attorney. Why, what's you're opinion?"

"I hate to burst your bubble, Lars, but I think they're trying to buy a New York Senator."

"Don't be ridiculous, Michael," Lawrence said in an unconvincing tone.

Michael could see that he had touched a nerve. He ate the last of the sandwich, wiped his mouth, and laid the napkin on the table. "Let me ask you something, Lars. Really, don't you think that it's just the least bit curious that Lugano asked you? You're Irish, a war hero on his way to becoming a Senator of one of the most important states in the union." He paused. "Aren't you the least bit curious?"

Lawrence waited to answer, shaking his head as if he were talking to himself. "I still don't believe your theory," he mumbled, "Lugano wouldn't go to that much trouble—I mean, if he wants to buy my favor—" He hesitated, thinking about the fee he had called generous when Lugano offered it.

Michael could see that Lawrence was becoming convinced.

"Once you take their money you're hooked, they'll own you. You're not that stupid to think that this will be the end. I wouldn't doubt for a moment that the verdict has already been determined. Lugano has bought the jury or the judge, or both, and you're just along for the ride." Michael realized that his voice had risen, and people were staring. He leaned forward, speaking softly.

"Dear God, Lars, you're better than all that. Protecting criminals you know to be guilty is disgraceful—I know two people at least who won't be very proud and in case you didn't notice, I'm concerned for your safety myself."

"Ahh, now I'm beginning to see my brother's motives, *Michael, qui tolis pecata mundi.*"

"No, Lawrence, I'm just concerned about your sins."

"You don't want to hear about my sins," Lawrence said defensively. Michael knew that when Lawrence attacked him personally, he was getting through to his brother.

"Let me ask you something, Lars—and I want an honest answer, okay?"

Lawrence leaned forward on folded arms and looked deferential. "Fine. Shoot."

"Do you believe the fee you've been offered to—well, let's say, to be a lot more than one might expect—even exorbitant?"

"I suppose it is a lot, yes."

"And do you think that it would be easier for Lugano to buy the jury than depend on your expertise—assuming of course that some of the witnesses were willing to come forward?" Lawrence was becoming uncomfortable, knowing where his brother was going.

"Maybe you should have been the attorney and me the priest."

"Please, Lawrence, just humor me. If you agree that Lugano can fix the jury, why do you think he needs to pay you a ton of money?"

Lawrence was silent.

"If you ask me, my learned brother, it's because Lugano wants to own a Senator. I don't believe—with all due respect—that he wants you as a lawyer. He wants a New York Senator in his back pocket."

Lawrence hated his brother's judgmental position; reluctantly, he nodded in agreement. "Well, if you're right, I've been a real dimwit, haven't I?"

"I happen to think you're a better lawyer than that, Lars." Michael placed his hand on his brother's and knew it was time now to bolster Lawrence's ego. "And you're going to make a great Senator. This case will not make you popular with honest people." Lawrence ignored the attempt at reconciliation.

"And all the time I thought they wanted me for my brains. Damn!" He struck the table with his fist so loud that some of the patrons looked their way. "Damn," he repeated in lowered voice.

After Lawrence left his brother, he felt like a drink and directed the cab driver to take him to his office. It was shortly after three p.m. when he reached in the bottom drawer of his desk and produced a bottle of Power's whiskey. He poured himself a tall drink, rested his feet on the desk, and thought about how he was going to refuse Lugano's offer. By the time the glass was drained he was ready to make the call. The phone rang twice and a woman answered. Soon the familiar deep voice he recognized as Lugano's sounded in his ear. "Lugano."

Lawrence's silence prompted him to repeat himself.

"This is Giovanni Lugano. Who is this?"

"Lawrence Riordan here, Mr. Lugano."

"Ah, Riordan. Good to hear from you. I hope you're calling with—how should I put it—worthy news."

Lawrence was glad now that he'd had a drop of courage.

"I want you to know I'm honored that you asked me to represent Mr. Di Angelo—I'm afraid, though, that I'm going to have to decline your offer. I wouldn't do him justice, not with all the campaigning I have to do." He didn't care for the silence and went on. "You understand, don't you?" More silence. "Mr. Lugano?"

"If it's more money you need…"

"No, it's not the money."

"You know we'll be most helpful lending our influence to assure your nomination."

"I have no doubt, Mr. Lugano…"

"Seventy-five grand—and a guarantee that you'll be the next Senator of our great state, Mr. Riordan." This time Lawrence was voiceless.

"Well, what will it be?" Lugano said.

"I'm going to have to refuse. I just don't believe I could spend the time on the case. I think it would be better to ask a lawyer with more time to better represent your friend."

"One hundred thousand dollars, and that's my final offer, Mr. Riordan. If you say no—well you know where I stand on my loyalties in the Senate race. Nothing personal, it's just that I'm a believer in quid pro quo. You can understand that, can't you?"

Lawrence thought about the conversation with his brother. Michael was right. It all made sense now. Lugano was buying his way to the Senate. He wasn't sure if it was the Powers, but it was finally a good feeling saying no to one of the most powerful men in New York.

One week later, Francis Bickford, the firm's senior partner, came into Lawrence's office. Francis Bickford was working toward his retirement, which meant hardly working at all. In his day, he was a powerful trial attorney, a strong defender of blue-collar workers who had little or no money to fight the big companies. All his life he had visions of going into politics but delayed too long. Now in his mid-sixties, grossly overweight and tired most of the time, all he wanted to do was settle back and take the grandkids fishing.

He asked Lawrence if he had time to spend with a lady who had been referred to them. Lawrence nodded, and soon he was being introduced to an older woman who, Bickford explained, was recently widowed. He knew that Bickford wouldn't have introduced her unless she had a healthy trust account or representing her would prove to be politically advantageous. In any event, she seemed distraught.

Phyllis Boylan had been fleeced. Every sound investment she owned, solid securities, all of her late husband's life savings, were gone. Bickford explained that after her husband's death she had been persuaded to sign everything—stocks, bonds, bank accounts—over to a trust managed by a local investment firm. Unfortunately, the trust director churned her investments. Costs ate up all of the couple's trust. She lost everything. Lawrence shook his head, realizing that companies such as this one, operating within the law, had been furnished a license to legally steal, preying on rich widows, among them Phyllis Boylan. Bickford whispered to Lawrence that this was a case that would do well for him in the newspapers. Lawrence nodded and smiled, thinking that there wasn't a case anywhere that didn't have political implications.

The woman, in her sixties, was petite. Her lips were tight; although she appeared fearful, her blue eyes were bright, curious, and still youthful. Lawrence thought that she was probably very pretty when she was younger. She seemed nervous, uncomfortable in this office. Her husband, she said, had handled all the couple's investments.

Bickford opened the door. "Shall I have Carol hold your calls?"

"Yes, that would be fine, thank you, Francis."

He left them alone, closing the door behind him.

As she talked about the looting of her account by the investment firm, Lawrence became infuriated. If there was ever a case showing the need for decency and probity, Lawrence knew that this was it. He was enraged at the actions of depraved individuals in business who thought nothing of stealing all this poor woman's savings. There was a statute of limitations. If he was going to help, he would have to work fast. He was enthusiastic about pressing ahead, bringing the case to court. Political implications receded as motivation. His political aspirations were becoming more distant each day. He had less than a week to prepare. It meant a lot of library time for research. He promised Mrs. Boylan that he would do everything in his power to recover her money. He was shaking her hand when Bickford appeared again after knocking briefly.

"Excuse me, Lawrence," he gestured to Phyllis Boylan, "Pardon my intrusion, Mrs. Boylan." He turned back to Lawrence. "Carol had to go to the post office. I'm filling in, though not nearly as good looking." His humor fell flat. "This seems to be your day for contributing to the pages of justice. There's a gentleman to see you. He didn't have an appointment but says it's very important that he discuss a very delicate matter with you. Your partners are beginning to feel like second-class lawyers here," he joked again. Lawrence gave a laid-back smile. "Shall I have him wait?"

"That's all right, Francis, we were just finished. What's his name?"

"Mr. Kenny, er, David I believe, David Kenny." Lawrence thought for a moment, then dismissed the idea that he knew anyone by that name. He turned to Phillis Boylan.

"I'll call you mid-week, Mrs. Boylan," he said, "and don't worry, we'll find some way to get back your savings." She thanked him and left. In a moment he was shaking hands with a tall, thin man with a white mustache that gave him a sophisticated look. His left hand clutched an impressive briefcase.

"Mr. Riordan, it's a pleasure to meet you," McIntee said. Bickford excused himself, shutting the door. Lawrence asked the older man to take a seat, then he returned to his black-leather chair behind the desk.

"I'm afraid I can't place the name, it's not familiar," Lawrence said curiously, his brow furrowed. "What can I do for you, Mr. Kenny?"

"I apologize for not calling and making an appointment," McIntee said. "Mind if I smoke?" McIntee offered the pack to Lawrence.

"No, thank you…and no, I don't mind." McIntee lit the cigarette with an expensive gold Cartier. He took a deep drag and talked on the exhaled smoke.

"I'm afraid my intentions are not what your colleague outside thought them to be. I've managed to see you under false pretenses, you might say."

"I'm not sure I understand."

"Let's just say I'm a voice out of the past. In a way, your past."

"I still don't get it—I can tell you have a slight Irish accent." His eyes lit, his face looked less puzzled. "Are you a friend of the family?"

"You could say that, yes, a friend of the family. On your mother's side," McIntee said, enjoying the cat-and-mouse game.

Lawrence was becoming impatient. "I'm afraid I'm very busy. Why don't you just state your business Mr. —"

"Kenny," McIntee said, "David Kenny."

"Kenny—yes, if you could come to the point we'll see if there's something I can do for you."

"Fair enough, Mr. Riordan," McIntee said, his large, bony hands putting the briefcase on the desk. "I'd like to show you something that I'm sure will be of interest." He opened the briefcase, unfolded the yellowed newsprint and laid it right-side up toward Lawrence. Initially Lawrence showed no emotion. He stared at the paper, not believing that this was happening. "Does the picture bring back some fond memories, Mr. Riordan?"

Lawrence gazed in disbelief at the double-truck page that occupied most of the desk top. His mouth was agape for a long time, his eyes staring blankly, reading the headline over and over. It was obvious the men in the photo were friends; he hoped that the story would identify them only as friends. His thoughts returned to the day the picture was taken, regretting the event then and even more now. Subheads struck him like giant hammers pounding, making his heart race. Key words in the text had been high-lighted: *homosexual, affairs, unknown American serviceman,* all reverberating in his mind, conjuring up ghosts of the past. He first assumed that Lugano was behind this blackmail threat. He recalled Lugano's insinuation: if he wasn't on the team, Lugano would have to go with the competition. His voice was mute. McIntee relaxed, slumping back into the chair, his mouth pursed, making smoke rings.

"Of course you recognize the other man?" There was no response.

"Let me restate that, Mr. Riordan. You obviously recognize the other queer in the photo, don't you?" Lawrence's mouth was tight with anger. "You bastards will stop at nothing," he managed to say.

"Bastards?" McIntee said with a derisive grin. "That's a whole other subject we can discuss later."

"Well, you can tell your friend Lugano to get fucked," Lawrence said quickly, rising to his feet. "Now you can get the fuck out of here before I forget I'm half your age and stuff your goddamn head in the waste basket—and set it on fire." McIntee slowly stood and extinguished the cigarette on the desk ashtray, closed the briefcase and moved toward the door. He turned before opening the door.

"You're making a big mistake, Mr. Riordan. I can go, if that's the way you want it—I just don't think that this article spread all over tomorrow's *New York Times* is going to do much for your shot at the Senate—to say nothing of your law career. By the way, you can keep the article. The *London Times* has another copy on file." He opened the door. Lawrence stopped him.

"Wait." Lawrence's tone changed. "Please, you have to understand my anger," he pleaded. "Please, Mr. Kenny, let's at least hear what you have to offer. That's what Lugano wants, isn't it, for us to talk?"

McIntee returned and sat. He lit another cigarette, this time without permission. Lawrence stood and glared out the window, looking at his own reflection. He needed time to gather his senses, time to reason out this mess, for if a story based on this article appeared in the tabloid newspapers, the scandal would ruin his family. He turned to face McIntee.

"What does Mr. Lugano want me to do?" he asked tentatively. McIntee didn't understand Lawrence's reference to Lugano. He decided that allowing Lawrence to continue believing that this man Lugano had something to do with the blackmail would subvert his plan.

"My being here has nothing to do with this Lugano you keep referring to. This is just between you and me." Lawrence sat down slowly. The look on his face changed from surprise to confusion and eventually anger.

"Who the hell are you then—and what are you doing with this?" Lawrence threw the paper at him.

"You don't deny then what the article suggests, that you had an affair with this McCabe fag?"

"Would you believe that we were just good friends, Mr. Kenny?" McIntee was slow to answer.

"I really don't think so, Mr. Riordan." He leaned toward Lawrence. "Why don't we leave that proposition for nosy newspaper reporters to clear up? They'll lock onto this like pit-bulls."

Lawrence realized that he was right. If there was ever a time to test this blackmailer, it was now. "First, I have a hunch your name isn't Kenny, is it?"

McIntee's response was curt. "That's not important, is it Mr. Riordan? Any more than you may not be who you think you are."

Lawrence determined to remain calm. "It would be easier for me to cooperate if I knew who you really are and what you want."

"Who I am isn't important. Let's just leave it that I'm an old friend of your mother. As for what I want?" He played the game for all it was worth. "A hundred and fifty grand should keep this"—he pointed a bony finger at the paper—"from becoming tomorrow's headlines."

"You're out of your fucking mind," Lawrence said, his face taking on a red glow. His fist came down hard on the desk.

"Fine then," McIntee said, unperturbed. He stood and grasped the briefcase. "If I go out the door this time, Mr. Riordan, the story gets printed." Lawrence rubbed his hands together nervously.

"Where in the hell do you think I'm going to come up with that kind of money—there's no way in hell."

"How about this Lugano you keep mentioning—sounds to me like he'd like a piece of whatever you have to offer. Maybe he just wants a piece of your ass," McIntee said bitterly. "On the other hand, you might have something of more value. You're a bright young man. Let me leave you with this thought. I don't give a good fuck where you get the money. I would strongly suggest that you explore all possibilities."

McIntee had no idea that things would go this well. He pursued a notion. "What do you think Mr. Lugano would give to have this information?"

Lawrence chewed on his lower lip, cursing himself for allowing the photo to be taken. Lugano could exploit secrets. Consequences might be worse. Answer a question with a question, he thought.

"It might help—what I mean is—well, if we're going to enter into an agreement, it might help if I knew how you came by this—information, Mr. Kenny. How do I know this is legitimate? It would help me decide to cooperate if there was—shall we say, authentication. For example, you said you were a friend of my mother's." Lawrence felt more at ease asking questions that would reveal McIntee's identity.

"Good try, Mr. Riordan. Let's just leave things the way they are for now, shall we?" He rose from the chair and dragged the briefcase from the table.

"Tell you what I'll do. I'm going to be very generous here and give you until the end of the month." He walked again to the door. He held his hand on the brass door knob and turned to face Lawrence, "Oh, about that bastard business?" he continued. "On top of all this, you're a bastard."

Lawrence was weak and angry. This couldn't be happening. He would wake up soon and find this a bad dream.

"Think about it. Naturally that includes your brother, the priest. I'll call you in a day or two to see how your pursuit of the payment is going." McIntee chortled as he opened the door. "Both of you—bastards."

The words trailed and Lawrence sat in silence, staring into space. The horrible notion that he might be who Kenny said he was absorbed all reasoning—a bastard. Talking to his mother was out of the question. Calling his brother was an option he entertained, but he thought it best to wait. Committing suicide seemed an easier solution. He looked for consolation. Lugano didn't seem part of the blackmail; however, he looked like the only source for the payoff to Kenny.

CHAPTER FIFTY-NINE

AUGUSTIN FLEMMING WAS growing impatient. He had been attending mass regularly, always with Michael Riordan presiding. He had become more of a Catholic than McIntee could ever have envisaged. He tithed such a substantial amount to the parish that the secretary made it a point to seek him out after mass and smile appreciatively. In return, he doffed his hat, after which he was always invited to join the parishioners for coffee and donuts in the parish hall. He managed never to overstay his welcome or be too talkative. He believed that he had made inroads with Michael Riordan.

Early on, he made it a point to ask Michael if he wouldn't mind hearing his confession openly. Without being anonymous, he could gain the priest's confidence. He enjoyed lying. There weren't many sins he had to invent; however, it was important that he give the priest the impression that he was a good man. All the sins were menial, or as the Catholics said, venial. There was some small degree of truth only when he talked about his wife's death. He felt responsible. He wasn't lying when he told Michael that he just wasn't around as much as he should have been. His love for business had taken all his time, especially looking after his investments in the stock market. Becoming a very rich man was no substitution for his lost family.

When the confession concluded, Flemming was amazed at his sense of appreciation for Michael's words. He felt better because everything he had done to hurt his family was forgiven by this holy man. As the months passed, Flemming's time confessing to Michael lasted only a few minutes.

His dramatic performance was showing signs of working. Michael began to confide in him after listening to his theories of successful investing.

Flemming met with McIntee every Monday night, always at a different location. This Monday night was routine. He arrived at Mickey O'Doul's Public House in Brooklyn twenty minutes early and ordered a beer. McIntee was on time. He looked tired and dropped into the seat across from Flemming.

"Well, my portly friend, how are the confessions coming along?" When the waiter returned, McIntee ordered an Irish neat. Flemming delayed his answer until the waiter left.

"I'm down to no sins at all—just maintenance."

"I'm not talkin' about your goddamn sins. Has he said anything to you about maybe you helping him out?"

"Not exactly, well other than information. He does seem to confide in me that way but so far he hasn't asked for any money."

"You're sure you conveyed to him that you were filthy rich. You got that across?"

"I told you that a long time ago. He knows I'm loaded."

McIntee gulped the whiskey and shook his head. "Maybe the time is right—maybe it's time to give him the ol' sickness routine. Do you think he's ready to believe that you would leave the church that much money?"

"I have no doubt that he believes I have no family. I know he thinks I'm a good Catholic. I've also led him to believe that since I've lost my wife and family because of my preoccupation with money, I'm more than willing to leave it to a just cause. I mentioned many times that I'm considering leaving it to some children's organization."

"And what does he say to that?"

"It's just a feeling, mind you, but I think, well, sometimes I get the impression he wants to talk about it—like maybe he has other ideas."

McIntee looked excited. "Like feathering his nest a little maybe."

When the waiter returned, they ordered another round.

"You've done a fine job," McIntee said euphorically. "Do you think he's ready for the death scene?"

"Frankly, I thought he'd have gone for it a while back—yep, I'd say he's more than ripe."

"Do you still think you can pull this thing off without him calling your doctor? That could really fuck things up."

"I'm sure. Remember, after I donate the stocks, I'm still goin' to be around. I'm dying but I'm not dead yet. I'm still his friend, even helping with the idea of borrowing on the investment."

"That's the most important thing, Gus. You have to convince him to borrow money against the stock, okay?"

"Don't worry. I'm actually looking forward to this acting job. Ya know what I really get a kick out of?"

"What's that?"

"When he forgives me—now I'm lookin' forward to him feeling really sad because I'm dying."

"Make sure you tell him that this is a private matter—just between you and him, okay?"

"Okay."

"That's very important. I don't want anyone getting ideas about looking out for your goddamn interest. They love you so fukken much I wouldn't put it past some do-gooder widow lookin' for a second opinion from some other doctor in the parish. I can't stress the importance of this being kept between you and the priest."

McIntee looked pensive. "You're sure he's ready to bite on the deal, Gus?"

"One thing for sure, I've learned—at least about this priest, aside from his obvious intelligence: he's honest, trusting, gullible and greedy. From what I can figure out, the Cardinal's put him in a bit of a hot seat. I have exactly what this poor bastard needs and I'm certain he's goin' to buy off on the deal."

"Timing is everything," McIntee said seriously.

Flemming agreed. They had another round. He filled McIntee in on the tremendous profits the print shop was making. Ignoring Flemming's outpourings, McIntee formulated images of the priest's demise. Soon now he would get to play his part in the game, the injured party. He couldn't wait to see the priest's face torn with disbelief when he would tell him that the stocks he held were counterfeit. He would surely have spent or committed the borrowed money to some cause or other, and, unable to return it, would be looking at some very harsh punitive damages. Hell, he might even be the cause of bankrupting the Archdiocese of New York. The Catholic Church would do anything rather than let that happen, he thought. They might even sacrifice a priest. McIntee hadn't heard a word Flemming said. He was still smiling when they left the warmth of the pub and ventured into the cold darkness, where it had begun to rain. God, what better time for all this tragedy to befall the priest than the Christmas season, he thought.

Almost a month had passed and McIntee was soon to include Kathleen Thornton in the scheme. The sun hadn't yet emerged to warm the morning. McIntee mentioned to the cabbie that it was getting cold and asked him to turn on the motor. He had been waiting for over an hour for Ryan to leave. He lit a cigarette and checked the time again. It was a few minutes after seven. He looked back impatiently toward the house and mumbled something to himself about running late. At last the front door opened and Ryan appeared. He hurried, giving Kathleen a quick peck on the cheek and rushing to his car. This was the first time McIntee had seen her in over thirty years. From what he could tell, she was still beautiful.

After Ryan started his car, he drove away, not waiting to warm it. McIntee was surprised that Ryan didn't pay more attention to the cab as he passed. Before he stepped out of the cab, he waited awhile longer to make sure Ryan hadn't forgotten something and returned to the house. He handed the cabbie a twenty and told him to go somewhere for coffee for two hours.

McIntee looked like a friendly, well-to-do gentleman in his fawn cashmere overcoat and Homburg. His brown-leather gloves had been chosen with an eye for style. He walked up the steps to the front door and rang the bell.

"I'm coming, darlin'," he heard her say, the latch quickly turning to unlock the door, which she opened broadly. Embarrassed, she groped at the collar of her robe, and she narrowed the opening of the door.

"Oh, my, I'm awfully sorry. My husband was running a little late; I just thought he was —"

"Kathleen," McIntee said, raising his gloved hand to stop her rambling. "Kathleen Barrett, or should I say Thornton?"

She shook her head. "I'm terribly sorry, Mr —"

"Sean McIntee—have I changed that much?"

Her mouth opened, but no words came forth.

"Well—are you just goin' to stand there and leave me out in the cold or do I get a bit of a hug for auld time's sake."

"Oh, my God, I don't believe it," she said, opening the door wide, "Come on in—and how is Bridget?" she said, all in one breath. She remembered the last time she heard mention of his name. Jailed for what was it? Mobster activity of some kind or other. She looked blankly past him as he embraced her, and she allowed him to kiss her cheek.

"Bridget is always askin' for ye," he said, removing his hat.

"Here, let me take that," she offered, trying to appear hospitable. After she put his hat and overcoat on hangers, she rushed about clearing the table of all signs of breakfast.

"I'm sorry the place is such a mess," she said, breathlessly trying to reorganize the morning paper. She gestured to the easy chair by the unlit fireplace. "Please, Sean, make yourself at home." McIntee took notice of family pictures on the mantel. On either side of the ornate clock, miniature gold-framed photos gave a capsule summary of the family's history. He picked one up and held it for closer scrutiny.

"So this must be your husband?"

"Yes—his name's Ryan," she said over clattering dishes in the sink. "That picture was taken a long time ago. He was a policeman in Boston at the time." She dried her hands and filled the kettle. "How about a cup of tea?"

"If it's not too much trouble," he said, easing into the chair.

"God, I can't believe it's you," she said, "after all these years. What have you been doing with yourself? Last time I heard, you were…" She hesitated. It was important to have her mind put at rest before she would feel comfortable enough to talk openly about other things.

"Jail?" he said, finishing her thoughts. She looked mortified. "I'm really sorry, Sean," she said, flummoxed, "if it's any consolation at all, I was horrified when I heard the news. I don't know if it helped any but I said a lot of prayers."

"Well, then," he smiled, "that must have been the reason I survived, eh! Would you believe they put me away for doing what I'd been brought up to do in Dublin—selling whiskey." His smile and apparent rectitude seemed to set her at ease. "The difference here was that it was illegal." He reached into his inside jacket pocket and took a cigarette from the case without offering one to her. She waved away his apology. "So you never took up the habit?"

"Never even had the urge."

"You're the lucky one then. Mind if I…"

"Please," she said, "dear God I must look awful." She changed the subject. "While we're waiting for the kettle to boil, I think I'll take a moment to change into something decent."

"You look great to me," he said, blowing smoke from the corner of his mouth. She turned and walked into what he presumed was the bedroom. After she closed the door, he stood to examine the photos on the mantelpiece. He recognized Lawrence in the photo by his Army Air Force uniform. He quickly passed over the photo of Maggie, remembering Bridget having mentioned something about a daughter who died. A sinister grin coincided with the thought that fate had taken care of one member of the family. He moved over to the roll-top desk and opened the center drawer. Brushing aside bills, he eyed an envelope with a familiar name in the return address: William Hamilton, New York. He took out the letter, put it in a pocket, and returned to the chair. He contemplated her appearance. He hoped to find that she still possessed that flirtatious manner. The whistling kettle brought him to attention and announced her presence. She rushed to remove the noisy kettle.

"It's like a timer in my life—this kettle, always going off when I'm in the middle of something." After she made the tea, she finished buttoning the white blouse and turned to face him. "There," she said, "how's that? Is there any resemblance to what I used to be, Sean?" She twirled like a school girl.

"You haven't changed a bit," he said, walking toward her. He held her hands.

"You look as beautiful as you did when I last saw you in Dublin." He wanted to kiss her again, this time on the lips. She drew away politely and sat at the table.

"Take this chair," she said eagerly, "sit and tell me what's going on in your life. I want to hear everything. I'm dying to know what Bridget's been up to."

They talked over tea for an hour. Memories of their innocent youth, first communion, confirmation, childhood games, relievio, and spin the bottle. He spoke of the times when they explored one another's physical differences. She always turned the subject off sex. He reminded her of the time he ran alongside while she rode the bicycle. The only way he could keep up was to have her sit on his hand while he held fast to the saddle. Her face reddened at his ramblings. Many times she attempted to change the conversation, but he continued with his preoccupation, raking memories that were beginning to bother her. He reminded her how he was mad with jealousy when she looked at another boy. He also reminded her that they had been chosen by their parents for marriage.

He allowed her to discuss her past. Now it was his turn again. It was time to direct his attention to what he came for.

"I remember when my life changed," he said bitterly. Unexpectedly, he pushed the cup and saucer aside. "You don't happen to have a drink in the house, do you? I mean something other than tea." Kathleen wished that he would leave; his mood swings frightened her. She considered telling him that there was no liquor and decided that to do so might make him even more belligerent. Dutifully, she took the half bottle of Powers and poured some into a small glass.

"Do you want anything with it, Sean?"

"No, thanks, good Irish whiskey is like a good Scotch, it's always much tastier neat." She handed him the glass and sat down.

"Aren't you having one then?" he said, hoisting the glass.

"It's a little early for me, Sean. Besides," she looked at the clock on the wall, "in a moment I'm going to have to prepare something for Ryan's lunch." McIntee restrained a smile. He knew her husband never came home for lunch. She was not at ease. She was frightened by his presence. He felt powerful.

"It's strange, isn't it, how people's destinies can be changed just like that?" He snapped his fingers.

"I'm not sure I understand," she said quizzically.

He took his time answering. After lighting another cigarette, he brushed the cloud of smoke away with his hand.

"I'm talking about Liam Riordan." He stopped to get her reaction. She stayed silent and acted surprised.

"When Liam Riordan or…" he faltered, "William Hamilton, wasn't it?" Silence. "The day he came on the scene my life changed. You can't imagine what a pain that man has been to me, Kathleen. First he takes you away from me…" He gulped the whiskey.

"And I know you'll find this real hard to believe. The bastard shows up fifteen years later at the other end of the world, no less, and sends me to Alcatraz."

"I'm very sorry about that, Sean, but you're wrong about Liam Riordan. I had nothing to do with him," she said, "I thought at the time that he had turned my father over to the British, remember?"

"Ah, you lie so sweetly, me darlin' Kathleen."

"Excuse me," she managed defiantly, "I think your presence here is no longer welcome." She pushed the chair back and stood. Her face was flushed. "Maybe your little sojourn in Alcatraz has left you with no affinity for the liquor—I think it's gone to your head." McIntee didn't budge. He enjoyed her fear. He waited to see what she was going to do now that he had refused to leave.

"Why don't we get together later, Sean." She tried a more calming overture, moving closer to him, extending her hand, "Sean, our friendship is too important to leave on angry feelings." A sneer crossed his face. He enjoyed her attempt at bravery as he held her hand. He could feel her fear, sensing her slight tug, an effort to make him stand, hoping he would leave. He relished watching her bosom heave. He applied more pressure.

"Please, Sean," she whispered, "please leave now—before Ryan comes home."

He pulled her to his lap and held her tight. She turned away, repulsed by his breath. His right arm wrapped her, restricting the movement of her arms. "Now, now, Kathleen, you're not afraid of little auld Sean, are you?" His left hand moved from her thigh, roaming, fingers touching the underside of her breast. She tried desperately to pull away from the viselike grip.

"He touched you like this, didn't he?" He unbuttoned her blouse. "He fucked you, didn't he, Kathleen?"

She shook her head. Her body trembled as he groped her. "No, Sean, please, don't do this—our friendship…"

"Bullshit," he hollered in her ear. "He fucked you an' got you pregnant. You had the bastards in Boston, didn't you?" He continued, exploring, ripping at her brassiere. "You never did marry Riordan or that fuck Hamilton, did you?"

Tears streamed, she threw her head back, wishing this would end. There was no use trying to make him believe that Ryan was coming home for lunch. He knew that wouldn't be happening.

"Did you? Answer me, you little whore!"

"No," she whispered.

"They're your little bastards, aren't they?" She just shook her head, salt from the tears filling her mouth. "Aren't they?" His mouth was too close.

"Yes."

"And I'd bet your ass that your hubby, Ryan, has no fukken idea whose kids they are. I'd lay you odds that hubby has no idea that your friend Hamilton is the father, has he?"

He had amused himself with her breasts long enough and moved his hand between her legs.

"Stop it!" she screamed and used the only weapon she had left. Drawing her head back as far as it would go, she brought it down furiously, striking him squarely on the bridge of his nose. She could feel it split under the weight of her forehead. Warm blood spewed over them both. He jumped to his feet, immediately releasing her. His hands covered his face; blood oozed through his fingers. Blinded, he groped the air with one hand.

"You fukken bitch—you've broken my goddamn nose." He stumbled toward the front door, stopped, and faced her. "That'll cost you a little more than I was going to ask," he muttered.

Kathleen took the opportunity to grab a carving knife from the drainer and waved it in his direction. "You vile bastard—take one more step toward me, Sean McIntee, and so help me God—I—I promise—I'll carve you like the pig that you are."

Her voice was enraged; he knew that she could. His eyes welled. He laughed nervously, adjusting his position to what he could see of her. He felt nauseated. From his pocket he produced a handkerchief and held it with one hand to his nose, which had an opening across the bridge, the likes of which a bare knuckled pugilist would have been proud to have administered. He cursed silently for allowing his sexual urges to jeopardize his intentions. One stupid moment of stimulation might have endangered all his well-laid plans.

"Get out!" Her voice rose. "Now—I mean it—out!"

"I'll leave after I tell you what I came to tell you and not before," he said nasally.

"Then I'd strongly recommend you get yourself to a whorehouse, Sean McIntee. If I tell my husband what happened here—he'll..."

"He won't do a goddamn thing, Kathleen, and you know it. He's an FBI agent, a law-abiding man. Hell, he can't afford to act like a crazy hoodlum—an asshole like me. No, Kathleen, I think you'd better listen to what I have to say before you make any more stupid statements."

She raised the knife when he began to move closer. He put up his hands defensively. Blood still poured from the gash and he returned the saturated handkerchief to cover his nose. "What I came to talk to you about was your sons," he said in a muffled tone, "and from what I've been reading their futures look—I suppose one could say, promising." She saw that her entire family was threatened. He hadn't come for sex; that was an impulsive act. He had attempted to rape her, but worse, he showed that he was ready to reveal to her husband the identity of her sons' father. He had the power to destroy the life she had made, her marriage, her children, by exposing the original lie.

"I have nothing to say to you about my sons," she said defiantly. It didn't bother her in the least, that when he attempted to say something, he coughed a thick red glob into the handkerchief, which he examined curiously through clouded eyes. He could have choked to death, for all she cared. He cleared his throat. She wished she had the guts to use the knife. She knew that no one would have blamed her. Her actions would have been justified. He had tried to rape her.

"What do you think would happen if it became public?" He coughed again. "That the popular young New York Senator-to-be is a queer?" He assumed by her silence that he would gain by continuing. "I don't suppose it would hurt the other one much—what's his name?"

"Michael," she said, dejected, "Father Michael." She couldn't believe she was having a conversation with this miserable excuse for a human being.

"I suppose Bridget told you about the boys?"

"She did."

"And by any chance did she also tell you who their father was?" she asked.

"She did—it's not what you think."

"How do you know what the hell I think?" she said angrily.

"Bridget is a born gossip," he said. "You should have known that. It wasn't her intention to see this used against you. No, I'm sure my dear sister would be very upset at me right now. Did you also know that at least one of your sons is queer, Kathleen?" Her silence gave him a chance to continue. "Well, of course you did—what mother wouldn't know that her son was an arsehole bandit?"

She placed the knife on the counter and sat at the kitchen table. She realized that he was here to show he knew this secret. What he called her son and the way he said it hurt her. If he wanted to ruin her life, he was being far more successful taking this direction than he would have been by inflicting physical pain. She hadn't felt this disheartened since Maggie's death.

"What do you want of me? If you have proof of all this, why don't you just go to the authorities—the newspapers? Why tell me?"

"Now that wouldn't do me much good, would it? Imagine the fun I'd have giving all this information to your husband, Ryan. How do you think Ryan would feel"—he emphasized the name—"knowing that his devoted little wife was best of friends with William Hamilton, also known in earlier times as Liam Riordan?" Her reaction showed that she hadn't told Ryan about Hamilton.

"I still can't imagine why you haven't gone to the newspapers?" She shouted. Her eyes flared. She raised her head to face him. "If you think for one moment that I would give myself to you—in return for your bloody silence…"

"Don't flatter yourself, Kathleen. If I wanted a good piece of arse it wouldn't be your broken down quim I'd be wantin'."

"What is it then, money? Do I look like I have money to give you?"

"Let's just say that you might have some sources for money—you know, to come up with somethin' reasonable."

"And just what would you consider a reasonable amount of money—speaking of which you do realize that my husband despises extortionists?"

"More than he would despise a wife who lied—who fucked his colleague?"

"That's not true," she shouted again, "that's a lie."

"Try to convince him of that after he finds out you've been seeing him!" He couldn't wait to read the letter in his pocket, hoping it would back up some of his accusations.

"How about an even fifty thousand?"

She stood, shocked by the demand. "How do you expect me to come up with that kind of money? You're out of your mind! And what makes you think I would satisfy your demands—even if I could?"

"Because, Kathleen—you've lived this lie too long. You have to save your son from public knowledge of his embarrassing, perverse, lecherous activities. Also, your husband won't be too understanding of William Hamilton. No, darlin', I think you'll find the money."

She knew he was right. Ryan would never understand, nor did the threat of ruining her son's career look like a real choice. She reluctantly conceded to entertain his demands.

"If I did agree with you—that is—if I had no other options, would you expect the money all at once? And how could I be sure you wouldn't come back for more?" His nose had stopped bleeding, and he put the handkerchief in his pocket. He removed the coat and hat from behind the door and turned to face her.

"You don't," he said, and left her with the rest of the day to shape her thoughts and deal with more lies that would soon follow.

Ryan paid no attention to the speedometer, which was approaching ninety miles an hour. He tried to analyze the phone call he had received after lunch. Kathleen must have been suffering a nervous breakdown. She pleaded with him to come home, yet not once did she say why. He reasoned that she was alone and for the time being, at least, she was not physically harmed. When he asked about Lawrence and Michael, she said that they were not the issue. It could have been bad news from home, her mother, maybe. He thought that even her mother's death wouldn't have made her this despondent. What in the hell was it then? What was it that was so important that it couldn't wait until he got home after work? He nosed the Packard sedan around a slow-moving car, then returned to his lane and back around a truck. He swerved to the far left shoulder to avoid the oncoming car. He could see the fear on the occupants' faces in the other vehicle, an older couple asking what kind of maniac was behind the wheel of the Packard. He was alone again on the road. His mind stopped racing. He looked at the speedometer and slowed the car. It wasn't like her to call him this way, desperate to talk to him right away. He had not the slightest idea what was wrong. He turned the wheel hard and came to a quick stop, knocking over the garbage cans in the driveway. He rushed up the stairs; she opened the door to greet him. She was shaking. Tear stains blotted her cheeks. Blood covered her white blouse. He held her trembling body.

"It's all right, Kathleen—it's all right, I'm here now. You're going to be just fine." He held her until she stopped shaking.

"There—everything's going to be all right." He walked her inside and kept one arm around her. She did not seem to be cut anywhere. He looked to see where the blood came from. He helped her sit and noticed the two cups, whiskey, and empty glass on the table.

"Who was here, Kathleen?" he said, gently kneeling beside her. He waited.

"Sean McIntee was here," she said, yielding.

His eyes squinted. "McIntee—isn't he the one—your Irish friend, the one that William put away over twenty years ago? He was here?"

"Yes, he came back—let him in thinking that…" Her voice trailed and tears welled in her eyes. "I thought he was—well, a friend, you know?"

"I know," he said. "Where did all the blood come from—did he hurt you?" It was the first time she smiled. "No, but I think I hurt him." Ryan took his time. "Did he try to hurt you? Do you think you should see a doctor?"

"No—the blood is his, he tried to rape me." Her body shuddered. "He tried to rape me, Ryan—so I used my head."

"That's my girl." She saw that he was trying to pacify her.

"No, I mean it! He had my arms pinned, so I used my head—I think I broke his nose."

Ryan was furious with himself for not being there. His face grew tense. "That swine," he said under his breath, holding back the urge to stand and shout that he wanted to kill the bastard.

"Let's get you into the shower and then to bed. You're sure you don't need to see a doctor?"

"He never touched me—not that way."

After she showered and put on clean clothes, they sat quietly in the living room and he poured two straight whiskeys and handed her one.

"While you were getting cleaned up, Kathleen, I put in a call to New York."

"New York?" she asked curiously.

"Yes. I made a call to William. He knows more about this thug than anyone. Don't you worry. We'll get him—and this time he won't get out. He'll go away for good."

"No, you mustn't Ryan," she said emphatically. "What I mean is, he's not worth it."

"You're worth it," he said. "As soon as William calls me back…"

"No, Ryan." Her tone was resigned. "We can't—look, Ryan, there's something I have to tell you." She had concluded that there was no good time to tell him about her secrets. She had withheld the truth about her love for Hamilton from him all these years and he had a right to know. He had to know of her shame, her parents' need to send her away to have the baby, and her need to create a marriage that never existed. She began at the beginning. She spoke of the young man who came into her life, Liam Riordan. As she spoke, he nodded approvingly, understanding most of the history. It was when she mentioned that Liam Riordan and William Hamilton were one and the same that he stopped her. He shook his head, staring at her, his face frozen.

"Whoa—wait a minute, you're going too fast for me. Are you telling me that Michael and Lawrence are…"

"That's right, William Hamilton's sons." There, she'd said it. She didn't care anymore. It really didn't seem all that difficult and she silently wished she'd come forward much earlier. Ryan was silent. He stared at the ceiling, all sorts of disturbing thoughts occupying his mind. He couldn't believe what he had heard. All these years, his good friend William Hamilton was the father of his boys. At least that's how he thought of them. The look on his face told her that this wasn't working as well as she had hoped. He was first to break the silence.

"I don't believe this—my wife of more than thirty years and my best friend—Jesus Christ, Kathleen, how could you keep this from me all these years—and why in the hell didn't you tell me this before?"

"Don't you see, Ryan? After a while it seemed so unimportant, after all, it happened so long ago. I still doubt that all this would be necessary if Sean McIntee wasn't going to blackmail me. I have no doubt that he is going to tell the papers about Lawrence's homosexuality. I'm sure of that, unless—unless we can come up with fifty thousand dollars."

"Fifty thousand! Christ, why didn't he ask for a million?" He sprang up abruptly and paced the room.

"How long did this little affair of yours go on?" he asked, in short-tempered tones. It was her turn to be upset. "That kind of question may be the reason I didn't bother to tell you the truth in the first place."

"So you do admit to lying."

"You're twisting my words."

"Well—why don't you try putting yourself in my goddamn place—I've just been told by my wife that she was having an affair with my best friend."

"There's no need for profanity, Ryan Thorton, and it wasn't an affair."

"Well just what the hell do you call it when your wife screws your best friend?" Her face flushed, she stared at him, her eyes zeroing in on his. She stood, walked into the bedroom and turned the lock. He stopped pacing and tried opening the door.

"Kathleen, open the door. Open the door, Kathleen, this conversation isn't finished." He listened for a response. "Kathleen," he said louder.

"Open the goddamn door so we can talk this through." Still no response. "I knew there was something going on. Nobody hangs around a married couple like that without something going on. It isn't natural. I could kill that bastard." He heard the door unlock and she threw it open.

"You're getting all upset over the wrong man. God Almighty! I don't understand you anymore. Sean McIntee comes into my home and nearly rapes me and you're thinking about killing our best friend."

"Correction, my dear, your best friend. He's the one who's been deceiving me all these years—after you, that is."

"You bastard," she said vehemently, "you lousy bastard. You don't really care about my feelings at all, do you? I'm like a piece of property." He had never before seen her so angry. He wanted to hold her, stop all this nonsense. He wanted things to return to the way they were. He pulled her to him and held her. She locked her arms around his waist.

"My God, what's happening to us?" he whispered.

"We seem to be having one of the very worst quarrels of our lives," she whispered. They stayed that way for a long time, holding on to one another, knowing things would never be the same. For Ryan, too many questions were unanswered. He was remembering times they'd been together as a threesome. All the times he tried to set Hamilton up with a date and every time it was a failure. He had considered the possibility that his good friend might be of another persuasion. He couldn't leave it alone that his wife may have been the reason for his indifference when it came to other women.

"Do the twins know?" He posed his question as politely as he could. "Know what?"

"You know—that Hamilton's their father?"

"No, they think he died in the war."

"I wish he had died in the war."

She pulled back. "Ryan Thornton, that's a terrible thing to say."

"Well, it's true, isn't it? If he had died we wouldn't be having this problem, would we?" She remained silent, and he thought awhile before posing the next question.

"Did you still love him when we got married?" Nothing. "Somehow I had the feeling you did." He waited. No response. He continued the policeman tactics. "I know this is as hard for you as it is me, but I have to know." His voice was gentle. "Do you still love him?"

She turned away and stared out the kitchen window. How could she explain her love for two men? She could not in this moment of turmoil.

He seemed to be pursuing her apparent infidelity instead of concentrating attention on the man who was trying to ruin their lives. She could not respond to his questions.

He walked behind her and placed his hands on her hips. He could see her reflected face in the window. "If you can't answer my questions, Kathleen, I can only assume that you still love him. Is that what you want me to believe?"

She folded her arms like a disobedient child. He could see her jaw line tighten. The reflection looked unsympathetic. He removed his hands. She didn't wish to dignify his insults with an answer and yet didn't quite know what to expect of his silence. She wanted to say something, anything, but she knew that a word would lead to further questions. He would never believe the decision that both she and William had made not to see one another in that way again. That decree would lead to other questions, like the time Hamilton had him sent out of town on a case so that he could be alone with her. My God, she thought, that would drive him away for sure. Where was she going to draw the line on the truth? It seemed to her now that there were so many questions that would hurt him. She turned only after she saw his reflection rotate away and move toward the door.

"Ryan, please try to understand," she said weakly, "I do love you." Mindful of his torment, she looked for a sign that his love for her was stronger than his anger. He never turned back to face her, and she did not see the hate and misery in his eyes.

CHAPTER SIXTY

P HYLLIS BOYLAN AND Lawrence sat at the same time-worn mahogany table where they were seated when the jury had delivered a decision in her favor just ten days earlier. To their left the same two silk-suited lawyers conversed in loud whispers with the defendants from the bond firm of McRae and Webber Securities. They had contested the jury's decision and now all waited for the judge to hear their plea for review of the verdict. Soon the sound of a door opening announced the entrance of Benjamin Alexander Caplin. He entered the courtroom briskly, his destination the tall, black, diamond-tufted leather chair like some great throne awaiting his presence. Caplin was in his late fifties, slightly built with thick, silver-colored hair. He was a Jew who practiced his faith judiciously and kept kosher. Prior to becoming a judge, he was a principal with one of the most prestigious anti-trust law firms in New York, and widely respected for his adherence to high standards. Lawrence reasoned that after the trial, when the jury foreman announced the guilty verdict, Judge Caplin had an agreeable look on his face and would no doubt uphold their decision.

"Please rise." The robust voice came from the bailiff, a giant of a man with a clean-shaven head. "The New York State Supreme Court is now in session." Caplin strode up the few steps to the great seat, lifted the robe and sat.

"All may be seated," the bailiff continued, and noisy seats shuffled as the parties at the tables adjusted their bodies for the arguments. Caplin took time to put on reading glasses and sorted the papers on the desk. To renew familiarity with the parties arguing the case, he looked at the plaintiff and her attorney, then fixed his gaze on Rich Calvo, remembered as the dominant silk suit, the man whom he found irritating with his annoying nervous habit of tapping his pencil on the table. Caplin felt disgust for the man whose face, he remembered, gleamed of mocking self-satisfaction when an argument terminated in his favor. How well he remembered Calvo, with his black, slicked-back hair and over-confident air.

"Counselor, I've read your brief on the motions raised, to wit, to reverse the verdict, grant a new trial, or reduce the amount specified in the verdict on the basis of passion and prejudice." Caplin's eyes never left Calvo, and his voice was stern. "How do you wish to handle this, Mr. Calvo?" Rich Calvo pushed back his chair and stood.

"If the court pleases." He cleared his throat. "Your Honor, I'd like to talk about the issues chronologically." Caplin, slowly removing his glasses with one hand, nodded for Calvo to continue. "Proceed, Mr. Calvo." The man with the slicked-back hair took five minutes to review the jury selection.

"And therefore, Your Honor, we feel that passion and prejudice were factors in this case from the beginning."

"The beginning?" Caplin looked curious.

"That's right, Your Honor, from the time the jury was selected."

"I'm not sure I know what you mean."

"Our contention is, Your Honor, that counsel's client, a very lovely lady, is the image of everybody's mother, and we feel that a jury composed of twelve men with no offsetting safeguards, having women jurors, for example, resulted in every juror feeling like…well, like a son, if you will. It was implicit in the way they received her testimony and we feel that the verdict reflects passion and prejudice."

The Judge, seeing that Calvo had completed his statement, turned to Lawrence. "Mr. Riordan?"

Lawrence stood. "Thank you, Your Honor," he said ingratiatingly. "Correct me if I'm wrong, but if my recollection serves me, I believe in the voir dire proceedings," he turned his attention to Calvo, "counsel excused three women jurors. Your Honor, the only inference I can draw from this is that counsel didn't want any women jurors. The only conclusion we could assume from this at the time, Your Honor, was that the women, women excused by Mr. Calvo, might have been of an age to identify with my client in a daughterly way and therefore might side with the plaintiff, Mrs. Boylan." Lawrence looked directly at Calvo, who was beginning to rap his pencil on the table. "Given those assumptions, I can see why they dismissed all the women jurors. I think it's a little late now to claim passion and prejudice." He looked back to Caplin. "I don't profess to know what was on counsel's mind, Your Honor, but for the record he excused three female jurors, and now he's bemoaning the fact that there were no women on the jury." Lawrence sat and waited for a response. He knew by Caplin's expression that the judge agreed.

"Do you have a reply, Mr. Calvo?"

Calvo cupped his hand and listened as his associate whispered something in his ear. He nodded, accepting what his colleague had to say, and stood. He looked at the wall and said something inaudible.

"I didn't hear that, Mr. Calvo."

"I said—I said, 'No,' Your Honor. We don't wish to continue discussing the subject of an absence of women on the jury at this time."

"Nor, I hope, at any other time, counselor." Caplin slowly put on his glasses, and after taking a moment to review the other issues, he turned the page. Once more he removed his glasses and sat back in the great chair. "Very well then, counselor, let's move on to the next matter, shall we?"

Calvo stood again after shuffling papers. "We did file on some evidentiary rulings by this Court." Calvo cleared his throat. "But for the record we're not going to pursue those. After careful study of the objections and the Court's rulings in toto, and after deliberation, we find them not prejudicial in that regard."

"I respect counsel's right to question this Court's rulings, and I find in your decision not to pursue them an indication that you applied a broad perspective to your review," Caplin said, acerbity punctuating every word. Lawrence scratched something on a pad and pushed it toward Phyllis. She studied it and smiled. It read, *two down and winning.*

"Next, Mr. Calvo." Benjamin Caplin appeared to be getting impatient with the defendant's attorney. "What's next?"

"The verdict, Your Honor."

Lawrence broke the silence with a snicker and covered his mouth. He knew that Caplin was looking his way and this was no time to incite the Judge. "Excuse me, Your Honor...I had something caught in my throat." Caplin glared for a while then turned back to Calvo.

"What is it about the verdict, Mr. Calvo, that you didn't comprehend?"

Calvo nervously rotated the pencil and rapped a drum cadence on the table.

"Although there's substantial evidence to support the figure of $250,000 invested with my client by the plaintiff, a matter by the way that we're also leaning toward appealing; however, more importantly, we do contend that the punitive damages of two-point-five million dollars granted by the jury— in proportion ten times the amount of the general damages—to be exorbitant. We feel that this, this enormous figure, speaks for itself as to passion and prejudice." He gestured to where Phyllis Boylan sat. "This elderly woman, Your Honor—being close to seventy—I mean what's her life expectancy?"

"Pardon me, counsel…"

Calvo ignored the Judge. "I mean how much time…"

"Counsel!" Caplin interrupted furiously, bringing the gavel down over and over until there was silence. The silence seemed to last forever.

"Your Honor—all we're trying to convey to the Court is that the life expectancy of…"

"I said no, counselor," Caplin said, "no, absolutely no. This Court is not going to let you pursue that avenue."

Lawrence knew it was over for the defendants. He clutched Phyllis Boylan's hand and in a moment Caplin's distinctive voice broke the silence.

"This is a case that cried to heaven for vengeance, to use a biblical term." Caplin gestured to Phyllis Boylan. "This poor woman lost all of her husband's hard-earned life savings by institutionalized corruption—based on the evidence presented to this Court. My personal feelings aside," he waved his arm as though to include all the men at the defendant's table, "the punitive damages of two and a half million dollars could have been five, and this Court, gentlemen, would not have reversed one iota of that verdict. I hope this sends a message to those organizations involved in the care of elderly people's investments. In short, counsel, your motion for a new trial because of passion and prejudice is denied." He brought the gavel down once more and dismissed the parties. He stood, then left the Court to murmurings of disapproval at the defendant's table.

Mrs. Boylan hugged and thanked Lawrence. He extended his hand to Calvo, who shook it reluctantly. After explaining the ramifications of the Judge's ruling, Lawrence said goodbye to Phyllis Boylan. She left the courtroom, met her sister, waiting in the corridor, and walked to the elevator. Her jubilant voice trailed as she excitedly explained the Judge's decision to her sister.

Lawrence, pushing open the doors to the street, was shocked to see Michael coming toward him, taking the steps two at a time.

"If you came to see your brother in action you're a little late," Lawrence said, hugging Michael, who pulled back to get his breath.

"I rushed over. Your office said I could find you here," he said breathlessly, his chest heaving between words. Lawrence recognized immediately that his brother was disturbed. Michael's face was white; Lawrence set his jubilance aside and thought the worst.

"What's wrong, Michael? Is Mother all right?" he asked, as though a telepathic suggestion was at work. Their ability to communicate without saying anything was incredible. Michael stopped to regain his breath; his hand rested on his knee.

"It's Dad—Mother called about half an hour ago—she said she tried to get hold of you. Mr. Bickford said you were in court." Michael's words came in short bursts.

"What about Dad, Michael? What's happened? Is he all right?"

"He's had a terrible accident—Mother said that he was in a coma."

"A coma? What on earth happened?"

"A car wreck, his car hit a telephone pole. Mother said he does seem to come in and out of a coma—I guess that's a good thing." They hurried down the courthouse steps.

"Mother said that we should come right away, Lawrence."

"That doesn't sound good. It doesn't sound good at all."

At street level they hailed a cab and headed directly for La Guardia, not bothering to pack. Lawrence did not mention his court victory.

They arrived at National Airport in early evening. Lawrence had called Ryan's office before boarding the plane and an agent met them at the airport to drive them to the hospital. Agent Robert Cox recognized them, introduced himself, then rushed the twins to a waiting vehicle.

After seating them, he took the driver's seat and speedily left the airport headed for the hospital. He breezed through traffic. Lawrence leaned forward, arms resting over the front-passenger seat.

"Mother said it was a car accident. Was anybody in the car with my dad when it happened, Mr. Cox?"

"No. I believe he was alone in the car. That's what I understand."

"He must have been pursuing someone. How did it happen?"

"I'm not sure exactly, Mr. Riordan. The investigating officers said that his car skidded out of control and hit a telephone pole. I didn't have an opportunity to read the report. I'm sure agent Hamilton will have more to tell you."

"He was chasing someone then?" Michael said.

"If he was, we're not sure who it would have been, Father."

"He was going fast then?" Lawrence asked.

"The report said that he was doing about ninety," Cox said reluctantly.

Lawrence sat back and loudly expelled a whistle of air.

"Dad was a hell of a driver—it just isn't like him."

"Unless something went wrong with the car," Michael said.

"We're looking into that, Father. The Bureau has the car. We're going to go over it with a fine-tooth comb."

Cox dropped them off at the entrance to the hospital and said he would be available if they needed him. Inside they were told that their father was in intensive care.

"Room 306," the receptionist said. "You can take the elevator." They double timed past orderlies and nurses to 306 and found the door ajar.

Michael moved inside ahead of Lawrence. Kathleen was at one side of the bed and William Hamilton the other. The room was quiet except for the sound of the ventilator. Nothing was recognizable about the person in the bed, not even the eyes, which stared blankly below the gauze dressing. Ryan's chest heaved with every air-escaping sound of the ventilator. Kathleen was relieved to see her sons. In a dramatic gesture, she rushed into the open arms of Michael. They stayed entwined, saying nothing. He could feel her body heave with every sob. Lawrence joined them for a moment, then broke away to shake hands with Hamilton.

"I'm glad you could be here for Mom, William."

"It's good to see you too, Lawrence. I wish the circumstances could be different."

"How is he?" Lawrence asked, touching the bandaged hand.

Hamilton's expression was enough to suggest that the prognosis did not look good. Michael slowly disengaged himself from Kathleen and knelt by Ryan. He blessed himself and prepared to administer the last rites to his father.

"Have you talked to the doctor, Mother?" Lawrence asked. He found his brother's actions a little theatrical.

"He should be by shortly, Lawrence. He was with another patient." She gestured for him to step outside. The three walked to the corridor, leaving Michael to pray alone for his father.

"I didn't want to say anything in there," Kathleen said quietly, "I don't want your father to hear anything negative."

Lawrence looked surprised. "He can hear?"

"We're not sure, Lawrence," Hamilton said.

"The doctor thought that given his condition, it wouldn't be unusual for Ryan to be going in and out of a coma," Kathleen said.

"And what condition would that be?"

"He's seeking another opinion—just to be sure."

Lawrence noticed a doctor coming their way. "Is this the doctor, Mother?"

Kathleen turned in the direction of the heavy footsteps, her blue eyes alight, shining with anxiety and hope. "Yes," she said.

"Doctor Travers, I'd like you to meet my son Lawrence. He just arrived with his brother from New York."

Travers, a tall, handsome young man with a square, powerful build and an honest, intelligent face, shook Lawrence's hand. "It's good to meet you. Your mother told me you'd be arriving from New York. I didn't know you'd get here this fast."

"We were lucky, Doctor, we got to the airport just before the plane left," Lawrence said. "I'm curious to know about my father, Doctor. Mother here doesn't seem to know what the prognosis is."

Travers hesitated, then he said, "I wish I could be more encouraging. The truth is your father's got a tough fight ahead. I've consulted with another neurosurgeon, and we both agree that your father has a very serious epidural hematoma."

Lawrence shrugged. "In English, Doctor, please put that in words we can deal with."

"I'm sorry," Travers raised his hand to the left side of his head just above and to the front of his ear. "Your father has a massive head injury, Lawrence, besides having five broken ribs, a ruptured spleen and a compound fracture in his right arm. This fracture in his left temporal bone is the real issue."

"Can you operate, Doctor? Is it something that you can fix?" Lawrence questioned, with a determined air. Kathleen put her hand on his arm.

"Please forgive our impatience, Doctor, it's just that we're very concerned for Ryan."

"I understand completely, Mrs. Thornton." He turned to face Lawrence. "We've already elevated the fractured area." He could see that Lawrence was still confused. He continued, "The fracture caved in on the brain, if you will, and caused a great deal of hemorrhaging. We had to first elevate the fracture." Once again he saw the puzzlement on Lawrence's face. He made a pulling gesture with his hand. "We removed the dent in his head." Lawrence nodded. "Then we had to tie off the meningeal artery." He paused. "Now, having conferred with Doctor Brummel, we are concerned about the possibility of a clot."

Hamilton broke in. "How do you explain his recovery, Doctor? Mrs. Thornton and I were talking to him just a few hours ago—before the surgery, and he sounded fine. He understood what we were saying and even responded."

"It's not unusual for a patient to show momentary improvement after the accident, Mr. Hamilton. There's always the remote chance that he'll recover—but it's doubtful that he will be in and out of a coma. Chances are he'll stay comatose."

"Are you saying..." Kathleen stammered, "that there's no hope for Ryan then?"

"There's always hope, Mrs. Thornton—and prayer."

"Prayer?" Lawrence muttered, and the corridor was quiet.

They stayed at the hospital, talking about times when things looked better and praying until darkness replaced the twilight. A night nurse interrupted them and mentioned politely that visitation hours had long ago passed. It took a lot of persuasion to get Kathleen to leave.

"Come on, Mother." Michael took her arm. "You look exhausted. Let's go home. We can all get a good night's sleep and return early in the morning."

It was a little after midnight when they arrived in Suitland. Kathleen turned the key in the latch and entered the dark house. Her thoughts returned to the circumstances that led to Ryan's catastrophe. The police investigating the accident told her that he was clocked at speeds over ninety miles an hour. She could not understand what he had been thinking and could not understand where he was headed at such great speed. Was he looking for McIntee? Or was he on his way to confront William? She had called Hamilton immediately after Ryan had rushed in anger from their home. After the police phoned and informed her of the accident, she called Hamilton again, and he came at once. She trembled with the thought that Ryan would never be with her in this house again. She could not escape the sense of dread. She calmed slightly when Michael spoke to her.

"Mother, are you all right?" He gave her a compassionate smile.

"Yes. Of course I'm all right," she said, leaving them in the front room and heading for the kitchen. In a moment the sound of the kettle filling with water told them that they were not going to bed without a *cuppa.*

The four sat around the table exchanging stories. Joy and sorrow, talking, laughing and crying combined as they drank tea and chatted into the night. Their tired bodies, crying for sleep, reawakened with telling of stimulating stories of the past. There were moments when Kathleen's silent reveries left her completely oblivious to the conversation of the three men at the table, moments when she was jogged to reality by a burst of collective laughter. Lawrence was the one intent on trying to understand what happened, always the one coming back to the present, the basis of his father's condition. Lawrence, with his lawyer's inquisitiveness, out of the blue, asked Kathleen if something had happened between them, before his father left. She looked surprised. Michael stepped in.

"Lawrence! I don't think that's any of our business."

Hamilton agreed. "Your brother's right, Lawrence. What happens between your mother and father is nobody's business but theirs."

"I'm not being accusatory, for Christ's sake. It's just that father might have said something—something that might explain his actions, where he was going so fast. Had he received a phone call before he left?" He waited for his mother to answer. She could refuse to answer, but that would only lead to more doubts. She rotated the teacup, examining the pattern of the tea leaves, remembering how, when she was young, Nora McIntee used to come to her house and examine their empty cups, predicting the future. Without raising her head, she said in a soft tone that she and Ryan had an argument. She prayed that Lawrence would leave it at that. Hamilton, who was sitting next to her, placed a sympathetic hand over hers. Lawrence apologized immediately. He rubbed his brow, and as if to eliminate the inquiry, he reached and touched her other hand.

"Please forgive me, Mother—it's just that I really thought that Father might have said something pertinent—a clue or something that would have given us insight to the accident."

Kathleen shook her head, tears welled in her tired eyes. "Of course you're right, Lawrence..." She looked downward as if embarrassed by what she would say next. "What really hurts is that our last words were... were so painful." She placed both hands to her face, her body convulsed, and she wept. Michael stood and went to her side. He knelt and held her trembling body.

"If...If only I hadn't told him."

"There...there, Mother, it's not important now. Why don't we get you to bed." He made an attempt to move her, but she drew back.

"No, Michael," she rubbed her eyes, "Lawrence is right—something did happen." Her mind awakened to the need for an explanation that could risk the loss of her sons' respect. The thought of their feeling of disappointment, even the possibility of their contempt for her, began to slowly ebb. She felt a sense of relief.

"Really, Mother—Michael is right," Lawrence said. "Why don't we get you to bed? We can talk tomorrow." Hamilton agreed, knowing that this was not the best time to talk about what he thought she might be contemplating. In his mind, they shared a lie rather than a secret.

"Please—I'm all right now—please." She looked compassionately at Hamilton. "I really do feel that because of the circumstances..." She hesitated and turned to face Lawrence. "Your father came home early because I called him. I called him because a man—a man out of my past, came to the house after your father had left for work." She swallowed hard and her body quivered. "His name is Sean McIntee. You may have heard me make mention of the McIntees. They were our neighbors in Dublin. We talked for hours—oh, little things at first, then he demanded money or he would blackmail me. Before he left—when I resisted..." She struggled awkwardly with an explanation of what happened next. "Anyway—before he left he—he tried to rape me."

For a moment, Michael held her shaking body tight. Lawrence was speechless. Hamilton wasn't surprised since she had told him about the attack earlier.

"What's sad is we were really good friends," she went on. "We grew up together in Dublin."

"Raped?" Lawrence said unbelievably. "Dear God, Mother, I had no idea—I'm sorry I pried—but why didn't you call the police?"

"I did, I called the best policeman I know, Lawrence."

"Sorry, I wasn't thinking—of course you did," he said in a patronizing tone. "You don't have to talk about this now."

"I'm just answering your question, Lawrence."

"That's not necessary, Mother..."

"Whether you like it or not, I'm determined to tell you something that has been tormenting me for over thirty years."

"Are you sure, Kathleen," Hamilton broke in, "that this is a good time?" Lawrence and Michael looked curiously at one another.

"Shall I begin at the beginning, William?"

"You know best, Kathleen," he said, aware that she would tell the boys at last. She demanded that Michael return to his chair and asked the twins to listen carefully. She moved the chair back and went into the bedroom. Michael and Lawrence, positioning themselves to listen, looked curiously at Hamilton, who shrugged. In a moment she returned with the small box fashioned like a chest, sat, and placed it on the table. She began with an explanation of the first time she set eyes on Liam Riordan. She told the story unhesitatingly until she came to the part about her visit to Dublin to see if Father Donnelly could help her with a marriage certificate.

"I believed that the only man I would ever love—the man whose children I would bear, had drowned when his ship was torpedoed by a German U-Boat." Slowly she drew back the lid and brought out a tin-type photo. She handed the photograph to Lawrence first. He studied it for a while then looked directly at Hamilton.

"Christ, it's—it's you!" Lawrence allowed Michael to take the photo. "I don't believe this—all this time, you've been my father!" Michael sat back, rubbed his forehead, and mumbled. "I don't know why you felt that you couldn't tell us, Mother—after all…"

"Don't you see, Michael, the times in which I grew up were very different than they are now. Unmarried women in Ireland were giving up their children to orphanages, many were sold to rich families in America. Besides, I thought that Liam Riordan had died—and what was wrong anyway about wanting to keep you for myself?"

Michael nodded in agreement. Lawrence seemed reluctant.

"When did you find out that Liam Riordan…" he turned to Hamilton… "or William, here, wasn't dead?"

She went on with the story, sometimes allowing Hamilton to interject details he remembered. He recounted his conversation with his boss and his decision to resign and marry her. He gave an account of her father's imprisonment, the escape from Kilmainham prison, the sinking of his ship, and later the justification for not correcting the reports of his death at sea. Kathleen was hearing details of events in his life for the first time. She was especially interested in his tales of those early days in Chicago, where he encountered Sean McIntee. Lawrence and Michael listened intently, not interrupting, hanging on every word.

When Lawrence excused himself for having too many cups of tea, he asked for complete silence until he returned. Michael was so engrossed he had to admit that he sometimes had an urge to have a cigarette. Kathleen was surprised to see him light up and take a deep drag. Hours later Kathleen ended the story that had been locked up for so long. The room was quiet.

"Well," Kathleen broke the silence, "now you know who your real father is."

The silence continued.

"You must think we're awful for keeping this a secret." More silence.

"You have to understand, I did it for you. I thought that it was better to create a father than leave you…" She couldn't say the word.

Michael said it for her. "Bastards?"

"Yes, I couldn't do that to you."

"It had to be awful for you both," Michael said compassionately. "It's hard to believe that Father never suspected anything."

"We never gave your father a reason to suspect anything."

"I wasn't implying that you did, Mother."

Lawrence, numbed by what he had heard, said, "I find that hard to believe, Mother."

Hamilton was stonefaced. "What do you find hard to believe, Lawrence?"

"It just sounds to me—a little unbelievable that there wasn't something going on between you two. I can't believe that Father didn't suspect something was going on and…"

Hamilton brusquely stood and leaned to face Lawrence.

"Frankly, your attitude is beginning to piss me off, Lawrence. Apologize to your mother…" Kathleen grabbed Hamilton's arm.

"Please, William, Lawrence doesn't mean anything. He's naturally shocked by all this and…"

"Shocked! What do you expect, for Christ's sake," Lawrence said sharply, "it's not every day you find out your mother is having an affair with…" He never got to finish the sentence. He saw the tremor of anger in her face as she stood and struck him. Kathleen stayed standing long after the loud slap resonated in the silence. Lawrence was conscious of having blundered. In an effort to put her and himself at ease, he slowly rose and went to her.

"I'm sorry, Mother…It was an ugly thing to say." He held her. "Please forgive me." He reached around her to Hamilton and the three locked in an embrace. Hamilton also apologized, and the three sat. Michael suggested that they go to bed. All stood but Lawrence, who looked deep in thought.

"Are you coming, Lawrence?" Kathleen asked.

"In a moment, Mother. I'll be along in a moment."

"I'm sorry I slapped you, Lawrence, I don't know what possessed me."

"It's not that, Mother. I have this awful feeling that we're being…well, manipulated…like puppets." Hamilton looked concerned and sat on the edge of the chair.

"What do you mean, Lawrence? I sensed that something other than what you've heard here tonight has been bothering you."

"This Sean McIntee…" Lawrence turned to Kathleen. "You said that his intention seemed to be more to do with blackmail than coming to… what I mean is his actions…his attempt at rape was more of an impulsive reaction. His real reason for seeing you was to extort money for keeping quiet about our births."

"That's what I believe—yes."

"By any chance was McIntee a tall, rather thin man—gray hair, mustache, slight Irish accent, a well-dressed gentleman type?"

"Why yes, Lawrence, that's exactly what he looked like," she said, bewildered.

"You sound like you know the man," Hamilton said, puzzled by the coincidence.

"Oh I know the bastard all right." Lawrence was not ready to tell his mother of threats to expose his homosexuality. He felt that enough had been said for one night. "He blackmailed me also—said that he had proof that I was a bastard."

"Dear God, he's bent on ruining this family." Kathleen was furious.

"Did you give him any money, Lawrence?" Hamilton asked.

"Not right away—but I couldn't have him spreading in the newspapers the story that I was a bastard."

"I'm not sure that it would have affected your career that much, Lawrence. It sounds like you eventually capitulated to his demands."

"Eventually, yes," he said, dejected. "The problem is I sold my services to…to a mob boss."

"Not Giovanni Lugano?" Michael's steel eyes flashed. "You told me you wouldn't take his offer."

"I had to come up with a hundred and fifty grand, Michael," he shot back. "Where else do you think I was going to get that kind of money? Certainly not from anyone here."

"Hold it—just a minute, let's not get all bent out of shape," Hamilton commanded. "This is exactly what this asshole…" He turned to apologize to Kathleen… "Please excuse my language, but I don't know what else to call this low-life. We'll figure something out if we just put our minds to it."

He looked at Michael. "How about you? It seems to me that McIntee is out to get us all. Did he approach you?" Michael pursed his lips, his eyes darted back and forth, suggesting that his brain was searching for anything that resembled offers of blackmail. "I can't say that anyone has tried to put the squeeze on me for anything."

"Can you think of anything out of the normal…unusual requests?" Hamilton persisted. "Have there been any offers of tithing, for example, in return for favors? Think, Michael."

Michael mumbled something and Hamilton asked him to repeat it.

"I didn't hear you, Michael. What did you say?"

"I said stocks." His face had drained of blood and turned white. "Oh God, what have I done?" He appeared to be addressing himself. "I've ruined the Archdiocese."

"What are you talking about, Michael?" Kathleen couldn't believe what she heard. Distant past and recent past were turning into a nightmare.

"What about the stocks, Michael?" Hamilton asked. "Did someone sign over some stock to you, or the Church?"

"A man named Kenny—David Kenny…"

Lawrence stopped him. "David Kenny? That's the same name that McIntee used when he approached me."

"But this man was nothing like you described...He was short and balding, stout, maybe in his late sixties."

"Yet he called himself Kenny?" Lawrence asked.

"Then there are two of them," Hamilton said.

"Two of them?" Lawrence waited for an explanation.

"That's right. McIntee is obviously working with a partner." He looked at Michael. "How much stock did he sell you?"

"He sold me nothing...He gave it to me, a donation, five million dollars." He ran his hands nervously through his dark, curly hair. "Oh, dear God, what have I done?"

Lawrence whistled. "Five million bucks for nothing, and you don't press for information?"

"Not exactly for nothing...I put a million dollars of the Church's money into a trust account for his son's family."

"You gave him a million bucks, and you didn't ask questions?"

"You don't understand, Lawrence. He didn't ask me for the money. I was the one who made the offer. After all, he was donating five million... The man's a parishioner. He's dying and this was his last wish."

"Michael, you'll have to agree that it sounds like a ruse," Hamilton said anxiously.

"The problem is the Archdiocese has already borrowed against the stock. I would guess that we've paid off loans and made commitments amounting to two and a half million." He put his hands over the sides of his face, and his eyes filled with tears.

Hamilton, sensing the pain in his son, vowed to put an end to McIntee once and for all. He glanced at his watch. "Look, it's time we got some sleep. Tomorrow I'll check with Bureau records. I have no doubt that I can find his accomplice. He's probably another felon, someone who was with McIntee in the slammer. With your help, Michael, we'll nail this guy." He placed his hand on Michael's shoulder and turned to Lawrence. "This situation with Lugano is a bit of a predicament, but I don't want you to worry about that either. I work for an organization that enjoys locking horns with scum like that." Hamilton gave him an encouraging smile.

"I hope you're right, William, and I do apologize for..."

Hamilton stopped him mid-sentence. "Enough for now, let's get some shut-eye."

Kathleen rose. She felt relieved. All was out in the open—no more dark secrets. "I believe that something good will come from this," she said to the three, closing her bedroom door.

The following day they sat with Ryan, who was still in a coma. Dr. Travers joined them thirty minutes before noon. Although he showed a positive attitude, he was careful to avoid giving Kathleen too much confidence in Ryan's recovery. When she tossed back her black hair and suggested that surely there were cases like Ryan's where patients recovered, he agreed. He didn't deflate her optimism, nor did he tell her that the damage to Ryan's brain would leave him cataleptic and no doubt lead to his death. Kathleen stayed at Ryan's side, talking to him as if he could hear, holding his hand, waiting for a reaction. Sometimes her eyes lit, sure that he had squeezed a little or responded to something she said by moving a finger. It was shortly after noon when Lawrence suggested that they go for lunch. Kathleen did not join them. Michael said that she had to eat something and he would bring her a sandwich.

In the hospital cafeteria, the combination of carbolic cleaners and food odors caused Lawrence to lose his appetite. After lunch, Hamilton said goodbye to Kathleen to return to New York. In a professional tone, he told Lawrence and Michael to call him immediately on their return to the city. Since the stocks had been transferred, the first urgent business was finding McIntee's accomplice. They would have to go through Bureau mugshots. Out of respect for their feelings, Hamilton did not pursue the issue. At that moment they were mourning Ryan's condition and consoling their mother.

McIntee's cautious eyes moved with flickering sureness. He had two major concerns, first that the envelope would not look suspicious, and most importantly, that the detonator would operate properly. He had already placed the iron and aluminum filings in the center of the double-layered manila envelope and now carefully placed the magnesium in the outer layer. While he slowly assembled the letter bomb, his obsessive hatred of William Hamilton filled his thoughts. He remembered the first time he saw and hated the man. It was at Ned Morriarty's wake when Hamilton was posing as the great American writer and had the gall to dance with his girl.

Later, as the years passed in Chicago, he had become indifferent to those troublesome days in Dublin and had almost forgotten Hamilton until the day of his arrest. His deep loathing of the man intensified after the trial and during his incarceration. Impulses of revenge kept him mindful of his goal: Hamilton's demise. Feeling the loss of Kathleen, he floated from present hatred to past joy. Days of their youth sparked images of the hoolies with singing and dancing the night away, times when the black porter flowed and no one had a care in the world. It was a time when the manufacturing of home-made bombs was part of the game, fighting for Ireland's independence. The explosives he made in those days were even more elemental, such as beer bottles filled with petrol and soap powder. He had even learned to apply some ancient Greek explosive formulas, building devices using charcoal, sulfur and potassium nitrate. Never had he been given the opportunity to use them.

His preoccupation with the past ended when he saw that he had to concentrate to finish what he was doing. For the second time that afternoon he had left the chemicals on the table to sit in the easy chair and review the meticulous plan for the death of Hamilton and the ruination of his bastard twins. He lit a cigarette, blew smoke, and smiled. He thought how lucky he was that Ryan Thornton was in a coma and not expected to live. Two articles sat on the table beside him. One was the letter he had stolen from Kathleen's bureau, the other was a folded Washington newspaper reporting the tragic accident of Agent Thornton. McIntee had called the hospital numerous times, hanging up until he was sure that it was Michael who answered. Posing as an FBI Agent from Ryan's office, he learned all he needed to know from the bereaved priest. Ryan's accident was a bonus he hadn't counted on. Everything was going better than he had planned. He had the first payment of extortion money from Lawrence Riordan, who naively believed that it would be the last time he would see his blackmailer. All had gone well with the priest in the exchange of the counterfeit stock.

McIntee could concentrate now on removing Hamilton from the equation. He massaged his chin as he considered steps that would have to go without error. It seemed too easy, yet it was the simplicity of this part of the plan that would annihilate Hamilton. Once Hamilton was gone, McIntee's triumph would build on the public outcry following reports of the wretched priest who engaged in stolen stocks.

He crunched the cigarette into the ashtray and picked up the phone. He took a deep breath and dialed. After waiting a moment, he said, with a mild Brooklyn accent, "Hello—yeah, I'd like to talk with Agent Hamilton." He reached for another cigarette while the woman at the other end asked him to give his name and to please state his business.

"Yeah—well, I'm afraid at the moment I can't do that," he said through tight lips as he lit the cigarette.

"Tell him it's very urgent, and giving him my name at this time would not be—shall we say, prudent." There was a silence. A bead of sweat formed on his brow. He took a deep breath and exhaled the smoke out of the side of his mouth. The nicotine kicked in and he relaxed. It would be natural to appear nervous, he thought. After all, he was volunteering to be a witness in the trial of the century. At last a man's voice answered.

"Hello," McIntee said. "Is this Agent Hamilton?" He paused. Hamilton demanded to know his name.

"Yeah—well I don't feel too comfortable givin' you my name right now, okay?" Silently, McIntee wiped the sweat from his lower lip.

"All I can say right now is that I hold a fairly decent position with the union." There was another lull.

"Yeah, Teamsters. What I'm calling about is this Di Angelo trial comin' up. You might say that I happen to have some information that, shall we say, could be damagin' to the defendant."

McIntee listened for a while and sucked in more smoke. He blew it away from the mouthpiece, as if out of some kind of courtesy to the voice on the other end.

"That's right," he said, "I actually saw the guy beat him to a pulp." He hesitated, "Yeah, a baseball bat. My testimony could put the guy away for a long time, maybe even the chair." McIntee paused, then said, "Yeah, I know who he works for. I have enough on the both of them. Lugano owns the union. The information I have is goin' to cost someone, if you know what I mean."

"Right. Look, I'll call you back, okay?" He waited.

"No, I'll call you." He hesitated again. "Better yet, I'll deliver an envelope, then we can talk."

He hung up and sighed. It was done, the hook was set. Hamilton was interested in getting information that would put the mob boss away for good and had insufficient time to trace the call. McIntee's next call would be from a pay phone. McIntee returned to the table. He had left the difficult and most dangerous part till last, the fuse. He wiped the sweat from his brow and carefully mixed the iodine crystals and ammonia hydroxide into a crystalline structure about one inch long and put it at the top of the envelope. Without applying too much pressure, he glued the flap and chuckled out loud. There was not a hint of remorse for all the agony he was going to bring about; the thought that he would cause a great sorrow in Kathleen's life made him jubilant.

The following day, Hamilton sat in his office looking over the skyline. The first thing he attended to was a check on the address of Michael's pudgy philanthropist. He wasn't surprised when the address turned out to be a condemned house that no one had occupied for years. There was not the slightest doubt in his mind now that Michael's stock certificates were fraudulent. After running into a dead end on the address, Hamilton paid a visit to the D.T.C and discovered that the stock, all purchased in

1935, was indeed registered to a David Kenny. There had been no action in the portfolio in twenty years. Further, the brokers had no record of David Kenny. Research told him that payments of annual taxes on the stock earnings had been issued from a bank in London. He noted the address of the bank.

Getting personal information outside the U.S. was going to be a little more complex. It was difficult to attend to Bureau matters knowing what Kathleen was going through. The last thing he wanted to do was leave her, but he thought it prudent to depart. Sensitive, life-shattering secrets had been revealed. Lawrence and Michael would need some time to themselves. Leaving the family alone would enhance his relationship with the twins. Besides, she promised to call him if there were any changes. He turned and faced the glass door to his office and for a moment watched the woman in the blue dress go about her work.

Mary Gallagher had been assigned as a secretary to Hamilton from the moment of his arrival at the New York field office. She had been with the Bureau for almost twenty years. A career woman who had never married, she loved her work. More than once she was heard to declare around the office that romance wasn't important. This declaration intrigued most of the single men in the office, drawn to this tall and attractive woman with a sophisticated air that said look but don't touch. Hamilton and Mary had a deep respect for each other. He trusted her advice, and over the months he had disclosed aspects of his past impossible to tell to anyone else. She had become a sounding board and check on his conscience. She was sensitive to his relationship with Lawrence and Michael; however, she was not aware of the most recent developments.

Raised in a family that observed its Irish heritage, Mary was a strong practicing Catholic and frequently reminded him of an old Irish adage that she truly believed. *There was a natural order to things, and in the end, everything worked out for the best.* If circumstances had been different, if he had never met Kathleen Barrett. If Ryan Thornton had gone into some other occupation and he hadn't met her again. If these things never happened, Mary Gallagher and William Hamilton might have made a great couple. The years defined the limits of their mysterious bond to a deep and ardent friendship. From outside the glass facade that separated his office from the busy bull pens around her, she could see that he appeared strained. She picked up the receiver and pushed the intercom.

"Yes, Mary?"

"Can I get you a cup of coffee, sir?"

"Sounds like a plan," he said. "Thanks."

Soon she returned and placed the filled cup on his desk.

"I don't wish to appear forward," she said, "but you look like you could use a friendly ear. Is it something you want to talk about?"

"You're too damned intuitive for your own good, you know," Hamilton said. She attempted to smile.

"I'm always a good listener," she said, concerned, his anxiety transferred to her. He sipped on the coffee and gestured for her to take a seat.

"Have you ever had a premonition that something," he wavered, "bad was about to happen?"

She smiled indulgently. "I'm Irish. What do you think?" Her eyes brightened. "Actually, all the time, sir. 'Course nothing ever comes of it. Thank God I have more false alarms than realities."

"I don't have these feelings very often," he said, imitating her tone. He stroked his chin. "This one really bothers me though," he admitted.

"Anything to do with the phone call you just got?" she asked.

"Everything," he said. "He's called twice now. Each call just long enough to avoid a tracer. Says he has information on this Di Angelo trial coming up. The D. A.'s preparing the case now with federal help. This is a case where my—Lawrence Riordan is going to be representing the defendant. I don't know—the whole thing's weird."

"If this man has information that would help your case, what's so weird about that? What would seem awkward to me," she said, "would be having a good friend represent the man you're trying to prosecute." He leaned back and locked his hands behind his neck.

"Uh huh," he muttered, "I guess you're right, Mary—maybe I'm just being paranoid."

"Did he say he'd see you personally? Or is it one of those anonymous types who wants to stay out of the limelight?"

"I suppose you're right," he said again. "In his last phone call, he suggested that he bring me the package personally. That was just a few hours ago." She smiled at him admiringly.

"See, you're worrying about nothing. I have a feeling that it's other things you have on your mind creating all the stress. By the way, how is Agent Thornton?"

"There's no change," he said solemnly. His uneasy expression gladdened and she recognized the change as an eagerness to get back to work.

"I'm expecting a call from Mrs. Thornton," he said.

"I'll put it right through," she said dutifully, walking toward the door, "right now I have some memos to file."

Later that afternoon, Hamilton returned from a long lunch with one of his agents. Before entering his office he asked Mary if there were any messages.

"Sorry," she said, looking up briefly from the typewriter, "Nothing from you know who."

"Thanks," he said, closing the door. He once again reviewed the notes he had written of his conversation with Lawrence and Michael. With the real David Kenny a mystery, everything depended on Michael's recognizing the extortionist. If he did, Hamilton believed that it wouldn't be difficult to locate the man—providing he hadn't left town. Hamilton considered having a lab check the validity of the stock that had been transferred to the Church; however, this could tip off the Church officials and Michael would be asked embarrassing questions. He thought it better to wait.

He needed Michael and Lawrence to help identify the short, portly man who would guide them to Sean McIntee. However, it seemed doubtful to him that they would leave their mother during this crisis. He was anxious to get this thing solved. Hamilton thought of a myriad of scenarios. For a moment he hated himself, ashamed of what he was thinking. Ryan's passing would certainly speed things up. He felt such self-deprecation that his clenched fists turned white. Still he thought it ironic that the capture of Sean McIntee was contingent on Ryan's expeditious recovery—or departure. He angrily threw the pencil on the desk and eased back with a great sigh. *Damn!* He thought. *This investigation is going nowhere until Michael returns.*

Mary knocked and entered. She put the manila envelope on the desk.

"Is this something you've been waiting for?" she said.

Still deep in thought, he acknowledged with a nod. He gazed absentmindedly at the envelope. The white label seemed official enough. It was typed and it read, Agent William Hamilton, Personal. It had the Bureau address. That was it. There was no return address, nor was there any indication of who the sender was. Mary Gallagher had just closed the door behind her when he jumped up and loudly called her name.

"Mary! Mary!" He laid the envelope on the corner of the desk and moved quickly, opening the door. Not wanting to alarm her, he lowered his voice.

"Who delivered the envelope, Mary?" he asked. "Where's the man who delivered it?" Mary stood and automatically stroked the wrinkles from her blue dress. "It wasn't a man, sir," she corrected herself. "It was a young man—a teenager."

"Teenager?" he said, alarmed. "I was expecting an adult. Where did he go?" Mary looked confused. "He just left the building."

"Damn! You should have had him wait 'till I had a chance to talk with him," he said sternly. Moving past her, he walked briskly to the elevator.

Just before the doors closed, he could see the young man inside. He looked frightened when he saw Hamilton hurrying toward the elevator and appeared relieved when the doors shut. In his frustration, Hamilton pushed at the button over and over, as if frantic actions would bring the elevator back up.

He rushed to the stairs, took them two at a time, ignoring the feeling of pins in his leg, brushing people out of the way. Those who worked for Hamilton stared after him in amazement. He believed the delivery boy and the manila envelope had more to do with Sean McIntee than the upcoming trial. Breathlessly he reached the foyer. The elevator was already on its way up again. The glass front doors had just closed and the top of the boy's head quickly disappeared down the steps. He was close, yet he reasoned that when the boy hit the familiar city streets, his territory, there would be little hope of finding him. Outside the building Hamilton anxiously looked up and down the avenue. Nothing. Not a sign of the boy. He bent over, recovering his breath, regretting the lost opportunity. With great effort of will, he returned to the building, feeling helpless, cursing his bad leg. He went up the steps one at a time.

Inside the foyer, he asked the man at the desk if he remembered what the boy looked like.

"What boy?"

Hamilton waved away the question. "Forget it!" he said, dejected.

He took to the stairs again; his pace picked up. He contemplated the envelope. He concluded that its contents could lead to identification of the telephone caller. The questions came faster than answers. Why would someone call him, specifically him, about the case? Why didn't the man personally deliver the information as he had led him to believe he would? Why didn't the boy stick around?

As doubts about the envelope grew, he sensed doom. Why did the envelope look and feel suspicious? He stopped momentarily. His body arched as if calling upon a superior being for explanations. "God damn it!" he muttered. Doom threatened once again. "Christ! It's a bomb!" he said louder. He drove forward as a sprinter might from the starting blocks and pushed past the people on the stairs. His determined expression alone frightened them. When he reached the office, those standing outside their cubicles stepped aside, giving him room in the tight companionway. He was ten feet or so from the glass-walled office and could clearly see Mary Gallagher inside. He was just seconds from touching her, yet it was as if he were dreaming. He felt that he had lead weights on his feet. He wanted to burst forward but couldn't.

Those last moments of Mary Gallagher's life would be indelibly emblazoned on his mind. Her smile had turned to concern when she saw him, as if she knew that she was about to die. The letter-opener in her hand sliced through the envelope even as she realized she was doing the wrong thing. The blinding flash preceded the explosion. As he felt the suffocating percussion, he saw her pretty face disappear. After that moment he remembered nothing.

He regained consciousness in the recovery room, looking into an oversized eye. The doctor put the magnifying glass back in his top pocket. Before going back to sleep, Hamilton heard the doctor say, "He has a bad concussion—but he'll survive."

Three days passed and Ryan's condition hadn't improved. Hamilton, in the same time, had healed, at least physically. He pledged to avenge the death of Mary Gallagher. He was glad that he did not remember much after the explosion. The photos were difficult enough to examine. The office had been immediately repaired after all the evidence was secured. Hamilton sat in the new leather chair, his gaze momentarily fixed on his new secretary. He vowed that this woman would never get so close to him as to think for a moment that she could open mail marked *personal*. He would like to know what had possessed Mary to open the envelope, especially after he had expressed so much concern at finding the messenger. He sighed deeply and rested back in the big chair. In the remoteness of the room, her smiling face, her special attention, fretting over his every need, just being, weaved in and out of his thoughts. Kathleen had called earlier with news of Ryan. She had convinced the twins to return to New York to help locate McIntee and his accomplice. He didn't tell her of the attempt on his life. Right now, he thought that Ryan was receiving all of the compassion she could muster. He slowly eased himself out of the chair. The old leg injury seemed to be sympathetic to his latest disaster and he limped from the office. He told his new secretary that he was going down to data processing.

"I'm expecting one man, possibly two, within the next hour or so. Michael and Lawrence Riordan, you can't mistake them, they're identical twins. Would you mind having someone escort them down to data processing as soon as they get here?" Within four hours from the time they left D.C., the brothers were entering the FBI building in downtown Manhattan. As ordered, his secretary had them escorted to a lower floor, where Hamilton greeted them. He shook their hands decorously as if to compensate for their learning that he was their father.

He told them about the bomb and the explosive letter. Michael seemed more aware of the consequences had Hamilton been killed. Lawrence, in contrast, believed his own position to be indefensible and Hamilton's death, although regretful, wouldn't have had much effect on his life one way or the other. Hamilton turned talk away from the attempt to kill him and began to explain the identification process. In a businesslike manner, he demonstrated the capabilities of the gigantic I.B.M processors that reached the ceiling. Hamilton realized the formality with which he was treating the twins was unnecessary and found it interesting that he related better to them when they thought of him as a friend. He sensed that they too felt awkward. Hamilton introduced them to an operator who, after being given some dates by Hamilton, placed a bundle of cards in a tray and shut the processor door.

"What institution did you say?" the man asked indifferently.

"Alcatraz," Hamilton said. They left the operator to the task of locating Michael's extortionist. Hamilton led them to a smaller adjacent room appointed sparsely with a table and four chairs. Along one wall stood a series of cathode ray tubes. Hamilton pushed the button that illuminated one of the large screens. He asked them to take a seat and told them that he would return in a minute. Lawrence and Michael sat in silence for a while in awe of the sophisticated equipment. Michael blessed himself and placed his hands on the side of his face.

"Don't tell me you're praying?" Lawrence said, irritated. "It seems that the more you pray the worse things get!"

Michael ignored him until he had finished. He blessed himself again.

Maybe if you helped with prayer instead of constantly ridiculing what everyone is trying to accomplish to solve our family's dilemma..." Hamilton's entrance stopped him from finishing the sentence.

"Is everything okay here?" he asked. They were silent. "You know it's going to take all our cooperation to solve this problem—this asshole isn't playing games," he said sternly. "McIntee is out to get this family." He raised his voice, "And who knows what he has planned for your mother." The room was silent and both nodded in agreement.

"Good," Hamilton continued in a more level tone. He told them that he had ordered something to eat and drink.

"This usually takes longer than people think. What we're going to do, Michael, is bring up photos on the screen. The cards we just pulled represent every suspect that was in Alcatraz the same time as McIntee. If there's anyone that you recognize, even close," he shrugged, "and Lawrence, you too, anyone you might have seen—say within the past year, jump in, okay?"

"Okay," Lawrence said seriously. Hamilton pushed a button on the control unit in his hand and the first picture appeared. Hamilton zoomed in and out of the photo, explaining the capabilities of the processor.

"Understand that these photos were taken at the time of their incarceration. Not only were the felons younger, they were also photographed with equipment that wasn't exactly today's state of the art." The hours passed. To Michael, every mugshot seemed to blend into one great ugly dismal expression. Hamilton suggested they take a break and eat something. Michael rubbed his weary eyes, tired from the intense concentration. He took a small bite of the pastrami sandwich and followed it with some milk.

"Who are all these people, anyway?" he asked Hamilton.

"Felons. Mostly forgers, counterfeit men, some printers in a former life." He bit into the sandwich and chewed for a moment. "Men who obviously weren't happy with what they were being paid."

"I suppose they could make more money—in a literal sense—working for themselves," Lawrence said, smiling.

"Yes! I suppose you could say that," Hamilton responded. He faced Michael. "I felt that there was not even the slightest recognition of our man."

"So far, no," Michael said disconsolately.

They continued for hours, going over the photo files again. Hamilton could see he had exhausted Michael's ability to concentrate.

"Before we pack it in for the night, there's one more mugshot I want you to look at, okay?"

"Fine," Michael said, but after this I'm going to have to get some sleep. I haven't slept in two days."

"I'm sorry, Michael," Hamilton said apologetically, I should have been more considerate and asked if…"

"No, that's all right," Michael interrupted, "it finally hit me, that's all." He gestured to the C.R.T. "Show us this last photo." Hamilton clicked the button and Michael immediately shook his head. Lawrence, who had turned from the screen, glanced back and jumped to his feet.

"That's him!" he hollered, "that's him, Kenny—that's David Kenny."

He was excited. After five hours of watching face after face, he finally had recognized someone. He sat down and stared at the face on the monitor. "But there's no mustache, and—and he looks younger, a lot younger."

"You're absolutely sure?" Hamilton asked.

"I'd bet my life on it."

"Good. The man you see here on the screen is McIntee in a photo taken twenty years ago." Lawrence whistled through closed teeth.

"Christ, he hasn't changed all that much. Older maybe, but it's definitely him."

Hamilton turned to Michael.

"You've never seen this man before?"

"Never," Michael said. "I wanted to be absolutely sure, Lawrence, that the man you thought was Kenny is really McIntee."

"I understand," Lawrence said.

"I happen to believe that the man Michael knows as David Kenny was also among the photos we went through tonight." Michael was shaking his head. Hamilton went on. "What's happened here is that McIntee stayed slim, his features didn't become distorted. They just got older. For example, he kept his hair. It turned gray. On the other hand, his accomplice became obese, distorting his features, he lost his hair. Now this man wouldn't be nearly as easy to recognize, would he?"

"That makes sense, William," Michael said, stroking his chin, "Do you want me to go over them again? I'd be happy to if I thought it would help."

"No. Why don't we call it a night."

He walked them to the door. "I'll have to see you out."

"What time do you want to see us in the morning?" Lawrence asked as they descended the stairs.

"Why don't we make it the afternoon, let's say around two. That should give you a chance to catch up on some sleep." Michael was about to interrupt when Hamilton went on, "Besides, I have an idea that might take me all morning to work on."

"Two o' clock it is then," Michael said as they entered the darkness to hail a taxi.

When they returned a few minutes before two o'clock the next day, they were escorted directly to Hamilton's office. He came from behind the chair to greet them.

"Well, you two look wide awake and ready for action."

"I'm more ready than I was yesterday," Michael said. "I'm ready for another go round of those photos and this time..."

"This time," Hamilton broke in, "I hope it won't be necessary."

"I don't understand."

"I have just one photo for you to look at, Michael, and I'm hoping it's our man."

Michael looked confused until Hamilton opened the folder on his desk and showed him an eight-by-ten glossy.

"Well?" Hamilton asked anxiously. "Is that your David Kenny?"

"Yes—yes, it's him, this photo is definitely a younger version—younger maybe but it's him. Dear God, William, how did you find him?"

Hamilton beamed. "I told you I had a plan. Early this morning I investigated printers in New York who had been granted a business license to operate a print shop in the past eighteen months. Actually there weren't as many as I thought. I passed all the names through the lab and guess what?"

"What's his real name?" Michael asked.

"Augustin Flemming. I went back through the photos we looked at last night," he hesitated, "and I can see why you did not recognize the man."

"Look." Hamilton handed Michael a photo taken at the time of Flemming's incarceration. Lawrence looked over his brother's shoulder.

"Christ," he said. "I doubt if his own goddamn mother would have recognized him." Michael, ignoring the profanity, handed the glossy back to Hamilton.

"Unbelievable," he said, "how did you manage to change the man's appearance?"

"It was all based on your input, Michael; the description you gave us was all we needed. Our lab boys did the rest. We know what our man looks like—and better yet," Hamilton boasted, "we know where he has his shop." Hamilton laid out a simple plan that called for Michael's help. Although Lawrence was eager to assist, there wasn't much that he could contribute. Hamilton suggested that Lawrence go back to taking care of his business.

Kathleen had set up residence at the hospital. She seldom left Ryan's side. Michael had called the room just a few moments earlier and filled her in on the progress of locating McIntee. As he was told, he made no mention of the attempt on Hamilton's life. She was relieved that he still seemed deferential to Hamilton. She thanked God that they were trying to accept the reality that William was their father. The twilight hours had allowed a chill to settle in; Kathleen rose to close the window. She returned and held Ryan's hand. If there was ever a hope that he might come out of the coma, even for a brief moment, she wanted to be with him. The haunting thought persisted that she would not have the opportunity to say she was sorry. Sorry now for not allowing him to know about a past, which, at the time, she felt was sullied. Why she hadn't told him was an enormous question that plagued her. The torment extinguished all other thoughts. She talked to him constantly and squeezed his hand, hoping for some response. She told him quietly how much she loved him. She whispered softly in his ear and tried to describe her feelings for William Hamilton. How could she deny her first love? It was as if she had been a widow all these years. Does a woman forget the love of her first husband? She thought that being asked to forget would be unreasonable. It wasn't her fault that Hamilton had appeared again after she was long married.

She went on and on justifying her feelings toward the two men who had awakened her most intimate desires. Seeing him now with tubes extending from his arms, tubes in his nose, and an oxygen mask to keep him alive, tore at her heart. She silently prayed that God would not judge her too harshly for her actions in the closing scene. The idea that her one slip from virtue caused this tragedy consumed her. It was an indiscretion almost commonplace. She wished she had been with Ryan; that she too could be in a coma, far away from the self-doubt, the culpability. Thoughts of the twins gladdened her and brought an encouraging smile. Their futures were promising. William Hamilton would not let that animal, Sean McIntee, hurt them.

At seven a.m. sharp, Hamilton and Michael turned off the headlights and stopped the car. Across the street, the print shop was dark and empty. Hamilton turned the engine off and eased back in the seat.

"Looks like we got here first," Hamilton said, reaching into his pocket for the pack and offering Michael a cigarette.

"I didn't think you smoked."

"I just picked it up again." Michael took a cigarette and commented on the silver case.

"Remind me to tell you about it sometime, Michael," Hamilton said, reaching to light Michael's cigarette.

"Does it have something to do with Mother?" Michael drew in the smoke.

"It was a short time after we'd first met—your mother didn't like the idea of me smoking so she took the last five cigarettes I had, case and all."

"She obviously wanted to keep you healthy—she must have loved you very much." Hamilton didn't respond; his thoughts returned to the Hill o'Howth, and Michael allowed him the retrospection. It was forty-five minutes before a man showed up and opened the door of the print shop.

"Anyone you recognize?"

"No—it's not him."

"Don't worry, it's a good sign, at least the shop isn't closed."

By eight-thirty more individuals had arrived. Still there was no one that resembled their pudgy friend. They spent the rest of the morning talking about their lost years. It was as though they had just been separated by a rarity of fate, as some people are separated by the insurmountable consequences of war or incarceration. Michael looked at his watch and sighed.

"It doesn't look like anyone's coming," he said, dejected.

"In this business you have to be patient. Remember, he's the owner. He can come and go as he pleases. Otherwise, I'd be as worried as you are."

"Whatever you say. Actually, I'm glad," a smile crossed Michael's face, "it did give us some time to talk alone."

"As your mother would say, there's a reason for everything."

Michael smiled and looked past him. His expression changed. His eyes widened, and although his mouth opened, nothing he said made sense.

"Oh my God," he said finally, "that's him." Hamilton ducked and pushed Michael down in the seat.

"You're sure it's him?"

"Positive," Michael whispered, "it was him."

"He didn't see you, did he?"

"No, he wasn't looking this way."

"Good," Hamilton said, "I want you to stay here. When we come out…" Hamilton hesitated, "you can drive, I hope?"

"Of course I can drive," Michael assured him.

"Good. When I bring him out we'll get in the back seat. I want you to drive, okay?"

"I understand," he said.

Hamilton checked for traffic before crossing. The entrance door had a small 'For Sale' sign in red, block letters. He felt lucky. Flemming obviously had plans to leave town. The shop was wide open, every inch filled with some kind of machinery, some run by large belts extending down from idlers in the ceiling that turned great flywheels, which in turn operated other pieces of equipment. To the right of the reception desk a small glassed-in office was occupied by the man who had entered the shop a short time before him. Hamilton's expression did not expose his exhilaration. His right hand moved surreptitiously, checking for the 38-special on his right hip. He was greeted by a middle-aged woman with a Brooklyn accent.

"Mornin'," she checked with the clock on the wall. "I guess it's afternoon," she corrected. "What can we do for ya?" Hamilton barely heard her over the thumping of lead moving as an operator pressed keys of a Linotype machine just a few feet behind her.

"Hello," he found himself shouting over the noise. "I'm interested in your company printing our brochures. We're a large corporation with a multitude of printing needs." She nodded as if for him to go on.

"I'd very much like to talk to your boss, if I may." He gestured toward the office. "Is that your boss—Mister…?"

"Flemming," she said. He was glad she had broken in.

"That's right, Mr. Flemming was the name of the man I was supposed to see—good references," he said, smiling.

She buzzed his office and the voice said, "Yes, what is it?"

"There's a gentleman out here to see ya, says he wants us to do some printing." She glanced up at Hamilton. "Says we come highly recommended." Flemming looked at him steadily through the glass.

"Send him in," he said eventually. Hamilton went inside and closed the door behind him. He introduced himself as George Blades, with Blades and Feldon Marketing. Flemming stood and offered him a chair. Hamilton sat and unbuttoned his jacket, making it easy to reach the revolver.

"So," Flemming said, "we have been highly recommended to your firm?"

"That's right, Mr. Flemming. Do you mind if I call you Gus?"

Flemming looked stunned. He hadn't responded to that name in years, not since the pen. Flemming stammered.

"I always go by Augustin—but I suppose that would be okay." He appeared nervous and changed the subject.

"Who referred us to you, mister?"

"Blades—but you may call me George." Hamilton was enjoying the game. "Actually, a number of people are aware of your fine talent, Gus. I've always admired your work."

Flemming stood and, looking troubled, said, "I think you'd better leave, Mr. Blades—or whatever your name is." His attempt at being firm wasn't persuasive. He began to stutter. "Look—look here—mister…"

"Sit your ass down, Gus, and don't even think about making a scene." Hamilton pulled his jacket back, exposing the gun on his hip.

Flemming slowly sat and forced himself to say something. "Who are you—what do you want from me?"

"I want McIntee," Hamilton said, to the point. "I want McIntee and you're the only one who knows where he is, Gus."

"McIntee? I don't believe I know anyone by…" Hamilton broke in, raising his voice.

"Cut the shit, Gus. You know goddamn well where he is and if you don't tell me I'll settle just as easy for your ass. Let me help refresh your memory." Hamilton held up his right hand and pointed to his forefinger. "One! How about being in possession of stolen stocks? Two! Forgery, extortion, and this one should have you facing attempted murder," he said, holding up his middle finger.

"That's right, Gus—finally, murder." Flemming was flustered.

"Murder? I never hurt anyone in my life—no, no, you're not pinning a murder rap on me. I never…"

"You murdered my secretary," Hamilton rushed in.

"Fuck you! You don't have anything on me—just who the hell do you think you are anyway?"

"Hamilton, the name's Agent William Hamilton with the FBI," he said sternly, displaying the badge. The room was quiet for a while and Flemming sat down. The intercom crackled and the Brooklyn twang broke the silence.

"Are you okay in there, Mr. Flemming—should I call someone?"

Hamilton looked at Flemming.

"The ball's in your court, Gus." Flemming sat back down and stared at Hamilton. His eyes surrendered.

"Its okay, Wanda," he said, yielding to Hamilton's demands.

"Where's McIntee?"

"I don't know." Hamilton stood. "Okay. That's it; let's go, you can take all the responsibility if that's the way you want it."

"No—I'm telling you the truth, I have no idea where he is."

Hamilton sat down. "You worked with him on this caper, didn't you?"

"Only the stock deal—believe me, I never knew about the—the murder. I remember reading about it in the paper, but so help me God I knew nothing about it. How do you know it was McIntee?"

"We just do," Hamilton asserted. He felt that Flemming was holding something back.

"You know then that Father Riordan has a twin?" Flemming tried to look surprised. Hamilton shook his head slowly. "You'd better come clean, Gus," he said, "If I find that you're not telling me everything, I'll throw your ass in the slammer that quick." He snapped his fingers. He waited for Flemming, who appeared frightened, to respond.

"Yes, he told me he had a twin brother," Flemming stammered. He asked me to engrave a phony newspaper article…"

"Phony newspaper article?"

"He had a photo—it was an old photo of the other twin. He was with some guy. McIntee said he was queer—wanted me to compose a double-truck cabaret page for a London paper. Make it look like a scandal, he said."

Hamilton was beginning to realize why Lawrence chose not to talk about his private life. Everything was beginning to make a little more sense.

"You admit to working with him," Hamilton said. "Why don't you know where he is? You must have had meetings."

"Yes, but he always called the meeting—we met in different places each time." Hamilton stroked his chin.

"Where does this David Kenny fit in? How did you get hold of his stock?"

"McIntee is David Kenny." He implied that Hamilton should have known. Hamilton looked confused.

"McIntee is David Kenny?"

"That's right. I guess he assumed that name just before he went into the slammer. He invested in some stock. He had some new identification papers made out. It's all legit, I guess. I believe his sister took care of the stock."

"Sister?"

"Yeah, she lives in England—I don't know that much about that end of things—he didn't talk much about her. I do know that he returned here from England legally—with this new name."

Hamilton took a moment to sort things out.

"Let me see if I get this. McIntee is in this country legally as David Kenny. He has millions in legal stock. He then makes counterfeit copies of his own stock and donates the stock to the Catholic Archdiocese of New York..."

"For a million real dollars," Flemming butted in. "That's right."

"Right," Hamilton went on, "then what does he do?" Hamilton answered before Flemming had a chance. "Screams bloody murder. And gets the priest he hates up there—Father Riordan—into serious trouble. So the stock registered to Kenny is real," Hamilton mused.

Flemming saw that he had an opportunity. *I have the real stock just behind me in the safe.* What he was thinking was worth a try.

"I suppose if you could get your hands on the stock it would mean a lot, wouldn't it?"

Hamilton sensed by Flemming's tone that he knew exactly where to find the stock. "Let me put it this way. If you have information, you'd better tell me now."

"I'm just a small fry in all this, Hamilton, and you know it. What happens to me in all this? Let's say, for instance, that I could get you the stock."

Nothing that Hamilton was doing now was within the established procedures of the Bureau. For the first time in his career, he was acting outside the Bureau's lines. He owed it to Kathleen, he owed it to his sons. "Mr. Flemming, I'm going to make you one hell of a deal."

Flemming's eyes brightened. "I'm listening."

"You find me the stock, do exactly as you are told, and I'll turn my back on the sale of this business you have here. I'll let you leave the country with your little stash."

Hamilton extended his hand and Flemming shook it vigorously. Flemming then stood and turned the combination lock on the safe behind him.

"It's in there?" Hamilton asked, surprised.

"Yes." The fat man smiled wryly. "He'd kill me for sure if he knew what I was doing."

"If you have the stock, there were definitely going to be more meetings."

"I didn't say there weren't. All I said was that I didn't know where he was. He always calls me for a meeting."

Hamilton examined the stock, holding it up to the light.

"Well, Gus, where does he call you? Here?"

"Usually, yeah."

Hamilton picked up the certificates. "Are you sure *this* is the real stock?"

"Absolutely. I signed the phony stuff over to the priest."

Hamilton put the certificates back into the envelope. Without being asked, Flemming reached inside the safe and handed Hamilton the double-truck page. Hamilton scanned the paper and gave an appreciative sigh. He folded the paper and placed it in his inside pocket.

"How many copies did you make?"

"This was the only one."

"If you're lying…"

"I'm telling the truth. This is the only copy."

"How about the photo?"

Flemming reached down to open a drawer in the desk and Hamilton moved fast, grasping the man's sleeve. The drawer was empty except for a white folded envelope, and he allowed Flemming to hand him the original.

"I want you to come with me," Hamilton ordered.

"Where are we going?"

"Never mind that, just bring the same pen you signed the forgeries with. Let's go." When they reached the car, Hamilton put Flemming in the back seat and followed to sit beside him. Michael looked at the man in the rear-view mirror.

"Hello, David," Michael said evenly. "You're looking healthy—have you been to Lourdes?"

"Look, Father—it was nothing personal. I'm really sorry you had to get hurt by this."

"We don't have time for talk right now," Hamilton declared.

"Michael, I want you to drive us to the bank where you have the counterfeit stock. Mr. Flemming here is going to be good enough to turn over the real stock to the Church. Isn't that right, Mr..." He hesitated, "Mr. Kenny?"

"I don't understand," Michael said. "Wouldn't we be stealing the stock—from the real Mr. Kenny, I mean...?"

"Mr. Flemming is the real Mr. Kenny, aren't you?" Hamilton glared at Flemming.

"That's right—I have the authority to do that, Father," Flemming, despondent, said.

Later that day, Michael arrived by cab at Lawrence's office. He rushed past Francis Bickford, who was having a conversation with the secretary. Looking at Michael as he passed, Bickford became confused. Bickford couldn't tell one twin from the other, even when one wore clerics. He opened his mouth to say something, but Michael had already opened the door to Lawrence's office.

"That's all right, I'll just let myself in," Michael said, looking back over his shoulder. Lawrence was on the phone, seated with his back to the door. When he heard Michael, he rotated the swivel chair to face his brother. Michael closed the door and hurriedly sat. Lawrence hushed his brother's apprehensive behavior with a wave.

"Yes, yes, that's right," Lawrence said, cupping the mouthpiece. "I have their word—yes, for all that's worth. It's my understanding that we should be seeing the first installment sometime this week." The room was quiet.

"Yes—and thank you, Mrs. Boylan—yes, later then." He ended the call.

"Well, where have you been? I've been trying to get hold of..." Michael jumped in.

"You wouldn't believe what happened to me today. Well actually, it all started early this morning." Lawrence made an effort to interrupt, but once Michael began to unload there seemed no stopping him. He began with the early morning surveillance, explaining every detail of what Hamilton had done in Flemming's office. From there he related how they had gone to the bank and, in the privacy of the vault, exchanged the fraudulent with the real stock. Each time Lawrence tried to say something, Michael silenced him with his hand.

"You should have seen how William used his influence," Michael said admiringly, his manner more like a high-school sycophant than the priest, nor did he resemble what one might expect of a prelate holding a high position in the Archdiocese. "You should have been there, Lawrence. He forced Flemming to sign over the real stock."

"Real stock?" Lawrence finally got to say something.

"That's right. As it turns out, Flemming was really David Kenny. Can you believe it?"

"Michael—that's all great, but…"

"Great! It's a Godsend. It means that the Church won't lose anything—and I'm in the clear." Michael recalled that Lawrence was also in trouble, and here he was, reveling in all his glory. *Poor Lawrence, how thoughtless I am.*

"Don't worry, Lawrence, William is going to take care of your problem. Now that my…"

"Would you just shut the hell up for one second, Michael!" Lawrence shouted the words so loudly that his secretary knocked and entered.

"Can I bring either of you something—tea maybe?"

"Thank you, no, Carol," Lawrence said in a civil tone. She waited awhile before closing the door.

"What's gotten into you," Michael said soberly, "I thought you'd be…"

"All I keep hearing about is goddamn Hamilton. Hamilton this and Hamilton that," Lawrence said angrily. "I'm getting just a little bit tired of hearing about all the shit that he's doing to help us out of, a mess that wouldn't have happened had it not been for him in the first place."

Michael stood and said nothing. Lawrence looked up at him with glassy eyes, eyes that just a moment ago were full of fire.

"Father died this morning at six-thirty," Lawrence said, his head cast down. The room was silent and Lawrence raised his head.

"Mother called you first, then she called me. I've been looking for you all day to tell you."

Michael slowly collapsed into the chair. Conscious of having blundered, he lost his enthusiasm and his expression changed to remorse. He no longer felt the relief of being redeemed. A great black cave took shape in his mind; in it Lawrence's words echoed cruelly. Thoughts returned, accelerating the self reproach. *I came in blurting out the good news of my own selfish predicament and my father is dead.* His remorse turned to embarrassment.

"I'm sorry I had to be so blunt, Michael, but damn it you didn't give me a chance—all I kept hearing was how great Hamilton was. I'm sorry."

"That's all right, Lawrence—I had it coming. I had no right to be so—so flippant. All I was thinking about was myself."

"It was your turn to act like an asshole. It's usually me." Lawrence managed a smile. In all their growing up years they never stayed mad at each other for more than a few moments. When one felt hurt, both suffered. Forgiveness was immediate. Michael placed his hands on his head and wept. Lawrence walked to him and placed his hand on his shoulder.

"It's okay," he said, "I got mine out of the way this morning."

Michael wiped his eyes.

"How's Mother?"

"Better than we are, I think."

"I think she expected the worst, don't you?"

"She sounded fine on the phone. You should call her. She really wanted to talk to you—about the services and everything."

Michael stood and moved toward the phone on Lawrence's desk.

"Mind if I call from here?"

"Not at all. That way we can both talk," Lawrence said.

CHAPTER SIXTY-ONE

ICHAEL CONCELEBRATED THE Funeral Mass with Father Rafferty. The church was full to overflowing. Kathleen observed familiar persons who usually appear only for "wakes an' weddin's," as they said in Ireland. She didn't realize they had so many friends. It looked as though all the FBI took time off to pay their respects. After the Gospel, Michael and Lawrence talked about their father. Michael spoke with great difficulty, breaking down as he related stories of his boyhood days, always the klutz when it came to sporting events with his father. He spoke of a very patient father who persevered and never chastised him for not catching the ball in his mitt or swinging wildly at air as the ball floated by from a slow, indulging underhanded pitch. Lawrence, on the other hand, although remorseful, showed less emotion.

After the mass, a two-mile parade of cars followed the funeral hearse to the graveyard. Father Rafferty was the first to arrive following the hearse. He wore a black soutane and white surplice. When all the mourners were present, he placed a stole over his shoulders and opened the well-worn black breviary.

Kathleen didn't remember much of the service at the graveside. Her thoughts rambled to Maggie's death. The revelation that she was going to have company was of some consolation. Oh, she knew that Maggie loved her, that theirs was a relationship that involved daily episodes of physical therapy, always the intent to stay healthy. She knew that it was different with a father and daughter. Theirs was a special relationship. Ryan never had to be the disciplinarian. Maggie had loved her dad more than anyone else and more than anything else in the world. As the coffin passed from Kathleen's sight, great streams of tears traced her cheeks. She truly believed that they were together again. Before the grave was filled, they walked away, leaving a lone piper playing *The Minstrel Boy*. She sat in the back seat of the car between her sons. As the car drove to the house where a rosary would be said, she quietly hummed.

The food was a magnificent display of meats, vegetables, salads, breads and potatoes in all varieties. One of Ryan's associates took care of the spirits. Later the piper returned and played away from everyone in a remote corner of the room. Altogether it was a solemn occasion. Soon the piper rested and a group gathered behind Katy Thornton as she played the piano. After a while, when the songsters, led by Father Rafferty, took a break, Katy was left alone and quietly played some of her favorite Chopin nocturnes. Kathleen tuned out the conversations and listened. The music opened her mind to all the good memories of Ryan. Tears began to well again as she listened to one of Ryan's favorites, Chopin's Etude No. 3. She knew by the way Katy played the piece, soft and with great expression, that her thoughts were also like some immense flood, engulfed in images of her son.

"A penny for your thoughts." Kathleen turned instantly. It was Madge.

"That's what Dennis used to ask me," Kathleen said pensively.

"I know," Madge said.

"To answer your question, I was thinking about a lot of things, especially the St. Patrick's party. It was the first time we kissed." She raised her shoulders and tilted her head. "I really did love him from the start, you know." She said it as if to diminish an offense.

"I know you did, Kathleen."

Over Kathleen's shoulder, Madge saw him coming.

Kathleen's eyes were covered.

"Guess who?" the deep voice said. It sounded exactly like Dennis Noonan.

"How's my favorite cousin?"

"Oh my God—James." She turned and almost disappeared in his arms.

"I'm so sorry, Kathleen. Ryan was a great guy, we all loved him."

She stayed in his arms while she collected herself. Then she held him at arm's length.

"God, you not only sound like your father, you look the spittin' image of him."

The three talked at length about the interim years until Father Rafferty came around again asking for the songsters to reunite. Joseph Kortner eventually managed to steal a little of her time. Since his retirement, his wife had passed away and he was considering going back to Austria. While they talked, she caught a glimpse of William Hamilton speaking with Michael and the Whale, who had flown in from Washington State. Hamilton had limited his talk with Kathleen to an expression of sympathy. He looked at her and smiled. He seemed to be excusing himself and worked his way through the crowd.

"Thanks for coming," she said, "I don't know how to thank you for what you did for Michael. He told me all about it."

"It was nothing," he said. "Besides, we still have to find you know who."

"You're always saving someone, aren't you? First my father, now my sons—our sons," she corrected herself.

"Thanks," he said. He reached into his inside pocket and took a cigarette from the case. "Mind if I smoke?"

"It's very bad for your health, you know."

"Who's worried?"

"I am," she said.

Hamilton turned and blew a cloud of smoke. "I'm determined to get McIntee," he said, ignoring her concerns, "and what I'm going to do with him I'm not sure yet. He could still talk—talk about us." He perked up. "But not about Lawrence."

She looked confused. "I thought that Lawrence…"

"It was all contrived," he interrupted, "a forged page in a newspaper that suggested something that happened a long time ago in Europe. It alluded to him being born out of wedlock," he lied. "It was totally without one iota of evidence."

"That reminds me," she said, "wait right here; I have something for you."

He looked surprised. "I won't move an inch."

She turned and maneuvered through the crowd to the bedroom and closed the door. He sipped on the ginger ale and for a moment wished it was something stronger. As his gaze fixed on the picture of Ryan on the mantelpiece, he felt a rush of grief. Her return interrupted his thoughts.

"Here," she said, handing him the tattered folder, "this is something I want you to have." It took him a moment to recognize the folder.

"Well, I'll be…"

"Father Donnelly sent it to me years ago. I just thought it might help you, that's all."

"Did you read what was in here?" he asked.

"No," she said, "I wasn't curious. Besides, it never was really necessary, was it?"

"Thanks—I do appreciate that." She looked around clandestinely and whispered. "I don't want you doing anything unlawful, William Hamilton—not for me or anyone."

"Kathleen, you know what this—this beast is capable of?"

She looked away again, then turned back to him. "Promise me you won't do anything stupid."

He shrugged.

"Promise," she said sternly.

"I promise I won't do anything stupid," he said, smiling.

She cocked her head. It was an expression that reminded him of their youth. He loved her then; he loved her more now. She looked around, then she moved closer to him. Somehow I feel that the promise you made gives you a great deal of latitude."

"Why don't we leave it that way. I need lots of latitude," he said, as they were joined by Father Rafferty.

"A little of your time, you two," he said, "We could use a few more singers."

Hamilton loved to listen to music of all kinds but could not carry a tune. Everyone but Kathleen was happy when Hamilton was called to the phone. Although she continued singing with the rest of the group, her eyes never left him. He said something and nodded a few times. She became concerned by his serious expression. He wasn't on the phone long. When he ended the call, he glanced at his watch and moved quickly to his Macintosh, hanging by the front door. He raised his hand, catching her attention. Kathleen excused herself and ventured toward him.

"You have to leave so soon?"

"Sorry, Kathleen, that was a man named Flemming, McIntee's accomplice, calling from New York. I told him to call me as soon as he heard something from McIntee." He looked again at his watch. "They're having a meeting this evening. I tried to have him stall McIntee, but Flemming said he seemed anxious to meet him tonight." He glanced once more at his watch. "At six this evening, he said. God, I hope I can get there in time."

"Time for what?"

"McIntee," he said. "I have an opportunity to get the bastard and I don't want to lose it."

She touched his arm tenderly. "Promise you'll be careful."

"I will—and by the way, there's no need to tell Michael or Lawrence yet. I want to surprise them," he said, closing the door.

CHAPTER SIXTY-TWO

H AMILTON HAD A chance to review the Dublin reports on the plane. He wished he'd had the portfolio the day he returned to the Barretts' home. So much would have been different. He would not have botched the attempt to tell Kathleen's mother about Mick's arrest. As the report pointed out, as a British agent he would not have needed a disguise to turn in Mick. He would not have spoken with an Irish accent. He shrugged and continued reading. *Hell, those people would have killed me anyway just for being a British agent*, he thought. His eyes widened. He pulled aside the letter from Nora McIntee addressed to Father Donnelly:

Dear Father Donnelly, As you know I don't have very much time left in this world. I have tried dearly to recount these things I'm about to describe in the confessional. I just couldn't bring myself to talk of my son as an informer.

Hamilton raised an eyebrow. *Christ!* He thought, *this asshole pervaded Kathleen's life and my life from the very beginning.*

He continued reading:

You reminded me that if there was something bothering me, so much that I couldn't bring myself to tell you face to face, I could put it in writing. It's not much easier to write about it, Father, but at least I can write and cry at the same time. All these years I've harboured the awesome lie that it was Kathleen Barrett's American boyfriend who was responsible for Mick Barrett's imprisonment. We were all so shocked to learn that he was a British spy it was easy to transfer the blame to him. All these years, Father, living that terrible lie. Even now it's hard to mention it. After all, wasn't Liam Riordan killed at sea? Who cared anymore? What difference did it make? My soul has been so plagued with guilt that I'm not about to take this awful lie to the grave. Sean, God forgive him, was the one who betrayed Mick. He didn't do it for the money, although that's what got him to America. God bless him, he didn't do it so much out of hate for Mick, as out of love for Kathleen.

I'm so ashamed I can't face anyone. Can you forgive me, Father, I mean without my presence in the confessional?

Nora McIntee

Hamilton lit a cigarette and put the portfolio away. He reviewed the question of dealing with McIntee. It would be easy to put McIntee away for forgery and extortion, but he could still talk. Who would be the legal holder of the stock? What would Lawrence's chances of becoming a Senator be if it was known that he was a homosexual or born out of wedlock or withholding the truth? Hamilton's reveries were suspended by the captain's voice instructing passengers to please fasten their seat belts and extinguish all cigarettes. They would be landing in about ten minutes. He looked at his watch. *Damn,* he thought, *I'll never make it to Brooklyn by six.*

Even though he had shown his credentials to the cabbie and told him to ignore the speed limits, it was doubtful that the taxi would reach the print shop before seven. The cabbie spent most of the trip laying on the horn and slowing down only to go through red lights. They wove their way through Brooklyn traffic. Hamilton could have sworn they rode on two wheels. Maybe it was better to survive than to be on time. He thanked the cabbie for his heroic effort, but for Christ's sake don't kill us. The cabbie, who was having more fun than he'd ever had before, reluctantly slowed when Hamilton demanded that he ease off.

"Turn here," Hamilton said, leaning over the front seat. When they turned, they saw that the area around the print shop was alive with police officers, flashing red lights, and an ambulance. The cab screeched to a halt and Hamilton paid and thanked the cabbie. He tried to rush past officers. They immediately stopped him. He thrashed about impatiently, swapping the folder from one hand to the other, looking for his identification. He flashed it to one of the officers, who apologized and allowed him to pass through. Inside, he stopped briefly by the woman who was sitting and sobbing loudly. He recognized her as the secretary he had talked to a few days earlier. She was being questioned by one of the plainclothes detectives. Hamilton flashed the badge again and introduced himself. The detective, Flannigan, the ultimate career cop, appeared to be in his early sixties. A cigar stub dangled from the side of his mouth. He wore a slovenly gray suit. While he hunkered down beside the woman, his weighty paunch labored his breathing.

"I didn't know this was a Federal situation," he said.

Hamilton ignored him and bent down on one knee. He looked at the woman, whose mascara streaked her cheeks. She was hysterical as she looked at him through watery eyes.

"You!" she said vehemently. "This is probably all your doing—ever since you came along…" Her fits returned. She did not finish the sentence. Hamilton rose and addressed Flannigan.

"What's happened? Where's Flemming?"

"He's in his office—with the coroner."

Hamilton rushed into the office. A photographer was taking pictures of the body while a short, skinny man with thick glasses was dusting for prints. Another man Hamilton assumed was the coroner leaned over Flemming, slumped against the wall as if asleep. The man was speaking inaudibly into a dictaphone. Flemming's head was bent down, resting on his unmoving chest. The white shirt was saturated with so much blood it was difficult to say if the shirt was meant to be red or white. Hamilton bent over to talk to the coroner.

"Hamilton, FBI. How was he killed?" The coroner pushed back on Flemming's forehead, revealing a deep incision running from ear to ear. He pushed more and the wound gaped, resembling a puppet's mouth. Hamilton thought he could see the man's vertebrae. He looked away.

"This was a vicious bastard that did this," the man said, "almost cut off his goddamn head."

"How long ago?" Hamilton asked.

"Well, the blood hasn't had time to congeal. Could be half an hour or so." Hamilton looked at his watch. It showed seven o'clock. "Damn," he said under his breath. He walked to the wall safe. When he found it locked, he made his way to the open doorway.

"Do you know the combination to the safe?" He was looking directly at the secretary, who now seemed under control.

"No, Mr. Flemming's the only one who had access. He didn't give the combination to no one."

Hamilton turned to Flannigan. "Do you have anyone who can open the damn thing?"

"Sure," he said sarcastically, "but I thought you hot shots had all the answers." Hamilton sighed. "Look, just get someone over here pronto, okay?"

A team with an acetylene torch worked forty-five minutes to open the safe. Hamilton bent to the opened door. He reached around feverishly through the smoke-filled safe and found nothing.

"Gone," he said under his breath. Hamilton felt stumped.

"Were you looking for something in particular?" Flannigan asked.

"Yeah, stock certificates."

"Counterfeit stuff?" Hamilton nodded.

"So that's why you guys are involved?"

Hamilton didn't answer. He walked stone-faced to where the woman sat with her pudgy hands clasped to her face. He was thinking his way through his next moves. Having arrived late, he expected to find Flemming alone and learn that McIntee had come and gone. It would have been difficult for Flemming to detain McIntee. Hamilton's face flushed and he slammed his fist on the counter beside the distraught woman. She jolted to life.

"Damn! Damn it all to hell," he said angrily.

Seeing his despair, Flannigan seemed less confrontational. "Wish I could be of some help, Hamilton."

"Maybe you can, Flannigan." He turned to the woman, who appeared to be more controlled, more approachable.

"Do you know anything about this?"

"Wanda, my name's Wanda Miles."

"Wanda, were you here when this happened?"

"No, I came back because I had forgotten something and found..."

"I understand, Wanda," Hamilton said quietly. "Tell me, what time was it when you left?"

"I was the last to leave—it was about quarter to six. Mr. Flemming was having a meeting with the man who loaned him the money to buy the shop. He never wanted me around when they had meetings."

"I see." Hamilton offered her a cigarette and lit one for himself.

"So you never saw this man who met with Mr. Flemming? Did you know his name?"

"Kenny...I don't know his first name."

"And you're sure you never saw the man?"

"That's right. We only talked on the phone. He called early this morning—said he needed to meet with Mr. Flemming. It was the second time he called in a week."

"Did you have any conversation with this man—anything that might help us locate him?"

"No," she said, "just answered his questions about whether Mr. Flemming was here so I could bring him to the phone. Nothing more."

"Let me decide if it was important—any conversation—anything."

"Well it was the same day you were here, remember?"

"Yes, yes, go on," Hamilton said anxiously.

"It was just a short time after you left with Mr. Flemming. I told him that Mr. Flemming had gone out with you."

"Me! And how did you describe me?"

"I just described you—you know. I told him that you two appeared to have an argument or something. You remember! Then I told him you both left to get into a car driven by the priest."

"You described the priest driving the car?"

"Sure—I followed you two to the sidewalk, I saw him clearly."

Hamilton took a last drag and extinguished the butt in the ashtray. It was clear enough. McIntee recognized the description of Michael. He knew that Flemming was talking to the FBI. Hamilton tried to out-think McIntee's next move. He turned to Flannigan.

"You want to help find this bastard?"

"I'll do what I can, Hamilton."

"Good," Hamilton said excitedly, "I want you to help me check all the airlines that have flights leaving for England. I believe that this murderer has already bought or will shortly buy a ticket." Hamilton was busy writing a description of McIntee. He also wrote his own address. He handed the paper to Flannigan.

"Here's the man you're looking for, Sean McIntee, and he may be traveling under an alias, David Kenny. He's dangerous, so tell your men to be very careful." Flannigan took the paper.

"We'll get to it right away," he said. "Is this your number?"

"Call me any time. It's my office," Hamilton said, smiling. "I owe you one."

"Think nothing of it—it's a feather in my cap to do something for the Bureau."

They shook hands and Hamilton left.

Later that evening, Hamilton was reviewing the folder again when the phone rang. He picked it up before the second ring.

"Hamilton," he said apprehensively. It was Flannigan.

"He just departed. David Kenny left on a Pan Am flight that's arriving in Heathrow at ten o'clock in the morning, London time."

"Fantastic—did you ask that the plane be returned?"

"They wouldn't do that without a court order...said our best bet was to contact the British authorities. I thought that might be more your bailiwick."

"That's okay, Flannigan. You did great. I'll take care of it from here." He wrote down the flight number and hung up. At least he knew where McIntee was...somewhere between New York and London at 30,000 feet. The first thing he had to do was get hold of some old friends at M15. He would have to wait until seven-thirty or so London time. In the meantime, he called Kathleen. He apologized for the late call and explained as much as he wanted her to know. She was curious why he wanted her brother's address in London.

"I don't understand what Paddy would have to do with all this," she said. "Do you know he belongs to..." She hesitated. "Well it's not an organization I'd care to be naming."

"I understand that, Kathleen, it's just that I remember you saying something about Paddy being a member of the..."

She broke in. "Not on the phone, William, please. My God, if any conversation was being taped it would be your office."

"All right, Kathleen. I won't mention the group," he humored her. "But would you mind giving me his address? I need a favor, that's all."

"What kind of favor?" she asked curiously.

"Just a small favor. Look, it's something he won't mind doing."

"You won't get him into any trouble now, will you?"

"I promise, at least no more than he's probably already in." He waited a moment while she found Paddy's address. When she returned, he jotted it down.

"Yes," he said, "I know where Paddington is." She was silent for a moment.

"You'll be careful?" she said. Her voice indicated concern.

"I'll be very careful," he said, "See ya," and hung up the phone.

As the plane taxied to be spotted next to the terminal, McIntee was smiling to himself. He felt safe. He had slept through most of the flight. *It was too bad things had to get botched up,* he thought, *but I was lucky to get out when I did.* Hamilton had come too close for comfort.

Although he didn't quite pull off his convoluted plan, he told himself that things could have been worse. At least he frightened the hell out of the bastard twins. His little visit to Kathleen resulted in the death of her husband. He still had all his stocks. The Church was still in possession of counterfeit stocks. There was no evidence that he killed Flemming. He relaxed, knowing that he could stay with Bridget for a while, cash in the stocks, and who knows where he might end up? He thought that some small island in the Mediterranean might be nice. His thoughts returned to his years of seclusion, when he browsed through dog-eared magazines with color photos of beautiful paradise-island retreats. Now that was possible. With the money from the stocks, he could buy an island.

The flight attendant interrupted his musings. "Mr. Kenny, we're ready to disembark."

"Yes, of course," he said, "I must have dozed off again."

One of the last to leave the plane, he followed the rest of the passengers through customs. He hadn't time to call Bridget before he left and decided to take a taxi. He felt elated and reckoned that it would be a nice surprise for his big sister. Initially he didn't think it unusual when a uniformed customs agent asked him to step aside with his suitcase.

"Would you mind terribly, sir," the man said, "we'd like to check your luggage, if you would be so kind—just a precautionary routine."

"Sure, happy to oblige," McIntee said, trying to appear unconcerned.

He was ushered into a private room, where two men waited in civilian clothes. The customs agents closed the door behind them and offered McIntee a seat. He declined the invitation to sit.

"I'd like you to meet Inspector Hawkins from Scotland Yard and Mr. Phillips from Intelligence." McIntee put the case down. He had a sudden lapse of speech. A lump had formed in his throat, making it difficult to swallow.

"It looks like you won't be seeing much of our fair city, Mr. Kenny… or should I say McIntee?"

McIntee didn't respond. His legs felt like putty. He stared past the agent, trying to regain his senses. Dryness thickened his tongue. He was dumbfounded. *Concentrate,* he thought. *Deny everything they accuse me of. I have to get a hold of myself.* "I'm sorry, Mr. Phillips, was it?"

"That's right," Phillips said.

"I'm afraid I don't know what you're talking about. I have no idea why you suspect me of being this other man—McIntee, did you say?"

"We have reason to believe, sir," Hawkins said, "that you—let us say for the time being, sir, that we wish to explore the possibility that you may be this man, McIntee. Anyway, we've been asked to hold you, sir."

McIntee said, "I am an American citizen. I demand to see someone from the American Embassy. I know my rights."

"Would you mind opening the briefcase, sir?" said the agent.

"Why? I have nothing but personal papers in here."

"We have reason to believe that you are in possession of stolen stocks, Mr. McIntee," Hawkins said.

"Kenny—I told you my name's Kenny, not McIntee." Hawkins grabbed at the valise. McIntee pulled back. McIntee was no match for the three men. During the brief struggle, his hands were handcuffed behind his back. Phillips, discovering that the briefcase was locked, demanded the key.

"You're making this more difficult on yourself, you know. Be a good man and just give me the key," Phillips said politely. "If the stocks are in your name, Mr. McIntee, you'll have nothing to worry about, will you?" McIntee remained resolute.

"I happen to know my rights—you can't…"

"Take him away, inspector." Phillips had had enough. Hawkins, a big man, easily escorted McIntee from the office. McIntee turned before the door closed on the two men inside.

"Where is this man taking me? I demand to know where I'm going."

"You're going to Brixton, Mr. McIntee. I'm sure you'll be very familiar with the accommodations, though from what I hear, they're not quite as comfortable as Alcatraz." McIntee's jaw dropped. His persistent demands trailed as the door closed behind him.

Hamilton was thinking more clearly, refreshed by the little sleep he had on the flight. He had allowed McIntee to sweat it out for twenty-four hours in London's infamous Brixton prison. He stopped by Phillips' office first to say hello. Phillips was an old friend, someone he knew during his duty at the house in Roehampton. Hamilton stayed for an hour, reliving their early days of espionage. He thanked Phillips and left with the briefcase. He had business to attend to before picking up McIntee. He was going to visit Kathleen's little brother in Paddington.

It was past eight p.m. when he arrived at Brixton prison. It was indeed everything he had heard said about it. Great thick stone walls, impossible, he thought, to penetrate, even with a jack-hammer. He touched bars that seemed much larger than he'd ever seen before. A musty, damp odor permeated the air. He displayed paperwork from Inspector Hawkins to a guard, giving him permission to pick up the prisoner, McIntee. He remembered the time that he and Father Donnelly released Kathleen's father from Kilmainham. This was of a different order of satisfaction. There was no risk. He couldn't wait to see McIntee's face when he saw who was picking him up. It all seemed worth it now. *At last,* he thought, *I'm going to put this bastard away for good.* He was asked to wait while they *fetched,* as they put it, the prisoner. At seeing Hamilton, McIntee looked unhappy. He was unshaven and wearing the clothes he had on when admitted; he smelled bad. His hands were handcuffed behind his back. Hamilton spoke first.

"Well, if it isn't Sean McIntee. It's been a long time. Would you say, twenty or so years?" McIntee was mute. His expression showed repugnance.

"How have the Brits been treating you?"

"Fuck you!"

"I guess that means—not so well." Hamilton smiled.

"You know, if you take me back, I'll tell all about your fag son—the fukken bum boy. You know which one that is, don't you? He'll never stand a chance of becoming a Senator. Shit, I don't think his career will be worth a goddamn thing when I'm through talkin'."

"And what about your life expectancy? You know that murder carries a death sentence, the chair."

"Maybe we could make a deal, you an' me—I don't talk and for my silence—shall we say, freedom. Hell, I'll even throw in a million or so. That kind of money could keep a mug like you extremely attractive to Kathleen now, wouldn't it?" Hamilton felt his blood boil. The thought of this vermin mentioning her name, touching her, made him want to reach out and strangle the bastard. He held back the urge to kill him.

"Let's go," Hamilton said, "We can finish this conversation on the ride to the airport." Hamilton dragged him past the guard at the front desk, where he signed out for the prisoner. Outside, the breeze was cold but a welcome relief from the stench inside. McIntee had difficulty adjusting his eyes to the dark of the street. Hamilton pulled him to the waiting car, where a man got out and followed McIntee into the back seat. Hamilton got in the front passenger seat and the car slowly moved into traffic. One of the men wrapped a piece of duct tape tightly over McIntee's mouth.

Hamilton turned around, facing McIntee. "Allow me to introduce you to some old friends, Sean." McIntee's eyes showed fear.

"Maybe you know some of them." He pointed to the man who'd gotten out of the car. This is Seamus O'Connor. He's a son of a dear friend of your mother. And this other gentleman," he gestured to McIntee's right, "is John Murphy, another friend of your dear, dead mother." McIntee squirmed and Murphy smacked him on the head with the handle of his revolver. McIntee was making muffled sounds through the tape. His eyes looked to Hamilton, pleading for mercy. Hamilton did not know if the tears were from the knot on the side of his temple or the thought of where he was being taken. Hamilton was having the time of his life.

"Oh, please forgive my manners. Our driver here is none other than Paddy." Paddy gave a quick glance over his shoulder. He smiled broadly and nodded.

"How are ye, Sean?" he said. McIntee was shaking his head. His eyes suggested he didn't know the man from Adam.

"Oh, there I go again, forgetting to introduce everyone properly. If you will—it's Paddy Barrett, you remember, Mick's son, Kathleen's little brother. You might not have remembered him, he was a little younger than you. He does know all about you though, like the time you informed on his father." McIntee was making muttering sounds again and shaking his head furiously. Hamilton held up the tattered folder.

"It's all here, Sean, including a very damaging letter from your own mother. She said you used the money to go to America."

Hamilton smiled. McIntee's eyes now said that he had given up all thoughts of ever seeing daylight.

"I also told Paddy about how you paid his sister a visit. I believe it ended with you attempting to rape her. It's not something that friends do when they pay a visit, is it Sean?" McIntee shook his head violently and his eyes flashed in agreement.

"Good," Hamilton said, "very good." He changed the subject. "I'll bet you'd like to make a deal with that stock of yours, wouldn't you?" Hamilton opened the manila envelope and held the certificates so that McIntee could see them clearly.

"You'd like to strike up a deal maybe?" McIntee nodded furiously and the eyes continued to agree. Yes, yes, he seemed to be saying, pleading. Hamilton waited a moment then tore the stock certificates in half. "You mean with this stock, you'd like to bargain for your life." He ripped halves into quarters. McIntee looked terrified. He pulled forward, making a futile effort to stop Hamilton. John Murphy stopped him again, this time drawing blood from the same bruise. McIntee grunted and slumped forward.

"You wouldn't get far with this stock, Sean. You see, this is the phony stock, the stock you had Flemming duplicate."

McIntee looked up. His eyelids sagged over lifeless eyes. It appeared that he had given up all hope.

Hamilton went on: "I didn't want you to think that there was the slightest possibility that your miserable crime would succeed. It's a consolation you will never come to appreciate. Your stock, the real stock, was signed over to the Church. I'm surprised you didn't remember that Flemming had the authority to do that." Hamilton lit a cigarette and offered it to McIntee. "Oh, sorry about that," he teased, taking a deep drag and blowing the smoke into McIntee's dead eyes.

"And as for Lawrence's situation, that piece of slander was destroyed. I'm surprised you didn't notice it was missing from the envelope." He inhaled, enjoying the moment. "Then again, I suppose you were in such a hurry to catch a plane you didn't notice."

Hamilton taunted McIntee until the car stopped at Heathrow.

"Well, here we are, Liam," Paddy said. Hamilton shook his hand hard. It was a long time since anyone had called him Liam.

"Say hello to Kathleen when you see her."

"I'll do that." He said goodbye to Murphy and O'Connor. Before he closed the door, he looked into McIntee's begging eyes and patted him on the cheek.

"Goodbye, Sean, and remember, if you're really—I mean truly sorry for all the shit you've caused people in this world—they might make your death a little less painful."

CHAPTER SIXTY-THREE

HAMILTON WAS HAPPY, happier than he'd been in years. The awful tragedy that had struck Kathleen and the twins had brought them closer. But trouble remained for Lawrence. Hamilton had to develop a plan that would release Lawrence from Lugano's payroll. He would have to work out the plan when he got back to the U.S. He spent the following day visiting friends who had been with him at the house in Roehampton. He learned that the Colonel had died years earlier, just before the outbreak of the Second World War. Later that day, he found himself drawn to Victoria Station. Amid the sounds of echoing doors shutting, air brakes, departure and arrival announcements, and the multitude of conversations, he found the ticket counter.

"Return ticket to Putney, please."

"Platform three, leaves at four-thirty." The little man behind the glass barrier had a monotonous voice and handed him the ticket without looking up. Hamilton thanked him and searched for platform three. From the train he saw the vast damage inflicted by the war. Some scenes, never changing, looked as though he had just passed them yesterday. His ruminations came to a sharp halt as the train slowed and he caught sight of the station sign. He decided to walk to the house where he had spent the last years of the first great war in seclusion. Little had changed. He recognized many of the shops and houses and remembered similar evenings when the shadows were long and purple and the buildings bathed in a rosy sunset. The walk was good. It allowed him to reminisce. As he retraced his steps, he centered on the early years when he was dead to Kathleen. He thought those were the years when she probably hated him.

When he reached the house, his thoughts of unchanging scenes were upset. He found it vacant, dilapidated, festooned with ivy, every window shattered. Some windows still had shutters, askew and ready to fall with the next wind. What was once a beautiful English Tudor, filled with life, men and women expending every effort to outwit the Kaiser, now awaited the demolition ball. The beautiful English garden looked like a jungle, completely overgrown with moss, morning glory, and weeds. He pushed the wrought-iron gate and after a few attempts it finally screeched open. When he reached the front door, it was half open. He stepped inside and brushed away the cobwebs. He looked through the open double doors. What was left of the blackboard hung crookedly from one screw. His gaze fixed on the fireplace; conversations of the past reverberated in his mind. What had become of the savants and professionals who had once occupied this room? His thoughts were jolted by the cry of a wild bird flying through a broken window.

Outside again, he breathed in the moist air and walked the old path, now covered with overgrowth. It was a walk he had made often with Colonel Lynch. The wrought-iron bench was still there. He stopped, sat, and lit a cigarette. He contemplated his life. Most people would have given anything to have experienced half of what he had. He had lived the life he had chosen, one rich with excitement, but the excitement came at a high price, too high a price. He had missed the most important aspect of all. He asked himself if he would have given up the excitement of chasing criminals for a boring nine-to-five job that would have enabled him to spend those years with Kathleen. Thinking about her made him want to be with her. He threw the half-smoked Winston on the ground and left for Heathrow.

When he disembarked the plane at La Guardia, he called Kathleen. After four rings, he was ready to hang up the phone when the familiar voice answered, sounding as though she had just been awakened from a deep sleep.

"Hello." She whispered, as if to avoid disturbing the caller.

"It's me, William. I guess I caught you at a bad time. You were sleeping, weren't you?"

"That's okay—really, I had just gone to bed." She asked eagerly, "How was the trip? Did you find McIntee?—and Paddy, did you…?"

"Whoa, one question at a time," he broke in.

"Sorry," she whispered, "it's just that you've been gone for three days—I was worried about you."

"I'm sorry, I guess I could have called sooner with the good news."

"Good news?" she repeated excitedly.

"McIntee is in the past tense."

"What do you mean, past tense, you didn't…"

"No, I didn't," he said, not allowing her to finish the thought.

"Just leave it at that. He's out of our—your life for good."

"I can't believe it. You mean Michael and Lawrence are no longer indebted **to him.**"

"Michael is completely in the clear. I'm sure the Archdiocese sees him as a hero. Lawrence took the money from Lugano, so now the mob's got their hooks in him. That's something I hope to change."

She said nothing. He momentarily despised himself and blamed his bluntness on lack of sleep.

"It's not as bad as it seems, Kathleen."

"I'm sorry, but the idea of Lawrence being part of—of the mob doesn't sound all that good to me, William."

"I don't want you to worry, Kathleen. I'll think of something."

"I don't wish to sound like an ingrate. I really do appreciate all that you have done," she said. "Now, how about Paddy, did you get to see him?"

"Yes, I spent half a day with Paddy. He turned out to be a fine man. You'd be proud of him. I didn't have time to meet his family—another trip maybe."

"That's great, William. I'm so happy that the boys are safe from that monster McIntee—and I can get some sleep now, knowing that you're home safe." Hamilton told her to go to bed and mentioned he would be in touch with her as soon as he worked something out with Lugano.

"Thanks again," she said. "I'll look forward to your call." He put the receiver down and took a deep breath. He was glad that he had called and discerned that she still had feelings for him. Outside, he hailed a cab.

"Queens," he said to the cabbie—"and take your time."

Michael sat in the small restaurant Lawrence had picked; he ordered a refill of coffee from the overly friendly waitress. He wasn't aware of her attraction to him; his inattentive composure she considered a challenge. She returned almost immediately with the coffee pot.

"Waitin' for someone, Father?" she asked resolutely.

"As a matter of fact, I am."

"Must be someone awful important," she said. "You've been waitin' a long time. This is your third refill."

"I wasn't counting," he said, checking the time. "It's my brother, he has no respect for other people's time."

"That's his problem. Personally, Father, I don't mind taking care of you 'till he gets here." She hardly took her eyes from him as she poured the coffee. "Can I get you something while you're waiting—besides coffee, I mean?"

"Thank you, no, you're very kind, but I think I'll wait."

She turned, swinging her hips suggestively. He finally realized her flirtatious manner was on his behalf and smiled to himself. She must know how foolish she looks. Since Hamilton's return several days earlier, he had thought of nothing but Lawrence's dilemma with Giovanni Lugano. Hamilton reminded them that it would take time to solve this one. Time and a great deal of planning. In the meantime, Lawrence would have to try the Di Angelo case.

There were many in the Church, and not just priests, but Monsignors and even Cardinals, who believed that men like Lawrence were being punished by God for their lifestyle and sexual prediliction. Michael preferred to believe that God wouldn't punish Lawrence for something he had no control over and it was just a coincidence that his own predicament was resolved for the better. He felt that Lawrence's assertive skepticism lately seemed to be shaken.

For nearly half an hour Michael waited; he was ready to leave when Lawrence burst into the restaurant, scanned the room, and pushed toward Michael. He dragged the chair back, causing many of the patrons to turn their way. Michael started to say something but was halted.

"God, I'm sorry," he said, out of breath, "I've been on the phone with Lugano most of the morning." Michael forgave him immediately. Urges of reprisals for his brother's tardiness vanished.

"Is everything okay? You look flustered."

"Flustered, hell; I'm goddamn angry. When this guy says move, he means now. Do you know what that—that…" He couldn't say *bastard*. "He wants me to work with some dirtbag detective. Develop some scandal involving Julio Martinez, he says, destroy his character by finding some bribable bitch to say he's been paying her on a regular basis to get screwed." Lawrence was furious. "Oh, yes, and we mustn't forget the union payoffs; that's an easy fix. Louie Garboni, that's the dirtbag's name, is supposed to be a pro at this sort of thing." The waitress's return halted his tirade.

"Oh, my God," she said, "two of a kind. Don't tell me you're a priest too?"

"No," he said curtly, upset at the interruption.

"Don't tell me. You're married."

"No, I won't," he said, becoming more upset with her familiarity. "I'm a homosexual!"

To her, his comment seemed absurd, impertinent. Michael appeared bewildered. Some of the patrons had overheard the remark and stared their way. Lawrence stared back and they returned to what they were doing.

"Well, aren't we the happy one," she said. "What can I get you, cheerful?" Lawrence threw out his arms. The belligerence faded from his face.

"Look—I apologize. You just caught me at a bad moment, that's all. I'd like a cup of coffee."

"No," she smiled wryly, "you *need* a cup of coffee." She turned with the same swagger and left.

"You know, Lawrence, sometimes I'd like to wring your infernal neck and right at this moment that's something devoutly to be wished." Michael pushed back in the chair. "I wish you hadn't tied yourself with Lugano. If only you'd waited."

"Oh, you mean like you waited?" Lawrence was silent. He reached for the pack of cigarettes and stuck the Winston in the side of his mouth.

"I'll have one of those," Michael said. Lawrence lit his first, then Michael's.

"Have you talked with William?" Michael asked, blowing smoke out of puffed cheeks like an amateur.

"This morning."

"And?"

"He told me to stick to it. That was before all this other stuff came down."

"Maybe you should call him back. Tell him what's happened. He could help you through this, Lawrence, I know he could."

"And in the meantime, I have to work with this weasel Garboni."

"Maybe you could stall him," Michael said doggedly.

"You don't say no to Lugano, Michael, especially when you've taken a hundred and fifty grand of his money." The waitress placed his cup in front of him and pulled back.

"There," she said, forcing a laugh, "are we being more polite now?"

"Depends," he said, smiling, "on how long you want to stick around." When she left, Michael picked up the conversation.

"You're not going to call William, are you?"

"Look, Michael, I know how you like him. You've really accepted him as your father. I'm not sure I can handle that, okay?"

"I've never heard him say that he was our father once, never. On the contrary, in case you haven't noticed, he seems to avoid any and all dialogue to do with his fatherhood. I believe that he's as clumsy with the subject as we are. I think you should call him."

"I'll call him when I'm ready."

"What if you talked to Lugano and told him you had changed your mind about the whole thing?" Michael was becoming more excited. "What if you told him you'd like to pay him back. You could make installments." Lawrence laughed out loud.

"You know, Michael, sometimes your lack of worldly knowledge amazes me. Besides, where in the hell am I going to come up with that kind of money?"

"Why does it have to come from hell? Why not heaven? I just procured five million dollars for the Archdiocese. I imagine a measly hundred and fifty thousand dollars wouldn't be much to ask of the Cardinal. It could be a loan."

"Oh, that's great. We could make installments. After all this mess, I'll be lucky to go to work for an ice-cream vendor, and you... Hell, you couldn't pay back the interest on that much money in a hundred years."

Lawrence looked furious again.

"I wouldn't hear of it, Michael. No way. You're in the clear in all this, and we're going to keep it that way. I'll work some other angle. Anyway, do you think for a moment that Lugano would settle for what he gave me? Don't you know anything about interest, Michael? Hell, the interest rates with these guys is probably fifty percent, at least."

They weren't in a mood to eat anything and spent the rest of the afternoon talking about better times. Michael made every effort to impress on his brother the awesome power of God.

Hamilton sat back in the leather chair with his feet on the desk and his hands locked behind his head. He stared vacantly at the city through the window. A black cloud covered what was left of the setting sun. Two busy days had passed since his return. Although he still had a field office to run, he justified as entitlement his efforts to solve Lawrence's predicament, especially given that Lugano was an enemy of the people. Hamilton was determined to liberate Lawrence from his torment. However, presently, it seemed a resolve without promise of an early fulfillment. The intercom directed his attention to the glass partition, where Mrs. Morgan, his new secretary, was gesturing to Lawrence.

"There's a gentleman named Mr. Riordan here to see you, sir. He says it's important." Lawrence was smiling apologetically.

"Thank you, Mrs. Morgan. Send him in, will you?" Hamilton said, waving to Lawrence. She opened the door, leading him inside, and offered to bring them coffee. Hamilton thanked her and gestured for Lawrence to take a seat.

"Sorry I didn't call you in advance," Lawrence said.

"No, really, it's okay. As a matter of fact, I was just thinking about you." Lawrence looked appreciative.

"I wanted to thank you for all you've done," he said, "I hope I'm not causing you too much trouble."

"Not at all," Hamilton said.

"I also wanted to know if you had any ideas about how to handle my situation with Lugano."

"Nothing so far. When it's to do with Lugano, I've learned to employ a good deal of patience. You'd be doing the Bureau a favor if you were willing to participate in whatever plan we manage to concoct. We've been trying to get something on him for years. Look at it this way, we now have—if you're willing, that is, a man on the inside, so to speak." Lawrence showed no hesitation.

"Of course I'm willing," he said.

"It could be dangerous." Hamilton's face was grave.

"That's something not totally unfamiliar to me."

"I understand." Hamilton remembered Lawrence's war record and smiled.

"Do you have something specific in mind?" Lawrence asked.

Hamilton shook his head.

"Not yet—I'll think of something though. How about you? Any ideas?"

"Not yet," Lawrence said, "When you formulate one, I'll be ready though."

"Good, that's what I wanted to hear."

Lawrence asked if he could smoke.

"If you need to, go ahead," Hamilton said, pulling an ashtray from one of the desk drawers. Lawrence flicked the Zippo lighter and lit the wick in one motion. He took a deep drag.

"Actually, I came today for two reasons. First I came to apologize and secondly I came because I'm worried about Michael."

"Apologize! For what?"

"For being an ass, I suppose. This thing with you and Mother—I guess I took the news badly. I might have been more understanding."

"I wouldn't expect you to take it any other way."

"Michael was understanding, wasn't he?" Lawrence said.

"Michael's a priest, Lawrence, they're trained differently than you and me. Forgiveness is their stock and trade."

"Still—I feel bad about the way I treated you and Mother."

Hamilton stood, walked to the window with his hands behind his back and stared out at the city. The black cloud still loomed.

"For what it's worth, Lawrence, you assumed rightly. I never stopped loving your mother…"

Lawrence interrupted. "You really don't have to explain anything to me. It's not necessary."

"I want to, Lawrence," he said, turning away from the window.

"I want you to know that as much as I loved her, I respected her marriage. I know you'll find this hard to believe, but—well, it's hard to say about another man, but I loved your father. He was a very close friend."

Lawrence reached for the ash tray and laughed. "You'll get no argument from me on that one."

Hamilton turned and smiled. "I wish men were more understanding," Hamilton said. "I think we have a lot to learn about real love, eh. Take Michael, for instance. Now there's a good example of a man who loves all other men, totally without inhibition."

"Even before he was a priest he was always tolerant, considerate of everyone's feelings," Lawrence said. "Now, I…"

"Don't sell yourself short." Hamilton stopped him. "There's more goodness in you than you're willing to give yourself credit for. Michael told me all about that pro bono case, the older woman who was being swindled by that investment firm. I heard you did a marvelous job of getting back her money."

"It was good for my political career."

"Don't bullshit me, Lawrence. I know you don't believe that."

"You've been spending too much time with your other son," Lawrence said, smiling laconically. "He probably won't be satisfied 'till he has you converted. You see, he really believes that one has to be in a state of grace to enter heaven. You have to be baptized and confirmed—and you'd better be baptized into the Catholic faith. He can't stand the thought of those he loves, friends—and now you, dying with original sin. It's the thought that we all might end up in hell that fuels his great passion. It's what drives him to save us."

Hamilton eased into the chair. He stared briefly at the ceiling and said, "I find your remarks—well, somewhat psychic, Lawrence."

"And how's that, William?"

"I have been in so many covert cases where priests have been involved—always helpful. Would you believe I have even been to confession?"

Lawrence shook his head in disbelief.

Hamilton continued. He recounted the time he went to see Father

Donnelly and his eventual friendship with the Irish priest. He explained his relationship with Father Potocsnak and his valuable support to put away Sean McIntee.

"I've had this relationship—this vicarious relationship with the Catholic Church, if you will—so much so that I've been strongly considering taking those classes...what do you call them?"

"Confraternity classes?" Lawrence said, bewildered. "You're going to become a Catholic?"

"What the hell's so strange about that? Thousands of people do it every day, for Chrissake," Hamilton said defensively.

"I'm just shocked, that's all—and you're going to have to watch out for that profanity," he said, grinning. "Michael chastises me constantly."

They were quiet while Mrs. Morgan brought and poured the coffee. When she left, Lawrence sipped the hot brew and spoke first.

"Anyway, speaking of Michael, that's what I really came here to talk about."

Hamilton raised an eyebrow.

"Michael is in the clear, he has nothing to be afraid of. McIntee is history. So is Mr. Kenny, for that matter. You're the one now we should be concentrating on, Lawrence."

"It's just something he said the other day. It's not in his character to do what he was talking about."

"What's that?"

"He was talking about borrowing money from the Church to pay back Lugano."

"Pay back Lugano? That's not the way these guys operate. Hell, they don't need the money, they've got you. That's all they wanted."

"I know that and you know that," Lawrence said, dismayed.

"You don't think he'd do anything stupid, do you?" Hamilton asked. "I mean really stupid, like try to pay them back?"

"I called him around three p.m. today. We were supposed to meet for lunch. It's not like him not to show up, although, God knows, I'd deserve being stood up. He just sounded different—remote. He said that there was something important to do. I couldn't put my finger on it, but I just felt that he was hiding something, you know."

"If someone knew that Michael was hiding something, Lawrence, that someone would be you."

"I guess that's what bothers me. I'm glad we talked. Really, I've wanted to talk with you about—well, about us, the family and all, but really it has been Michael's behavior that brought me here."

"Do you want me to go over there? I don't mind paying a visit."

"I'd appreciate that," Lawrence said. "I hope it's nothing. One of those telepathic hallucinations gone awry."

Hamilton went to the closet and put on the Macintosh.

"Let's hope you're right, Lawrence," he said apprehensively.

Hamilton drove. He didn't find it necessary to use the red light. Within half an hour they arrived at the chancery. A middle-aged woman greeted them from behind a turn-of-the-century rosewood-paneled desk.

"How may I help you, gentlemen?" Believing Lawrence to be Father Michael, she apologized.

"Excuse me, Father, I remember seeing you here before."

"I'm not Father Michael," Lawrence said.

The woman looked confused for a moment, then she smiled knowingly. "Then you must be his twin brother," she said.

"Yes, my name's Lawrence Riordan and this is Agent Hamilton of the FBI." She smiled and Hamilton nodded.

"Is Father Michael in?" Hamilton asked.

"No, he left about…" She turned to check the clock on the wall. "He's been gone for about an hour and a half. What's curious is it was the first time I've seen him without his clerics. That's why I was so confused when I saw you. I thought he'd changed again."

"Did he say where he was going?" Hamilton inquired.

"He didn't say a word, just walked right past me. It wasn't like him not to say something."

"Is the Cardinal in?" Hamilton asked.

"Cardinal Spellman? I can call up there. Please wait a moment. You can take a seat…"

"You don't understand, Mrs…?"

"Dougherty, Mildred."

"Well, Mildred, this is of extreme importance, and we don't have time to sit. I'd appreciate it if you'd call His Eminence now. Tell him Agent Hamilton of the FBI is here to see him on important business."

She picked up what looked like a special phone and spoke to someone. It didn't sound as though she was talking directly to the Cardinal. She waited a moment. Then she turned to Hamilton and asked if he had any I.D.

Soon they were escorted by a young priest up a spacious staircase with an ornate, dark-stained balustrade. After they waited a moment in the foyer, a door opened and the two were ushered into the room. Cardinal Spellman came from behind the desk to greet them. He extended his hand, and Hamilton shook it firmly.

"My name's Hamilton, Your Eminence, I'm with the FBI, and this is Lawrence Riordan, Father Michael's twin brother."

Lawrence genuflected on one knee and kissed the ring.

"What an amazing likeness," the Cardinal said, "I'd never tell you apart. Believe it or not, Lawrence, I've been following your political career and I must say we need more men like you and Jack Kennedy working on the Catholic issues."

"Thank you, Your Eminence."

He looked directly at Hamilton. "And what, pray God, brings the Federal Bureau here? Not to arrest someone, I hope."

Hamilton smiled. "It's nothing like that, Your Eminence. As a matter of fact, it may turn out to be nothing at all."

"How may I be of help then?"

"It's about Father Michael. By any chance…" Hamilton hesitated. "This is an awkward question…"

"Go on, ask."

Lawrence was becoming impatient with Hamilton and jumped in.

"Has my brother been to see you today?"

"Does it have to do with the money?" Spellman said casually. Lawrence dropped down into one of the overstuffed chairs and placed his hands on his head. Spellman looked concerned.

"It's really all right. I allowed him the money. I have to tell you, though, that there isn't another person in the world I would have done this for. He's a very special young man. I trust him implicitly. The money was for someone very special. I didn't ask."

"How much did he ask for, Your Eminence?" Hamilton asked.

"Two hundred thousand."

"It was a check, I hope."

"No. I did find that rather curious. He brought along a briefcase."

"You mean he left here with two hundred thousand dollars in a briefcase, and you don't—you don't find that irresponsible? On his part I mean." Hamilton was becoming irritated.

"As I said before, Father Michael was responsible for bringing the Church a great deal of money. What he asked for was not for himself, I know that to be a fact."

"What time did he leave with the money?"

The Cardinal reflected for a moment and looked at the clock on the wall, then he said, "It was five-thirty, about an hour ago."

Lawrence sighed. He seemed to be talking to no one in particular. "I don't believe he did it," he murmured.

Hamilton put his hand on Lawrence's shoulder to get his attention.

"I thought you said the amount was one hundred and fifty thousand dollars?"

"It was. I told Michael the other day that even if they were paid back they would be demanding interest."

Cardinal Spellman's confusion was now turning to annoyance. "Would someone care to tell me what's going on here?"

Hamilton apologized. "We're really sorry about all this. Well, it's a long story and we don't have a great deal of time right now. You're absolutely right about Father Michael, though. All I can say now is that he's attempting to do a very brave thing."

"Obviously something to do with the FBI?" the Cardinal said.

"Yes, but it also involves the Church," Hamilton lied. "If he succeeds he'll save the Church a great embarrassment."

"If this involves the Church I should be informed. I demand that you tell me."

"I promise you, Your Excellency. I'll tell you as soon as we know the outcome. It's a matter of—of national security." He turned to face Lawrence. "That's why Mr. Lawrence Riordan is involved. Your Father Michael is doing a great service for the Church and his country. Would you mind if we took a look in Father Michael's office?"

The cardinal looked suspicious. "Should I be asking for a warrant or are you being truthful that all this is in Father Michael's best interest?"

"Do you think that his twin brother," Hamilton gestured to Lawrence, "would be involved in his brother's ruination?"

"The Bible is full of such parables, Agent Hamilton," Spellman said, smiling. The smile faded, replaced with apparent trepidation. "I'll have Manzini take you to his office right away."

Hamilton reached for the confused Cardinal's hand and clumsily kissed the ring. The Cardinal then showed them into Michael's office and left them alone. Hamilton hastily examined papers on the desk.

"What exactly are we looking for, William?"

"Before Michael went, he had to do some investigating: a name, an address, anything. I'm assuming he had no idea where Lugano could be located." He opened a black datebook and scanned it quickly.

"He had to write something down. Look for impressions on blank paper."

Lawrence picked up the waste basket and casually pulled out a crumpled piece of paper. After he read it, he handed it to Hamilton.

"Is there anything to this?"

Hamilton examined the wrinkled page.

"Falzoni Construction," he said, "This may be it."

There were two numbers next to the name, one discernible and the other smudged. In the top-right corner a number seven had been drawn over many times, embellished with radiating boxes. "Here," he handed the paper back to Lawrence. "It's smudged. Can you make it out?"

Lawrence looked at the number and shook his head while Hamilton dialed the number as he made it out. After a moment he said:

"Is this the Lugano residence? I see—and by any chance is Mr. Lugano there?" He waited again. "Do you happen to know where he is. It's very important."

Silence again.

"No, that's okay, I'll call him tomorrow." He hung up the phone.

"Any luck?" he asked, turning to Lawrence.

"First couple o' digits. That's it." Hamilton scanned the room looking for a phonebook. Lawrence finally found it in the lower drawer of the desk. Hamilton took it and traced with his finger until he came across Falzoni Construction Company.

"It's in Westchester County, New Rochelle, North Avenue and Beechmont."

"How do you know that's where he went?"

"Would you throw away an address and phone number if you planned to continue the relationship? Besides, it wasn't an accident that it was on the same page as Lugano's home number. It's about an hour drive at best, and we have a half hour to get there. I'll answer any questions you have on the way." Then he pulled Lawrence from the room and rushed down the stairs past Mrs. Dougherty, whose jaw had dropped at the strange manner of the two men.

There is no greater evidence of oversight in dealing with the criminal mind than a failure to apply the science of deduction to the patterns of corruption. Michael was failing to apply one to the other, yet he was feeling both elated and perplexed when he stepped from the car. He explored the area and looked back at the cab that brought him. The sound of the engine faded before the red tail-lights dissolved into the evening mist. It was a dark and eerily quiet neighborhood just north of the Bronx. He checked the mailbox. Lugano had suggested that they meet at Falzoni Construction Company. After verifying the name, he ascended the steps and pressed the doorbell button. A burly man with an unusually white face and a thick accent greeted him. "You musta be Riordan?" the man said contemptuously.

"That's right. I'm Mr. Lugano's new consigliere."

The man opened the door wider to allow Michael to enter a crudely furnished reception area. Michael was about to take a seat when the man stopped him.

"I have to make-a-sure you don't have a piece."

Michael obliged him by raising his arms. The man was thorough. He gestured for Michael to sit and attempted to open the briefcase.

"Here's the key," Michael said, then offhandedly he asked, "Mr. Lugano must have a fair number of enemies?"

The man opened the briefcase and carried out a perfunctory search.

"Most are dead," he said dryly. He lifted some of the bills to make sure there wasn't a hidden weapon. "De boss is wid someone right now."

"That's all right, I don't mind waiting," Michael said.

The man sat across from him and lit a cigar.

"It's a Havana." He blew a great puff of smoke "Would you like-a-one?" The offer appeared to come as a reaction to a childhood lesson in manners.

"No thanks, I think I'll pass." Michael thought about all the businesses that Lugano ruled and the ills New York suffered by allowing him a monopoly on construction. He dominated all the concrete and steel construction bids in the city. It seemed to Michael that he was even more powerful than the Mayor. He was remembering their conversation on the phone. Michael had called Lugano at home and was severely scolded. It was at that moment that he nearly decided not to go through with the charade. He was here, eager to do this for Lawrence. After a while the incomprehensible voices behind the closed door were quiet. The door opened and a well-dressed older man walked past him. He looked embarrassed when he saw Michael. Lugano stood in the doorway, smiling.

"Have you met my new attorney? I'm sure you've come across one another, being that you're in the same line of business." The man stopped and shook Michael's hand. It was obvious that the man recognized him.

"Judge Alexander, I'd like you to meet Lawrence Riordan. He's a sure shot at the Senate this time around."

"Your Honor," Michael said.

It was evident that the judge was humiliated. He couldn't wait to leave. The big man locked the door after him and Lugano asked Michael to come into the office. He was introduced to a man named Alfredo, who looked emaciated and offered a limp handshake.

"I'm trying to get him appointed to the Supreme Court," he said casually, motioning toward the judge. "Please, Alfredo, Mr. Riordan and myself need to talk business for a while. Lawrence, take a seat." Alfredo left the room. Lugano returned to the diamond-tufted leather chair behind the desk.

"Now, what's so important that it couldn't wait 'till later?"

"First, let me apologize for bothering you at home."

"And I'm sorry I had to treat you so harshly, Lawrence. You have to understand I'm a very private man. You have to respect the need to keep my family away from my business matters."

"I do," Michael said, smiling.

"Good," Lugano said, "what can I do for you?"

"I'll come right to the point, Mr. Lugano."

"I appreciate brevity."

"I've had a good deal of time to think about your very generous job offer."

"And?"

"I'm not sure that I'm the man you need."

"Unless I'm mistaken, Lawrence, I believe the offer was already accepted. We shook hands on it."

Michael had no idea what had transpired between Lawrence and the mob boss.

"I'll be the first to admit that I'm not the lawyer you think I am. If you think for a moment that I have the expertise to represent Mr. Di Angelo, you're being overly confident of my abilities. I'd be doing you and the defendant a terrible disservice."

"Lawrence, is that what you're worried about? Not winning the case?" He rose, walked around the desk, and placed a fatherly hand on Michael's shoulder.

This wasn't going the way Michael wanted. Lugano was smooth as silk.

"Lawrence, I want you to know that I appreciate what you're feeling. Your sense of loyalty—you don't want to let me down. That's admirable, but you shouldn't be so virtuous." He took a cigarette from the silver case on the desk and offered it to his visitor.

Michael accepted the cigarette and allowed Lugano to light it. A drink would have been more appropriate. He knew it was going to be difficult to convince Lugano, he just didn't know how difficult.

"You and I have much bigger fish to fry, Lawrence. I'm going to see to it that you, my friend, will occupy the next seat for our fair state in the Senate."

"I really do appreciate that, Mr. Lugano, but I guess what I'm trying to say is that—well, that I really want out of our arrangement." He'd said it.

Lugano said nothing. He focused on Michael an uncomfortable, sinister gaze. Michael couldn't face him. Finally it was the fear of losing the battle that forced Michael to raise his head and glare back. Lugano's eyes widened. He grinned.

"Why don't you take some more time to think about it, Lawrence? I know the trial's coming up, but maybe you should take a short vacation—the Bahamas perhaps. Get yourself a good-looking woman." He clicked his teeth.

"I don't think that's going to change how I feel," Michael said. He opened the briefcase and placed it on the desk in front of Lugano.

"There's fifty thousand more than you gave me in there, Mr. Lugano. I'd like you to take it back."

Lugano's jaw tightened, his eyes narrowed, and for the first time, Michael was fearful. He wished he'd listened to his brother. He could pretend to take Lugano's offer and get out of there. He was going to have to lie as believably as he had ever done before.

"Maybe I am being hasty. It's this—my father died last night…" He despised himself for bringing his father into this exchange.

"Well, now," Lugano said sympathetically, "I can imagine how you feel—and here I thought that you were beginning to be disenchanted with our partnership. I have to admit you had me going there for a bit." He held the cigarette delicately between his middle finger and thumb. "I'd still like you to take some time off though—and no need to worry, I'll make it right with the firm."

Michael was momentarily elated. He had survived. Next time he would most definitely listen to his brother in these matters. He reached across the desk and closed the briefcase.

"I appreciate your understanding—I'll be all right as soon as things get back to normal," he said nervously. Michael stood. He reached for the briefcase. Lugano placed a big hand over his.

"That's okay, Lawrence. I respect your right to have a change of mind. If you decide not to continue our relationship, a conviction I find thoroughly plausible, wouldn't it be best to leave the money? That way if you have a—shall we say, change of heart—we'll have no need for another meeting, right?"

Michael was confused. He had an awful feeling that he was going to lose two hundred thousand dollars of the Church's money and Lawrence was still going to be indebted to this man. "I don't think that will be necessary, Mr. Lugano. I feel much better now that we've had this talk." He pulled on the handle of the briefcase. Lugano pulled it to his side of the desk. Michael looked devastated.

"Don't worry, Lawrence, I'm not about to run away with such a paltry sum. You'll get it back when you make up your mind."

Michael wanted dearly to believe him.

"Do you mind if I call a cab?" he said, dejected.

"Did someone bring you then?" Lugano asked.

"I came by cab." The moment he said it, Michael realized that he had just lost an opportunity. He silently cursed his honesty.

Lugano knew now that Lawrence hadn't informed anyone about this trip. He saw fear. He rejoiced in it.

"I'd be happy to have Vincent take you back, but if it makes you feel better, I can call you a cab."

Michael nodded and felt relieved when Lugano looked through the phone directory and dialed.

"Yes, I'd like a cab sent to North Avenue and Beechmont in New Rochelle, please." He pursed his lips.

"Uh huh," he muttered.

"That's right, yes New Rochelle—could you hold a moment please?" He looked at Michael and cupped his hand over the mouthpiece.

The action raised no questions with Michael.

"They won't have a cab available for another couple of hours." He checked his watch. "I'm afraid I'll be long gone by then. I promised the kids I'd get home early—you're welcome to wait for the cab."

Michael shrugged. "Well, I guess —"

"Look, why don't you just go with Vincent. You're not putting him out. He lives in the Bronx." He held out the phone. "It's up to you, Lawrence. Besides, no sense spending money on cabs if you don't have to, is there?"

Michael was less distressed, believing that Lugano had made an effort. He smiled and nodded in agreement.

"Very well," he said, "if Vincent doesn't mind."

"Vincent does gladly what I ask him to do," he said, smiling broadly. He didn't see that Lugano had a finger holding down the receiver. Lugano pushed a buzzer on the desk. "Vincent, would you mind very much taking Mr. Riordan back to his apartment in the city."

"Sure ting, boss." The door opened instantly.

Vincent held the door, and Michael moved past him to the reception area, failing to see the knowing nod that Lugano gave the ashen-faced man.

Hamilton leaned hard on the accelerator, sending the car surging forward; the burst of speed pressed Lawrence back against the seat.

"You might have warned me," Lawrence said, "I would have packed a chute."

"I believe Michael's meeting was at seven. If he left the Chancery at five-thirty, he's probably there by now. I hate to think of Michael being used as a decoy, but maybe this is what we've needed to do to apprehend Lugano."

"Do you really think that he might…" Lawrence couldn't finish his train of thought.

"Attempt to eliminate Michael?" Hamilton interjected, "He might, if he thought that Michael—you, that is, was thinking of getting out. I don't want to frighten you. At the same time. I don't want to give you any optimistic illusions." He swerved to avoid hitting another car. "Nobody has ever quit the mob." He pulled the wheel hard to the left, turning north onto Hutchenson River Parkway.

"Don't worry, we'll get there in time. It's a little before seven and they still have to talk, right?"

It was seven-twenty when they pulled into the driveway of Falzoni Construction. Lugano was locking the front door and looked around at the stopped car. Hamilton told Lawrence to stay where he was, and although possessed of an intuitive tragic curiosity, Lawrence obeyed him. Hamilton had his coat pushed back, ready if he needed to use his pistol.

"Agent Hamilton, FBI—I want to have a word with you."

Lugano couldn't tell if there was anyone else in the car and realized that if there was ever a time to remain in control, it was now. Hamilton continued walking toward him.

"Are you Giovanni Lugano, by any chance?"

Lugano placed the briefcase on the porch, leaving his hands free. "Why don't you just state your business and I'll see if I can be of any help."

Hamilton glanced downward at the briefcase then back to Lugano. He could sense the man's apprehension.

"Either you, sir, are going to tell me what it is that you want or I intend to leave."

"You are Lugano, aren't you?"

"And what if I am."

"That briefcase," Hamilton pointed downward. "Now, I'm no Houdini, but I'd lay you good odds that there's about two hundred thousand dollars in the case."

"That's the most preposterous thing I've ever heard," Lugano said, picking up the briefcase. He attempted to walk around Hamilton, pushing him to one side. Hamilton slammed him against the front door. He was so absorbed with Lugano, he failed to see Alfredo, whose black clothes had merged into the darkness. Lawrence, seeing the specular of light reflecting off the gun's barrel, rushed from the car.

"William, look out!"

Even before Lawrence shouted, as if guided by some telepathic suggestion, Hamilton drew and fired at the black outline in the bushes. Two bursts of fire resonated in the quiet evening. One bullet lodged in the front door and the other struck its mark.

Simultaneously, Lugano had reached to his inside pocket for his concealed Italian Beretta. Hamilton grabbed the gun handle and turned it outwards, away from Lugano's body, and dropped him to the ground. In quick, practiced moves, Hamilton cuffed Lugano's hands behind his back and dragged him to his feet. Lawrence came up to the porch and stared at Lugano.

"Where's my brother, you asshole?" Lugano shook his head in disbelief.

"I'm his twin brother, you dipshit, now where the hell is he?"

Hamilton handed Lawrence the Beretta and told him to check on the man in the bushes. Then he turned his attention back to Lugano.

"Where's Lawrence Riordan?" he said, shaking Lugano. He hadn't been this enraged with anyone since McIntee.

"Answer me, you piece of shit, or so help me God you'll never see morning."

While he waited for Lugano to say something, Lawrence returned. "He's dead," he said casually.

Lugano had begun to shake, but still he remained silent. Lawrence reached inside Lugano's shirt collar and twisted until the man's face looked as though it was about to burst. "Here. Let me have the bastard for just two seconds…"

Hamilton pulled him off.

"Look, I'm not going to stand here much longer, Lugano. I have just so much patience then I'm going to turn you over to his brother."

"Riordan told me…" He swallowed hard. "He told me his brother was a—a priest," Lugano said, sucking air. "You're not like any priest I ever…"

"Right at this moment I'm a mad fucking priest, okay! Now tell me where my brother is or I'll end up sacrificing your ass right here to the gods."

"Get this lunatic away from me—I have my rights."

"You have no rights," Hamilton said harshly.

"You're mistaken, Agent—whatever your name is."

"Hamilton. The name's Hamilton—look, let bygones be bygones—we'll begin fresh. All we wish to know is where Lawrence Riordan is. We know you had a meeting with him tonight. If something's happened to him— we'll have you to blame, won't we?"

"You'll just have to find him first—won't you?" Lugano sneered.

Lawrence had had enough. In one swift motion he thrust the gun down the front of Lugano's pants and cocked the trigger.

"I'm counting to three, asshole, then I'm going to blow your prick to hell. If that doesn't make you talk, I'm going to blow off your fucking nose. I'll send you to your wife in so many fucking pieces you'll look like a jig-saw puzzle.

"One."

"You're a priest," Lugano said nervously, "you could never do it."

"Two."

"You wouldn't…"

Lugano never heard the three. He was stopped mid-sentence by the explosion between his legs. He dropped onto his knees. A small pool of blood formed on the porch.

Hamilton was shocked. He didn't believe that Lawrence would fire.

"There's a school under construction—it's—it's by the nature woods, about two miles—on Beechmont, you can't…" He passed out before he could say another word.

Hamilton dragged Lugano over to where the other man lay. He wiped the Beretta clean and placed it in his hand. He would call Flannigan as soon as he could and tell him there'd been a shoot-out. He seized the briefcase.

Hamilton, upset with Lawrence's behavior, barely gave him time to get into the car.

"That's some interrogating technique you have."

"Thank you. You think the FBI could use me then?"

"Actually I had the Nazi Stormtroupers more in mind," he said impatiently. "You didn't have to shoot him. It's what makes us different from them. There are ways…"

"Oh yeah," Lawrence interrupted, "you were really beginning to make him talk." He pushed his fingers through his hair.

"Look, I know you're upset, but do it my way, okay?"

Lawrence mumbled something beyond understanding.

Lugano's directions had been accurate. In moments they were turning onto the jobsite he had described. The project sign said that a new modern high school was coming soon. Hamilton turned off the headlights and put the car in neutral, allowing the vehicle to creep down the dirt road. He waited for his eyes to adjust to the dark. There were no signs of life. The car came to a stop.

He and Lawrence surveyed the site, made up of half-finished buildings. The black structures looked vaguely ominous against the dark-blue evening. Hamilton grew worried. Either Michael was dead or they were chasing a shadow set by Lugano. Hamilton was beginning to believe the latter when he paused at the end of a cluster of buildings. At first he saw the light, then, focusing, he discerned the shape around it.

"The job shack," he whispered loudly, "I hope they're still there."

They were startled by the sound of the approaching truck. It was difficult to identify because of the blinding headlights.

"Damn it all to hell." Hamilton's face grew grave. Quickly he reached into his jacket pocket, pulled out a leather folder, and handed it to Lawrence. "Here, take this and tell them you're FBI. Find out what they want—and don't let them go any farther."

"Supposing they're Lugano's soldiers—how the hell do you expect me to detain them without a gun?"

"Usually the badge is enough. Keep your other hand in your inside pocket—like you have one. It works almost every time."

"The *almost* bothers me," Lawrence said, talking back over his shoulder. Lawrence waved his arms and stood menacingly in front of the truck. When it finally came to a halt, he approached the driver's side, displaying the badge. He was shocked when he saw the truck's profile, a concrete drum, revolving, and heard the gravel mix sliding in the tub. His mind was in a vortex of frightening images of Michael being buried somewhere in the school's foundation. The surly voice of the driver returned him to the present.

"Are you the guy I'm supposed to deliver this load to?"

Lawrence pushed the badge closer, almost touching the man's face. He did exactly as Hamilton directed.

"FBI! Don't try anything stupid."

The man took his hands off the wheel.

"Honest t'God, all's I'm doin' is what I been asked by Mr. Falzoni. He calls and tells me to deliver five yards o' concrete to the school, see."

"You work for Falzoni?"

"Yeah—ya might say that. I been subcontractin' for over a year."

"And didn't you think it odd to be asked to deliver concrete at this time of night—in this temperature?"

"When it comes to Falzoni, you learn not to ask questions."

Lawrence ordered the man out of the truck.

"I'll take it from here," he said. "I want you to start walking."

"That's a twenty-mile walk, mister…"

"Now," Lawrence said, drawing his wallet half way from his inside pocket.

"All right—all right," the driver said, turning. He muttered something about the law as Lawrence got into the truck and put it in gear. Lawrence pulled the truck alongside Hamilton, who was surprised to see him in the driver's seat.

"What in…"

Lawrence cut him off.

"The driver's on his way back to town. I guess Falzoni must have received orders from Lugano to deliver five yards of concrete to the school here. Sounds like they might be expecting us, eh?"

Hamilton smiled.

"Good. Turn off the lights and drive up to within about ten yards of the shack. When I give you the word, turn them on, okay."

"Roger," Lawrence said, giving Hamilton a salute.

Lawrence rounded the corner and pointed the truck at the shack as he had been ordered. Hamilton placed himself behind one of the open doors. He drew his gun and shouted.

"Hey—anybody in there?—I got the concrete that Mr. Lugano ordered."

The shack went dark and the door opened. A black shape filled the doorway.

"It's about goddamn time."

"Now!" Hamilton shouted. Lawrence hit the lights and illuminated the small building. Hamilton had raised the gun to shoot, but there were two men frozen in the doorway. The big, white-faced man had Michael around the neck with one hand and a gun in the other. Lawrence, seeing his brother alive, jumped from the truck and ran toward them. He called out his name.

"Michael! It's me, Lawrence." Hamilton called for him to stop. The ashen-faced man fired blindly in Lawrence's direction. Michael pulled away and Hamilton found his mark. The man's upper chest burst and the impact forced him to reel back inside the shack. Hamilton rushed to where he thought Lawrence was.

"Lawrence—Lawrence are you all right?"

"I'm fine—he just grazed me."

Michael, his feet and hands tied, hobbled toward them. "Lars—Thank

God you're okay." Within arm's reach of Lawrence, Michael fell, hit by a bullet in his back.

Hamilton instantly fired at the man in the shack. The round struck him between his eyes. "Aw, Christ," Hamilton said, broken hearted as Michael fell into his brother's arms. "Goddammit!"

Lawrence was terror stricken as he gently laid Michael on the ground. Hamilton untied Michael's hands and placed his jacket under his head. Then he tore away some clothing to get a better look at the wound. The bullet had shattered the upper part of the sternum. Pieces of bone thrust upwards from the wound. Hamilton figured by the way the blood pumped that the bullet had hit a major artery. He had to turn away from the torment on Lawrence's face and hurried to the shack, where he knew he could find a phone.

"Listen to me, Michael," Lawrence said, stroking his brother's white face. "Don't give up." He raised his head. "God, why him? Why not me? He's the one you had all the plans for. You can't let him die."

"Lars," his voice was barely audible. "Lars, please tell Mother…"

"Don't talk, Michael. Try to conserve your energy. William has phoned for an ambulance—just lie still."

"It's all right, Lars—I know I'm dying—really, I don't mind."

"Don't say that."

"I don't mind—I do want you to know that—I'm going to miss you terribly, Lars—even though you've been a scoundrel."

"And you haven't?"

Lawrence smiled and tasted the salt from his tears. "How about the time we put the pillows on the clappers? You were part of that, you know. And how…"

Michael squeezed Lawrence's arm. "It's okay, Lars—I don't have much time—my mouth is so dry…"

Lawrence spit in his handkerchief and moistened his brother's lips.

Michael smiled. "Please—do me a favor."

"Anything, anything at all."

"Remember what Mother always says—there's a reason for everything. Don't go blaming God for this." He squeezed harder. "Please, Lars."

"I promise."

"With feeling—like you mean it."

"I promise."

Michael managed a smile. "I love you, you know. That's okay, Lars, I know deep down you feel the same way—you've just—never been able to say it, that's all."

More tears streamed down Lawrence's face and his mouth felt as though it couldn't form the words. He took a deep breath. "I love you, Michael," he said, and Michael's face gleamed. As Lawrence recited the Act of Contrition, Michael squeezed his hand and seemed to smile. He closed his eyes and died.

CHAPTER SIXTY-FOUR

New York, 1960

E VEN NOW, REMINISCING, he thought that the absurdity of his situation made some sense. He had taken Michael's identity, this time forever, it seemed. Lawrence wiped his moist eyes. That night would forever haunt his reveries. He always felt that eulogies were overly commendatory of the deceased. His were certainly no exception. Few, as far as is known, while lying in state have themselves heard their virtues extolled. People stood before the congregation and praised him for good behavior and described humorous events that he was learning about for the first time.

He questioned now how things might have gone had Hamilton not suggested that he take Michael's place. He would have, without a doubt, lived a life of fear, since Lugano's indictment in Michael's death had ended in a mistrial. The Mafia boss's lawyers made a strong case of distinguishing the real killers from Lugano, described as a good family man and benefactor to the City of New York. Alfredo and Vincent had already been eliminated by the FBI. He also remembered how relieved the Cardinal felt when he returned with the money.

Hamilton, who wrote him often during his sabbatical, mentioned that Lugano had died of a heart attack in 1959. A glow of pleasure crossed Lawrence's face as he revived mental pictures of Lugano living the little time he had left as half a man; for this unclean thought Lawrence would have to perform some plenary indulgence.

Now that he was no longer dominated by the strict rules of the monastery, his life would be more bearable.

Prior to leaving Spain, Father Riordan had been elevated to the rank of

Monsignor, at the recommendation of the Cardinal. His Abbot had found Father Riordan unworthy, given his faults. Father Riordan was forever breaking the rules, especially the rule of silence. He took a moment to reflect on what the Abbot would have done had he known that he wasn't ordained. The Abbot would have had a solution to his frustration with Father Riordan.

He pondered the state of his penitents' souls. Had he really given them absolution? He believed that he had. He was elevated to the office of Monsignor, despite the Abbot's report. He was no longer simply a priest. He knew that Michael would have believed that these parishioners were forgiven. It wasn't their fault that he wasn't an ordained priest. He deduced that if the Church believed that individuals dying and incapable of communication could be absolved by a Catholic lay person reciting the Act of Contrition on their behalf, then surely he could do so. He thought that these were times in which all his confessions would be deemed an emergency.

He became aware of the silence on the other side of the screen. Someone was obviously awaiting judgment.

"Is that everything?" he said.

"Yes, Father—I've been waiting for you to give me my penance."

Lawrence hardly remembered giving absolution.

"Ten Our Fathers and five Hail Marys," he said authoritatively.

He checked the time, peered through the small opening in the door, and sighed. He saw just one more penitent. He heard the door close and waited for the person to kneel. He slowly moved the door, exposing the obscured face.

"Bless me, Father, for I have sinned. It's been two weeks since my last confession. I accuse myself of thoughts of anger, Father."

"Anger is one of those normal sins that may not be all that bad." He thought a moment, then he elaborated, "unless it's directed at another person."

"It's good to have you home, Michael," the voice said offhandedly.

"Mother!" He realized he was projecting. He lowered his voice. "Mother—what in the world...?"

"I'm having my confession heard, if that's all right?"

"Of course it's all right," he said, flustered. "I just got back into town. I was going to call you." He waited for her to respond. When she did not, he went on: "You could have come by the rectory."

"This is my confession, Michael." She seemed to smile. "I'll hear yours later."

"You don't have to confess anything to me, Mother. As a matter of fact,

I'd feel more comfortable if you went to one of the other priests—and not to me."

"I want to talk to you about Lawrence," she said seriously.

"Lawrence?"

"Yes. After the funeral, you left so fast we hardly had time to talk. And you somehow lost your ability to write. I understood your need to go on a sabbatical—you loved him so much. You were closer to him than anyone else. Sometimes I thought that the two of you were one. Other times, most of the time, I saw you as—well, complete opposites. As much as I tried to treat you both the same, Lawrence…" She searched for the right words. "Lawrence was always the one to get into trouble. I don't think he felt that I loved him as much as you."

"Mother, you don't have to tell me these things—it seems so pointless now. Besides, God has forgiven you any…"

"It's not God that I want to forgive me right now; it's you, Michael. I want you to know that I loved you just a little more, I guess. Somehow I feel that your forgiveness—well, in so many ways you were much alike," she sighed. "Lawrence wasn't always the most likable child, you know." In the silence that followed, he wanted to tell her everything. He wanted to tell her he was sorry. It was what she said next that prompted him to hold his tongue.

"I prayed that he could be more like you. Now I realize that he wasn't you, Michael. He had a personality of his own, a life he had to pursue. He could never have been like you and it took me too long to recognize your differences."

He knew that he wasn't as engaging as Michael. She reminded him of the times when his actions were defiant. She recounted the incidents that reflected their differences. Lawrence had no response. Listening to her made him sad. He recognized he had hurt her.

"You understand now why I had to see you."

"I understand, Mother. I also know that although there were times when Lawrence seemed most insufferable, he never, not for an instant, stopped loving you. You must know that."

"I suppose my real concern is that he knew that I never stopped loving him."

"I can say with confidence, Mother, that he died knowing that."

For a moment, she was silent.

"And you would know that, wouldn't you, Michael?"

"I do know that!"

"Good. I feel better already." She seemed to perk up. "Let's get together later—when you're through with confessions. William and I would like to take you to dinner."

"That's good, Mother. And how is he these days? He wrote me a lot while I was in Spain."

"More than you wrote to me, I'll bet," she said derisively. "By the way, we're thinking of getting married." Her comment was so cavalier it caught him by surprise.

"Well, I'll be…"

"We wanted to ask you first."

"Why ask me, Mother? If that's something you guys want to do you don't have to get my permission."

"Thank you, Michael."

"Is he going to be willing to take the classes?"

"He's actually looking forward to them. Can you believe that?"

"So, William's going to become a Catholic—I just think that's great, Mother. I'm very happy for you. Give me about an hour or so. I'll meet you somewhere."

"At the rectory then," she said excitedly, "in about half an hour."

"Good," he said.

He was speechless.

She broke the silence. "Well!"

"Yes, Mother?"

"Aren't you going to give me absolution?"

He smiled. "If you are truly sorry and promise never to come here again…"

"Michael, you're making a mockery," she said ceremoniously. "So help me, you sound more like your brother…"

He stopped her and agreed to be more decorous, then he gave her absolution as she recited the Act of Contrition. When she left, he sighed deeply. He had survived their first intimate conversation and she had no idea that he wasn't Michael. He was elated.

Outside the church, Hamilton stood by the railing smoking a cigarette. When she came down the steps, he thought that she was just as beautiful and graceful as when he first saw her. She wore a green skirt and jacket over a white blouse. The black, curly hair was now streaked with gray, but her face was as youthful and vibrant as ever. He flicked the cigarette and took her hand.

"Well," he said anxiously, "how did it go?"

"How did it go?" she echoed.

"Your confession? Was he surprised?" She cocked her head back and seemed amused at his curiosity.

"One of the first things you'll have to learn about the confessional, William, is it's absolute privacy."

"Oh, come on, Kathleen, I just want to know if he—well, seemed okay with us?"

"I am willing to admit I worried how he was going to take the news of our marriage."

"And?" he asked, persevering.

"He took it well," she said. "He did laugh though at the idea of you taking confraternity classes."

"I know how important this confidentiality thing is, but did you mention that you knew?"

"You mean that he isn't Michael? No." She appeared to be concentrating intensely. "I rather like Lawrence as a priest."

"I find it amazing how you assumed right away that Lawrence had taken Michael's identity."

"Not **assumed**, William, **knew**. Remember, a mother doesn't need medals or birthmarks to tell her sons apart." He placed his arm around her waist and pulled her close.

"You know, I've never once stopped loving you. All those years, even when I had no idea where you were or what you were doing. You were all I thought about." She was surprised when he took her hand and placed the ring on her finger.

"The bairin breac ring!" she exclaimed, and looking up at him, smiled with youthful impetuosity.

"You couldn't have given me a better gift," she said, reaching up to kiss him. The walk toward the rectory was interrupted by her childlike skipping over the pavers. She hummed an Irish melody that carried him back through the years.

"That song, Kathleen, it sounds so familiar."

She sang the words:

Oh, the ring of the piper's tune,
Oh, for one of those hours of gladness,
Gone, alas, like my youth too soon.

Acknowledgments

THANKS TO ALL of you named here.

I must begin by thanking my family who lived closest to me during these past nearly 15 years as I labored writing this book.

To Mig, my wife, you are incredibly patient. Anita, Dan, Peter, Pat, Maggie, Catie, Erin, and Willie, you are my inspiration. I hope that, in return, I can inspire you to keep growing, learning, and dreaming about what might be.

A special thanks to our close friend Sandy Good, a terribly creative lady, who is the only other person I know who equals my crazy need to express "creative juices." Soon after we hatched the idea for this book in the 1990s, it became obvious that Sandy wouldn't be able to continue an active part in writing. She was still busy with a large, young family, an elderly mother and an aging, ill aunt, all of whom needed her daily attention.

A special thanks also to my good friend, now deceased, Judge John Wilson. John grew up in Hell's Kitchen, New York, and was a great legal mind. I relied on him for his take as the characters became entangled in the legal and illegal ways of life in Boston and, earlier, in Ireland. Because John revered his Irish lineage, he was particularly interested in my book, and as we would walk for miles in north Everett, we would discuss the characters as though they were truly alive.

I miss John a great deal and will always be grateful to him for his time, talent, and friendship.

Because I am not a medical mind, I relied on the help of friend Dr. Sanford Wright and son-in-law Jim Potocsnak, P.A., for their knowledge of all things medical.

I know even less about the world of finance, so I relied on Bill O'Neil for his expertise in the complicated world of stocks and bonds.

Much of this book was written in longhand. I would write everywhere. I confess, I even spent many a Sunday writing, when I probably should have been paying attention to the priest and the sermon he was delivering.

I would write during business meetings, waiting in a doctor's office for an appointment, stalled in traffic on the freeway, anywhere that I was stopped long enough to pick up a pencil and paper.

I did not own a computer until I was into this book for over a year. Then I not only needed to acquaint myself with the ins and outs of the computer but also needed to teach myself to type. Lord, was this frustrating! My characters were coming alive and wanting to be noticed, and here I was unable to put them to paper as quickly as I needed. Over and over I hit the keys and before long the process became less difficult. Soon the procedure was almost comfortable, and the book continued.

Many folks helped clean up my mess of typing and punctuation. Among those are Erin Fraser, Mary Henry, Maggie Potocsnak, and Georgia Dee McCleod. In early editing, Beth Wood, Florence Clarke, and Mig (of course) provided help.

At times when I wanted to send my computer flying, our good friend and computer guru, Sandy Oberg, would set me on a path to recovery. And son-in-law and creative designer Dan Fraser was a godsend when it came to putting this book to bed.

This brings me to Denzil Walters. A gentler man you couldn't meet. His patience is legendary. And he needed every ounce of that patience dealing with me. There is so much I didn't know about the business of editing a book. He has been able to guide me through the final process of bringing this work to you. Thanks for being such a good friend to me and Mig. You are one of our many earthly treasures.

Finally, Dennis Peters, friend and brother-in-law. He doesn't know it, but he has mentored me since we met 50 years ago. His hunger for knowledge has always been an inspiration, and at 72 he continues to inspire his students, his children, grandchildren and me. Thanks, Dennis.

Reading Background

A s THE STORY in this book took shape, I drew upon scores of books and articles for reliable information about men who played a significant part in the rebellion in Dublin, two world wars, the criminal gangs that defied the FBI, and the agents who fought them in the years of prohibition. I think of my reading as directed and undirected. Before the thought of writing this novel occurred to me, I read fiction and non-fiction that in time contributed to my understanding of the conditions surrounding characters I created. In this group I put James Joyce's *The Dubliners*, the biography of W.B. Yeats, by John Jakes, Thomas Cahill's *How the Irish Saved Civilization*, Devin Garrity's *Irish Short Stories*, works of Graham Green, and Barbara Tuchman's *Guns of August*. When I turned to writing scenes that called for specific details about individuals who played a part in the action I describe, I went to the most recent channels to expand on what I had come to know through earlier reading. These on-line sources included Wikipedia, which provided information about Dion O'Bannion, Hymie Weiss and Earl Wojciechowski, the Rev. William Montgomery and the Room 40 Cryptographers, and Boston's history. Through the historylearningsite.co/uk I found answers to my questions about the Easter uprising and James Connolly. I depended on *The Baltimore Catechism* for accurate spelling of phrases that I had heard and some I had spoken but had not put in writing until the moment came for a character to say them in this story.

About the Author

AUSTIN DWYER WAS born in Thurles, County Tipperary, Ireland, in 1938. He studied music composition and music theory and learned to play the piano, flute, and uilleann pipes in classes at the Municipal School of Music in Dublin. Music classes followed a full day at the Christian Brothers School. Music was an easy love, since his mother and father were both musicians. His mother played the banjo and sang; his father played the fiddle.

After graduating, Dwyer, like many others of his generation, worked at jobs "going nowhere." With his mother's encouragement, he packed his few belongings and set out for the United States.

As a nineteen-year-old ready to see the world, he joined the U.S. Air Force. The Air Force took him back to Europe, where he had studied art.

In the service he became a friend of a fellow Air-Force member, Ron Peters, whose maternal grandmother was from Ireland. Austin invited Peters to visit the Dwyer family in Ireland. Ron, in turn, invited Austin to visit the Peters family in Everett, Washington, after their enlistment term ended in 1961. In the Peters home he met Ron's sister Mig. Two years later they were married.

Establishing a household with Mig in Everett began with work in a paper mill to pay for the expenses of attending the Burnley School of Professional Art in Seattle. He was recognized early as a student with extraordinary artistic skills. He would go on to teach commercial art and illustration for fourteen years at Burnley.

With a growing family of eight children, Dwyer took on free-lance art jobs to supplement his teaching income. He later founded with a partner the Cohen/Dwyer marketing and advertising agency.

While work, his family, church, painting, and household projects filled his days, he began turning a distant dream of writing a novel into a reality in 1995.

As a painter, Dwyer has won honors and awards that have earned recognition from coast to coast, Connecticut to San Diego, and in the United Kingdom. His works today are signed with a distinguishing title, an honor awarded by master painters: ASMA, American Society of Maritime Artists. His paintings are shown in the Mystic Maritime International Exhibit, the San Diego Museum of Maritime Art, the Coos Museum, Oregon, and the Kirsten Gallery, Seattle. Calendar prints of his oil paintings showing Foss tugs at work moving U.S. Navy aircraft carriers and container ships in roiling seas hang in offices and homes along the U.S. coastline.

He is a painter's painter: Other artists come to him for solutions to difficult questions in perspective. He amiably shows the way to the solutions. His art tours in Ireland attract professional artists looking for the landscapes, city scenes, and community pub activities that have become familiar through movies, songs, poetry, histories, novels, and short stories.

He is invited to high school and college classes to talk about art and the work of the professional artist. His life serves as an inspiration for students choosing a path to success in writing and business as well as art.

Teaching appeals to the aspect of his nature represented in the words of Mary Gallagher, the secretary of William Hamilton in *The Ring of the Piper's Tune*. She believed there was a natural order to things, "and, in the end, everything worked out for the best." Still, she hedged her conviction. Experience gave rise to second thoughts, reducing her risk in investing in the belief as an absolute, a good bet every day. Asked if she had ever had a premonition that something bad was about to happen, she said, "I'm Irish. What do you think?"

Teaching, writing, painting, framing a new work for a gallery, singing, playing the piano, Dwyer increases the odds of good coming from one direction or another.

CPSIA information can be obtained
at www.ICGtesting.com
Printed in the USA
BVOW08*2355201017
498274BV00001B/1/P

9 781440 174780